JUSTINE,
PHILOSOPHY IN THE BEDROOM
AND OTHER WRITINGS

JUSTINE, PHILOSOPHY IN THE BEDROOM AND OTHER WRITINGS

Marquis de Sade

ARROW BOOKS

Arrow Books Limited
20 Vauxhall Bridge Road, London SW1V 2SA

An imprint of the Random Century Group

London Melbourne Sydney Auckland Johannesburg
and agencies throughout the world

Originally published by Grove Weidenfeld,
a division of Wheatland Corporation.
Arrow edition 1991

Printed and bound in Great Britain by
The Guernsey Press Co. Ltd
Guernsey, C.I.

ISBN 0 09 982160 5

Acknowledgments

The essay by Jean Paulhan, "The Marquis de Sade and His Accomplice," was originally published as a preface to the second edition of *Les Infortunes de la Vertu* published in 1946 by *Les Editions du Point du Jour*, copyright 1946 by Jean Paulhan. The essay was later reprinted, under the title *"La Douteuse Justine ou les Revanches de la Vertu,"* as an introduction to the 1959 edition of *Les Infortunes de la Vertu* published by Jean-Jacques Pauvert. It is here reprinted by permission of the author. The essay "Sade" by Maurice Blanchot forms part of that author's volume entitled *Lautréamont et Sade,* copyright 1949 by *Les Editions de Minuit,* and is here reprinted by permission of the publisher. The editors wish to thank Grove Press, Inc. for permission to include certain information in the Chronology in the form of both entries and notes, taken from *The Marquis de Sade, a Definitive Biography,* by Gilbert Lely, copyright © 1961 by Elek Books Limited. This work is a one-volume abridgment of the two-volume *La Vie du Marquis de Sade* by the same author, to which the editors have referred in their Foreword, wherein further acknowledgments have also been made. Finally, the editors wish especially to thank Miss Marilynn Meeker for the meticulous job of editing, and for the number and diversity of her suggestions.

Contents

My manner of thinking, so you say, cannot be approved. Do you suppose I care? A poor fool indeed is he who adopts a manner of thinking for others! My manner of thinking stems straight from my considered reflections; it holds with my existence, with the way I am made. It is not in my power to alter it; and were it, I'd not do so. This manner of thinking you find fault with is my sole consolation in life; it alleviates all my sufferings in prison, it composes all my pleasures in the world outside, it is dearer to me than life itself. Not my manner of thinking but the manner of thinking of others has been the source of my unhappiness. The reasoning man who scorns the prejudices of simpletons necessarily becomes the enemy of simpletons; he must expect as much, and laugh at the inevitable. A traveler journeys along a fine road. It has been strewn with traps. He falls into one. Do you say it is the traveler's fault, or that of the scoundrel who lays the traps? If then, as you tell me, they are willing to restore my liberty if I am willing to pay for it by the sacrifice of my principles or my tastes, we may bid one another an eternal adieu, for rather than part with those, I would sacrifice a thousand lives and a thousand liberties, if I had them. These principles and these tastes, I am their fanatic adherent; and fanaticism in me is the product of the persecutions I have endured from my tyrants. The longer they continue their vexations, the deeper they root my principles in my heart, and I openly declare that no one need ever talk to me of liberty if it is offered to me only in return for their destruction.

—THE MARQUIS DE SADE, IN A LETTER TO HIS WIFE

Foreword

That the Marquis de Sade also wrote books is a fact now known to almost everyone who reads. And knowledge of Sade as a writer ordinarily ends there. For of his immense and incomparable literary achievement, and of his capital importance in the history of ideas, hardly a suspicion has been conveyed by occasional collections of anodyne fragments culled from his writings or by more frequent and flagrantly spurious "adaptations." (Of the two, cheap-paperback pastiche and more tastefully contrived anthology of excerpts, the latter, equally meretricious, is hardly the less dishonest.) To date, this is Sade bibliography in the United States. To date, Sade remains an unknown author.

For this, censorship, Puritan morality, hypocrisy, and lack of cultivation may be blamed, although not very usefully, since Sade sought condemnation. Ultimately, the fault for it is all his own, and the fate of his books is his triumph. Strange? To be and to stay an unknown author, that has always been his status and his destiny, that was the status he coveted, that was the destiny he created for himself, not by accident or unwittingly, but deliberately and out of an uncommon perversity. To write, but to go unread—this has happened to many writers. To write endlessly and under the most unfavorable conditions and as though nothing mattered more than to write, but to write in such a way, at such length, upon such subjects, in such a manner and using such language as to render oneself unapproachable, "unpublishable," "unknown," and yet upon succeeding generations to exert the most intense and enduring influence—this, it will be admitted, is rare indeed.

Secrets cannot survive their disclosure; to bare Sade to the public would seem to be rendering him a disservice. Against this "betrayal"—a graver one by far than any accomplished by the obscure tradesmen who from time to time get out a child's version of *Justine*—Sade has a defense: it consists in maintaining the reader at a distance, not merely at arm's length but at a remove one is tempted to call absolute. Or, to put it more simply, in forcing every reader—every so-called reasonable reader—to reject him.

Thus, the present attempt—which is the first to be made in the United States—to provide the basis for a serious understanding of Sade is in a certain sense bound to fail. In this sense: the "reasonable" man (we repeat) can come to no understanding with this exceptional man who rejects everything by which and for which the former lives—laws, beliefs, duties, fears, God, country, family, fellows—everything and the human condition itself, and proposes instead a way of life which is the undoing of common sense and all its works, and which from the point of view of common sense resembles nothing so much as death; and which is, of course, impossible. Such must be the judgment of the "reasonable" man—of him who builds, saves, increases, continues, and thanks to whom the world goes round.

Even so, however firmly he be established in the normality that makes everyday life possible, still more firmly established in him and infinitely more deeply—in the farther reaches of his inalienable self, in his instincts, his dreams, his incoercible desires—the impossible dwells, a sovereign in hiding. What Sade has to say to us—and what we as normal social beings cannot heed or even hear—already exists within us, like a resonance, a forgotten truth or like the divine promise whose fulfillment is finally the most solemn concern of our human existence.

Whether or not it is dangerous to read Sade is a question that easily becomes lost in a multitude of others and has never been settled except by those whose arguments are rooted in the conviction that reading leads to trouble. So it does; so it must, for reading leads nowhere but to questions. If books are to be burned, Sade certainly must be burned along with the rest. But if, ultimately freedom has any meaning, any meaning profounder than the facile utterances that fill our speeches and litter the columns of our per odicals, then, we submit, they should not. At any rate, it is not our intention to enter any special plea for Sade. Nor to apologize for one of our civilization's treasures. Disinterred or left underground, Sade neither gains nor loses. While for us . . . the worst poverty may be said to consist in the ignorance of one's riches.

* * *

Great writing needs no justification, no complex exegesis: it is its own defense. Still, the special nature of Sade's work, the legend attached to his name, and the unusual length of time intervening between the writing and the present publication seemed to call for some introduction, both critical and biographical. Thus, Part One of the present volume aims at situating Sade in his times and among his familiars. For the brief biography in the form of a Chronology, the editors have relied primarily upon, and are indebted to, Maurice Heine's outline for a projected *Life* contained in Volume I of his *Œuvres choisies et Pages Magistrales du Marquis de Sade*. We also owe a particular debt to Gilbert Lely, Heine's close friend and heir to the great scholar's papers. The extent of both their contributions to the establishment of a valid Sade biography, and to a fuller understanding of both the man and his work, is detailed elsewhere.

Sade's letters are particularly revealing. We have included seven, ranging over an almost thirty-year period from the year of his marriage when he was twenty-three to the time of his release from the Monarchy's dungeons by the Revolutionary government, when he was over fifty. Letter I is from an unpublished manuscript, and is cited in Volume I of Lely's biography; Letters II, III, IV, and V are from *L'Aigle Mademoiselle* . . .;[1] Letters VI and VII are from Paul Bourdin's *Correspondance*.

We have included two exploratory essays on Sade. The first, by Jean Paulhan, was written in 1946 as the Preface for a second edition of *Les Infortunes de la Vertu* published that year. The second, by Maurice Blanchot, forms part of that author's volume

---

[1] For full details of publication, see the Bibliography.

entitled *Lautréamont et Sade* which was published by *Les Editions de Minuit* in 1949. They form part of a growing body of perceptive Sade criticism which has developed over the past two or three decades.

The "Note Concerning My Detention" was first published in *Cahiers personnels* (*1803–1804*). Sade's "Last Will and Testament" has only recently been published in its entirety in French,[2] and is here offered in English for the first time.

If, through the material in Part One, we have tried to situate Sade, we have not attempted to conceal the singularity of his tastes or in any wise to depict him other than he was. He was a voluptuary, a libertine—let it not be forgotten that the latter term derives from the Latin *liber:* "free"—an exceptional man of exceptional penchants, passions, and ideas. But a monster? In his famous *grande lettre* to Madame de Sade, dated February 20, 1781, and written while he was a prisoner in the Bastille, Sade declares:

> I am a libertine, but I am neither *a criminal* nor *a murderer* [italics Sade's], and since I am compelled to set my apology next to my vindication, I shall therefore say that it might well be possible that those who condemn me as unjustly as I have been might themselves be unable to offset their infamies by good works as clearly established as those I can contrast to my errors. I am a libertine, but three families residing in your area have for five years lived off my charity, and I have saved them from the farthest depths of poverty. I am a libertine, but I have saved a deserter from death, a deserter abandoned by his entire regiment and by his colonel. I am a libertine, but at Evry, with your whole family looking on, I saved a child—at the risk of my life—who was on the verge of being crushed beneath the wheels of a runaway horse-drawn cart, by snatching the child from beneath it. I am a libertine, but I have never compromised my wife's health. Nor have I been guilty of the other kinds of libertinage so often fatal to children's fortunes: have I ruined them by gambling or by other expenses that might have deprived them of, or even by one day foreshortened, their inheritance? Have I managed my own fortune badly, as long as I had a say in the matter? In a word, did I in my youth herald a heart capable of the atrocities of which I today stand accused? . . . How therefore do you presume that, from so innocent a childhood and youth, I have suddenly arrived at the ultimate of premeditated horror? no, you do not believe it. And you who today tyrannize me so cruelly, you do not

---

2 In Volume II of Lely's biography.

believe it either: your vengeance has beguiled your mind, you have pro-
ceded blindly to tyrannize, but your heart knows mine, it judges it more
fairly, and it knows full well it is innocent.[3]

It was as a libertine that Sade first ran afoul of the authorities.
It was society—a society Sade termed, not unjustly, as "thoroughly
corrupted"—that feared a man so free it condemned him for half
his adult life, and in so doing made of him a writer. If there is a
disparity between the life and the writings, the society that immured
him is to blame. With his usual perception about himself, Sade once
noted in a letter to his wife that, had the authorities any insight,
they would not have locked him up to plot and daydream and make
philosophical disquisitions as wild and vengeful and absolute as any
ever formulated; they would have set him free and surrounded him
with a harem on whom to feast. But societies do not cater to strange
tastes; they condemn them. Thus Sade became a writer.

In presenting Sade the writer, in Parts Two and Three of the
present volume, we made a number of fundamental decisions at the
outset. We first decided to include nothing but complete works.
Otherwise, in our opinion, the endeavor was pointless. Further, as
Sade was a writer both of works he acknowledged and works he
disclaimed (and who is to say which of the two types most fairly
represents him?) it seemed essential to offer examples of both sorts.
Without which, again, the endeavor was pointless—and hypocritical. Finally, in making our selections we have obviously chosen
works we believe represent him fairly and are among his best.

Part Two consists of two of his philosophical dialogues. The
first, *Dialogue between a Priest and a Dying Man*, written in 1782
and until recently thought to be Sade's earliest literary effort, was
not published until 1926. The present translation is from the original edition. The second, *Philosophy in the Bedroom*, was first published in 1795, not under Sade's name, or only by inference: it
appeared simply as "by the Author of *Justine*." It is a major work,
represents a not unfair example of the clandestine writings, and
contains the justly famous philosophical-political tract, "Yet Another Effort, Frenchmen, If You Would Become Republicans,"
which is as good, as reasonably concise a summation of his view-

---

[3] Marquis de Sade: *L'Aigle, Mademoiselle* . . .

point as we have. It is a work of amazing vigor, imbued throughout with Sade's dark—but not bitter—humor, and creates a memorable cast of Sadean characters. Although Lely deems it the "least cruel" of his clandestine writings, *Philosophy* will reveal what all the clamor is about. The translation is from the 1952 edition published by Jean-Jacques Pauvert.

Two of Sade's moral tales make up Part Three. *Eugénie de Franval,* which dates from 1788, is generally judged to be one of the two or three best novella-length works which Sade wrote and is, in the opinion of many, a minor masterpiece of eighteenth-century French literature. The translation is from the 1959 edition of *Les Crimes de l'Amour* published by Jean-Jacques Pauvert. Finally, the inclusion of *Justine,* here presented for the first time in its complete form, was mandatory. It is Sade's most famous novel, although there are several more infamous. It is the work, too, which bridges the gap between the avowed and the clandestine, and is thus of special interest. For if it is true that, consciously or unconsciously, Sade was seeking condemnation, with *Justine* he was seeing to what lengths he could go and remain read. The translation is from the 1950 edition published by *Le Soleil Noir,* which contains a preface by Georges Bataille.

Each of the four works presented is directly preceded by a historical-bibliographical note which will, we trust, help situate it.

It is our hope that this volume will contribute to a better understanding of a man who has too long been steeped in shadow. If it does, it will be but slight retribution for the countless ignominies to which Sade was subjected during his long, tormented, and incredibly patient life, and during the century and a half since his death.

In his will, Sade ordered that acorns be strewn over his grave, "in order that, the spot become green again, and the copse grown back thick over it, the traces of my grave may disappear from the face of the earth, as I trust the memory of me shall fade out of the minds of men. . . ." Of all Sade's prophecies small or splendid, this one, about himself, seems the least likely to come true.

R.S., A.W.

Publisher's Preface

Donatien-Alphonse-François de Sade, better known to history as the Marquis de Sade, has rarely, if ever, had a fair hearing. A good portion of his adult life was spent in the prisons and dungeons and asylums of the sundry French governments under which he lived—Monarchy, Republic, Consulate, and Empire. During his lifetime, or shortly after his death, most of his writings were destroyed either by acts of God or by acts of willful malice, not only by Sade's enemies but also by his friends and even his family—which was chiefly concerned with erasing his dark stain from its honored escutcheon. As recently as World War II, some of Sade's personal notebooks and correspondence, which had miraculously been preserved for over a century and a quarter, fell into the hands of the pillaging Germans and were lost, rendered unintelligible by exposure to the elements, or simply destroyed. Of Sade's creative work—excepting his letters and diaries—less than one fourth of what he wrote has come down to us.

"Come down to us" is hardly an apt description, for though this quarter has indeed survived, only a small fraction has ever been made public, at least until very recently. The aura of infamy about the author's name has been such that even the most innocent—meaning "relatively non-scandalous," for in Sade nothing is wholly innocent—of his works has often been proscribed by the censors or by acts of self-censorship on the part of scholars and publishers. Although he was far from forgotten throughout the nineteenth century—as Jean Paulhan notes in his now classic essay on *Justine,* Sade was read and consulted by many of the most significant writers of the preceding century—he was relegated and confined to a nether region, to a clandestinity from which, it seemed tacitly to be agreed, he should never emerge. If, as many, including the editors of the present volume, tend to believe, this scandalous neglect—or neglect due to scandal—was the fate to which Sade truly aspired, then the nineteenth century represents the zenith of his triumph, for it was the nadir of his influence. Dominated as it was in spirit by the plump, prim figure of Victoria *Regina,* this age would doubtless have echoed the lofty sentiments expressed by Charles Villiers, who issued the following exemplary challenge to his compatriots:

> Let all decent and respectable people conspire together to destroy as many copies of *Justine* as they can lay their hands upon. For myself, I am going to purchase the three copies which are still at my booksellers and consign them to the fire. May my action serve as a general alarm.[1]

As the century waned, however, a few influential voices were raised in dissent, not only refusing to share the prevailing opinion but daring to take issue with it. "It is necessary," wrote Baudelaire, "to keep coming back to Sade, again and again." Swinburne publicly acknowledged his debt to Sade:

> I deplore with all my heart this incurable blindness, this reiterated, philistine stubbornness which yet holds you in the chains of the goddess Virtue and prevents you from appreciating the true worth of this Great Man to whom I am indebted (and what, indeed, do I not owe to him?) for whatever I have inadequately been able to express with regard to my sentiments toward God and man. I am compelled to believe that God has hardened your heart; I can find no other explanation for your indifference to the singular but surprising merits of the Marquis.

He then went on to prophesy ecstatically:

> The day and the century will come when statues will be erected to him in the walls of every city, and when at the base of every statue, sacrifices will be offered up unto him.[2]

While that day, and that century, are not yet at hand, our own era has witnessed an evolution, if not a revolution, in the attitude of at least the more enlightened, regarding both the life and writ-

---

[1] Maurice Nadeau: "Exploration de Sade," in *Marquis de Sade: Œuvres, Textes choisies par Maurice Nadeau,* La Jeune Parque, Paris, 1947.

[2] Gilbert Lely: *Morceaux choisis de Donatien-Alphonse-François Marquis de Sade,* Pierre Seghers, Paris, 1948.

ings of the Marquis de Sade (for both have been condemned, and as the name of the author affects one's attitude toward the work, so the work affects and colors the legend of the life).

In 1909, the amazingly eclectic Guillaume Apollinaire, as a result of his research in the *Enfer* of the Bibliothèque Nationale in Paris, published a selection of Sade's work and, in his Introduction, proclaimed him to be "the freest spirit that ever lived." In the ensuing half-century, an increasing number of voices were raised in Sade's behalf; writers and critics not only extolled him vaguely, but were reading him, examining his work as it had never been examined before. Among them were André Breton, Jean Paulhan, Maurice Blanchot, Pierre Klossowski, Simone de Beauvoir, and Maurice Nadeau, all of whom applied themselves diligently to discovering the secret of this extraordinary man, the likes of whom the world had never seen either before or since. However much these critics may differ as to their conclusions, they are all agreed on one fundamental point: Sade is a writer of the first importance, and one who must be taken seriously. As Maurice Blanchot aptly notes: It is not incredible to think that, in Sade, we have the most absolute writer who has ever lived, and, yet, for a century and a half, we have chosen to ignore him? And is not this choice voluntarily to ignore him, on the grounds that his work and doctrine are too somber, too anarchistic, too blasphemous, too erotic—the charges vary with the censor—both doubtful and dangerous, a choice on the side of darkness?

None of this serious criticism and intellectual speculation would have been possible, however, without the work, during the third and fourth decades of this century, of that exemplary Sade scholar, Maurice Heine. For fifteen years, with painstaking care, he sifted through the mountain of manuscripts entombed in the Bibliothèque Nationale in Paris and in a dozen other libraries and museums throughout France, constantly revealing new material that had been believed lost, meticulously comparing various manuscripts and published versions and thus restoring to their pristine state works that had been truncated or emasculated. Thanks to him, during the ten-year span from 1926 to 1935, the following works of Sade were published:

Historiettes, Contes et fabliaux, in 1926;

Dialogue entre un prêtre et un moribond, also in 1926;

Les Infortunes de la Vertu, being the original draft of *Justine,* in 1930;

Les 120 Journées de Sodome, ou l'École du Libertinage, the "lost manuscript of the Bastille" miraculously recovered and finally published, in three volumes, from 1931 to 1935.

Since Heine's death in 1940,[3] his work has been carried on with equal devotion and unflagging enthusiasm by Gilbert Lely, who had first met the elder scholar in 1933, and from almost the moment of that first encounter took up the torch which he still bears today.[4] Lely's definitive, two-volume biography, *La Vie du Marquis de Sade,* was published by Librairie Gallimard in 1952 and 1957, and offers a more complete and detailed view of Sade than has ever before been available. Moreover, Lely's research led him to discover, in the Condé-en-Brie château of Count Xavier de Sade, an unhoped-for collection of previously unknown Sade material, including more than a hundred and fifty letters—most of which are addressed to the Marquis' wife—which the author wrote between 1777 and 1786, while he was a prisoner in Vincennes and the Bastille. To date, Lely has published ninety-one of these letters, in three different volumes;[5] they form a remarkable record of Sade's existence during this crucial and yet so productive period of his life and, together with the earlier correspondence, offer a formi-

---

[3] Maurice Heine, 1884–1940. A poet as well as a scholar, Heine has often been described as "the inventor of Sade." André Breton, in his eulogy to Heine, published in 1948, makes mention of him as a man sprung "from the depths of the eighteenth century, with his encyclopedic culture . . . a man so lost among us." (*Cahiers de la Pléiade,* Summer, 1948).

[4] Much, one might add, as Heine took up the torch from Apollinaire. Heine, in his Preface to *Historiettes, Contes et fabliaux,* relates that, shortly before Apollinaire's death, the two men met and decided that together they would "search out and publish the *disjecta membra* of Sade." Apollinaire's premature death put an end to the joint project, but Heine, in spite of poor and failing health, devoted himself for the next twenty years to the task.

[5] The three volumes are: *L'Aigle, Mademoiselle . . . ,* George Artigues, Paris, 1949; *Le Carillon de Vincennes,* Arcanes, Paris, 1953; *Monsieur le 6,* Juillard, Paris, 1954.

dable record of, and cast new light upon, this much maligned and misunderstood man.

To this constantly increasing store of newly discovered material has been added new editions, based on sound documentation, of Sade's major writings. In France, over the past fifteen years, a courageous young publisher, Jean-Jacques Pauvert, has systematically brought out the complete works of Sade, in twenty-seven volumes, prefaced by the most cogent of contemporary essays. More recently, in Scandinavia, integral editions of the major Sade writings have begun to appear, and in tiny Denmark a project similar to Pauvert's pioneering effort is underway.

In English, however, there is still precious little material available, and, as the editors have indicated, even that, at best, is in the form of largely innocuous fragments carefully culled so as not to offend; at worst, and this is a more recent development, totally spurious editions of Sade have appeared—what the editors have referred to as the "cheap-paperback pastiche"—baldly proclaiming to be complete. One can only lament that these gross misrepresentations may yet accomplish what all the censors and calumniators have thus far failed to do over the past two hundred years: these shoddy, and indeed execrable rehashes of his work may yet bury Sade.

We boast that we have shrugged off the hypocritic coils of Victorianism, that the last bastions of censorship are on the verge of falling, and yet Sade still remains locked in the library keeps of the world. "I address myself only to those persons capable of hearing me," Sade once remarked. To date we have never allowed his works to seek that audience of hardy "capables," preferring to judge and sentence them without a public hearing. Thus today we only know him by the words he contributed to the language: sadism, sadistic, sadist. But to know him and judge him by these epithets alone is to ignore what Sade is and means. He is, for example, much more than that shunned and restricted pillar of pornography on which his reputation rests, for it has been adequately demonstrated that nothing dates more quickly than real obscenity, in whatever sphere, and Sade has steadfastly refused to date or die. To endure, a writer cannot rely or base his work upon that dubious foundation, and those writers over the span of the past century who have been attacked as too coarse or too candid for public consumption and who have survived—Baudelaire, Flaubert, Zola among the late-nineteenth-century French notables; Joyce, D. H. Lawrence, and Henry Miller more recently and in our own language—have survived precisely because of other qualities. So is it with Sade.

What is strange, and worth investigating, is how, given the neglect, the quasi-total condemnation of his writings—how has Sade survived? What is there in his work that has caused it so to endure? Its eroticism? To be sure. Its shock qualities, based on a philosophy of negation which, as the editors note, no "reasonable man can understand, much less accept? No doubt. Its imaginative power, which is of such scope and magnitude as to create an entire universe, a self-contained world not of human comedy but of human (and super-human) tragedy, surreal rather than real, a writhing, insensate universe at the pole opposite Gethsemane and Golgotha? Yes, that too. And yet, to date, we have preferred to immure the man and ignore his writings, fearing his absolute vision.

To profit from that extraordinary vision, however, we do not have to subscribe to it. But if we ignore it, we do so at our own risk. For to ignore Sade is to choose not to know part of ourselves, that inviolable part which lurks within each of us and which, eluding the light of reason, can, we have learned in this century, establish absolute evil as a rule of conduct and threaten to destroy the world.

Now, twenty years after the end of the world's worst holocaust, after the burial of that master of applied evil, Adolph Hitler, we believe there is added reason to disinter Sade. For though his works speak for themselves and need no apology, they will also serve to remind us, in an age which legislates billions to construct bigger and better doomsday machines, bombs that can wipe out entire populations and missiles to deliver them with incredible swiftness and unerring aim, of the absolute evil of which man is capable. Surely, if we can accept to live with the daily specter of the absolute bomb, we can accept as well to live with the works of this possessed and exceptional man, who may be able to teach us a trifle more about ourselves.

THE PUBLISHER

The
Marquis
de Sade

Part
One

Critical
&
Biographical

The Marquis de Sade
and His Accomplice

by Jean Paulhan, of l'Académie Française

I. THE SECRET

Over the past few years we have come to understand what has made for the greatest best seller of all time, the success of the New Testament. It is because this book has its secret. On every page, in every line, this book implies something never flatly stated, but which intrigues and involves us all the more on that account. And since in this piece we shall not have anything further to say about the Gospel, nothing need prevent us from disclosing its secret.

It is that Jesus Christ is light of heart. As shown us by the New Testament, he is solemn and rather pensive, irritated sometimes, at other times in tears, and always very serious. But we detect something else, something the New Testament does not tell us: that Jesus is not against an occasional joke. That he is full of humor. That he now and again talks without rhyme or reason, just to see what will happen (when he addresses the fig trees, for instance). In short, that he enjoys himself.

I would not like to hurt anyone's feelings by comparing the Gospel of Good with the most ingenious, and also the most extensive, of all Gospels of Evil which a clear-minded and eminently sane rebel once composed. But I still must say it: if *Justine* deserved to be favorite reading—at least during a certain period of their lives—with Lamartine,

3

Baudelaire, and Swinburne, with Barbey d'Aurevilly and Lautréamont, with Nietzsche, Dostoevski, and Kafka (or, on a slightly different plane, with Ewerz, Sacher-Masoch, and Mirbeau) it is because this strange although apparently simple book, which the writers of the nineteenth century—hardly ever designating it by name—spent their time plagiarizing, utilizing, applying, refuting, this book which posed a question so grave that to answer it and to fall short of answering it completely was as much as an entire century could achieve, this book contains its secret too. I shall come back to it. But first let's settle the question of immorality.

II. CONCERNING CERTAIN DANGEROUS BOOKS

Is there anything to be added to what has already been said about the advantage and need of punishment for the wrongdoer? There are a thousand opinions on the subject, and a hundred thousand treatises have been written; and yet it seems to me that the crux of the matter has been neglected, possibly because it is too obvious, because it goes without saying. Well, saying it will make it better still.

The first point is only too evident: that criminals are a menace, that they imperil society and are a threat to the human race itself, from whose standpoint, for example, it would be better if there were no murderers. If the law left each of us at liberty to kill his neighbors (as often we would like to do) and his parents (which the psychoanalysts claim is what we basically desire), there would not be many people left alive on earth. Only friends would be left. Not even friends would be left, for finally—though this is a detail we usually forget to consider—our friends are themselves the fathers, sons, or neighbors of somebody. I move on to the second point, which is equally obvious once one gives it a little thought.

This second point is that criminals are in general curious people, more curious than law-abiding people: I mean unusual, giving more food for thought. And though it may happen that they utter nothing but banalities, they are more surprising to listen to—owing precisely to this contrast between the dangerous content within and the inoffensive appearance without. Of all this the authors of detective stories are very aware: no sooner do we begin to suspect the honest country lawyer or the worthy pharmacist of having once upon a time poisoned a whole family, than the slightest thing he says warrants our most avid attention, and he needs but predict a change in the weather for us to sense he is meditating some new crime. Moralists declare that it suffices to have brought an end, even through negligence, to a single human life in order to feel oneself utterly changed. And moralists are imprudent in saying so, for all of us desire to feel such a change in ourselves. It's a wish as old as the world; it's more or less the story of the Tree of Good and Evil. And if discretion ordinarily restrains us from changing ourselves to this extent, we nevertheless have the keen desire to frequent those who have undergone the experience, to befriend them, to espouse their remorse (and the Knowledge that comes thereof). The only point to remember here is the conviction I referred to earlier that an assassin is not someone to encourage; and that through admiring him we participate in some vast plot against man and society. And here is where even those among us who are not overly scrupulous find themselves all of a sudden betwixt and between, torn by conflicting feelings, deprived alike of the advantages of a good conscience and of a bad. Here is where punishment intervenes.

Shortcomings and merits of criminals

I may safely assert that it straightens out everything. As of the moment the thief is robbed in his turn—if not always of his money, at least of some years of his life, which are worth money and a good deal more besides—and the assassin assassinated, we may without hesitation associate with them, and for example, while they are still alive, bring them oranges in prison; we may become fond of them, enamored of them, we can even feast upon their words: *they are paying, they have paid.* This we know; it was yet better known by the kings and queens and saints who in

Advantages of punishment

olden days used to accompany criminals up to the scaffold, and who would even, like Saint Catherine, catch a few drops of their blood to save. (And who today is not stirred by gratitude toward the handful of men who teach us, as they pay the extreme penalty, the danger and the very meaning, which had become lost to us, of treason?[1])

This is what I have been driving at: for one hundred and fifty years it has been the custom to frequent Sade through the intermediary of other authors. We do not read *Les Crimes de l'Amour*, instead we read *L'Auberge de l'ange gardien;* nor do we read *Philosophy in the Bedroom* but *Beyond Good and Evil;* nor *Les Infortunes de la Vertu,* but *The Castle* or *The Trial;* nor *Juliette,* but *Weird Women;* nor *La Nouvelle Justine,* but *Le Jardin des supplices;* nor *Le Portefeuille d'un homme de lettres* (which has, moreover, been lost) but *Les Mémoires d'outre-tombe.* And in such timidity one can find little else than the effect of the scruples I mentioned earlier. Yes, it is true that Sade was a dangerous man: sensual, violent-tempered, a knave upon occasion, and (in his dreams if not elsewhere) atrociously cruel. For not only does he invite us to slay our neighbors and our parents, he would have us kill our own wives. He would go even further: he would with pleasure see the whole of mankind done away with, to make room for some new invention of Nature. He was not particularly sociable; nor social either. He cared about liberties. He had liberties on the brain. But these are scruples we can set at rest.

For Sade paid, and paid dearly. He spent thirty years of his life in various bastilles, fortresses, or keeps of the Monarchy, then of the Republic, of the Terror, of the Consulate and of the Empire. "The freest spirit," said Apollinaire, "that has ever lived." The most imprisoned body at any rate. It has sometimes been maintained that to all his novels there is a single key, and that it is cruelty (and that, I would maintain, is to take a simple view of them). But fa-

---

[1] This essay dates from 1946.—*Tr.*

more surely, to all his adventures and to all his books there is a single end, and that is prison. There is even a mystery in so many arrests and internments.

Let us see how well the crime corresponds to the punishment. It seems established that Sade gave a spanking to a whore in Paris: does that fit with a year in jail? Some aphrodisiac sweets to some girls in Marseilles: does that justify ten years in the Bastille? He seduces his sister-in-law: does that justify a month in the Conciergerie? He causes no end of bother to his powerful, his redoubtable in-laws, the President and the Presidente de Montreuil: does that justify two years in a fortress? He enables several moderates to escape (we are in the midst of the Terror): does that justify a year in Madelonnettes? It is acknowledged that he published some obscene books, that he attacked Bonaparte's entourage; and it is not impossible that he feigned madness. Does that justify fourteen years in Charenton, three in Bicêtre, and one in Sainte-Pélagie? Would it not strongly appear as if, for a whole string of French governments, any and every excuse sufficed for clapping him behind bars? and, who knows, as if Sade did about all he could to get himself imprisoned? Perhaps; one thing however is certain: we know that Sade ran his risks; that he accepted them—that he multiplied them. We also know that in reading him we are possibly running risks of our own. Here am I, free to think what thoughts I will about that descendant of the chaste Laure de Noves,[2] to wonder what there may have been that was good in him, and at any rate delightful; to muse upon that extreme distinction, upon those blue eyes into which, when he was a child, ladies liked to look; upon that faint hint of effeminacy about his figure, upon those sparkling teeth;[3] upon those wartime triumphs; upon that

Sade paid, and paid more than his share

[2] Wife of Paul de Sade, whom she married in 1325. Famous for her beauty, she was the "Laura" of Petrarch's Sonnets. Whether she was actually Petrarch's mistress or not has never been proved.—*Tr.*

[3] Of Sade not a single portrait from life has come down to us. I borrow these details from letters, from police descriptions, also from the image Sade gives of himself in *Aline et Valcour*.

violent bent for pleasure; upon those repartees, impetuous but subtle and perhaps tinged with something of cockiness and vainglory; upon the young Provençal nobleman whose vassals come to do him homage, and who is accompanied wherever he goes by the too faithful love, the love-in-spite-of-everything of that tall and somewhat equine and rather boisterous Renée—his wife—at bottom a good and gentle woman.

III. The Divine Marquis

I shall leave aside the special efficacity Duclos had in mind when he spoke of "those books you read with only one hand." Not that it isn't interesting, and to a certain extent sensational: more than one very serious and even abstruse writer has dreamed that his writings might exert a similar influence, generate similar repercussions (on other levels, of course). But touching all this there is not much to be said, since such results are usually unpredictable. Then, too, it is usually agreed that veiled language and allusion (or if you prefer, teasing and smuttiness) are more apt to produce them than forthright and unadorned obscenity. Now, veiled language and allusion are rare in Sade, and smuttiness non-existent. Indeed, that may be what is held against him. Nothing is further from him than that kind of smug smile, of malicious innuendo which Brantôme displays in his tales of thoroughbred distractions, which Voltaire or Diderot show in their spicy passages, and that mincing deviousness which Crébillon, in his stories of alcoves and sofas, brings to discouraging perfection. There is in literature a free-masonry of pleasure, whose winks and nods and half-spoken enticements and ellipses are known to all its members. But Sade breaks with these conventions. He is as unhampered by the laws and rules of the erotic novel as was ever an Edgar Allan Poe by those of the detective story, a Victor Hugo by those of the serialized novel. He is unceasingly direct, explicit—tragic too. If at all costs he had to be classified, it would be among those authors who, as Montaigne once said, castrate you. Surely not among those who titillate you. And there is another sort of device he spurns.

It is the one we must term the literary device. Many a famous work owes its value—and in any case its renown —to the incorporation of an intricate system of literary allusions. Voltaire in his tragedies, Delille in his poems evoke in every line, and take credit in evoking, Racine or Corneille, or Virgil, or Homer. To cite only the nearest rival of Sade (and, as it were, his competitor in the domain of Evil) it is fairly obvious that Laclos is steeped to satura- tion in a literature—whereof, moreover, he makes the cleverest, the most intelligent use. *Les Liaisons dangereuses* is the joust of courtly love (for everything consists in find- ing out whether Valmont will succeed in meriting Madame de Merteuil), waged by Racinian heroines (neither Phaedra nor Andromache is lacking) within the lists of the facile society painted by Crébillon, by Nerciat, by Vivant-Denon (for everything proceeds straight and briskly to the bed- chamber—everything at least is envisaged with this denoue- ment in view). Such is the key to its mystery: discreetly wrapped up inside *Les Liaisons* is a little course on the history of literature for grownups. For the most mysterious authors are generally the most literary, and the strangeness in their writings is owing precisely to the disparate elements they contain, to this yoking together of characters come from the remotest milieux—and works—who are quite astonished to encounter one another. Laclos, moreover, was never able to reproduce his prodigious feat again.

Neither a pornographer nor a littéra- teur

But Sade, with his glaciers and his gulfs and his terrifying castles, with the unremitting onslaught he de- livers against God—and against man himself—with his drumming insistence and his repetitions and his dreadful platitudes, with his stubborn pursuit of a sensational but ex- haustively rationalized action, with this constantly main- tained presence of all the parts of the body (not a one of them but somehow serves), of all the mind's ideas (Sade had read as widely as Marx), with this singular disdain for literary artifices but with this unfaltering demand for the truth, with this look of a man forever animated and entranced by one of those undefinable dreams that sometimes take rise in the instinct, with these tremendous squanderings of energy and these expenditures of life which evoke redoubtable primitive festivals—or great modern wars, festivals of another sort perhaps—with these vast raidings of the world or, better still, this looting he is the first to perpetrate on man, Sade has no need of analyses or of alternatives, of images or of dramatic turns of events, of elegance or of amplifications. He neither distinguishes nor separates. He repeats himself over again. His books remind one of the sacred books of the great religions. From them emanates, for brief instants caught in some maxim—

One of those dreams whose source is in instinct

> Dangerous moments there are when the physical self is fired by the mind's extravagances. . . .

> There is no better way to familiarize oneself with death than through the medium of a libertine idea.

> They declaim against the passions without bothering to think that it is from their flame philosophy lights its torch. . . .

—(and what maxims they are!) that mighty and obsessing murmur which sometimes arises from literature, and is perhaps its justification: Amiel,[4] Montaigne, the Kalevala, the Ramayana. If it be objected that these I include among sacred books have never had their religion nor their faithful, I shall begin my reply by saying that it is a very good thing and that we should be glad (thereby being in a freer position to judge the books on their own merits instead of by their effects). Upon further thought, I shall add that I am not so sure after all, and that the religion in question was by its very nature condemned to clandestinity—but able, from hiding, to address an appeal to us now and then: three lines out of Baudelaire:

> Who hide a whip under their trailing robes
> And mingle, in the dismal wood and lonely night,
> The foam of pleasure with the flow of tears.

---

[4] Of all Amiel wrote only a twentieth has so far been published.

Joseph de Maistre's remark: "Woe unto the nation that were to ban torture";[5] Swinburne's phrase "the martyred Marquis"; Lautréamont's "Cruelty's delights! They are delights that endure"; Pushkin's observation upon "the joy we are hurled into by whatever heralds death." As for Chateaubriand—I am wary of the somewhat murky pleasure that Chateaubriand, among others, derives from the death of women who once loved him, of regimes he fought for, of the religion he believes the true one. And there are reasons, though they are not easily elucidated reasons, why Sade has so often been designated as the Divine Marquis. Whether or not he actually was a marquis is open to question; but there is no question that a certain number of persons, and apparently respectable persons, held him to be divine—or properly diabolical, which is something akin.

Sade divine if not a marquis

Still, on this score a doubt does assail me. I wonder, when today I behold so many writers struggling so hard and so consciously to avoid literary artifice in their treatment of an indescribable event of whose erotic and at the same time frightful character we are given every assurance, mindful in all circumstances to misconstrue Creation, and busy looking for the sublime in the infamous, the great in the subversive, demanding furthermore that every work commit and compromise its author forever in keeping with a kind of efficacity (which is not without its resemblance to the wholly physiological and local efficacity I referred to earlier), I wonder if one is not compelled to recognize, in a terror so extreme, less an invention than a remembrance, less an ideal than a nostalgia, and in short if our contemporary literature, in that area where it seems to us most alive —most aggressive, in any case—is not oriented entirely toward the past and, to be precise, dominated, determined by Sade as eighteenth-century tragedy was by Racine.

But my aim was only to talk about *Justine*.

---

[5] Cf. "The submission of the people is never due to anything other than violence and the frequent use of torture. . . ." (*La Nouvelle Justine,* Book IV.)

IV. THE SURPRISES OF LOVE

Well, Justine possesses every virtue, and for each of them she finds herself punished. Compassionate Justine is robbed by a beggar. Pious, she is raped by a monk. Honest, she is fleeced by a usurer. She refuses to become the accomplice in a larceny, a poisoning, an armed assault (for ill luck and poverty cast her into strange company), and it is she, the clumsy one, who is charged with theft, with brigandage, with murder. And so it goes with her throughout. And yet, against villainies of every description the only weapons Justine knows how to use are a pure heart and a sensitive soul. They prove inadequate: to whomever abuses her she brings good fortune, and the monsters who torment her become a minister, surgeon to His Majesty, a millionaire. Here's a novel which bears every resemblance to those edifying works in which vice is seen punished every time, and virtue rewarded. Except that in *Justine* it's the other way around; but this novel's failing, strictly from the viewpoint of the novel (which is our viewpoint), remains the same: the reader always knows how things are going to end. Now *Justine*'s ending fails even of the triteness which finally made an unduly virtuous conclusion one of the conventions of the novel, a convention hardly less tried and true than a novel's division into chapters or episodes. Sade, from all evidence, takes his unhappy denouements extremely seriously, and shows himself taken unaware by them every time. And the strangest thing of all is that they take us unaware too.

The riddle of the Gothic novel

This surprise ending poses a singular problem. Singular, for Sade will have none of the facilities that were commonly being employed at about the same period by his rivals, the Gothic novelists. Amazing the reader is too easy when, like Mrs. Radcliffe or Matthew Lewis, you enlist the help of phantoms, supernatural events, infernal machineries, all inherently startling. However, it is with man alone Sade wishes to deal; and, he specifies, with natural man such as he had been painted by, for example, Richardson or Fielding.[6] Therefore no ogres or wizards, no angels or demons—above all no gods!—but rather the human faculty which forges these gods, angels, or demons, rather the vices or virtues which, when they lead us into startling situations, set this faculty to work. The riddle thus posed has two or three words, the first of them being a very plain and every-day one: modesty.

It is a curious thing that the eighteenth century, to which we owe the most cynical descriptions of manners in our literature, also gave us two great portraitists of modesty: one of them, as everybody knows, was Marivaux. The other, and it is beyond me why everybody persists in not knowing it, was Sade. It is curious, or rather it is not curious at all. So much fear and trembling in the face of love and so much defiance of fear, so many self-respects to preserve and so many withdrawals into the self, and this refusal to use one's eyes and ears which reveals and at the same time protects everything that was finally to go under the title of *marivaudage*—for Marivaux shares with Sade the dubious distinction of having left his name to a certain form of amorous behavior: and I am not sure, indeed, that the attribution is any more correct or better understood in the case of Sade than in that of Marivaux; that shyness and that dread of being hurt are only explicable, only understandable if there are chances of being hurt and if, in sum, love is a perilous affair. Marivaux' heroines are modest to such a degree one would think they had read *Justine*. While Justine herself . . .

Sade, painter of modesty

Whatever befalls her, Justine is unprepared for it. Experience teaches her nothing. Her soul remains ignorant, her body more ignorant still. One cannot even allow her an occasional flutter of the eyelashes, a hint of a smile. Never will she take the first step. Even when in love, it does not occur to her to kiss Bressac. "Although my imagi-

---

[6] Cf. "Idée sur les romans," Sade's preface to *Les Crimes de l'Amour*.

nation," she says, "may sometimes have strayed to these pleasures, I believed them to be chaste as the God who inspired them, given by Nature to serve as consolation to humans, engendered of love and of sensibility; very far was I from believing that man, after the example of beasts . . ." Each time she is amazed when upon her are performed operations whose meaning she scarcely suspects, and whose interest she fails totally to comprehend. She is the image of the most heart-rending virtue—and, alas, of virtue most heartlessly rent. "Modesty," they used to say in those days, "is a quality you put on with pins. . . ." But as worn by Justine, the pins go through into her flesh and bring forth blood when her dress is removed. Shall it be said that it requires considerable good grace on the part of the reader to let himself be surprised and hurt along with her? No; for that reader is free to interpret as moral and sentimental anguishes all the very physical anguishes displayed before him. In its movement *Justine* is kin to those fairy tales where we are told Cinderella is shod in glass slippers—and we understand immediately (unless we are a little dull) that Cinderella walks with infinite caution. And then too we live on the verge of the strange. What, when you come down to it, is more strange than at the end of one's arms to have these queer prehensile organs, reddish and wrinkled, one's hands, and little transparent gems at the divergent extremities of these hands? Sometimes we catch ourselves in the act of eating, wholly absorbed in grinding fragments of dead animals between the other gems that stud our mouth. So it is with the rest; and among all the things we do there is perhaps not a single one which will brook prolonged attention. However, there exists a domain wherein strangeness enters neither by chance nor exceptionally, but where it is constant and the rule.

For, when all is said and done, we are not greatly bewildered by eating: we have (vaguely) the impression that our present meal is the sequel to a thousand past meals, which it strongly resembles and which serve as its guarantee. Whereas each time we fall in love again, it seems to us—so incomparable and so indescribable is every feature of our beloved—that we have never loved before. Poets speak of cool fountains, of bowers of bliss, of hyacinths and roses; they speak in vain, for they evoke hardly more than a faint reflection of the greatest surprise life reserves for us.

Love and pleasure are unpredictable

On another plane, the same surprise stamps the expressions and proverbs used when in common speech the secret organs are referred to as "little brother," "little man," "little friend," "the little creature that lives under a bush and lives on seed." What in the world can they have done to us, these organs, that we are thus unable to talk about them simply? Ah, they do at least this: they refuse to be treated with familiarity. In such sort that the prose writer, regarding them, can only record surprise and bewilderment?

Yes, doubtless. Or else he may each time vary and renew the reasons for this surprise, so that it is ever fresh for the reader and never, instead of suggesting the wonderful to him, imposes bewilderment upon him. Thus does Sade proceed, in his own manner. For what finally do such a multitude of approaches to pleasure and so many different and curious ways of making love signify if not that the ways of love and pleasure perpetually amaze us, are perpetually unpredictable? *Justine,* I have said, reads—or should be read—like a fairy tale. We may add that it is a tale solely concerned with that particular feature of love, paradoxical and in itself nigh unto incredible, which drives lovers, as Lucretia put it, to ravage the bodies of those they love.

However, there is one final word to the riddle.

V. JUSTINE, OR THE NEW OEDIPUS

Sade did not wait until he reached prison before beginning to read. He devoured the favorite books of his age. He knew the *Encyclopedia* by heart. For Voltaire and Rousseau his feelings were a mixture of sympathy and aversion. The aversion was on grounds of logic: Sade considered those two thinkers incoherent. Inconsequent, that was the word for it then. But he accepted their exactingness, their principles—and their prejudices. Of which this is the gist.

The eighteenth century had just made a discovery, and was not a little proud of it, that a mystery is not an explanation. No, and that a myth isn't an explanation either. On the contrary, it was noticed that no sooner is a myth forged than, in order to stand, it needs another myth to support it. The Indians hold that it is upon the back of a tortoise that the world is carried. So be it; but upon whose back is the tortoise borne? It is God that created the world. All right; but who created God? To be sure, this discovery (if it deserves the name of one) had been made earlier; but the Encyclopedists now excel in giving it this popular and, at the same time, fashionable form. Henceforth, all talk of God will be for memory's sake; and it will be of a God against whom Voltaire—and later Sade—range man alone, man (they go on to say) who is nothing other than man. Man (Voltaire adds) who is not noble. Natural man, man minus the Fable.

Sade, disciple of the Encyclopedia

This was to reject straight off all the current charm—all the perennial facilities—of literature. This was also to lay oneself open to a new difficulty. For, you know, this lonely man did after all have to go and invent God, and the spirits, and the satyrs, and the Minotaur. Now you'll not be very far advanced toward acquaintance with him until you have managed—by consulting nothing outside the bounds of human nature—to account for not just our real societies and the passions that agitate them, but also for those vast fantastic societies which accompany them like their shadow. Such is the weight with which, all of a sudden, the death of God falls upon Letters. Voltaire is human, I know. He even belongs among the better specimens of common everyday man. However, there is no getting away from the fact that there have been wars and great religions, migrations and

Empires, the Inquisition and human sacrifice—and that, in fine, men have not very often resembled Voltaire.

"Never mind," replies the *Encyclopedia*. "We are not presumptuous. We shall have the necessary patience. We already have man for a start: he is right here, we have him before our eyes. We are companions in exile (if it be a question of exile). We have but to observe man objectively, to submit him to our investigations. Sooner or later he'll come clean. Should he contrive to hide (for he is crafty) some one or other of his penchants from us, our grand-children will get at them. Time is on our side. For the present, let us compile our notes and assemble our collections."

Sade belongs to his age. He too begins with analyzing and patient collecting. That gigantic catalogue of perversions, *The 120 Days of Sodom,* was for a long time taken to be the summit and conclusion of his work. Not at all; it is the foundation of his work, and the breaking of ground for it. Such a beginning would have won approval from the *Encyclopedia.* Indeed, for rigorousness Sade outdoes any of the Encyclopedists, who (thought he) all fall more or less rapidly into dishonesty: some, like Rousseau, because they are weak-natured and prone to tears, forever being embarrassed by things as they are, always ready to shrink from the sight, from the touch, from the sound of man such as their senses perceive him to be, and to chase instead after some sort of kindly savage (whose existence the history of peoples denies a thousand times over). Others, like Voltaire, because of their hardheadedness and unemotional character, being quite incapable of believing in the truth of passions they themselves do not experience. Or still others, like Diderot, brilliant but frivolous, skipping from one idea to the next. Voltaire's version of man may explain how humankind came to invent the spade; Jean-Jacques', the hayloft; Diderot's, conversation. But ogres and inquisitions and wars? "Eh," replies Voltaire, "those poor people were mad. We shall correct all that." "That is exactly what I call cheating," rejoins Sade; "we set out to understand man, and

Where Voltaire and Jean-Jacques cheat

before we have even begun you are already trying to change him."

This rigor—I am much tempted to say, this heroism—might, it cannot be denied, have played Sade false and led him astray (as it did, at about the same period, that hot-blooded little fool and very able writer, Restif de la Bretonne). Such was not the case. Reiterating them through ten volumes and supporting them with a thousand examples, a Krafft-Ebing was to consecrate the categories and distinctions the Divine Marquis traced. Later, a Freud was to adopt Sade's very method and principle. There has not, I think, been any other example, in our Letters, of a few novels providing the basis, fifty years after their publication, for a whole science of man. It must surely be agreed that, before he was deprived of his liberty, Sade must have been an even keener observer than he was a tireless reader. Or else that a certain fire in him caused him to feel—and also enabled him to intuit—the broadest range of passions. And to me it seems strange that this has not earned him more gratitude. That said, it is all too obvious that scientific rigor, in such matters, entails its danger: it usually leads to awarding overmuch and too exclusive importance, in the study of the passions, to the physical aspect of love (as, in social economy, it leads to overemphasis upon individual interest). For the existence of the soul, even the existence of the mind, may be easily denied; but not copulation.

Another facility; and Sade refuses it no less severely. That which is common to most erotic books, and which is absent from his, is, as we have noted, a certain superior tone (and it could just as well be called an inferior tone), a certain air of sufficiency (or insufficiency, if you prefer to call it that). More precisely, a certain stiltedness, an aloofness of style, a certain abrupt divergence of style from content. For literature halts, and so almost does language, before an event (which is sometimes called animal, or bestial) wherewith the mind seems to have nothing to do; and which one therefore confines oneself to ascertaining and recording, either—like Boccaccio or Crébillon—with an amused satisfaction, or with a few reservations, like Margaret of Navarre or Godart d'Aucourt. But this divorce they establish, this distance they preserve is unacceptable to Sade. "Man is all of a piece," says he, "and lucid. There is nothing he does but he does it as a reasoning being." Whence it is his heroes accept themselves for what they are, constantly, down to their last aberrations, and keep themselves under their mind's survey. "We buggers," one of them declares (but all the others speak in the same vein), "pride ourselves upon our frankness and upon exactitude in our principles." Speeches and reflections are what set them in action.

Man undertakes nothing that is not subject to the scrutiny of his reason

Therein resides their weakness. For reflections and speeches could then also appease them. No argument, however wise, does not accept in advance to bow before a rebuttal if in the latter it recognizes wisdom superior to its own. Thus does the Léonore of *Aline et Valcour* more than once elude rape by means of the excellent pretexts she invents on the spur of the moment. Justine herself is again and again invited to refute her persecutors. There is never any deviation from the rule: "No transports," she is told. "Give me arguments. I'll cede to them if they are good." Now, Justine has a head on her shoulders. The problem presented to her is so honestly presented—so detailed, so explicit—that we expect her to find the solution to it at any moment. One word and the riddle would be solved. Justine, or the new Oedipus.

VI. Three Riddles

Most of these riddles have provided no end of diversion since Sade's time. The danger is that we today tend to consider them separately whereas Sade poses them simultaneously and in combined form; the danger is also that, detached from one another, they are too familiar to us, and the answer to them—or the difficulty of answering them— too evident. But let's have a close look at the texts.

The unique and its property

"First of all," says Sade, "the exact details. Who are you, and what are you after in this world? Only too often I behold you asleep, inert, or just barely alive, coming and going like some organic statue. This statue—is it you? No, you would have yourself a conscious being, as conscious as possible, and rational. You seek happiness, which increases consciousness tenfold. What happiness? Ordinarily it is located in pleasure and in love. All well and good. But one thing: avoid confusing the two. To love and to taste pleasure are essentially different; proof thereof is that one loves every day without tasting pleasure, and that one still more frequently tastes pleasure without loving. Now, while an indisputable pleasure goes with the gratification of the senses, love, you will admit, is accompanied by nuisances and troubles of every sort. 'But moral pleasures,' do you say? Indeed. Do you know of a single one that originates anywhere but in the imagination? Only grant me that freedom is this imagination's sole sustenance; and the joys it dispenses to you are keen to the extent the imagination is unhampered by reins or laws. What? Fix some a priori rule upon the imagination? Why, is it not imprudent merely to speak of rules? Leave the imagination free to follow its own bent.

"Pleasure, that was what we were discussing. Here we still have to distinguish the pleasure you sense from that which you think you bestow. Now, from Nature we obtain abundant information about ourselves, and precious little about others. About the woman you clasp in your arms, can you say with certainty that she does not feign pleasure? About the woman you mistreat, are you quite sure that from abuse she does not derive some obscure and lascivious satisfaction? Let us confine ourselves to simple evidence: through thoughtfulness, gentleness, concern for the feelings of others we saddle our own pleasure with restrictions, and make this sacrifice to obtain a doubtful result. Rather, is it not normal for a man to prefer what he feels to what he does not feel? And have we ever felt a single impulse from Nature bidding us to give others a preference over ourselves?"

"Still in all," Justine replies, "the moral impera-
tive . . ."

"Ah, morals," Sade goes on, "a word or two about
morals, if you like. Are you then unaware that murder was
honored in China, rape in New Zealand, theft in Sparta?
That man you watch being drawn and quartered in the
market place, what has he done? He ventured to acquit himself in Paris of some Japanese virtue. That other whom we
have left to rot in a dank dungeon, what was his crime? He
read Confucius. No, Justine, the vice and virtue they shout
about are words which, when you scan them for their meaning, never yield anything but local ideas. At best, and if you
consider them rightly, they tell you in which country you
should have been born. Moral science is simply geography
misconstrued."

"But we who were born in France," says Justine.

"I was coming to that. It is indeed true that, from
earliest childhood, we hear nothing but lectures on charity
and goodness. These virtues, as you know, were invented by
Christians. Do you know why? The answer is, that being
themselves slaves, powerless and destitute, for their pleasures—for their very survival—they could look nowhere but
to their masters' bounty. Their whole interest lay in persuading those masters to behave charitably. To that end
they employed all their parables, their legends, their sayings, all their seductive wiles. Those masters, great fools
that they were, let themselves be taken in. So much the worse
for them. But we philosophers, with more experience behind
us, we shall, by pursuing pleasure in the manner we wish and
pursuing it with all our might, do exactly what your beloved
slaves practiced, Justine, and not what they preached."

*A slaves'
morality*

"And remorse?" Justine timidly asks. "What shall you
do about remorse?"

"Haven't you already noticed? The only deeds man is
given to repent are those he is not accustomed to performing. Get into the habit, and there's an end to qualms and
regrets; whereas one crime may perhaps leave us uneasy,
ten, twenty crimes do not."

"I have never tried."

"Why not try it and find out? Furthermore, it is
vouched for by the innumerable examples offered to us day
in, day out by those thieves and brigands who, most appro-
priately, are called hardened criminals. The further one
sinks into stupidity, the better disposed one becomes for
faith; similarly, oft-repeated crime renders one callous.
There you have the very best proof that virtue is but a
superficial principle in man."

"However," Justine insinuates, "had there formerly
been some agreement entered into by men, some understanding binding man to man, which our honor or our well-
being might enjoin us to uphold—"

"Ah, ha," says Sade, "you raise there the entire question of the social contract."

"Perhaps I do."

"And I fear you misunderstand it. But let us see. You
claim that in the earliest stage of their societies men concluded a pact along these lines: 'I shall do you no ill so long
as you do me none.' "

"It could have been a tacit arrangement," Justine remarks. "Anyhow, I fail to see how, without some such
thing, any society could be founded or last one day."

"All right. A pact, and one which must constantly receive fresh adherents, one which must be reindorsed by each
of us."

"Why not?"

"I would simply draw your attention to one thing, that
a pact of this kind presupposes the equality of the contract-
ing parties. I renounced doing you harm; which means I was
free to harm you up until then. I renounce harming you
now; this means I have been free to harm you up until now."

"Well?"

"Imagine however that you are delivered utterly into
my power the way a slave is into his master's, the way a man
condemned to die is handed over to his executioner. How
could it possibly occur to me to strike a bargain with you
whereby you acquire illusory rights through my foregoing

*The social
contract*

real rights? If you are unable to hurt me, why in the world should I fear you and deprive myself for your sake? But let us go still further. You will grant me that everybody draws his pleasure from the exercise of his particular faculties and attributes: like the athlete from wrestling, and the generous man from his benevolent actions; thus also the violent man from his very violence. If you are completely in my power, it is from oppressing you that I am going to reap my greatest joys."

"Is it possible?" wonders Justine. "Is it human?"

"That man be human is not something I'd stake my life on. However, observe this also: as the mighty man takes pleasure from the exercise of his strength, so does the gentle or the weak man profit from his compassion. He too has a good time. It is his own way of having a good time; and that is his business. Why the devil must I further reward him for the enjoyment he gives himself?"

"Thus you see," says Justine, "that there are a thousand varieties of weakness and strength."

"I don't doubt that. Civilization has changed the aspect of Nature; civilization nonetheless respects her laws. The rich of today are just as ferocious in their exploitation of the poor as the violent used to be in their vexation of the helpless. All these financiers, all these important personages you see would bleed the entire population dry if they fancied its blood might yield a few grains of gold."

"It is indeed dreadful," Justine admits, "and I must own I have seen some examples of it."

VII. THREE MORE RIDDLES

That religion, conventional morality, society itself are among those malignant inventions which enable certain individuals, they being none other than the most powerful individuals, to victimize the lower classes—this is a proposition contradicted by no eighteenth-century writer concerned with ideas. The wise, the modest Vauvenargues himself ap-

peals in the name of Nature. Voltaire simply finds religion
to blame for the state of affairs, Rousseau blames society,
Diderot the going morality. And Sade blames them all at
the same time. Aye, the laws are harsh, their enforcement
is implacable, the authorities are despotic. (We are rushing,
says Sade—and Sade is the only one saying it—toward
Revolution.[7]) Very well. What is left for him to do who
has grasped this truth, and who is nevertheless powerless to
put a speedy end to so many oppressions?

If nothing else he can at least free himself of them,
inwardly defeat their influence upon him. Grimm, Diderot,
Rousseau, Mademoiselle de Lespinasse or Madame d'Epi-
nay cleave, as regards morality, to a single tenet which they
sometimes proclaim openly, sometimes conceal: that one
must in every case discover and then heed the heart's first
and most spontaneous prompting; by dint of patience and
of weeding out obstructions, restore the primitive man in
oneself; and in oneself restore—they add—natural goodness.

Of the various *Savages of Tahiti, Bougainville's Voyages, Histoire des Sévérambes, Supplements to the Voyages*

Primitive and *Supplements to the Supplements,* which toward 1760
mentality were the fare of sensitive souls, modern sociology has left
nothing intact. Nothing except the yarns. It could have been
expected.

For I see very well that Tahitian savages know nothing
of our laws and of our moral codes. But what if they know
others, no less severe or, who can tell, crueler still? Shall
we go a little further? I can see very well that they do not
have our coaches or our cannons. And if this were deliberate? What if they had known our civilization, and then
given it up (as you are tempted to do)? It is said, after all,
that the Chinese invented gunpowder long ago, and the
Romans the elevator. The Tahitians you behold are perhaps
the last vestiges of a glorious and prosperous society, which
had its palaces and its pomp—and then came to know the
vanity of riches and of display. Regarding languages, Meillet

---

[7] In *Aline et Valcour.*

points out that there is no particular one about which we can say with certainty that it is closer to its origins than others. Likewise, not a single people exists that we can with complete honesty call *primitive*.

"Why," Jean-Jacques replies, "as for this primitive man, it's enough for me to experience him in myself. And I know he is good."

"I'm not so sure of it," says Sade.

Everybody has complained, and rightly enough, that there are too many tortures in *Justine*—and in *La Nouvelle Justine* a hundred times too many. Too many strappadoes and needles, gibbets and pulleys, whips and irons. All the same, let's not be hypocrites. Our European literature includes another work, a greatly esteemed one, which contains (together with illustrations) more tortures by far than all of Sade's writings, and in its tortures more refinements, and in its refinements more ingenuity: not thirty or forty, but one hundred thousand women bundled in dry straw and then slowly burned alive (after having first been gagged, to reduce the level of their screaming); and other women spread-eagled on nail-studded beds, and raped in front of their impaled husbands; and princes and princesses grilled over live coals; and peasant women in chains (those sweet, lamb-like creatures, says the author) lashed and clubbed while dying of systematic starvation. At the end of which it isn't by the dozen (as in *La Nouvelle Justine*) the victims are counted, but by the million. Twenty million, according to the author. He is a respectable author, and reliable historians (such as Gomara and Fray Luis Bertram) are there to confirm his allegations to within a round million; for this we are referring to is no novel but a piece of pure and simple reportage: the *Brief Relation of the Destruction of the Indies* of Father Bartolomé de Las Casas, whom no one is likely to accuse of designing to flatter our wicked instincts. Nor were the Spanish soldiers who set out for the New World selected for their cruelty. Who were they? Sightseers, ordinary adventurers, like you and me. What happened? Why, native populations were turned over to them.

About the pleasures of cruelty

That man is able to derive the liveliest pleasure from cutting man (and woman) to pieces, and first—and perhaps especially—from the idea of cutting them to pieces, this is a fact, an obvious fact which we customarily hide from ourselves out of I don't know what sort of cowardice. I do not know because, so far as I can see, there is nothing in all this that could for one minute conflict with Christian belief—nor moreover with Moslem or Taoist—which maintains that man once upon a time parted ways with God. And as for the unbeliever, by what right could he refuse to observe that man with unbiased eyes?

Yet refuse he does once he is in a hurry to build, to slap together, a natural philosophy—the nineteenth century's term for it will be "a lay ethic"—untrammeled by laws and by authority, untrammeled by God. And as of now integrity is of slight importance to him. Well! how precious Sade thus becomes to us in his refusal of lies, in his refusal to seek short cuts, in his refusal to cheat! His refusal is a little too vehement? Ah, Sade is not a patient man. And do you suppose he is not exasperated by the others, with their ecstasies before Nature, their weepings over waterfalls, their quiverings upon the soft greensward? To so much sottishness an antidote was needed.

"A queer antidote," Justine murmurs. "So pray tell me: what life shall be mine to lead?"

"An absurd life," answers Sade. "But let's have a look at it."

The absurd world

The scene is usually laid in some awesome and almost inaccessible castle. Or in some monastery lost in the depths of a forest. Justine is there, a captive, and locked in the tower with her are three girls, the sober Omphale, the addle-brained Florette, Cornélie the inconsolable, all slaves of the perverse monks. Are they alone? No, everything would indicate that within the walls of the cloister there are other towers, other women. Sometimes this or that slave vanishes. What becomes of her? Everything leads to the suspicion that in leaving the monastery she takes leave of life. For what reason is she taken away? It is impossible to know. Her age has no bearing upon it: "I have seen a seventy-year-old woman here," Omphale tells Justine, "and during the time they retained her in service I saw more than a dozen girls dismissed who were under sixteen." Nor is her behavior a factor. "I have seen some who flew to do their every desire, and who were gone within six weeks; others, sullen and temperamental, whom they kept a good many years." Well-clothed girls, well-fed. If they but knew where they stood, and what conduct . . . but no. "Here, ignorance of the law is no excuse. You are forewarned of nothing, and you are punished for everything. . . . Yesterday, though you made no mistakes, you were given the whip. You shall soon receive it again for having committed some. Above all, don't ever get the idea that you are innocent." (Thus are the themes of the castle and of the trial interwoven throughout *Justine.*) "The essential thing," Omphale goes on to say, "is never to refuse anything . . . to be ready for everything, and even so, though this be the best course to follow, it does not much insure your safety. . . ."[8]

What remedies for so many ills? There is but one. The miserable can take consolation in the fact they are surrounded by others who are equally miserable, tormented by the same enigmas, victims of the same absurdity.

But it would be naive to suppose that in this adventure Sade's sole concern is the fate of four little lambs.

VIII. SADE'S DISAPPOINTMENT

In 1791 Sade was to have his hour, and his months, of triumph.

For the Revolution, which recognized in him one of its Fathers, made him a free and honored man. At the Théâtre Molière his *Le Comte Oxtiern* is being played; in the streets the people hum a *Cantata to the Divine Marat* whose author is the Divine Marquis. The brilliance of his

---

[8] *Les Infortunes de la Vertu.*

conversation, the breadth of his learning, the force of his hatred, everything about Sade spells a shining and safe career ahead. With his new friends he differs upon not more than one or two points: for example, like Marat, he favors a communist State,[9] but he would also like to retain a Prince to oversee the application of the new laws. Graver however is this: these new laws are to be mild and moderate. Capital punishment is ruled out of them. Though the heat of his passions may sometimes justify an individual's crime, nothing can excuse crime's presence in the legal codes "which are by their very definition rational and of a dispassionate nature. But here we have one of those delicate distinctions which escape a great many people, who are manifestly unable either to think clearly or to count. You put a man to the gallows, my good friends, for having killed another man: and lo! that makes two men the less instead of one."[10]

The President of Piques

Thus, and not without insolence, speaks Citizen-Secretary Brutus Sade before a meeting of the Section of Piques. How does he sound? how does he look? He stands not so straight as he used to, after his years in the tyrant's dungeons; and he has put on weight, too. But ever the grand style, and the gracious air, the same warmth of personality. A hint of obsequiousness. An engaging smile.

He smiles, as all disappointed people do. He is disappointed. To be free, to be in the midst of life again, that's not everything. Troubles, problems are beginning to beset him from all sides. There's his notary, that insect Gaufridy, demanding money; his sons, behaving as though their father did not exist; his castles in Provence, threatened with demolition, and being pillaged in the meantime. Right here in the Section he sees himself closely watched by his fellow citizens. They expected something else from the ferocious Sade. Something else than this level-headedness, these cantatas, this politeness (at a time when the enemy besets us from

---

9 The theories put forward by Zamé in *Aline et Valcour* seem fairly exactly to represent Sade's own political views.

10 Cf. *Philosophy in the Bedroom,* "Yet Another Effort, Frenchmen, If You Would Become Republicans."

without while from within the fifth column saps our finances and seeks to starve us into submission). Secretary—and even, a little later, President—of Piques: very nice, but one must still earn one's living. He files a request for a head librarian's post. No reply. The theaters turn down his new plays which, it would appear, are lacking in civism. "So they want civism, do they? I'll give them all they can swallow," Sade mutters, seated behind his President's desk. It's at that point that a little old gentleman sneaks into his office on tiptoe, somebody with an aristocratic past who'd like, thinks the Secretary, to become one of the boys; who sits down off in a corner. Who positively looks, thinks the Secretary, as if he were pissing in his pants. Who sits there fiddling stupidly with his cane; who plainly deserves nothing better than to be purged, with his face of a weasel. Why, good heavens, if it isn't the President de Montreuil! The Enemy, the Persecutor to whom Sade is indebted for some thirteen years in jail.

Well, Sade simply goes over and shakes hands with him. And cheers him up a bit. No need to worry, they'll admit him into the Section. And, you know, it's not all fun and frolic at the Section. Poor Montreuil puts on a big grin all the same. Three days later an officer in the Army of the Somme, one Major Ramand, is brought before Sade. "You have aided *émigrés* to escape?" Sade demands. "I have." "That means death, you realize." "I realize it," says the good Major. "Bah," says Sade. "Here's three hundred *livres* and some identity papers. Off with you."[11] Another three days later, Ramand is safe somewhere in the countryside and Sade is behind bars in Les Madelonnettes. If he misses being executed it's by a hairsbreadth and because Robespierre is sent to the guillotine. Sade is released from prison; but he'll be back there shortly. This time it is for having printed a pamphlet against Josephine. Why a pamphlet, why against Josephine? Probably for the same reason he treated Montreuil as a friend and released the Major.

Wherein Sade returns to prison

---

[11] "They wanted me to commit an inhumane act. I have never wanted to," Sade will later write in a letter to Gaufridy.

The simplest explanation is the first one that comes to mind. In prison Sade had become a writer. To be sure, he'd already scribbled a little, prior to then, here and there. Indeed, he'd shown himself able to wield a pretty pen, as they say; in the Troubadour manner (of course; for he is Provençal). But in prison writing had been accompanied by a sort of revelation.

It is impossible to measure, even to glimpse, the whole extent of an achievement of which a bare fourth has survived the effects of persecution; the rest having been burned, pulped, lost. Rather, if you wish to obtain an idea of the fury—of the rage—with which Sade proceeds, consider how for *Les Infortunes de la Vertu* he works out a meticulous outline, then writes the novel a first time, then writes it again, then writes it yet again, each time expanding upon each detail, correcting the least phrase or, better still, reinventing it; and the second version is twice the length of the first; the third—fifteen hundred pages long—three times the length of the second. With Sade, writing is worse than a vice or a drug. It has simultaneously to do with passion and with duty. Now, directly he is set at large, everything conspires against continuing—politics, children, business. How is one to keep afloat while writing? Parasite, pimp, blackmailer—as we know only too well, for him who has the need to write, it's write by hook or by crook. And the unlucky individual who has acquired—for the sake of his independence, says he—some "second trade" (but what then was his first?) has hardly—journalist, civil servant, insurance salesman—any other resource: he has himself put down as sick. For his part, Sade puts himself down as guilty. They're jailing rebels this year? He's a rebel. The indulgent are in trouble? "I am free to let off fools if I so please." Plotters? Why not be a plotter? The impious and the libertine? There's a category I fit into perfectly. When all else fails, there's always madness. You could read, nothing stood in the way of your writing—and your fury at being held captive didn't hurt—in the madhouses and prisons of the eighteenth century, fairly mild places, furthermore, for a nobleman up on nobody knew exactly what count. "What's that one in here for?" Sade's jailers used to wonder. "Seems like they got him for conspiracy against God." "Ever heard the like of it?"

Yes, the argument is plausible. But shall we look a little farther? Sometimes a man will pursue fame, love, independence with such fervor that he overshoots the mark, with such passion that his passion will sometimes come to scorn what at first it sought, to deride the meager products of such efforts. The glory you strove so hard after, was it this tattle in the press, these silly interviews, this being elected to Academies, and this popular tune whose author nobody knows? Liberty, was it this (scanty) applause from the front rows; these defiant approbations; these votes which tomorrow will swing against you? No, in order to be satisfied with a pittance, pride is not enough, you need vanity of the most stupid sort. Vanity, and also a fondness for being shortchanged, a desire to be cuckolded. At this point the driving forces within a man undergo a mysterious change in direction; and the victor senses he has been vanquished by his victory; and the lover flees his mistress, and for the spirit that lusted after riches, poverty is now the mark of well-being. Our hero delights in and at the same time is exasperated by the silence his extravagant pretensions create around him; the lover of liberty turns around and goes back to prison. Totally disgusted.

Causes of a disappointment

Yes, the explanation is plausible. However, I cannot say that it greatly pleases me. Let us return to our ill-starred lambs.

IX. SADE HIMSELF, OR THE SOLUTION TO THE RIDDLE

Sadism did not used to be much talked about. Nowadays it is, in the newspapers and in serious books. The change is for the better. For this is an entirely natural and immediate trait in man, a trait he has possessed since the very beginning and which, when you come down to it, may be summed up in a few words: we demand to be happy; we also demand that others be rather less happy than we. That this trait may, under the pressure of circumstances, degenerate into frightful manias—this is a matter upon which psychiatrists are qualified to speak, not I. Whether Sade was a sadist or not I don't know: the trial records shed little light upon the question. In the case we are best acquainted with—the Marseilles affair—Sade figures as a masochist, which is the very opposite. I see that at least once he flatly refused to be sadistic in spite of all sorts of encouragement: his past grievances, his feelings of the moment, and the chorus of the Section of Piques. But it could be argued that the true sadist is the one who declines to practice sadism on easy terms, who will not stand to be told when and where to give expression to his idiosyncrasy. Each of us is proud in his own way.

Masochism is incomprehensible

Over the last fifty years or so we have got into the habit of talking about *masochism* (which is what I have just done) as we do about sadism. With the same naturalness, in the same matter-of-fact way. As if it were a human characteristic no less simple, no less necessary than sadism; and no less susceptible of becoming a mania either. I have no objection to that. But if it is a natural characteristic, you'll admit it is a very queer one; queer almost to the point of being incredible; and that to call it natural requires considerable forbearance on our part.

If I take the eye, for example, I note that it is subject to a wide range of anomalies. It can be farsighted, or myopic. It can present yet rarer and (like sadism) yet more distinguished defects: amaurosis or diplopia. It is sometimes able to put its faultiness to profit: it can be nyctalopic, and content to be so. (Just as a sadist turns his sadism to advantage; after all, a well-ordered society can hardly do without public executioners; at any rate, without judges and nurses and surgeons.) So far so good. But never, never has there been found an eye that was afflicted by buzzings, hyperacusia or colored audition. Well, that, all else being equal, is what some claim in behalf of masochism.

When pain experienced by others gives me pleasure, this pleasure I feel is obviously an unusual feeling; and doubtless a reprehensible one. In any case it is a clear and comprehensible feeling, and an article upon it can be included in the *Encyclopedia*. But that my *own* pain be pleasure to me, that my humiliation be to me a dignification —this is no longer reprehensible or unusual, it is simply obscure, and it is only too easy for me to reply that if it is pain, it isn't pleasure, if it's dignification, then it's not humiliation. If it's . . . And so on and so forth. Yet, however that may be, there does indeed exist, nobody will deny it, something which can be rightly termed masochism. To be more precise, there do indeed exist men, and women also, whom we must call masochists.

For there are some who seek nothing so eagerly as mockery and ridicule, and who thrive better on shame than on bread and wine: Philip of Neri, who used to caper in the streets and shave only one side of his face, preferred to pass for a madman than for a saint; the sheik Abu Yazid al Bisthami would give urchins a couple of walnuts in exchange for a slap. There is no lack of persons who to their friends —and to those foremost among all their friends, themselves —fondly wish "suffering, abandon, infirmity, ill-treatment and dishonor and profound self-contempt and the martyr-dom of self-distrust."[12] And others too who say with the Portuguese nun: "Increase the number of my afflictions." To anyone contending that behind whatever it may appear to be this amounts to a clever attempt to assure oneself of the weal which follows after woe, and the honor which follows dishonor, and the triumph of esteem which follows after the ordeal of disdain, in keeping with some natural law of compensation, the reply would have to be that he had not very well grasped the question. But let me continue.

Masochism is a universal trait

We see other persons who steer a steady course toward vexations and abuse, who, no matter where they happen to be, are extraordinarily alert and, through the workings of some unerring instinct, as if sensitized to the presence of a

---

[12] Nietzsche: *The Will to Power*.

possible source of mistreatment and as if fascinated in advance, attracted, summoned by the cruel potentialities they have somehow detected in a man everybody else sees as a decent and unexceptional chap. (Thus Justine . . .) Or else, of their own accord, with peculiar willfulness march straight to where prison, trials, and death await them. (Thus Sade . . .)

Let there be no mistake: I do not pretend to be clearing up the mystery, I do not in the least claim to be explaining a difficult fact, a truly mysterious fact, which defies analysis now and has never yielded to it in the past. No. Instructed by experience, my inclination would instead be to acknowledge that in masochism we are dealing with something veritable but incomprehensible; with, to put it more vaguely, an *occurrence*—a frequent occurrence, perhaps, but at any rate an obscure one, and one which remains impenetrable to my intelligence. (After all, why these people are the way they are is more than I can fathom.) In short, I concede to mystery its share in all this—and, doing so, I am at once rewarded for my modesty. I venture no comments about proud spirits who seek silence or greedy spirits who seek poverty (for I must own that the explanation I offered a little while ago was, while banal, rather farfetched: that the proud spirit, the greedy or the libertarian spirit, having been acquainted beforehand with the signs of glory, wealth, liberty, were in a poor position to complain afterward).

For if it happens that man sometimes experiences that which is not altogether human, and to which no familiar habits or everyday usages apply—but natural man is not *other* than civilized man, nor I *other* than other human beings, nor kindliness *other* than perfidy, nor pain *other* than pleasure—sadism, in the final analysis, is probably nothing else than the approach to and, as it were the (perhaps maladroit and certainly odious) testing of a truth so difficult and so mysterious that once it is acknowledged as such, the problems we have been helpless to resolve—and the very riddles Sade puts to Justine—become instantly and miraculously transparent. It is as though it were enough for

The riddles find their solution

me, in order to be able to see clearly (to see my way clearly through questions and a world both mightily confused and absurd), to have once and for all taken obscurity into account.

Here it will be said to me, and very justly said, that the truth we are seeking is too inaccessible, and is as foreign to our language as to our understanding. So indeed it is, and it should be plain that, rather than express it, I am simply endeavoring, once having set aside a space for it to occupy, to encircle it, to surround it. Though he fails to formulate it in thought or speech, the man who has suffered it one time and a thousand times, who has experienced it, still retains the resource of living it, of being it. And I finally understand in what sense Sade, like Pascal, Nietzsche, or Rimbaud, *paid;* in what sense also he was able to merit the title of *divine* as it was conferred upon him by a popular idiom which sometimes is of greater justness than the judgments of critics, sometimes rings truer than the lines of poets.

There is another resource, however.

X. THE ACCOMPLICE

In a curious book by Crébillon, *The Letters of the Marquise de M.,* tender affection and jealousy, the need for love and ensuing regrets, desire and coquetry are rendered with great subtlety, with such subtlety that at no stage in the story does the reader ever know for sure whether or not the Marquise and the Count have been to bed together. But in *Justine* it's quite the reverse. And Justine's amorous adventures—very diverse, very involuntary—are shown us in the greatest detail without our ever having an inkling of what it might be our heroine is feeling—desire, love, loathing, indifference. Truly, it is difficult to say. And Sade knows it only too well. He knows it only too well because Justine is Sade himself.

That is Justine's secret. A strange secret. A hard secret to get at, but not because it is nameless or unnamable. Hard to get at because, on the contrary, it already has its name because it has, if anything, been identified a little too often, under the name of that good Austrian novelist who came into the world a hundred years after Sade, and who gave his cruel heroines a riding crop to wield and sometimes a mink coat to wear. Well I know that Nature encompasses every taste, every mania. This particular one is no more harmful or more unpleasant than any other. Nor is it any less. But for mysteriousness it is not to be surpassed. It is the sole passion that cannot be thwarted without encouraging it, punished without rewarding it. Perfectly incomprehensible: absurd. What remains to be said? Only that the critic can turn this absurdity into a rationale.

It is now her turn to speak, the discreet, modest, satiated Justine Sade chose for his accomplice.

Sade

by Maurice Blanchot

A hundred and fifty years ago there appeared in Holland *La Nouvelle Justine, ou les Malheurs de la Vertu, suivie de l'Histoire de Juliette, sa soeur.* This monumental work, which had been preceded by several shorter versions, had grown longer with each successive revision until it reached the gigantic proportions of four thousand pages in this final form. This almost endless, overwhelming work immediately horrified the world.

If there is an *Enfer* in libraries—a special section for works deemed unfit for human consumption—it is for such a book. No literature of any period has seen a work so scandalous, one which has so profoundly wounded the thoughts and feelings of men. Today, when the writings of Henry Miller cause us to quake and quail, who would dare to compete with Sade's licentiousness? Yes, the claim can be made: we have here the most scandalous work ever written. Is this not reason enough for us to turn our attention to it? What! You mean to say we have here the opportunity to acquaint ourselves with a work beyond which no other writer, at any time, has ever managed to venture; we have, so to speak, a veritable absolute in our hands, in this relative world of letters, and we make no attempt to question or consult it? You mean to say it does not occur to us to ask *why* it is unique, why it cannot be exceeded, what there is about it which is so outrageous, so eternally too strong for man to stomach? Curious neglect. But can it be that the purity of the scandal is solely dependent upon this neglect? When one considers the precautions that history has taken to make a prodigious enigma out of Sade, when one thinks of those twenty-seven years behind bars, of that fettered and forbidden existence, when the sequestration affects not only a man's life but his afterlife—so much so that the condemnation of his work to seclusion seems to condemn him as well, still alive, to some eternal prison—then one is led to wonder whether the censors and judges who claim to immure Sade are not actually serving him instead, are not fulfilling the most fervent wishes of his libertinage, he who always aspired to the solitude of the earth's entrails, to the mystery of a subterranean and reclusive existence. In a dozen different ways, Sade formulated the idea that man's wildest excesses call for secrecy, for the obscurity of the farthest depths, the inviolable solitude of a cell. Now, the strange thing is that it is the guardians of morality who, by condemning Sade to solitary confinement, have thereby made themselves the most faithful accomplices of his immorality. It was Sade's mother-in-law, the prudish Madame de Montreuil, who, by turning his life into a prison, at the same time made of it a masterpiece of infamy and debauchery. And, similarly, if today, a hundred and fifty years later, *Justine and Juliette* still seems to us the most scandalous, the most subversive of books, it is because it is almost impossible to read it: every possible measure has been taken—by the author, the publishers, and with the added help of universal Morality—to make certain this book remains a secret, a wholly unreadable work, as much for its length, the way it was written, and its endless repetitions, as for the force of its descriptions and its ferocious indecency, all of which could not help but secure its damnation. A scandalous, scarcely approachable book, which no one can render public. But a book which also shows that there is no scandal where there is first no respect, and that wherever the scandal is extraordinary the respect is extreme. Who, indeed, is more respected than Sade? How many people, still today, profoundly believe that all they have to do is hold this accursed book in their hands for a few moments for Rousseau's arrogant warning to come true: Any girl who reads but a single page of this book will be lost? Such respect is indeed a great treasure for a literature and a civilization. One can therefore not refrain from making this one discreet request, addressed to all Sade's publishers present and future: when dealing with Sade, at least respect the scandalous aspect.

Luckily, Sade defends himself rather well. Not only his work but his thinking remains impenetrable—and this in spite of the fact that both abound in detailed theories, which he expounds and repeats over and over again with disconcerting patience, and in spite of the fact that he reasons with impeccable clarity and not inconsiderable logic. He has a penchant—and even a passion—for systems. He expounds and affirms and offers proof; he comes back to the same problem a hundred times over (and a hundred is a conservative figure), he studies it from every angle, he considers every possible objection and answers them all, then manages to come up with some further objections and replies to them as well. And since what he says is usually simple enough, since his language is rich but precise and firm, it would seem that nothing should be more simple in dealing with Sade than to elucidate the ideology which, in his case, is inseparable from passion. And yet, what *is* the gist of Sade's thought? What in fact *did* he say? What is the scheme, the order of this system? Where does it begin and where does it end? Is there, indeed, more than the shadow of a system in the probing of this mind, so obsessed as it is with reason? And why is it that so many well co-ordinated principles fail to form the solid whole which they ought to and which, at least on the surface, they in fact seem to? That too remains unclear. Such is the first peculiar characteristic of Sade: his theories and ideas are constantly generating and unleashing irrational forces to which they are bound. These forces simultaneously animate and thwart the theories, in such a way that the theories resist at first but then eventually yield; they seek to dominate the insurgent force, finally do, but only after they have unleashed other obscure forces, which bear the theories further along, deflect them from their course, and distort them. The result is that everything which is said is clear, but seems to be at the mercy of something left unsaid, and a little later on what has not been explicitly stated does indeed appear and is reintegrated by logic; but then this in its turn succumbs to the influence of some other, still hidden force, until finally everything *is* expressed, is revealed, but also everything is plunged back again into the obscurity of unformulated and inexpressible thoughts.

The reader is often ill at ease when faced with this thought which is made clear only by a further thought which, for the present, cannot be clarified; and he becomes even more uncomfortable as he realizes that Sade's stated principles—what we may term his basic philosophy—appears to be simplicity itself. This philosophy is one of self-interest, of absolute egoism: Each of us must do exactly as he pleases, each of us is bound by one law alone, that of his own pleasure. This morality is based upon the primary fact of absolute solitude. Sade has stated it, and repeated it, in every conceivable form: Nature wills that we be born alone, there is no real contact or relationship possible between one person and another. The only rule of conduct for me to follow, therefore, is to prefer whatever affects me pleasurably and, conversely, to hold as naught anything which, as a result of my preferences, may cause harm to others. The greatest pain inflicted on others is of less account than my own pleasure. Little do I care if the price I have to pay for my least delight is an awesome accumulation of atrocious crimes, for pleasure flatters me, it is within, while the effects of crime, being outside me, do not affect me.

These principles are clear. We find them reiterated and developed in a thousand ways through some twenty volumes. Sade never tires of them. What he infinitely enjoys is to square them against the prevailing theories of the time, the theories of man's equality before Nature and the law. He then proposes this kind of reasoning: Since all men are equal in the eyes of Nature, I therefore have the right, because of this identity, not to sacrifice myself for the preservation of others, their ruin being indispensable to my happiness. Or else he will propound a kind of Declaration of the Rights of Eroticism, with this axiom—equally valid for men and women alike—as a fundamental precept: Give yourself to whomsoever desires you, take from whomever you please. "What evil do I do, what crime do I commit when, upon meeting some lovely creature, I say: 'Avail me of that part of you which can give me a moment's satisfaction and, if you wish, make full use of that part of mine which may prove agreeable to you'?" To Sade, such propositions seem irrefutable. For pages on end he invokes the equality of individuals and the reciprocity of rights, without ever realizing that his arguments, far from being buttressed by these lofty principles, are becoming meaningless because of them. "Never can an act of possession be exercised on a free person," he declares. But what conclusion does he draw from this? Not that he has lost the right to perpetrate violence on anyone or to abuse such a person for his own pleasure, against that person's will, but rather that no one, in order to refuse himself to Sade, may invoke exclusive attachments, a right of "possession." For Sade, the equality of all human beings is the right to equal use of them all, freedom is the power to bend others to his own will.

To see formulas of this sort piling up on top of each other leads one to conclude that there is something missing in Sade's reasoning process, some lacuna or madness. One has the feeling of grappling with the product of a profoundly disturbed mind, strangely suspended over the void. But suddenly logic reasserts itself, the objections vanish, and little by little the system takes shape. Justine, who, we recall, represents Virtue in Sade's world— Virtue which is tenacious, humble, continually wretched and oppressed but never convinced of its errors—suddenly declares in a most reasonable manner: Your principles presuppose power. If my happiness consists in never taking into account the interests of others, in exploiting every opportunity to hurt or injure them, there will perforce come a day when the interests of others will likewise consist in doing me harm; in the name of what shall I then protest? "Can the person who isolates himself do battle with the whole world?" To this classic objection, Sade's protagonist replies, both explicitly and implicitly, in a number of ways, and these replies gradually lead us into the heart of his universe. Yes, he starts off by saying, my right is the right of power. And indeed Sade's cast of characters is composed primarily of a tiny number of omnipotent men who have had the energy and initiative to raise themselves above the law and place themselves outside the pale of prejudice, men who feel that Nature has singled them out and, feeling themselves worthy of this distinction, strive to assuage their passions by any and all means.

These peerless men generally belong to a privileged class: they are dukes and kings, the Pope, himself issued from the nobility; they benefit from the advantages of their rank and fortune, and from the impunity which their high station confers upon them. To their birth they owe the inequality which they are content to exploit and perfect by the exercise of an implacable despotism. They are the most powerful because they belong to a powerful class. "I call people," says one of them, "that vile and reprehensible class which manages to survive only by dint of sweat and toil; all who breathe must join together against this abject class."

Nonetheless, there can be no doubt that, although these sovereigns of debauchery generally concentrate in themselves and to their own advantage the full inequality of classes, this is but a historical circumstance to which Sade, in his value judgments, pays not the slightest heed. Sade discerned clearly that, at the time he was writing, power was a social category, that it was part and parcel of the organization of society such as it existed both before and after the Revolution. But he also believes that power (like solitude, moreover) is not merely a state but a choice and a conquest, and that only he is powerful who by his own will and energy knows how to make himself so. Actually, Sade's heroes are recruited from two opposing milieux: from among the highest and the lowest, from among the mighty of the world and, at the opposite pole, fished up from the sewers and cesspools of the lower depths. At the outset, both these groups have something extreme working for them, for the extreme of poverty is as powerful a stimulus as are the dazzling possibilities that fortune offers. When one is a Dubois or a Durand, one revolts against the law because one is too far beneath it to be able to conform to the law without perishing. And when one is a Saint-Fond or the Duc de Blangis, one is too far above the law to be able to submit to it without debasement. This is why, in Sade's works, the apology for crime derives from two contradictory principles: for some men, inequality is a fact of Nature; certain persons are necessarily slaves and victims, they have no rights, they are nothing, against them any act, any crime is permitted. Whence those frenzied eulogies to tyranny, those political constitutions bent on making it forever impossible for the weak to seek vengeance or the poor to grow rich. "Let it be clearly understood," says Verneuil,

> that 'tis among Nature's intentions that there necessarily be a class of individuals who by their birth and inherent weakness shall remain essentially subject to the other class.

> The laws are not made for the people. . . . The basic precept of any wise government is to make certain that the people shall not encroach upon the authority of the masters.

And Saint-Fond:

> The people shall be kept in a state of slavery which will make it quite impossible for them ever to attempt to dominate the wealthy or debase their properties and possessions.

Or again:

> All that goes under the name of crimes of libertinage shall never be punished, save in the slave castes.

Here, it would seem, we have the most blatant, the wildest theoretical apology for absolute despotism ever formulated. But suddenly the perspective shifts. And what does Dubois say?

> Nature has caused us all to be equals born; if fate is pleased to intervene and upset the primary scheme of things, it is up to us to correct its caprices and, through our own skill, to repair the usurpations of the strongest. . . . So long as our good faith and patience serve only to double the weight of our chains, our crimes will be as Virtues, and we would be fools indeed to abstain from them when they can lessen the yoke wherewith their cruelty bears us down.

And she adds: for the poor, crime alone can open the doors to life; villainy is the recompense for injustice, just as theft is the revenge of the dispossessed. Thus the lines are clearly drawn: equality, inequality; freedom to oppress, revolt against the oppressor; these are merely provisional arguments by which Sadean man, depending on his position in the social hierarchy, asserts his right to power. Actually, the distinction between those who require crime in order to survive and those for whom crime is the sole source of pleasure, will soon vanish. Madame Dubois becomes a baroness. Madame Durand, a fourth-rate poisoner, ascends to a higher station than that occupied by the selfsame princesses whom Juliette unhesitatingly sacrifices to her. Counts become bandit chieftains, the head of a group of highwaymen (as in *Faxelange*), or else innkeepers, the better to despoil and murder fools. Most of the victims of libertinage, however, are selected from among the aristocracy; they must be of noble birth. It is to his mother, the Countess, that the Marquis de Bressac declares with superb contempt: "Thy days belong to me, and mine are sacred."

Now, what happens? A few men have become powerful. Some were bequeathed power by birth, but they have also demonstrated that they deserve it by the way in which they have accrued it and enjoyed it. Others have risen to power, and the sign of their success is that, once having resorted to crime to acquire power, they use it to acquire the freedom to commit any crime whatsoever. Such then is Sade's world: a few people who have reached the pinnacle, and around them an infinite, nameless dust, an anonymous mass of creatures which has neither rights nor power. Let us see what now happens to the rule of absolute egoism. I do whatever I please, says Sade's hero, all I know, all I recognize is my own pleasure, and to make certain I get it I torture and kill. You threaten me with a like fate the day I shall happen to meet someone whose happiness is dependent on torturing and killing me. But I have acquired power precisely in order to raise myself above this threat. Whenever Sade comes up with answers such as these, we can feel ourselves slipping toward an area of his thought which is sustained solely by the obscure forces which lurk therein. What is this power which fears neither chance nor law, which exposes itself disdainfully to the terrible risks of a rule conceived in these terms: I shall do you all the harm I please, you may do me all the harm you can—under the assumption that such a rule will invariably operate to its advantage? Now, the point is that all it takes is a single exception for these principles to disintegrate and collapse: if the Powerful One, whose sole purpose is pleasure, ever once encounters misfortune, if in the exercise of his tyranny he once becomes a victim, he will be lost, the law of pleasure will appear a sham, a lie, and man, instead of wishing to triumph through excess, will once again revert to that mediocrity that ever casts a worried eye in fear of the slightest evil which may befall him.

Sade knows this. "And what if luck should turn against you?" Justine asks him. Sade's reply is to delve deeper into his system and demonstrate that to him who casts his lot wholeheartedly with evil, nothing evil can ever happen. This is the basic tenet, the very cornerstone of his work: to Virtue, nothing but misfortune; to Vice, the reward of constant prosperity. There are times, especially in the early versions of *Justine,* when this assertion seems to be a simple meretricious hypothesis which the author, always adroitly maneuvering the tale to suit his own needs, advances as proof. One has the impression that Sade is spinning fables and being taken in by them when he entrusts matters to a black Providence whose function it is to shower blessings on all those who have opted for evil. But in *La Nouvelle Justine* and in *Juliette* everything changes. There can be no doubt that Sade is profoundly convinced of at least this: that the man of absolute egoism can never fall upon evil days; better, that he will, without exception, be forever happy, and happy to the highest degree. A mad idea? Perhaps. But with Sade the idea is allied to forces so violent that they finally render irrefutable, in his eyes, the ideas they support. In actual fact, the translation of this conviction into doctrine is not at all that simple. Sade resorts to several solutions, he tries them endlessly, although none can really ever satisfy him. The first is strictly verbal: it consists in repudiating the social contract which, according to Sade, is the safeguard of the weak and, theoretically, constitutes a grave menace for the powerful. In practice, however, the Powerful One knows full well how to utilize the law to consolidate his advantages. But if he does this, then he is powerful only through the law, and it is the law which, in principle, incarnates power. Except in time of war, or during a period of anarchy, the Sovereign is merely the sovereign, for even if the law helps him to crush the weak, it is nevertheless through an authority created in the name of the weak that he becomes master, substituting the false bond of a pact for the naked strength of man. "My neighbors' passions frighten me infinitely less than do the law's injustices, for my neighbors' passions are contained by mine, whilst nothing constrains, nothing checks the injustices of the law." Nothing checks the inequities of the law for the simple reason that there is nothing above it, hence it is always superior to me. This is why, even if it serves me, it also oppresses me. This is also why Sade, whatever affinity he may have had for the Revolution and however much he was able to identify himself with it, was drawn to it only to the extent that it constituted for a short time the possibility of a regime without law, since it represented a transition period from one set of laws to the other. Sade gave voice to this idea in the following curious observations:

> The rule of law is inferior to that of anarchy: the most obvious proof of what I assert is the fact that any government is obliged to plunge itself into anarchy whenever it aspires to remake its constitution. In order to

abrogate its former laws, it is compelled to establish a revolutionary regime in which there is no law: this regime finally gives birth to new laws, but this second state is necessarily less pure than the first, since it derives from it. . . .

Actually, Power adapts itself to, and refuses to acknowledge the authority of, any regime; in the midst of a world denatured by law, it creates for itself an enclave in which all law is silenced, a closed place wherein all legal sovereignty is ignored rather than contested. In the statutes of the *Société des Amis du Crime*, there is one article which prohibits all political activity.

> The Society respects the government under which it lives, and if it places itself above the law it is because one of its principles specifies that man does not have the power to make laws in conflict with the laws of Nature; but the disorders of the Society's members, being always interior, must never scandalize either the governed or the governments.

And if in Sade's writings it sometimes does come to pass that the Power undertakes some political action or becomes involved in a revolution—as is the case with Borchamps who conspires with the Loge du Nord to overthrow the Swedish monarchy—the reasons which lead him to do so are quite unrelated to any desire to emancipate the law. "Why do you so loathe Swedish despotism?" one of the conspirators is asked. "Jealousy, ambition, pride, despair at the thought of being dominated, my own desire to tyrannize others." "But does the happiness of the people have no bearing upon your opinions?" "All I am interested in is my own."

If pressed, Power can always maintain that it has nothing to fear from the ordinary man, who is weak, and likewise nothing to fear from the law, which it refuses to recognize as being legitimate. The real problem is the relationship of the powerful among themselves. These peerless men, who come from the highest as well as the lowest echelons of society, necessarily meet: the similarity of their tastes brings them together; the fact that they are exceptions, by setting them both apart, also brings them together. But what relation can there be between exceptions? Sade certainly pondered this question at great length. As always, he moves from one possible solution to another until finally, at the end of his chain of logic, he brings forth from this enigma the only word that matters to him. When he devises a secret society governed by strict conventions, the purpose of which is to curb excesses, he can cite the precedent of numerous similar societies then much in vogue. For Sade lived at a time when the freemasonry of libertinage and free-masonry itself led to the emergence, in the midst of a society in ruins, of a great number of secret societies, clandestine "colleges" founded on the complicity of passions and on a mutual respect for dangerous ideas. The *Société des Amis du Crime* is an effort of this kind. Its statutes, studied and analyzed at great length, forbid its members from indulging in any displays of ferocious passion among themselves, stipulating that these passions can only be sati-ated in two seraglios which are to be peopled by members of the virtuous classes. When they are in each other's company, the mem-bers must "give themselves over to their freest fantasies, and do everything"; but, says Sade, "no cruel passions allowed." We can easily see why: it is a question of avoiding at all costs the encounter, on a terrain where evil would become their undoing, of those who expect only pleasure from evil. Superior libertines are allies, but never meet.

Such a compromise cannot satisfy Sade. It must therefore be pointed out that, although the heroes of his books are constantly drawn into close alliance with one another by the conventions which determine the limits of their power and superimpose order on chaos, the possibility of betrayal is forever present: between ac-complices there is a constantly mounting tension, so much so that they ultimately feel themselves less bound by the oath that unites them than by the mutual need to violate this oath. This situation makes the final part of *Juliette* extremely dramatic. Juliette is a woman of principle. She respects libertinage, and when she meets an accomplished criminal, the perfection of the crime for which he is responsible and the power of destruction which he represents not only induce her to join forces with him but, what is more, lead her to spare his life if she can, even when this alliance becomes dangerous for her. Thus, even though she is in danger of being killed by the monster Minski, she refuses to have him murdered. "This man is too great a scourge to humanity for me to deprive the world of him," she says. And then there is another character, the author of veritable masterpieces of lubricity: yes, him she finally does destroy, but only because she has noticed that, upon emerging from these orgies of blood, he has developed the habit of retiring to a chapel to purify his soul. Is the perfect criminal therefore presumed to be exempt from the passions in which he indulges? Can it be that there is a principle, an ultimate principle, which guarantees that the libertine can never be either the object or the victim of his own libertinage? "You have told me a hundred times," Madame de Donis says to Juliette, "that libertines never harm one another. Do you care to refute this maxim?" The reply is clear: Juliette does indeed refute it; Madame de Donis is sacrificed. And gradually the most beloved confederates in crime, the most respected companions of debauchery perish, victims either of their own fidelity or their perjury, or of the lassitude or the ardor of their feelings. Nothing can save them, nothing excuses them. Scarcely has Juliette sent her best friends to their death than she turns toward new allies and exchanges with them vows of eternal confidence. Vows they themselves find risible, since they know full well that the only reason they assign any limitations to their excesses is in order to be in a position to harvest the pleasure which comes from exceeding them.

The following exchange of conversation among several masters of crime fairly describes this situation. One of the criminals, Gernand, says of his cousin Bressac: "You know, he is my heir. And yet I dare say he is not in any hurry for my life: we have the same tastes, we think in the same way, he knows that he has a sure friend in me." That's all very true, says Bressac, I shall never harm a hair on your head. And yet this Bressac points out that another of their relatives, d'Esterval, who makes a specialty of slitting the throats of passing travelers, had come close to murdering him. "Yes," says d'Esterval, "but as a relative, never as a companion in debauchery." But Bressac remains skeptical, and, indeed, they concur that this consideration almost failed to stop Dorothée, d'Esterval's wife. And what does this Dorothée reply? "Your praise is in your death warrant. The terrible habit I have of immolating the men who please me means that your sentence is passed and inscribed right next to my declaration of love." All of which is quite clear. But under these conditions what becomes of Sade's proposition concerning happiness through Evil? What happens to that certainty that the man of all vices will always be happy, as he who has but a single virtue will perforce be plagued by misfortune? Actually, Sade's work is strewn with the corpses of libertines struck down at the very pinnacle of their glory. Justine is not alone in her wretchedness; misfortune strikes the strongest and most energetic of Sade's heroines as well, the superb Clairwill, as it strikes Saint-Fond, murdered by Noirceuil, and the licentious Borghese, who is hurled headlong into the crater of a volcano; as, indeed, it strikes literally hundreds of perfect criminals. Strange denouements, singular triumphs for these perverse men! How can Sade's mad reason remain blind to all these many contradictions it contains? But it is precisely these contradictions which, for Sade, provide him with his proof, and this is why:

A cursory reading of *Justine* can be deceiving; one may erroneously think it no more than a rather coarse and vulgar piece of fiction. We see this virtuous girl who is forever being raped, beaten, tortured, the victim of a fate bent on her destruction. And when we read *Juliette* we follow a depraved girl as she flies from pleasure to pleasure. It is hardly likely that we shall be convinced by such a plot. But the point is that we have overlooked the book's most important aspect: the reader who is merely attentive to the sadness of one and the satisfaction of the other has neglected to remark that the two sisters' stories are basically identical, that everything which happens to Justine also happens to Juliette, that both go through the same gantlet of experiences and are put to the same painful tests. Juliette is also cast into prison, roundly flogged, sentenced to the rack, endlessly tortured. Hers is a hideous existence, but here is the rub: from these ills, these agonies, she derives pleasure; these tortures delight her. "How delicious are the irons wrought by the crime one adores." Not to mention those uncommon tortures which are so terrible for Justine and which, for Juliette, are a source of pure delight. In one scene set in the château of a wicked magistrate, poor Justine is subjected to tortures which are truly execrable. Her pain is indescribable. The reader is taken completely aback by such injustice. And then what happens? A thoroughly depraved girl who has witnessed the scene and become inflamed by the spectacle demands that the same torture be inflicted on her, right there on the spot. And from it she derives the most exquisite pleasure. Thus it is true that Virtue is the source of man's unhappiness, not because it exposes him to painful or unfortunate circumstances but because, if Virtue were eliminated, what was once painful then becomes pleasurable, and torments become voluptuous.

For Sade, sovereign man is impervious to evil because no one can do him any harm. He is a man possessed of every passion, and his passions are slaked by any and every thing. We have had a tendency to take Jean Paulhan's conclusions that Sade's sadism conceals a contrary propensity as a paradox too witty and too clever to be true.[1] But we can see that this idea is the very heart of Sade's system. The absolute egoist is he who is able to transform everything disagreeable into something likable, everything repugnant into something attractive. Like the bedroom philosopher, he declares: "I love everything, I enjoy everything, my desire is to commingle all kinds and contraries." And this is why Sade, in his *Les 120 Journées,* has set himself the gigantic task of drawing up the complete inventory of anomalies and aberrations, listing every kind of human possibility. In order to be at the mercy of nothing, it was necessary for him to experience everything.

> You shall know nothing if you have not known everything, and if you are timid enough to stop with what is natural, Nature will elude your grasp forever.

One understands why the sorrowful Justine's objection: "And what if luck should turn against you?" cannot upset the criminal soul. For if indeed luck does reverse itself and turn into misfortune, the latter will actually be no more than another facet of fortune itself, as much to be desired and as satisfying as the former. But you are risking the gallows! You may end in the most ignominious of deaths. "That," replies the libertine, "is my most cherished desire." "Ah, Juliette," Borghese says,

> if only my transgressions can lead me like the last of creatures to the fate to which their wild abandon conducts them. The gallows itself would be for me a voluptuous throne, and there would I face death by relishing the pleasure of expiring a victim of my crimes.

And another:

---

[1] M. Blanchot is referring, of course, to Paulhan's "The Marquis de Sade and His Accomplice" which appeared three years before his own study on Sade.

The true libertine loves even the reproaches he receives for the unspeakable deeds he has done. Have we not seen some who loved the very tortures human vengeance was readying for them, who submitted to them joyfully, who beheld the scaffold as a throne of glory upon which they would have been most grieved not to perish with the same courage they ha.. displayed in the loathsome exercise of their heinous crimes? There is the man at the ultimate degree of meditated corruption.

Against a Power such as this, what can the law do? It believes it is punishing him, and actually it is rewarding him; it exalts him by debasing him. Similarly, what can the libertine do, what injury inflict upon his peer? He may one day betray and destroy him, but this betrayal is the source of savage pleasure to him who is the victim of it and who views such a betrayal as the confirmation of all his suspicions and can die reveling in the thought that he has been the occasion for yet a new crime (not to mention other joys).

One of Sade's most curious heroines is named Amélie. She lives in Sweden, and one day she seeks out Borchamps, the conspirator whom we have already mentioned. Borchamps, hoping for a gigantic massacre, has just betrayed all his fellow plotters and delivered them into the hands of the king. This betrayal has fired Amélie's enthusiasm. "I love your ferocity," she tells him.

Swear to me that I shall one day be your victim. Since the age of fifteen, my mind has been ablaze, obsessed with the idea of perishing a victim of libertinage's most cruel passions. I do not wish to die tomorrow, no doubt; my extravagance does not go that far. But in no other manner do I wish to die: to become, in expiring, the occasion of a crime is an idea that makes my head spin.

Strange head, full worthy of this reply: "I love your mind to the point of madness, and I believe that you and I will do splendid things together." Then: "There's no denying it: she's rotten, putrified."

Thus, everything begins to grow clear: to the integral man, who is at his fullest, there is no possible evil. If he injures others, the result is voluptuous; injury endured at their hands is sheer delight. Virtue pleases him because Virtue is weak and he crushes it; Vice pleases him because he finds pleasure in the chaos that results from it, even though it be at his expense. If he lives, there is no circumstance, no event that he cannot turn into happiness.

And if he dies, he finds an even greater happiness in his death, and in the knowledge of his destruction he sees the crowning achievement of a life whose sole justification lay in the need to destroy. He is therefore inaccessible to others. He is impervious to all attacks, nothing can rob him of his power to be himself and to enjoy himself. That is the primary meaning of his solitude. Even if he in his turn seemingly becomes a victim and a thrall, the violence of the passions he knows how to slake in any situation assures him of his sovereignty and makes him feel that in any circumstance, in life as in death, he remains omnipotent. It is for this reason that, despite the analogy of the descriptions, it seems only fair to leave to Sacher-Masoch the paternity of masochism, and the paternity of sadism to Sade. The pleasure Sade's heroes find in degradation never lessens their self-possession, and abjection adds to their stature. Shame, remorse, a penchant for punishment— all such feelings are foreign to them. When Saint-Fond says to Juliette: "My pride is such that I should like to be served by persons kneeling, and never speak to that vile scum called people save through an interpreter," she replies, without a trace of irony, by asking: "But don't the caprices of libertinage compel you to come down from such heights?" To which Saint-Fond replies: "For minds as organized as ours, that humiliation serves as an exquisite flattery to our pride." And Sade adds in a note: "This is readily understood; one does what no one else does; one is therefore unique." On the moral level, the same prideful satisfaction in the feeling that one is an exile from humanity:

> The world must tremble upon learning of the crimes we shall have committed. Men must be made to blush and feel ashamed at belonging to the same species as we do. I demand that a monument be raised to commemorate this crime and signal it to the whole world, and that our names be graven upon it by our own hands.

To be unique, unique among one's own species, is indeed the sign of true sovereignty, and we shall see to what absolute limits Sade has taken this category, and what absolute meaning he has given it.

The whole scheme is beginning to be even clearer. And yet at the stage to which we have progressed we also feel that it is also becoming very dark indeed. This deft movement by which the

Unique Being eludes the influence and control of others is far from crystal clear. In certain respects, it is a sort of stoic insensibility, which seems to assume man's perfect autonomy with respect to the world. But at the same time it is the exact opposite, for the Unique Being, being independent of all the others who are incapable of harming him, immediately declares complete dominion over them. And it is not because others are powerless against him that torture, the stab of the dagger, and debasing maneuvers they devise against him leave him intact, but because he can do whatever he wishes to others that even the pain others cause him affords him the pleasure of power and helps him exercise his sovereignty. Now, this situation becomes very embarrassing. For the moment that "to be master of myself" means "to be master of others," the moment my independence does not derive from my autonomy but from the dependence of others upon me, it becomes obvious that I remain bound to the others and have need of them, if only to reduce them to nothing. Sade's commentators have often pointed out this difficulty. It is far from certain whether Sade himself was aware of it, and one of the original aspects of this "exceptional" philosophy perhaps comes from this fact: when one is not Sade there is a crucial problem created, through which the relations of mutual solidarity between master and slave are reintroduced; but if one *is* Sade, there is no problem and, furthermore, it is impossible even to imagine one in this connection.

It is impossible for us to examine, as we should, the large number of texts (with Sade, everything is always infinitely numerous) which relate to this situation. Actually, there is a plethora of contradictions. Sometimes the most ferocious libertinage seems as though haunted by the contradiction of its pleasures. The libertine derives his most exquisite pleasure and joy from the destruction of his victims, but this joy ruins itself, is self-destructive, since it annihilates what causes it. "The pleasure one gets from killing a woman," says one of them,

> is soon past; once dead, she feels nothing further; the pleasure of making her suffer disappears with her life. . . . Brand her (with a red-hot iron); sully and soil her; from this debasement she will suffer to the very last moments of her life and our lust, infinitely prolonged, will as a result be even more delicious.

Similarly, Saint-Fond, not content with tortures that are too simple, dreams of a kind of infinitely protracted death for everyone; it is for this reason that he conceives of an undeniably ingenious system whereby he would avail himself of Hell and arrange to use, in this upper world, Hell's inexhaustible resources for torturing victims of his choice. Here we can surely discern what inextricable bonds oppression creates between the oppressor and the oppressed. Sade's heroes draw their sustenance from the deaths they cause, and there are times when, dreaming of everlasting life, he dreams of a death he can inflict eternally. The result is that the executioner and the victim, set eternally face to face, find themselves endowed equally with the same power, with the same divine attribute of eternity. It would be impossible to claim that such a contradiction does not exist in Sade's work. But even more often he attempts to by-pass it by the use of arguments that give us a much clearer and more profound picture of the world that is his. Clairwill chides Saint-Fond for what she terms his unpardonable excesses, and to restore him to the right path she advises him thus:

> Get rid of that voluptuous idea which works you up to such a white-hot pitch—the idea of indefinitely prolonging the agonies of the creature you have selected to kill—get rid of it and replace it by a greater abundance of murders. Do not concentrate on killing the same person over a long period, which is an impossibility, but murder a whole host of others, which is entirely feasible.

Increased numbers is indeed the more correct solution. To consider human beings from the viewpoint of quantity kills them more completely than does the physical act of violence which annihilates them. It may well be that the criminal is inextricably bound to and involved with the person he murders. But the libertine who, as he immolates his victim, feels only the need to sacrifice a thousand others, seems strangely free of all involvement with him. In his eyes, the victim does not of itself exist, he is not a distinct individual but a mere sign, which is indefinitely replaceable in a vast erotic equation. When we read statements such as this: "Nothing is so amusing, nothing so stimulates and excites the brain as do large numbers," we comprehend more fully why Sade utilizes the concept of equality so often to buttress his arguments. To declare that all men are equal is equivalent to saying that no one is worth more than any other, all are interchangeable, each is only a unit, a cipher in an infinite progression. For the Unique Person, all men are equal in their nothingness, and the Unique One, by reducing them to nothing, simply clarifies and demonstrates this nothingness.

That is what makes Sade's world so strange. Scenes of savagery are followed by more scenes of savagery. The repetition is as extraordinary as it is endless. It is not unusual for a libertine to slaughter four or five hundred victims in a single session; then he starts in again the following day; then again that same evening with a new ceremony. The arrangements and positions may vary slightly, but once again things work up to a fever pitch and hecatomb succeeds hecatomb. But is it not eminently clear that those who perish in these gigantic butcheries no longer possess the slightest reality, and if they disappear with such ludicrous ease it is because they have previously been annihilated by a total, absolute act of destruction, because they are present and die only to bear witness to this kind of original cataclysm, this destruction applicable not only to themselves but to everyone else as well? What is especially striking is the fact that the world in which the Unique One lives and moves and has his being is a desert; the creatures he encounters there are less than things, less than shades. And when he torments and destroys them he is not wresting away their lives but verifying their nothingness, establishing his authority over their non-existence, and from this he derives his greatest satisfaction. What in fact does the Duc de Blangis say to the women who, at the dawn of the first of the hundred and twenty days, have been gathered together as the pleasure pawns for the four libertines?

> Consider your circumstances, remember who you are and who we are, and let these reflections cause you to tremble and shudder with horror. You are outside the borders of France, in the heart of an uninhabited forest, far beyond the steep mountains whose paths and passages have been obliterated behind you the minute you crossed over them; you are sealed in an impregnable citadel, no one in the world has the slightest idea where are you, you are beyond the reach of both your friends and your family: so far as the world is concerned, *you are already dead.*

This last should be taken quite literally. These women are already dead, suppressed, enclosed in the absolute void of a bastille into which existence no longer dares to enter, a bastille where their lives serve only to make manifest this quality of "already dead" with which they are commingled.

We shall leave aside the tales of necrophilia which, while there is no dearth of them in Sade's writings, seem at some remove from the "normal" inclinations of his heroes. We should, moreover, point out that whenever Sade's heroes exclaim: "Ah, the lovely corpse!" and wax ecstatic at the insensibility of death, they have generally begun their careers as murderers, and it is the effects of this capacity for aggression that they are striving to prolong beyond the grave. It is undeniable that what characterizes Sade's world is not the desire to become one with the cadaver's immobilized and petrified existence, nor is it the attempt to slip into the passivity of a form representing the absence of forms, of a wholly real reality, shielded and protected from life's uncertainties and yet incarnating the very essence of irreality. Quite the contrary: the center of Sade's world is the urgent need for sovereignty to assert itself by an enormous negation. This negation, which cannot be satisfied or adequately demonstrated on the plane of the particular, requires large quantities, for it is basically intended to transcend the plane of human existence. It is in vain that Sadean man imposes himself on others by his power to destroy them: if he gives the impression of never being dependent on them, even in the situation where he finds himself obliged to annihilate them—if he invariably seems capable of doing without them, it is because he has placed himself on a plane where he and they no longer have anything in common, and he has done this by setting himself such goals and lending his projects a scope which infinitely transcends man and his puny existence. In other words, insofar as Sadean man seems surprisingly free with respect to his victims—upon whom, however, his pleasures depend—it is because violence, as it applies to and is used upon them, is not aimed at them but at something else, something far beyond them, and all Sade's violence does is to authenticate—frenziedly, and endlessly in each particular case—the general act of destruction by which he has reduced God and the world to nothing.

Clearly, with Sade the criminal instinct stems from a nostalgic, transcendental vision which the miserable practical possibilities are forever debasing and dishonoring. The most glorious crime which this poor world is capable of providing is a wretched nothing which makes the libertine blush with shame. Like the monk Jérôme, there is not one among them who is not overwhelmed with shame at the thought of how mediocre his crimes are, and all seek a crime superior to any of which man is capable in this world. "And unhappily," says Jérôme, "I cannot find it. All we do is but the pale image of what we dream of doing." And Clairwill says:

> What I should like to find is a crime the effects of which would be perpetual, even when I myself do not act, so that there would not be a single moment of my life, even when I were asleep, when I was not the cause of some chaos, a chaos of such proportions that it would provoke a general corruption or a disturbance so formal that even after my death its effects would still be felt.

To which Juliette offers this reply, calculated to please the author of the *La Nouvelle Justine:* "Try your hand at a moral crime, the kind one commits in writing." Although Sade, in his doctrine, reduced to a strict minimum the part played by intellectual pleasures, although he eliminated almost entirely intellectual eroticism (because his own erotic dream consists in projecting, onto characters who do not dream but really act, the unreal movement of his pleasures: Sade's eroticism is a dream eroticism, since it expresses itself almost exclusively in fiction; but the more this eroticism is imagined, the more it requires a fiction from which dream is excluded, a fiction wherein debauchery can be enacted and lived), and although Sade does however, and in an exceptional sense, exalt the imaginary, it is because he is wonderfully well aware of the fact that the basis for many an imperfect crime is some impossible crime that only the imagination can comprehend. And that is why he allows Belmore to say:

> Ah, Juliette, how delightful are the pleasures of the imagination! In these delectable moments, the whole world is ours; not a single creature resists us, we devastate the world, we repopulate it with new objects which, in turn, we immolate. The means to every crime is ours, and we employ them all, we multiply the horror a hundredfold.

In his volume of essays *Sade mon prochain,* wherein the boldest ideas are advanced on Sade and also on the problems Sade's existence can help to clarify, Pierre Klossowski explains the extremely complex character of the relations the Sadean consciousness entertains with God and with its fellow men. He shows that these are negative, but that, inasmuch as this negation is real, it re-introduces the concept it rejects: the concept of God and of one's fellow man are, Klossowski says, indispensable to the libertine consciousness. This is a point we could discuss endlessly, for Sade's work is a welter of clear ideas wherein everything is stated but wherein everything is also concealed. Nevertheless, Sade's originality seems to us to reside in his extremely firm claim to found man's sovereignty upon a transcendent power of negation, a power which in no wise depends upon the objects it destroys and which, in order to destroy them, does not even presuppose their previous existence because, at the instant it destroys them, it has already previously, and without exception, considered them as nothing. A dialectic such as this finds both its best example and, perhaps, its justification, in the stance Sade's Omnipotent One assumes with respect to divine omnipotence.

Maurice Heine has emphasized Sade's extraordinary steadfastness of purpose when it comes to atheism.[2] But how right Klossowski is to remind us that Sade's is not a cold-blooded atheism. The moment the name of God is interjected into even the mildest discussion or plot, the language is instantly ignited, the tone becomes haranguing and the words are infused with and overwhelmed by hate. It is surely not in the scenes of luxury and lust that Sade's passion is revealed; but whenever the Unique One finds the slightest vestige of God in his path, then are the violence and scorn and heat of pride and the vertigo of power and desire immediately awakened. In a way, the notion of God is man's inexpiable fault, his original sin, the proof of his nothingness, the thing which justifies and authorizes crime, for when one is dealing with a person who has accepted to prostrate himself before God and declare himself as worthless in God's eyes, one cannot resort to too extreme or too energetic measures against him. "The notion of God is the one fault I cannot forgive in man," writes Sade. A decisive thought, and one of the keys of his system. The belief in an omnipotent God who only grants to man the reality of a wisp of straw, an atom of nothingness, makes it incumbent upon the integral man to retrieve this superhuman power and exercise himself, on behalf of

    [2] Sade: *Dialogue entre un prêtre et un moribond, avec un avant-propos et des notes par Maurice Heine.* Paris, Stendhal et Cie., 1926.

man and at the expense of men, the sovereign right which they have granted to God. When the criminal kills, he is God-on-earth, because he effects between his victim and himself a relationship of subordination wherein the latter sees the concrete definition of divine sovereignty. The moment a true libertine detects, be it in the mind of the most corrupt debauchee, the slightest trace of religious faith, he immediately decrees him dead: for the miscreant debauchee has destroyed himself, by having abdicated into the hands of God. To do so means that he considers himself as nothing, so that he who kills him is simply rectifying a situation which is only thinly veiled by appearances.

Sadean man denies man, and this negation is achieved through the intermediary of the notion of God. He temporarily makes himself God, so that there before him men are reduced to nothing and discover the nothingness of a being before God. "It is true, is it not, prince, that you do not love men?" Juliette asks. "I loathe them. Not a moment goes by that my mind is not busy plotting violently to do them harm. Indeed, there is no race more horrible, more frightful. . . . How low and scurvy, how vile and disgusting a race it is!" "But," Juliette breaks in, "you do not really believe that you are to be included among men? . . . Oh, no, no, when one dominates them with such energy, it is impossible to belong to the same race." To which Saint-Fond: "Yes, she is right, we are gods."

Still, the dialectic evolves to further levels: Sade's man, who has taken unto himself the power to set himself above men—the power which men madly yield to God—never for a moment forgets that this power is completely negative. To be God can have only one meaning: to crush man, to reduce creation to nothing. "I should like to be Pandora's box," Saint-Fond says at another point, "so that all the evils which escaped from my breast might destroy all mankind individually." And Verneuil: "And if it were true a God existed, would we not be his rivals, since we destroy thus what he has made?" This is the way an ambiguous conception of the Omnipotent is gradually fashioned, and yet there can scarcely be any doubt about the ultimate meaning. Klossowski refers often to the theories of this same Saint-Fond, some of whose views we have cited and who, among all Sade's heroes, is the only one to believe in a Supreme Being. But the God in whom he believes is not terribly benign, but "extremely vindictive, very barbaric, very wicked, most unjust, and very cruel." He is the Supreme Being of wickedness, the God of malfeasance. From this idea Sade deduced all kinds of brilliant theories. He imagines a Last Judgment which he describes with all the resources of savage humor which he possesses. We hear God upbraiding the good in these terms:

> When you saw that everything was vicious and criminal on earth, why did you stray into the paths of virtue? Did not the perpetual misery with which I covered the universe suffice to convince you that I love only disorder and chaos, and that to please me you must irritate me? Did I not daily provide you with the example of destruction? Seeing which, Fool, why did you not destroy, why did you not do as I did?

But having recalled this, it is obvious that the conception of an infernal God is but a way station of the dialectic according to which Sade's superman, after having denied man in the guise of God, next advances to meet God and will in turn deny him in the name of Nature, in order finally to deny Nature by identifying it with the spirit of negation. In the evil God, the negation which has just exterminated the notion of man rests as it were for a few moments before launching a new attack, this time against itself. In becoming God, Saint-Fond by the same stroke compels God to become Saint-Fond, and the Supreme Being, into whose hands the weak have committed themselves in order to force the strong to commit themselves as well, no longer asserts Himself except as the gigantic constraint of a rocklike transcendence which crushes each in proportion to his frailty. This is hatred of mankind hypostasized, raised to its highest degree. But no sooner has the spirit of negation attained the pinnacle of absolute existence than it is compelled to become aware of its own infinitude and can only turn against the affirmation of this absolute existence, which now is the sole object worthy of a negation grown infinite. It is the hatred of men that was embodied in God. Now it is the hatred of God which liberates from God hatred itself—a hatred so violent that it seems to be constantly, moment by moment, projecting the reality of what it is denying, the better to assert and justify itself. "If that existence— if God's existence," says Dubois,

> should prove to be true, the mere pleasure of baiting and annoying the person so designated would become the most precious compensation for

the necessity I would then find myself in to acknowledge some belief in him.

But does a hate so intense and searing as this not indicate, as Klossowski would seem to believe, a faith which had forgotten its name and resorted to blasphemy as a means of forcing God to break his silence? That seems quite unlikely to us. On the contrary, everything suggests that the only reason this powerful hatred has shown such a predilection for the deity is because it has found in him both a pretense and a privileged sustenance. For Sade, God is clearly nothing more than a prop for his hate. That hatred is too great to be concerned about any particular object; being infinite, and as it is constantly transcending any limits, it tends to delight in itself and to wax ecstatic over that infinitude to which it lends the name of God ("The sole source of your system," Clairwill says to Saint-Fond, "is your profound hatred for God."). But it is hate and hate alone which is real, and in the end it will turn itself with the same intensity and fearlessness against Nature as against the non-existent God it loathes.

Actually, if Sade's most tempestuous passions are unleashed by things religious, by the name of God and by his priests, whom Sade terms "God-makers," it is because the terms *God* and *religion* embody virtually every form of his hatred. In God, he hates the nothingness of man, who has fashioned such a master for himself, and the thought of this nothingness irritates and inflames him to such an extent that all he can do is join forces with God to sanction this nothingness. And he also hates God's omnipotence, in which he recognizes what should properly belong to him, and God becomes the figure and embodiment of his infinite hate. And finally, what he hates in God is God's poverty, the nullity of an existence which, however much it may posit itself as existence and creation, is nothing, for what is great, what is everything, is the spirit of destruction.

This spirit of destruction, in Sade's system, is identified with Nature. This point proved to be a thorny one for Sade, and he found himself forced to grope his way along, and in fact had to repudiate the then fashionable atheistic philosophies for which he could not help but feel a certain sympathy and from which his reason, always eager for supporting opinions, could draw an inexhaustible supply. But to the extent that he was able to pass beyond naturalistic ideology and that he was not taken in by external analogies, he proves to us that in him logic has proceeded to its ultimate limits without ever abandoning the field to the obscure forces which supported it. "Nature" is one of those words Sade, like so many eighteenth-century authors, delighted in writing. It is in the name of Nature that he wages his battle against God and against everything that God stands for, especially morality. There is no need to emphasize this point: Sade emphasizes it over and over again; his material on the subject is truly staggering. According to him, this Nature is first of all universal life, and for hundreds and hundreds of pages his whole philosophy consists in reiterating that immoral instincts are good, since they are the facts of Nature, and the first and last appeal must be to Nature. In other words, no morality: the fact reigns. But subsequently, bothered by the equal value he sees himself obliged to accord both to good and evil instincts and impulses, he attempts to establish a new scale of values with crime at the summit. His principal argument consists in maintaining that crime conforms more closely to the spirit of Nature, because it is movement, that is life; Nature, he says, which wishes to create, needs crime, which destroys: all this is set forth in the greatest detail and at incredible length, and sometimes with rather striking proof. Nevertheless, by dint of talking about Nature, by being constantly faced with this frame of reference, ubiquitous and commanding, the Sadean protagonist becomes gradually annoyed, his anger mounts, and before long his hatred for Nature is such that Nature, unbearable in his eyes, is the target for his anathemas and negations. "Yes, my friend, yes indeed, I loathe Nature." There are two deep-seated reasons for this revolt. On the one hand, he finds it quite intolerable that the incredible power of destruction which he represents has no other purpose than to authorize Nature to create. And on the other hand, insofar as he himself belongs to Nature he feels that Nature eludes his negation, and that the more he insults and defiles it the better he serves it, the more he annihilates it the more he is submitting to its law. Whence those cries of hatred, that truly insane revolt:

Oh thou, blind and insensate force, when I shall have exterminated all the creatures on the face of the earth I shall still be far indeed from my goal, for I shall have served thee, cruel master, whereas all I aspire to is to revenge myself for the stupidity and evil which thou makest men to experience by refusing them the means to indulge themselves freely in the frightful predilections which thou dost inspire in them.

Therein lies the expression of a primordial and elementary feeling : to insult and outrage Nature is man's most deep-rooted exigency, one which is a thousand times stronger than his need to offend God.

In everything we do there are nothing but idols offended and creatures insulted, but Nature is not among them, and it is she I should like to outrage. I should like to upset her plans, thwart her progress, arrest the wheeling courses of the stars, throw the spheres floating in space into mighty confusion, destroy what serves Nature and protect what is harmful to her; in a word, to insult her in her works—and this I am unable to do.

And once again, in the above passage, Sade allows himself to confuse Nature with its great laws, and this enables him to dream of a cataclysm such that it could destroy them; but his logic rejects this compromise and when, elsewhere, he envisions an engineer inventing a machine to pulverize the universe, he is forced into the following admission: no one will have been more deserving of Nature than he. Sade was perfectly well aware of the fact that to annihilate everything is not to annihilate the world, for the world is not only universal affirmation but universal destruction as well, and can be represented alike by the totality of being and the totality of nonbeing. It is for this reason that the struggle with Nature represents, in man's history, a far more advanced dialectical stage than his struggle with God. We can safely state, without fear of unduly modernizing Sade's thought, that he was one of the first thinkers of his century to have recognized and incorporated into his world view the notion of transcendence: since the notion of nothingness, of nonbeing, belongs to the world, one cannot conceive of the world's nonbeing except from within a totality, which is still the world.

If crime is the spirit of Nature, there is no crime against Nature and, consequently, there is no crime possible. Sade states this, at times with the most profound satisfaction, and then again with the deepest resentment and rage. For to deny the possibility of crime allows him to deny morality and God and all human values;

but to deny crime is also to renounce the spirit of negation, to admit that this spirit can suppress itself. This is a conclusion against which he protests most vigorously, and one which leads him little by little to withdraw all reality from Nature. In the last volumes of *La Nouvelle Justine,* (especially in Volumes VIII and IX), Juliette repudiates all her previous conceptions and makes amends in the following terms:

> Fool that I was, before we parted I was still involved with the notion of Nature, but the new systems which I have since adopted have removed me from her. . . .

Nature, she says, has no more reality, no more truth or meaning than God:

> Ah, bitch, perhaps thou dost deceive me too, as in times past I was deceived by the vile deific chimera to which thou art, we were told, submissive; we are no more dependent upon thee than upon him; perhaps the causes are not essential to the effects. . . .

Thus Nature disappears, although the philosopher had placed all his trust in her and although he would greatly have loved to make a formidable death machine of universal life. But mere nothingness is not his goal. What he has striven for is sovereignty, through the spirit of negation, carried to its extreme. Putting this negation to the test, he has alternately employed it on men, God, and Nature. Men, God, and Nature: the moment each of these notions comes in contact with negation it seems to be endowed with a certain value, but if one considers the experiment as a whole, these moments no longer have the slightest reality, for the characteristic of the experiment consists precisely in ruining and nullifying them one after the other. What are men, if before God they are nothing? What is God when compared to Nature? And what in fact is Nature, which is compelled to vanish, driven to disappear by man's need to outrage it? Thus the circle is closed. With man we started, we now end up with man. Except that he now bears a new name: he is called the Unique One, the man who is unique of his kind.

Sade, having discovered that in man negation was power, claimed to base man's future on negation carried to the extreme. To reach this ultimate limit, he dreamed up—borrowing from the vocabulary of his time—a principle which, by its very ambiguity, represents a most ingenious choice. This principle is: Energy. Energy is, actually, a completely equivocal notion. It is both a reserve of forces and an expenditure of forces, both potential and kinetic, an affirmation which can only be wrought by means of negation, and it is the power which is destruction. Furthermore, it is both fact and law, axiom and value.

One thing quite striking is that Sade, in a universe full of effervescence and passion, suppresses desire and deems it suspect rather than emphasizing it and raising it to the highest level of importance. The reason he does so is that desire denies solitude and leads to a dangerous acknowledgment of the world of others. But when Saint-Fond declares:

> My passions, concentrated on a single point, resemble the rays of a sun assembled by a magnifying glass: they immediately set fire to whatever object they find in their way,

we can see very clearly why "destruction" and "power" may appear synonymous, without the destroyed object deriving the slightest value from this operation. This principle has another advantage: it assigns man a future without saddling him with any feeling of indebtedness to any transcendental concept. For this all honor is due Sade. He has claimed to overthrow the morality of Good, but despite a few provocative affirmations he has been very careful not to replace it with a Gospel of Evil. When he writes: "All is good when it is excessive," he can be reproached for the uncertainty of his principle, but he cannot be charged with wanting to establish the supremacy of man over the supremacy of ideas to which man would be subordinated. In this doctrine, no conduct is granted any special privileges: one can choose to do whatever one likes; the important thing is that, in doing them, one should be able to render coincident the maximum of destruction and the maximum of affirmation. Practically speaking, that is exactly what happens in Sade's novels. It is not the degree of Vice or Virtue that makes people happy or unhappy, but the energy they put to use, for, in Sade's words:

> Happiness is proportionate to the energy of principles; no one who drifts endlessly would ever be capable of experiencing it.

Juliette, to whom Saint-Fond proposes a plan by which two-thirds of France would be decimated by starvation, has a moment's hesitation and is overawed at the prospect: immediately she is threatened. Why? Because she has shown signs of weakness, her vital temper is slackened, and the greater energy of Saint-Fond prepares to make her its prey. This is even clearer in the case of Durand. Durand is a poisoner completely incapable of the slightest virtue; her corruption is total. But one day the government of Venice asks her to disseminate the plague. The project frightens her, not because of its immoral character but because of the dangers she would expose herself to. Straightway she is condemned. Her energy failed her and she found her master; and that master is death. In leading a dangerous life, says Sade, what really matters is never "to lack the strength necessary to forge beyond the furthermost limits." One might say that this strange world is not made up of individuals, but of systems of vectors, of greater or lesser tensions. Wherever or whenever the tension falls, catastrophe inevitably ensues. Futhermore, there is no reason to distinguish between Nature's energy and the energy of man: luxury and lust are a kind of lightning flash, as lightning is the lubricity of Nature; the weak will be the victim of both and the mighty will emerge triumphant. Justine is struck by lightning; Juliette is not. There is nothing providential about this denouement. Justine's weakness attracts the same lightning which Juliette's energy deflects away from her. Similarly, everything that happens to Justine makes her unhappy, because everything that affects her diminishes her; we are told of Justine that her inclinations are "virtuous but base," and this must be taken in the strict sense of the phrase. On the contrary, everything that befalls Juliette reveals her own power to her, and she enjoys it as she would some increment of herself. This is why, were she to die, her death would carry her to the very apogee of power and exaltation, for it would enable her to experience total destruction as the total release of her enormous energy.

Sade was clearly aware of the fact that the supremacy of energetic man, insofar as he achieves this supremacy by identifying himself with the spirit of negation, is a paradoxical situation. The integral man, who asserts himself completely, is also completely destroyed. He is the man of all passions, and he is without feeling. First he destroyed himself as man, then as God, and then as Nature; thus did he become the Unique Being. Now he is all-powerful, for the negation in him has vanquished everything. To describe his formation, Sade resorts to an extremely curious concept to which he gives the classical name: *apathy*.

Apathy is the spirit of negation applied to the man who has chosen to make himself supreme. In a way, it is both the cause and the principle of energy. Sade, it would seem, reasons about as follows: the individual of today represents a certain quantum of force; generally he squanders and disperses his forces, by estranging them, to the benefit of those simulacra which parade under the names of "other people," "God," or "ideals." Through this dispersal, he makes the mistake of exhausting his possibilities, by wasting them, but what is worse, of basing his conduct on weakness, for if he expends himself on behalf of others it is because he believes he needs them as a crutch to lean upon. This is a fatal lapse: he weakens himself by spending his strength in vain, and he expends his energies because he deems himself weak. But the true man knows that he is alone, and he accepts it; everything in him which relates to others—to his whole seventeen centuries' heritage of cowardice —he repudiates and rejects: for example, pity, gratitude, and love are all sentiments he crushes and destroys; by destroying them, he recuperates all the strength that he would have had to dedicate to these debilitating impulses and, what is even more important, from this labor of destruction he draws the beginning of a true energy.

It must be well understood that apathy does not only consist in ruining "parasitical" affections, but also in opposing the spontaneity of any passion at all. The vicious person who immediately abandons himself to his vice betrays a flaw that will be his undoing. Even debauchees of genius, perfectly endowed to become monsters if they simply content themselves with following their bent, will end in disaster. Sade is adamant: in order to convert passion into energy, it must be compressed and mediatized by passing through a necessary moment of insensibility, after which it will attain its apogee. During the early stages of her career, Juliette is constantly reprimanded by Clairwill, who reproaches her for committing crimes only out of enthusiasm, of lighting the torch of crime only from the torch of passion, and who also accuses her of valuing lust and the effer-

vescence of pleasure above everything else. These are dangerous
and facile tendencies. Crime matters more than lust, and the cold-
blooded, the premeditated crime is greater than the crime committed in the heat of passion. But most important is the somber, secret
crime "committed by a conscious hardening of sensitivity," because
it is the act of a soul which, having destroyed everything within
itself, has accumulated an immense strength which will completely
identify itself with the act of total destruction which it prepares. All
these mighty libertines who live solely for pleasure are mighty only
because they have eliminated in themselves all capacity for pleasure.
This is why they resort to terrifying and hideous anomalies, for
otherwise the mediocrity of normal pleasures would suffice for
them. But they have made themselves insensitive: they claim to
enjoy their insensibility, their rejected and annihilated sensibility,
and they become ferocious. Cruelty is nothing more than the negation of self, carried so far that it is transformed into a destructive
explosion; insensibility makes a tremor of the whole being, says
Sade, and adds:

> The soul assumes a kind of apathy which is soon metamorphosed into
> pleasures a thousand times more exquisite than those which weakness and
> self-indulgence would procure for them.

It is understandable that, in this world, principles play a major
role. The libertine is "pensive, deeply introspective, incapable of
being moved by anything whatsoever." He keeps to himself, cannot
tolerate either noise or laughter; nothing must divert his attention;
"apathy, unconcern, stoicism, solitude within oneself—these are the
conditions he requires in order to attain a proper state of the soul." A
transformation such as this, involving a labor of self-destruction,
is not accomplished without the most extreme difficulty. *Juliette* is
a kind of *Bildungsroman,* an apprentice's manual in which we
gradually learn to recognize the slow transformation of an energetic
soul. On the surface, Juliette is thoroughly depraved from the very
start. But in reality, at that stage, she is only equipped with a few
penchants, and her mind is yet intact; she has a tremendous effort yet
to make, for, as Balzac once remarked: *n'est pas detruit qui veut.*
Sade notes that there are extremely dangerous moments in this effort
to achieve apathy. It may happen, for example, that insensibility can

put the libertine into such a state of prostration that he may at any moment revert to morality: he believes himself hardened, while actually he is only weakened, a perfect prey for remorse. Now, a single gesture of virtue, by revalorizing the universe of man and God, is enough to bring down his entire power structure; however lofty he may be, that universe crumbles and, generally, this fall is his death. If, however, while in this state of prostration wherein he feels nothing more than a tasteless repugnance for the worst excesses, he finds one final increment of strength with which to augment this insensibility by dreaming up new excesses which repel him even more, then he will evolve from a state of prostration and dereliction to one of omnipotence, from induration and indifference to the most extreme voluptuousness and, "shaken to the very fiber of his being," the supreme enjoyment of the self will transport him a sovereign, beyond all imaginable limits.

One of the most surprising aspects of Sade and his fate is that, although scandal has no better symbol than he, all that is daring and scandalous in his thinking has for so long remained unknown. There is no need to list and classify the themes he discovered— themes which the most adventurous minds of future centuries will apply themselves to developing and reaffirming. We have touched upon them in passing, and even so we have limited ourselves to depicting the main elements of his thought by stressing the basic doctrine. We could just as easily have discussed his concept of dreams, which he views as the work of the mind restored to instinct and thus delivered from the influences of waking morality. Or we might have dwelled upon all that part of his thinking in which he proves himself the precursor of Freud, as for example when he writes:

> It is in the mother's womb that are fashioned the organs which must render us susceptible of this or that fantasy; the first objects which we encounter, the first conversations we overhear, determine the pattern; do what it will, education is incapable of altering the pattern.

In Sade there is also something of the traditional moralist, and it would be a simple matter to make a collection of his maxims which would make those of La Rochefoucauld seem weak and hesitant by comparison. Sade is often accused of having written badly, and, in fact, he often did write in extreme haste and with a prolixity that tries the patience. But he is also capable of a strange humor, his style reveals an icy joviality and, in its extravagance, a kind of cold innocence which one may find preferable to the full range of Voltaire's irony and which, in fact, is not to be found in the work of any other French writer. All these are exceptional merits, but they were in vain. Until the day when Apollinaire and Maurice Heine —and when André Breton, with his sixth, divinatory sense of the hidden forces of history—opened the way toward him, and even later, until the recent studies of Georges Bataille, Jean Paulhan, and Pierre Klossowski, Sade—the master of the great themes of modern thought and sensibility—continued to glitter like an empty name. Why? Because this thought is the work of madness, because it was molded by a depravity which the world was incapable of facing squarely. What is more, Sade's doctrine is presented as the theory of that depravity, a blueprint of his personal penchant, a doctrine which attempts to transpose the most repugnant anomaly into a complete *Weltanschauung*. For the first time, philosophy is openly conceived of as being the product of an illness,[3] and it has the effrontery to present as a logical and universal theory a system the sole guarantee for which is the personal preferences of an aberrant individual.

This again is one of Sade's most important and original contributions. One may safely say that Sade performed his own psychoanalysis by writing a text wherein he consigns everything which relates to his obsessions and wherein, too, he seeks to discover what logic and what coherence his remarks reveal. But, what is more, he was the first to demonstrate, and demonstrate proudly, that from a certain personal and even monstrous form of behavior there could rightfully be derived a world view significant enough so that some eminent thinkers concerned only with the human condition were to do nothing more than to reaffirm its chief perspectives and provide added proof of its validity. Sade had the courage to assert

---

3 Sade does not mind in the least admitting it: "The man endowed with singular tastes is a sick man."

that by fearlessly accepting the singular tastes that were his and by taking them as the point of departure and the very principle of all reason, he provided philosophy with the solidest foundation it could hope to have, and advanced himself as the means to a profound interpretation of human destiny taken in its entirety. Such pretension is doubtless no longer of a sort to terrify us, but, in all fairness, we are only beginning to take it seriously, and for a long while this pretension was enough to turn away from Sade's thinking even those who were interested in Sade.

First of all, what was he exactly? A monstrous exception, absolutely outside the pale of humanity. "The unique thing about Sade," Nodier once remarked, "is his having committed a crime so monstrous that one could not characterize it without danger." (In a sense, this was one of Sade's ambitions: to be innocent by dint of culpability; to smash what is normal, once and for all, and smash the laws by which he could have been judged.) Another contemporary, Pitou, writes in a rather terrifying manner: "Justice had relegated him to a corner of the prison and offered every prisoner a free hand to rid the world of this burden." When, later, there was recognized in Sade an anomaly to be found in certain other people too, he was quickly and carefully sealed up inside this unnamable aberration to which, indeed, no other than this unique name could be applied. Even later, when this anomaly was held to reflect credit on Sade, when he was seen as a man free enough to have invented a new science and, in any event, as an exceptional man both by his destiny and his preoccupations, and when, finally, sadism was seen as a possibility of interest to all humanity—even then Sade's own thought continued to be neglected, as if there could be no doubt that there was more originality and authenticity in sadism than in the way in which Sade himself had been able to interpret it. Examining it more closely, however, we see that it is not negligible and that, amidst all its teeming contradictions, there emerges, on the problem which Sade's name illustrates, insights more significant than anything the most learned and illuminated minds have come up with on the subject to this day. We do not say that this philosophy is viable. But it does show that between the normal man who imprisons the sadistic man in an impasse, and the sadist who turns the impasse into a way out, it is the latter who is closer to the truth, who knows more about the logic of his situation and has the more profound understanding of it, and it is he who is in a position to be able to help the normal man to self-understanding, by helping him to modify the bases of all comprehension.

Chronology

1740

June 2—In the Condé mansion on the rue de Condé,[1] in Paris, the Countess de Sade, nee (1712) Marie-Eléonore de Maillé de Carman, lady-in-waiting to the Princess de Condé, gives birth to a son, during the seventh year of her marriage to Jean-Baptiste-Joseph-François (born 1702), Count de Sade, lord of the manors of Saumane and La Coste and co-lord of Mazan, Lieutenant-General of the provinces of Bresse, Bugey, Valromey, and Gex, then Ambassador from Louis XV to the Elector of Cologne.[2]

June 3—In the absence of both his godparents (his godfather being his maternal grandfather Donatien de Maillé, Marquis de Carmen, and his godmother Louise-Aldonse d'Astoaud de Murs, his paternal grandmother), the infant is held out over the baptismal font in the parish church of Saint-Sulpice by two retainers of the Sade household. For Christian names he is given Donatien-Alphonse-François instead of those apparently intended for him, Louis-Aldonse-Donatien, a mishap which is to plague him with the authorities throughout his life, and especially under the Republic.

[1] The Condé mansion actually occupied most of the area today enclosed by the rue de Condé, the rue de Vaugirard, the rue Monsieur-le-Prince, and the Carrefour d'Odéon.

[2] Sade's father also subsequently served as Louis XV's Ambassador to Russia, and then to London. Perhaps the best portrait of the Count de Sade is the following description by Paul Bourdin: "He was a meticulous and rather grim person, stiff both in manner and language, as pompous to his family as to his servants, most jealous of his rights, rigid to the point of narrowness, yet liberal to the point of prodigality." (Paul Bourdin, ed., *Correspondance inédite du Marquis de Sade, de ses proches et de ses familiers,* Paris, Librairie de France, 1929.)

1744. Aet. 4

August 16—The municipal council of Saumane sends its consuls and secretary to Avignon "to compliment My Lord the Marquis de Sade, son of the Lord Count of this place, on his happy arrival at Avignon and to wish him long and happy years as heir apparent. . . ."

1745. Aet. 5

January 24—A paternal uncle of the Marquis, Jacques-François-Paul-Aldonse (born at the château de Mazan on September 21, 1705), moves to the Benedictine monastery of Saint-Léger d'Ebreuil, to which he has been named abbot. Entrusted with the education of his nephew, he shares with him two homes, his residence at d'Ebreuil and another at Saumane, a seigneury of which he has life-long tenure.

1750. Aet. 10

. . . .—The Marquis returns to Paris to enter Louis le Grand Collège, a Jesuit school. He is given a personal tutor, Abbé Jacques-François Amblet.[3]

1754. Aet. 14

May 24—Young Sade obtains from the genealogist Clairambault a certificate of nobility in order to be received into the training school attached to the Light Horse Regiment of the Royal Guards.

1755. Aet. 15

December 14—He is appointed sub-lieutenant without pay in the King's Own Infantry Regiment.

---

[3] In what has generally been taken to be an autobiographical passage in *Aline et Valcour*, Sade describes his teacher in the following terms: "I returned to Paris to study under the guidance of a man who was both severe and intelligent, one who would probably have exerted a good influence on my youth, but unfortunately I did not keep him long enough."

1757. Aet. 17

January 14—The Marquis de Sade is granted a commission as Cornet (Standard Bearer) in the Carbine Regiment, Saint-André Brigade, and participates in the war against Prussia.[4]

April 1—He is transferred, with the same rank, to the Malvoisin Brigade.

1759. Aet. 19

April 21—He is promoted to the rank of captain in the Burgundy Horse.

1763. Aet. 23

Late February—Sade, it would appear, is engaged to two young ladies simultaneously: Mademoiselle Renée-Pélagie de Montreuil and Mademoiselle Laure de Lauris. Of the two, Sade prefers the latter, with whom he is wildly in love, but his father is intent on arranging an alliance between his son and the wealthy Montreuil family, doubtless because of the seemingly delicate financial situation in which he then finds himself.[5]

March 15—Sade is discharged with the rank of cavalry captain, the Paris Treaty having to all intents and purposes ended the Seven Years' War.

Late April—Only a scant two weeks before the date set for his marriage to Mlle. de Montreuil, Sade is still in Avignon, trying to win the hand of Laure de Lauris, despite the fact that she apparently has broken off the engagement. Sade's father is angry and

---

[4] Writing of the campaign, again in *Aline et Valcour,* Sade notes: "I am sure I gave a good account of myself. The natural impetuosity of my character, that fiery Soul with which Nature endowed me, served but to enhance that unflinching savagery which men call courage and which—quite wrongly I am sure—is considered the one indispensable quality in our make-up.

[5] In a letter dated at the end of 1762, the Count wrote his brother, Abbé de Sade: "Everything here has been seized"; in another letter he complained that he was dying of poverty—which was, to say the least, an exaggeration. But that his fortunes were precarious there seems to be little doubt, and there is every indication that the Count was a poor manager of his own affairs and properties.

concerned by the Marquis' conduct, which is compromising the proposed alliance with the Montreuil family; nonetheless, young Sade appears to have been so persuasive or eloquent that the Count at one point consents to his marrying Lady Laure.[6]

May 1—The King, the Queen, and the royal family give their consent to the proposed marriage between the Marquis de Sade, allied through the Maillé family to the royal blood of the Condés, and Renée-Pélagie Cordier de Launay de Montreuil (born in Paris December 3, 1741), eldest daughter of the President Claude-René de Montreuil and of Marie-Madeleine Masson de Plissay (married August 22, 1740).

May 15—The marriage contract is signed by the parties in the town house of the President, situated rue Neuve-du-Luxembourg. The future husband signs it Louis-Aldonse-Donatien.

May 17—The marriage is celebrated in the church of Saint-Roch.

October 29—By order of the King, the Marquis de Sade is committed to Vincennes fortress for excesses committed in a brothel which he has been frequenting for a month.

November 13—The order to free the Marquis is delivered, but the King commands him to withdraw to Echauffour Manor, a property owned by the Montreuils, and to remain there.

1764. Aet. 24

May 4—The King authorizes Sade to go to Dijon, with the provision that he remain there only long enough to address the Burgundy Parliament in his capacity of Lt.-General of the King for the provinces of Bresse, Bugey, Valromey, and Gex.

September 11—The King completely revokes the order restricting Sade's residence to Echauffour Manor.

---

[6] Elsewhere in the present volume is the only letter, discovered in 1948 in the Bibliothèque Nationale in Paris, from Sade to Laure de Lauris, a letter revealing many facets of the author's character: passion, instability, brilliance, and a touch of the scoundrel.

December 7—In a report, Police Inspector Marais notes that M. de Sade is in Paris and adds that he (Marais) has asked La Bris-sualt[7] "to refrain from providing the Marquis with girls to go to any private chambers with him."

1765. Aet. 25

. . . .—Sade has taken as mistress an actress-prostitute who is the toast of all the young fops in Paris, Mlle. Beauvoisin.

June–July—Sade is at La Coste with Mlle. Beauvoisin, passing her off as his wife's relative or at times even as his wife. Sade's mother-in-law, Lady Montreuil, has had wind of the affair, but apparently it has been kept from his wife.

September—Sade is back in Paris, but spending more time at La Beauvoisin's house than at his own. His alleged reason for remaining in Paris is that he must settle his debts, which amount to 4500 *livres*.

1766. Aet. 26

November 4—Sade pays a M. Lestarjette the sum of two hundred *livres* as four and a half months' rent on a furnished cottage in the suburb of Arcueil. This little retreat is to be associated with important events in Sade's life.

1767. Aet. 27

January 24—Jean-Baptiste-François-Joseph, Count de Sade, dies at Montreuil, near Versailles, at the age of sixty-five, leaving his son the Marquis de Sade as his sole heir.

April 16—The Marquis de Sade is promoted to Captain Commander in the du Mestre Cavalry Regiment, with orders to assemble his company without delay. Lady Montreuil's reaction is one of delight, for, as she notes, "it means at least a short period of peace."

---

[7] The proprietress of a famous Paris brothel.

April 20—Sade leaves for Lyons to rejoin Mlle. de Beauvoisin, leaving his wife, who is five months pregnant, in Paris.

June 21—Debate and deliberation by the community of La Coste, which results in a favorable reply to the demands of the Marquis for due recognition of his rank and for a memorial service for his deceased father in the church.

August 27—In the parish of the Madeleine de la Ville-l'Evêque in Paris, Louis-Marie, Count de Sade, the Marquis' first son is born.

October 16—Inspector Marais reports on M. de Sade's unsuccessful attempts to induce Mlle. Rivière of the Opéra—where she is a member of the ballet—to live with him. He "has offered her 25 *louis* a month on condition that whenever she is not performing she will spend her time with him at his *maisonette* in Arcueil. The young lady has refused, but M. Sade is still pursuing her."

1768. Aet. 28

January 24—Louis-Marie de Sade is baptized in the private chapel of the Condé mansion, the Prince de Condé and the Princess de Conti being his godparents.

April 3—On Easter Sunday, at about nine o'clock in the morning on the Place des Victoires, the Marquis de Sade accosts Rose Keller, the widow of one Valentin, a pastry cook's assistant. A cotton spinner by trade, out of work for a month and now reduced to begging alms, she accepts to accompany Sade in a cab to Arcueil. There, in his rented cottage, he orders her to undress, threatens her with a knife, and flogs her. He then locks her in a room from which, however, she shortly manages to escape. Reaching the village—it now being about four in the afternoon—Rose Keller encounters three local women to whom she recounts her adventure and exhibits her wounds. The women take her to the authorities. Her statement is recorded[8] and she is examined at once by the village doctor, Pierre Paul Le Comte.

---

8 The Arcueil magistrate being absent, her statement is actually taken by the Constabulary Brigadier of neighboring Bourg la Reine, who has been summoned for that purpose.

April 7—Madame de Sade summons Abbé Amblet and M. Claude Antoine Sohier to her residence at the rue Neuve-du-Luxembourg and dispatches them to Arcueil to determine whether Rose Keller can be prevailed upon to drop the charge she has made to the local magistrate. The emissaries obtain her agreement in return for 2400 *livres,* plus a payment of seven gold *louis* for dressings and medication.

April 12—Sade sets out for Saumur castle in the company of Abbé Amblet, having been granted the privilege of not being conducted there under police escort.

April 15–23—Concerned by the rumors circulating, the Paris Council orders the case taken out of the hands of the local magistrate and transferred to those of the criminal court of La Tournelle, which proceeds to a thorough examination of the evidence and declares the accused under arrest.

April 30—Inspector Marais appears at Saumur castle to transfer the Marquis to Pierre-Encise prison near Lyons, where discipline is not so lax.

June 2—The King signs two Royal Orders, one authorizing the transfer of the Marquis to the Conciergerie du Palais where the High Court is to ratify the previously issued Royal Letters of Annulment, the other ordering his transfer back to Pierre-Encise.

June 10—The accused is interrogated and admits to the principal allegations, but insists that Rose Keller was fully aware of what would be expected of her at Arcueil. He presents the Letters of Annulment granted him by the King. That same day, the High Court of Paris, meeting *in pleno,* pronounces for ratification of the annulment and directs the Marquis "to refund the sum of one hundred *livres* relative to the board of prisoners in the Conciergerie du Palais prison."

June 11 or 12—The Marquis is returned to Pierre-Encise.

August—At the request of her husband, the Marquise arrives in Lyons, where she will remain until the Marquis recovers his freedom.

November 16—Two Royal Orders are issued, one instructing the supervisor of Pierre-Encise to release Sade, the other enjoining Sade to retire to his estates at La Coste. The Marquise, perhaps because she is again pregnant, returns to Paris shortly after the release of her husband, while he proceeds to Provence as ordered.

1769. Aet. 29

June 27—Birth in Paris of Donatien-Claude-Armand, Chevalier de Sade, the Marquis' second son, who is christened the following day at the parish church of Madeleine de la Ville-l'Evêque.

1770. Aet. 30

August—Sade reports to resume his military duties as a Captain Commander in the Burgundy Regiment. After some difficulties caused by the deputy commander of the regiment, who at first places Sade under arrest and forbids the quartermaster to take any orders whatsoever from the newly arrived captain, he is fully reinstated in his duties.

1771. Aet. 31

March 13—Sade applies to the Minister of War, requesting the rank of colonel, without stipend, which application is granted on March 19.

April 17—Birth in Paris of Madeleine-Laure, daughter of the Marquis de Sade.

May 27—The Marquis, who has recently arrived in Provence, orders the public officials of Saumane, of which he is the lord of the manor, to do him homage.

June 1—The Marquis is authorized to draw 10,000 *livres* as the fee payable upon his cession to the Count d'Osmont of the regimental colonelcy.

September 9—Sade leaves Fort l'Evêque prison, where he has spent a week for debts. To obtain his release he pays a sum of 3000 francs in cash and the remainder in a promissory note dated October 15.

November 7—Sade's sister-in-law, Mademoiselle Anne-Prospère de Launay de Montreuil, joins the Sades at La Coste.

1772. Aet. 32

January 20—In the theater at La Coste, Sade presents a comedy of which he is the author.

Mid-June—With his manservant Armand, known as Latour, Sade sets out for Marseilles for the purpose of collecting some monies due him.

June 25—Having several days to spend in Marseilles, Sade sends Latour out in search of some girls with whom to entertain himself.

June 27—Latour arranges a rendezvous with four girls—Marianne Laverne, Mariannette Laugier, Rose Coste, and Mariette Borelly—at Mariette's place at the corner of the rue des Capucins. The girls range in age from eighteen to twenty-three, Marianne being the youngest and Mariette the eldest (Sade has several times specified to Latour that he is to look for "very young girls"). In the course of the morning, during which Sade and Latour sequester themselves together with each of the girls singly, then with some jointly, the Marquis offers at least two of the girls some aniseed sweets, the sugar of which had been soaked with Spanish fly extract, or cantharides. The orgy lasts throughout the morning. That same evening, Sade's last in Marseilles, Latour procures him another prostitute, Marguerite Coste, to whom he also gives a number of the same sweets.

June 30—The Royal Prosecutor attached to the Seneschal's Court of Marseilles is informed that one Marguerite Coste, after consuming an excessive number of sweets pressed upon her by a stranger, has been so racked with intestinal pains as to indicate that she has been poisoned. The Prosecutor calls for an investigation.

The Lt.-General for criminal matters, Chomel, records Marguerite Coste's accusations, a doctor is appointed to examine her, and a pharmacist to analyze the matter vomited.

July 1—Mariette Borelly and the three other prostitutes make a statement to the Lt.-General and the Royal Prosecutor, Marianne ascribing her digestive troubles during and after the morning bout to the aniseed offered her by the Marquis. All four girls profess indignation at the attitude of the Marquis and his valet whom they accuse of "homosexual sodomy," at the same time claiming to have refused to accede to Sade's and Latour's "unnatural advances."[9]

July 4—Medical reports on Marguerite Coste and Marianne Laverne are completed and deposed. The Lt.-General signs the submission to the Royal Prosecutor of the ten statements made. The Royal Prosecutor decrees the arrest of both Sade and Latour.

July 4 (?)—The Marquis, either fearing trouble or being unofficially informed of his impending arrest, flees from La Coste château accompanied by his sister-in-law, Anne.

July 5—The pharmacists who have analyzed both the matter thrown up by Marguerite Coste and the uneaten candy found in Mariette Borelly's room, conclude that they have found no trace of arsenic, nor any corrosive sublimate in the specimens.

July 11—Acting upon the warrant of July 4, the bailiff of Apt with three mounted men and a brigadier from the Constabulary, go to La Coste and are advised that Sade and Latour have departed a week before. Further warrants are then issued for their arrest, as are summons for them to appear before the court two weeks from that date. The possessions of the two fugitives are impounded and listed.

Mid-July—The Marquise de Sade goes to Marseilles to appeal her husband's case before the magistrates.

August 8 and 17—Marguerite Coste and Marianne Laverne appear before a Marseilles lawyer and drop their charges against Sade and Latour.

---

9 Given that the eighteenth-century penalty for sodomy, for either party involved, was death, the girls' denials are understandable.

August 26—The Royal Prosecutor orders special proceedings against the accused and missing persons and stipulates that the re-examination of witnesses shall require confrontation.

August 29—The President de Montreuil joins his daughter, the Marquise de Sade, at La Coste, the younger sister Anne being in flight with the Marquis.

September 3—Final verdict: Sade and Latour, being declared contumacious and defaulting, are found guilty, the former of the crimes of poisoning and sodomy and the latter of the crime of sodomy, and are condemned to expiate their crimes at the cathedral porch before being taken to the Place Saint-Louis "for the said Sade to be decapitated . . . and the said Latour to be hanged by the neck and strangled . . . then the body of the said Sade and that of the said Latour to be burned and their ashes strewn to the wind."

September 11—Judgment at the bar of the High Court of Provence (the chamber summoned during the summer vacation) confirms and renders executive the sentence of the Seneschal's Court of Marseilles.

September 12—Sade and Latour are executed in effigy on the Place des Prêcheurs, in Aix.

October 7—The Canoness, Lady Anne de Launay, returns to La Coste and remains there with her sister.[10]

October 27—Leaving his luggage at Nice, Sade reaches Chambéry, traveling under the name of the Count de Mazan. With him are Latour, another footman named Carteron, and his sister-in-law, Lady Anne.

Early November—After putting up for a few days at the Pomme d'Or, Sade rents a country house for six months, the house being outside the city gates. About the same time, having discovered her son-in-law's whereabouts, Lady de Montreuil prevails upon the Duke d'Aiguillon to ask the King of Sardinia's ambassador to issue

---

[10] Some accounts have it that Lady Anne did not long remain with her sister, but that by mid-October she herself had decamped again to rejoin the Marquis, her brother-in-law. (Cf. Lely: *La Vie du Marquis de Sade,* Vol. I, Paris, Librairie Gallimard, 1952, p. 355.)

a Royal Order "for the arrest and imprisonment of the Count de Mazan, a French nobleman in retreat at Chambéry."

December 8—Major de Chavanne and two adjutants, acting upon the order of His Majesty the King of Sardinia, Duke of Savoy, arrest Sade and Latour at Sade's Chambéry residence.

December 9—The Marquis is driven by post chaise, escorted by four cavalrymen, to the Fort Miolans prison, where he signs a pledge to the commander of the fort, M. de Launay, not to attempt to escape. Latour constitutes himself a voluntary prisoner, joining his master behind bars.

December 18—A family council convening in Avignon declares before a notary public that, given the absence of the Marquis, the education of his children and the administration of their property shall be confided to the Marquise, who is appointed their guardian *ad hoc*.

1773. Aet. 33

January 1—Commandant de Launay, in a letter to the Governor of Savoy, describes his prisoner as "unreliable as he is hot tempered and impulsive . . . capable of some desperate action" and suggests that Sade be transferred to a more secure prison. Over the ensuing weeks, de Launay reiterates this request and several times over disclaims responsibility for the security of Sade.

March 6—The Marquise, having left Paris a week or so before, arrives by post chaise at Chambéry, disguised in masculine clothing and accompanied by a friend and confidant, Alberet.

March 7–14—Repeated attempts by the Marquise to see her husband, which de Launay, in constant contact with the Governor of Savoy, steadfastly refuses. Finally giving up all hope of seeing her husband, Madame de Sade leaves by post chaise for Lyons.

March 18—Back at La Coste, the Marquise writes both to the Count de la Tour and to the King of Sardinia[11] imploring each to

---

[11] There was now a new king, Charles Emmanuel III, who had been ruling at the time of Sade's imprisonment, having died on February 20, 1773. His son Victor Amadeus III succeeded him.

intercede on behalf of her husband. To the latter she notes: "My husband is not to be classed with the rogues of whom the universe should be purged. . . . Bias against him has turned [a misdemeanor] into a crime," which she dismisses as a "youthful folly that endangered no life nor honor nor the reputation of any citizen. . . ."

April 30—At approximately 8:30 P.M., Sade, the Baron de l'Allée (a fellow prisoner), and Latour climb out of the only unbarred window of the fortress and, aided by a local farmer, Joseph Violin, head for the French frontier.

May 1—Walking all night, the fugitives reach the village of Chapareillant by sunup, but by the time a search party sent out by de Launay arrives at the French border Sade is well on his way to Grenoble. How long he remained in Grenoble and exactly where he hid out remain unknown, but sometime before the end of 1773 he returns clandestinely to join his wife at La Coste.

December 16—Lady de Montreuil obtains a court order to have the Marquis incarcerated anew in Pierre-Encise prison.

1774. Aet. 34

January 6—Inspector Goupil of the Paris police, armed with the court orders of December 16 and accompanied by four bowmen and a troup of mounted constables from Marseilles, force their way at night into La Coste castle, but find only the Marquise. Goupil searches the place, and especially the Marquis' study, whose papers he confiscates or burns.

March 25—The Minister of the Royal Household, the Duke de la Vrillière, in transferring the King's orders relative to the Marquis de Sade to the Governor of Provence, suggests that it would be best to arrest him not under his own roof but while he is out making the rounds in the neighborhood.

April 12—The Governor replies to the Duke de la Vrillière that Sade is not at La Coste and promises to undertake a discreet investigation.

July 14—At 3:00 A.M. Lady Anne writes to the Abbé de Sade to inform him of her sudden departure, together with her sister, for Paris.[12]

November 17—Lady Anne, in Paris, reproaches the Abbé for not having replied to her. About this same date, Madame de Sade returns to La Coste, whether or not in the company of the Marquis is not clear. But it is clear that they had been together in Lyons, and were together later at La Coste. Throughout the winter the Sades remain at La Coste, seldom venturing abroad and seeing very few people.

1775. Aet. 35

January—Very little is known of the "young girls' scandal" which dates from this winter. On their way back from Paris in November of the preceding year, the Marquise, either alone or in concert with the Marquis, hired seven new servants: one was a young maid named Nanon, five other girls fifteen years of age, and a secretary (male) a trifle older. Some of the parents claimed the girls had been taken without their consent, and in January at least three of the parents filed a complaint. Criminal proceedings were instituted at Lyons, and the Marquise voyaged there to try and quash the affair. One of the girls was secretly taken to the Abbé de Sade and another placed in a nunnery, whence she escaped several months later.

January 21—Sade prepares a formal refutation of the accusations made against him by the girl presently with his uncle and also against the accusations made by the Abbé himself.

February 11—Lady de Montreuil sends the first of a long series of letters to the notary Gaufridy of Apt, Sade's recently appointed legal adviser. She entreats him to assume the responsibility for promptly returning, in person and with all guarantees, these girls to their parents in Lyons and Vienne, including the girl presently at the Abbé de Sade's at Saumane.

---

[12] Exactly how long Lady Anne had been at La Coste, and what her precise relationship with her brother-in-law was by now, is not clear from any extant records.

February 15—The Marquise does not want to return the girls until they have first been examined by a doctor who will furnish them with an appropriate medical certificate. She begs the Abbé not to let the girl in his charge be seen.

May 3—From Aix-en-Provence, the President Bruny d'Entrecastaux simultaneously informs the heads of both junior branches of the family, the Count de Sade-Eyguières and Count Sade-Vauredone, the provost of Saint-Victor of Marseilles, that he has it firsthand that the Marquis de Sade is at La Coste, where he indulges in excesses of every kind with young people of both sexes whom he kidnaps especially from Lyons, in which city charges have been deposed against him.

May 11—Anne Sablonnière, known as Nanon, chambermaid at La Coste, gives birth at Courthézon to a baby girl, Anne Elizabeth, the certificate of baptism attributing the paternity to her husband Barthélemy Fayère, but "some people maintain it was conceived by the work of the Lord of the Manor."

May 18—The Abbé de Sade requests the capture of his nephew, who is presently at La Coste, and demands that he be incarcerated as a madman.

June 20—Alexandre de Nerclos, Prior of the Jumiège convent, informs the Abbé de Sade that he has lately opened his door to a young girl who has escaped from La Coste, whence three servants of the Marquis have come to seize her on the pretext that she had stolen forty *livres*. He turns her over to the Abbé's confidant so that he can place her under his protection as he has with the others from the manor.

June 21—The Marquise brings a complaint against Nanon, charging her with the theft of some household silver. This is merely a maneuver to hold Nanon in check pending the arrival of a Royal *lettre de cachet* which Lady Montreuil has said was forthcoming, for the Sades now consider Nanon the source of all their trouble with the other girls and are apprehensive lest she go to Lyons and stir up the whole business again.

June 22—The Prior de Nerclos assures the Abbé de Sade that he believes he has stifled any unfortunate rumors, but adds that the

Marquis must be shut up for the rest of his days. He is also convinced that "the Marquise is no better than her husband, for he knows that no one in their house went to confession on Easter Sunday and Lady de Sade allows her servants to have dealings with a married Lutheran woman."

July 5—The Minister of the Royal Household informs Madame de Montreuil that he has just issued the necessary Royal Orders for Nanon to be imprisoned at Arles.

July 30—Nanon's daughter, Anne Elizabeth, dies at La Coste, her wet nurse, being six months pregnant, having no more milk.

August—Sade is traveling incognito in Italy under the name of the Count de Mazan. In Florence, he steeps himself in the works of art of the Grand Duke's "superb gallery."

September 29—The Marquis arrives in Rome.

October 6—One of Sade's bailiffs is instructed to visit Nanon in the house of constraint at Arles. She threatens to kill herself if she is not set free, and relates to the bailiff "a thousand horrors."

October 17—The Marquise thanks the Abbé for persuading the Isle-sur-Sorgue hospital to accept the girl he had been keeping in his charge. She agrees to pay the expenses but asks that the girl not be allowed to speak to anyone.

November 10—The Abbé de Sade reports to the notary Gaufridy that the girl is completely well again and that he intends to take her out of the hospital and give her to the care of one of the Marquis' farmers in Mazan, Ripert by name, where she will be better off than at Saumane and less likely to talk to strangers.

1776. Aet. 36

End of January—The Marquis is at Naples, where the French chargé d'affaires, M. Beranger, mistakes him for a certain M. Tessier, cashier of a Lyons store who has absconded with eighty thousand *livres*. To exculpate himself, he is obliged to reveal his real identity, produce supporting documents and agree to be presented t court in his colonel's uniform. He writes both to Gaufridy and to his wife asking whatever he would do if, because of his reputation, he was recognized and attacked.

March 15—The Marquise learns that one of the girls involved in the La Coste scandal has left the Caderousse convent for Lyons, in the company of two young men who have come for her, one of whom declares he is her godfather. About the same time, Sade writes to his wife proposing to return to La Coste, but she dispatches Sade's valet Carteron, known as La Jeunesse, to Naples, to dissuade him from such a risky undertaking.

May 4—M. de Mazan leaves Naples, and on June 1 arrives at Rome.

End of June—Sade reaches Grenoble, via Bologne and Turin; from Grenoble he sends Carteron ahead to La Coste to prepare his return by mid-July.

July 26—Sade is now at home, and rumors circulate that he has turned religious—one rumor even has it that he had been received by the Pope—none of which the Marquise tries to quash. Meanwhile, the girl placed in farmer Ripert's care also flees, but before returning to Vienne she spends a week at Orange making a deposition there to the local magistrate.

November 2—Father Durand, recollect monk, is charged by Sade, who is in Montpellier, to find him a cook for La Coste. Catherine Trillet (or Treillet) is suggested, and the monk vouches to her father, a coverlet weaver, for the standing of La Coste and assures him that, as far as morals go, it is "like a nunnery." Her father consents, and the twenty-two-year-old Catherine, who is described as "very pretty," is driven to La Coste by Father Durand.

November 4—The Marquis is back at La Coste. Money is an increasingly serious problem: the forty thousand *livres* due the Marquis as Lt.-General of Bresse are under sequester. At her daughter's request, Lady Montreuil sends 1200 *livres* not directly to her daughter but to the lawyer Gaufridy, with strict orders for him to spend it only on pressing domestic needs.

Mid-December—Sade has written to Father Durand to engage four servants for La Coste. On December 13 or 14, there arrive a secretary named Rolland, a wigmaker, a chambermaid named Cavanis and a kitchenmaid "of foreign origin." The following morning three of the four—all but the kitchenmaid—return to Montpellier where they inform M. Trillet what has transpired at the manor.[13] Trillet, worried about his daughter, demands that Father Durand write to Sade requesting that he return Catherine to her father.

Late December—Gaufridy receives an anonymous letter notifying him that an officer and ten horsemen have been ordered to go to the Ste.-Clair fair at Apt and arrest the Marquis. Thus forewarned, Sade avoids the fair.

1777. Aet. 37

January 14—Marie-Eléonore de Maillé de Carman, Dowager Countess de Sade, dies at the Carmelite convent in the rue Enfer in Paris, aged sixty-five.

January 17—Toward one o'clock M. Trillet comes to La Coste to claim his daughter, who is known in the château as Justine. During an argument with the Marquis, Trillet fires a pistol shot at him almost point blank, but misses. He runs off to the La Coste township where he babbles about what has happened. At about five o'clock Catherine sends someone to find her father, who returns to the château. There she tries to calm him, but Trillet, who has brought four other men back with him, flies into another rage and fires a second shot into a courtyard where he thinks Sade to be. All five men then flee.

January 18—The junior magistrate at La Coste, learning of the attempted murder the previous day, begins to hear witnesses.

January 20—Trillet leaves La Coste, after professing to Messrs. Paulet and Vidal that he feels "the sincerest emotions of friendship and attachment for the Marquis."

---

13 What actually did transpire is not clear, but it would appear that Sade was accused by the new domestics of having tried during the night to have his way with each of them, an allegation that Sade categorically denied, as might be expected.

Late January—In Aix, Trillet enters a charge, backed by a state-ment outlining what had transpired a month before at La Coste with the newly hired servants. Upon their return to Montpellier, according to Trillet, the three domestics had told him that the Mar-quis had, during the night, "tried to have his way with them by of-fering them a purse of silver." His decision to take back his daughter, Trillet adds, was reinforced by the fact that the superior of Father Durand's monastery, having learned of the affair, ex-pelled Durand from the monastery. In his denial, Sade claims that he never asked Father Durand to hire these servants for him, hav-ing no need of them, and that it was for this reason he had them returned the following day to Montpellier. Sade adds that he found all "these people frightfully prepossessing" and notes that one would have to be an "arch fool" to have aggravated "their ill hu-mor brought about by their pointless trip" by trying to "outrage them during the night." Moreover, he notes, how could he have tried to bribe them with money, since he had none?

January 30—The Attorney General of Aix makes known, through the intermediary of the Aix lawyer Mouret, his opinion as to the Trillet affair, which is that the father should be given im-mediate satisfaction. After so many other imperfectly quashed af-fairs, the consequences of the present one might become most serious.

February 1—Sade, en route for Paris,[14] reaches Tain, near Va-lence. Sade is traveling with La Jeunesse, while the Marquise is with Catherine Trillet, who has begged Madame to take her along and not send her back to Montpellier.

February 8—The Sades reach Paris and learn of the Dowager Countess' death in mid-January. Sade puts up at his former tutor's, Abbé Amblet, who gives him a warm reception.

February 10 or 12—Madame de Sade decides that the time has come for her to inform her mother that her husband is in Paris.

---

[14] Perhaps alarmed by news of the Dowager Countess' state of health. The Sades did not learn of the Dowager's death until their arrival in Paris on February 8, thus three weeks after the event.

February 13—The Marquis de Sade is arrested by Inspector Marais at the Hôtel de Danemark on the rue Jacob and taken to Vincennes fortress where, at 9:30 that night, he is formally entered as a prisoner.

Late February—Sade writes his wife his first letter as a prisoner (she still does not know in which prison he has been incarcerated): "I feel it completely impossible to long endure a condition so cruel. I am overwhelmed with despair. . . . My blood is too hot to bear such terrible restriction. . . . If I am not released in four days, I shall crack my skull against these walls." All Lady Sade's applications to see her husband are denied.

April 18—Sade to his wife: "I am in a tower closed in by nineteen iron doors, with light reaching me only through two little windows, each with a score of iron bars." He complains that in over the two months he has been in prison he has been allowed only five walks of one hour each, "in a sort of tomb about forty feet square surrounded by walls more than fifty feet high."

June 24—Madame de Sade is now aware that her husband is being held at Vincennes.

September 1—Sade, in a letter to his wife, expresses the horror of his situation and says that, before experiencing it, he would never have believed it. Such cages should be reserved for savage beasts, he notes, not for human beings.

September 23 and 24—Both Lady de Montreuil and Lady de Sade write to the Minister of the Royal Household in favor of the quashing of the sentence of 1772 and requesting that this be formally submitted to the King in his Council of Dispatches of the 26th inst.

1778. Aet. 38

Early February—Nanon is set free, on condition that she not come within three leagues of Lyons or Vienne.

April 30—Jean-Baptiste-Joseph-David, Comte de Sade d'Eyguières, obtains from the King the post of Lt.-General of the provinces of Bresse, Bugey, Valromey and Gex formerly held by the Marquis de Sade, which has been in suspense for the past five years.

May 23—Faced with the choice of having recourse to the plea of insanity or of personally appearing before the High Court of Provence (in connection with the Marseilles affair of 1772), Sade opts for the second choice.

May 27—The King grants the Marquis de Sade papers of *ester à droit* to appeal the sentence of the High Court of Provence, despite the expiration of the legal period of five years.

June 14—Escorted by Inspector Marais, Sade leaves Vincennes to journey to Aix, arriving there on the evening of Saturday, June 20.

June 30—A crowd of 200 gathers at the door of the Jacobin monastery where the High Court holds its sessions, in anticipation of seeing the Marquis de Sade, but the prisoner both arrives and departs in a sedan chair with curtains drawn, thus thwarting their curiosity. Plaintiff's Counsel Joseph-Jérôme Siméon and the Royal Attorney, General d'Eymar de Montmeyan, both speak eloquently in Sade's behalf, and the Court, after deliberation, declares the Marseilles trial null and void for absolute lack of evidence of any poisoning. The Court also orders a new investigation of the allegations of libertinage and pederasty alone, and the hearing of witnesses.

July 7–10—Cross-examination of Sade. The following day the Court issues a decision ordering a special trial. On July 10 there is a re-examination of the witnesses and confrontation with the accused.

July 14—The Marquis is cross-examined publicly in the High Court chambers, returning shortly thereafter for the judgment, which finds Sade guilty of acts of debauch and excessive libertinage. The Court orders that "Louis-Aldonse-Donatien de Sade be admonished behind the bench in the presence of the Attorney General in future to be of more seemly conduct," and prohibits him "to live in or frequent the city of Marseilles for three years." Further, he is condemned to pay fifty *livres* applicable to the prison fund and the cost of justice.

July 15—Sade leaves Aix, escorted by Marais, Marais' younger brother Antoine and two junior guards, on his way back to Vincennes where, in spite of his legal victory, he is still a prisoner of the King's by virtue of the *lettre de cachet* of February 13, 1777.

July 16—At Valence, where the party has stopped at an inn overnight, the Marquis makes his escape. In spite of a thorough search of the immediate vicinity, no trace is found of Sade, who described what happened in his "Story of My Imprisonment": "I had taken refuge about half a mile out of town in a shanty near a farmer's threshing floor. Then two local countrymen guided me. We first went toward Montelimar, but after a league we changed our minds and returned to the Rhône, intending to cross it, but we could not find a boat. Finally, just as day was breaking, one of us crossed the river to Vivarais where he found a boat that was suitable and this, for a *louis,* took me down to Avignon." At Avignon, Sade goes to a friend's house, has supper, and orders a carriage to take him that same night to La Coste.

July 18—Sade reaches La Coste, where he spends a quiet month, with Mlle. Dorothée de Rousset acting as housekeeper.

July 27—Madame de Sade has only recently learned from her mother of the verdict of the High Court of Aix (but she has not yet learned of Sade's escape). Upon being informed that her husband, although cleared at Aix, must nevertheless return to his cell at Vincennes, she "completely loses control of herself" in the course of a terrible scene with her mother.

August 19—Warned of the presence of suspicious characters in the region, the Marquis takes to hiding out at various places in the neighborhood of La Coste.

August 23—Sade, in spite of strong pleas by his friend Canon Vidal, returns to take up residence at La Coste.

August 26—At 4:00 A.M. the door to Sade's chamber is forced by a group of armed men, whose leader covers the culprit, before witnesses, with the foulest insults.

September 7—After thirteen days' travel by post chaise then further travel by stage coach, Sade arrives at 8:30 P.M. at Vincennes, where he is locked in cell No. 6.

November 6—Mlle. de Rousset arrives in Paris to stay with the Marquise.

December 7—After three months' solitary confinement, Sade is allowed to have pen and paper and to write as he please, and is given permission to take exercise twice a week.

1779. Aet. 39

January—Sade sends season's greetings in verse to Mlle. de Rousset, whom he now addresses as "Saint" Rousset, because of her boundless goodness toward him.

March 29—Sade's exercise periods are increased to three a week.

July 15—He now enjoys five exercise periods a week.

November 9—Mlle. de Rousset, to whom Sade has been writing letters full of unjust reproaches and complaints, breaks off her correspondence with him, although she remains devoted to him and continues her unflagging efforts on his behalf.

1780. Aet. 40

April 21—Sade is visited by M. Le Noir[15] who informs him that he will soon be permitted to receive a visit from his wife.

April 25—Sade's exercise periods become daily.

June 26—An altercation with a jailer, whom Sade maintains was extremely insolent to him, results in the suspension of his daily exercise periods.

June 28—The Captain of the Guard, M. de Valage, who comes to inform the prisoner officially of the suppression of his walks, is

---

[15] Charles Le Noir (1732–1807), Chief of Police of Paris for approximately a ten-year period ending in August, 1785. He is best remembered for his work in improving the hospitals and abolishing torture. He was generally known as a kind, just person, qualities rarely found in the men occupying such a position.

threatened and berated by Sade. According to the report of the warden, M. de Rougemont,[16] Sade then begins to shout at the top of his voice trying to arouse the other prisoners. Spying a fellow prisoner whom he detested, Mirabeau, down below in the prison yard taking exercise, Sade shouts at him out of his cell window, calling him the Commandant's (*i.e.* de Rougemont's) catamite, blaming him for his, Sade's, being deprived of his walks, suggesting he might go kiss the warden's ass. Sade dares him to answer, adding for good measure that he intends, once free, to lop off Mirabeau's ears. To which Mirabeau replies: "My name is that of a man of honor who has never either dissected or poisoned any women, a man who will be only too pleased to write his name on your shoulders with a razor, if only you're not broken on the wheel before I have a chance to do so, a man you inspire with one fear only, and that is that you might put him in mourning à la Grève." (The square where executions are then taking place.)

July 24—The motives for holding Sade prisoner are debated at Versailles, and the First Minister orders that all information relating to the Marquis' case be gathered and given him for examination.

December 13—Mirabeau, leaving Vincennes prison, endorses his official discharge on the back of the record of Sade's arrival there on February 13, 1777.

1781. Aet. 41

March 9—After thirty-six weeks, the prisoner's exercise periods are restored.

May 10—Lady Anne de Launay, Sade's sister-in-law, falls ill with smallpox, the first signs of the disease appearing this Thursday evening.

---

16 Charles de Rougemont was the bastard son of the Marquis d'Oise, his mother being an English woman named Mrs. Hatt. Sade, who loathed the man, often referred to him is "that quarter Englishman" or simply "that mongrel." He also had more highly descriptive epithets for de Rougemont, one of which was "a toad in breeches." He was, wrote Sade, one of those men "so robot-like, so idiotic, so dimwitted that he could never think of any way to refuse a request but by saying 'It has never been done before, I've never known it to be done before.'"

May 13—Lady Anne dies at 1:00 P.M.

June—Mlle. de Rousset is back at La Coste, where she once again corresponds with the Marquis.

July 13—Sade receives his first visit from his wife, after a separation of four years and five months. They are allowed to meet only in the presence of a witness.

Early October—M. Le Noir suspends the visits of the Marquise because of the violent attacks of husbandly jealousy to which Sade was subject. To counter Sade's suspicions—most probably completely without foundation—Lady de Sade moves from her apartment on the rue de la Marche and withdraws into the convent of Sainte-Aure.

1782. Aet. 42

July 12—Sade completes the manuscript of his *Dialogue between a Priest and a Dying Man.*

August 6—Sade is deprived of all books because they "overheated his head" and led him to write "unseemly things."

September 25—Resumed after January, the Marquise's rare visits are again suspended because of the prisoner's poor conduct.

1783. Aet. 43

February—Sade, suffering from eye trouble, is treated by the oculist Grandjean.

April 1—Madame de Sade informs her husband of the marriage of her younger sister, Françoise-Pélagie, born October 12, 1760, to the Marquis de Wavrin, the wedding having taken place toward the end of January.

. . . . —Louis-Marie de Sade, the Marquis' eldest son, is named sub-lieutenant in the Rohan-Soubise Regiment. Sade, wanting him to wear the same cavalry uniform he had worn, is furious and writes his wife, categorically objecting to the appointment.

1784. Aet. 44

January 25—Mlle. de Rousset, who has long been suffering from tuberculosis, dies at La Coste, aged forty years and nineteen days.

February 29—Excerpt from the *Répertoire ou Journalier du château de la Bastille:* "M. Surbois, inspector of police, has taken the Marquis de Sade from Vincennes at nine o'clock in the evening. The Royal Order, counter signed by Breteuil, is dated January 31: he is lodged in second Liberty.[17]

March 3—M. Le Noir writes to the Governor of the Bastille recommending that Sade, like two other noblemen recently transferred from Vincennes to the Bastille, be allowed to take periodic walks at the latter prison.

March 8—Sade, in a letter to his wife, complains of conditions at the Bastille, maintaining they are far worse than at Vincennes.

March 16—Madame de Sade pays her first visit to the Bastille, bringing him six pounds of candles. She is allowed to visit him twice monthly.

July 16—Le Noir authorizes Grandjean, the oculist, to attend to the Marquis.

1785. Aet. 45

October 22—The Marquis begins the final revision of his draft of a major work, *The 120 Days of Sodom or The School for Libertines.*

---

[17] That is, on the second floor of Liberty Tower. When Sade was imprisoned in the Bastille, Liberty Tower consisted of two dungeon cells, six rooms one above the other and a circle of narrow cells. Sade's room, on the second floor, like the one below it and the four above, was some fifteen feet in diameter and about eighteen feet high.

November 12—In twenty evenings of work, between seven and ten, he covers one side of a twelve-meter-long roll of paper which he has prepared for this purpose.

November 28—After thirty-seven days of work Sade completes the second side of the famous manuscript of *The 120 Days* in the form in which it has come down to us.

. . . . —Cardinal de Rohan is imprisoned in the Bastille. The presence of the Church dignitary stops all private visits to all prisoners.

1786. Aet. 46

July 13—Madame de Sade's visits, at the rate of one a month, are reinstated.

1787. Aet. 47

May 23—The prisoner, who hitherto has been allowed a one-hour walk only every second day, is now provisionally given an hour's walk daily.

May 25—Madame de Sade writes to Gaufridy that M. Sade is in fair health but getting "very fat."

June 21—A simple decree of the Châtelet in Paris provides for the administration of the properties of the Marquis de Sade, he "being absent for the past ten years."

July 8—Sade completes *Les Infortunes de la Vertu,* a philosophical story 138 pages long which he wrote in two weeks, in spite of the fact that, as he pencils in the margin of the last page, "All the time I was writing this my eyes bothered me."

October 7—Owing to the arrival of a prisoner just as he was supposed to begin his walk, Sade's exercise hour is suspended, and he has what the official report describes as a "violent outburst."[18]

---

[18] Letter of October 10, 1787, from Major de Losme-Salbry to the Chief of Police.

October 10—Sade berates the Governor and his aide who come to announce to him the suspension of his exercise periods.

October 23—Sade's exercise right is restored.

1788. Aet. 48

March 1—Sade begins work upon his short novel *Eugénie de Franval*, which he completes in six days.

June 5—Sade's exercise period again having been suspended "for impertinence" and he having so been informed in writing, the prisoner nonetheless attempts to descend at his regular hour to the yard and, according to de Losme, "it was only when the officer [stationed at his door] pointed his gun at him that he retreated, swearing loudly."

October 1—Sade draws up the *Catalogue raisonné* of his writings. By now, apart from his clandestine works, he has the contents of fifteen octavo volumes.

October—At Madame de Sade's request, the Lt.-General of police authorizes the prisoner to read magazines and newspapers.

1789. Aet. 49

January–June—Authorized on November 24 of the preceding year to visit her husband weekly rather than bi-weekly, Madame de Sade pays her husband twenty-three visits during the first half of 1789.

July 2—The Bastille logbook notes that "The Count de Sade" shouted several times from the window of the Bastille that the prisoners were being slaughtered and that the people should come to liberate them."

---

[19] Although Sade is known as, and bore the title of, Marquis, he was also often referred to as "Count." In a letter to his wife written early in 1784, Sade in fact announced his intention to pass on the title of Marquis to his eldest son Louis-Marie, and himself assume the title of Count, "following the custom of all [noble] families."

July 4—At 1:00 A.M., as a result of a report made to Lord de Villedeuil on the Marquis' conduct on July 2, he is transferred to Charenton Asylum by Inspector Quidor.[20]

July 9—Sade signs the authorization requested by Commissaire Chenot to have his Bastille cell, which was placed under seals on July 4, opened in the presence of his emissary, Madame de Sade.

July 14—Awakened by the quickening pace of events, Madame de Sade, who has not yet carried out her commission relative to Sade's personal belongings left behind in the Bastille, sends her authorization to Commissaire Chenot and then leaves town for the country. The Bastille is stormed and Sade's cell sacked, his furniture, his suits and linen, his library and, most important, his manuscripts, are "burned, pillaged, torn up and carried off."

July 19—Madame de Sade informs Commissaire Chenot that, for personal reasons, she cannot consider herself responsible for the papers and effects of the Marquis de Sade.

October 5—Madame de Sade escapes from Paris, accompanied by her daughter and a maid, to avoid being "dragged out by the women of the lower classes who are forcing all the women in the town houses to march with them through the rain and mud to Versailles to seize the King." She then relates that the King has been brought from Versailles to Paris, "the heads of his two bodyguards set on pikes before him," and that "Paris is in a state of intoxication."

1790. Aet. 50

March 13—The Constituent Assembly adopts a projected decree concerning the *lettres de cachet* stipulating that all prisoners detained by such Royal Orders will be released save for those condemned to death, indicted or judged insane.

---

[20] An asylum run by the charity order of friars known as the Petits Pères. According to Sade's own description, his transfer from the Bastille to Charenton was effected by six men who, pistol in hand, entered his cell and tore him from his bed. He was allowed to take nothing with him, neither his books nor manuscripts.

March 18—Sade is visited at Charenton by his two sons, whom he has not seen in fifteen years and who have come to inform him of the decree of the Assembly.

April 2—On this day, Good Friday, Sade recovers his liberty and leaves Charenton, without a penny. He goes directly to see the man who is handling his affairs, M. de Milly, attorney at the Châtelet Court, who provides him with a bed to sleep in and six *louis*.

April 3—Madame de Sade, a resident of the convent of Sainte-Aure, refuses to see her husband from whom she has decided to separate.

April 28—Madame de Sade formally applies to the Châtelet Court for a separation order. Sade, who claims he has already seen her attitude changing toward him, tends to blame it upon the influence of her Father Confessor.

June 9—The Châtelet Court issues a separation order and instructs the Marquis de Sade to restore to his wife 160,842 *livres* received as marriage settlement.

July 1—Sade obtains an identity card as "an active citizen" of the Place Vendôme Section, later to be known as the Piques Section.

August 3—The Théâtre Italien accepts his one-act verse play, *Le Suborneur*.

August 17—Sade gives a reading at the Comédie-Française of his one-act play in free verse, *Le Boudoir ou le mari crédule*. A week later the play is rejected, but a second reading agreed to, providing the author makes some changes.

August 25—Sade forms a liaison with a young actress, Marie-Constance Renelle, her husband Balthazar Quesnet having deserted her and left her with their one child. This liaison, which Sade will describe many times as "less than platonic," but founded on mutual love and attachment, will last the rest of his life.[21]

---

[21] In a letter to Reinaud, his Aix attorney, Sade writes: "Nothing was ever more virtuous than my little nest. To begin with, there is not a hint of love-making. She is just a decent, kindly, matronly person, sweet and good and with a keen mind. . . ." (Letter of January, 1791.)

September 16—Sade's five-act play, *Le Misanthrope par amour ou Sophie et Desfrancs,* is "unanimously accepted" by the Comédie-Française.

November 1—Sade moves into a house with garden at No. 20, rue Neuve-des-Mathurins, off the Chaussée d'Antin.

1791. Aet. 51

March 5—Sade writes to Reinaud telling him that he will send the four volumes of his novel, *Aline et Valcour,* which are to be printed by Easter. He also remarks that he now has five plays accepted by various theaters.

June 12—Sade notes, in a letter to Reinaud, that his novel *Justine ou les Malheurs de la Vertu* is being printed, adding that it is "too immoral a work for so religious and modest a man as yourself."

October 22—First performance, at the Théâtre Molière on the rue Saint-Martin, of Sade's *Le Comte Oxtiern ou les effets du libertinage.* A second performance is given two weeks later, on November 4, which gives rise to a disturbance and causes Sade to suspend further performances.

November 24—Sade gives a reading to the Comédie-Française of his *Jeanne Laisné ou le Siège de Beauvais,* which is rejected by an eight-to-five vote.

1792. Aet. 52

March 5—At the Théâtre Italien, a Jacobin cabal, all wearing red bonnets with the point forward, makes so much noise that *Le Suborneur* cannot be completed and the performance is halted after the fourth scene. The reason given for the demonstration: the author was an aristocrat.

May—Sub-Lieutenant Donatien-Claude-Armand de Sade, aide-de-camp of the Marquis de Toulongeon, deserts.

August 18—Sade solemnly disavows his sons' emigration, a necessary step taken to save himself, the Republic having issued a decree making parents responsible for the actions of their children.

September 3—During the massacres,[22] Sade is for the first time the secretary of his section.

September 17–21—A crowd of people from La Coste—men, women and children—force their way into the château and ransack it, destroying or carting away most of the furniture. The municipal guard is helpless to cope with the mob, but the municipality does its best to save what remains of Sade's furniture and effects and has them housed in the vicarage, until they are carted away a week later by two bailiffs from Apt who arrive with a requisition order and abuse their limited authority to load all pieces of value onto four wagons, over the protests of the La Coste municipal council.

October 17—Sade is a soldier in the 8th Company of the Piques Section and commissaire for the organization of the cavalry in that section.

October—Sade in possession of the first copies of his political pamphlet *Idées sur le mode de la sanction des Loix,* which is published by his own section and sent to the other forty-seven sections of Paris for their study and opinion.

November 4—Sade is called by the Piques Section to do twenty-four hours' guard duty commencing at 9:00 A.M.

December 13—Under the name Louis-Alphonse-Donatien Sade, the Marquis' name is entered—whether by error or willful malice—on the list of *émigrés* of the Bouches-du-Rhône department.

1793. Aet. 53

January 21—"Louis Capet, thirty-nine, profession: last King of the French" is guillotined on the Place de la Revolution at 10:22 A.M.

---

[22] On September 3, ten thousand prisoners were slaughtered. "Nothing can equal the horror of the massacre," Sade wrote to Gaufridy on September 5. "The former Princess de Lamballe was one of the victims. Her head, stuck on a pike, was shown to the King and Queen and her body, after being subjected to the most savage debauchery, was dragged through the streets for eight hours. . . ."

February 26—Together with Citizens Carré and Desormeaux, Sade signs the report he has drawn up concerning their inspection of five hospitals which the Hospital Commission had entrusted them with on January 17.

April 13—In a letter to Gaufridy, Sade announces that he has been appointed court assessor. "I have two items of news which will surprise you. Lord Montreuil has been to see me![23] And guess the other! I would give you a hundred guesses! I am appointed magistrate, yes, magistrate! By the prosecution! Who, my dear lawyer, would have told you that fifteen years back? You see how wise my old head is becoming in its old age...."

June 15—Citizen Sade, secretary of the assembly of the sections of Paris, is appointed one of the four delegates who the following day are to present an address to the Convention calling for an annulment of the decree which established a Parisian army of six thousand men at forty *sous* a day.

June 26—A new department, the Vaucluse, is created out of the former Bouches-du-Rhône department, but in submitting the list of *émigrés* to the new department Sade's name, which has been ordered from the list, still appears there, a fact which is later to have grave consequences for him.

July 23—Sade has been appointed chairman of the Piques Section, and he announces the news with elation to Gaufridy.

August 2—At a stormy session of the Piques Section, Sade gives up the chair to the vice-chairman, refusing to act as chairman for a proposal he deems "horrible . . . utterly inhuman."

September 29—The General Assembly of the Piques Section, "approving the principles and vigor" of Sade's pamphlet entitled *Discours aux mânes de Marat et de Le Peletier,* decides to print it and send it to the National Assembly.

November 15 (25 Brumaire, Year II)—Sade is the leader of seven other delegates who appear before the bar of the National

---

[23] The former President de Montreuil had come to visit his son-in-law, whom he had not seen in fifteen years, at the Piques Section of which Sade was secretary. Sade was obviously pleased by the deferential visit.

Convention to read the *Petition of the Piques Section to the Representatives of the French People,* of which Sade is the author.[24]

December 8 (18 Frimaire, Year II)—A warrant is issued for Sade's arrest based on a letter Sade had written two years earlier, and he is arrested at his house on the rue Neuve-des-Mathurins and taken to Madelonnettes prison.[25]

1794. Aet. 54

January 13 (23 Nivôse, Year II)—The police department of Paris orders the transfer of the prisoner Sade to the Carmelite convent on the rue de Vaugirard.[26]

January 22 (3 Pluviôse, Year II)—By order of the police department dated 1 Pluviôse, Sade is transferred to the Saint-Lazare prison.[27]

February 12 (24 Pluviôse, Year II)—Sade's name is again (by error?) placed on the list of *émigrés,* under the Christian names of Louis-Alphonse-Donatien, with the mention "Vaucluse, Apt, December 13, 1793."

March 8 (18 Ventôse, Year II)—Sade submits a report in his defense to the Committee of Public Safety defending his conduct since 1789. In it he maintains he was overjoyed when the King ("the most immoral rascal and the most outrageous tyrant") was

[24] The petition proposed the idolatrous worship of the Virtues at the deserted altar of Catholicism. It was received favorably by the Convention, who decided to pass on the proposal to the Committee on Public Education.

[25] Sade's letter, which he could only lamely explain ("I had no idea how scandalously that guard had been formed"), was to the Duc de Brissac, commander of Louis Capet's Guard. Sade's letter fell into the hands of Citizen Pache, former Mayor of Paris.

[26] During the Revolution this convent (the building of which still stands at No. 70, rue de Vaugirard) was made a prison. In it, a year and half earlier, on September 2, 1792, one hundred and fifty priests were murdered.

[27] Originally built in 1632 as a Lepers' Hospice. It was sacked in 1789 but sufficiently repaired to house prisoners five years later. Until its destruction in 1940 it served both as a hospital and women's prison. The building at No. 107, rue du Faubourg Saint-Denis stands on the site today.

beheaded and draws attention to his many activities and increasing responsibility in the Piques Section.[28] He further denies that he or his family before him were ever aristocrats, claiming they were either in business or cultivating the land.

March 27 (7 Germinal, Year II)—For reasons of illness, Sade is transferred to Picpus Hospice, a prison hospital only recently opened.[29]

July 27 (9 Thermidor, Year II)—Sade's name appears eleventh on a list of twenty-eight prisoners to be brought to trial. For some reason not wholly explained, the court bailiff fails to take Sade and returns with only twenty-three of the twenty-eight. All but two are guillotined the same day on a square only a few hundred yards from the Picpus prison where Sade was held.[30]

July 28 (10 Thermidor, Year II)—Beginning at 7:30 P.M., Robespierre and twenty-two other terrorists are executed; thunderous cheering from the crowd.

October 13 (22 Vendémiaire, Year III)—The Committee of General Safety signs the order freeing Citizen Sade immediately.

October 15 (24 Vendémiaire, Year III)—After 312 days of detention, Sade is released and authorized, in spite of his being a former nobleman and in view of his patriotic work, to reside in his house on the rue Neuve-des-Mathurins.

---

[28] It is to be noted, however, that in spite of his plea for support, none of his former colleagues dared come forth in support of their former chairman. Later, after the execution of Robespierre and a slackening if not end of the Terror, his colleagues signed a statement in his behalf, on August 25, 1794.

[29] Called Coignart House, this property had formerly been the convent of the Canoness of Saint Augustine, who had been ordered to vacate it in 1792. Two "humane" citizens, Riedain and Coignard, decided to set up a prison hospice there for the care of prisoners who were ill and whose purses were sufficient to purchase their health, and at the same time save their necks from the guillotine.

[30] Sade describes it thus (letter of November 19, 1794): "An earthly paradise, a lovely building, a magnificent garden, choice company, charming women, then all at once the guillotine is set up directly under our windows [the inhabitants of the Place de la Concorde had complained that the stench of blood had become impossible from the guillotine there, and it had thus been removed to the Place du Trône Renversé near the Picpus Hospice], and they began to dispose of the dead in the middle of our garden. . . . We buried 1,800 in thirty-five days."

1795. Aet. 55

January (Nivôse-Pluviôse, Year III)—Death of the former President de Montreuil about six months after his release from the prison where he and his wife had been kept during the Reign of Terror.

May (Floréal-Prairial, Year III)—Sade's son, Louis-Marie, is back in Paris. Since neither he nor his brother has ever appeared on any list of *émigrés*, a story is concocted according to which Louis has been traveling through France studying botany and gravure; as for Donatien-Claude-Armand, he is in Malta where he is on duty with a foreign power allied to France.

1796. Aet. 56

October 13 (22 Vendémiaire, Year V)—Sade sells La Coste, "both buildings and furniture," to the representatives of M. and Mme. Rovère for 58,400 *livres*, which sum will never be paid to him in its entirety.

October (Vendémiaire, Year V)—Sade is living in the town of Clichy.

December 1 (11 Frimaire, Year V)—Sade gives as his new address the house of Citizeness Quesnet, 3, Place de la Liberté in Saint-Ouen.

1797. Aet. 57

May–June (Floréal-Prairial, Year V)—Sade, together with Mme. Quesnet, visits Provence, paying calls on Gaufridy in Apt, and going to La Coste, Bonnieux and Mazan.

October (Brumaire, Year VI)—Sade and Mme. Quesnet return to Saint-Ouen.

November (Brumaire, Year VI)—Having learned that he is listed in Vaucluse as an *émigré* and thus not only liable to arrest but subject to having his property and possessions confiscated, Sade sets about filing a protest with the police, complete with substantial documentation.

1798. Aet. 58

September 10 (24 Fructidor, Year VI)—Sade and Mme. Quesnet are, for lack of funds, compelled to leave Saint-Ouen: she puts up with friends and he finds refuge in Beauce with one of his farmers.

November (Brumaire, Year VII)—The sellers of the properties at Malmaison and Granvilliers, which Sade has purchased with money realized from the sale of La Coste, having not yet been paid in full, secure an injunction on the transfer of said properties. Sade's farmer thus refuses to lodge him any longer, and he is obliged to move from place to place, wherever he can find a bed or a meal.

1799. Aet. 59

January 24 (5 Pluviôse, Year VII)—Sade goes to live with Mme. Quesnet's son for the winter, their residence being an unheated attic.[31]

February 13 (25 Pluviôse, Year VII)—Sade earns forty *sous* a day working as an employee in a Versailles theater, with which miserable sum he is supporting not only himself but "feeding and raising" Madame Quesnet's son.

June 28 (10 Messidor, Year VII)—A decree forbidding the names of ex-nobles to be stricken from the list of *émigrés* reduces Sade to despair: "Death and misery, this then is the recompense I receive for my everlasting devotion to the Republic."

---

[31] Sade to Gaufridy: "My dear one's [Mme. Quesnet's] boy and I live here at the back of a barn, subsisting on a few carrots and beans and warming ourselves (not every day but whenever we can) with some kindling which we generally buy on credit. . . ."

August 5 (18 Thermidor, Year VII)—The municipal administration of the canton of Clichy issues Sade a certificate of residence and citizenship, countersigned by Commissioner Cazade, who is in charge of his security.

December 10 (19 Frimaire, Year VIII)—Following the example of the Vaucluse authorities, who had earlier lifted the sequester on Sade's properties, the Bouches-du-Rhône department does likewise.

December 13 (22 Frimaire, Year VIII)—Revival of Sade's play *Oxtiern ou les malheurs du libertinage* on the stage of the Société Dramatique of Versailles, the author playing the role of Fabrice. This is the same play performed eight years earlier at the Théâtre Molière, but Sade slightly revised the title.

1800. Aet. 60

January 26 (6 Pluviôse, Year VIII)—Sade is in the public infirmary of Versailles, "dying of cold and hunger" as he writes Gaufridy in an attempt to elicit some money from him.

February 20 (1 Ventôse, Year VIII)—Commissioner Cazade comes to Versailles to inform Madame Quesnet and Sade that two bailiff's men at twelve francs a day have been placed in their Saint-Ouen house, since they had failed to make their payments. That same day Sade is threatened with debtors' prison if he fails to pay two outstanding bills before the 9 *Ventôse*. Fortunately for Sade, Cazade is most helpful and solicitous, and maintains that since Sade is in his care, he cannot be taken to jail unless he, Cazade, takes him.

April 5 (15 Germinal, Year VIII)—Sade is back at Saint-Ouen, and Commissioner Cazade writes to Gaufridy, whose indifferent manner of running Sade's business affairs and his slowness in replying to letters is characterized as criminal by the Marquis.

May (Floréal-Prairial, Year VIII)—Sade has previously accused Gaufridy of accepting bribes and threatened him with legal action. Gaufridy now resigns his post as Sade's steward.

June (Prairial-Messidor, Year VIII)—Mme. Quesnet, armed with legal powers to inspect the Sade estates and examine his accounts, goes to Provence to investigate the situation. "It is impossible, after thirty years of stewardship, for things to be in more of a mess."

July (Messidor, Year VIII)—The publication of *Zoloé*, a pamphlet, unsigned, attacking Josephine, Mmes. Tallien, and Visconti, Bonaparte, Tallien and Barras. It was long thought that Sade was the author of *Zoloé*, and this pamphlet has often been cited as the reason for Sade's arrest in 1801. It has now been clearly established that Sade was not the author.

October 22 (30 Vendémiaire, Year IX)—In the *Journal de Paris*, an article by the critic Villeterque appears, violently attacking Sade's *Les Crimes de l'Amour*, which has just been published. In the article Villeterque refers to Sade as the author of *Justine*.

1801. Aet. 61

January 16 (26 Nivôse, Year IX)—The Minister of Police issues a certificate of amnesty making it possible to raise the sequester on Sade's property.[32]

March 6 (15 Ventôse, Year IX)—Sade, along with his publisher Nicolas Massé, is arrested in the latter's office, Sade just happening to be there when the police arrive. They make a search of Massé's premises and find various manuscripts and printed works either in Sade's hand or, in the case of the printed works, annotated by him, including *Juliette* and *La Nouvelle Justine*. Simultaneously, two other searches are made, one at the house of a friend of Sade's, which uncovers nothing, and the other at the house in Saint-Ouen where Sade possesses a secret study where there was hung a piece of tapestry depicting "the most obscene subjects, most of which were drawn from the infamous novel *Justine*." The tapestry is taken to the Prefecture.

March 7 (16 Ventôse, Year IX)—Sade and Massé are interrogated. The latter, upon the promise of liberty, reveals where the

---

[32] His name has still not been struck from the list of *émigrés*, however, a fact which his family will continue to use against him.

stock of *Juliette* is held and turns it over, almost in its entirety, to the police. Sade admits to knowing of the manuscript, but claims he is only the copyist.

April 2 (12 Germinal, Year IX)—Prefect Dubois, in agreement with the Minister of Police, decides that a "trial would cause too much of a scandal which an exemplary punishment would still not make worthwhile." It is therefore decided to "place" Sade in Sainte-Pélagie prison[33] as "administrative punishment" for being the author of "that infamous novel *Justine*" and of that "still more terrible work *Juliette*."

April 5 (15 Germinal, Year IX)—Sade is incarcerated in Sainte-Pélagie.

1802. Aet. 62

May 20 (30 Floréal, Year X)—From Sainte-Pélagie, where he is still held, Sade writes to the Minister of Justice saying that as a captive in the "most frightful prison in Paris," he demands to be freed or tried. He swears he is not the author of *Justine*.

1803. Aet. 63

March 14 (23 Ventôse, Year XI)—Sade is transferred to Bicêtre prison.

April 27 (7 Floréal, Year XI)—At the instigation of Sade's family, the prisoner is transferred from Bicêtre ("a frightful prison") to the Charenton Asylum, under the escort of a policeman. His family agrees to pay his board at Charenton, which is set at 3000 francs annually.[34]

---

[33] A former convent founded in 1662, Sainte-Pélagie became a political prison during the Revolution.

[34] Sade had already spent some time in Charenton, having been transferred there out of the Bastille ten days before the latter was stormed. Closed in 1795, the Directory ordered it rehabilitated and reopened in 1797 as an asylum for the care and treatment of the insane of both sexes. It was under the direct control of the Ministry of the Interior.

1804. Aet. 64

May 1 (11 Floréal, Year XII)—The Prefect orders an examination of Sade's papers and has the prisoner informed that if he continues to show himself rebellious he will be sent back to Bicêtre.

June 20 (1 Messidor, Year XII)—Sade sends the newly constituted Senatorial Commission for Individual Liberty a strong protest against his arbitrary detention, noting that he has now spent four years in prison without coming to trial. Six weeks later[35] he repeats the plea in a letter to M. Fouché, Minister of Police.

September 8 (21 Fructidor, Year XII)—The Prefect of Police Dubois submits a statement to the Minister of Police in which he describes Sade as an "incorrigible man" who was in a state of "constant licentious insanity" and of a "character hostile to any form of constraint." His conclusion is that there is good reason to leave him in Charenton where his family pays his board and where they desire he remain, to safeguard the family honor.

1805. Aet. 65

April 14 (24 Germinal, Year XIII)—On this Easter Sunday, Sade takes communion and takes up the collection in the parish church of Charenton-Saint-Maurice.

May 17 (27 Floréal, Year XIII)—Prefect Dubois, learning of this liberty granted Sade, reprimands the director of Charenton, M. de Coulmier, warning him that Sade is a prisoner who must "under no circumstances be allowed out without express authorization from me" and asking: "Moreover, did it not occur to you that the presence of such an individual [in church] could not fail to inspire a feeling of horror and cause public disturbances?"

August 24 (6 Fructidor, Year XIII)—Sade draws up and signs a memorandum outlining the final conditions to which he will agree

---

[35] On August 12 (24 *Thermidor,* Year XII). "The laws and regulations concerning individual liberty have never been as openly defied as in my case," wrote Sade, "since it is without any sentence or any other legal act that they persist in keeping me under lock and key."

to his family's proposed purchase of all his property (save Saumane) in return for a life annuity.

1806. Aet. 66

January 30[36]—Sade draws up his last will and testament.[37]

March 5—He begins the final draft of his *Histoire d'Emilie.*

July 10—He completes the first volume which he entitles *Mémoires d'Emilie de Valrose, ou les Egarements du libertinage.*

October 14—Louis-Marie de Sade takes part in the battle of Jena, on the staff of General Beaumont.

1807. Aet. 67

April 25—After thirteen months and twenty days work, Sade completes the revision of *Histoire d'Emilie,* which occupies seventy-two notebooks and forms the four final volumes of a large ten-volume work, the general title of which, "definitively decided upon today," is: *Les Journées de Florbelle, ou la Nature dévoilée, suivies des Mémoires de l'abbé de Modose et des Aventures d'Emilie de Volnange.*

June 5—The police seize several manuscripts in Sade's room at Charenton, presumably *Les Journées de Florbelle* which Sade is never to see again and which will be burned shortly after his death.

1808. Aet. 68

June 14—Louis-Marie de Sade is wounded at Friedland. His valorous conduct earns him mention in the military dispatches.

June 17—Sade writes to Napoleon, describing himself as the father of a son who has distinguished himself on the battlefield and requesting liberation.

---

36 The Gregorian calendar was re-established on January 1, 1806.

37 The full text appears at the end of Part One.

August 2—The Chief Medical Officer of Charenton, Antoine-Athanase-Royer-Collard, describes to the Minister of Police all the disadvantages that the presence of "the author of that infamous novel *Justine*" entails. "The man is not mad," Royer-Collard notes. "His only madness is that of vice. . . . Finally, it is rumored that he is living in the asylum with a woman[38] whom he passes off as his daughter." He recommends the suppression of the theater which Sade has organized at Charenton, maintaining it is dangerous for the patients,[39] and requests that Sade be transferred to some prison or fortress.

September 2—In spite of Coulmier's intervention on Sade's behalf,[40] the Minister decides to transfer the Marquis to Ham prison.

September 12—M. de Coulmier pays a personal call upon the Minister to appeal against the decision to transfer Sade out of Charenton, at least until such time as Sade's family makes up the back payments due for Sade's board and keep.[41]

September—Dr. Deguise, the Charenton surgeon, states that in Sade's plethoric condition, to transfer him would endanger his life.

---

[38] Mme. Quesnet, who has on her own initiative moved into Charenton to be with Sade.

[39] With Charenton inmates as the actors, Sade staged and directed his own plays in an improvised theater in the asylum.

[40] M. de Coulmier is described as "a man of intelligence and influence," having once sat in the Constituent Assembly. "Everyone liked him," wrote Dr. Ramon, a Charenton doctor during the period of Sade's incarceration there. "[He] ruled despotically, though there was never anything rigorous or austere about his rule." Except for the early months of Sade's detention, when he was inclined to be demanding and difficult, M. de Coulmier generally took his part against the harsh interdictions of the authorities. When in September, 1808, the Prefect of Police wrote the Minister of the Interior concerning Sade's involvement with the theatrical events at Charenton, he noted that M. de Coulmier "says that in this matter he is much obliged to de Sade, for, seeing in light drama a therapeutic method for the deranged he thinks himself fortunate to have in the asylum a man capable of giving stage training to those he wishes to treat by this therapy." It is obvious from the above observation that the Director of Charenton was well ahead of his era in the treatment of the insane.

[41] Knowing Coulmier's sympathetic attitude toward and understanding of Sade, it would appear that his request for a delay of transfer on the grounds of delinquent back payments was but a thinly veiled pretext to keep his patient at Charenton.

November 11—Sade's family requests a postponement of his transfer, and the Minister agrees to defer it to April 15, 1809.

1809. Aet. 69

April 21—The transfer is postponed indefinitely.

June 9—Louis-Marie de Sade, Lieutenant in the 2nd Battalion of the Isembourg Regiment, is ambushed near Mercugliano on the road to Otranto, where he is on way to rejoin his regiment, and is killed.

1810. Aet. 70

July 7—At about 10:00 A.M., Madame de Sade, who has been blind for some time, dies at Echauffour Castle.

August 28—Sade sells his Mazan estates to Calixte-Antoine-Alexandre Ripert for the sum of 56,462 francs 50 centimes, which is collected by Sade's children as their mother's heirs.

October 18—The Count de Montalivet, Minister of the Interior, issues a harsh order: "Considering that M. de Sade . . . is suffering from the most dangerous of insanities, contact between him and the other inmates poses incalculable dangers, and for as much as his writings are no less demented than his speech and conduct . . . I therefore order the following: That Monsieur de Sade be given completely separate lodging so that he be barred from all communication with others . . . and that the greatest care be taken to prevent any use by him of pencils, pens, ink, or paper. The director of the asylum is made personally responsible for the execution of this order."

October 24—M. de Coulmier acknowledges receipt of the Minister's order and, noting that he does not have at his disposal at Charenton an isolated area such as the Minister requests for Sade, asks that Sade be transferred elsewhere. He further points out to Count Montalivet that "he credits himself with being the head of a humanitarian establishment" and would find it humiliating to see himself become "a jailer" or one given to the persecution of a fellow creature.

1811. Aet. 71

February 6—A police report against two booksellers, Clémendot and Barba, who are selling *Justine* both in the provinces and in Paris, and against the former who is accused of secretly printing and distributing a set of one hundred engravings for *Justine* that had come into his possession.

March 31—Sade is interrogated at Charenton.

July 9—Napoleon, sitting in Privy Council, decides to keep Sade in detention at Charenton.

November 14—Sade is again questioned at Charenton, this time by Count Corvietto; in contrast to the March interrogation, when he was treated very rudely, Corvietto is "very gentle and decent."

1812. Aet. 72

June 9—The Minister of Police informs M. de Coulmier that he may inform the interested party that the Emperor, in meetings of the Privy Council of April 19 and May 3, has decided to continue Sade's detention.

October 6—Some occasional verses, of which Sade is the author, are sung to His Eminence Cardinal Maury, Archbishop of Paris, who is visiting the Charenton Hospice.

1813. Aet. 73

March 31—Sade is subjected to a third interrogation, "very severe but very short."

May 6—A ministerial order prohibits any further theatrical spectacles at Charenton.

May 9—Sade begins to put the finishing touches on his *Histoire secrète d'Isabelle de Bavière,* which he completes four months later.

. . . .—Publication of the two-volume work *La Marquise de Gange,* of which Sade is the anonymous author.

1814. Aet. 74

April 11—Napoleon abdicates.

May 3—Solemn entry into Paris of Louis XVIII.

May 31—M. de Coulmier is replaced as Director of Charenton by M. Roulhac de Maupas.

September 7—M. Roulhac de Maupas calls the attention of the Minister of the Interior, Abbé de Montesquiou, to the necessity of removing from Charenton the Marquis de Sade who cannot be properly guarded and whose age and state of health do not permit seclusion. He further notes that, in spite of his commitments to pay for his father's board undertaken at the time of his transfer from Bicêtre to Charenton, M. de Sade *fils* has refused to pay arrears on the board amounting to 8934 francs, although he has acquired his father's properties which guaranteed the dowry of his late mother, and denies that he owes his father's creditors anything, maintaining all these debts antedated his own mortgage.

October 21—The Minister of the Interior invites Count Beugnot, Director-General of the Police, to make a decision concerning M. de Sade, who cannot remain at Charenton without grave consequences and who should be removed to a State prison.

December 1—Sade, whose health has been failing for several months, ceases to be able to walk.

December 2—This day, a Saturday, Sade's son Donatien-Claude-Armand, comes to visit his father and asks the newly appointed student-doctor, L.-J. Ramon, to spend the night with him. On his way to the appointment, Dr. Ramon meets Abbé Geoffrey on his way out of Sade's room, Sade having made an appointment with the

Abbé for the following morning. Ramon reports Sade's breathing as "noisy and labored" and he helps him take a few sips of herbal tea to help ease the pulmonary congestion from which Sade is suffering. Shortly before ten, the old man dies without a murmur, either from the above-named pulmonary congestion or from an "adynamic and gangrenous fever," according to the official report made to the director and to the police.

In spite of the strict instructions to the contrary in his will, Sade is buried in the Charenton cemetery. The burial costs sixty-five *livres,* of which twenty for the cross, ten for the coffin, six for the chapel, nine for candles, six for the chaplain, eight for the bearers, and six for the gravedigger.

Seven Letters (1763–1790)

LETTER I (1763)

To Mademoiselle de L...[1]

At Avignon, this 6th April 1763.[2]

Perjurer! ungrateful wretch! pray tell what has happened to those sentiments of lifelong devotion? who compels you to inconstancy? who obliges you to break the bonds which were to unite us forever? Did you take my departure for flight?[3] Did you believe that I could exist and flee from you? 'Tis doubtless from your own that you were judging the sentiments of my heart. I obtain the consent of my parents; my father, with tears in his eyes, asks of me naught but one last favor, and that is to come to Avignon to be married. I leave; I am assured that all efforts will now be bent toward persuading your father to bring you to these parts. I arrive, God knows with what alacrity and eagerness, in this region which is to become the witness of my happiness, a lasting happiness, a happiness that nothing will ever again be able to trouble. . . . But what is to become of me—dear God! can I ever survive this sorrow? —what is to become of me when I learn that, inspired by some noble impulse, you cast yourself at your father's knees to ask him to give up all further thought of this marriage, saying that you have no wish to be forced into any alliance. Vain and foolish reason, dictated by perfidy, O thou ungrateful, faithless wretch! You were afraid of being united to someone who adored you. These bonds of an everlasting chain were becoming a burden to you, and your heart, which is seduced by fickleness and frivolity alone, was not discerning or sensitive enough to be conscious of all the charms such bonds entailed. 'Twas the thought of leaving Paris that frightened you; my love was not enough for you; I was unable to make it last. Fie, monster, born to make my life miserable, stay there in Paris forever! May it one day become, through the deceitfulness and knavery of the scoundrel who will replace me in your heart, as odious to you as your own double dealing has made it in my eyes! . . . But what am I saying? Oh, my dear, my divine friend! the sole support of my heart, the only love of my life, where, my beloved, is my despair leading me? Forgive the outpourings of a poor wretch who no longer knows himself, for whom death, after the loss of what he loves, is the sole recourse. Alas! I draw near to it, this moment which will deliver me from the day I detest; my only wish now is to see it arrive. What can make me cling to a life whose sole delight was you? I lose you; I lose my existence, my life, I die, and by the cruelest of deaths. . . . My mind wanders, my love, I am no longer myself; let the tears which becloud my eyes, flow. . . . I cannot survive such misfortunes.—What are you doing? . . . what has become of you? . . . What am I in your eyes? An object of horror? of love? . . . Tell me, how do you view me? How can you justify your conduct? Good Heavens, perhaps mine cannot be justified in your eyes! Ah, if you will love me, if you love me as you have always loved me, as I love you, as I adore you, as I shall adore you all my life, pity our misfortunes, pity the crushing blows of fortune, write me, try and justify your actions. . . . Alas! it will not be all that difficult: what most pains and racks my heart is to find you guilty. Oh, how greatly 'tis relieved when it recognizes its error! If you love me, I do not for a moment doubt that you have opted for the convent. The last day I saw you, you remember, the day of all our misfortunes, you told me you would be delighted if they sent you to a convent. If you want us to be able to see each other, you know 'tis the only decision for you to take; for you know full well that it will be impossible for me to see you at your house. My father, when he sent me word of your action, gave me the choice of remaining here as long as I liked or rejoining him immediately. 'Tis your reply which will decide me; let it not languish; I shall count the days. Grant me the means of seeing you upon my arrival. I do not for a moment doubt that I shall find them in your letter. Whatever does not seem positive I shall take as a refusal; any refusal will be clear proof of your inconstancy, and your inconstancy my most certain sentence of death. But I cannot believe you have changed. What reason could bring you to? Perhaps this voyage of mine alarmed you: but, alas, let us be quite clear as to the veritable reasons for it. They blinded me, they made me believe I was rushing into the arms of happiness, whereas all they were trying to do was remove me from it. . . .[4] My dear love, do not abandon me, I beseech you; earnestly request the convent. As soon as I receive your letter I shall be off, and at your side. What tender moments we shall relive! . . . Take care of your health; I am working to restore my own. But no matter what the state of yours may be, nothing will keep me from offering you the most tender proof of my love. Throughout this affair, I believe you have had good reason, and will again, to be satisfied with my discretion. But I have merely done my duty; 'tis not that I am giving myself credit. . . . Beware of inconstancy; I do not deserve it. I confess to you that I shall be furious, and there is no horror I shall not commit. The little business of the c . . .[5] ought to make you be sparing of me. I confess that I shall not conceal it from my rival, nor will that be the only secret I shall confide to him. There are no lengths—this I swear to you—to which I shall not go, no horrors to which I shall not stoop. . . . But I blush to think of employing these means to keep you. I wish to, and must, talk to you only of your love. Your promises, your oaths, your letters which I read incessantly every day, alone should keep you bound to me; I appeal only to them. I beg of you not to see . . . . . .; he is unworthy to appear before you. In a word, my dear love, let me count upon your constancy! My absence will not be long; I await only your letter to depart. . . . Let it be good and kind, I beg of you, and may I find the means to see you when I arrive. I desire, I think of, I crave only you. . . . No, I am not afraid of being effaced from your heart; I have not deserved it. Love me still, my dear, and trust in time. And perhaps there will come a time, a time not far off, when you will not be so afraid to come into my family. When I am the head of it, my wishes will dictate my choice, and perhaps I shall then find you more determined. I need to be comforted and consoled, to be reassured, to receive proof of your constancy: everything alarms me. Your heroic act has dealt a blow to me. I assure you and give you my word of honor that nothing is more certain than what I am writing you, that I await naught but your reply to set out. My father has sent for me again; do not think that it is for a marriage. My mind is fully made up not to marry, and never have I aspired to do so. I am employing every means necessary, and those I deem the best, to make certain this letter reaches you. Do not fail to give the woman who delivers it to you a receipt, in your own hand, formulated in these terms: *I acknowledge receipt of a letter from such-and-such a person.* Follow this formula to the letter, for she is not to be paid what is promised her until she delivers the receipt into my hands. If you care to see me, do not delay your reply. I am counting the days. Try to make certain I receive it promptly, and that I find the means to see you when I arrive. Love me always; be faithful to me, if you do not wish to see me expire of sorrow. Adieu, my beloved child, I adore you and love you a thousand times more than life itself. Come, now, say what you will, but I swear that we shall never be aught but one for the other.[8]

LETTER II (1777)

To Madame la Présidente de Montreuil

This the 13th March 1777.[1]

If in a person capable of having violated at one stroke all of the most sacred sentiments mortals are given in trust: those of humanity in having a son arrested beside the coffin of his dead mother,[2] those of hospitality in betraying someone who had just cast himself into your arms, those of Nature in respecting not even the sanctuary taken by him who sought refuge in your daughter's embrace; if, I say, in one such person there could yet exist some trace of compassion, I would perhaps endeavor to excite it through a description at once authentic and frightful of my horrible plight. But these complaints were useless; independently of that fact, I have yet pride enough, low though I am laid, not to ornament your triumph with my tears, and even in these depths of misfortune I have courage enough to refrain from pleading with my tyrant.

To place before you a few simple considerations will then be the sole purpose of this letter. You will set upon them what value you please; these few remarks, then no more, so that in silence you will be able for some short while at least to savor the pleasure you reap from my woes.

For a long time, Madame, I have been your victim; but do not think to make me your dupe. It is sometimes interesting to be the one, always humiliating to be the other, and I flatter myself upon as much penetration as you can claim deceit. I pray you, Madame, let us at all times maintain the very clearest distinction between two separate things, my case and my imprisonment: for my chil-

125

dren's sake you are seeking the favor of the courts, and imprisonment, which you allege indispensable to that end and which is certainly not at all, is not and cannot be anything but the effect of your
vengeance. Of all the opinions heard so far, the gloomiest, the
most terrifying, that of M. Siméon[3] of Aix, said positively that it
was altogether possible to obtain a judgment whereby *exile would
serve as prison to the accused*. Those are Siméon's own words. A
lettre de cachet banishing me out of the realm, would that not have
answered the same purpose?—Of course—but it would not so well
have satisfied your fury.

Was it then you, all by yourself, who hatched and had enacted
the scheme of having me locked away between four walls? And
how on earth could the wise magistrates today governing the State
have let themselves be hoodwinked to the point of believing they
were promoting the interests of a family when the whole matter
was patently of slaking a woman's thirst for revenge? Why, I repeat, am I behind bars? why is an imprudence on my part construed
as a crime? why is there opposition to allowing me to prove to my
judges the difference between the two? and why does that opposition come from you? So many questions to which, unless I am much
mistaken, Madame is not disposed to reply. Ten or a dozen bolts
and locks presently answer in your stead; but this tyranny's argument, to which law is formally opposed, is not eternally triumphant.
In this I take comfort.

Fixing our attention upon my case alone, is it to clear my
name that you have me punished? and are you so deluded as to believe that this punishment shall go unknown? Do you fancy that
they who eventually get wind of it shall fail to see a misdeed somewhere, punishment being so evident? Be it meted out by the King,
be it meted out by judges, 'tis punishment nonetheless, and the public—which is neither indulgent nor overly curious to ferret out the
truth—, is the public going to make this frivolous distinction? and
will it not always see prior crime where punishment has ensued?
And how then my enemies shall exult! what splendid opportunities
you ready for them in the future! and how tempted they shall be to
have at me anew, since the results correspond so nicely to their intentions! All your five years of slandering me have provided the
foundation for this attitude and behavior in my regard, and you

have at all times been aware of it from the cruel situation you have seen me in during this whole period, constantly the target of fresh calumnies which sordid interest based upon the unhappiness of my situation. How would you have a man thought anything but guilty after the public authorities come three or four times knocking at his door, and when he is finally clapped into jail once he is got hold of? Whom do you hope to convince I have not been in confinement when such a long time has passed since I've been seen or heard from? After all the maneuvers employed to seize me, and then after my disappearance—what else do you suppose anyone could think save that I had been arrested? And from this, what advantage shall be gleaned? My reputation lost forever and new troubles arising at every turn. That is what I shall owe to your superior manner of handling my affairs.

But let us consider matters from another viewpoint. Is this a personal chastening I'm getting? and as if I were a naughty little boy, the idea is to spank me into good behavior? Wasted efforts, Madame. If the wretchedness and ignominy to which I have been reduced by the Marseilles judges' absurd proceedings, who punished the most commonplace of indiscretions as though it were a crime, have failed to make me mend my ways, your iron bars and your iron doors and your locks will not be more successful. You ought by now to know me well enough to realize that the mere suspicion of dishonor is capable of withering me to the heart, and you are clever enough to understand that a fault whose origin is in hot-bloodedness is not corrected by bringing that blood to a boil, by firing the brain through deprivation and inflaming the imagination through solitude. What I advance here will be supported by every reasonable being who has some acquaintance of me and who is not infatuated with the idiotic notion, that to correct or punish a man you must encage him like a wild beast; and I challenge any sane spirit not to conclude that from such usage the only possible result for me is the most certain organic disturbance.

If then neither my conduct nor my reputation stand to gain from this latest piece of kindness in my regard—if, on the contrary, everything loses thereby, and it crazes my brain—what purpose shall it have served, Madame? It shall have served your vengeance, no? Yes, 'tis all too obvious, everything leads back to that starting point; and all I've just written is quite beside the point, all that matters not in the slightest, only one thing does: that I be sacrificed . . . and you satisfied. Indeed, you very surely say to yourself, *the greater the damage wrought, the more content I'll be*. But ought you not have been amply contented, Madame, by the six months I had of prison in Savoy *for the same cause?* Were five years of afflictions and stigmas insufficient? and was this appalling denouement absolutely necessary?—especially after I gave you the demonstration of what lengths this sort of maltreatment could drive me to, by risking my life to escape from it! Own that, knowing what you know, 'tis evidence of no little barbarity on your part to have the same thing inflicted upon me again, and with episodes a thousand times crueler than before and which, sickening me into total revolt, will at any moment have me dashing my head against the bars confining me. Do not reduce me to despair, Madame; I cannot endure this horrible solitude unscathed, I sense the worst coming. Remember: never shall any good come to you from bestializing my soul and rendering my heart immune to feeling, the only possible results of the frightful state you have had me put in. Give me time to repair my errors, do not make yourself responsible for those into which perhaps I shall again be swept by the dreadful disorder I feel brewing in my mind.

I am respectfully, Madame, your very humble and very obedient servant.

DE SADE

P. S.—If the person from Montpellier[4] returns, I hope it will not be without the most urgent recommendation not to breathe a word about the scandalous scene to which you shrewdly made him a witness, a blunder which, considering the circumstances of his father's affairs, is assuredly quite inexcusable.

LETTER III (1783)

To Madame de Sade[1]

Be so good as to tell me which of the two it is, Goodie *Cordier*[2] or Gaffer *Fouloiseau*,[3] who is against my having any shirts. You can deny clean linen to the inmates of a hospital; but I do not intend to go without it. How your meanness, that of your origin and that of your parents, shines forth in your every act! My dove, the day I so far forgot what I was that I could be willing to sell you what I am, it may have been to get you under the covers—but it wasn't to go uncovered. You and your crew, keep what I say there well in mind until I have the chance to bring it out in print.

If I go through as much linen as I do, blame it on the laundress who every day either loses or tears to shreds everything of mine she can get her hands on, and rather than remonstrate with me, enjoin his lordship the Warden to issue orders remedying this state of affairs. Not a month passes but all this costs me eight or ten francs. Should such things be allowed?

At any rate, I declare to you that if inside the next two weeks the linen I request is not forthcoming, I shall interpret this as proof positive that I am on the eve of deliverance, and shall pack my baggage; only my imminent release can possibly justify your stupid refusal to send me something to put on my back. Let them but remove the madmen from this establishment and one will be less loath to use what the house provides, one could then forgo asking to have things sent all the time from home. This place was not intended for the insane; Charenton is where they are to be put, not here, and the disgraceful greed that led to keeping them locked

129

away there seems now to have been set aside by the police, the result being that those who are not mad risk becoming so by contagion. But the police are tolerant, tolerant of everything except discourtesy toward whores. You may render yourself guilty of every possible abuse and infamy so long as you respect the backsides of whores:[4] that's essential, and the explanation is not far to seek: whores pay, whereas we do not. Once I am out of here I too must contrive to put myself a little under the protection of the police: like a whore I too have an ass and I'd be well pleased to have it shown respect. I will have *M. Fouloiseau* take a look at it—even kiss it if he'd like to, and I am very sure that *moved* by such a prospect, he will straightway record my name in the book of protégés.

The story was told to me that upon arriving in Paris (when you had me arrested) it was thus you went about having yourself *certified*. Before anything else the question was of determining whether the said ass had or had not been outraged—because my good mother-in-law claimed I was *an outrager of asses*. Consequently she wanted *an examination by an expert*. There she was, as I understand it, telling them *You see, gentlemen, you see, he's a little devil, full of vices; he might even . . . perhaps . . . who knows? there's so much libertinage in that head of his. . . .* And, as I understand it, there you were, lifting your petticoats. Magistrate Le Noir adjusts his spectacles, Albaret[5] is holding the lamp, Le Noir's alguazils have got pen and paper. And a report upon the state of the premises was writ out in these terms:

"*Item*, having betaken ourselves to the said Hôtel de Danemark at the requisition of *Dame Montreuil* nee *Cordier, Marie-Magdeleine*,[6] we did uncover the said *Pélagie du Chauffour*,[7] daughter to the aforementioned, and having with care made proper and thorough examination we proclaim the said *du Chauffour* well and duly provided with a set of two very fair buttocks, excellently formed and intact within and without. We did ourselves approach and have our assistants as nearly approach the said member. They, at their risk and peril, did pry, spread, sniff, and probe, and having like ourselves observed naught but health in these parts, we have delivered these presents, whereof usage may be made in conformance to the law; and do furthermore, upon the basis of the exhibition described above, grant the said *Pélagie du Chauffour* access to the Tribunal and in future to our powerful protection.

"*Signed:* Jean-Baptiste Le Noir, trifler extraordinary in Paris and born protector of the brothels in the capital and surroundings."

Well? Is that how it went? Come, be a friend, tell me about it. . . . *In addition* or, if you prefer, *in spite of it all,* you have not sent me a quarter of the things I need.

To begin with, I need linen, most decidedly I must have linen, otherwise I make ready my departure; then four dozen meringues; two dozen sponge cakes (large); four dozen chocolate pastille candies, vanillaed, and not that infamous rubbish you sent me in the way of sweets last time.

What, will you tell me, are these twelve quarter-quires of paper? I asked for no quires of anything; I asked you for a copybook to replace the one containing the comedy I had conveyed to you. Send me that copybook and don't prattle so, it's very tiresome. So acknowledge receipt of my manuscript. It is not at all of the sort I'd like to have go astray. It belongs safely in a drawer for the time being; later, when it goes to the printer, it can be corrected. Until then it need not get lost. With manuscripts you delete, you amend, you tinker, they are meant for that; but they are never meant to be stolen.

For God's own sake, when will you finally be tired of truckling? Had you ever noticed one of your servilities to meet with success, I'd let it pass; but after close on to seven years of this, where has it brought you? Come, speak up. You aim at my undoing? You would unsettle my brain? If so, you are all going to be wonderfully rewarded for your efforts, for by everything that is most holy to me I swear to pay every one of your farces back and with good measure; I assure you I shall grasp their spirit with an artfulness that will stun you, and shall compel you all to recognize for the rest of your days what colossal imbeciles you have been. I confess I was a long while believing your Le Noir had no hand in these abominations, but since he continues to suffer them, that alone proves he has his part in them and convinces me that he is no less a damned fool than the others.

Do not forget the nightcap, the spectacles, the six cakes of wax, Jean-Jacques' *Confessions* and the coat M. de Rougemont claims that you have. I am returning a boring novel and vols. 4 and 6 of Velly. With these I send a hearty kiss for your nether end and am, devil take me, going to give myself a flick of the wrist in its honor! Now don't run off and tell the Presidente so, for being a good Jansenist, she's all against the *molinizing* of wives. She maintains that M. Cordier has never *rammed* anything but her *vessel of propagation* and that whoever steers any other course is doomed to sink in hell. And I who had a Jesuit upbringing, I who from Father Sanchez learned that one must avoid *plunging in over one's depth,* and look hard lest one *leap into emptiness* because, according to Descartes, *Nature abhors a vacuum,* I cannot put myself in accord with *Mamma Cordier.* But you're a philosopher, you have a countercharming *countersense,* much counterplay and narrowness in your *countersense* and heat in *the rectum,* whence it is I am able to accord myself very well with you.

I am yours indeed, in truth your own.

Directly this letter reaches you, will you please go in person to the shop of M. Grandjean, oculist, rue Galande by Place Maubert and tell him to send straight to M. de Rougemont the drugs and instruments he promised to furnish to the prisoner he visited in Vincennes; and while you are about it you will go to see *your protector Le Noir,* and tell him to arrange to have me enjoy a little fresh air. He enjoys plenty of it, does Le Noir, although a wickeder man than I by far: I've paddled a few asses, yes, I don't deny it, and he has brought a million souls to the brink of starvation. The King is just: let His Majesty decide between Le Noir and me and have the guiltier broken on the wheel, I make the proposal with confidence.

In addition to the neglected errands and to those requested above, attend, if you please, to procuring for me one pint of eau de Cologne, a head-ribbon and a half-pint of orange-water.

LETTER IV (1783)

To Madame de Sade[1]

My queen, my amiable queen, they are forsooth droll fellows and insolent, the lackeys you have in hire. Were it anything less than certain that your numbers are riddles (squaring nicely, by the way, with my manner of thinking)[2] your errand boys would be in line for a sound caning one of these days. Ah, would you hear the latest? They are giving me their estimates upon how much longer I am to remain here! Exquisite farce! It's for you, charming princess, it is for you who are on your way to sup and dicker with Madame Turnkey (at the hospital today), I say it's for you, my cunning one, to take the temperature of my captors, for you to divine just when it is going to suit them to unkennel me, for you to learn their pleasure of my lordships Martin,[3] Albaret, Fouloiseau, and the other knaves of that breed whom you will deign to permit me, for my part, to consider so many cab horses fit for whipping or to serve the public convenience at whatever hour and in any kind of weather.

To refuse me Jean-Jacques' *Confessions*, now there's an excellent thing, above all after having sent me Lucretius and the dialogues of Voltaire; that demonstrates great judiciousness, profound discernment in your spiritual guides. Alas, they do me much honor in reckoning that the writings of a deist can be dangerous reading for me; would that I were still at that stage. You are not sublime in your methods of doctoring, my worthy healers of the soul! Learn that it is the point to which the disease has advanced that determines whether a specific remedy be good or bad for the patient, not the remedy in itself. They cure Russian peasants of fever with arsenic; to that treatment, however, a pretty woman's stomach does not well respond. Therein see the proof that everything is relative. Let that be your starting point, gentlemen, and have enough common sense to realize, when you send me the book I ask for, that while Rousseau may represent a threat for dull-witted bigots of your species, he is a salutary author for me. Jean-Jacques is to me what *The Imitation of Christ* is for you. Rousseau's ethics and religion are strict and severe to me, I read them when I feel the need to improve myself. If you would not have me become better than I am, why, 'tis high time you told me so. The state one is in when one is good is an uncomfortable and disagreeable state for me, and I ask no more than to be left to wallow in my slough; I like it there. Gentlemen, you imagine your pons asinorum must be used and must succeed with everybody; and you are mistaken, I'll prove it to you. There are a thousand instances in which one is obliged to tolerate an ill in order to destroy a vice. For example, you fancied you were sure to work wonders, I'll wager, by reducing me to an atrocious abstinence in the article of *carnal sin*. Well, you were wrong: you have produced a ferment in my brain, owing to you phantoms have arisen in me which I shall have to render real. That was beginning to happen, you have done naught but reinforce and accelerate developments. When one builds up the fire too high under the pot, you know full well that it must boil over.

Had I been given Mr. 6[4] to cure, I'd have proceeded very differently, for instead of locking him up amidst cannibals I would have cloistered him for a while with girls, I'd have supplied him girls in such good number that damn me if after these seven years there'd be a drop of fuel now left in the lamp! When you have a steed too fiery to bridle you gallop him over rough terrain, you don't shut him up in the stable. Thereby might you have guided Mr. 6 into the *good way*, into what they call the *honorable path*. You'd have brought an end to those *philosophical subterfuges*, to those devious practices Nature disavows (as though Nature had anything to do with all this), to those *dangerous* truancies of a too ardent imagination which ever in hot pursuit of happiness and never able to find it anywhere, finishes by substituting illusions for reality and *dishonest detours* for lawful pleasure. . . . Yes, in the middle of a harem Mr. 6 would have become *the friend of woman;* he would have discovered and *felt* that there is nothing so beautiful, nothing so *great* as her sex, and that outside of her sex there is no salvation. Occupied solely in serving ladies and in satisfying their dainty desires, Mr. 6 would have sacrificed all his own. Susceptible of none but decent ones, with him decency would have become a habit, that habit would have accustomed his mind to quelling penchants which had hitherto prevented him from pleasing. The whole treatment would have ended with our sufferer appeased and at peace; and lo! see how out of the depths of vice I would have enticed him back to virtue. For once again, a little less of vice is virtuousness in a very vicious heart. Think not that 'tis child's play, to retrieve a man from the abyss; your mere proposal to rescue him will cause him to cling tight to where he is. Content yourself with having him conceive a liking for things milder in their form but in substance the same as those he is wont to delight in. Little by little you will gradually hoist him up from the cloaca. But if you hurry him along, jostle him, if you attempt to snatch everything away from him all at once, you will only irritate him further. Only by slow steps is a stomach accustomed to a diet; you destroy it if you suddenly deprive it of food. True enough, there are certain spirits (and of these I have known one or two) so heavily mired in evil, and who unfortunately find therein such charm, that however slight it were, any reform would be painful for them; 'twould seem they are at home in evil, that they have their abode there, that for them evil is like a natural state whence no effort to extricate them might avail: for that some divine intervention would be necessary and, unhappily, heaven, to whom good or evil in men is a matter of great indifference, never performs miracles in their behalf. And, strangest of all, profoundly wicked spirits are not sorry for their plight; all the inquietudes, all the nuisances, all the cares vice brings in its train, these, far from becoming torments to them, are rather delights, similar, so to speak, to the rigors of a mistress one loves dearly, and for whose sake one would be aggrieved not to have sometimes to suffer. Yes, my fairest of the fair, by God's own truth, well do I know a few spirits of this kind. Oh, and how dangerous they are! May the Eternal spare us, thou and me, ever from resembling them, and to obtain His mercy let us both before we lay us in our beds, kneel down and recite a *Paternoster* and an *Ave Maria* with an *Oremus* or two in honor of Mr. *Saint* [*lacuna in MS.*]. ('Tis a signal.)

With a great kiss for each of your buttocks.

I would remind you that you have sent me beef marrow in the past when the weather was just as warm as it is at present, and that I have none left; I beseech you to send me some without fail by the 15th of the month. Also, two night-ribbons, so as not to have to wait when one needs replacing: the widest and darkest you are able to find.

Herewith the exact measurements for a case I would be obliged if you would have made for me, generally similar to the other you sent me but with these dimensions, to be observed to the sixteenth of an inch and with a top that screws on three inches from the end. No loops, no ivory clasps like the last time, because they don't hold. This case (since your confessors must have an explanation for everything) is to store rolled up plans, prints and several little landscapes I've done in red ink. And I believe indeed [*one or two words obliterated in MS.*] were it for a nun, ought to put [*several words obliterated in MS.*]. Kindly attend to this errand as soon as possible; my plans and drawings are floating loose everywhere about, I don't know where to stick them.

Those who tell you I have enough linen are wrong. I am down to four wearable shirts and am completely without handkerchiefs and towels. So send me what I have requested, will you please, and put a stop to your silly joking upon this subject. Send me linen, plenty of linen—bah, never fear, I've plenty of time ahead of me to wear it out.

LETTER V (1783)

To Madame de Sade[1]

Good God, how right he is when M. Duclos tells us on page 101 of his *Confessions*[2] that *the witticisms of barristers always stink of the backstairs.* Allow me to go him one better and say that *they smell of the outroom, of the outhouse:* the brainless platitudes your mother and her *Keeper of the Tables* invent are of an odor not to be suffered in any proper salon. And so you never weary of their drivel and their pranks! and so we are to have buffoonery and lawyers to the bitter end! Well, my chit, feed on that stuff to your heart's content, gorge yourself on it, drink yourself high with it. I am wrong to wish to teach you nice manners, quite as wrong as were he who would attempt to prove to a pig *that a vanilla cream pasty is better than a t. . . .* But if you give me examples of obstinacy, at least forbear from criticizing me for mine. You cleave to your principles, eh? And so do I to mine. But the great difference between us two is that my systems are founded upon reason while yours are merely the fruit of imbecility.

My manner of thinking, so you say, cannot be approved. Do you suppose I care? A poor fool indeed is he who adopts a manner of thinking for others! My manner of thinking stems straight from my considered reflections; it holds with my existence, with the way I am made. It is not in my power to alter it; and were it, I'd not do so. This manner of thinking you find fault with is my sole conolation in life; it alleviates all my sufferings in prison, it composes all my pleasures in the world outside, it is dearer to me than

137

life itself. Not my manner of thinking but the manner of thinking of others has been the source of my unhappiness. The reasoning man who scorns the prejudices of simpletons necessarily becomes the enemy of simpletons; he must expect as much, and laugh at the inevitable. A traveler journeys along a fine road. It has been strewn with traps. He falls into one. Do you say it is the traveler's fault, or that of the scoundrel who lays the traps? If then, as you tell me, they are willing to restore my liberty if I am willing to pay for it by the sacrifice of my principles or my tastes, we may bid one another an eternal adieu, for rather than part with those, I would sacrifice a thousand lives and a thousand liberties, if I had them. These principles and these tastes, I am their fanatic adherent; and fanaticism in me is the product of the persecutions I have endured from my tyrants. The longer they continue their vexations, the deeper they root my principles in my heart, and I openly declare that no one need ever talk to me of liberty if it is offered to me only in return for their destruction. I say that to you. I shall say it to M. Le Noir. I shall say it to the entire earth. Were the very scaffold before me, I'd not change my tune. If my principles and my tastes cannot consort with the laws of this land, I don't for a moment insist upon remaining in France. In Europe there are wise governments which do not cast dishonor upon people because of their tastes and which do not cast them into jail because of their opinions. I shall go elsewhere to live, and I shall live there happily.

The opinions or the vices of private individuals do not harm the State; through their morals only public figures exert any influence upon the general administration. Whether a private person believes or does not believe in God, whether he admires and venerates a harlot or treats her with kicks and curses, neither this form of behavior nor that will maintain or shake the constitution of a State. But let the magistrate whose duty is to see the victualing of a town double the price of commodities because the purveyors make it worth his while, let the treasurer entrusted with public funds leave hirelings to go unpaid because he prefers to turn those pennies to his own account, let the steward of a royal and numerous household leave the luckless troops to die of hunger whom the King has introduced into his palace, because that officer would have a hearty feed at home the Thursday before Shrove Tuesday—and from one end of the country to the other the effects of this malversation will be felt; everything falls to pieces. And nonetheless the extortioner triumphs while the honest man rots in a dungeon. *A State approaches its ruin,* spake Chancellor Olivier[3] at the Bed of Justice held in Henry II's reign, *when only the weak are punished, and the rich felon gets his impunity from his gold.*

Let the King first correct what is vicious in the government, let him do away with its abuses, let him hang the ministers who deceive or rob him, before he sets to repressing his subjects' opinions or tastes! Once again: those tastes and opinions shall not unsteady his throne, but the indignities of those near to it will overthrow it sooner or later.

Your parents, you tell me, dear friend, your parents are taking measures to prevent me from ever being in a position to claim anything from them. This extraordinary sentence is all the more so for demonstrating that either they or I must be knaves. If they think me capable of asking them for anything beyond your dowry, I am the knave (but I am not; knavery has never had entrance among my principles, it's too base a vice); and if, on the contrary, they are taking measures in order never to give me that upon which my children must naturally count, then they are the knaves. Kindly decide which it is to be, the one or the other, for your sentence leaves no middle ground. You point your finger at them? I am not surprised. Neither am I surprised at the trouble they encountered marrying you off, or at the remark one of your suitors made: *The daughter, I'm nothing loath; but spare me from the parents.* My surprise shall cease at the fact they have been paying me your dowry in vouchers that lose two-thirds on the market; no more shall I marvel that those who were concerned for my interests always used to warn me: *Have a care there, you've no idea whom you are dealing with.* People who take measures not to pay the dowry promised to their daughter, none of the doings of such people ought to cause surprise; and I have long suspected that the honor of having sired three children upon you was going to be my ruin. It's doubtless to secure it that your mother has so often had my house entered and my *papers* filched. It won't cost her but a few *louis* to have some documents now disappear out of the notaries' files, to have some notes to Albaret falsified: and when at last I emerge from here I shall be perfectly able to beg in the streets. —Well, what's to be done in the face of that? To me three things shall always remain as consolation for everything: the pleasure of informing the public, which is not fond of the foul tricks lawyers play upon noblemen; the hope of advising the King by going and casting myself at his feet if need be, to ask restitution for the roguery of your parents; and should all that fail, the satisfaction, to me very sweet, of possessing you for your own sake, my dear friend, and of devoting the little that shall still be mine to your needs, to your desires, to the charm unto my heart unique of seeing you owe everything to me.

DE SADE

LETTER VI (1790)

To Monsieur Gaufridy[1]

The 12th of April 1790

I came out of Charenton (whither I had been transferred from the Bastille) on Good Friday. The better the day the better the deed! Yes, my good friend, 'twas upon that day I recovered my freedom; wherefore have I decided to celebrate it as a holiday for the rest of my life and instead of those concerts, of those frivolous promenades custom has irreligiously sanctified at that time of year, when we ought only to moan and weep, instead, I say, of all those mundane vanities, whenever the forty-fifth day after Ash Wednesday brings us around to another Good Friday, you shall see me fall to my knees, pray, give thanks . . . make resolutions to mend my ways, and keep them.

Now to the facts, my dear lawyer, for I see you about to echo what everybody tells me: *It's not talk we want, Sir, but facts*—to the facts then: the facts are that I landed in the middle of Paris without a *louis* in my pocket, without knowing where to go, where to lodge, where to dine, where to procure any money. M. de Milly, procurator at the Châtelet, and who has been supervising my interests in this part of the country for twenty-six years, was kind enough to offer me a bed, his board and six *louis*. Unwilling to overstay my welcome or become a burden, after four days at M. de Milly's, with three *louis* left of the original six, I had to set forth and find for myself everything—inn, domestic, tailor, my meals, etc. —with three *louis*.

My circumstances being what they were I made request of

141

Madame la Présidente de Montreuil, which lady graciously consented to instruct her notary to advance me a few *louis* upon condition I write to you at once for the wherewithal first to reimburse the borrowed sum, and second to stay alive. I do therefore conjure you, my good lawyer, to dispatch to me without delay of any sort the *preliminary* sum of one thousand crowns, the sum I asked you for the other day and whereof my need is no less extreme than the promptitude of your response to it essential.

LETTER VII (1790)

To Monsieur Gaufridy

I have just this instant come into receipt of your letter of the fourteenth: as it arrives too soon to be in answer to mine, I am master of my disappointment at not encountering here one of those charming notes which by far outvalue love letters, and with which one obtains money immediately.

You must not doubt that if I did not write to you during my detention, 'twas because I lacked the means to do so; I cannot well forgive you for supposing my silence due to anything else. I'd not have bothered about business details, what would have been the use in my position? But I would have inquired after your news, I would have given you my own, upon the chains lading me we might have dropped an occasional flower. But my captors would not have it so; I did venture a letter to you in that vein, it was returned to me, *flung* back at me, after that I wrote no more. Therefore, my dear lawyer, I repeat it, I cannot forgive you for having doubted my feelings in your regard. We have known one another since childhood, I need not remind you of it; a long-standing friendship made it natural that it be you in whom I placed my trust when long ago I besought you to take on the management of my affairs; what motive could I have had for changing my attitude? 'Twas not your fault I was arrested at La Coste, 'twas mine, I was too sure I was in safety there and I knew not with what an abominable family I had to contend. It goes without saying, and I assume you will have understood already, that when I speak here of family I am referring to the Montreuils; you have not, cannot have, the faintest conception of

143

the *infernal* and *anthropophagical* manner in which these people have conducted themselves with me. Had I been the last of the living and the lowliest, nobody would have dared treat me with the barbarity I have suffered thanks to them; in fine, it has cost me my eyesight and my chest; for lack of exercise I have become so enormously fat I can scarce stir my body; prison slew in me the very faculty of sensation; I have no more taste for anything, no liking, no love; the society I so madly regretted looks so dull to me today, so forlorn and sad! There are moments when I am moved by a wish to join the Trappists, and I cannot say but what I may go off some fine day and vanish altogether from the scene. Never was I such a misanthrope as since I have returned into the midst of men; and if in their eyes I now have the look of a stranger, they may be very sure they produce the same effect upon me. I was not idle during my detention; consider, my dear lawyer, I had readied fifteen volumes for the printer;[1] now that I am at large, hardly a quarter of those manuscripts remains to me. Through unpardonable thoughtlessness, Madame de Sade let some of them become lost, let others be seized; thirteen years of toil gone for naught! The bulk of those writings had remained behind in my room at the Bastille when on the fourth of July, I was removed from there to Charenton; on the fourteenth the Bastille is stormed, overrun, and my manuscripts, six hundred books I owned, two thousand pounds worth of furniture, precious portraits, the lot is lacerated, burned, carried off, pillaged: a clean sweep, not a straw left: and all that owing to the sheer negligence of Madame de Sade. She had had ten whole days to retrieve my possessions; she could not but have known that the Bastille, which they had been cramming with guns, powder, soldiers, was being prepared either for an *attack* or for a *defense*. Why then did she not hasten to get my belongings out of harm's way? my manuscripts?—my manuscripts over whose loss I shed tears of blood! Other beds, tables, chests of drawers can be found, but ideas once gone are not found again. . . . No, my friend, no, I shall never be able to figure to you my despair at their loss, for me it is irreparable. Since then, the sensitive and delicate Madame de Sade holds me at arm's length, won't see me. Another would have said *He is unhappy, we must dry his tears away;* this logic of feelings has not been hers. I have not lost enough, she wishes to ruin me, she is asking for a separation. Through this inconceivable proceeding she is going to legitimate all the calumnies that have been spewed against me; she is going to leave her children and me destitute and despised, and that in order to live, or rather to *vegetate deliciously,* as she phrases it, in a convent[2] where some *confessor* is doubtless consoling her, giving her to see the merits and the practicability of the path of crime, of horror, and of indignity down which her behavior is going to drive us all. When 'tis my most mortal enemy who has her ear, the advice my wife is receiving could not possibly be worse, nor more disastrous.

You will have no trouble realizing, my dear lawyer, that having now to answer out of my assets for the sums drawn from my wife's dowry (one hundred sixty thousand *livres*), this separation is going to be my financial finish, which is what these monsters are after. Alas, great God! I'd thought seventeen miserable years, thirteen of them in horrible dungeons, would expiate a few rash follies committed in my youth. You see how mistaken I was, my friend. The rage of Spaniards is never appeased, and this execrable family is Spanish. Thus could Voltaire write in *Alzire: What? You have a Spaniard's look—and you have the capacity to forgive?*

NOTES TO LETTERS

LETTER I

1. Laure-Victoire-Adeline de Lauris, born in Avignon on the 8th of June, 1741, was exactly one year younger than Sade. Hers was one of the most illustrious houses of Provence, tracing its lineage back to the thirteenth century. Although it has long been known that, prior to 1763, the year of his marriage, the fiery-tempered Sade had not often lacked for objects of his amatory dalliance or affection, the existence of Mademoiselle de Lauris as one of them remained unknown to Sade scholars and students until recently. It was the indefatigable Gilbert Lely who, in 1949, discovered the present letter among the unpublished correspondence of the Sade family which Maurice Heine bequeathed to the Bibliothèque Nationale in Paris.

2. Sade was married to Mademoiselle de Montreuil on May 17th of this same year. Thus his ardent letter to Mademoiselle de Lauris predates his marriage by less than six weeks.

3. Sade had gone to Avignon, ostensibly to await the arrival of his mistress and wife-to-be. But following his departure from Paris, either Mlle. de Lauris had a change of heart or, perhaps, family pressures were brought to bear against the marriage.

4. Although Sade's father apparently acquiesced to his son's demands to marry Mademoiselle de Lauris, it is known that he far preferred the much more advantageous alliance with the Montreuil family. Sade's sentence here would seem to suggest that someone, perhaps his father acting alone or in collusion, sent him to Avignon under false pretenses, the real motive being to separate him from Laure.

5. Lely speculates, not unreasonably, that the "c . . ." may refer to the "picturesque term which, still today, is used in popular language to designate gonorrhea. Indeed, in a letter from the Count de Sade to his sister, the Abbess de Saint-Laurent (Bibliothèque Nationale MS. 24384, no. 1936) mentions that the Marquis is 'more in love than ever' with Mlle. de Lauris, who apparently '*made him ill*.' And there would seem to be little doubt about the matter when one compares this remark to the allusions earlier in Sade's letter

where he admonishes Laure: 'Take care of your health; I am working to restore my own. . . . ' "

6. The fact is that Laure de Lauris never married. There is also evidence that Sade's feelings for her persisted long after his marriage to Mademoiselle de Montreuil, as suggested by a letter Sade subsequently wrote to Laure's father, reproaching him for not inviting Sade to a ball Monsieur Lauris was giving. In this letter, Sade speaks of "My absolutely irreproachable conduct since everlasting bonds [i.e., his marriage to another] have prevented me from forming those which were destined to make my happiness." Lely further speculates, without the slightest evidence however, that Sade may have had a later liaison with Laure, after his marriage, during the years he was living at La Coste. The only basis for his speculation is the proximity of La Coste and Vacqueyras, the seigneury of the Lauris family, which were only twenty miles apart.

LETTER II

1. One month to the day after Sade was incarcerated in Vincennes Keep.

2. From 1773, when he escaped from the fortress of Miolans, until his arrest on February 13, 1777, in Paris, Sade was either traveling incognito abroad or hiding in France. In late January of 1777, by means of messages reporting the grave state of his mother's health, Madame de Montreuil succeeded in luring Sade to Paris: arriving there (on February 8) he learned the Dowager Countess had died three weeks previously. And on the 13th, Inspector Marais, armed with a *lettre de cachet* obtained by Madame de Montreuil, arrested the Marquis in his hotel and conducted him to Vincennes.

3. Joseph-Jérôme Siméon of Aix-en Provence was attorney for the defense when in 1778 Sade appeared before the Parliament of Aix to face charges of having poisoned some prostitutes in Marseilles in 1772. Inculpated that same year, the Aix court had condemned Sade—then in flight—to be burned in effigy. The search for him continued: he was at last overtaken at Chambéry. It was in connection with the Marseilles episode that Sade was imprisoned at Miolans, and then in Vincennes.

4. To our knowledge, the identity of the person in question has so far eluded all Sade scholars.

LETTER III

1. Undated letter which from internal evidence would seem to have been written in July, 1783. It was dispatched from Vincennes where, after standing trial in Aix, Sade had been imprisoned (for the third time) since September 7, 1778.

2. Goodie *Cordier:* Madame de Montreuil.

3. *Fouloiseau* was Madame de Montreuil's factotum.

4. In another letter, cited by Lely, Sade remarks: " 'Tis for having taken disrespectful liberties with the ass of a whore that the father of a family, separated from his children, must risk the loss of their affection, must be snatched from the arms of his wife, from the care of his lands, must be robbed, ruined, dishonored, doomed, must be prevented from bringing up his children to enter into the world, and from appearing in it himself, must be the plaything of a gang of jailers, the prey of three or four other villains, must waste his lifetime, lose his health, be despoiled of his money, and be for the past seven years shut up like a lunatic in an iron cage."

5. Albaret: another of Madame de Montreuil's factotums.

6. The Presidente's full name was: Marie-Madeleine Masson de Plissay, Dame Cordier de Launay de Montreuil.

7. Madame de Sade's Christian name was, as we have noted, Renée-Pélagie. The Montreuils owned a property called d'Echauffour.

LETTER IV

1. Letter written from Vincennes, undated but clearly belonging to the same period as Letter III.

2. Concerning the "numbers," the "signals," the "ciphers" Sade again and again refers to in his letters (and in his "Note Concerning My Detention") Gilbert Lely writes (*L'Aigle, Mademoiselle* . . . , pp. 153–54) : "In almost all of Sade's letters of this period one meets with allusions to more or less comprehensible numbers which he often calls *signals.* What does this curious arithmetic signify? Imprisoned in Vincennes by *lettre de cachet,* that is, utterly at the mercy of his persecutors' discretion, Sade found himself in tragic ignorance of how long his detention was to last; wherewith he contrived a system of deduction based upon calculations which, while they may appear ludicrous to us, were in his mind of a nature to reveal the wildly yearned for day of his liberation. . . . Actually, the Marquis' troubling arithmetical operations constitute a kind of defense mechanism, a partly unconscious struggle to ward off the despair which, he dreaded, were it to gain the upper hand, would lead to the overthrow of his reason. Absolutely in the dark as to his captors' concrete intentions, Sade is led 'to ferret out the most unexpected points of departure for his calculations,' writes Maurice Heine. 'To his eye everything has the look of a hint of his fate, or perhaps of a mysterious indication that has escaped the censor's notice. His mind fastens desperately upon the number of lines in a letter, upon the number of times such and such a word is repeated

even upon a consonance which, spoken aloud, suggests a figure.' But his efforts are not confined to trying to discover the date of his return to freedom; he also seeks for clues regarding his life while in prison: upon exactly what day will he again be allowed to take exercise? When will Madame de Sade visit him? His wife's letters are the major source from which he mines the elements for his reckonings, and sometimes when the deductions he extracts from them have a baneful or contradictory look, he accuses Madame de Montreuil of having suggested to the Marquise such *signals* as might demoralize or throw him into perplexity."

An example: "This letter has 72 syllables which are the 72 weeks remaining. It has 7 lines plus 7 syllables which makes exactly the 7 months and 7 days from the 17th of April till the 22nd of January, 1780. It has 191 letters and 49 words. Now, 49 words plus 16 lines makes 59 [*sic*], and there are 59 weeks between now and May 30. . . ."

Another: "On March 28 he sent to borrow 6 candles from me; and on April 6, 6 others whereof I lent only 4. . . . Thursday the 6th of January, 9 months after the borrowing of the candles, on exactly the same day 25 were returned to me instead of the 10 I had lent, which seems very plainly to designate another 9 months in prison, making 25 in all."

And finally: "I know of nothing that better illustrates the sterility of your imaginations, your dearth of imagination, than the unbearable monotony of your insipid signals. What! nothing but valets forever sick of cleaning boots! or else workers reduced to enforced idleness! And most recently, because you had to find a 23 from somewhere, this: promenades restricted to between 2 and 3. Presto! there's your 23. —Astounding! Sublime! What! What quickness of wit, what genius, what brilliance! But, these signals of yours, if you must make them, at least do so with an honest intent and not as so many vexations."

3. Martin: a police sheriff.

4. Mr. 6: that is, Sade himself. He occupied Cell No. 6 at Vincennes.

LETTER V

1. Written from Vincennes, probably in early November, 1783.

2. *Les Confessions du comte de* ***, published in 1742, is less a novel than a gallery of portraits and a collection of anecdotes.

3. François Olivier (1493–1560), Chancellor of France under François I and Henri II.

LETTER VI

1. Gaufridy was a notary public and procurator in the little town of Apt near La Coste, Sade's favorite residence in Provence. Gaufridy's father had handled business affairs for the Comte de Sade; the Marquis entrusted his own to the younger Gaufridy, who for twenty years supervised the management and finances of his estates at Mazan, Saumane, and Arles as well as at La Coste.

LETTER VII

1. Sade is referring to his *Catalogue raisonné des œuvres de l'auteur,* which he had drawn up in the Bastille on October 1, 1788, and to which we refer elsewhere in the present volume.

2. In 1781 Madame de Sade had taken up quarters at Sainte-Aure, a Carmelite convent in Paris, where she was to remain up until and after the time of her legal separation from the Marquis.

Note Concerning My Detention

I observed that the situation wherein I was being kept and the pranks being played upon me were forcing me to mistake true and authentic happenings for events produced by the imbecile spitefulness of the scoundrels who had me at their mercy; the effort to render myself insensible to those arranged by artifice had the further result of rendering me insensible to those of fate or of Nature, in such wise that for the sake of my inward peace, I preferred to credit nothing and to adopt an attitude of indifference toward everything. Whence there developed the terrible and dangerous situation of being ever ready to discount as a deliberate falsehood any announcement of some unpleasant truth, and in the interest of tranquillity, to rank it among the lies that were multiplied to foster or give rise to situations; nay, it may fairly be said that nothing did greater hurt both to my heart and to my character. To undo my mind was the aim of all this. It failed; knowing me well, my persecutors ought to have known that my mind was too strong and too philosophical to yield to such nonsense. But it did nonetheless have a hardening effect upon my heart, a souring effect upon my character: effects both pernicious and harmful to produce, and which testified to naught but the crass stupidity of these teasings, worthy of the crass dolts who inflicted and who recommended them. And what were the dire effects further produced upon me by the denial of the good books I wanted to read, by the obstacles created to hinder me from composing the good books I wanted to write! But what had one not to expect from people who, forming ciphers and signals, had, through sending me to Bicêtre, sacrificed my honor and my reputation?

151

That system of signals and ciphers those rogues utilized while I was in the Bastille and during the last of my detentions, wrought yet another and grave damage upon me through accustoming me to cling to any such fantastic notion or phantom as might shore up my hope and to any conjecture capable of nourishing it. Thus did my mind take on the sophistical cast I am reproached for in my writings.

By way of final remark, how, I wonder, can inconsistency be carried to the point of saying that if I wrote *Justine,* 'twas at the Bastille, and of thrusting me back into a situation worse still than the one in which I, as it is alleged, composed the work in question? Here is the plainest demonstration that everything done and uttered concerning me proceeded from the fanaticism of pious idiots and from the flagrant stupidity of their henchmen. . . . Oh, how right was Sophocles when he said: *A husband almost always meets with his downfall either in the woman he takes for his wife or in the family he allies himself to.*

Consecutive to the foregoing remarks I think it best to join a few touching on *Justine,* remarks I submit to the thick-skulled Ostrogoths who had me imprisoned on account of it.

Only a small amount of common sense were needed (but have incarcerators any at all?) to be convinced that I am not and could not be the author of that book. But, unfortunately, I was in the clutches of a flock of imbeciles who always use fetters for arguments and bigotry instead of philosophy, and that for the great good reason that it is always much easier to impound than to ponder and to pray to God than to be useful to mankind. In the one case some virtues are required; only hypocrisy is required in the other.

After having been once upon a time suspected of a few extravagances of the imagination similar to those depicted in *Justine,* I ask whether it were possible to believe that I would go and put pen to paper in order to reveal turpitudes which would necessarily bring my own to be recollected. I am guilty of those turpitudes, or else I am not: it must be the one or the other. Had I committed them, assuredly I would wrap them in the thickest silence all the rest of my life; and if I am only suspected of them without ever having committed them, what have I to gain from divulging them when this piece of folly would have for its unique result to draw questioning eyes my way? It would be the height of stupidity. And my hatred for my tormentors is such I am unwilling to resemble them in that respect.

But still another more powerful reason will, I hope, speedily convince anyone that I cannot be the author of this book. Read it attentively and one will see that through inexcusable clumsiness, through a manner of proceeding that was bound to set the author at loggerheads with wise man and fool alike, with the good as well as with the wicked, all the philosophical personages in this novel are villains to the core. However, I myself am a philosopher; everyone acquainted with me will certify that I consider philosophy my profession and my glory. . . . And can anyone for one instant, save he suppose me mad, can anyone, I say, suppose for one minute that I could bring myself to present what I hold to be the noblest of all callings, under colors so loathsome and in a shape so execrable? What would you say of him who were deliberately to go befoul in the mire the costume he was fondest of and in which he thought he struck the finest figure? Is such ineptness even conceivable? Is the like anywhere to be seen in my other works? On the contrary, all the villains I have described are devout because the devout are all villains and all philosophers decent folk, because most decent folk are philosophers. Let me be permitted a reference to the works I speak of. Is there in *Aline et Valcour* a betterbehaved, more virtuous, more dutiful creature than Léonore? And at the same time is there a more philosophical? Is there anyone in the world more devout than my Portuguese? And does the world contain a greater villain? All my fictional persons have this tint; I have never departed from this principle. However, I repeat it, the complete opposite is manifest in *Justine*. Therefore it is not true that *Justine* is my doing. I go farther: it cannot possibly be. That is what I have just proven.

I shall here add something better still: how very odd it is that all the pietistic rabble, all the Geoffroys, the Genlis, the Legouvés, the Chateaubriands, the La Harpes, the Luce de Lancivals, the Villeterques, how odd that all these trustees of the shaveling corporation should have flown furiously out at *Justine,* when that book does nothing but plead in their favor. Had they paid some-one to write a work denigrating philosophy, they'd not have been able to buy anything so well done. And by all that I hold dear in the world I swear I shall never forgive myself for having been useful to individuals whom I so prodigiously despise.

No greater error could there be than to attribute to me a book . . . a book violating all my principles and of which, by all conceivable evidence, I cannot be the author; and, what is more, to make such a to-do over a work which, rightly considered, is but the final paroxysm of a diseased imagination with the ravings whereof they stupidly excite everyone's mind by crying it up as they do.

Stung by this inculpation, I have just prepared two works in four volumes[1] each where I have assailed, toppled, demolished the insidious sophistries in *Justine,* pulverized them from first to last. But since it is written on high, according to our friend Jacques the Fatalist,[2] that men of letters are to be the perpetual victims of stupidity and of folly, my writings are being held, their publication is being delayed (and perhaps even prevented) while new editions of *Justine* pour from the press every other week. Bravo, my friends! there'd be no understanding your motions were you to cease your opposition to good and your encouragements to evil. In vain did we *revolution* ourselves to achieve the contrary, 'twas written on high that the most violent abuses are ever to hold sway in our France and that so long as any French soil is left on the globe, it will be recognizable by the corruption practiced upon it.

---

[1] These would very probably be *Marcel ou le Cordelier* and *Conrad ou le jaloux en délire,* never published and the MSS. of which have never been found. That of *Conrad,* a novel dealing with the history of the Albigensians, was reported to have been among the papers of the Marquis that were "seized at the time he was being taken to Charen-ton."

[2] The main character in a novel by Diderot.

Last Will and Testament

OF DONATIEN-ALPHONSE-FRANÇOIS SADE

Man of Letters

For the execution of the clauses mentioned here below, I rely upon the filial piety of my children, desiring that their own may act with regard to them as they will have done with regard to me.

First: Wishing to give evidence to demoiselle Marie-Constance Reinelle, wife of Monsieur Balthasar Quesnet, believed deceased, wishing, as I say, to give evidence to this lady, insofar as my poor powers permit, of my extreme gratitude for the care she has given me and the sincere friendship she has shown me from the twenty-fifth of August, seventeen hundred ninety, to the day of my death, sentiments proffered by her not only with the utmost tact and disinterest, but, what is even more, with the most courageous energy, since, during the Reign of Terror, she saved me from the revolutionary blade all too surely suspended over my head, as everyone knows; and therefore, for the reasons outlined above, I hereby will and bequeath to the said lady Marie-Constance Reinelle, wife of Quesnet, the sum of eighty thousand *livres* in cash from the Tours mint, in whatsoever currency is then in usage in France at the time of my demise, wishing and understanding that this sum be deducted from the freest and most unattached portion of my legacy, charging my children to deposit it, within the space of a month from the day of my decease, with Monsieur Finot, notary at Charenton-Saint-Maurice, whom for this purpose I name the executor of my will and whom I charge to utilize the said sum in the manner the most secure and advantageous to Madame Quesnet, and in a manner susceptible to provide her with an income sufficient for her food and support, which income shall be promptly remitted to her on a quarterly basis, shall be transferable and not attachable by any person whatsoever, desiring, moreover, that the principal and the sale of the above-mentioned bequest be revertible to Charles Quesnet, son of the said dame Quesnet, who shall become the proprietor of the total, but only following the demise of his worthy mother.

And this desire which I here express concerning the bequest I make to Madame Quesnet, I beseech my children, in the unlikely case that they should seek to evade or shirk their responsibility, I beseech them to remember that they had promised the said dame Quesnet a sum roughly similar in recognition of the care she took of their father, and as this present document merely concurs with and anticipates their initial intentions, any doubt as to their acquiescence to my final wishes is forever banished from my mind and will never for a moment trouble it further, especially when I reflect upon the filial virtues which have never ceased to characterize them and make them full worthy of my paternal sentiments.

Second: I further leave and bequeath to the aforementioned Madame Quesnet all the furniture, effects, linen, clothing, books or papers which are in my chambers at the time of my decease, with the exception, however, of my father's papers, which shall be indicated as such by labels placed upon the bundles, which papers shall be handed over to my children.

Third: It is equally my intention and the expression of my last will that the present bequest in no wise deprive Madame Marie-Constance Reinelle, wife of Quesnet, of any rights, claims, or levies that she may care to make upon my estate, whatever the grounds may be.

Fourth: I leave and bequeath to Monsieur Finot, the executor of my last will and testament, a ring valued at twelve hundred *livres*, in return for the trouble which the execution of the present act shall have occasioned him.

Fifth: Finally, I absolutely forbid that my body be opened upon any pretext whatsoever. I urgently insist that it be kept a full forty-eight hours in the chamber where I shall have died, placed in a wooden coffin which shall not be nailed shut until the prescribed forty-eight hours have elapsed, at the end of which period the said coffin shall be nailed shut; during this interval a message shall be sent express to M. Le Normand, wood seller in Versailles, living at number 101, boulevard de l'Egalité, requesting him to come in his own person, with a cart, to fetch my body away and to convey it under his own escort and in the said cart to the wood upon my property at Malmaison near Epernon, in the commune of Emancé where I would have it laid to rest, without ceremony of any kind, in the first copse standing to the right as the said wood is entered from the side of the old château by way of the broad lane dividing it. The ditch opened in this copse shall be dug by the farmer tenant of Malmaison under M. Le Normand's supervision, who shall not leave my body until after he has placed it in the said ditch; upon this occasion he may, if he so wishes, be accompanied by those among my kinsmen or friends who without display or pomp of any sort whatsoever shall have been kind enough to give me this last proof of their attachment. The ditch once covered over, above it acorns shall be strewn, in order that the spot become green again, and the copse grown back thick over it, the traces of my grave may disappear from the face of the earth as I trust the memory of me shall fade out of the minds of all men save nevertheless for those few who in their goodness have loved me until the last and of whom I carry away a sweet remembrance with me to the grave.

Done at Charenton-Saint-Maurice in a state of reason and good health this thirtieth day of January in the year one thousand eight hundred six.

D. A. F. Sade

The Marquis de Sade

Part Two

Two Philosophical Dialogues

Dialogue between a Priest and a Dying Man
(1782)

U*ntil the recent discovery of Volume I of Sade's mis-*
cellaneous works (œuvres diverses), *which contains his*
early occasional prose and verse, as well as his one-act play,
Le Philosophe soi-disant, *and an epistolary work,* Voyage de
Hollande, *the* Dialogue *between a Priest and a Dying Man*
was his earliest known work to be dated with certainty.
Sade completed it, or completed the notebook which con-
tains it, on July 12, 1782, during the fourth year of his
second imprisonment in Vincennes. It is one of the most in-
cisive works of Sade, who is not especially noted for his
concision, and is contemporary to The 120 Days of Sodom,
upon which it is known that he was hard at work that same
year. Like The 120 Days, *the* Dialogue *between a Priest*
and a Dying Man did not figure in Sade's 1788 Catalogue
raisonné, *which was limited to works he wished publicly to*
acknowledge.

The Dialogue *did not appear until more than a century*
after Sade's death. In the course of the nineteenth century,
the notebook containing it was sold and resold on a number
of occasions at various auctions of autograph manuscripts,
and in 1920 Maurice Heine was fortunate enough to be
able to purchase it at a sale held on November 6 at Paris'
Hôtel Drouot. Six years later he published it with an ex-
haustive introduction.[1] *Since it is included in a notebook*
containing primarily rough drafts, notes, and jottings, Lely

---

[1] Dialogue entre un prêtre et un moribond, *par Donatien-Alphonse-Fran-*
çois, marquis de Sade, publié pour la première fois sur le manuscrit auto-
graphe inédit, avec un avant-propos et des notes par Maurice Heine. Paris,
Stendhal et Cie., 1926.

raises the question as to whether this work was ever polished or reworked to the author's satisfaction. Heine's observation, however, that the manuscript was written in a "firm, legible hand, with few words crossed out" would indicate that Sade may well have been satisfied with its composition. In any event, the work needs no apology.

What may most astonish the reader about the Dialogue is the author's failure to acknowledge it. For, compared to much of his other writing, it seems tame indeed, despite the ferocity of its attack on the deity and the clerical establishment. As Heine points out, however, one may tend to give the Age of Reason, from the vantage point of the present century, more than its due. In fact, Sade's position on the subject of religion was far more radical than that of most of his contemporaries, even the most enlightened. When, in the Encyclopedia *of 1751, and under their own signatures, Diderot and d'Alembert can pronounce themselves in the following terms, it is easier to understand Sade's reticence:*

> *Even the more tolerant of men will not deny that the judge has the right to repress those who profess atheism, and even to condemn them to death if there is no other way of freeing society from them. . . . If he can punish those who harm a single person, he doubtless has as much a right to punish those who wrong an entire society by denying that there is a God. . . . Such a man may be considered as an enemy of all men.[2]*

In the light of the above, one reads the Dialogue *with a wider respect for the audacity and uncompromising nature of Sade's mind.*

---

[2] Ibid.

PRIEST—Come to this the fatal hour when at last from the eyes of deluded man the scales must fall away, and be shown the cruel picture of his errors and his vices—say, my son, do you not repent the host of sins unto which you were led by weakness and human frailty?

DYING MAN—Yes, my friend, I do repent.

PRIEST—Rejoice then in these pangs of remorse, during the brief space remaining to you profit therefrom to obtain Heaven's general absolution for your sins, and be mindful of it, only through the mediation of the Most Holy Sacrament of penance will you be granted it by the Eternal.

DYING MAN—I do not understand you, any more than you have understood me.

PRIEST—Eh?

DYING MAN—I told you that I repented.

PRIEST—I heard you say it.

DYING MAN—Yes, but without understanding it.

PRIEST—My interpretation—

DYING MAN—Hold. I shall give you mine. By Nature created, created with very keen tastes, with very strong passions; placed on this earth for the sole purpose of yielding to them and satisfying them, and these effects of my creation being naught but necessities directly relating to Nature's fundamental designs or, if you prefer, naught but essential derivatives proceeding from her intentions in my regard, all in accordance with her laws, I repent not having

165

acknowledged her omnipotence as fully as I might have done, I am only sorry for the modest use I made of the faculties (criminal in your view, perfectly ordinary in mine) she gave me to serve her; I did sometimes resist her, I repent it. Misled by your absurd doctrines, with them for arms I mindlessly challenged the desires instilled in me by a much diviner inspiration, and thereof do I repent: I only plucked an occasional flower when I might have gathered an ample harvest of fruit—such are the just grounds for the regrets I have, do me the honor of considering me incapable of harboring any others.

PRIEST—Lo! where your fallacies take you, to what pass are you brought by your sophistries! To created being you ascribe all the Creator's power, and those unlucky penchants which have led you astray, ah! do you not see they are merely the products of corrupted nature, to which you attribute omnipotence?

DYING MAN—Friend—it looks to me as though your dialectic were as false as your thinking. Pray straighten your arguing or else leave me to die in peace. What do you mean by Creator, and what do you mean by corrupted nature?

PRIEST—The Creator is the master of the universe, 'tis He who has wrought everything, everything created, and who maintains it all through the mere fact of His omnipotence.

DYING MAN—An impressive figure indeed. Tell me now why this so very formidable fellow did nevertheless, as you would have it, create a corrupted nature?

PRIEST—What glory would men ever have, had not God left them free will; and in the enjoyment thereof, what merit could come to them, were there not on earth the possibility of doing good and that of avoiding evil?

DYING MAN—And so your god bungled his work deliberately, in order to tempt or test his creature—did he then not know, did he then not doubt what the result would be?

PRIEST—He knew it undoubtedly but, once again, he wished to leave to man the merit of choice.

DYING MAN—And to what purpose, since from the outset he knew the course affairs would take and since, all-mighty as you tell me he is, he had but to make his creature choose as suited him?

PRIEST—Who is there can penetrate God's vast and infinite designs regarding man, and who can grasp all that makes up the universal scheme?

DYING MAN—Anyone who simplifies matters, my friend, anyone, above all, who refrains from multiplying causes in order to confuse effects all the more. What need have you of a second difficulty when you are unable to resolve the first, and once it is possible that Nature may all alone have done what you attribute to your god, why must you go looking for someone to be her overlord? The cause and explanation of what you do not understand may perhaps be the simplest thing in the world. Perfect your physics and you will understand Nature better, refine your reason, banish your prejudices and you'll have no further need of your god.

PRIEST—Wretched man! I took you for no worse than a Socinian—arms I had to combat you. But 'tis clear you are an atheist, and seeing that your heart is shut to the authentic and innumerable proofs we receive every day of our lives of the Creator's existence—I have no more to say to you. There is no restoring the blind to the light.

DYING MAN—Softly, my friend, own that between the two, he who blindfolds himself must surely see less of the light than he who snatches the blindfold away from his eyes. You compose, you construct, you dream, you magnify and complicate; I sift, I simplify. You accumulate errors, pile one atop the other; I combat them all. Which one of us is blind?

PRIEST—Then you do not believe in God at all?

DYING MAN—No. And for one very sound reason: it is perfectly impossible to believe in what one does not understand. Between understanding and faith immediate connections must subsist; understanding is the very lifeblood of faith; where understanding has ceased, faith is dead; and when they who are in such a case proclaim they have faith, they deceive. You yourself, preacher, I defy you to believe in the god you predicate to me—you must fail because you cannot demonstrate him to me, because it is not in you to define him to me, because consequently you do not understand him—because as of the moment you do not understand him, you can no longer furnish me any reasonable argument concerning him, and because, in sum, anything beyond the limits and grasp of the human mind is either illusion or futility; and because your god having to be one or the other of the two, in the first instance I should be mad to believe in him, in the second a fool. My friend, prove to me that matter is inert and I will grant you a creator, prove to me that Nature does not suffice to herself and I'll let you imagine her ruled by a higher force; until then, expect nothing from me, I bow to evidence only, and evidence I perceive only through my senses: my belief goes no farther than they, beyond that point my faith collapses. I believe in the sun because I see it, I conceive it as the focal center of all the inflammable matter in Nature, its periodic movement pleases but does not amaze me. 'Tis a mechanical operation, perhaps as simple as the workings of electricity, but which we are unable to understand. Need I bother more about it? when you have roofed everything over with your god, will I be any the better off? and shall I still not have to make an effort at least as great to understand the artisan as to define his handiwork? By edifying your chimera it is thus no service you have rendered me, you have made me uneasy in my mind but you have not enlightened it, and instead of gratitude I owe you resentment. Your god is a machine you fabricated in your passions' behalf, you manipulated it to their liking; but the day it interfered with mine, I kicked it out of my way, deem it fitting that I did so; and now, at this moment when I sink and my soul stands in need of calm and philosophy, belabor it not with your riddles and your cant, which alarm but will not convince it, which will irritate without improving it; good friends and on the best terms have we ever been, this soul and I, so Nature wished it to be; as it is, so she expressly modeled it, for my soul is the result of the dispositions she formed in me pursuant to her own ends and needs; and as she has an equal need of vices and of virtues, whenever she was pleased to move me to evil, she did so, whenever she wanted a good deed from me, she roused in me the desire to perform one, and even so I did as I was bid. Look nowhere but to her workings for the unique cause of our fickle human behavior, and in her laws hope to find no other springs than her will and her requirements.

PRIEST—And so whatever is in this world, is necessary.

DYING MAN—Exactly.

PRIEST—But if everything is necessary—then the whole is regulated.

DYING MAN—I am not the one to deny it.

PRIEST—And what can regulate the whole save it be an all-powerful and all-knowing hand?

DYING MAN—Say, is it not necessary that gunpowder ignite when you set a spark to it?

PRIEST—Yes.

DYING MAN—And do you find any presence of wisdom in that?

PRIEST—None.

DYING MAN—It is then possible that things necessarily come about without being determined by a superior intelligence, and possible hence that everything derive logically from a primary cause, without there being either reason or wisdom in that primary cause.

PRIEST—What are you aiming at?

DYING MAN—At proving to you that the world and all therein may be what it is and as you see it to be, without any wise and reasoning cause directing it, and that natural effects must have natural causes: natural causes sufficing, there is no need to invent any such unnatural ones as your god who himself, as I have told you already, would require to be explained and who would at the same time be the explanation of nothing; and that once 'tis plain your god is superfluous, he is perfectly useless; that what is useless would greatly appear to be imaginary only, null and therefore non-existent; thus, to conclude that your god is a fiction I need no other argument than that which furnishes me the certitude of his inutility.

PRIEST—At that rate there is no great need for me to talk to you about religion.

DYING MAN—True, but why not anyhow? Nothing so much amuses me as this sign of the extent to which human beings have been carried away by fanaticism and stupidity; although the prodigious spectacle of folly we are facing here may be horrible, it is always interesting. Answer me honestly, and endeavor to set personal considerations aside: were I weak enough to fall victim to your silly theories concerning the fabulous existence of the being who renders religion necessary, under what form would you advise me to worship him? Would you have me adopt the daydreams of Confucius rather than the absurdities of Brahma, should I kneel before the great snake to which the Blacks pray, invoke the Peruvians' sun or Moses' Lord of Hosts, to which Mohammedan sect should I rally, or which Christian heresy would be preferable in your view? Be careful how you reply.

PRIEST—Can it be doubtful?

DYING MAN—Then 'tis egoistical.

PRIEST—No, my son, 'tis as much out of love for thee as for myself I urge thee to embrace my creed.

DYING MAN—And I wonder how the one or the other of us can have much love for himself, to deign to listen to such degrading nonsense.

PRIEST—But who can be mistaken about the miracles wrought by our Divine Redeemer?

DYING MAN—He who sees in him anything else than the most vulgar of all tricksters and the most arrant of all impostors.

PRIEST—*O God, you hear him and your wrath thunders not forth!*

DYING MAN—No my friend, all is peace and quiet around us, because your god, be it from impotence or from reason or from whatever you please, is a being whose existence I shall momentarily concede out of condescension for you or, if you prefer, in order to accommodate myself to your sorry little perspective; because this god, I say, were he to exist, as you are mad enough to believe, could not have selected as means to persuade us, anything more ridiculous than those your Jesus incarnates.

PRIEST—What! the prophecies, the miracles, the martyrs—are they not so many proofs?

DYING MAN—How, so long as I abide by the rules of logic, how would you have me accept as proof anything which itself is lacking proof? Before a prophecy could constitute proof I should first have to be completely certain it was ever pronounced; the prophecies history tells us of belong to history and for me they can only have the force of other historical facts, whereof three out of four are exceedingly dubious; if to this I add the strong probability that they have been transmitted to us by not very objective historians, who recorded what they preferred to have us read, I shall be quite within my rights if I am skeptical. And furthermore, who is there to assure me that this prophecy was not made after the fact, that it was not a stratagem of everyday political scheming, like that which predicts a happy reign under a just king, or frost in wintertime? As for your miracles, I am not any readier to be taken in by such rubbish. All rascals have performed them, all fools have believed in them; before I'd be persuaded of the truth of a miracle I would have to be very sure the event so called by you was absolutely contrary to the laws of Nature, for only what is outside of Nature can pass for miraculous; and who is so deeply learned in Nature that he can affirm the precise point where her domain ends, and the precise point where it is infringed upon? Only two things are needed to accredit an alleged miracle, a mountebank and a few simpletons; tush, there's the whole origin of your prodigies; all new adherents to a religious sect have wrought some; and more extraordinary still, all have found imbeciles around to believe them. Your Jesus' feats do not surpass those of Apollonius of Tyana, yet nobody thinks to take the latter for a god; and when we come to your martyrs, assuredly, these are the feeblest of all your arguments. To produce martyrs you need but have enthusiasm on the one hand, resistance on the other; and so long as an opposed cause offers me as many of them as does yours, I shall never be sufficiently authorized to believe one better than another, but rather very much inclined to consider all of them pitiable. Ah my friend! were it true that the god you preach did exist, would he need miracle, martyr, or prophecy to secure recognition? and if, as you declare, the human heart were of his making, would he not have chosen it for the repository of his law? Then would this law, impartial for all mankind because emanating from a just god, then would it be found graved deep and writ clear in all men alike, and from one end of the world to the other, all men, having this delicate and sensitive organ in common, would also resemble each other through the homage they would render the god whence they had got it; all would adore and serve him in one identical manner, and they would be as incapable of disregarding this god as of resisting the inward impulse to worship him. Instead of that, what do I behold throughout this world? As many gods as there are countries; as many different cults as there are different minds or different imaginations; and this swarm of opinions among which it is physically impossible for me to choose, say now, is this a just god's doing? Fie upon you, preacher, you outrage your god when you present him to me thus; rather let me deny him completely, for if he exists then I outrage him far less by my incredulity than do you through your blasphemies. Return to your senses, preacher, your Jesus is no better than Mohammed, Mohammed no better than Moses, and the three of them combined no better than Confucius, who did after all have some wise things to say while the others did naught but rave; in general, though, such people are all mere frauds: philosophers laughed at them, the mob believed them, and justice ought to have hanged them.

PRIEST—Alas, justice dealt only too harshly with one of the four.

DYING MAN—If he alone got what he deserved it was he deserved it most richly; seditious, turbulent, calumniating, dishonest, libertine, a clumsy buffoon, and very mischievous; he had the art of overawing common folk and stirring up the rabble; and hence came in line for punishment in a kingdom where the state of affairs was what it was in Jerusalem then. They were very wise indeed to get rid of him, and this perhaps is the one case in which my extremely lenient and also extremely tolerant maxims are able to allow the severity of Themis; I excuse any misbehavior save that which may endanger the government one lives under, kings and their majesties are the only things I respect; and whoever does not love his country and his king were better dead than alive.

PRIEST—But you do surely believe something awaits us after this life, you must at some time or another have sought to pierce the dark shadows enshrouding our mortal fate, and what other theory could have satisfied your anxious spirit, than that of the numberless woes that betide him who has lived wickedly, and an eternity of rewards for him whose life has been good?

DYING MAN—What other, my friend? that of nothingness, it has never held terrors for me, in it I see naught but what is consoling and unpretentious; all the other theories are of pride's composition, this one alone is of reason's. Moreover, 'tis neither dreadful nor absolute, this nothingness. Before my eyes have I not the example of Nature's perpetual generations and regenerations? Nothing perishes in the world, my friend, nothing is lost; man today, worm tomorrow, the day after tomorrow a fly; is it not to keep steadily on existing? And what entitles me to be rewarded for virtues which are in me through no fault of my own, or again punished for crimes wherefor the ultimate responsibility is not mine? how are you to put your alleged god's goodness into tune with this system, and can he have wished to create me in order to reap pleasure from punishing me, and that solely on account of a choice he does not leave me free to determine?

PRIEST—You are free.

DYING MAN—Yes, in terms of your prejudices; but reason puts them to rout, and the theory of human freedom was never devised except to fabricate that of grace, which was to acquire such importance for your reveries. What man on earth, seeing the scaffold a step beyond the crime, would commit it were he free not to commit it? We are the pawns of an irresistible force, and never for an instant is it within our power to do anything but make the best of our lot and forge ahead along the path that has been traced for us. There is not a single virtue which is not necessary to Nature and conversely not a single crime which she does not need and it is in the perfect balance she maintains between the one and the other that her immense science consists; but can we be guilty for adding our weight to this side or that when it is she who tosses us onto the scales? no more so than the hornet who thrusts his dart into your skin.

PRIEST—Then we should not shrink from the worst of all crimes.

DYING MAN—I say nothing of the kind. Let the evil deed be proscribed by law, let justice smite the criminal, that will be deterrent enough; but if by misfortune we do commit it even so, let's not cry over spilled milk; remorse is inefficacious, since it does not stay us from crime, futile since it does not repair it, therefore it is absurd to beat one's breast, more absurd still to dread being punished in another world if we have been lucky to escape it in this. God forbid that this be construed as encouragement to crime, no, we should avoid it as much as we can, but one must learn to shun it through reason and not through false fears which lead to naught and whose effects are so quickly overcome in any moderately steadfast soul. Reason, sir—yes, our reason alone should warn us that harm done our fellows can never bring happiness to us; and our heart, that contributing to their felicity is the greatest joy Nature has accorded us on earth; the entirety of human morals is contained in this one phrase: *Render others as happy as one desires oneself to be,* and never inflict more pain upon them than one would like to receive at their hands. There you are, my friend, those are the only principles we should observe, and you need neither god nor religion to appreciate and subscribe to them, you need only have a good heart. But I feel my strength ebbing away; preacher, put away your prejudices, unbend, be a man, be human, without fear and without hope forget your gods and your religions too: they are none of them good for anything but to set man at odds with man, and the mere name of these horrors has caused greater loss of life on earth than all other wars and all other plagues combined. Renounce the idea of another world; there is none, but do not renounce the pleasure of being happy and of making for happiness in this. Nature offers you no other way of doubling your existence, of extending it. —My friend, lewd pleasures were ever dearer to me than anything else, I have idolized them all my life and my wish has been to end it in their bosom; my end draws near, six women lovelier than the light of day are waiting in the chamber adjoining, I have reserved them for this moment, partake of the feast with me, following my example embrace them instead of the vain sophistries of superstition, under their caresses strive for a little while to forget your hypocritical beliefs.

NOTE

The dying man rang, the women entered; and after he had been a little while in their arms the preacher became one whom Nature has corrupted, all because he had not succeeded in explaining what a corrupt nature is.

Philosophy
in the Bedroom
(1795)

T*he year 1795 was a fruitful and auspicious one for Sade. Almost miraculously, he had survived the Reign of Terror and, just six weeks after the execution of Robespierre, was once again set free, on October 15, 1794. Sade's printer, Girouard, who had published* Justine *and, before his arrest under the Terror had been preparing* Aline et Valcour *for publication, had not been so lucky: on January 8, 1794, he went to the guillotine.*

After Sade regained his freedom, he managed to retrieve that portion of Aline et Valcour *which Girouard had already printed prior to his arrest, and by mid-summer of 1795 the first edition of this four-volume work, which Sade acknowledged, was published.*

This same year there also appeared a small format, two-volume work, of anonymous authorship, enticingly entitled La Philosophie dans le boudoir. *Although anonymous, it was offered as a "posthumous work by the author of* Justine," *a subterfuge Sade was to utilize two years later for the publication of* La Nouvelle Justine. *The place of publication of the original edition was given as* Londres, aux dépens de la Compagnie, *and besides an allegorical frontispiece, it contained four erotic engravings. The epigraph of the original edition is* La mère en préscrira la lecture à sa fille (*Mothers will make this volume mandatory reading for their daughters*). *A second edition, in two octavo volumes of 203 and 191 pages respectively, appeared ten years later, in 1805, with the added subtitle—for which Sade, then in the Charenton asylum, can scarcely have been responsible—*ou les Instituteurs immoraux (*or The Immoral Teachers*). *Curiously, the epigraph of this second* *edition appeared—whether the change was intentional or not is a moot point—as* La mère en *proscrira* la lecture à sa fille (*Mothers will* forbid *their daughters to read it*).

Together with the Dialogue between a Priest and a Dying Man, *the* Philosophy in the Bedroom *is the only other nontheatrical work of Sade's written in the form of dialogue. Consisting of seven "Dialogues," in which philosophical speculations and dissertations on morality, history, and religion commingle with typical Sadean sexual fantasies, this work is one of the most specific, eloquent, and least redundant of Sade's major fictions. The four protagonists are Eugénie de Mistival, a chaste fifteen-year-old, a virgin and neophyte who is to be initiated into the mysteries of sensual pleasure; twenty-six-year-old Madame de Saint-Ange, a woman "of extreme lubricity"; her brother, the Chevalier de Mirvel, also a debauchee of considerable talents but who, unlike his sister and the fourth protagonist, Dolmancé ("The most corrupt and dangerous of men"), draws the line at the boundary of cruelty. All three of the initiators, with the possible exception of the Chevalier, who is still wrestling with his soul on the question of inflicting cruelty, would qualify as Sade's Unique Beings, of whom Maurice Blanchot makes mention in his Introduction. And, by the end of the day, Eugénie too, the aptest of pupils, is well on her way along the path of libertinage, that is (in Sade s canon), of freedom.*

The economy and disposition of the four principal characters enable Sade to expound his views both positively and negatively, for teaching, initiating the neophyte, is not only instructing but also disabusing: one must rid Eugénie's pretty little head of all the false notions of religion, morality, and virtue which a hypocritical mother and false society have instilled in her since birth.

The long "Fifth Dialogue" of this work contains the well-known "Yet Another Effort, Frenchmen, If You Would Become Republicans," which Le Chevalier reads aloud. Although it may detract from the otherwise considerable unity of the work, this "pamphlet"[1] is a work of considerable force, and perhaps the most eloquent refutation to those who accuse Sade of, or simplistically assimilate him to, the forces of evil and darkness which our century has spawned: fascism. The scope and complexity of Sade's ideas—independently of their individual merit or lack of merit—are such that they abound in contradictions and paradoxes, and may be quoted to prove or demonstrate a vast spectrum of opinion. But one thing is certain: Sade was for fewer laws, not more; for less restrictive social restraints on the individual, not more oppressive ones. As Maurice Heine has noted:

> It is with the individual, with the countless individuals who go to make up human societies, that Sade has placed the only organic strength these societies may possess. . . . He offers a withering criticism of any social restraints which reduce to whatever slight degree the activity of the incoercible human element. In his eyes, the only thing which will lead him to accept not a social pact but a social compromise—which can be denounced and renewed at any time—is the self-interest of the individual. For him, any society which fails to understand this fundamental truth is destined to perish.

In the light of Krafft-Ebing, Freud, or the detailed case histories of Wilhelm Stekel, the Philosophy in the Bedroom may appear somewhat less audacious than it did to previous generations (or those select few of the earlier generations who clandestinely were able to read it). That it is one of Sade's most seminal and compelling works there can be no doubt. It possesses another virtue: from one end to the other, there reigns a humor—a black and often grotesque humor, admittedly—which one looks for in vain in his strictly theatrical productions, and which perhaps exists nowhere else in his writing with such éclat, save in his extraordinary letters.

---

[1] During the Revolution of 1848, it was detached from the larger work and widely disseminated as a stirring work of great patriotic import.

TABLE OF CONTENTS

TO LIBERTINES

Voluptuaries of all ages, of every sex, it is to you only that I offer this work; nourish yourselves upon its principles: they favor your passions, and these passions, whereof coldly insipid moralists put you in fear, are naught but the means Nature employs to bring man to the ends she prescribes to him; harken only to these delicious promptings, for no voice save that of the passions can conduct you to happiness.

Lewd women, let the voluptuous Saint-Ange be your model; after her example, be heedless of all that contradicts pleasure's divine laws, by which all her life she was enchained.

You young maidens, too long constrained by a fanciful Virtue's absurd and dangerous bonds and by those of a disgusting religion, imitate the fiery Eugénie; be as quick as she to destroy, to spurn all those ridiculous precepts inculcated in you by imbecile parents.

And you, amiable debauchees, you who since youth have known no limits but those of your desires and who have been governed by your caprices alone, study the cynical Dolmancé, proceed like him and go as far as he if you too would travel the length of those flowered ways your lechery prepares for you; in Dolmancé's academy be at last convinced it is only by exploring and enlarging the sphere of his tastes and whims, it is only by sacrificing everything to the senses' pleasure that this individual, who never asked to be cast into this universe of woe, that this poor creature who goes under the name of Man, may be able to sow a smattering of roses atop the thorny path of life.

DIALOGUE THE FIRST

MADAME DE SAINT-ANGE,
LE CHEVALIER DE MIRVEL

MADAME DE SAINT-ANGE—Good day, my friend. And what of Monsieur Dolmancé?

LE CHEVALIER—He'll be here promptly at four; we do not dine until seven—and will have, as you see, ample time to chat.

MADAME DE SAINT-ANGE—You know, my dear brother, I *do* begin to have a few misgivings about my curiosity and all the obscene plans scheduled for today. Chevalier, you overindulge me, truly you do. The more sensible I should be, the more excited and libertine this accursed mind of mine becomes—and all that you have given me but serves to spoil me. . . . At twenty-six, I should be sober and staid, and I'm still nothing but the most licentious of women. . . . Oh, I've a busy brain, my friend; you'd scarce believe the ideas I have, the things I'd like to do. I supposed that by confining myself to women I would become better behaved . . . ; that were my desires concentrated upon my own sex I would no longer pant after yours: pure fantasy, my friend; my imagination has only been pricked the more by the pleasures I thought to deprive myself of. I have discovered that when it is a question of someone like me, born for libertinage, it is useless to think of imposing limits or restraints upon oneself—impetuous desires immediately sweep them away. In a word, my dear, I am an amphibious creature: I love everything, everyone, whatever it is, it amuses me; I should like to combine every species—but you must admit, Chevalier, is it not the height of extravagance for me to wish to know this unusual Dolmancé who in all his life, you tell me, has been unable to see a woman according to the prescriptions of common usage, this Dolmancé who, a sodomite out of principle, not only worships his own sex but never yields to ours save when we consent to put at his disposal those so well beloved charms of which he habitually makes use when consorting with men? Tell me, Chevalier, if my fancy is not bizarre! I want to be Ganymede to this new Jupiter, I want to enjoy his tastes, his debauches, I want to be the victim of his errors. Until now, and well you know it, my friend, until now I have given myself thus only to you, through complaisance, or to a few of my servants who, paid to use me in this manner, adopted it for profit only. But today it is no longer the desire to oblige nor is it caprice that moves me, but solely my own penchants. I believe that, between my past experiences with this curious mania and the courtesies to which I am going to be subjected, there is an inconceivable difference, and I wish to be acquainted with it. Paint your Dolmancé for me, please do, that I may have him well fixed in my mind before I see him arrive; for you know my acquaintance with him is limited to an encounter the other day in a house where we were together for but a few minutes.

LE CHEVALIER—Dolmancé, my dear sister, has just turned thirty-six; he is tall, extremely handsome, eyes very alive and very intelligent, but all the same there is some suspicion of hardness, and a trace of wickedness in his features; he has the whitest teeth in the world, a shade of softness about his figure and in his attitude, doubtless owing to his habit of taking on effeminate airs so often; he is extremely elegant, has a pretty voice, many talents, and above all else an exceedingly philosophic bent to his mind.

MADAME DE SAINT-ANGE—But I trust he does not believe in God!

LE CHEVALIER—Oh, perish the thought! He is the most notorious atheist, the most immoral fellow. . . . Oh, no; his is the most complete and thoroughgoing corruption, and he the most evil individual, the greatest scoundrel in the world.

MADAME DE SAINT-ANGE—Ah, how that warms me! Methinks that I'll be wild about this man. And what of his fancies, brother?

LE CHEVALIER—You know them full well; Sodom's delights are as dear to him in their active as in their passive form. For his pleasures, he cares for none but men; if however he sometimes deigns to employ women, it is only upon condition they be obliging enough to exchange sex with him. I've spoken of you to him; I advised him of your intentions, he agrees, and in his turn reminds you of the rules of the game. I warn you, my dear, he will refuse you altogether if you attempt to engage him to undertake anything else. "What I consent to do with your sister is," he declares, "an extravagance, an indiscretion with which one soils oneself but rarely and only by taking ample precautions."

MADAME DE SAINT-ANGE—*Soil oneself! . . . Precautions! . . .* Oh, how I adore the language those agreeable persons use! Between ourselves, we women also have exclusive words which like these just spoken, give an idea of the profound horror they have of all those who show heretical tendencies. . . . Tell me, my dear, has he had you? With your adorable face and your twenty years, one may, I dare say, captivate such a man?

LE CHEVALIER—We've committed follies together—I'll not hide them from you; you have too much wit to condemn them. The fact is, I favor women; I only give myself up to these odd whimsies when an attractive man urges me to them. And then there's nothing I stop at. I've none of that ludicrous arrogance which makes our young upstarts believe that it's by cuts with your walking stick you respond to such propositions. Is man master of his penchants? One must feel sorry for those who have strange tastes, but never insult them. Their wrong is Nature's too; they are no more responsible for having come into the world with tendencies unlike ours than are we for being born bandy-legged or well-proportioned. Is it, however, that a man acts insultingly to you when he manifests his desire to enjoy you? No, surely not; it is a compliment you are paid; why then answer with injuries and insults? Only fools can think thus; never will you hear an intelligent man discuss the question in a manner different from mine; but the trouble is, the world is peopled with poor idiots who believe it is to lack respect for them to avow one finds them fitted for one's pleasures, and who, pampered by women—themselves forever jealous of what has the look of infringing upon their rights—, fancy themselves to be the Don Quixotes of those ordinary rights, and brutalize whoever does not acknowledge the entirety of their extent.

MADAME DE SAINT-ANGE—Come, my friend, kiss me. Were you to think otherwise, you'd not be my brother. A few details, I beseech you, both with what regards this man's appearance and his pleasures with you.

LE CHEVALIER—One of his friends informed Monsieur Dolmancé of the superb member wherewith you know me provided, and he obtained the consent of the Marquis de V*** to bring us together at supper. Once there, I was obliged to display my equipment: at first curiosity appeared to be his single motive; however, a very fair ass turned my way, and with which I was invited to amuse myself, soon made me see that penchant alone was the cause of this examination. I had Dolmancé notice all the enterprise's difficulties; he was steadfast. "A ram holds no terrors for me," he said, "and you'll not have even the glory of being the most formidable amongst the men who have perforated the anus I offer you." The Marquis was on hand; he encouraged us by fingering, dandling, kissing whatever the one or the other of us brought to light. I took up my position. . . . "Surely some kind of priming?" I urged. "Nothing of the sort," said the Marquis, "you'll rob Dolmancé of half the sensations he awaits from you; he wants you to cleave him in two, he wants to be torn asunder." "Well," I said, blindly plunging into the gulf, "he'll be satisfied." Perhaps, my dear sister, you think that I met with a great deal of trouble . . . not at all; my prick, enormous as it is, disappeared, contrary to all my expectations, and I touched the bottom of his entrails without the bugger seeming to feel a thing. I dealt kindly with Dolmancé; the extreme ecstasy he tasted, his wrigglings and quiverings, his enticing utterances, all this soon made me happy too, and I inundated him. Scarcely was

I withdrawn when Dolmancé, turning toward me, his hair in disarray and his face red as a bacchante: "You see the state you've put me in, my dear Chevalier," said he, simultaneously presenting a pert, tough rogue of a prick, very long and at least six inches around, "deign, O my love, deign to serve me as a woman after having been my lover, and enable me to say that in your divine arms I have tasted all the delights of the fancy I cherish supremely." Finding as little difficulty in the one as in the other, I readied myself; the Marquis, dropping his breeches before my eyes, begged me to have the kindness to be yet a little of the man with him while I played wife to his friend; and I dealt with him as I had with Dolmancé, who paid me back a hundredfold for all the blows wherewith I belabored our third; and soon, into the depths of my ass, he exhaled that enchanted liquor with which, at virtually the same instant, I sprayed the bowels of V***.

MADAME DE SAINT-ANGE—You must have known the most extreme pleasure, to find yourself thus between two; they say it is charming.

LE CHEVALIER—My angel, it is surely the best place to be; but whatever may be said of them, they're all extravagances which I should never prefer to the pleasure of women.

MADAME DE SAINT-ANGE—Well, my chivalrous friend, as reward for your touching consideration, today I am going to hand over to your passions a young virgin, a girl, more beautiful than Love itself.

LE CHEVALIER—What! With Dolmancé . . . you're bringing a woman here?

MADAME DE SAINT-ANGE—It is a matter of an education; that of a little thing I knew last autumn at the convent, while my husband was at the baths. We could accomplish nothing there, we dared try nothing, too many eyes were fixed upon us, but we made a promise to meet again, to get together as soon as possible. Occupied with nothing but this desire, I have, in order to satisfy it, become acquainted with her family. Her father is a libertine—I've enthralled him. At any rate, the lovely one is coming, I am waiting for her; we'll spend two days together . . . two delicious days; I shall employ the better part of the time educating the young lady. Dolmancé and I will put into this pretty little head every principle of the most unbridled libertinage, we will set her ablaze with our own fire, we will feed her upon our philosophy, inspire her with our desires, and as I wish to join a little practice to theory, as I like the demonstrations to keep abreast of the dissertations, I have destined to you, dear brother, the harvest of Cythera's myrtle, and to Dolmancé shall go the roses of Sodom. I'll have two pleasures at once: that of enjoying these criminal lecheries myself, and that of giving the lessons, of inspiring fancies in the sweet innocent I am luring into our nets. Very well, Chevalier, answer me: is the project worthy of my imagination?

LE CHEVALIER—It could not have risen in another: it is divine, my sister, and I promise to enact to perfection the charming role you reserve for me. Ah, mischievous one, how much pleasure you are going to take in educating this child; what pleasure you will find in corrupting her, in stifling within this young heart every seed of virtue and of religion planted there by her tutors! Actually, all this is too roué for me.

MADAME DE SAINT-ANGE—Be certain I'll spare nothing to pervert her, degrade her, demolish in her all the false ethical notions with which they may already have been able to dizzy her; in two lessons, I want to render her as criminal as am I . . . as impious . . . as debauched, as depraved. Notify Dolmancé, explain everything to him immediately he gets here so that his immoralities' poison, circulating in this young spirit together with the venom I shall inject, will in the shortest possible time wither and still all the seeds of virtue that, but for us, might germinate there.

LE CHEVALIER—It would be impossible to find a better man: irreligion, impiety, inhumanity, libertinage spill from Dolmancé's lips as in times past mystic unction fell from those of the celebrated Archbishop of Cambrai. He is the most profound seducer, the most corrupt, the most dangerous man. . . . Ah, my dear, let your pupil but comply with this teacher's instructions, and I guarantee her straightway damned.

MADAME DE SAINT-ANGE—It should certainly not take long, considering the dispositions I know her to possess. . . .

LE CHEVALIER—But tell me, my dear sister, is there nothing to fear from the parents? May not this little one chatter when she returns home?

MADAME DE SAINT-ANGE—Have no fears. I have seduced the father . . . he's mine. I must confess to you, I surrendered myself to him in order to close his eyes: he knows nothing of my designs, and will never dare to scan them. . . . I have him.

LE CHEVALIER—Your methods are appalling!

MADAME DE SAINT-ANGE—Such they must be, else they're not sure.

LE CHEVALIER—And tell me, please, who is this youngster?

MADAME DE SAINT-ANGE—Her name is Eugénie, daughter of a certain Mistival, one of the wealthiest commercial figures in the capital, aged about thirty-six; her mother is thirty-two at the very most, and the little girl fifteen. Mistival is as libertine as his wife is pious. As for Eugénie, dear one, I should in vain undertake to figure her to you; she is quite beyond my descriptive powers . . . satisfy yourself with the knowledge that assuredly neither you nor I have ever set eyes on anything so delicious, anywhere.

LE CHEVALIER—But at least sketch a little if you cannot paint the portrait, so that, knowing fairly well with whom I am to deal, I may better fill my imagination with the idol to which I must sacrifice.

MADAME DE SAINT-ANGE—Very well, my friend: her abundant chestnut hair—there's too much of it to grasp in one's hand—descends to below her buttocks; her skin is of a dazzling whiteness, her nose rather aquiline, her eyes jet black and of a warmth! . . . Ah, my friend, 'tis impossible to resist those eyes. . . . You've no idea of the stupidities they've driven me to. . . . Could you but see the pretty eyebrows that crown them . . . the extraordinary lashes that border them. . . . A very small mouth, superb teeth, and, all of it, of a freshness! . . . One of her beauties is the elegant manner whereby her lovely head is attached to her shoulders, the air of nobility she has when she turns. . . . Eugénie is tall for her age: one might think her seventeen; her figure is a model of elegance and finesse, her throat, her bosom delicious. . . . There indeed are the two prettiest little breasts! . . . Scarcely enough there to fill the hand, but so soft . . . so fresh . . . so very white! Twenty times have I gone out of my head while kissing them; and had you been able to see how she came alive under my caresses . . . how her two great eyes represented to me the whole state of her mind. . . . My friend, I ignore the rest. Ah! but if I must judge of her by what I know, never, I say, had Olympus a divinity comparable with this. . . . But I hear her . . . leave us; go out by way of the garden to avoid meeting her, and be on time at the rendezvous.

LE CHEVALIER—The portrait you have just made for me assures my promptness. . . . Ah, heaven! to go out . . . to leave you, in the state I am in . . . Adieu! . . . a kiss . . . a kiss, my dear sister, to satisfy me at least till then. (*She kisses him, touches the prick straining in his breeches, and the young man leaves in haste.*)

DIALOGUE THE SECOND

MADAME DE SAINT-ANGE, EUGENIE

MADAME DE SAINT-ANGE—Welcome, my pet! I have been awaiting you with an impatience you fully appreciate if you can read the feelings I have in my heart.

EUGENIE—Oh, my precious one, I thought I should never arrive, so eager was I to find myself in your arms. An hour before leaving, I dreaded all might be changed; my mother was absolutely opposed to this delightful party, declaring it ill became a girl of my age to go abroad alone; but my father had so abused her the day before yesterday that a single one of his glances was quite enough to cause Madame Mistival to subside utterly, and it ended with her consenting to what my father had granted me, and I rushed here. I have two days; your carriage and one of your servants must without fail take me home the day after tomorrow.

MADAME DE SAINT-ANGE—How short is this period, my dearest angel, in so little time I shall hardly be able to express to you all you excite in me . . . and indeed we have to talk. You know, do you not, that 'tis during this interview that I am to initiate you into the most secret of Venus' mysteries; shall two days be time enough?

EUGENIE—Ah, were I not to arrive at a complete knowledge, I should remain. . . . I came hither to be instructed, and will not go till I am informed. . . .

MADAME DE SAINT-ANGE, *kissing her*—Dear love, how many things are we going to do and say to one another! But, by the way, do you wish to take lunch, my queen? For the lesson may be prolonged.

EUGENIE—I have no need, dear friend, than to listen to you; we lunched a league from here; I'll be able to wait until eight o'clock this evening without feeling the least hunger.

MADAME DE SAINT-ANGE—Then let's go into my boudoir, where we will be more at our ease. I have already spoken to the servants. You may be certain no one shall take it into his head to interrupt us. (*They enter the boudoir, linked arm in arm.*)

DIALOGUE THE THIRD

In a Delightful Boudoir

MADAME DE SAINT-ANGE,
EUGENIE, DOLMANCE

EUGENIE, *greatly surprised to find in this room a man whom she had not expected*—Great God! Dearest friend, we are betrayed!

MADAME DE SAINT-ANGE, *equally surprised*—Strange, Monsieur, to find you here. Were you not expected at four?

DOLMANCE—One always hastens the advent of that happiness which comes of seeing you, Madame. I encountered Monsieur, your brother—he anticipated the usefulness of my presence at the lessons you are to give Mademoiselle, and knew this to be the lyceum where they would be given. Unperceived, he introduced me into this chamber, far from imagining you might disapprove; and as for himself, aware his demonstrations will only be necessary after the dissertations on theory, he will not make his appearance until later.

MADAME DE SAINT-ANGE—Indeed, Dolmancé, this is an unforeseen turn. . . .

EUGENIE—By which I am not deceived, my good friend; it is all your work. . . . At least, you should have consulted me . . . instead of exposing me to this shame. It will certainly prejudice all our projects.

MADAME DE SAINT-ANGE—Eugénie, I protest—my brother is responsible for this, not I. But there's no cause for alarm: I know Dolmancé for a most agreeable man, and he possesses just that degree of philosophic understanding we require for your enlightenment. He can be of nothing but the greatest service to our schemes. As for his discretion, I am as willing to answer for it as for my own. Therefore, dear heart, familiarize yourself with this man who in all the world is the best endowed to form you and to guide you into a career of the happiness and the pleasures we wish to taste together.

EUGENIE, *blushing*—Oh! I still find all this most upsetting. . . .

DOLMANCE—Come, my lovely Eugénie, put yourself at ease. . . . Modesty is an antiquated virtue which you, so rich in charms, ought to know wonderfully well how to do without.

EUGENIE—But decency . . .

DOLMANCE—Ha! A Gothicism not very much defended these days. It is so hostile to Nature! (*Dolmancé seizes Eugénie, folds her in his arms, and kisses her.*)

EUGENIE, *struggling in his embrace*—That's quite enough, Monsieur! . . . Indeed, you show me very little consideration!

MADAME DE SAINT-ANGE—Eugénie, listen to me: let's both of us cease behaving like prudes with this charming gentleman; I am not better acquainted with him than are you, yet watch how I give myself to him. (*She kisses him indecently on the mouth.*) Imitate me.

EUGENIE—Oh, most willingly; where might I find better examples? (*She puts herself in Dolmancé's arms; he kisses her ardently, tongue in mouth.*)

DOLMANCE—Amiable, delicious creature!

MADAME DE SAINT-ANGE, *kissing her in the same way*—Didst think, little chit, I'd not have my turn as well? (*At this point Dolmancé, holding first one in his arms, then the other, tongues both, each for a quarter of an hour, and they both tongue one another and him.*)

DOLMANCE—Ah, such preliminaries make me drunk with desire! Mesdames, upon my word, it is extraordinarily warm here; more lightly attired, we might converse with infinitely greater comfort.

MADAME DE SAINT-ANGE—You are right, sir; we'll don these gauze negligees—of our charms, they'll conceal only those that must be hidden from desire.

EUGENIE—Indeed, dear one, you lead me to do things! . . .

MADAME DE SAINT-ANGE, *helping her undress*—Completely ridiculous, isn't it?

EUGENIE—Most improper at the very least, I'd say. . . . My! how you kiss me!

MADAME DE SAINT-ANGE—Pretty bosom! . . . a rose only now reaching full bloom.

DOLMANCE, *considering, without touching, Eugénie's breasts*—And which promises yet other allurements . . . infinitely to be preferred.

MADAME DE SAINT-ANGE—Infinitely to be preferred?

DOLMANCE—Oh yes, upon my honor. (*Saying which, Dolmancé appears eager to turn Eugénie about in order to inspect her from the rear.*)

EUGENIE—No, I beg of you!

MADAME DE SAINT-ANGE—No, Dolmancé . . . I don't want you yet to see . . . an object whose sway over you is so great that, the image of it once fixed in your head, you are unable thereafter to reason coolly. We need your lessons, first give them to us—and afterward the myrtle you covet will be your reward.

DOLMANCE—Very well, but in order to demonstrate, in order to give this beautiful child the first lessons of libertinage, we will require willing co-operation from you, Madame, in the exercise that must follow.

MADAME DE SAINT-ANGE—So be it! All right then, look you here—I'm entirely naked. Make your dissertations upon me as much as you please.

DOLMANCE—Oh, lovely body! 'Tis Venus herself, embellished by the Graces.

EUGENIE—Oh, my dear friend, what charms! delights! Let me drink them in with my eyes, let me cover them with my kisses. (*She does so.*)

DOLMANCE—What excellent predispositions! A trifle less passion, lovely Eugénie, for the moment you are only being asked to show a little attention.

EUGENIE—Let's continue, I'm listening. . . . But how beautiful she is . . . so plump, so fresh! . . . Ah, how charming my dear friend is. Is she not, Monsieur?

DOLMANCE—Beautiful, assuredly . . . she is wondrous to see; but I am persuaded you yield to her in nothing. . . . Well, now, my pretty little student, either you pay attention to me or beware lest, if you are not docile, I exercise over you the rights amply conferred upon me by my title as your mentor.

MADAME DE SAINT-ANGE—Oh, yes, yes indeed, Dolmancé, I put her into your safekeeping. She must have a severe scolding if she misbehaves.

DOLMANCE—It is very possible I might not be able to confine myself to remonstrances.

EUGENIE—Great heaven! You terrify me . . . what then would you do to me, Monsieur?

DOLMANCE, *stammering, and kissing Eugénie on the mouth*—Punishments . . . corrections . . . I might very well hold this pretty little ass accountable for mistakes made by the head. (*He strikes the former through the gauze dressing gown in which Eugénie is presently arrayed.*)

MADAME DE SAINT-ANGE—Yes, I approve of the project but not of the gesture. Let's begin our lesson, else the little time granted us to enjoy Eugénie will be spent in preliminaries, and the instruction shall remain incomplete.

DOLMANCE, *who, as he discusses them, one by one touches the parts of Madame de Saint-Ange's body*—I begin. I will say nothing of these fleshy globes; you know as well as I, Eugénie, that they are indifferently known as *bosoms, breasts, tits.* Pleasure may put them to profitable use: while amusing himself, a lover has them continually before his eyes: he caresses them, handles them, indeed, some lovers form of them the very seat of their pleasure and niche their member between these twin mounts of Venus which the woman then squeezes together, compressing this member; after a little management, certain men succeed in spreading thereupon the delicious balm of life whose outpouring causes the whole happiness of libertines. . . . But this member of which we shall be obliged to speak incessantly—should we not be well advised, Madame, to give our student a lecture upon it?

MADAME DE SAINT-ANGE—Verily, I do think so.

DOLMANCE—Very well, Madame, I am going to recline upon this couch; place yourself near me. Then you will lay hands upon the subject and you will yourself explain its properties to our young student. (*Dolmancé lies down and Madame de Saint-Ange demonstrates.*)

MADAME DE SAINT-ANGE—This scepter of Venus you have before your eyes, Eugénie, is the primary agent of love's pleasure: it is called the *member:* there is not a single part of the human body into which it cannot introduce itself. Always obedient to the passions of the person who wields it, sometimes it nests there (*She touches Eugénie's cunt.*), this is the ordinary route, the one in widest use, but not the most agreeable; in pursuit of a more mysterious sanctuary, it is often here (*She spreads wide Eugénie's buttocks and indicates the anus.*) that the libertine seeks enjoyment we will return to this most delicious pleasure of them all; there are as well the mouth, the breasts, the armpits which provide him with further altars upon which to burn his incense. And finally whatever be the place among all these he most prefers, after a few instants of agitation the member may be seen to vent a white and viscou liquor, whose flowing forth plunges the man into a delirium intense enough to procure for him the sweetest pleasures he can hope to have in life.

EUGENIE—How much I should like to see this liquor flow!

MADAME DE SAINT-ANGE—I need but vibrate my hand—you see how the thing becomes irritated the more I chafe and pull on it. These movements are known as *pollution,* and in the language of libertinage this action is called *frigging.*

EUGENIE—Oh, please, dear friend, allow me to frig this splendid member!

DOLMANCE—Look out! I'll not be able . . . don't interfere with her, Madame, this ingenuousness has got me horribly erected.

MADAME DE SAINT-ANGE—No good will come of this excitement. Be reasonable, Dolmancé: once that semen flows, the activity of your animal spirits will be diminished and the warmth of your dissertations will be lessened correspondingly.

EUGENIE, *fondling Dolmancé's testicles*—Ah, my dear friend, how sorry I am you resist my desires! . . . And these balls, what might be their purpose? What are they called?

MADAME DE SAINT-ANGE—The technical term is *genitals, male genitals . . . testicles* belongs to art, the *balls* are the reservoir containing the abundant semen I have just mentioned and which, expelled into the woman's matrix, or womb, produces the human species; but we will not stress these details, Eugénie, for they relate more to medicine than to libertinage. A pretty girl ought simply to concern herself with *fucking,* and never with *engendering.* No need to touch at greater length on what pertains to the dull business of population, from now on we shall address ourselves principally, nay, uniquely to those libertine lecheries whose spirit is in no wise reproductive.

EUGENIE—But, dear friend, when this enormous member I can scarcely grip in my hand, when this member penetrates, as you assure me it can, into a hole as little as the one in your behind, that must cause the woman a great deal of pain.

MADAME DE SAINT-ANGE—Whether this introduction be wrought before or behind, if she is not yet accustomed to it a woman always suffers. It has pleased Nature so to make us that we attain happiness only by way of pain. But once vanquished and had this way, nothing can equal the joy one tastes upon the entrance of this member into our ass; it is a pleasure incontestably superior to any sensation procured by this same introduction in front. And, besides, how many dangers does not a woman thus avoid! Fewer risks to her health, and none at all of pregnancy. For the present I'll say no more about this delight—your master and mine, Eugénie, will soon award it a full analysis, and by uniting practice with theory will, I trust, convince you, my precious one, that amongst all the bedroom's pleasures, that is the only one for which you should have a preference.

DOLMANCE—I beg you to speed your demonstrations, Madame, for I can no longer restrain myself; I'll discharge despite my efforts, and this redoubtable member, reduced to nothing, will be unable to aid your lessons.

EUGENIE—What! It would be reduced to nothing, dear heart, if it were to lose this semen you speak of! . . . Oh, do allow me to help him lose it, so that I may see what happens to it. . . . And besides, I should take such pleasure in seeing it flow!

MADAME DE SAINT-ANGE—No, no, Dolmancé, up with you. Remember that this is the payment of your labors, and that I'll not turn her over to you until you've merited her.

DOLMANCE—So be it; but the better to convince Eugénie of all we are going to relate concerning pleasure, would it be in any way prejudicial to Eugénie's instruction if, for instance, you were to frig her in front of me?

MADAME DE SAINT-ANGE—Why, doubtless not, and I shall do so all the more happily since I am certain this lubricious episode will only enrich our lessons. Onto the couch, my sweet.

EUGENIE—Oh dear God! the delicious niche! But why all these mirrors?

MADAME DE SAINT-ANGE—By repeating our attitudes and postures in a thousand different ways, they infinitely multiply those same pleasures for the persons seated here upon this ottoman. Thus everything is visible, no part of the body can remain hidden: everything must be seen; these images are so many groups disposed around those enchained by love, so many delicious tableaux wherewith lewdness waxes drunk and which soon drive it to its climax.

EUGENIE—What a marvelous invention!

MADAME DE SAINT-ANGE—Dolmancé, undress the victim yourself.

DOLMANCE—That will not be difficult, since 'tis merely a question of removing this gauze in order to discern naked the most appealing features. (*He strips her, and his first glances are instantly directed upon her behind.*) And so I am about to see this divine, this priceless ass of which I have such ardent expectations! . . . Ah, by God! What fullness of flesh and what coolness, what stunning elegance! . . . Never have I seen one lovelier!

MADAME DE SAINT-ANGE—Rascal! How clearly your initial homages betray your tastes and pleasures!

DOLMANCE—But can there be anything in the world to equal this? . . . Where might love find a more divine altar? . . . Eugénie . . . sublime Eugénie, let me overwhelm this ass of yours with the softest caresses. (*He fingers and kisses it, transported.*)

MADAME DE SAINT-ANGE—Stop, libertine! . . . You forget Eugénie belongs to me only. She's to be your reward for the lessons she awaits from you; but you'll not have your recompense before she has been given those lessons. Enough of this ardor or you'll anger me.

DOLMANCE—Scoundrel! It's your jealousy. . . . Very well. Pass me yours and I'll pay it a similar homage. (*He raises Madame de Saint-Ange's negligee and caresses her behind.*) Ah, 'tis lovely, my angel, 'tis delicious too! Let me compare them both. . . . I'd see them one next to the other—Ganymede beside Venus! (*He lavishes kisses upon each.*) In order to have the bewitching spectacle of so much beauty constantly before my eyes, Madame, could you not, by interlacing yourselves, uninterruptedly offer my gaze these charming asses I worship?

MADAME DE SAINT-ANGE—Perfectly well! There . . . are you satisfied? . . . (*They intertwine their bodies in such a manner that both asses confront Dolmancé.*)

DOLMANCE—It could not be better: 'tis precisely what I asked for. And now agitate those superb asses with all the fire of lubricity; let them sink and rise in cadence; let them obey the proddings whereby pleasure is going to stir them. . . . Oh, splendid, splendid, 'tis delicious! . . .

EUGENIE—Ah, my dearest one, what pleasures you give me. . . . What is it you call what you are doing now?

MADAME DE SAINT-ANGE—Frigging, my pet, giving oneself pleasure. Stop a moment; we'll alter our positions. Examine my cunt . . . thus is named the temple of Venus. Look sharply at that coign your hand covers, examine it well. I am going to open it a little. This elevation you notice above it is called the *mound,* which is garnished with hair, generally, when one reaches the age of fourteen or fifteen, when, that is, a girl begins to have periods. Here above is a little tongue-shaped thing—that is the clitoris, and there lies all a woman's power of sensation. It is the center of all mine; it would be impossible to tickle this part of me without seeing me swoon with delight. . . . Try it. . . . Ah, sweet little bitch, how well you do it! One would think you've done nothing else all your life! . . . enough! . . . stop! . . . No, I tell you, no, I do not wish to surrender myself. . . . Oh, Dolmancé, stop me! . . . under the enchanted fingers of this pretty child, I am about to go out of my mind.

DOLMANCE—You might be able to lower the temperature of your ideas by varying them: frig her in your turn; keep a grip on yourself, and let her go to work. . . . There, yes, in this position, in this manner her pretty little ass is between my hands, I'll pollute it ever so lightly with a finger. . . . Let yourself go Eugénie, abandon all your senses to pleasure, let it be the one object, the one god of your existence; it is to this god a girl ought to sacrifice everything, and in her eyes, nothing must be as holy as pleasure.

EUGENIE—Nothing in the world is so delightful, I do feel that. . . . I am beside myself . . . I no longer know what I am saying, nor what I am doing. . . . What a drunkenness steals through all my being!

DOLMANCE—Look at the little rascal discharge! And squeeze! . . . Her anus nearly nipped off the end of my finger . . . how splendid it would be to bugger her at such a moment! (*He stands and claps his prick to the girl's ass.*)

MADAME DE SAINT-ANGE—Yet another moment's patience. The dear girl's education must be our sole occupation! . . . How pleasant it is to enlighten her!

DOLMANCE—Well then, Eugénie, you observe that after a more or less prolonged pollution, the seminal glands swell, enlarge, and finally exhale a liquid whose release hurls the woman into the most intense rapture. This is known as *discharging*. When it pleases your good friend here, I'll show you, but in a more energetic and more imperious manner, how the same operation occurs in a man.

MADAME DE SAINT-ANGE—Wait, Eugénie, now I'm going to teach you a new way to drown a woman in joy. Spread your thighs. . . . Dolmancé, you see how I am adjusting her, her ass is all yours. Suck it for her while my tongue licks her cunt, and between the two of us let's see if we can get her to swoon three or four times. Your little mound is charming, Eugénie, how I adore kissing this downy flesh! . . . I see your clitoris more clearly now; 'tis but somewhat formed, yet most sensitive. . . . How you do quiver and squirm! . . . Let me spread you. . . . Ah! you're a virgin indeed! . . . Describe what you feel when our two tongues run at once into your two apertures. (*They do as they have said.*)

EUGENIE—Ah, my dear, it thrills me so; it is a sensation impossible to depict! I'd be hard put to say which of your tongues plunges me further into my delirium.

DOLMANCE—In this posture, Madame, my prick is well within your reach. Condescend to frig it, I beg of you, while I suck this heavenly ass. Thrust your tongue yet further, Madame; don't be content to suck her clitoris; make your voluptuous tongue penetrate into her womb: 'tis the surest way to hasten the ejaculation.

EUGENIE, *stiffening*—I cannot bear it any more! oh, I'm dying! Don't abandon me, dear friends, I am about to swoon. (*She discharges between her two initiators.*)

MADAME DE SAINT-ANGE—Well, my pet! What think you of the pleasure we have given you?

EUGENIE—I am dead, exhausted . . . but I beg you to explain two words you pronounced and which I do not understand. First of all, what does *womb* signify?

MADAME DE SAINT-ANGE—'Tis a kind of vessel much resembling a bottle whose neck embraces the male's member, and which receives the fuck produced in the woman by glandular seepage and in the man by the ejaculation we will exhibit for you; and of the commingling of these liquors is born the germ whereof result now boys, now girls.

EUGENIE—Oh, I see; this definition simultaneously explains the word *fuck* whose meaning I did not thoroughly grasp until now. And is the union of the seeds necessary to the formation of the fetus?

MADAME DE SAINT-ANGE—Assuredly; although it is proven that the fetus owes its existence only to the man's sperm, this latter, by itself, unmixed with the woman's, would come to naught. But that which we women furnish has a merely elaborative function; it does not create, it furthers creation without being its cause. Indeed, there are several contemporary naturalists who claim it is useless; whence the moralists, always guided by science's discoveries, have decided—and the conclusion has a degree of plausibility—that, such being the case, the child born of the father's blood owes filial tenderness to him alone, an assertion not without its appealing qualities and one which, even though a woman, I should not be inclined to contest.

EUGENIE—It is in my heart I find confirmation of what you tell me, my dear; for I love my father to distraction, and I feel a loathing for my mother.

DOLMANCE—But there is nothing unusual about that predilection; I have always thought as you. I still lament my father's death;

when I lost my mother, I lit a perfect bonfire from joy. . . . I detested her. Be unafraid, Eugénie, and adopt these same sentiments; they are natural: uniquely formed of our sires' blood, we owe absolutely nothing to our mothers. What, furthermore, did they do but co-operate in the act which our fathers, on the contrary, solicited? Thus, it was the father who desired our birth, whereas the mother merely consented thereto. As regards sentiment, what a difference!

MADAME DE SAINT-ANGE—Yet a thousand more reasons in your favor, Eugénie, if it is a mother still alive. If in all the world there is a mother who ought to be abhorred she is certainly yours! Superstitious, pious, a shrew, a scold . . . and what with her revolting prudery I dare wager the fool has never in her life committed a faux pas. Ah, my dear, how I hate virtuous women! . . . But we'll return to that question.

DOLMANCE—And now would it not be fitting for Eugénie, directed by me, to learn to pay back what you have just done in her behalf? I think she might frig you before me.

MADAME DE SAINT-ANGE—I applaud the suggestion—and while she frigs me, would not you, Dolmancé, relish the sight of my ass?

DOLMANCE—Are you able to doubt, Madame, of the pleasure with which I will render it my gentlest homages?

MADAME DE SAINT-ANGE, *presenting her buttocks to him*—Do you find me suitable thus?

DOLMANCE—Wonderfully! I should never find a better manner to render you all the services Eugénie found so enormously to her liking. And now, my little wildcat, station yourself for a moment between your friend's legs, so, and with that pretty little tongue of yours, care for her as she has for you. Why, bless me! This way I shall be able to manage both your asses: I'll fondle Eugénie's while sucking her lovely friend's. . . . There, admirable . . . How agreeably we are all together.

MADAME DE SAINT-ANGE, *swooning*—Good God, I'm dying. . . . Dolmancé, how I love to handle your prick while I discharge. . . . I'd have it drown me in fuck, so frig it! Suck me! Oh, heavenly fuck! How I love to play the whore when my sperm flows this way! . . . It's done, finished, I cannot go on. . . . You've ruined me, both of you. . . . I think I have never had so much pleasure in my life.

EUGENIE—And how happy I am to be its cause! But, dear friend, you have just uttered another unfamiliar word. What do you understand this expression *whore* to mean? Forgive me, but you know I'm here to learn.

MADAME DE SAINT-ANGE—My most lovely one, in such wise are called the public victims of the debauchery of men, creatures prepared at all times to surrender their persons, whether from temperament or for reward; happy and deserving creatures common opinion assails but whom license crowns and who, far more necessary to the society which they strive to serve than are prudes, forgo the esteem an unjust society denies them. All hail to those in whose eyes this title is an honor! Such are truly lovable women, the only authentic philosophers! As for myself, dear heart, I, who for twelve years have endeavored to merit the laurel, I assure you that if I do not work as a whore, I always play as one. Better still, I love thus to be named when I am fucked: 'tis a vilification that fires my brain.

EUGENIE—My dear, I fancy I too should not be sorry to be called a whore, though 'tis true I scarcely merit the name; but is not virtue opposed to such misconduct, and does it not reproach us for behaving as we do?

DOLMANCE—Ah, Eugénie, have done with virtues! Among the sacrifices that can be made to those counterfeit divinities, is there one worth an instant of the pleasures one tastes in outraging them? Come, my sweet, virtue is but a chimera whose worship consists exclusively in perpetual immolations, in unnumbered rebellions against the temperament's inspirations. Can such impulses be natural? Does Nature recommend what offends her? Eugénie, be not the dupe of those women you hear called virtuous. Theirs are not, if you wish, the same passions as ours; but they harken to others, and often more contemptible. . . . There is ambition, there pride, there you find self-seeking, and often, again, it is a question of mere constitutional numbness, of torpor: there are beings who have no urges. Are we, I ask, to revere such as them? No; the virtuous woman acts, or is inactive, from pure selfishness. Is it then better, wiser, more just to perform sacrifices to egoism than to one's passions? As for me, I believe the one far worthier than the other, and who heeds but this latter voice is far better advised, no question of it, since it only is the organ of Nature, while the former is simply that of stupidity and prejudice. One single drop of fuck shed from this member, Eugénie, is more precious to me than the most sublime deeds of a virtue I scorn.

EUGENIE—(*Calm being to some degree re-established during these expositions, the women, clad again in their negligees, are reclining upon a couch, and Dolmancé, seated in an armchair, is close by.*) But there is more than one species of virtue. What think you of, for example, pity?

DOLMANCE—What can it be for whosoever has no belief in religion? And who is able to have religious beliefs? Come now, Eugénie, let's reason systematically. Do you not call religion the pact that binds man to his Creator and which obliges him to give his Creator evidence, by means of worship, of his gratitude for the existence received from this sublime author?

EUGENIE—It could not be better defined.

DOLMANCE—Excellent! If it is demonstrated that man owes his existence to nothing but Nature's irresistible schemes; if man is thus proven as ancient in this world as is ancient the globe itself, he is but as the oak, as grain, as the minerals to be found in the earth's entrails, who are bound only to reproduce, reproduction being necessitated by the globe's existence, which owes its own to nothing whatsoever; if it is demonstrated that this God, whom fools behold as the author and maker of all we know there to be, is simply the *ne plus ultra* of human reason, merely the phantom created at the moment this reason can advance its operations no further; if it is proven that this God's existence is impossible, and that Nature, forever in action, forever moving, has of herself what it pleases idiots to award God gratuitously; if it is certain that this inert being's existence, once supposed, he would be of all things the most ridiculous, since he would have been useful only one single time and, thereafter and throughout millions of centuries, fixed in a contemptible stillness and inactivity; that, supposing him to exist as religions portray him to us, this would be the most detestable of creatures, since it would be God who permits evil to be on earth while his omnipotence could prevent it; if, I say, all that is admitted to be proven, as incontestably it is, do you believe, Eugénie, that it is a very necessary virtue, this piety which binds man to an idiotic, insufficient, atrocious, and contemptible Creator?

EUGENIE, *to Madame de Saint-Ange*—What! Then you mean to say, dear friend, God's existence is an illusion?

MADAME DE SAINT-ANGE—And without doubt one of the most deplorable.

DOLMANCE—To believe therein one must first have gone out of one's mind. Fruit of the terror of some and of the frailty of others, that abominable phantom, Eugénie, is of no use to the terrestrial scheme and would infallibly be injurious to it, since the will of God would have to be just and should never be able to ally itself to the essential injustices decreed by Nature; since He would constantly have to will the good, while Nature must desire it only as compensation for the evil which serves her laws; since it would be necessary that he, God, exert his influence at all times, while Nature, one of whose laws is this perpetual activity, could only find herself in competition with and unceasing opposition to him. Am I to hear in reply, that God and Nature are one? 'Tis an absurdity. The thing created cannot be the creative being's equal. Might the pocket watch be the watchmaker? Very well then, they will continue, Nature is nothing, it is God who is all. Another stupidity! There are necessarily two things in the universe: the creative agent and the being created; now, to identify this creative agent is the single task before us, the one question to which one has got to provide a reply.

If matter acts, is moved by combinations unknown to us, if movement is inherent in Nature; if, in short, she alone, by reason of her energy, is able to create, produce, preserve, maintain, hold in equilibrium within the immense plains of space all the spheres that stand before our gaze and whose uniform march, unvarying, fills us with awe and admiration, what then becomes of the need to seek out a foreign agent, since this active faculty essentially is to be found in Nature herself, who is naught else than matter in action? Do you suppose your deific chimera will shed light upon anything? I defy anyone to prove him to me. It being supposed that I am mistaken upon matter's internal faculties, I have before me, at least, nothing worse than a difficulty. What do you do for me when you offer your God to me? Nothing but offering one more god. And how would you have me acknowledge as cause of what I do not understand, something that I understand even less? Will it be by means of the Christian religion that I shall examine . . . that I shall obtain a view of your appalling God? Then let us cast a glance upon the God Christianity propounds. . . .

What do I see in the God of that infamous sect if not an inconsistent and barbarous being, today the creator of a world of destruction he repents of tomorrow; what do I see there but a frail being forever unable to bring man to heel and force him to bend a knee. This creature, although emanated from him, dominates him, knows how to offend him and thereby merit torments eternally! What a weak fellow, this God! How able he was to mold all that we know and to fail to form man in his own guise! Whereunto you will answer, that had man been created so, man would have been little deserving of his author; what a platitude this is! and what necessity is there that man be deserving of his God? Had man been formed wholly good, man should never have been able to do evil, and only then would the work be worthy of a god. To allow man to choose was to tempt him; and God's infinite powers very well advised him of what would be the result. Immediately the being was created, it was hence to pleasure that God doomed the creature he had himself formed. A horrible God, this God of yours, a monster! Is there a criminal more worthy of our hatred and our implacable vengeance than he! However, little content with a task so sublimely executed, he drowns man to convert him; he burns him; he curses him.

Nothing in all that alters man one jot. More powerful than this villainous God, a being still in possession of his power, forever able to brave his author, the *Devil* by his seductions incessantly succeeds in leading astray the flock that the Eternal reserved unto himself. Nothing can vanquish the hold this demon's energy has upon us. But picture, in your own terms, the frightful God you preach: he has but one son; an only son, begot of some passing strange commerce; for, as man doth *fuck,* so he hath willed that his Lord *fucketh* too; and the Lord didst detach and send down out of Heaven this respectable part of himself. One perhaps imagines that it is upon celestial rays, in the midst of an angelic cortege, within sight of all the universe this sublime creature is going to appear ... not at all; 'tis upon a Jewish whore's breast, 'tis in a proper pigsty that there is announced the God who has come to save the earth! Behold the worthy extraction accorded this personage! But his mission is honorable—will he disabuse us? Let us have a close look at him for an instant. What does he say? What is it he does? What is his sublime mission? What mystery is he about to reveal? What is the dogma he is going to prescribe for us? What will be the act wherein at last his grandeur will shine?

I see, first of all, an obscure childhood, a few doubtless very libertine services this smutty fellow renders the priests at the Temple of Jerusalem; next, a fifteen years' disappearance during which the scoundrel goes to poison himself with all the reveries of the Egyptian school, which at length he fetches back to Judea. Scarcely does he reappear when his raving begins: he says he is the son of God, his father's peer; to this alliance he joins another phantom he calls the Holy Ghost, and these three persons, he swears, must be but one! The more this preposterous mystery amazes the reason, the more the low fellow declares there is merit in swallowing it ... and danger in refusing it. It is to save us one and all, the imbecile argues, that he has assumed a fleshly shape although he is *God,* mortally incarnate in the breast of a child of man; and the glittering wonders one is about to see him perform will speedily convince all the world of it. During a ribald supper indeed, the cheat transforms, so they say, water into wine; in a desert he feeds a few bandits upon the victuals previously hidden there by his devoted confederates; one of his cronies plays dead, our impostor restores him to life again; he betakes himself to mountain and there, before two or three of his friends only, he brings off a jugglery that would cause the worst among our contemporary mountebanks to redden with shame.

Roundly damning, moreover, all those who do not accredit him, the scoundrel promises the heavens to whatever fools will listen. He writes nothing, for he is ignorant; talks very little, for he is stupid; does even less, for he is weak; and, finally, completely exhausting the patience of the magistrates with his seditious outbursts, the charlatan has himself fixed to the cross after having assured the rogues who follow him that, every time they invoke him, he will descend to them to get himself eaten. He is put to torture, he puts up with it. Monsieur his Papa, that sublime God whence he dares affirm he descends, succors him not in the least, and there you have him, this scoundrel, used like the last of the outlaws of whom he was such a fitting chief.

His henchmen assemble: "It's all up with us," they say, "and all our hopes are perished lest we save ourselves with a quick piece of cunning. We'll besot the guard set to watch over Jesus; then make off with his body, bruit it abroad he is risen: the trick's sure; if we manage to get this knavery believed, our new religion's founded, propagated; it'll seduce all the world. . . . To work!" The blow is struck, it succeeds. In how many blackguards has not boldness occupied the place of merit! The corpse is filched, fools, women, children bawl out "Miracle!" at the top of their lungs; nevertheless, in this city where such great prodigies have just been wrought, in this city stained with a God's blood, no one cares to believe in this God; not a single conversion is operated there. Better yet: so little worthy of transmission is the event that no historian alludes to it. Only this impostor's disciples think they have something to gain from the fraud; but not at the hour.

This detail is crucial; let's note it well. They permit several years to pass before exploiting their artifice; at length, they erect upon it the shaky edifice of their unwholesome doctrine. Men are pleased by any novelty. Weary of the emperors' despotism, the world agrees to the need for a revolution. These cheats are heard, they make a very rapid progress; 'tis the story of every error. Soon the altars of Venus and Mars are changed to those of Jesus and Mary; the life of the impostor is published, the insipid fiction finds its dupes; he is represented as having said a hundred things which never came into his head; some few of his own drivelings instantly become the basis of his morality, and as this romance is preached to the poor, charity becomes its foremost virtue. Weird rites are instituted under the name of *sacraments*; the most offensive and the most abominable of them all is the one whereby a priest, covered with crimes, has, notwithstanding, thanks to a few magical words, the power to bring God back in a morsel of bread. Let there be no mistake: at its very birth, this shameful cult might have been utterly destroyed had one but employed against it those weapons of the contempt it deserved; but men took it into their heads to employ persecution; the cult throve; 'twas inevitable.

Even today were one to cover it with ridicule, it would fall. The adroit Voltaire never used any other arm, and among all writers he is the one who may congratulate himself upon having the greatest number of proselytes. Such, in a few words, Eugénie, is the history of God and of religion; consider the treatment these fables deserve, and adopt a determined attitude toward them.

EUGENIE—My choice is unperplexed; I scorn the lot of these unhealthy reveries, and this God himself, to whom I lately clove through weakness or through ignorance, is henceforth nothing for me but an object of horror.

MADAME DE SAINT-ANGE—Swear to me to think no more of him, never to be concerned for him, never to invoke him at any moment in your life, and so long as breath be in you never to return to him.

EUGENIE, *flinging herself upon Madame de Saint-Ange's breast*—I pledge it in your arms! How readily I see that what you demand is for my own good, and that you would never have such reminiscences disturb my tranquillity!

MADAME DE SAINT-ANGE—What other motive could I have?

EUGENIE—But, Dolmancé, it seems to me it was the analysis of virtues that led us to the examination of religions. Let us now return to the former. Might there not exist in this religion, completely ridiculous though it is, some virtues prescribed by it, whose cultivation could contribute to our happiness?

DOLMANCE—All right, let us see. Shall chastity be that virtue your own eyes destroy, Eugénie, although you and all about you are the very image of it? Are you going to respect the obligation to combat all Nature's operations, will you sacrifice them all to the vain and ludicrous honor of never having had a weakness? Be fair and answer me, pretty little friend: think you to find in this absurd and dangerous purity of soul all the pleasures of the contrary vice?

EUGENIE—No, I'm bound to declare I see nothing there; I do not feel the least inclination to be chaste, but rather the most compelling urge to the opposite vice. But, Dolmancé, might not charity and benevolence bring happiness to some sensitive souls?

DOLMANCE—Begone those virtues which produce naught but ingratitude! But, my charming friend, be not at all deceived: benevolence is surely rather pride's vice than an authentic virtue in the soul; never is it with the single intention of performing a good act, but instead ostentatiously that one aids one's fellow man; one would be most annoyed were the alms one has just bestowed not to receive the utmost possible publicity. Nor, Eugénie, are you to imagine that, as is the popular view, this action has only excellent consequences; for my part I behold it as nothing other than the greatest of all duperies; it accustoms the poor man to doles which provoke the deterioration of his energy; when able to expect your charities, he ceases to work and becomes, when they fail him, a thief or assassin. On all sides I hear them ask after the means to suppress mendicity, and meanwhile they do everything possible to encourage it. Would you have no flies in your bed chamber? Don't spread about sugar to attract them into it. You wish to have no poor in France? Distribute no alms, and above all shut down your poorhouses. The individual born in misfortune thereupon seeing himself deprived of these dangerous crutches, will fend for himself, summoning up all the resources put in him by Nature, to extricate himself from the condition wherein he started life; and he will importune you no longer. Destroy, with entire unpity, raze to the ground, those detestable houses where you billet the progeny of the libertinage of the poor, appalling cloacas, wherefrom there every day spews forth into society a swarm of new-made creatures whose unique hope resides in your purse. What purpose, I ask, is there in preserving such individuals with so much care? Does anyone fear France's depopulation? Ha! dread not.

One of the foremost of this nation's defects consists in a population by far too numerous, and much is wanting when such overabundances become considered the State's riches. These supernumerary beings are like unto the parasitical branches which, living only at the trunk's expense, always bring it to final decline. Remember that in no matter what political organization, whenever the size of the population exceeds what is strictly necessary to its existence, that society languishes. Examine France well, and you will observe that to be her situation. What results of it? 'Tis clear. The Chinese, wiser than we, are most careful to avoid the perils of excessive numbers. No asylum for the shameful fruit of debauchery: it is not preserved, it is abandoned, just as are the aftermaths of digestion. No establishments for poverty: such a thing is totally unknown in China. There, everyone works: there, everyone is happy; nothing saps the poor man's energy and everyone can say, as did Nero, *Quid est pauper?*

EUGENIE, *to Madame de Saint-Ange*—Beloved friend, my father thinks exactly as Monsieur Dolmancé: never in his life has he performed a good work, and he is continually abusing my mother for the money she spends in such practices. She belonged to the *Maternal Society,* to the *Philanthropic Club;* I have no idea of what association she is not a member; he obliged her to stop all that by promising her he would reduce her to the narrowest pension were she to relapse into similar follies.

MADAME DE SAINT-ANGE—There is nothing more ludicrous and at the same time more dangerous, Eugénie, than all these sodalities; it is to them, to free public schools, and to charitable establishments we owe the terrible disorder in which we presently live. Never give alms, my dear, I beseech you.

EUGENIE—Nothing to fear on that score; it was long ago my father put me under the same obligation, and I am too little tempted to benevolence to disregard his orders . . . my heart's impulses, and your desires.

DOLMANCE—Nature has endowed each of us with a capacity for kindly feelings: let us not squander them on others. What to me are the woes that beset others? have I not enough of my own without afflicting myself with those that are foreign to me? May our sensibility's hearth warm naught but our pleasures! Let us feel when it is to their advantage; and when it is not, let us be absolutely unbending. From this exact economy of feeling, from this judicious use of sensibility, there results a kind of cruelty which is sometimes not without its delights. One cannot always do evil; deprived of the pleasure it affords, we can at least find the sensation's equivalent in the minor but piquant wickedness of never doing good.

EUGENIE—Dear God, how your discourses inflame me! I believe I would now sooner suffer death than be made to perform a good act!

MADAME DE SAINT-ANGE—And were the opportunity presented to do an evil one, would you be ready to commit it?

EUGENIE—Be still, temptress; I'll not answer that until you have completed my instruction. In the light of all you tell me, it seems, Dolmancé, that there is nothing on earth as indifferent as the committing of good or evil; ought not our tastes, our temperament alone counsel us?

DOLMANCE—Ah, be in no doubt of it, Eugénie, these words *vice* and *virtue* contain for us naught but local ideas. There is no deed, in whatever the unusual form you may imagine it, which is really criminal, none which may be really called virtuous. All is relative to our manners and the climate we inhabit; what is a crime here is often a virtue several hundred leagues hence, and the virtues of another hemisphere might well reverse themselves into crimes in our own. There is no horror that has not been consecrated somewhere, no virtue that has not been blasted. When geography alone decides whether an action be worthy of praise or blame, we cannot attach any great importance to ridiculous and frivolous sentiments, but rather should be impeccably armed against them, to the point, indeed, where we fearlessly prefer the scorn of men if the actions which excite it are for us sources of even the mildest voluptuousness.

EUGENIE—But it would however appear to me that there must be actions in themselves so dangerous and so evil that they have come to be considered from one end of the earth to the other as generally criminal.

MADAME DE SAINT-ANGE—There are none, my love, none, not even theft, nor incest, neither murder nor parricide itself.

EUGENIE—What! such horrors are somewhere tolerated?

DOLMANCE—They have been honored, crowned, beheld as exemplary deeds, whereas in other places, humaneness, candor, benevolence, chastity, in brief, all our virtues have been regarded as monstrosities.

EUGENIE—I would have you explain that to me; I ask for a succinct analysis of each one of those crimes, but I beg you to begin by exposing your opinions upon libertinage in young girls, then upon the adultery of married women.

MADAME DE SAINT-ANGE—Then listen to me, Eugénie. It is absurd to say that immediately a girl is weaned she must continue the victim of her parents' will in order to remain thus to her dying day. It is not in this age of preoccupation with the rights of man and general concern for liberties that girls ought to continue to believe themselves their families' slaves, when it is clearly established that these families' power over them is totally illusory. Let us consult Nature upon so interesting a question as this, and may the laws that govern animals, in much stricter conformance with Nature, provide us for a moment with examples. Amongst beasts, do paternal duties extend beyond primary physical needs? Do not the offspring of animals possess all their parents' liberty, all their rights? As soon as they are able to walk alone and feed themselves, beginning at this instant, are they any longer recognized by the authors of their days? And do the young fancy themselves in any sense beholden to those whence they have received breath? Surely not. By what right, hence, are other duties incumbent upon the children of men? And what is the basis of these duties if not the fathers' greed or ambition? Well, I ask if it is just that a young girl who is beginning to feel and reason be submitted to such constraints. Is it not prejudice which all unaided forges those chains? And is there anything more ridiculous than to see a maiden of fifteen or sixteen, consumed by desires she is compelled to suppress, wait, and, while waiting, endure worse than hell's torments until it pleases her parents, having first rendered her youth miserable, further to sacrifice her riper years by immolating them to their perfidious cupidity when they associate her, despite her wishes, with a husband who either has nothing wherewith to make himself loved, or who possesses everything to make himself hated?

Ah! no. No, Eugénie, such bonds are quickly dissolved; it is necessary that when once she reaches the age of reason the girl be detached from the paternal household, and after having received a public education it is necessary that at the age of fifteen she be left her own mistress, to become what she wishes. She will be delivered unto vice? Ha! what does that matter? Are not the services a young girl renders in consenting to procure the happiness of all who apply to her, infinitely more important than those which, isolating herself, she performs for her husband? Woman's destiny is to be wanton, like the bitch, the she-wolf; she must belong to all who claim her. Clearly, it is to outrage the fate Nature imposes upon women to fetter them by the absurd ties of a solitary marriage.

Let us hope eyes will be opened, and that while we go about assuring the liberty of every individual, the fate of unhappy girls will not be overlooked; but should they have the great misfortune to be forgotten, then, of their own accord rising above usage and prejudice, let them boldly fling off and spurn the shameful irons wherewith others presume to keep them subjugated; they will rapidly conquer custom and opinion; man become wiser, because he will be freer, will sense the injustice that would exist in scorning whoever acts thus, and will sense too that the act of yielding to Nature's promptings, beheld as a crime by a captive people, can be so no longer amongst a free people.

Begin, therefore, with the legitimacy of these principles, Eugénie, and break your shackles at no matter what the cost; be contemptuous of the futile remonstrances of an imbecile mother to whom you legitimately owe only hatred and a curse. If your father, who is a libertine, desires you, why then, go merrily to him: let him enjoy you, but enjoy without enchaining you; cast off the yoke if he wishes to enslave you; more than one daughter has treated thus with her father. Fuck, in one word, fuck: 'twas for that you were brought into the world; no limits to your pleasure save those of your strength and will; no exceptions as to place, to time, to partner; all the time, everywhere, every man has got to serve your pleasures; continence is an impossible virtue for which Nature, her rights violated, instantly punishes us with a thousand miseries. So long as the laws remain such as they are today, employ some discretion: loud opinion forces us to do so; but in privacy and silence let us compensate ourselves for that cruel chastity we are obliged to display in public.

Let our young maiden strive to procure herself a companion who, unattached and abroad in the world, can secretly cause her to taste the world's pleasures; failing of that, let her contrive to seduce the Arguses posted round her; let her beg them to prostitute her, and promise them all the money they can earn from her sale; either those watchdogs alone, or the women they will find and whom one calls *procuresses,* will soon supply the little one's wants; then let her kick up the dust into the eyes of everyone at hand, brothers, cousins, friends, parents; let her give herself to everyone, if that is necessary to hide her conduct; let her even make the sacrifice, if 'tis required of her, of her tastes and affections; one intrigue which might displease her, and into which she would enter only for reasons of policy, will straightway lead her to another more agreeable; and there she is, *launched.* But let her not revert to her childhood prejudices; menaces, exhortations, duties, virtues, religion, advice, let her give not a damn for the one or the lot of them; let her stubbornly reject and despise all that which but tends to her re-entry into thralldom, and all that which, in a word, does not hie her along the road to the depths of impudicity.

'Tis but folly in our parents when they foretell the disasters of a libertine career; there are thorns everywhere, but along the path of vice roses bloom above them; Nature causes none to smile along virtue's muddy track. Upon the former of the routes, the one snare to fear is men's opinion; but what mettlesome girl, with a little reflection, will not render herself superior to that contemptible opinion? The pleasures received through esteem, Eugénie, are nothing but moral pleasures, acceptable to none but certain minds; those of *fuckery* please all, and their winning characteristics soon eclipse the hallucinatory scorn from which escape is difficult when one flouts the public's views at which several cool-headed women have so much laughed as therefrom to derive one pleasure the more. Fuck, Eugénie, fuck, my angel; your body is your own, yours alone; in all the world there is but yourself who has the right to enjoy it as you see fit.

Profit from the fairest period in your life; these golden years of our pleasure are only too few and too brief. If we are so fortunate as to have enjoyed them, delicious memories console and amuse us in our old age. These years lost . . . and we are racked by bitterest regrets, gnawing remorse conjoins with the sufferings of age and the fatal onset of the grave is all tears and brambles. . . . But have you the madness to hope for immortality?

Why, then, 'tis by fucking, my dear, you will remain in human memory. The Lucretias were soon forgot whereas the Theodoras and the Messalinas are subjects for life's sweetest and most frequent conversation. How, Eugénie, may one not elect an alternative which twines in our hair the flowers of this world and yet leaves us the hope of reverence when we are gone out of it? How, I say, may one not prefer this course to another which, causing us stupidly to vegetate upon earth, promises us nothing after our existence but scorn and oblivion?

EUGENIE, *to Madame de Saint-Ange*—Oh! my love, how these seductive words inflame my mind and captivate my soul! I am in a state hardly to be painted. . . . And, I pray, will you be able to acquaint me with some of these women . . . (*worried*) who will, if I tell them to, prostitute me?

MADAME DE SAINT-ANGE—For the moment and until you have become more experienced, the matter is entirely my concern, Eugénie; trust me and above all the precautions I am taking to mask your excesses; my brother and this solid friend instructing you will be the first to whom I wish you to give yourself; afterward, we will discover others. Be not disturbed, dear heart: I shall have you fly from one pleasure to the next, I'll plunge you in a sea of delights, I will fill your cup to overflowing, my angel, I will sate you.

EUGENIE, *throwing herself into Madame de Saint-Ange's arms* —Oh, my dearest one, I adore you; you will never have a more submissive scholar. But it seems to me you gave me to understand in our earlier conversations that it were a difficult thing for a young person to fling herself into libertinage without the husband she is to wed perceiving it later on?

MADAME DE SAINT-ANGE—'Tis true, my heart, but there are secrets which heal all those breaches. I promise to make them known to you, and then, had you fucked like Antoinette, I charge myself to render you as much a virgin as you were the day you were born.

EUGENIE—Oh, my delightful one! Come, continue to instruct me. Be quick then; teach me what should be a woman's conduct in marriage.

MADAME DE SAINT-ANGE—In whatever circumstances, a woman, my dear, whether unwedded, wife, or widow, must never have for objective, occupation, or desire anything save to have herself fucked from morning to night: 'tis for this unique end Nature created her; but if, in order to answer this intention, I require her to trample upon all the prejudices of her childhood, if I prescribe to her the most formal disobedience to her family's orders, the most arrant contempt for all her relatives' advice, you will agree with me, Eugénie, that among all the bonds to be burst, I ought very surely to recommend that the very first be those of wedlock.

Indeed, Eugénie, consider the young girl scarcely out of her father's house or her pension, knowing nothing, without experience: of a sudden she is obliged to pass thence into the arms of a man she has never seen, she is called to the altar and compelled to swear to this man an oath of obedience, of fidelity, the more unjust for her often having nothing in the depths of her heart but the greatest desire to break her word. In all the world, is there a more terrible fate than this, Eugénie? However, whether her husband pleases her or no, whether or not he has tenderness in store for her or vile treatment, behold! she is married; her honor binds her to her oaths: it is attainted if she disregards them; she must be doomed or shackled: either way, she must perish of despair. Ah, no! Eugénie, no! 'tis not for that end we are born; those absurd laws are the handiwork of men, and we must not submit to them. And divorce? Is it capable of satisfying us? Probably not. What greater assurance have we of finding the happiness in a later bondage that eluded us in an earlier?

Therefore, in secrecy let us compensate ourselves for all the restraint imposed by such absurd unions, and let us be certain indeed that this species of disorders, to whatever extreme we carry them, far from outraging Nature, is but a sincere homage we render her; it is to obey her laws to cede to the desires she alone has placed in us; it is only in resisting that we affront her. The adultery men deem a crime, which they have dared punish in us even with death, adultery, Eugénie, is hence nothing but an acquittance sanctioned by a natural law the whims of those tyrants shall never be able to abrogate. But is it not horrible, say our husbands, to lay us open to cherishing as our own children, to embracing as ours the fruit of your licentiousness? The objection is Rousseau's; it is, I admit, the only faintly specious one wherewith adultery may be opposed. Well! Is it not extremely simple to surrender oneself to libertinage without fear of pregnancy? Is it not easier yet to check it if through our oversight or imprudence it should occur? But, as we shall return to the subject, let's now but treat the heart of the matter: we will see that, however plausible it at first appears, the argument is chimerical nevertheless.

First, provided I sleep with my husband, provided his semen flows to the depths of my womb, should I see ten men at the same time I consort with him, nothing will ever be able to prove to him that the child I bear does not belong to him; it is quite as likely the child is his as not, and in a case of uncertainty he cannot justifiably disclaim his part in bringing about something which may perhaps have been all of his doing. Immediately it can be his, it is his; any man who vexes himself with suspicions upon this head seeks vexations, even were his wife a vestal he would plague himself with worries, for it is impossible to be sure of a woman, and she who has behaved well for years may someday interrupt her good behavior.

Hence, if this husband is suspicious, he will be so in any case: never, then, will he be convinced the child he embraces is really his own. Now, if he can be suspicious in any case, there can be no disadvantage in sometimes justifying his suspicions: with what regards his state of happiness or unhappiness, it will all be one; therefore, 'tis just as well things be thus. Well, suppose him in complete error: picture him caressing the fruit of his wife's libertinage: where is the crime in that? Are not our goods held in common? In which case, what ill do I cause by introducing into the ménage a child to whom must be accorded a share of these goods? 'Twill be my share the child will have; he'll steal nothing from my tender mate: I consider as a levy upon my dowry this portion to which the child will be heir; hence, neither it nor I take anything from my husband. Had this child been his, by what title would it have been a claimant to a part of my chattels and monies? Is it not by reason of the fact the child would have been my offspring? Very well, the child is going to inherit this part, rightfully the child's by virtue of the same intimate alliance. It is because this child belongs to me that I owe it a share of my wealth.

With what are you to reproach me? The child is provided for. "But you deceive your husband; thus to be false is atrocious." "No, it's tit for tat," say I, "and there's an end to it: I was the dupe in the first place of the attachments he forced upon me: I take my revenge: what could be more simple?" "But your husband's honor has suffered a real outrage." "What ludicrous notion is this! My libertinage in no wise affects my husband; mine are personal faults. This alleged dishonor signified something a century ago; we're rid of our illusions today, and my husband is no more sullied by my debauches than I might be by his. I might fuck with the whole wide world without wounding him in the slightest. This so-called hurt is therefore a mere fable whose authentic existence is impossible. Of the two things, one: either my husband is a brutal, a jealous man, or he is a delicate one; in the former hypothesis, the best course for me is to avenge myself for his conduct; in the latter, I should be unable to aggrieve him; the fact I am tasting pleasures will make him happy if he is honest; no man of refinement fails to relish the spectacle of the happiness of the person he adores." "But, were you to love him, would you wish him to do the same?" "Ah, woe unto the wife who decides to be jealous of her husband! Let her be content with what he gives her, if she loves him; but let her make no attempt to constrain him; not only will she have no success, but she will soon make herself detested. So long as I am reasonable, I shall never be afflicted by my husband's debauches; let him be thus with me, and peace will reign in the house."

Let us recapitulate: Whatever be adultery's issue, were it even to introduce into the home children who do not belong to the husband, because they are the wife's they have certain rights to a portion of that wife's dowry; if the husband has intelligence of the thing, he must consider them as he would children his wife might have had by an earlier marriage; if he knows nothing, he'll not be the worse for it, for one cannot be distressed by what one is unaware of; if the adultery is followed by no consequences and if it remain unknown to the husband, no jurist can prove, in this case, the existence of crime: here, adultery appears as an act of perfect indifference to the husband, who knows nothing of it, and perfectly splendid for the wife, whom it delights; if the husband discovers the adultery, 'tis no longer the adultery which is an evil, for it was not such a moment ago, and it could not have altered its nature: if evil there be, it is in the husband's discovery of it: well, that fault belongs only to him: it has nothing to do with his wife.

Those who in former times punished the adulterer were hence mere hangmen, tyrannical and jealous, who, viewing everything subjectively, unjustly imagined that in order to be criminal it was only necessary to offend them, as if a personal injury were always to be considered a crime, and as if one might justly describe as a crime an act which, far from outraging Nature or society, clearly serves the one and the other. There are, however, cases when adultery, easy to prove, becomes more embarrassing for the woman without for that reason being any more criminal; witness, for example, the case wherein the husband is found either impotent or subject to inclinations disfavorable to engendering. As she is susceptible of pleasure, and as her husband never is, her deportment doubtless then becomes more open; but ought she be disquieted on that account? Surely not. The one precaution she must take is to produce no children, or to have an abortion if these precautions should happen to fail her. If it is thanks to her husband's unseemly penchants that she is compelled to compensate herself for his neglect, she has first of all to satisfy him, without repugnance and according to his tastes, of whatever character they may chance to be; next, let her make it known to him that such complacencies entitle her to a counterpart; let her demand an entire liberty in return for the one she accords; thereupon, the husband refuses or else he consents: if he consents, as has mine, one puts oneself at his disposal and redoubles one's ministrations and condescensions to his caprices; if he refuses, then one perfects one's concealments and one fucks peacefully in their shadow. Is he impotent? Why, then one parts company; but, whatever may be the case, one gives oneself: one fucks, my lamb, the particular situation notwithstanding, because we are born to fuck, because by fucking we obey and fulfill Nature's ordinations, and because all man-made laws which would contravene Nature's are made for naught but our contempt.

A silly gull is the woman whom ties as absurd as those of wedlock inhibit from surrendering to her penchants, who dreads either pregnancy or the injury to her husband, or the yet more vain tarnishing of her reputation! You have just seen, Eugénie, yes, you have just sensed what a dupe she is when basely she immolates both her happiness and all life's joys to the most preposterous prejudices. Oh! let her fuck with impunity! Will a little false glory, a few frivolous religious anticipations balance the weight of her sacrifices? No; no, virtue, vice, all are confounded in the grave. A few years hence, will the public any more exalt the ones than it condemns the others? Why, no, once again, I say no, and the wretch who has lived a stranger to joy, dies, alas, unrewarded.

EUGENIE—How thoroughly you persuade me, my angel, what a straight way you make with my prejudices, what short work you make of all the false principles my mother planted in me! Oh, I would be married tomorrow in order immediately to put your maxims into use. How seductive they are, how true, and how much I love them! Only one thing troubles me, dear one, in what you have just said to me, and as I understand it not at all, I beg you to explain: your husband, you declare, does not, when he takes his pleasure with you, strike an attitude such as would produce children: what then, pray tell, does he do?

MADAME DE SAINT-ANGE—My husband was already advanced in years when I married him. On our wedding night he gave me notice of his fancies, the while assuring me that, for his part, never would he interfere with mine; I swore to obey him and we have always, since then, he and I, lived in the most delicious independence and mutual understanding. My husband's whim is to have himself sucked, and here is the most unusual practice joined as a corollary to that one: while, as I bend over him, my buttocks squarely over his face and cheerily pumping the fuck from his balls, I must shit in his mouth!... He swallows it down!...

EUGENIE—Now there's a most extraordinary notion!

DOLMANCE—None may be qualified thus, my dear: all are a part of Nature; when she created men, she was pleased to vary their tastes as she made different their countenances, and we ought no more be astonished at the diversity she has put in our features than at that she has placed in our affections. The fancy your friend has just mentioned could not be more à la mode; an infinite number of men, and principally those of a certain age, are prodigiously addicted to it; would you refuse your co-operation, Eugénie, were someone to require it of you?

EUGENIE, *turning red*—In accordance with the maxims wherewith I am being inculcated here, can I refuse anything? I only ask to be forgiven my surprise; this is the first time I have heard of all these lubricities: I must first of all visualize them; but between the solution of the problem and the execution of the act, I believe my tutors can rest assured there will never be but the distance they themselves impose. However all that may be, my dear, you won your liberty by acquiescing to this duty?

MADAME DE SAINT-ANGE—The most entire liberty, Eugénie. On my side, I did everything I wished without his raising any obstacles, but I took no lover: I was too fond of pleasure for that. Unlucky woman, she who is attached; she needs but take a lover to be lost, while ten scenes of libertinage, repeated every day, if she wishes, vanish into the night of silence instantly they are consummated. I was wealthy: I had young men in my pay, they fucked me incognito, I surrounded myself with charming valets, assured of tasting the sweetest pleasures with me upon condition of discretion, certain they would be thrown out-of-doors if they so much as opened their mouths. You have no idea, dear heart, of the torrent of delights into which, in this manner, I did plunge. Such is the conduct I will always urge upon every woman who would imitate me. During my twelve married years I have been fucked by upward of ten or twelve thousand individuals . . . and in the company I keep I am thought well-behaved! Another would have had lovers; by the time she exchanged the first for the second she would have been doomed.

EUGENIE—This seems the safest way of proceeding; most decidedly, it shall be mine; I must, like yourself, marry a rich man, and above all one with fancies. . . . But, my dear, your husband is strictly bound by his tastes? Does he never ask anything else of you?

MADAME DE SAINT-ANGE—Never in a dozen years has he been untrue to himself a single day, save when I am on an outing. A very pretty girl he very much wanted me to take into the house then substitutes for me, and things proceed exceeding well.

EUGENIE—But he doesn't stop there, surely? There are other objects, outside the house, competing to diversify his pleasures?

DOLMANCE—Be certain there are, Eugénie; Madame's husband is one of the greatest libertines of the day; he spends above one hundred thousand crowns a year upon the obscene tastes your friend described to you but a moment ago.

MADAME DE SAINT-ANGE—To tell the truth, I suspect the figure may be higher; but what are his excesses to me, since their multiplicity authorizes and camouflages my own?

EUGENIE—I beseech you, let us follow in detail the manners by which a young person, married or not, may preserve herself from pregnancy, for I confess I am made most timorous by dread of it, whether it be the work of the husband I must take, or the effect of a career of libertinage. You have just indicated one means while speaking of your husband's tastes; but this fashion of taking one's pleasure, which may be highly agreeable to the man, does not seem as pleasurable for the woman, and it is our dalliances, exempt from the risks I fear, that I desire you to discuss.

MADAME DE SAINT-ANGE—A girl risks having a child only in proportion to the frequency with which she permits the man to invade her cunt. Let her scrupulously avoid this manner of tasting delight; in its stead, let her offer indiscriminately her hand, her mouth, her breasts, or her ass. This last thoroughfare will yield her considerable pleasure, far more, indeed, than any other; by means of the others she will give pleasure.

In the first instance, that is to say, the one which brings the hand into play, one proceeds in the fashion you observed a short while ago, Eugénie; one shakes one's friend's member as if one were pumping it; after a little agitation, the sperm is emitted; meanwhile, the man kisses, caresses you, and with this liquid wets that part of your body whereof he is fondest. If one wishes to have it distributed over the breasts, one stretches upon the bed, the virile member is fitted between the two tits, they are compressed, and after a few passes the man discharges so as to flood you sometimes up to the height of your face. This manner is the least voluptuous of all and can only suit those women whose breasts, from repeated usage, have acquired that flexibility, that looseness needed to grip the man's member tightly when clamped between them. Pleasure incepted at the mouth is infinitely more agreeable, quite as much for the man as for the woman. The best way to go about it is for the woman to lie prone, contrariwise to her fucker and upon his body: he pops his prick into your mouth and, his head being lodged between your thighs, he repays in kind what you do for him, by introducing his tongue into your cunt or by playing it over your clitoris; when employing this attitude one must show spirit, catch hold of the buttocks, and the partners should finger and tickle each other's asshole, a measure always necessary to complete voluptuousness. Spirited lovers, those full of imagination, therewith swallow the fuck which squirts into their mouths, and thus delicately they enjoy the exquisite pleasure of mutually causing this precious liquid, mechanically diverted from its customary destination, to pass into their entrails.

DOLMANCE—Eugénie, 'tis a delicious method. I recommend to you its execution. Thus to cheat propagation of its rights and to contradict what fools call the laws of Nature, is truly most charming. The thighs, the armpits also sometimes provide asylum to the man's member and offer him retreats where his seed may be spilled without risk of pregnancy.

MADAME DE SAINT-ANGE—Some women insert sponges into the vagina's interior; these, intercepting the sperm, prevent it from springing into the vessel where generation occurs. Others oblige their fuckers to make use of a little sack of Venetian skin, in the vulgate called a condom, which the semen fills and where it is prevented from flowing farther. But of all the possibilities, that presented by the ass is without any doubt the most delicious. Dolmancé, to you I reserve the dissertations thereupon. Who better than you might be able to describe a taste in whose defense, were it to require any defense, you would lay down your life?

DOLMANCE—I acknowledge my weakness. I admit as well that in all the world there is no mode of pleasure-taking preferable to this; I worship it in either sex; but I'll confess a young lad's ass gives me yet more pleasure than a girl's. *Buggers* is the appellation designating those who are this fancy's adepts; now, Eugénie, when one goes so far as to be a bugger, one must not stop halfway. To fuck women in the rear is but the first part of buggery; 'tis with men Nature wishes men to practice this oddity, and it is especially for men she has given us an inclination. Absurd to say the mania offends Nature; can it be so, when 'tis she who puts it into our head? can she dictate what degrades her? No, Eugénie, not at all; this is as good a place to serve her as any other, and perhaps it is there she is most devoutly worshiped. Propagation owes its existence to her forbearance. How could she have prescribed as law an act which challenges her omnipotence, since propagation is but a consequence of her primary intentions, and since new constructions, wrought by her hand, were our species to be destroyed absolutely, would become again primordial intentions whose accomplishment would be far more flattering to her pride and to her power?

MADAME DE SAINT-ANGE—Do you know, Dolmancé, that by means of this system you are going to be led to prove that totally to extinguish the human race would be nothing but to render Nature a service?

DOLMANCE—Who doubts of it, Madame?

MADAME DE SAINT-ANGE—My God! wars, plagues, famines, murders would no longer be but accidents, necessary to Nature's laws, and man, whether instrumental to or the object of these effects, would hence no longer be more a criminal in the one case than he would be a victim in the other?

DOLMANCE—Victim he is, without doubt, when he bends before the blows of ill fortune; but criminal, never. We shall have more to say about all these things; for the moment, in the lovely Eugénie's behalf, let's analyze sodomistic pleasures, which presently are the subject of our discussion. In this mode of pleasure-seeking, the posture most commonly adopted by the woman is for her to lie belly down upon the edge of the bed, the buttocks well spread, the head as low as possible; after having mused for an instant upon the splendid prospect of a ready and beckoning ass, after having patted it, slapped it a bit, handled it, sometimes after having beaten or whipped it, pinched and bitten it, the rake moistens with his mouth the pretty little hole he is about to perforate, and prepares his entry with the tip of his tongue; in similar wise, he wets his engine with saliva, or with pomade, and gently presents it to the aperture he intends to pierce; he guides it with one hand, with the other he lays wide open the cheeks of his delight; immediately he feels his member penetrate, he must thrust energetically, taking all due care not to give ground; then it is, occasionally, the woman suffers, if she is new, or young; but, totally heedless of the pangs which are soon to change into pleasures, the fucker must be lively and drive his engine ahead, inch by inch, gradually, but with determination, till at last he is arrived at his objective, till, that is to say, his device's hairs precisely rub the anal rim of the embuggered party. Then may he give free rein to himself; all the thorns are plucked from out his path, there remain roses only there. To complete the metamorphosis into pleasures of what distresses his object still experiences, if it be a boy, let him seize his prick and frig it; let him twiddle her clitoris, if 'tis a girl; the titillations of the pleasure he will cause to be born will in turn work a prodigious contraction in the patient's anus, and will double the delight of the agent who, overwhelmed with comfort, will soon dart, to the very depths of the ass of his delight, a sperm quite as abundant as thick, thus determined by so many lubricious details. There are some who do not care to have the patient take pleasure in the operation; an attitude we will account for in good time.

MADAME DE SAINT-ANGE—Allow me to be the scholar for a moment, and let me ask you, Dolmancé, in what state the patient's ass must be in order to ensure the agent a maximum of pleasure?

DOLMANCE—Full, by all means; 'tis essential the object in use have the most imperious desire to shit, so that the end of the fucker's prick, reaching the turd, may drive deep into it, and may more warmly and more softly deposit there the fuck which irritates and sets it afire.

MADAME DE SAINT-ANGE—I fear the patient's pleasure is less.

DOLMANCE—Error! This method of pleasure-taking is such that there exists no possibility of the fucker's receiving hurt nor of the employed object's failing to be transported into seventh heaven. No other matches this in value, no other can so completely satisfy each of the protagonists, and they who have tasted of it know a great difficulty in abandoning it for another. Such, Eugénie, are the best ways of taking pleasure with a man if the perils of pregnancy are to be avoided; for one enjoys—and be very certain of it—not only offering a man one's ass, but also sucking and frigging him, etc., and I have known libertine ladies who often had an higher esteem for this byplay than for real pleasures. The imagination is the spur of delights; in those of this order, all depends upon it, it is the mainspring of everything; now, is it not by means of the imagination one knows joy? is it not of the imagination that there come the most piquant delights?

MADAME DE SAINT-ANGE—Indeed; but let Eugénie beware thereof; the imagination serves us not save when our mind is absolutely free of prejudices: but a single one will suffice to chill it. This capricious portion of our mind is so libertine nothing can restrain it; its greatest triumph, its most eminent delights come of exceeding all limits imposed upon it; of all regularity it is an enemy, it worships disorder, idolizes whatever wears the brand of crime; whence derived the extraordinary reply of an imaginative woman who was fucking coolly with her husband: "Why this ice?" quoth he. "Ah, truly," answered this singular creature, " *'tis all very dull, what you are doing with me.*"

EUGENIE—I adore the remark. . . . Ah, my dear, how great is my urge to become acquainted with these divine outbursts of a disordered imagination! You'd never believe it, but during our stay together . . . since the instant we met—no, no, my darling, never could you conceive all the voluptuous ideas my brain has caressed. . . . Oh, how well I now understand what is evil . . . how much it is desired of my heart!

MADAME DE SAINT-ANGE—May atrocities, horrors, may the most odious crimes astonish you no more, my Eugénie; what is of the filthiest, the most infamous, the most forbidden, 'tis that which best rouses the intellect . . . 'tis that which always causes us most deliciously to discharge.

EUGENIE—To how many incredible perversities must you not, the one and the other, have surrendered yourselves! And how I should relish hearing the details!

DOLMANCE, *kissing and fondling the young lady*—Beauteous Eugénie, a hundred times more would I love to see you experience all I should love to do, rather than to relate to you what I have done.

EUGENIE—I know not whether it would be too good for me to accede to everything.

MADAME DE SAINT-ANGE—I would not advise it, Eugénie.

EUGENIE—Very well, I spare Dolmancé his narrations; but you, my dear, pray tell me what they are, the most extraordinary things you have done in your life?

MADAME DE SAINT-ANGE—I engaged fifteen men, alone; in twenty-four hours, I was ninety times fucked, as much before as behind.

EUGENIE—Mere debauches, those, tours de force; I dare wager you have done yet more uncommon things.

MADAME DE SAINT-ANGE—I passed a term in a brothel.

EUGENIE—And what does that word mean?

DOLMANCE—Such are called the public houses where in consideration of a price agreed upon, each man finds young and pretty girls in good sort to satisfy his passions.

EUGENIE—And you gave yourself there, my dearest?

MADAME DE SAINT-ANGE—Yes; there I was, a perfect whore; there during an entire week I satisfied the whims of a goodly number of lechers, and there I beheld the most unusual tastes displayed; moved by a similar libertine principle, like the celebrated empress Theodora, Justinian's wife,[1] I waylaid men in the streets, upon public promenades, and the money I earned from these prostitutions I spent at the lottery.

EUGENIE—My dear, I know that mind of yours: you've gone still further than that.

MADAME DE SAINT-ANGE—Were it possible?

EUGENIE—Why, yes! Yes, and this is how I fancy it: have you not told me our most delicious moral sensations come of the imagination?

MADAME DE SAINT-ANGE—I did say so.

EUGENIE—Then, by allowing this imagination to stray, by according it the freedom to overstep those ultimate boundaries religion, decency, humaneness, virtue, in a word, all our pretended obligations would like to prescribe to it, is it not possible that the imagination's extravagances would be prodigious?

MADAME DE SAINT-ANGE—No doubt.

EUGENIE—Well, is it not by reason of the immensity of these extravagances that the imagination will be the more inflamed?

MADAME DE SAINT-ANGE—Nothing more true.

EUGENIE—If that is so, the more we wish to be agitated, the more we desire to be moved violently, the more we must give rein

---

[1] See the *Anecdotes* of Procopius.

to our imagination; we must bend it toward the inconceivable; our enjoyment will thereby be increased, made better for the track the intellect follows, and ...

DOLMANCE, *kissing Eugénie*—Delicious!

MADAME DE SAINT-ANGE—My, but how our little rascal has progressed, and in such a brief space! But, do you know, my charming one, that one can go very far by the route you trace for us.

EUGENIE—I understand it very nicely thus; and since I will subject myself to no inhibitions, you see to what lengths I suppose one may go.

MADAME DE SAINT-ANGE—To crime, vicious creature, to the blackest, most frightful crimes.

EUGENIE, *in a lowered and halting voice*—But you say no crime exists there ... and after all, it is but to fire the mind: one thinks, but one does not do.

DOLMANCE—However, 'tis very sweet to carry out what one has fancied.

EUGENIE, *flushing*—Well, then, carry it out. ... Would you not like to persuade me, dear teachers, that you have never done what you have conceived?

MADAME DE SAINT-ANGE—It has sometimes been given to me to do it. ...

EUGENIE—There we are!

DOLMANCE—Ah! what a mind.

EUGENIE, *continuing*—What I ask you is this: what have you fancied, and then, having fancied, what have you done?

MADAME DE SAINT-ANGE, *stammering*—Someday, Eugénie, I shall ... relate my life to you. Let us continue our instruction ... for you would bring me to say things ... things ...

EUGENIE—Ah, begone! I see you do not love me enough fully to open your soul to me; I shall wait as long as you say; let's get on with the particulars. Tell me, my dear, who was the happy mortal who intended at your beginnings?

MADAME DE SAINT-ANGE—My brother: from childhood on he adored me; during our earliest years we often amused each other without attaining our goal; I promised to give myself to him immediately I married; I kept my word; happily, my husband damaged nothing: my brother harvested all. We continue with our intrigue, but without hampering ourselves; we do not—he on his part, I on mine—plunge ourselves into anything but the most divine of libertinage's excesses; we even mutually serve one another: I procure women for him, he introduces me to men.

EUGENIE—Delightful arrangement! But, is not incest a crime?

DOLMANCE—Might one so regard Nature's gentlest unions, the ones she most insistently prescribes to us and counsels most warmly? Eugénie, a moment of reason: how, after the vast afflictions our planet sometime knew, how was the human species otherwise able to perpetuate itself, if not through incest? Of which we find, do we not, the example and the proof itself in the books Christianity respects most highly. By what other means could Adam's family[2] and that of Noah have been preserved? Sift, examine universal custom: everywhere you will detect incest authorized, considered a wise law and proper to cement familial ties. If, in a word, love is born of resemblance, where may it be more perfect than between brother and sister, between father and daughter? An ill-founded policy, one produced by the fear lest certain families become too powerful, bans incest from our midst; but let us not abuse ourselves to the point of mistaking for natural law what is dictated to us only by interest or ambition; let us delve into our hearts: 'tis always there I send our pedantic moralists; let us but question this sacred organ and we will notice that nothing is more exquisite than carnal connection within the family; let us cease to be blind with what concerns a brother's feelings for his sister, a father's for his daughter: in vain does one or the other disguise them behind a mask of legitimate tenderness: the most violent love

---

2 Adam was nothing, nor was Noah, but a restorer of humankind. An appalling catastrophe left Adam alone in the world, just as a similar event did Noah; but Adam's tradition is lost to us, Noah's has been preserved.

is the unique sentiment ablaze in them, the only one Nature has deposited in their hearts. Hence, let us double, triple these delicious incests, fearlessly multiply them, and let us believe that the more straitly the object of our desires does belong to us, the greater charm shall there be in enjoying it.

One of my friends has the habit of living with the girl he had by his own mother; not a week ago he deflowered a thirteen-year-old boy, fruit of his commerce with this girl; in a few years' time, this same lad will wed his mother: such are my friend's wishes; he is readying for them all a destiny analogous to the projects he delights in and his intentions, I know very well, are yet to enjoy what this marriage will bring to bear; he is young and he has cause to hope for the best. Consider, gentle Eugénie, with what a quantity of incests and crimes this honest friend would be soiled were there a jot of truth in the low notion that would have us define these alliances as evil. To be brief, in all these matters I base my attitude upon one principle: had Nature condemned sodomy's pleasures, incestuous correspondences, pollutions, and so forth, would she have allowed us to find so much delight in them? That she may tolerate what outrages her is unthinkable.

EUGENIE—Oh! My divine teachers, I see full well that, according to your doctrine, there are very few crimes in the world, and that we may peacefully follow the bent of all our desires, however singular they may appear to fools who, shocked and alarmed by everything, stupidly confuse social institutions for Nature's divine ordinations. And yet, my friends, do you not at least acknowledge that there exist certain actions absolutely revolting and decidedly criminal, although enjoined by Nature? I am nothing loath to agree with you, that this Nature, as extraordinary in the productions she creates as various in the penchants she gives us, sometimes moves us to cruel deeds; but if, surrendered to depravity, we were to yield to this bizarre Nature's promptings, were we to go so far as to attempt, let me suppose, the lives of our fellows, you will surely grant me, at least I do hope so, that such an act would be a crime?

DOLMANCE—Indeed, Eugénie, little good would it do for us to grant you anything of the sort. Destruction being one of the chief laws of Nature, nothing that destroys can be criminal; how might an action which so well serves Nature ever be outrageous to her? This destruction of which man is wont to boast is, moreover, nothing but an illusion; murder is no destruction; he who commits it does but alter forms, he gives back to Nature the elements whereof the hand of this skilled artisan instantly re-creates other beings: now, as creations cannot but afford delight to him by whom they are wrought, the murderer thus prepares for Nature a pleasure most agreeable, he furnishes her materials, she employs them without delay, and the act fools have had the madness to blame is nothing but meritorious in the universal agent's eye. 'Tis our pride prompts us to elevate murder into crime. Esteeming ourselves the foremost of the universe's creatures, we have stupidly imagined that every hurt this sublime creature endures must perforce be an enormity; we have believed Nature would perish should our marvelous species chance to be blotted out of existence, while the whole extirpation of the breed would, by returning to Nature the creative faculty she has entrusted to us, reinvigorate her, she would have again that energy we deprive her of by propagating our own selves; but what an inconsequence, Eugénie! indeed! an ambitious sovereign can destroy, at his ease and without the least scruple, the enemies prejudicial to his grandiose designs. . . . Cruel laws, arbitrary, imperious laws can likewise every century assassinate millions of individuals and we, feeble and wretched creatures, we are not allowed to sacrifice a single being to our vengeance or our caprice! Is there anything so barbarous, so outlandish, so grotesque? and, cloaking ourselves in the profoundest mystery, must we not amply compensate ourselves for this ineptitude, and have revenge?[3]

EUGENIE—Yes, of course . . . Oh, but your ethics seduce me, and how I savor their bouquet! Yet, wait, Dolmancé, tell me now, in good conscience, whether you have not sometimes had satisfaction in crime?

DOLMANCE—Do not force me to reveal my faults to you: their number and kind might bring me excessively to blush; Perhaps someday I'll confess them to you.

---

[3] This article will be treated exhaustively further on; for the time being, we limit ourselves to laying some of the bases for the system to be developed later.

MADAME DE SAINT-ANGE—While guiding the law's blade, the criminal has often employed it to satisfy his passions.

DOLMANCE—Would that I have no other reproaches to make myself!

MADAME DE SAINT-ANGE, *throwing her arms about his neck*—Divine man! . . . I adore you! . . . What spirit, what courage are needed to have tasted every pleasure, as have you! 'Tis to the man of genius only there is reserved the honor of shattering all the links and shackles of ignorance and stupidity. Kiss me—oh, you are charming!

DOLMANCE—Be frank, Eugénie, tell me: have you never wished the death of anyone?

EUGENIE—Oh, I have! Yes! there is every day before my eyes an abominable creature I have long wished to see in her grave.

MADAME DE SAINT-ANGE—Now, I dare say I have guessed her name.

EUGENIE—Whom do you suspect?

MADAME DE SAINT-ANGE—Your mother?

EUGENIE—Oh, let me hide myself upon your breast!

DOLMANCE—Voluptuous creature! in my turn I would overwhelm her with the caresses that should be the reward of her heart's energy and her exquisite mind. (*Dolmancé kisses her entire body and bestows light smacks upon her buttocks; he has an erection; his hands, from time to time, stray also over Madame de Saint-Ange's behind which is lubriciously tendered him; restored a little to his senses, Dolmancé proceeds.*) But why should we not put this sublime idea into execution?

MADAME DE SAINT-ANGE—Eugénie, I detested my mother quite as much as you hate yours, and I hesitated not.

EUGENIE—The means have been lacking to me.

MADAME DE SAINT-ANGE—The courage, rather.

EUGENIE—Alas! still so young.

DOLMANCE—But, Eugénie, now what would you do?

EUGENIE—Everything . . . only show me the way and you'll see!

DOLMANCE—It will be shown you, Eugénie, I promise it; but thereunto, I put a condition.

EUGENIE—And what is it? or rather what is the condition I am not ready to accept?

DOLMANCE—Come, my rascal, come into my arms: I can hold off no longer; your charming behind must be the price of the gift I promise you, one crime has got to pay for another. Come hither! . . . nay, both, the two of you, run to drown in floods of fuck the heavenly fire that blazes in us!

MADAME DE SAINT-ANGE—If you please, let us put a little order in these revels; measure is required even in the depths of infamy and delirium.

DOLMANCE—Nothing easier: the major object, so it appears to me, is that I discharge the while giving this charming girl all possible pleasure: I am going to insert my prick in her ass; meanwhile, as she reclines in your arms you will frig her; do your utmost; by means of the position I place you in, she will be able to retaliate in kind; you will kiss one another. After a few runs into this child's ass, we will vary the picture: I will have you, Madame, by the ass; Eugénie, on top of you, your head between her legs, will present her clitoris to me; I'll suck it: thus I'll cause her to come a second time. Next, I will lodge my prick in her anus; you will avail me of your ass, 'twill take the place of the cunt she had under my nose, and now you will have at it in the style she will have employed, her head now between your legs; I'll suck your asshole as I have just sucked her cunt, you will discharge, so will I, and all the while my hand, embracing the dear sweet pretty little body of this charming novice, will go ahead to tickle her clitoris that she too may swoon from delight.

MADAME DE SAINT-ANGE—Capital, my Dolmancé, but will not there be something missing?

DOLMANCE—A prick in my ass? Madame, you are right.

MADAME DE SAINT-ANGE—Let's do without it this morning: we'll have it in the afternoon: my brother will join us and our pleasures will be at their height. Now let's to work.

DOLMANCE—I think I'll have Eugénie frig me for a moment. (*She does so.*) Yes, quite, that's it . . . a bit more quickly, my heart . . . that rosy head must always be kept naked, never let it be covered over, the more 'tis kept taut the more you facilitate the erection . . . never, you must never cap the prick you frig . . . 'Tis very well done . . . thus you yourself put into a proper state the member that is to perforate you. . . . Notice how it responds, gets sturdily up. . . . Give me your tongue, little bitch. . . . Let your ass rest on my right hand, while my left goes on to toy with your clitoris.

MADAME DE SAINT-ANGE—Eugénie, would you like to cause him to taste the extremest pleasures?

EUGENIE—By all means . . . I wish to do everything to give him them.

MADAME DE SAINT-ANGE—Why, then take his prick in your mouth and suck it a few instants.

EUGENIE, *does it*—Thus?

DOLMANCE—Delicious mouth! what warmth! Worth as much to me as the prettiest ass! . . . Voluptuous, tactful, accomplished woman, never deny your lovers this pleasure: 'twill bind them to you forever . . . Ah! by God! ah, by God's own fuck! . . .

MADAME DE SAINT-ANGE—My, what blasphemies, my friend.

DOLMANCE—I'll have your ass, Madame, if you please. . . . Yes, give it me, let me kiss it while I'm sucked, and be not astonished at my language: one of my largest pleasures is to swear in God's name when I'm stiff. It seems then that my spirit, at such a moment exalted a thousand times more, abhors, scorns this disgusting fiction; I would like to discover some way better to revile it or to outrage it further; and when my accursed musings lead me to the conviction of the nullity of this repulsive object of my hatred, I am irritated and would instantly like to be able to re-edify the phantom so that my rage might at least fall upon some target; imitate me, charming women, and you will observe such discourses to increase without fail your sensibility. But, by God's very damnation, I say, I've got absolutely, whatever be my pleasure, I've got to retire from this celestial mouth . . . else I'll leave my fuck in it! . . . All right, Eugénie, move! let's get on with the scene I proposed and, the three of us, let's be plunged into the most voluptuous drunkenness. (*The positions are arranged.*)

EUGENIE—Oh, how I fear, dear one, that your efforts will come to naught! The disproportion is exceedingly strong.

DOLMANCE—Why, I sodomize the very youngest every day; just yesterday a little lad of seven was deflowered by that prick, and in less than three minutes. . . . Courage, Eugénie, courage! . . .

EUGENIE—Oh! You're tearing me!

MADAME DE SAINT-ANGE—A little management there, Dolmancé; remember, I am responsible for the creature.

DOLMANCE—Then frig her, Madame, she'll feel the pain less; but there! 'tis said, 'tis done! I'm in up to the hilt.

EUGENIE—Oh heaven! it is not without trouble . . . see the sweat on my forehead, dear friend. . . . Ah! God, I've never undergone such agonies! . . .

MADAME DE SAINT-ANGE—Yet there you are, dear heart, half deflowered, there you are, arrived at a woman's estate; 'tis well worth purchasing the glory at the cost of a little inconvenience; my fingers then do not soothe you at all?

EUGENIE—Could I have borne it without them! . . . Tickle away, rub, my angel. . . . I feel it, imperceptibly the pain metamorphoses into pleasure. . . . Push, Dolmancé! . . . thrust! thrust! oh, I am dying! . . .

DOLMANCE—O by God's holy fuck! thrice bloody fuck of God! Let's change! I'll not be able to hold . . . your behind, kind lady, I beseech you, your ass, quick, place yourself as I told you. (*Shift of attitude, and Dolmancé goes on.*) 'Tis easier so . . . how my prick penetrates . . . but, Madame, this noble ass is not the less delicious for that. . . .

EUGENIE—Am I as I should be, Dolmancé?

DOLMANCE—Admirably! I've got this little virgin cunt all to myself, delicious. Oh, I'm a guilty one, a villain, indeed I know it; such charms were not made for my eyes; but the desire to provide this child with a firm grounding in voluptuousness over-shadows every other consideration. I want to make her fuck to flow, if 'tis possible I want to exhaust her, drink her dry. . . . (*He sucks her.*)

EUGENIE—This pleasure will kill me, I can't resist it! . . .

MADAME DE SAINT-ANGE—I'm coming, I say! Oh fuck! . . . fuck! . . . Dolmancé, I'm discharging! . . .

EUGENIE—And I too, my darling! Oh, my God, how he does suck me! . . .

MADAME DE SAINT-ANGE—Then swear, little whore, curse! . . . Then cry an oath! . . .

EUGENIE—All right then, damn thee! I discharge! Damn thee! . . . I am so sweetly drunk! . . .

DOLMANCE—To your post! . . . Take up your station! . . . Eugénie! . . . I'll be the dupe of these handlings and shifts. (*Eugénie assumes her place.*) Ah, good! here again am I, at my original place and abode . . . exhibit your asshole, Madame, I'll pump it at my leisure. . . . Oh, but I love to kiss an ass I've just left off fucking. . . . Ah! lick up mine, do you hear, while I drive my sperm deep home into your friend's. . . . Wouldst believe it, Madame? in it goes, and this time effortlessly! Ah, fuck! fuck! you've no idea how it squeezes, how she clamps me! Holy frigging God, what ecstasy! . . . Oh, 'tis there, 'tis done, I resist no longer . . . flow! my fluid flows! . . . and I die! . . .

EUGENIE—He causes me to die also, my friend, I swear it to you. . . .

MADAME DE SAINT-ANGE—The wench! how promptly she's taken to it!

DOLMANCE—Yes, but I know countless girls of her age nothing on earth could force to take their pleasure otherwise; 'tis only the first encounter that taxes; a woman has no sooner tried that sauce and she'll eat no other cookery. . . . Oh heavens! I'm spent; let me get my breath, a few moments' respite, please.

MADAME DE SAINT-ANGE—There they are, my dear: men. A glance at us, no more, and their desires are satisfied; the subsequent annihilation conducts them to disgust, soon to contempt.

DOLMANCE, *coolly*—Why, what an insult, heavenly creature! (*They embrace.*) The one and the other of you are made for naught but homages, whatever be the state wherein one finds oneself.

MADAME DE SAINT-ANGE—Console yourself, Eugénie; while they may have acquired the right to neglect us because they are sated, have we not in the same way that to scorn them, when their conduct bids us to it? If Tiberius sacrificed to Caprea the objects that had just appeased his hungers,[4] Zingua, Africa's queen, also immolated her lovers.[5]

DOLMANCE—Such excesses, perfectly simple and very intelligible to me, doubtless, all the same ought never be committed amongst ourselves: "Wolves are safe in their own company," as the proverb has it, and trivial though it may be, 'tis true. My friends, dread nothing from me, ever: I'll perhaps have you do much that is evil, but never will I do any to you.

EUGENIE—No, my dear, I dare be held answerable for it: never will Dolmancé abuse the privileges we grant him; I believe he has the roué's probity: it is the best; but let us bring our teacher back to his theorems and, before our senses subside into calm, let us return, I beg of you, to the great design that inflamed us before.

MADAME DE SAINT-ANGE—What, dost think yet on that? I thought 'twas no more than a little intellectual effervescence.

EUGENIE—It is the most certain impulse of my heart, and I'll not be content till the crime is done.

---

[4] See Suetonius and Dion Cassius of Nicaea.
[5] See the *History of Zingua, Queen of Angola.*

MADAME DE SAINT-ANGE—Oh splendid! splendid! Let her off, though; consider: she is your mother.

EUGENIE—Noble title!

DOLMANCE—She is right: did this mother think of Eugénie when she brought her into the world? The jade let herself be fucked because she found it agreeable, but she was very far from having this daughter in mind. Let her act as she sees fit with what regards her mother; let's allow her complete freedom and we'll be content to assure her that, whatever be the extreme lengths she goes to, never will she render herself guilty of any evil.

EUGENIE—I abhor her, I detest her, a thousand causes justify my hate; I've got to have her life at no matter what the cost!

DOLMANCE—Very well, since your resolve is unshakable, you'll be satisfied, Eugénie, I give you my oath; but permit me a few words of advice which, before you act, are of the utmost necessity. Never let your secret go out of your mouth, my dear, and always act alone: nothing is more dangerous than an accomplice: let us always beware of even those whom we think most closely attached to us: "One must," wrote Machiavelli, "either have no confederates, or dispatch them as soon as one has made use of them." Nor is that all: guile, Eugénie, guile is indispensable to the projects you are forming. Move closer than ever to your victim before destroying her; have the look of sympathy for her, seem to console her; cajole her, partake of her sufferings, swear you worship her; do yet more: persuade her of it: deceit, in such instances, cannot be carried too far. Nero caressed Agrippina upon the deck of the very bark with which she was to be engulfed: imitate his example, use all the knavery, all the imposture your brain can invent. To lie is always a necessity for women; above all when they choose to deceive, falsehood becomes vital to them.

EUGENIE—Those instructions will be remembered and, no doubt, put into effect; but let us delve deeper into this deceit whose usage you recommend to women; think you then that it is absolutely essential in this world?

DOLMANCE—Without hesitation I say I know of nothing more necessary in life; one certain truth shall prove its indispensability: everyone employs it; I ask, in the light of that, how a sincere individual will not always founder in the midst of a society of false people. Now, if 'tis true, as they declare, that virtues are of some usefulness in civil life, how would you have someone unprovided with either will, or power, or the gift of any virtue, which is the case with many persons, how, I ask you, would you have it that such a personage be not essentially obliged to feign, to dissemble, in order to obtain, in his turn, a little portion of the happiness his competitors seek to wrest away from him? And, in effect, it is very surely virtue, or might it not be the appearance of virtue, which really becomes necessary to social man? Let's not doubt that the appearance alone is quite sufficient to him: he has got that, and he possesses all he needs. Since one does nothing in this world but pinch, rub, and elbow others, is it not enough that they display their skin to us? Let us moreover be well persuaded that of the practice of virtue we can at the very most say that it is hardly useful save to him who has it; others reap so little therefrom that so long as the man who must live amongst other men appears virtuous, it matters not in the slightest whether he is so in fact or not. Deceit, furthermore, is almost always an assured means to success; he who possesses deceit necessarily begins with an advantage over whosoever has commerce or correspondence with him: dazzling him with a false exterior, he gains his confidence; convince others to place trust in you, and you have succeeded. I perceive someone has deceived me, I have only myself to blame; and he who has conned me has done so all the more prettily if because of pride I make no complaint and bear it all nobly; his ascendancy over me will always be pronounced; he will be right, I wrong; he will advance, I'll recede; he is great, I am nothing; he will be enriched, I ruined; in a word, always above me, he'll straightway capture public opinion; once arrived there, useless for me to inculpate him, I'll simply not be heard; and so boldly and unceasingly we'll give ourselves over to the most infamous deceit; let us behold it as the key to every grace, every favor, all reputation, all riches, and by means of the keen pleasure of acting villainously, let us placate the little twinge our conscience feels at having manufactured dupes.

MADAME DE SAINT-ANGE—Having there infinitely more on the matter than, so it appears to me, is needed, Eugénie, well convinced, ought also to be reassured, encouraged: she will take action when she pleases. We had now better resume our dissertations upon men's various libertine caprices; the field should be vast; let's survey it; we've just initiated our student into a few of the practice's mysteries, let's not neglect theory.

DOLMANCE—The libertine details of masculine passions, Madame, have little therein to provide suitable stuff for the instruction of a girl who, like Eugénie, is not destined for the whoring profession; she will marry and, such being the hypothesis, one may stake ten to one on it, her husband will have none of those inclinations; however, were he to have them, her wiser conduct is readily to be described: much gentleness, a readiness ever to comply, good humor; on the other hand, much deceit and ample but covert compensation: those few words contain it all. However, were you, Eugénie, to desire some analysis of men's preferences when they resort to libertinage, we might, in order most lucidly to examine the question, generally reduce those tastes to three: *sodomy, sacrilegious fancies,* and *penchants to cruelty.* The first of these passions is universal today; to what we have already said upon it, we shall join a few choice reflections. It divides into two classes, active and passive: the man who embuggers, be it a boy, be it a woman, acquits himself of an active sodomization; he is a passive sodomite when he has himself buggered. The question has often been raised, which of the two fashions of sodomistic behavior is the more voluptuous? assuredly, 'tis the passive, since one enjoys at a single stroke the sensations of before and behind; it is so sweet to change sex, so delicious to counterfeit the whore, to give oneself to a man who treats us as if we were a woman, to call that man one's paramour, to avow oneself his mistress! Ah! my friends, what voluptuousness! But, Eugénie, we shall limit ourselves here to a few details of advice relating only to women who, transforming themselves into men, wish, like us, to enjoy this delicious pleasure. I have just familiarized you with those attacks, Eugénie, and I have observed enough to be persuaded you will one of these days make admirable progress in this career; I exhort you to pursue it diligently as one of the most delightful of the Cytherean isle, and am perfectly sure you will follow my counsel. I'll restrict myself to two or three suggestions essential to every person determined henceforth to know none but these pleasures or ones analogous. First of all, be mindful also of yourself, insist your clitoris be frigged while you are being buggered: no two things harmonize so sweetly as do these two pleasures; avoid a douche, let there be no rubbing upon the sheets, no wiping with towels, when you have just been fucked in this style; 'tis a good idea to have the breech open always; whereof result desires, and titillations which soon obviate any concern for tidiness; there is no imagining to what point the sensations are prolonged. Prior to sodomite amusements remember to avoid acids: they aggravate haemorrhoids and render introductions painful: do not permit several men to discharge one after the other into your ass: this mixture of sperms, however it may excite the imagination, is never beneficial and often dangerous to the health; always rid yourself of each emission before allowing the next to be deposited.

EUGENIE—But if they were to be made in my cunt, should that purging not be a crime?

MADAME DE SAINT-ANGE—Imagine nothing of the sort, sweet little fool; there is not the least wrong in diverting a man's semen into a detour by one means or by another, because propagation is in no wise the objective of Nature; she merely tolerates it; from her viewpoint, the less we propagate, the better; and when we avoid it altogether, that's best of all. Eugénie, be the implacable enemy of this wearisome child-getting, and even in marriage incessantly deflect that perfidious liquor whose vegetation serves only to spoil our figures, which deadens our voluptuous sensations, withers us, ages and makes us fade and disturbs our health; get your husband to accustom himself to these losses; entice him into this or that passage, let him busy himself there and thus keep him from making his offerings at the temple; tell him you detest children, point out the advantages of having none. Keep a close watch over yourself in this article, my dear, for, I declare to you, I hold generation in such horror I should cease to be your friend the instant you were to become pregnant. If, however, the misfortune does occur, without yourself having been at fault, notify me within the first seven or eight weeks, and I'll have it very neatly remedied. Dread not infanticide; the crime is imaginary: we are always mistress of what we carry in our womb, and we do no more harm in destroying this kind of matter than in evacuating another, by medicines, when we feel the need.

EUGENIE—But if the child is near the hour of its birth?

MADAME DE SAINT-ANGE—Were it in the world, we should still have the right to destroy it. In all the world there is no prerogative more secure than that of mothers over their children. No race has failed to recognize this truth: 'tis founded in reason, consecrated in principle.

DOLMANCE—The right is natural . . . it is incontestable. The deific system's extravagance was the source of every one of those gross errors. The imbeciles who believed in God, persuaded that our existence is had of none but him and that immediately an embryo begins to mature, a little soul, emanation of God, comes straightway to animate it; these fools, I say, assuredly had to regard as a capital crime this small creature's undoing, because, according to them, it no longer belonged to men. 'Twas God's work; 'twas God's own: dispatch it without crime? No. Since, however, the torch of philosophy has dissipated all those impostures, since, the celestial chimera has been tumbled in the dust, since, better instructed of physics' laws and secrets, we have evolved the principle of generation, and now that this material mechanism offers nothing more astonishing to the eye than the development of a germ of wheat, we have been called back to Nature and away from human error. As we have broadened the horizon of our rights, we have recognized that we are perfectly free to take back what we only gave up reluctantly, or by accident, and that it is impossible to demand of any individual whomsoever that he become a father or a mother against his will; that this creature whether more or less on earth is not of very much consequence, and that we become, in a word, as certainly the masters of this morsel of flesh, however it be animated, as we are of the nails we pare from our fingers, or the excrements we eliminate through our bowels, because the one and the other are our own, and because we are absolute proprietors of what emanates from us. Having had elaborated for you, Eugénie, the very mediocre importance the act of murder has here on earth, you have been obliged to see of what slight consequence, similarly, must be everything that has to do with childbearing even if the act is perpetrated against a person who has arrived at the age of reason; unnecessary to embroider upon it: your high intelligence adds its own arguments to support my proofs. Peruse the history of the manner of all the world's peoples and you will unfailingly see that the practice is global; you will finally be convinced that it would be sheer imbecility to accord a very indifferent action the title of evil.

EUGENIE, *first to Dolmancé*—I cannot tell you to what point you persuade me. (*Now addressing herself to Madame de Saint-Ange:*) But tell me, my most dear, have you ever had occasion to employ the remedy you propose to me in order internally to destroy the fetus?

MADAME DE SAINT-ANGE—Twice, and both times with total success; but I must admit I have had recourse to it only at pregnancy's outset; however, I am acquainted with two ladies who have used the same remedy at mid-term, and they assure me it all came out as happily with them. Should you be in need, count upon me, my dear, but I urge you never to allow yourself to fall into a state of having need. An ounce of prevention . . . But back we go, and on with the lubricious details we have promised this young lady. Pursue, Dolmancé; we've reached the sacrilegious fancies.

DOLMANCE—I suppose Eugénie is sufficiently disabused on the score of religious errors to be intimately persuaded that sporting with the objects of fools' piety can have no sort of consequence. Sacrilegious fancies have so little substance to them that indeed they cannot heat any but those very youthful minds gladdened by any rupture of restraint; 'tis here a kind of petty vindictiveness which fires the imagination and which, very probably, can provoke a moment or two of enjoyment; but these delights, it would seem to me, must become insipid and cold when one is of an age to understand and to be convinced of the nullity of the objects of which the idols we jeer at are but meager likenesses. The profanation of relics, the images of saints, the host, the crucifix, all that, in the philosopher's view can amount to no more than the degradation of a pagan statue. Once your scorn has condemned those execrable baubles, you must leave them to contempt, and forget them; 'tis not wise to preserve anything for all that but blasphemy, not that blasphemy has much meaning, for as of the moment God does not exist, what's the use of insulting his name? but it is essential to pronounce hard and foul words during pleasure's intoxication, and the language of blasphemy very well serves the imagination. Be utterly unsparing; be lavish in your expressions; they must scandalize to the last degree; for 'tis sweet to scandalize: causing scandal flatters one's pride, and though this be a minor triumph, 'tis not to be disdained; I say it openly, Mesdames, such is one of my secret delights: few are the moral pleasures which more actively affect my imagination. Try it, Eugénie, and you shall see what results from it. Above all, labor to articulate a prodigious impiety when you find yourself with persons of your own age who yet vegetate in superstition's twilight; parade your debauchery, announce your libertinage; affect a whorish air, let them spy your breast when you go with them into secluded places, garb yourself indecently; flauntingly expose the most intimate parts of your body; require of your friends that they do the same; seduce them, lecture them, cause them to see what is ridiculous in their prejudices; put them eye to eye with what is called *evil*; in their company swear like a trooper; if they are younger than you, take them by force, ply them with examples or with counsels, entertain them with all you can think of that is, in a word, most apt to pervert them, thuswise corrupt them; similarly, be extremely free with men; display irreligion and impudence to them; far from taking umbrage at the liberties they will take, mysteriously grant them everything which can amuse them without compromising yourself; let yourself be handled by them, frig them, get yourself frigged; yes, go even so far as to lend them your ass; but, since the fictitious honor of women is bound up with their anterior integrity, be in a less willing humor to have it demolished; once married, secure a lackey, not a lover, or pay a few reliable young men: from there on, all is to be masked, and is; no more peril to your reputation and without anyone ever having been able to suspect you, you have learned the art of doing whatever you please. Let us move on.

Cruel pleasures comprise the third sort we promised to analyze. This variety is today exceedingly common amongst men, and here is the argument they employ to justify them: we wish to be roused, stirred, they say, 'tis the aim of every man who pursues pleasure, and we would be moved by the most active means. Taking our departure from this point, it is not a question of knowing whether our proceedings please or displease the object that serves us, it is purely a question of exposing our nervous system to the most violent possible shock; now, there is no doubt that we are much more keenly affected by pain than by pleasure: the reverberations that result in us when the sensation of pain is produced in others will essentially be of a more vigorous character, more incisive, will more energetically resound in us, will put the animal spirits more violently into circulation and these, directing themselves toward the nether regions by the retrograde motion essential to them, instantly will ignite the organs of voluptuousness and dispose them to pleasure. Pleasure's effects, in women, are always uncertain; often disappointing; it is, furthermore, very difficult for an old or an ugly man to produce them. When it does happen that they are produced, they are feeble, and the nervous concussions fainter; hence, pain must be preferred, for pain's telling effects cannot deceive, and its vibrations are more powerful. But, one may object to men infatuated by this mania, this pain is afflictive to one's fellow; is it charitable to do others ill for the sake of delighting oneself? In answer thereto, the rascals reply that, accustomed in the pleasure-taking act to thinking exclusively of themselves and accounting others as nothing, they are persuaded that it is entirely reasonable, in accordance with natural impulsions, to prefer what they feel to what they do not feel. What, they dare ask, what do these pains occasioned in others do to us? Hurt us? No; on the contrary, we have just demonstrated that from their production there results a sensation delightful to us. For what reason then ought we to go softly with an individual who feels one thing while we feel another? Why should we spare him a torment that will cost us never a tear, when it is certain that from this suffering a very great pleasure for us will be born? Have we ever felt a single natural impulse advising us to prefer others to ourselves, and is each of us not alone, and for himself in this world? 'Tis a very false tone you use when you speak to us of this Nature which you interpret as telling us not to do to others what we would not have done to us; such stuff never came but from the lips of men, and weak men. Never does a strong man take it into his head to speak that language. They were the first Christians who, daily persecuted on account of their ridiculous doctrine, used to cry at whosoever chose to hear: "Don't burn us, don't flay us! *Nature says one must not do unto others that which unto oneself one would not have done!*" Fools! How could Nature, who always urges us to delight in ourselves, who never implants in us other instincts, other notions, other inspirations, how could Nature, the next moment, assure us that we must not, however, decide to love ourselves if that might cause others pain? Ah! believe me, Eugénie, believe me, Nature, mother to us all, never speaks to us save of ourselves; nothing has more of the egoistic than her message, and what we recognize most clearly therein is the immutable and sacred counsel: prefer thyself, love thyself, no matter at whose expense. But the others, they say to you, may avenge themselves. . . . Let them! the mightier will vanquish; he will be right. Very well, there it is, the primitive state of perpetual strife and destruction for which Nature's hand created us, and within which alone it is of advantage to her that we remain.

Thus, my dear Eugénie, is the manner of these persons' arguing, and from my experience and studies I may add thereunto that cruelty, very far from being a vice, is the first sentiment Nature injects in us all. The infant breaks his toy, bites his nurse's breast, strangles his canary long before he is able to reason; cruelty is stamped in animals, in whom, as I think I have said, Nature's laws are more emphatically to be read than in ourselves; cruelty exists amongst savages, so much nearer to Nature than civilized men are; absurd then to maintain cruelty is a consequence of depravity. I repeat, the doctrine is false. Cruelty is natural. All of us are born furnished with a dose of cruelty education later modifies; but education does not belong to Nature, and is as deforming to Nature's sacred effects as arboriculture is to trees. In your orchards compare the tree abandoned to Nature's ministry with the other your art cares for, and you will see which is the more beautiful, you will discover from which you will pluck the superior fruit. Cruelty is simply the energy in a man civilization has not yet altogether corrupted: therefore it is a virtue, not a vice. Repeal your laws, do away with your constraints, your chastisements, your habits, and cruelty will have dangerous effects no more, since it will never manifest itself save when it meets with resistance, and then the collision will always be between competing cruelties; it is in the civilized state cruelty is dangerous, because the assaulted person nearly always lacks the force or the means to repel injury; but in the state of uncivilization, if cruelty's target is strong, he will repulse cruelty; and if the person attacked is weak, why, the case here is merely that of assault upon one of those persons whom Nature's law prescribes to yield to the strong—'tis all one, and why seek trouble where there is none?

We may dispense with an explanation of cruelty in man's lubricious pleasure; you already have a faint idea, Eugénie, of the several excesses they tend to lead to, and your ardent imagination must easily enable you to understand that for a firm and stoical spirit, they should be restricted by no limits. Nero, Tiberius, Heliogabolus slaughtered their children to cause an erection; Maréchal de Retz, Charolais, Condé also committed murders of debauch; the first declared upon being questioned that he knew no delight more powerful than the one derived from the torture inflicted by his chaplain and himself upon infants of either sex. Seven or eight hundred sacrificed children were found in one of his Breton châteaux. All quite conceivable, I've just proven it to you. Our constitution, our scheme, our organs, the flow of liquids, the animal spirits' energy, such are the physical causes which in the same hour make for the Tituses and the Neros, the Messalinas or the Chantals; we can no longer take pride in the virtue that repents of vice, no more condemn Nature for having caused us to be born good than for having created us criminal: she acts in keeping with her designs, her views, her needs: let us submit to them. And so I will only examine, in what follows, female cruelty, which is always more active than male, by reason of the excessive sensibility of women's organs.

In general, we distinguish two sorts of cruelty: that resulting from stupidity, which, never reasoned, never analyzed, assimilates the unthinking individual into a ferocious beast: this cruelty affords no pleasure, for he inclined to it is incapable of discrimination; such a being's brutalities are rarely dangerous: it is always easy to find protection against them; the other species of cruelty, fruit of extreme organic sensibility, is known only to them who are extremely delicate in their person, and the extremes to which it drives them are those determined by intelligence and niceness of feeling; this delicacy, so finely wrought, so sensitive to impressions, responds above all, best, and immediately to cruelty; it awakens in cruelty, cruelty liberates it. How few are able to grasp these distinctions! ... and how few there are who sense them! They exist nonetheless. Now, it is this second kind of cruelty you will most often find in women. Study them well: you will see whether it is not their excessive sensitivity that leads them to cruelty; you will see whether it is not their extremely active imagination, the acuity of their intelligence that renders them criminal, ferocious; oh, they are charming creatures, every one of them; and not one of the lot cannot turn a wise man into a giddy fool if she tries; unhappily, the rigidity, or rather the absurdity, of our customs acts as no encouragement to their cruelty; they are obliged to conceal themselves, to feign, to cover over their propensities with ostensible good and benevolent works which they detest to the depths of their soul; only behind the darkest curtain, by taking the greatest precautions, aided by a few dependable friends, are they able to surrender to their inclinations; and as there are many of this sort, so there are many who are miserable. Would you meet them? Announce a cruel spectacle, a burning, a battle, a combat of gladiators, you will see droves of them come running; but these occasions are not numerous enough to feed their fury: they contain themselves, and they suffer.

Let's cast a rapid glance at women of this variety. Zingua, Queen of Angola, cruelest of women, killed her lovers as soon as they had had their way with her; often she had warriors contend while she looked on and was the victor's prize; to flatter her ferocious spirit, she had every pregnant woman under the age of thirty ground in a mortar.[6] Zoé, a Chinese emperor's wife, knew no pleasure equal to what she felt upon witnessing the execution of criminals; wanting these, she had slaves put to death, and the while would fuck with her husband, and proportioned her discharges to the anguishes she made these wretches endure. 'Twas she who, searching to improve the tortures she imposed upon her victims, invented the famous hollow column of brass one heats after having sealed the patient within. Theodora, Justinian's wife, amused herself seeing eunuchs made; and Messalina frigged herself while men were masturbated to death before her. The women of Florida cause their husband's member to swell and they deposit little insects upon the glans, which produces very horrible agonies; they league together to perform the operation, several of them attacking one man in order to be more sure of the thing. When the Spaniards came, they themselves held their husbands while those European barbarians assassinated them. Mesdames Voisin and la Branvilliers poisoned for the simple pleasure of committing crime. In a word, history furnishes a thousand thousand details of women's cruelty, and it is because of the natural penchant they have, because of their instincts for cruelty, that I should like to have them become accustomed to active flagellation, a means by which cruel men appease their ferocity. Some few among them have the habit already, I know, but it is not yet in use amongst women, at least to the point I should desire. By means of this outlet given women's barbarity, society would have much to gain; for, unable to be evil in one way, they are in some other, and, thus broadcasting their poison everywhere about, they cause their husbands and their families to despair. The refusal to perform a good action, when the occasion presents itself, and that to relieve misfortune, surely gives considerable impetus, if you wish, to that ferocity into which certain women naturally are led, but all this is pale, weak stuff, and often falls far short of the need they have to do yet worse. There would be without doubt other devices whereby woman, at once sensitive and ferocious, might calm her intemperate emotions, but, Eugénie, they are dangerous means, and I should never dare recommend them to you. . . . But, my stars! What is the matter with you, dear angel? Madame, look at the state your pupil is in!

---

[6] See the *History of Zingua, Queen of Angola,* written by a missionary.

EUGENIE, *frigging herself*—Oh Christ! you drive me wild! See what your frigging speeches do! . . .

DOLMANCE—To the rescue, Madame, help me if you will! Are we going to allow this lovely child to discharge without our aid? . . .

MADAME DE SAINT-ANGE—Oh, what an injustice 'twould be! (*Taking Eugénie in her arms.*) Adorable creature, never have I beheld a sensibility like yours, never so delightful a mind! . . .

DOLMANCE—Take care of the fore-end, Madame, I am going to glide over this pretty little asshole with my tongue, and give her a few light slaps on these cheeks; she must be made to discharge at least seven or eight times in this manner.

EUGENIE, *wild-eyed, beside herself*—Ah, by fuck! it won't be difficult!

DOLMANCE—In your present posture, ladies, you might be able to suck my prick, one after the other; thus excited, I could with much more energy advance to our charming pupil's pleasures.

EUGENIE—My dear, I dispute with you the honor of sucking this noble prick. (*She seizes it.*)

DOLMANCE—Oh, what delights! what voluptuous warmth! Eugénie, will you behave well at this critical instant?

MADAME DE SAINT-ANGE—She'll swallow, oh, I promise you, she'll swallow it down; yet . . . on the other hand, if she were through childishness . . . for I do not know what reason . . . were she to neglect the duties lubricity imposes upon her . . .

DOLMANCE, *greatly aroused*—I'd not forgive her, Madame, there would be no pardon for her! . . . An exemplary punishment . . . I swear to you she'd be whipped . . . whipped till her blood flowed. . . . Ah, damn the both of you, I discharge . . . my fuck's coming! . . . Swallow . . . swallow, Eugénie, let there not be one drop lost! and you, Madame, look to my ass; it's ready for you. . . . Do you see how it yawns? do you not see how it calls your fingers? By God's fuck! my ecstasy is complete . . . drive them in further, to the wrist! Ah, back on our feet, I can no more . . . this delicious girl has sucked me like an angel. . . .

EUGENIE—My dear, my adorable instructor, not a drop was lost. Kiss me, my love, your fuck is now in the depths of my bowels.

DOLMANCE—She is delicious . . . and how the wench discharged! . . .

MADAME DE SAINT-ANGE—She is inundated—but what's that I hear? Someone knocks? who can have come to trouble us? My brother . . . imprudent creature!

EUGENIE—But, my dear, this is treason!

DOLMANCE—Unparalleled, is it not? Fear not, Eugénie, we labor for naught but to procure you pleasures.

MADAME DE SAINT-ANGE—And we'll very soon convince her of it! Come in, dear brother, and have a laugh at this little girl's shyness; she's hiding herself so as not to be seen by you.

DIALOGUE THE FOURTH

MADAME DE SAINT-ANGE, EUGENIE, DOLMANCE, LE CHEVALIER DE MIRVEL

LE CHEVALIER—Lovely Eugénie, I beg you to be easy; my discretion is entire; there is my sister and there my friend, both of whom can be held answerable for me.

DOLMANCE—I see but one way to terminate this ridiculous ceremony: look here, Chevalier, we are educating this pretty girl, we are teaching her all a little girl of her age should know and, the better to instruct her, we join some practice to theory. She must have a tableau dressed for her: it must feature a prick discharging, that's where presently we are; would you like to serve as model?

LE CHEVALIER—Surely, the proposal is too flattering to refuse, and Mademoiselle has the charms that will very quickly guarantee the desired lesson's effects.

MADAME DE SAINT-ANGE—Then let's go on; to work!

EUGENIE—Oh, indeed, 'tis too much; you abuse my inexperience to such a degree . . . but for whom is Monsieur going to take me?

LE CHEVALIER—For a charming girl, Eugénie . . . for the most adorable creature I have ever laid eyes on. (*He kisses her;*

his hands rove over her charms.) Oh God! what fresh, what sweet attractions! . . . enchanting! . . .

DOLMANCE—Less prattle, Chevalier, let's act instead; I'll direct the scene, 'tis my right; the object here is to exhibit to Eugénie the mechanics of an ejaculation; but, since it should be difficult for her to observe such a phenomenon in cold blood, the four of us are going to group ourselves close together. You, Madame, will frig your friend, I'll be responsible for the Chevalier. When 'tis a question of a man's pollution, he would infinitely prefer to entrust the business to another man, not to a woman. As a man knows what suits himself, so he knows how to manage for another. . . . Well, off we go. Positions! (*They arrange themselves.*)

MADAME DE SAINT-ANGE—Are we not too close?

DOLMANCE, *who has already got his hands upon the Chevalier* —Impossible to be too close, Madame; we must have your friend's face and breast inundated by the proofs of your brother's virility; let him aim at her nose, as the saying goes. Master of the pump, I'll direct the stream in such wise she'll be covered quite absolutely. Meanwhile, frig her in every lubricious part of her body; Eugénie, give all of your imagination up to dwelling upon libertinage's ultimate extravagances; think that you are about to see its most splendid mysteries operated before your very eyes; cast away every restraint, spurn every one: never was modesty a virtue. Had Nature desired some part of our body to be hidden, she would have seen to the matter herself; but she created us naked; hence, she wishes that we go naked, and all contrary practice thoroughly outrages her laws. Children, who do not yet have any notion of pleasure and consequently of the necessity to render it more keen by modesty, exhibit all of themselves. One also sometimes meets with a yet stranger curiosity: there are countries where, although modesty of manners is not to be encountered, modesty of dress is in usage. In Tahiti, girls are clothed, and when one demands it, they strip. . . .

MADAME DE SAINT-ANGE—What I love about Dolmancé is that he wastes not a moment; all the while he discourses, observe how he acts, look how approvingly he inspects my brother's superb ass, how voluptuously he frigs the young man's handsome prick.

. . . Come, Eugénie, let's not tarry. There's the pump's nozzle in the air; it won't be long before we're flooded.

EUGENIE—Oh, dearest friend, what a monstrous member! . . . I can scarcely get my hand around it! . . . Dear God, are they all as big as this?

DOLMANCE—Eugénie, you know that mine is much inferior in size; such engines are redoubtable for a youngster; you are fully aware one such as this could not without danger perforate you.

EUGENIE, *already being frigged by Madame de Saint-Ange*— I'd brave anything to enjoy it!

DOLMANCE—And you would be right: a girl ought never be terrified by such a thing; Nature lends a helping hand, and the torrents of pleasure wherewith she overwhelms you soon compensate the slight inconveniences that precede them. I have seen girls younger than you sustain still more massy pricks: with courage and patience life's greatest obstacles are surmounted. 'Tis madness to think one must have a child deflowered by only very small pricks. I hold the contrary view, that a virgin should be delivered unto none but the vastest engines to be had, in order that, the hymeneal ligaments sooner burst, pleasure's sensations can more promptly occur in her. To be sure, once launched on this diet, she will have much to do to quit it for another less piquant, more meager; but if she is wealthy, lovely, and youthful, she'll find as many of this size as she can wish. Let her keep her wits about her: should something mediocre be offered her, and should she nevertheless have the desire to make use of it, let her put it in her ass.

MADAME DE SAINT-ANGE—Indeed, and to be still happier, let her employ the greater and the lesser at once; let the voluptuous jars wherewith she will agitate him who encunts her serve to precipitate the ecstasy of the other who buggers, and, drowned in the fuck of the two, let her loose her own as she dies of pleasure.

DOLMANCE—(*It should be pointed out that the pollutions continue throughout all of the dialogue.*) It seems to me two or three more pricks should figure in the picture you describe, Madame;

this woman of yours ought to have, don't you think, a prick in her mouth and another in each hand?

MADAME DE SAINT-ANGE—She might have some clapped under her armpits and a few in her hair, if it were possible she ought to have thirty ranged round her; under such circumstances, one must have, touch, devour nothing but pricks, be inundated by them all, at the same instant one discharges oneself. Ah, Dolmancé! libertine that you are, I defy you to equal me in these delicious combats of luxury. . . . On this head, I've done all that it is possible to do.

EUGENIE, *continuously frigged by her friend, as is the Chevalier by Dolmancé*—Oh, my sweet! . . . I grow dizzy! . . . Why, I too could procure myself such pleasures! . . . I could give myself . . . to a perfect army of men! . . . Ah, what delight! . . . How you frig me, dearest one . . . you are the very goddess of pleasure . . . and how this wondrous prick does swell . . . how its majestic head enlarges and grows red! . . .

DOLMANCE—He's not far from the denouement.

LE CHEVALIER—Eugénie . . . sister . . . approach. . . . Oh, what divine breasts! . . . what soft, plump thighs! Discharge! discharge both, my fuck will join yours! . . . It flows! leaps! Christ (*During the crisis, Dolmancé has carefully directed his friend's outpourings of sperm upon the two women and principally upon Eugénie, who finds herself drenched.*)

EUGENIE—Magnificent spectacle! how noble, how majestic it is . . . I'm completely covered! . . . it sprang into my very eyes! . .

MADAME DE SAINT-ANGE—Wait, dear heart, let me gather up these priceless pearls; I'll rub some upon your clitoris more speedily to provoke your own discharge.

EUGENIE—Ah! yes, my darling, yes! delicious idea . . . go ahead, and I'll come in your arms.

MADAME DE SAINT-ANGE—Divine child, kiss me a thousand times over . . . let me suck your tongue . . . let me breathe your voluptuous respiration all fired by pleasure's heat! Ah, fuck! discharge myself. . . . Brother, finish me, I beg you to finish me! . .

DOLMANCE—Yes, Chevalier . . . frig your sister.

LE CHEVALIER—I'd prefer to fuck her . . . I'm still in a state to.

DOLMANCE—Very well, press it in and give me your ass; I'll fuck you throughout this voluptuous incest. Eugénie, armed with this India rubber dildo, will bugger me. Destined someday to have enacted all the roles of lechery, she has got to strive, in the lessons we're giving here, to fulfill them all equally well.

EUGENIE, *rigging up the dildo*—Oh, willingly! You will never find me wanting when it is a question of libertinage; it is now my single god, the unique rule of my conduct, the single basis of all my actions. (*She buggers Dolmancé.*) In like wise, my dear master? Is it well done? . . .

DOLMANCE—Splendidly! . . . Truly, the little rascal buggers me mannishly! Fine! it seems to me we are all four perfectly attached one to the other; we have but to commence.

MADAME DE SAINT-ANGE—Oh, I'm dying, Chevalier! . . . I am incapable of becoming accustomed to the throbbing of your lovely prick! . . .

DOLMANCE—Ah, but this damned, this charming ass affords me pleasure! Oh fuck! fuck! all of us, let's discharge together! Christ, but I perish! I expire! Ah, in my life never have I come more voluptuously! Hast lost thy sperm, Chevalier?

LE CHEVALIER—Look you at this cunt: smeared, muddied up, is it not?

DOLMANCE—Oh, my friend, wouldst I had as much in my ass!

MADAME DE SAINT-ANGE—Rest, stop, I am dead.

DOLMANCE, *kissing Eugénie*—This matchless girl has fucked me like a god.

EUGENIE—In truth, I found it rather pleasurable.

DOLMANCE—All excesses procure it, provided one is libertine; and a woman is best advised to multiply those excesses even to beyond the possible.

MADAME DE SAINT-ANGE—I have deposited five hundred *louis* with a notary, and the purse will belong to any individual, whomsoever he be, who can teach me a passion I am ignorant of now, and who can plunge me into an ecstasy I have not yet enjoyed.

DOLMANCE—(*At this point the interlocutors, set to rights, have ceased to occupy themselves with all but conversation.*) The idea is strange, Madame, and I'd accept to try, but I am in doubt whether this uncommon desire after which you chase, resembles the delicate pleasures you have just tasted.

MADAME DE SAINT-ANGE—What indeed!

DOLMANCE—'Tis that, in honor, I know nothing so boring as enjoyment of the cunt and when once, Madame, one has, like yourself, tasted what the ass has to offer, I cannot conceive how one may forsake that pleasure for others.

MADAME DE SAINT-ANGE—They are old habits. When one thinks as I do, one wishes everywhere to be fucked and whatever the part an engine perforates, one is made happy upon feeling it there. However, I am wholly of your opinion and herewith attest to all voluptuous women that the pleasure they will experience of assfucking will always by much surpass the one they experience in having a man by the cunt. On this count let them refer to that woman who in all Europe has accomplished most in the one manner and in the other: I certify there is not the least comparison to be made, and that very reluctantly will they return to the fore after having put their behinds to the proof.

LE CHEVALIER—My thoughts are not entirely identical. I am prepared for anything that is expected of me, but, by taste, in women I really love only the altar Nature indicates for the rendering of an homage.

DOLMANCE—Why, to be sure, and it's the ass! My dear Chevalier, never did Nature, if you scrupulously examine her ordinations, never did Nature indicate another altar for our offerings than the asshole, but this latter she expressly commands. Ah, by God! were not her intention that we fuck assholes, would she have so exactly proportioned this orifice to fit our member? is not this aperture circular, like this instrument? Why, then! What person, no matter how great an enemy of common sense, can imagine that an oval hole could have been created for our cylindrical pricks! Ponder this deformity and you will at once apprehend Nature's intentions; we very plainly see that too frequent sacrifices made in this part, by increasing a propagation of which only her forbearance makes us capable, would displease her infallibly. But let us go on with our education. Eugénie has just, entirely at her leisure, contemplated the sublime mystery of a discharge; presently, I would like to have her learn how to direct its flow.

MADAME DE SAINT-ANGE—Considering your exhaustion, 'tis to expose her to a great deal of trouble.

DOLMANCE—To be sure; and that is why I should desire that we have, from your house or your fields, some robust young lad who could serve as a mannequin, and upon whom we could give our lessons.

MADAME DE SAINT-ANGE—I've precisely what you need.

DOLMANCE—It might not be, by chance, a young gardener, with a delicious aspect, of about eighteen years or twenty, whom I saw just a short while ago, working in your kitchen garden?

MADAME DE SAINT-ANGE—Augustin? Exactly, yes, Augustin, whose member measures fourteen inches in length and has a circumference of eight and an half!

DOLMANCE—Great heaven! what a monster! . . . and that discharges? . . .

MADAME DE SAINT-ANGE—Like a waterfall! . . . I'll go fetch him.

DIALOGUE THE FIFTH

DOLMANCE, LE CHEVALIER, AUGUSTIN, EUGENIE, MADAME DE SAINT-ANGE

MADAME DE SAINT-ANGE, *presenting Augustin*—Behold the man I mentioned. Let's on with it, friends, let's to our frolics; what would life be without its little amusements? Come hither, simpleton! Oh, the ninny! . . . Would you believe it, I have been six months struggling to turn this great pig into something fit for civilized society, and I've got nowhere with him.

AUGUSTIN—Aye, M'am, you speak sometimes like that, that I'm beginning not to get on so bad right now, and when there's a piece of ground lying fallow you always give it to me to till, I'm the one that gets it.

DOLMANCE, *laughing*—Oh, precious! . . . charming! . . . The dear boy, he's as frank as he is fresh. . . . (*Exhibiting Eugénie.*) Augustin, look sharp, my lad, there's a bed of flowers lying fallow; would you like to try your spade on it?

AUGUSTIN—Oh Jemmy, Sir! Such neat little oddments ain't made for such as me.

DOLMANCE—To it, Mademoiselle.

EUGENIE, *blushing*—Heavens! I am so ashamed!

266

DOLMANCE—Rid yourself of that weak-hearted sentiment; all actions, and above all those of libertinage, being inspired in us by Nature, there is not one, of whatever kind, that warrants shame. Be smart there, Eugénie, act the whore with this young man; consider that every provocation sensed by a boy and originating from a girl is a natural offertory, and that your sex never serves Nature better than when it prostitutes itself to ours; that 'tis, in a word, to be fucked that you were born, and that she who refuses her obedience to this intention Nature has for her does not deserve to see the light longer. You yourself, lower the young man's trousers to below his handsome thighs, roll his shirt up under his vest, so that his fore-end ... and his after, which, by the by, is damn fine, are at your disposal. ... Now, let one of your hands catch up that lank length of flesh, pendant now, but which, I wager, will soon amaze you in its new form, and with your other hand explore his buttocks, and, thus, tickle his rectal gap. ... Yes, in this manner ... (*To show Eugénie how 'tis to be done, he socratizes Augustin himself.*) Uncap this rubicund head; never, while you pollute it, never allow it to be covered over; keep it naked ... stretch the skin, yea, stretch it taut. ... Now there; dost see what effect my lesson has had already? ... And you, my boy, I beseech you, don't stand there holding your hands behind your back; isn't there something you might put them to? Let them stray about upon this superb breast, over these wondrous buttocks. ...

AUGUSTIN—Sir, couldn't I give this miss a smack or two, it would make me right happy.

MADAME DE SAINT-ANGE—Well, kiss her, imbecile, kiss her as much as you like; do you not kiss me when I'm in bed with you?

AUGUSTIN—Oh, jeez! Pretty little mouth, all fresh and nice-tasting! ... Seems like I've got my nose in the roses in our garden. (*Showing his rising prick.*) Look, Sir, that's what it does, d'ye see it?

EUGENIE—Good heaven! How it enlarges!

DOLMANCE—Attempt now to put rather more regularity in your motions, let them be more energetic. ... Here, yield me your place for an instant, and watch closely what I do. (*He frigs Augus-*

tin.) Do you observe? These movements are more purposeful and at the same time softer. There, begin again and above all keep the head bare . . . Good! there it is in its full vigor; now let's ascertain whether it's bigger than the Chevalier's.

EUGENIE—Be certain of it: you see very well I cannot get my hand around it.

DOLMANCE, *measuring*—Yes, right you are: fourteen long, eight and a half around. I've never seen a larger. 'Tis what is called a superb prick. And you, Madame, you say you employ it?

MADAME DE SAINT-ANGE—Regularly, every night I spend here in the country.

DOLMANCE—But not, I hope, in the ass?

MADAME DE SAINT-ANGE—Rather more often there than in the cunt.

DOLMANCE—Ah! my God! what libertinage! Upon my honor, I don't know whether I could manage it.

MADAME DE SAINT-ANGE—Don't pinch, Dolmancé, and he'll penetrate your ass as neatly as he does mine.

DOLMANCE—We shall see; I flatter myself in the belief our Augustin will do me the honor of casting a little fuck into my behind: I'll repay him in the same coin; but let's continue, we have lessons to give. . . . Look sharp, Eugénie, mind, the serpent is about to disgorge its venom: prepare yourself; fix your gaze upon the head of this sublime weapon; and when as the sign of its approaching spasm you see it inflate, take on a deeper, more purple hue, let your activities then become frenzied; let your fingers now tickling his anus dig as deep as possible, before the event occurs; give yourself entirely to the libertine who is amusing himself with you; seek out his mouth in order to suck it; let your charms fly, so to speak, to do your hands' bidding. . . . He discharges, Eugénie, 'tis the moment of your triumph.

AUGUSTIN—Aië! aië! Miss, it's killing me! I can't do no more! More, go on and do me more, harder, Miss, please, Miss! Ah, God a'mighty! I can't see straight! . . .

DOLMANCE—Redouble your efforts, Eugénie! Triple them! Caution to the winds, he's drunk and in his throes! . . . God, what abundance of sperm! . . . with what power it springs forth! . . . Behold the traces of the initial jet: it shot ten feet, nay, more! By God's fuck! the room's awash; Never have I seen a comparable discharge, and you tell me, Madame, this article fucked you last night?

MADAME DE SAINT-ANGE—Nine or ten times, I believe; we gave up counting long ago.

LE CHEVALIER—Lovely Eugénie, you're covered with it.

EUGENIE—Wouldst I were drowned in it. (*To Dolmancé:*) Tell me, my dear master, are you content?

DOLMANCE—Mightily, for a beginning; but there remain several episodes you have neglected.

MADAME DE SAINT-ANGE—Wait; they can mean nothing to her lest they are the fruit of experience; for my part, I confess I am exceedingly pleased with my Eugénie; the happiest dispositions are apparent in her, and I believe that we ought now to have her enjoy another spectacle. Let's have her witness the effects of a prick in the ass. Dolmancé, I am going to offer you mine; I shall be in my brother's arms; he will encunt me, I'll be buggered by you, and Eugénie will prepare your prick, will insert it in my ass, will supervise all the movements, will study them, all this in order to familiarize herself with this operation to which, afterward, she will submit; it will then be a question of this Hercules' fair prick.

DOLMANCE—I am passing eager to see this pretty little behind rent by brave Augustin's violent blows; but I agree to what you propose, Madame, provided we add one detail: Augustin, whom I'll have stiff again with two strokes of my wrist, will bugger me while I sodomize you.

MADAME DE SAINT-ANGE—I heartily approve the arrangement; I too gain thereby; and my scholar will benefit from two excellent lessons instead of one.

DOLMANCE, *seizing Augustin*—Come, my stalwart swain, I'll restore thee to life. . . . Eh, look how the brute responds! Kiss me, dear friend. . . . You are still all wetted over with fuck, and 'tis fuck I ask of thee. Ah, by God, I simply must pump his ass while frigging him! . . .

LE CHEVALIER—Approach, sister; to comply with Dolmancé's strictures and with yours, I am going to stretch out on this bed; you will lie in my arms, and expose your gorgeous buttocks to him, and very wide indeed you shall spread them. . . . Yes, just so: we're ready to begin.

DOLMANCE—No, not quite; wait for me; I must first of all enter your sister's ass, since Augustin whispers me to do it; next, I'll marry you: remember, let's not fall short of any of our principles and remember also that a student is observing us, and we owe her precise demonstrations. Eugénie, come frig me while I determine this low fellow's enormous engine; lend a hand with my own erection, pollute my prick, very lightly, roll it upon your buttocks. . . . (*She does so.*)

EUGENIE—Is this as it ought to be?

DOLMANCE—There is always too much of the timorous in your movements; far more tightly squeeze the prick you frig, Eugénie; if masturbation is agreeable at all it is because the member is more severely compressed then than in fucking, it is therefore necessary that the co-operating hand become, for the engine over which it works, an infinitely straiter passage than exists anywhere else in the body. . . . Better! Yes, that's better! Spread your behind yet a little more so that with each stroke the end of my prick can glide ahead to touch your asshole. . . . yes, very good, very good indeed! While waiting, Chevalier, frig your sister; we will be at your disposal in a minute. . . . Ah, excellent! there's my man stiffening! Now ready yourself, Madame; open that sublime ass to my impure ardor; Eugénie, guide the dart, it must be your hand that conducts it to the vent, your hand must make it penetrate; immediately it is in, get a grip on good Augustin here, and fill my entrails up with him; those are an apprentice's chores and thence there is much instruction to be had; that, my dear, is why I put you to this trouble.

MADAME DE SAINT-ANGE—Are my buttocks where you wish them, Dolmancé? Ah, my angel, if you but knew how much I desire you, how long I have been waiting to be buggered by a sodomite!

DOLMANCE—Thy will shall be done, Madame; but suffer me to halt an instant at my idol's feet; I would praise it before entering into the depths of the sanctuary. . . . What a divine ass is this! . . . let me kiss it! let me lick it, lick it a thousand times over and a thousand more! . . . Here, that's the prick you yearn for! . . . Dost feel it, bitch? Tell me, say, dost feel it penetrate? . . .

MADAME DE SAINT-ANGE—Oh, drive it to darkness in my bowels! . . . Oh sweet lechery, what is your empire!

DOLMANCE—'Tis an ass such as never in my days have I fucked; worthy of Ganymede himself! To it, Eugénie, be immediately attendant upon my buggering by Augustin.

EUGENIE—I bring him to you; there. (*To Augustin:*) Wake, sweet angel, do you spy the hole you've to pierce?

AUGUSTIN—Aye, I see it. Mother of God! there's a big one I say! I'll go in easier than into you, Miss. Kiss me a little so it will enter nice.

EUGENIE, *embracing him*—Oh, as much as you like, you are so fresh! . . . But push, do you hear! The head's out of sight—'twas quick, and I dare say the rest will follow close behind. . . .

DOLMANCE—Thrust, thrust, my good fellow . . . tear me, if so it must be. . . . Dost see my ass? Is it not ready? Doth it not beckon? Well, drive . . . ah, by Christ! what a bludgeon! never have I received one of such amplitude . . . Eugénie, how many inches remain outside?

EUGENIE—Scarcely two.

DOLMANCE—Then I have eleven in my ass! . . . What ecstasy! He cleaves me in twain, I can no more! Chevalier! Are you ready?

LE CHEVALIER—Feel, and give me your opinion.

DOLMANCE—Come hither, my children, let me wed thee . . . let me do all I may to expedite this heavenly incest. (*He introduces the Chevalier's prick into his sister's cunt.*)

MADAME DE SAINT-ANGE—Why, my dears, there I am fucked from either side! By Jesus! What a divine pleasure! No, there's none like it in all the world. Ah, fuck! how I pity the woman who has not tasted it! Rattle me, Dolmancé, smite away . . . let the violence of your movements impale me upon my brother's blade and you, Eugénie, do you contemplate me; come, regard me in vice; come, learn, from my example, to savor it, to be transported, to taste it with delectation. . . . Behold, my love, behold all that I simultaneously do: scandal, seduction, bad example, incest, adultery, sodomy! Oh, Satan! one and unique god of my soul, inspire thou in me something yet more, present further perversions to my smoking heart, and then shalt thou see how I shall plunge myself into them all!

DOLMANCE—Ah voluptuous creature, how you do stir up my fuck, how your sentiments and the uncommon temperature of your ass do excite it to discharge! 'Twill all have me coming in an instant. . . . Eugénie, fire my fucker's courage, belabor his flanks, pry apart his buttocks; you are now somewhat skilled in the art of reviving the desires in him who vacillates . . . your approach alone gives energy to the prick that fucks me. . . . I feel it, the strokes are more powerful . . . oh, thou bitch, I must yield to you what I should never have wanted but to owe to my own ass-end . . . wait for me! wait, dost hear? Oh, my friends, let us not discharge but in unison: 'tis life's single pleasure! . . .

MADAME DE SAINT-ANGE—Fuck! fuck! come when you wish . . . for I can withstand it no longer! Oh double name of God be-fucked! Sacred bugger-God! I come! . . . Inundate me, my friends, soak, drench, drown your whore! spray floods of your scum-fuck to the very seat of this blazing soul! it exists for naught but to be slaked, quenched by your tides! Aië! aië! aië! . . . fuck! . . . fuck! . . . what incredible excess of voluptuousness! . . . I am slain! . . . Eugénie, let me kiss thee, let me eat thee! let me consume, batten upon thy fuck as I loose my own! . . . (*Augustin, Dolmancé and the Chevalier act in chorus; the fear of appearing monotonous prevents us from recording expressions which, upon such occasions, are all very apt to resemble one another.*)

DOLMANCE—And there is one of the fairest fucks I have ever had. (*Showing Augustin to the others.*) This bugger glutted me with sperm! but, Madame, I consider I passed as much on to you.

MADAME DE SAINT-ANGE—Ah, speak not to me of it; I am sunk in it.

EUGENIE—I cannot say as much, not I! no! (*Casting herself playfully into her friend's arms.*) You say you have committed abundant sins, my dearest, but as for me, blessed God! not a one. Oh, if I have got to eat my soup cold this way, I'll have indigestion.

MADAME DE SAINT-ANGE, *bursting into laughter*—How droll the creature is!

DOLMANCE—But how charming! Come here, little one, I'd whip thee a bit. (*He strikes her ass.*) Kiss me, your turn is soon to come.

MADAME DE SAINT-ANGE—From now on we must occupy ourselves exclusively with her; consider her, brother, she's the prey; examine that charming maidenhead; 'twill soon belong to thee.

EUGENIE—Oh, no! not by the fore-end! 'twould hurt me overmuch; from behind as much as you please, as Dolmancé dealt with me a short while ago.

MADAME DE SAINT-ANGE—Naive and delicious girl! She demands of you precisely what one has so much difficulty obtaining from others.

EUGENIE—Oh, 'tis not without a little remorse; for you have not entirely reassured me upon the criminal enormity I have always heard ascribed to this, especially when it is done between man and man, as has just occurred with Dolmancé and Augustin; tell me, Monsieur, tell me how your philosophy explains this species of misdemeanor. 'Tis frightful, is it not?

DOLMANCE—Start from one fundamental point, Eugénie: in libertinage, nothing is frightful, because everything libertinage suggests is also a natural inspiration; the most extraordinary, the most bizarre acts, those which most arrantly seem to conflict with every law, every human institution (as for Heaven, I have nothing to say), well, Eugénie, even those are not frightful, and there is not one amongst them all that cannot be demonstrated within the boundaries of Nature; it is certain that the one you allude to, lovely Eugénie, is the very same relative to which one finds such a strange fable in the tasteless fictions of the Holy Writ, that tedious compilation of an untutored Jew during a Babylonian captivity; but the anecdote is false, wants all likelihood, all verisimilitude, when it is affirmed that in retribution for these depravities, those cities, those towns rather, perished by fire; having their site upon the craters of ancient volcanoes, Sodom, Gomorrah too, perished like the Italian cities Vesuvius' lavas submerged; and that's all there is to the miracle, yet, all the same, 'twas from this most simple event they departed in order barbarously to invent the torture of fire to be used against those unfortunate humans who, in one area of Europe, delivered themselves over to this natural fancy.

EUGENIE—Oh, 'tis natural?

DOLMANCE—Yes, natural, so I affirm it to be; Nature has not got two voices, you know, one of them condemning all day what the other commands, and it is very certain that it is nowhere but from her organ that those men who are infatuated with this mania receive the impressions that drive them to it. They who wish to denigrate the taste or proscribe its practice declare it is harmful to population; how dull-witted they are, these imbeciles who think of nothing but the multiplication of their kind, and who detect nothing but the crime in anything that conduces to a different end. Is it really so firmly established that Nature has so great a need for this overcrowding as they would like to have us believe? is it very certain that one is guilty of an outrage whenever one abstains from this stupid propagation? To convince ourselves, let us for an instant scrutinize both her operations and her laws. Were it that Nature did naught but create, and never destroy, I might be able to believe, with those tedious sophists, that the sublimest of all actions would be incessantly to labor at production, and following that, I should grant, with them, that the refusal to reproduce would be, would perforce have to be, a crime; however, does not the most fleeting glance at natural operations reveal that destructions are just as necessary to her plan as are creations? that the one and the other of these functions are interconnected and enmeshed so intimately that for either to operate without the other would be impossible? that nothing would be born, nothing would be regenerated without destructions? Destruction, hence, like creation, is one of Nature's mandates.

This principle acknowledged, how may I offend Nature by refusing to create? the which, supposing there to be some evil in it, would appear infinitely less evil, no question about it, than the act of destruction, which latter is numbered among her laws, as I have but a moment ago proven. If on the one hand I admit the penchant Nature has given me to fabricate these losses and ruins, I must examine, on the other hand, to see whether they are not necessary to her and whether I do not conform with her will when I destroy; thus considered, where then, I ask you, is the crime? But, the fools and the populators continue to object—and they are naught but one—this procreative sperm cannot have been placed in your loins for any purpose other than reproduction: to misuse it is an offense. I have just proven the contrary, since this misuse would not even be equivalent to destruction, and since destruction, far more serious than misuse, would not itself be criminal. Secondly, it is false that Nature intends this spermatic liquid to be employed only and entirely for reproduction; were this true, she would not permit its spillage under any circumstance save those appropriate to that end. But experience shows that the contrary may happen, since we lose it both when and where we wish. Secondly, she would forbid the occurrence of those losses save in coitus, losses which, however, do take place, both when we dream and when we summon remembrances; were Nature miserly about this so precious sap, 'twould never but be into the vessel of reproduction she would tolerate its flow; assuredly, she would not wish this voluptuousness, wherewith at such moments she crowns us, to be felt by us when we divert our tribute; for it would not be reasonable to suppose she could consent to give us pleasures at the very moment we heaped insults upon her. Let us go further; were women not born save to produce —which most surely would be the case were this production so dear to Nature—, would it happen that, throughout the whole length of a woman's life, there are no more than seven years, all the arithmetic performed, during which she is in a state capable of conceiving and giving birth? What! Nature avidly seeks propagation, does she; and everything which does not tend to this end offends her, does it! and out of a hundred years of life the sex destined to produce cannot do so during more than seven years! Nature wishes for propagation only, and the semen she accords man to serve in these reproducings is lost, wasted, misused wherever and as often as it pleases man! He takes the same pleasures in this loss as in useful employment of his seed, and never the least inconvenience! . . .

Let us cease, good friends, let us cease to believe in such absurdities: they cause good sense to shudder. Ah! far from outraging Nature, on the contrary—and let us be well persuaded of it —, the sodomite and Lesbian serve her by stubbornly abstaining from a conjunction whose resultant progeniture can be nothing but irksome to her. Let us make no mistake about it, this propagation was never one of her laws, nothing she ever demanded of us, but at the very most something she tolerated; I have told you so. Why! what difference would it make to her were the race of men entirely to be extinguished upon earth, annihilated! she laughs at our pride when we persuade ourselves all would be over and done with were this misfortune to occur! Why, she would simply fail to notice it. Do you fancy races have not already become extinct? Buffon counts several of them perished, and Nature, struck dumb by a so precious loss, doesn't so much as murmur! The entire species might be wiped out and the air would not be the less pure for it, nor the Star less brilliant, nor the universe's march less exact. What idiocy it is to think that our kind is so useful to the world that he who might not labor to propagate it or he who might disturb this propagation would necessarily become a criminal! Let's bring this blindness to a stop and may the example of more reasonable peoples serve to persuade us of our errors. There is not one corner of the earth where the alleged crime of sodomy has not had shrines and votaries. The Greeks, who made of it, so to speak, a virtue, raised a statue unto Venus Callipygea; Rome sent to Athens for law, and returned with this divine taste.

And under the emperors, behold the progress it made! Sheltered by the Roman eagle, it spread from one end of the earth to the other; with the Empire's collapse, it took refuge near the diadem, it followed the arts in Italy, it is handed down to those of us who govern ourselves aright. We discover a hemisphere, we find sodomy in it. Cook casts anchor in a new world: sodomy reigns there. Had our balloons reached the moon, it would have been discovered there as well. Delicious preference, child of Nature and of pleasure, thou must be everywhere men are to be found, and wherever thou shalt be known, there shall they erect altars to thee! O my friends, can there be an extravagance to equal that of imagining that a man must be a monster deserving to lose his life because he has preferred enjoyment of the asshole to that of the cunt, because a young man with whom he finds two pleasures, those of being at once lover and mistress, has appeared to him preferable to a young girl, who promises him but half as much! He shall be a villain, a monster, for having wished to play the role of a sex not his own! Indeed! Why then has Nature created him susceptible of this pleasure?

Let us inspect his conformation; you will observe radical differences between it and that of other men who have not been blessed with this predilection for the behind; his buttocks will be fairer, plumper; never a hair will shade the altar of pleasure, whose interior, lined with a more delicate, more sensual, more sensitive membrane, will be found positively of the same variety as the interior of a woman's vagina; this man's character, once again unlike that of others, will be softer, more pliant, subtler; in him you will find almost all the vices and all the virtues native to women; you will recognize even their weaknesses there; all will have feminine manias and sometimes feminine habits and traits. Would it then be possible that Nature, having thuswise assimilated them into women, could be irritated by what they have of women's tastes? Is it not evident that this is a category of men different from the other, a class Nature has created in order to diminish or minimize propagation, whose overgreat extent would infallibly be prejudicial to her? . . . Ah, dear Eugénie, did you but know how delicate is one's enjoyment when a heavy prick fills the behind, when, driven to the balls, it flutters there, palpitating; and then, withdrawn to the foreskin, it hesitates, and returns, plunges in again, up to the hair! No, no, in the wide world there is no pleasure to rival this one: 'tis the delight of philosophers, that of heroes, it would be that of the gods were not the parts used in his heavenly conjugation the only gods we on earth should reverence![7]

EUGENIE, *very much moved*—Oh, my friends, let me be buggered! . . . Here, my buttocks stand ready. . . . I present them to you! . . . Fuck me, for I discharge! . . . (*Upon pronouncing these words, she falls into the arms of Madame de Saint-Ange, who clasps her, embraces her, and offers the young lady's elevated flanks to Dolmancé.*)

MADAME DE SAINT-ANGE—Divine teacher, will you resist the proposal? Will you not be tempted by this sublime ass? See how it doth yawn, how it winks at thee!

DOLMANCE—I ask your forgiveness, beautiful Eugénie: it shall not be I, if indeed you wish it, who shall undertake to extinguish the fires I have lit. Dear child, in my eyes you possess the large fault of being a woman. I was so considerate as to forget much in order to harvest your virginity; deign to think well of me for going no further: the Chevalier is going to take the task in hand. His sister, equipped with this artificial prick, will bestow the most redoubtable buffets upon her brother's ass, all the while presenting her noble behind to Augustin, who shall bugger her and whom I'll fuck meantime; for, I make no attempt to conceal it, this fine lad's ass has been signaling to me for an hour, and I wish absolutely to repay him for what he has done to me.

EUGENIE—I accept the revision; but, in truth, Dolmancé, the frankness of your avowal little offsets its impoliteness.

DOLMANCE—A thousand pardons, Mademoiselle; but we other buggers are very nice on the question of candor and the exactitude of our principles.

MADAME DE SAINT-ANGE—However, a reputation for candor is not the one we commonly grant those whom, like yourself, are accustomed only to taking people from behind.

---

[7] A later part of this work promising us a much more extensive dissertation upon this subject, we have, here, limited ourselves to an analysis but roughly sketched and but boldly outlined.

DOLMANCE—We do have something of the treacherous, yes; a touch of the false, you may believe it. But after all, Madame, I have demonstrated to you that this character is indispensable to man in society. Condemned to live amidst people who have the greatest interest in hiding themselves from our gaze, in disguising the vices they have in order to exhibit nothing but virtues they never respect, there should be the greatest danger in the thing were we to show them frankness only; for then, 'tis evident, we would give them all the advantages over us they on their part refuse us, and the dupery would be manifest. The needs for dissimulation and hypocrisy are bequeathed us by society; let us yield to the fact. Allow me for an instant to offer my own example to you, Madame: there is surely no being more corrupt anywhere in the world; well, my contemporaries are deceived in me; ask them what they think of Dolmancé, and they all will tell you I am an honest man, whereas there is not a single crime whereof I have not gleaned the most exquisite delights.

MADAME DE SAINT-ANGE—Oh, you do not convince me that you have committed atrocities.

DOLMANCE—Atrocities . . . indeed, Madame, I have wrought horrors.

MADAME DE SAINT-ANGE—Fie, you are like the man who said to his confessor: "Needless to go into details, Sir; murder and theft excepted, you can be sure I've done everything."

DOLMANCE—Yes, Madame, I should say the same thing, omitting those exceptions.

MADAME DE SAINT-ANGE—What! libertine, you have permitted yourself . . .

DOLMANCE—Everything, Madame, everything; with a temperament and principles like mine, does one deny oneself anything?

MADAME DE SAINT-ANGE—Oh, let's fuck! fuck! . . . I can bear such language no longer; we'll return to it. But save your confessions for later, Dolmancé; to hear them best your auditors should be *clear-headed*. And when you have an erection, all the sincerity deserts what you say, you fall to uttering horrors and from you we get, in the guise of truths, the libertine glitterings of an inflamed imagination. (*They take their places.*)

DOLMANCE—One moment, Chevalier, one moment; I am the one who shall introduce it; but, by way of preliminary, and I ask the lovely Eugénie's pardon for it, she must allow me to flog her in order she be put in the proper humor. (*He beats her.*)

EUGENIE—I assure you, this ceremony has no purpose. . . . Admit, Dolmancé, that it satisfies your lewdness; but in doing it don't take on airs, I beg of you, and suppose you are doing anything in my behalf.

DOLMANCE, *whipping merrily away*—Ah, you'll have news for me in a moment! . . . You have yet no acquaintance with this pre-liminary's influences. . . . Come, come, little bitch, you'll be lashed!

EUGENIE—My God, how he does wax hot! And my buttocks too, they are all afire! . . . But, indeed, you're hurting me!

MADAME DE SAINT-ANGE—I'll avenge you, dear heart; I'll retaliate in kind. (*She takes up a whip and flogs Dolmancé.*)

DOLMANCE—With all my heart; I ask but one favor of Eugénie: that she consent to be flogged as vigorously as I myself desire to be; you notice how well within natural law I am; but wait, let's arrange it: let Eugénie mount your flanks, Madame, she will clutch your neck, like those children whose mothers carry them on their backs; that way, I'll have two asses under my hand; I'll drub them together; the Chevalier and Augustin, both will work upon me, striking my buttocks. . . . Yes, 'tis thus . . . Well, there we are! . . . what ecstasy!

MADAME DE SAINT-ANGE—Do not spare this little rascal, I beseech you, and as I ask no quarter, I want you to grant it to no one.

EUGENIE—Aië! aië! aië! I believe my blood is flowing!

MADAME DE SAINT-ANGE—'Twill embellish our buttocks by lending color to them. . . . Courage, my angel, courage; bear in mind that it is always by way of pain one arrives at pleasure.

EUGENIE—I can no more!

DOLMANCE, *halts a minute to contemplate his work; then, starting in again*—Another fifty, Eugénie; yes, precisely, fifty more on either cheek will do it. O bitches! how great shall now be your pleasure in fucking! (*The posture is dissolved.*)

MADAME DE SAINT-ANGE, *examining Eugénie's buttocks*—Oh, the poor little thing, her behind is all bloodied over! Beast, how much pleasure you take thus in kissing cruelty's vestiges!

DOLMANCE, *polluting himself*—Yes, I mask nothing, and my pleasures would be more ardent were the wounds more cruel.

EUGENIE—But you are a monster!

DOLMANCE—Indeed I am.

LE CHEVALIER—There's good faith in him at least.

DOLMANCE—Off with you, Chevalier. Sodomize her.

LE CHEVALIER—Hold her body and in three shakes 'twill be done.

EUGENIE—Oh heavens! Yours is thicker than Dolmancé's . . . Chevalier, you are tearing me apart! . . . go softly, I beg of you! . . .

LE CHEVALIER—Impossible, my angel, I must reach my objective. . . . Consider: I'm performing before my master's eyes; both his prestige and mine are at stake.

DOLMANCE—'Tis there! I prodigiously love to see a prick's pubic hair rub the border of an anus. . . . Come now, Madame, embugger your brother. Here we have Augustin's prick, in an admirable way to be introduced into you, and I promise you I'll spare your fucker nothing. . . . Excellent! it seems to me we've got our rosary well strung together; not another thought now but of discharging.

MADAME DE SAINT-ANGE—Cast an eye on this little tramp! How she quivers and wriggles!

EUGENIE—Is it my fault? I am dying from pleasure! That whipping . . . this immense prick . . . the amiable Chevalier who frigs me the while! My darling, my darling, I can no more!

MADAME DE SAINT-ANGE—Jesus! nor can I! I discharge! . . .

DOLMANCE—A little unity, my friends; grant me another two more minutes to overtake you and we shall all of us come together.

LE CHEVALIER—There's no time left; my fuck runs into lovely Eugénie's ass . . . I am dying! Ah sacred name of the fucking Almighty! what pleasure! . . .

DOLMANCE—I follow you, friends . . . I follow hard after you . . . I too am blinded by fuck. . . .

AUGUSTIN—Me too! . . . and me! . . .

MADAME DE SAINT-ANGE—What a scene! . . . This bugger has filled up my ass! . . .

LE CHEVALIER—To the bidet, ladies, to the bidet!

MADAME DE SAINT-ANGE—No, indeed, no, I like that, I do; I like the feeling of fuck in my ass, and keep it in me as long as I can.

EUGENIE—No more, enough. . . . My friends, tell me now if a woman must always accept the proposal, when 'tis made to her, thus to be fucked?

MADAME DE SAINT-ANGE—Always, dear heart, unfailingly. More, as this mode of fucking is delightful, she ought to require it of those of whom she makes use; but if she is dependent upon the person with whom she amuses herself, if she hopes to obtain favors from him, gifts or thanks, let her restrain her eagerness and not surrender her ass for nothing; cede it after being urged, besought, wheedled; there is not a man of all those who possess the taste who would not ruin himself for a woman clever enough to refuse him nothing save with the design of inflaming him further; she will extract from him all she wants if she well has the art of yielding only when pressed.

DOLMANCE—Well, little angel, are you converted? have you given over believing sodomy a crime?

EUGENIE—And were it one, what care I? Have you not demonstrated the nonexistence of crime? There are now very few actions which appear criminal in my view.

DOLMANCE—There is crime in nothing, dear girl, regardless of what it be: the most monstrous of deeds has, does it not, an auspicious aspect?

EUGENIE—Who's to gainsay it?

DOLMANCE—Well, as of this moment, it loses every aspect of crime; for, in order that what serves one by harming another be a crime, one should first have to demonstrate that the injured person is more important, more precious to Nature than the person who performs the injury and serves her; now, all individuals being of uniform importance in her eyes, 'tis impossible that she have a predilection for some one among them; hence, the deed that serves one person by causing suffering to another is of perfect indifference to Nature.

EUGENIE—But if the action were harmful to a very great quantity of individuals . . . and if it rewarded us with only a very small quantity of pleasure, would it not then be a frightful thing to execute it?

DOLMANCE—No more so, because there is no possible comparison between what others experience and what we sense; the heaviest dose of agony in others ought, assuredly, to be as naught to us, and the faintest quickening of pleasure, registered in us, does touch us; therefore, we should, at whatever the price, prefer this most minor excitation which enchants us, to the immense sum of others' miseries, which cannot affect us; but, on the contrary, should it happen that the singularity of our organs, some bizarre feature in our construction, renders agreeable to us the sufferings of our fellows, as sometimes occurs, who can doubt, then, that we should incontestably prefer anguish in others, which entertains us, to that anguish's absence, which would represent, for us, a kind of privation? The source of all our moral errors lies in the ridiculous acknowledgment of that tie of brotherhood the Christians invented in the age of their ill-fortune and sore distress. Constrained to beg pity from others, 'twas not unclever to claim that all men are brothers; how is one to refuse aid if this hypothesis be accepted? But its rational acceptance is impossible; are we not all born solitary, isolated? I say more: are we not come into the world all enemies, the one of the other, all in a state of perpetual and reciprocal warfare? Now, I ask whether such would be the situation if they did truly exist, this supposed tie of brotherhood and the virtues it enjoins? Are they really natural? Were they inspired in man by Nature's voice, men would be aware of them at birth. From that time onward, pity, good works, generosity, would be native virtues against which 'twould be impossible to defend oneself, and would render the primitive state of savage man totally contrary to what we observe it to be.

EUGENIE—Yet if, as you say, Nature caused man to be born alone, all independent of other men, you will at least grant me that his needs, bringing him together with other men, must necessarily have established some ties between them; whence blood relationships, ties of love too, of friendship, of gratitude: you will, I hope, respect those at least.

DOLMANCE—No more than the others, I am afraid; but let us analyze them, I should like to: a swift glance, Eugénie, at each one in particular. Would you say, for example, that the need to marry or to prolong my race or to arrange my fortune or insure my future must establish indissoluble or sacred ties with the object I ally myself to? Would it not, I ask you, be an absurdity to argue thus? So long as the act of coition lasts, I may, to be sure, continue in need of that object, in order to participate in the act; but once it is over and I am satisfied, what, I wonder, will attach the results of this commerce to me? These latter relationships were the results of the terror of parents who dreaded lest they be abandoned in old age, and the politic attentions they show us when we are in our infancy have no object but to make them deserving of the same consideration when they are become old. Let us no longer be the dupes of this rubbish: we owe nothing to our parents . . . not the least thing, Eugénie, and since it is far less for our sake than for their own they have labored, we may rightfully test them, even rid ourselves of them if their behavior annoys us; we ought to love them only if they comport themselves well with us, and then our tenderness toward them ought not to be one degree greater than what we might feel for other friends, because the rights of birth establish nothing, are basis to nothing, and, once they have been wisely scrutinized and with deliberation, we will surely find nothing there but reasons to hate those who, exclusively thoughtful of their own pleasure, have often given us nothing but an unhappy and unhealthy existence.

You mention, Eugénie, ties of love; may you never know them! Ah! for the happiness I wish you, may such a sentiment never approach your breast! What is love? One can only consider it, so it seems to me, as the effect upon us of a beautiful object's qualities; these effects distract us; they inflame us; were we to possess this object, all would be well with us; if 'tis impossible to have it, we are in despair. But what is the foundation of this sentiment? desire. What are this sentiment's consequences? madness. Let us confine ourselves to the cause and guarantee ourselves against the effects. The cause is to possess the object: spendid! let's strive to succeed, but using our head, not losing our wits; let's enjoy it when we've got it; let's console ourselves if we fail: a thousand other identical and often much superior objects exist to soothe our regrets and our pride: all men, all women resemble each other: no love resists the effects of sane reflection. O 'tis a very great cheat and a dupery, this intoxication which puts us in such a state that we see no more, exist no more save through this object insanely adored! Is this really to live? Is it not rather voluntarily to deprive oneself of all life's sweetness? Is it not to wish to linger in a burning fever which devours, consumes us, without affording us other than metaphysical joys, which bear such a likeness to the effects of madness? Were we always to love this adorable object, were it certain we should never have to quit it, 'twould still be an extravagance without doubt, but at least an excusable one. Does this happen, however? Has one many examples of these deathless liaisons, unions which are never dissolved or repudiated? A few months of doting and dalliance soon restores the object to its proper size and shape, and we blush to think of the incense we have squanderingly burned upon that altar, and often we come to wonder that it ever could have seduced us at all.

O voluptuous young women, deliver your bodies unto us as often and as much as you wish! Fuck, divert yourselves, that's the essential thing; but be quick to fly from love. There is none but physical good in it, said Buffon, and as a good philosopher he exercised his reason on an understanding of Nature. I repeat it, amuse yourselves; but love not at all; nor be any more concerned to make yourselves loved: to exhaust oneself in lamentation, waste in sighs, abase oneself in leering and oglings, pen billets-doux, 'tis not that which you must do; it is to fuck, to multiply and often change your fuckers, it is above all to oppose yourselves resolutely to enslavement by any one single person, because the outcome of constant love, binding you to him, would be to prevent you from giving yourself to someone else, a cruel selfishness which would soon become fatal to your pleasures. Women are not made for one single man; 'tis for men at large Nature created them. Listening only to this sacred voice, let them surrender themselves, indifferently, to all who want them: always whores, never mistresses, eschewing love, worshiping pleasure; it will be roses only they will discover in life's career; it will no longer be but flowers they proffer us! Ask, Eugénie, ask the charming woman who has so kindly consented to undertake your education, ask her what is to be done with a man after one has enjoyed him. (*In a lower voice, so as not to be heard by Augustin.*) Ask her if she would lift a finger to save this Augustin who, today, is the cause of her delights. Should it fall out that someone wished to steal him from her, she would take another, would think no more on this one and, soon weary of the new, would herself sacrifice him within two months' time, were new pleasures to be born of this maneuver.

MADAME DE SAINT-ANGE—Let my dear Eugénie be very sure that Dolmancé is describing the impulses of my heart, mine and that of every other woman, as if she were to unfold it to him herself.

DOLMANCE—The final part of my analysis treats the bonds of friendship and those of gratitude. We shall respect the former, very well, provided they remain useful to us; let us keep our friends as long as they serve us; forget them immediately we have nothing further from them; 'tis never but selfishly one should love people; to love them for themselves is nothing but dupery; Nature never inspires other movements in mankind's soul, other sentiments than those which ought to prove useful in some sort, good for something; nothing is more an egoist than Nature; then let us be egoists too, if we wish to live in harmony with her dictates. As for gratitude, Eugénie, 'tis doubtless the most feeble of all the bonds. Is it then for ourselves men are obliging to us? Not a bit of it, my dear; 'tis through ostentation, for the sake of pride. Is it not humiliating thus to become the toy of others' pride? Is it not yet more so to fall into indebtedness to them? Nothing is more burdensome than a kindness one has received. No middle way, no compromise: you have got to repay it or ready yourself for abuse. Upon proud spirits a good deed sits very heavily: it weighs upon them with such violence that the one feeling they exhale is hatred for their benefactors. What then, in your opinion, are now the ties which supply the isolation wherein Nature creates us? What are they, those which should establish relationships between men? By what title should we love them, those others, cherish them, prefer them to ourselves? By what right should we relieve them, who says that we must relieve them in misfortune? Where now in our souls is that cradle of the pretty and useless virtues of generosity, humanity, charity, all those enumerated in the absurd codes of a few idiotic religious doctrines, doctrines which, preached by impostors or by indigents, were invented to secure them their sustenance and toleration? Why, Eugénie, why do you yet acknowledge something sacred in men? Do you conceive some reasons for not always preferring yourself to them?

EUGENIE—What you say so thrills my heart that my mind can take no exception to it.

MADAME DE SAINT-ANGE—These precepts are grounded in Nature, Eugénie; the proof is that you approve them; freshly hatched from her womb, how could what you sense be the fruit of corruption?

EUGENIE—But if all the errors you speak of are in Nature, why do our laws oppose them?

DOLMANCE—Those laws, being forged for universal application, are in perpetual conflict with personal interest, just as personal interest is always in contradiction with the general interest. Good for society, our laws are very bad for the individuals whereof it is composed; for, if they one time protect the individual, they hinder, trouble, fetter him for three quarters of his life; and so the wise man, the man full of contempt for them, will be wary of them, as he is of reptiles and vipers which, although they wound or kill, are nevertheless sometimes useful to medicine; he will safeguard himself against the laws as he would against noxious beasts; he will shelter himself behind precautions, behind mysteries, the which, for prudence, is easily done. Should the fancy to execute a few crimes inflame your spirit, Eugénie, be very certain you may commit them peacefully in the company of your friend and me.

EUGENIE—Ah, the fancy is already in my heart!

MADAME DE SAINT-ANGE—What caprice agitates you, Eugénie? you may report it to us in confidence.

EUGENIE, *wild-eyed*—I want a victim.

MADAME DE SAINT-ANGE—And of what sex would you desire her to be?

EUGENIE—Of mine!

DOLMANCE—Well, Madame, are you content with your student? does she make sufficiently rapid progress?

EUGENIE, *as above*—A victim, my dearest, a victim! . . . Oh, God, that would cause my life's happiness! . . .

MADAME DE SAINT-ANGE—And what would you do with her?

EUGENIE—Everything! . . . everything! . . . all that could render her the most wretched of creatures. Oh, my dearest, my dearest, have pity on me! I can stand it no longer!

DOLMANCE—By God, what an imagination! . . . Come, Eugénie, you are delicious . . . come, let me bestow a thousand kisses upon you! (*He takes her in his arms.*) Look, Madame, do you see it? Do you see this libertine discharge *mentally*, without anyone having touched her? I must absolutely embugger her once again.

EUGENIE—And afterward will I have what I request?

DOLMANCE—Yes, mad creature! . . . yes, we assure you, you shall! . . .

EUGENIE—Oh, my friend, there is my ass! . . . do with it what you will! . . .

DOLMANCE—One moment, while I arrange this pleasure bout in a sufficiently lustful manner. (*As Dolmancé gives his orders, each person executes them, taking his post.*) Augustin, lie down on the bed; Eugénie, do you recline in his arms; while I sodomize her, I'll frig her clitoris with the head of Augustin's superb prick, and Augustin who must be sparing of his fuck will take good care not to discharge; the gentle Chevalier—who, without saying a word, softly frigs himself while listening to us—will have the kindness to arrange himself upon Eugénie's shoulders so as to expose his fine buttocks to my kisses: I'll frig him amain; so shall I have my engine in an ass and a prick in each hand, to pollute; and you, Madame, after having been your master, I want you to become mine: buckle on the most gigantic of your dildos. (*Madame de Saint-Ange opens a chest filled with a store of them, and our hero selects the most massive.*) Splendid! This, according to the label, is fourteen by ten; fit it about your loins, Madame, and spare me not.

MADAME DE SAINT-ANGE—Indeed, Dolmancé, you had best reconsider. I will cripple you with this device.

DOLMANCE—Fear not; push, my angel, penetrate: I'll not enter your dear Engénie's ass until your enormous member is well advanced into mine . . . and it is! it is! oh, little Jesus! . . . You propel me heavenward! . . . No pity, my lovely one . . . I tell you I am going to fuck your ass without preparations . . . oh, sweet God! magnificent ass! . . .

EUGENIE—Oh, my friend, you are tearing me. . . . at least prepare the way.

DOLMANCE—I'll do nothing of the sort, by God: half the pleasure's lost by these stupid attentions. Put yourself in mind of our principles, Eugénie: I labor in my behalf only: now victim for a moment, my lovely angel, soon you'll persecute in your turn. . . Ah, holy God, it enters! . . .

EUGENIE—You are putting me to death!

DOLMANCE—Ah God! I touch bottom! . . .

EUGENIE—Ah, do what you will, 'tis arrived . . . I feel nothing but pleasure! . . .

DOLMANCE—How I love to frig this huge prick on a virgin's clitoris! . . . You, Chevalier, show me a good ass. . . . Do I frig you well, libertine? . . . And you, Madame, do fuck me, fuck your slut . . . yes, I am she and wish to be . . . Eugénie, discharge, my angel, yes, discharge! . . . Despite himself, Augustin fills me with his fuck. . . . I receive the Chevalier's, mine goes to join him. . . . I resist no more. . . . Eugénie, wiggle your buttocks and grip my prick: I am going to jet a blazing fuck-stream deep into your entrails. . . . Ah! fucking bugger of a God! I die! (*He withdraws, the circle breaks.*) Behold, Madame, here's your little libertine full of fuck again; the entrance to her cunt is soaked with it; frig her, vigorously smite her clitoris all wet with sperm: 'tis one of the most delicious things that may be done.

EUGENIE, *palpitating*—Oh, my blessed one, what pleasure you give me! Ah, dear love, I burn with lubricity! (*The posture is assumed.*)

DOLMANCE—Chevalier, as 'tis you who'll deflower this lovely child, add your ministrations to those of your sister, that she may swoon in your arms, and strike the sodomite's attitude: I am going to embugger you while Augustin does the same to me. (*The disposition is effected.*)

LE CHEVALIER—Is my position satisfactory?

DOLMANCE—Your ass ever so gently raised, up with it, a fraction of an inch, my love; there, just so . . . without lubrication, Chevalier?

LE CHEVALIER—Why, bless my soul! as you damned well please; can I feel anything but pleasure in this delicious girl's womb! (*He kisses her, frigs her, burying a finger in her cunt while Madame de Saint-Ange strums Eugénie's clitoris.*)

DOLMANCE—As for myself, my dear, I, be assured of it, I take far more pleasure with you than with Eugénie; there is a immense difference between a boy's and girl's ass. . . . So bugger me, Augustin! what a bloody effort is required to get you to move!

AUGUSTIN—B'damn, Sir, it's because it's just been running and dripping a moment ago into this pretty little turtledove here and now you're wanting it to get right up for your bum there which really ain't so pretty,

DOLMANCE—Idiot! But why complain? 'Tis Mother Nature. Well, go on, trusty Augustin, go on with your indiscriminate penetrating, and when one day you have a little more experience, you will tell me whether one ass isn't worth thirty cunts. . . . Eugénie, deal fairly with the Chevalier; you are thoughtless of everyone but yourself; well, libertine, you are right; but in your own pleasure's interest, frig him, since he is to gather your first fruits.

EUGENIE—But I am frigging him, I do kiss him, I am going out of my head. . . . Aië! aië! aië! my friends, I can stand no more . . . pity my condition . . . I am dying . . . I discharge! Oh, God! I am in ecstasy! . . .

DOLMANCE—Now, as for myself, I have elected prudence and restraint: I wish merely to have this fine ass put me in form; the fuck that's being fired in me I am saving for Madame de Saint-Ange: 'tis wonderfully amusing to commence in one ass the operation one wishes to conclude in another. I say there, Chevalier, you seem nicely got up . . . shall we to the deflowering? . . .

EUGENIE—Oh, heavens! no, not by him, I'd perish from it; yours is smaller, Dolmancé: may it be you to whom I owe thanks for the operation, I beg of you!

DOLMANCE—'Tis out of the question, my angel; I've never fucked a cunt in my life and one cannot begin at my age. Your hymen belongs to the Chevalier: of us all here, he alone is worthy of its capture: do you not rob him of his just prize.

MADAME DE SAINT-ANGE—Refuse a maidenhead . . . as fresh, as pretty as this—for I defy anyone to say my Eugénie is not the loveliest girl in France—oh, Monsieur! Monsieur, indeed, that's what I call holding too closely to one's principles!

DOLMANCE—You say I am too scrupulous, Madame? 'Tis unkind. For there are multitudes of my colleagues, stricter in their worship than I, who most assuredly would not bugger you. . . . I, I've done it, and would do it again: it is not, thus, as you suspect, a question of carrying my worship to the point of fanaticism.

MADAME DE SAINT-ANGE—Well then Chevalier, the task is yours, proceed; but have a little care what you do; consider the narrowness of the channel you are going to navigate: what of the proportion between the contents and the container?

EUGENIE—Oh, 'twill kill me, I'm sure of it, 'tis inevitable. . . . But my furious desire to be fucked makes me chance it fearlessly. . . . Go on, penetrate, my dear, I abandon myself to you.

LE CHEVALIER, *taking a firm grip upon his rampant prick*— Fuck, yes! let it go in. . . . Sister, Dolmancé, each of you take one of her legs. . . . Ah, by God, what an enterprise! . . . Yes, yes, she must be split like a melon, halved, God and God again, yes, it's got to enter!

EUGENIE—Gently, gently, the pain is great. . . . (*She screams; tears roll down her cheeks.*) Help me! my good friend. . . . (*She struggles.*) No, I don't want him to do it! . . . I'll cry for help if you persist! . . .

LE CHEVALIER—Cry away as much as you please, little chit, I tell you it must go in even were it to shiver you into small pieces.

EUGENIE—What barbarity!

DOLMANCE—Fuck! is one expected to be a gentleman when one is stiff?

LE CHEVALIER—Ha! look! it's sunk . . . it's in! by God! . . . Fuck! there's the maidenhead blasted to the devil! . . . Look how it bleeds!

EUGENIE—Go on, tiger! . . . tear me to ribbons if you wish . . . I don't care a damn! . . . kiss me, butcher, I adore you! . . . Oh, 'tis nothing when it's inside: all the pains are forgot. . . . Woe unto girls who shy away from such an attack! . . . What tremendous pleasures they deny themselves at the cost of a little trouble! . . . Thrust! thrust! push! Chevalier, I am coming! . . . spray your fuck over the wounds and lacerations . . . drive it to the bottom of my womb . . . ah! suffering gives way to pleasure . . . I am ready to swoon! . . . (*The Chevalier discharges; while he fucked, Dolmancé toyed with his ass and balls, and Madame de Saint-Ange tickled Eugénie's clitoris. They dissolve their position.*)

DOLMANCE—'Twould be my opinion that, while the avenue is open, the little bitch might instantly be fucked by Augustin!

EUGENIE—By Augustin! . . . a prick of those dimensions! . . . ah, immediately! . . . While I am still bleeding! . . . Do you then wish to kill me?

MADAME DE SAINT-ANGE—Dear heart . . . kiss me, I sympathize with you . . . but sentence has been pronounced; there is no appeal, my dearest: you have got to submit to it.

AUGUSTIN—Ah, zounds! here I am, all ready: soon's it means sticking this bonny girl and I'd come, by God, all the way from Rome, on foot.

LE CHEVALIER, *grasping Augustin's mammoth device*—Look at it, Eugénie, look how it is erect . . . how worthy it is to replace me. . . .

EUGENIE—Oh merciful heaven, what a piece! . . . Oh, 'tis clear, you design my death! . . .

AUGUSTIN, *seizing Eugénie*—Oh no, Mam'selle, that's never killed anybody.

DOLMANCE—One instant, my fine boy, one instant: she must present her ass to me while you fuck her . . . yes, that's it, come hither, Madame; I promised to sodomize you, I'll keep my word; but situate yourself in such a way that as I fuck you, I can be within reach of Eugénie's fucker. And let the Chevalier flog me in the meantime. (*All is arranged.*)

EUGENIE—Oh fuck! he cracks me! . . . Go gently, great lout! . . . Ah, the bugger! he digs in! . . . there 'tis, the fucking-john! . . .

he's at the very bottom! . . . I'm dying! . . . Oh, Dolmancé, how you strike! . . . 'tis to ignite me before and behind; you're setting my buttocks afire!

DOLMANCE, *swinging his whip with all his strength*—You'll be afire . . . you'll burn, little bitch! . . . and you'll only discharge the more deliciously. How you frig her, Saint-Ange . . . let your deft fingers soothe the hurt that Augustin and I cause her! . . . But your anus contracts . . . I see it, Madame, I see it! we're going to come together. . . . Oh, 'tis I know not how divine thus to be, 'twixt brother and sister!

MADAME DE SAINT-ANGE, *to Dolmancé*—Fuck, my star, fuck! . . . Never do I believe I have had so much pleasure!

LE CHEVALIER—Dolmancé, let's change hands; be nimble: pass from my sister's ass to Eugénie's, so as to acquaint her with the intermediary's pleasures, and I will embugger my sister who meanwhile will shower upon your ass the very whip strokes wherewith you've just brought Eugénie's behind to blood.

DOLMANCE, *executing the proposal*—Agreed . . . there, my friend, hast ever seen a shift more cunningly effected?

EUGENIE—What! both of them on top of me, good heavens! . . . what will come next? I've really had enough of this oaf! . . . Ah, how much fuck this double pleasure is going to cost me! . . . it flows already. Without that sensual ejaculation, I believe I would be already dead. . . . Why, my dearest, you imitate me. . . . Oh, hear the bitch swear! . . . Discharge, Dolmancé, . . . discharge, my love . . . this fat peasant inundates me: he shoots to the depths of my entrails. . . . Oh, my good fuckers, what is this? Two at a time! Good Christ! . . . receive my fuck, dear companions, it conjoins itself with your own. . . . I am annihilated. . . . (*The attitudes are dissolved.*) Well, my dear, what think you of your scholar? . . . Am I enough of a whore now? . . . But what a state you do put me in . . . what an agitation! . . . Oh, yes, I swear, in my drunkenness, I swear I would have gone if necessary and got myself fucked in the middle of the street! . . .

DOLMANCE—How beautiful she is thus.

EUGENIE—You! I detest you: you refused me.

DOLMANCE—Could I contradict my dogmas?

EUGENIE—Very well, I forgive you, and I must respect the principles which lead us to wild conduct; how could I not acknowledge and adopt them, I who wish not to live save in crime? Let's sit down and chat a little; I'm exhausted. Continue my instruction, Dolmancé, and say something that will console me for the excesses to which I have given myself over; stifle my remorse; encourage me.

MADAME DE SAINT-ANGE—'Tis fair enough: as we say, a little theory must succeed practice: it is the means to make a perfect disciple.

DOLMANCE—Well then! Upon what subject, Eugénie, would you like to have a discussion?

EUGENIE—I should like to know whether manners are truly necessary in a governed society, whether their influence has any weight with the national genius.

DOLMANCE—Why, by God, I have something here with me. As I left home this morning I bought, outside the Palace of Equality, a little pamphlet, which if one can believe the title, ought surely to answer your question. . . . It's come straight from the press.

MADAME DE SAINT-ANGE—Let me see it. (*She reads:*) "Yet Another Effort, Frenchmen, If You Would Become Republicans." Upon my word, 'tis an unusual title: 'tis promising; Chevalier, you possess a fine organ, read it to us.

DOLMANCE—Unless I am mistaken, this should perfectly reply to Eugénie's queries.

EUGENIE—Assuredly!

MADAME DE SAINT-ANGE—Out with you, Augustin: this is not for you; but don't go too far; we'll ring when we want you back.

LE CHEVALIER—Well, I'll begin.

YET ANOTHER EFFORT,

FRENCHMEN,

IF YOU WOULD BECOME REPUBLICANS

RELIGION

I am about to put forward some major ideas; they will be heard and pondered. If not all of them please, surely a few will; in some sort, then, I shall have contributed to the progress of our age, and shall be content. We near our goal, but haltingly: I confess that I am disturbed by the presentiment that we are on the eve of failing once again to arrive there. Is it thought that goal will be attained when at last we have been given laws? Abandon the notion; for what should we, who have no religion, do with laws? We must have a creed, a creed befitting the republican character, something far removed from ever being able to resume the worship of Rome. In this age, when we are convinced that morals must be the basis of religion, and not religion of morals, we need a body of beliefs in keeping with our customs and habits, something that would be their necessary consequence, and that could, by lifting up the spirit, maintain it perpetually at the high level of this precious liberty, which today the spirit has made its unique idol.

Well, I ask, is it thinkable that the doctrine of one of Titus' slaves, of a clumsy histrionic from Judaea, be fitting to a free and warlike nation that has just regenerated itself? No, my fellow countrymen, no; you think nothing of the sort. If, to his misfortune, the Frenchman were to entomb himself in the grave of Christianity, then on one side the priests' pride, their tyranny, their despotism, vices forever cropping up in that impure horde, on the other side the baseness, the narrowness, the platitudes of dogma and mystery of this infamous and fabulous religion, would, by blunting the fine edge of the republican spirit, rapidly put about the Frenchman's neck the yoke which his vitality but yesterday shattered.

Let us not lose sight of the fact this puerile religion was among our tyrants' best weapons: one of its key dogmas was to *render unto Caesar that which is Caesar's*. However, we have dethroned

Caesar, we are no longer disposed to render him anything. Frenchmen, it would be in vain were you to suppose that your oath-taking clergy today is in any essential manner different from yesterday's non-juring clergy: there are inherent vices beyond all possibility of correction. Before ten years are out—utilizing the Christian religion, its superstitions, its prejudices—your priests, their pledges notwithstanding and though despoiled of their riches, are sure to reassert their empire over the souls they shall have undermined and captured; they shall restore the monarchy, because the power of kings has always reinforced that of the church; and your republican edifice, its foundations eaten away, shall collapse.

O you who have axes ready to hand, deal the final blow to the tree of superstition; be not content to prune its branches: uproot entirely a plant whose effects are so contagious. Well understand that your system of liberty and equality too rudely affronts the ministers of Christ's altars for there ever to be one of them who will either adopt it in good faith or give over seeking to topple it, if he is able to recover any dominion over consciences. What priest, comparing the condition to which he has been reduced with the one he formerly enjoyed, will not do his utmost to win back both the confidence and the authority he has lost? And how many feeble and pusillanimous creatures will not speedily become again the thralls of this cunning shavepate! Why is it imagined that the nuisances which existed before cannot be revived to plague us anew? In the Christian church's infancy, were priests less ambitious than they are today? You observe how far they advanced; to what do you suppose they owed their success if not to the means religion furnished them? Well, if you do not absolutely prohibit this religion, those who preach it, having yet the same means, will soon achieve the same ends.

Then annihilate forever what may one day destroy your work. Consider that the fruit of your labors being reserved for your grandchildren only, duty and probity command that you bequeath them none of those seeds of disaster which could mean for your descendants a renewal of the chaos whence we have with so much trouble just emerged. At the present moment our prejudices are weakening; the people have already abjured the Catholic absurdities; they have already suppressed the temples, sent the relics flying, and agreed that marriage is a mere civil undertaking; the smashed confessionals serve as public meeting places; the former faithful, deserting the apostolic banquet, leave the gods of flour dough to the mice. Frenchmen, an end to your waverings: all of Europe, one hand halfway raised to the blindfold over her eyes, expects that effort by which you must snatch it from her head. Make haste: *holy Rome* strains every nerve to repress your vigor; hurry, lest you give Rome time to secure her grip upon the few proselytes remaining to her. Unsparingly and recklessly smite off her proud and trembling head; and before two months the tree of liberty, overshadowing the wreckage of Peter's Chair, will soar victoriously above all the contemptible Christian vestiges and idols raised with such effrontery over the ashes of Cato and Brutus.

Frenchmen, I repeat it to you: Europe awaits her deliverance from *scepter* and *censer* alike. Know well that you cannot possibly liberate her from royal tyranny without at the same time breaking for her the fetters of religious superstition: the shackles of the one are too intimately linked to those of the other; let one of the two survive, and you cannot avoid falling subject to the other you have left intact. It is no longer before the knees of either an imaginary being or a vile impostor a republican must prostrate himself; his only gods must now be *courage* and *liberty*. Rome disappeared immediately Christianity was preached there, and France is doomed if she continues to revere it.

Let the absurd dogmas, the appalling mysteries, the impossible morality of this disgusting religion be examined with attention, and it will be seen whether it befits a republic. Do you honestly believe I would allow myself to be dominated by the opinion of a man I had just seen kneeling before the idiot priest of Jesus? No; certainly not! That eternally base fellow will eternally adhere, by dint of the baseness of his attitudes, to the atrocities of the *ancien régime;* as of the moment he were able to submit to the stupidities of a religion as abject as the one we are mad enough to acknowledge, he is no longer competent to dictate laws or transmit learning to me; I no longer see him as other than a slave to prejudice and superstition.

To convince ourselves, we have but to cast our eyes upon the handful of individuals who remain attached to our fathers' insensate worship: we will see whether they are not all irreconcilable enemies of the present system, we will see whether it is not amongst their numbers that all of that justly contemned caste of *royalists* and *aristocrats* is included. Let the slave of a crowned brigand grovel, if he pleases, at the feet of a plaster image; such an object is ready-made for his soul of mud. He who can serve kings must adore gods; but we, Frenchmen, but we, my fellow countrymen, we, rather than once more crawl beneath such contemptible traces, we would die a thousand times over rather than abase ourselves anew! Since we believe a cult necessary, let us imitate the Romans: actions, passions, heroes—those were the objects of their respect. Idols of this sort elevated the soul, electrified it, and more: they communicated to the spirit the virtues of the respected being. Minerva's devotee coveted wisdom. Courage found its abode in his heart who worshiped Mars. Not a single one of that great people's gods was deprived of energy; all of them infused into the spirit of him who venerated them the fire with which they were themselves ablaze; and each Roman hoped someday to be himself worshiped, each aspired to become as great at least as the deity he took for a model. But what, on the contrary, do we find in Christianity's futile gods? What, I want to know, what does this idiot's religion offer you?[8] Does the grubby Nazarene fraud inspire any great thoughts in you? His foul, nay repellent mother, the shameless Mary—does she excite any virtues? And do you discover in the saints who garnish the Christian Elysium, any example of greatness, of either heroism or virtue? So alien to lofty conceptions is this miserable belief, that no artist can employ its attributes in the monuments he raises; even in Rome itself, most of the embellishments of the papal palaces have their origins in paganism, and as long as this world shall continue, paganism alone will arouse the verve of great men.

Shall we find more motifs of grandeur in pure theism? Will acceptance of a chimera infuse into men's minds the high degree

---

[8] A careful inspection of this religion will reveal to anyone that the impieties with which it is filled come in part from the Jews' ferocity and innocence, and in part from the indifference and confusion of the Gentiles; instead of appropriating what was good in what the ancient peoples had to offer, the Christians seem only to have formed their doctrine from a mixture of the vices they found everywhere.

of energy essential to republican virtues, and move men to cherish and practice them? Let us imagine nothing of the kind; we have bid farewell to that phantom and, at the present time, atheism is the one doctrine of all those prone to reason. As we gradually proceeded to our enlightenment, we came more and more to feel that, motion being inherent in matter, the prime mover existed only as an illusion, and that all that exists essentially having to be in motion, the motor was useless; we sensed that this chimerical divinity, prudently invented by the earliest legislators, was, in their hands, simply one more means to enthrall us, and that, reserving unto themselves the right to make the phantom speak, they knew very well how to get him to say nothing but what would shore up the preposterous laws whereby they declared they served us. Lycurgus, Numa, Moses, Jesus Christ, Mohammed, all these great rogues, all these great thought-tyrants, knew how to associate the divinities they fabricated with their own boundless ambition; and, certain of captivating the people with the sanction of those gods, they were always studious, as everyone knows, either to consult them exclusively about, or to make them exclusively respond to, what they thought likely to serve their own interests.

Therefore, today let us equally despise both that empty god impostors have celebrated, and all the farce of religious subtleties surrounding a ridiculous belief: it is no longer with this bauble that free men are to be amused. Let the total extermination of cults and denominations therefore enter into the principles we broadcast throughout all Europe. Let us not be content with breaking scepters; we will pulverize the idols forever: there is never more than a single step from superstition to royalism.[9] Does anyone doubt it? Then let him understand once and for all, that in every age one of the primary concerns of kings has been to maintain the dominant religion as one of the political bases that best sustains the throne. But, since it is shattered, that throne, and since it is,

---

[9] Inspect the history of every race: never will you find one of them changing the government it has for a monarchical system, save by reason of the brutalization or the superstition that grips them; you will see kings always upholding religion, and religion sanctifying kings. One knows the story of the steward and the cook: *Hand me the pepper; I'll pass you the butter*. Wretched mortals! are you then destined forever to resemble these two rascals' master?

happily, shattered for all time, let us have not the slightest qualm about also demolishing the thing that supplied its plinth.

Yes, citizens, religion is incompatible with the libertarian system; you have sensed as much. Never will a free man stoop to Christianity's gods; never will its dogmas, its rites, its mysteries, or its morals suit a republican. One more effort; since you labor to destroy all the old foundations, do not permit one of them to survive, for let but one endure, 'tis enough, the rest will be restored. And how much more certain of their revival must we not be if the one you tolerate is positively the source and cradle of all the others! Let us give over thinking religion can be useful to man; once good laws are decreed unto us, we will be able to dispense with religion. But, they assure us, the people stand in need of one; it amuses them, they are soothed by it. Fine! Then, if that be the case, give us a religion proper to free men; give us the gods of paganism. We shall willingly worship Jupiter, Hercules, Pallas; but we have no use for a dimensionless god who nevertheless fills everything with his immensity, an omnipotent god who never achieves what he wills, a supremely good being who creates malcontents only, a friend of order in whose government everything is in turmoil. No, we want no more of a god who is at loggerheads with Nature, who is the father of confusion, who moves man at the moment man abandons himself to horrors; such a god makes us quiver with indignation, and we consign him forever to the oblivion whence the infamous Robespierre wished to call him forth.[10]

Frenchmen, in the stead of that unworthy phantom, we will substitute the imposing simulacra that rendered Rome mistress of the earth; let us treat every Christian image as we have the tokens of monarchy. There where once tyrants sat we have mounted emblems of liberty; in like manner we will place effigies of great men on the pedestals once occupied by statues of the knaves Christianity adored.[11] Let us cease to entertain doubts as to the effect of atheism

---

[10] All religions are agreed in exalting the divinity's wisdom and power; but as soon as they expose his conduct, we find nothing but imprudence, weakness, and folly. God, they say, created the world for himself, and up until the present time his efforts to make it honor him have proven unsuccessful; God created us to worship him, and our days are spent mocking him! Unfortunate fellow, that God!

[11] We are only speaking here of those great men whose reputation has been for a long while secure.

in the country: have not the peasants felt the necessity of the annihilation of the Catholic cult, so contradictory to the true principles
of freedom? Have they not watched undaunted, and without sorrow or pain, their altars and presbyteries battered to bits? Ah! rest
assured, they will renounce their ridiculous god in the same way.
The statues of Mars, of Minerva, and of Liberty will be set up in
the most conspicuous places in the villages; holidays will be celebrated there every year; the prize will be decreed to the worthiest
citizen. At the entrance to a secluded wood, Venus, Hymen, and
Love, erected beneath a rustic temple, will receive lovers' homages;
there, by the hand of the Graces, Beauty will crown Constancy.
More than mere loving will be required in order to pose one's
candidacy for the tiara; it will be necessary to have merited love.
Heroism, capabilities, humaneness, largeness of spirit, a proven
civism—those are the credentials the lover shall be obliged to
present at his mistress' feet, and they will be of far greater value
than the titles of birth and wealth a fool's pride used to require.
Some virtues at least will be born of this worship, whereas nothing
but crimes come of that other we had the weakness to profess. This
worship will ally itself to the liberty we serve; it will animate,
nourish, inflame liberty, whereas theism is in its essence and in its
nature the most deadly enemy of the liberty we adore.

Was a drop of blood spilled when the pagan idols were
destroyed under the Eastern Empire? The revolution, prepared
by the stupidity of a people become slaves again, was accomplished
without the slightest hindrance or outcry. Why do we dread the
work of philosophy as more painful than that of despotism? It is
only the priests who still hold the people, whom you hesitate to
enlighten, captive at the feet of their imaginary god: take the
priests from the people, and the veil will fall away naturally. Be
persuaded that these people, a good deal wiser than you suppose
them, once rid of tyranny's irons, will soon also be rid of superstition's. You are afraid of the people unrestrained—how ridiculous! Ah, believe me, citizens, the man not to be checked by the
material sword of justice will hardly be halted by the moral fear
of hell's torments, at which he has laughed since childhood; in a
word, many crimes have been committed as a consequence of your
theism, but never has it prevented a single one.

If it is true that passions blind, that their effect is to cloud our eyes to dangers that surround us, how may we suppose that those dangers which are remote, such as the punishments announced by your god, can successfully dispel the cloud not even the blade of the law itself, constantly suspended above the passions, is able to penetrate? If then it is patently clear that this supplementary check imposed by the idea of a god becomes useless, if it is demonstrated that by its other effects it is dangerous, then I wish to know, to what use can it be put, and from what motives should we lend our support in order to prolong its existence?

Is someone about to tell me that we are not yet mature enough to consolidate our revolution in so brilliant a manner? Ah, my fellow citizens, the road we took in '89 has been much more difficult than the one still ahead of us, and we have little yet to do to conquer the opinion we have been harrying since the time of the overwhelming of the Bastille. Let us firmly believe that a people wise enough and brave enough to drag an impudent monarch from the heights of grandeur to the foot of the scaffold, a people that, in these last few years, has been able to vanquish so many prejudices and sweep away so many ridiculous impediments, will be sufficiently wise and brave to terminate the affair and in the interests of the republic's well-being, abolish a mere phantom after having successfully beheaded a real king.

Frenchmen, only strike the initial blows; your State education will then see to the rest. Get promptly to the task of training the youth, it must be amongst your most important concerns; above all, build their education upon a sound ethical basis, the ethical basis that was so neglected in your religious education. Rather than fatigue your children's young organs with deific stupidities, replace them with excellent social principles; instead of teaching them futile prayers which, by the time they are sixteen, they will glory in having forgotten, let them be instructed in their duties toward society; train them to cherish the virtues you scarcely ever mentioned in former times and which, without your religious fables, are sufficient for their individual happiness; make them sense that this happiness consists in rendering others as fortunate as we desire to be ourselves. If you repose these truths upon Christian chimeras, as you so foolishly used to do, scarcely will your pupils have detected the absurd futility of its foundations than they will overthrow the entire edifice, and they will become bandits for the simple reason they believe the religion they have toppled forbids them to be bandits. On the other hand, if you make them sense the necessity of virtue, uniquely because their happiness depends upon it, egoism will turn them into honest people, and this law which dictates their behavior to men will always be the surest, the soundest of all. Let there then be the most scrupulous care taken to avoid mixing religious fantasies into this State education. Never lose sight of the fact it is free men we wish to form, not the wretched worshipers of a god. Let a simple philosopher introduce these new pupils to the inscrutable but wonderful sublimities of Nature; let him prove to them that awareness of a god, often highly dangerous to men, never contributed to their happiness, and that they will not be happier for acknowledging as a cause of what they do not understand, something they well understand even less; that it is far less essential to inquire into the workings of Nature than to enjoy her and obey her laws; that these laws are as wise as they are simple; that they are written in the hearts of all men; and that it is but necessary to interrogate that heart to discern its impulse. If they wish absolutely that you speak to them of a creator, answer that things always having been what now they are, never having had a beginning and never going to have an end, it thus becomes as useless as impossible for man to be able to trace things back to an imaginary origin which would explain nothing and do not a jot of good. Tell them that men are incapable of obtaining true notions of a being who does not make his influence felt on one of our senses.

All our ideas are representations of objects that strike us: what is to represent to us the idea of a god, who is plainly an idea without object? Is not such an idea, you will add when talking to them, quite as impossible as effects without causes? Is an idea without prototype anything other than an hallucination? Some scholars, you will continue, assure us that the idea of a god is innate, and that mortals already have this idea when in their mothers' bellies. But, you will remark, that is false; every principle is a judgment, every judgment the outcome of experience, and experience is only acquired by the exercise of the senses; whence it follows that religious principles bear upon nothing whatever and are not in the slightest innate. How, you will go on, how have they been able to convince rational beings that the thing most difficult to understand is the most vital to them? It is that mankind has been terrorized; it is that when one is afraid one ceases to reason; it is, above all, that we have been advised to mistrust reason and defy it; and that, when the brain is disturbed, one believes anything and examines nothing. Ignorance and fear, you will repeat to them, ignorance and fear—those are the twin bases of every religion.

Man's uncertainty with respect to his god is, precisely, the cause for his attachment to his religion. Man's fear in dark places is as much physical as moral; fear becomes habitual in him, and is changed into need: he would believe he were lacking something even were he to have nothing more to hope for or dread. Next, return to the utilitarian value of morals: apropos of this vast subject, give them many more examples than lessons, many more demonstrations than books, and you will make good citizens of them: you will turn them into fine warriors, fine fathers, fine husbands: you will fashion men that much more devoted to their country's liberty, whose minds will be forever immune to servility, forever hostile to servitude, whose genius will never be troubled by any religious terror. And then true patriotism will shine in every spirit, and will reign there in all its force and purity, because it will become the sovereign sentiment there, and no alien notion will dilute or cool its energy; then your second generation will be sure, reliable, and your own work, consolidated by it, will go on to become the law of the universe. But if, through fear or faintheartedness, these counsels are ignored, if the foundations of the edifice we thought we destroyed are left intact, what then will happen? They will rebuild upon these foundations, and will set thereupon the same colossi, with this difference, and it will be a cruel one: the new structures will be cemented with such strength that neither your generation nor ensuing ones will avail against them.

Let there be no doubt of it: religions are the cradles of despotism: the foremost amongst all the despots was a priest: the first king and the first emperor of Rome, Numa and Augustus, associated themselves, the one and the other, with the sacerdotal; Constantine and Clovis were rather abbots than sovereigns; Heliogabalus was priest of the sun. At all times, in every century, every age, there has been such a connection between despotism and religion that it is infinitely apparent and demonstrated a thousand times over, that in destroying one, the other must be undermined, for the simple reason that the first will always put the law into the service of the second. I do not, however, propose either massacres or expulsions. Such dreadful things have no place in the enlightened mind. No, do not assassinate at all, do not expel at all; these are royal atrocities, or the brigands' who imitate kings; it is not at all by acting as they that you will force men to look with horror upon them who practiced those crimes. Let us reserve the employment of force for the idols; ridicule alone will suffice for those who serve them: Julian's sarcasm wrought greater damage to Christianity than all Nero's tortures. Yes, we shall destroy for all time any notion of a god, and make soldiers of his priests; a few of them are already; let them keep to this trade, soldiering, so worthy of a republican; but let them give us no more of their chimerical being nor of his nonsense-filled religion, the single object of our scorn.

Let us condemn the first of those blessed charlatans who comes to us to say a few more words either of god or of religion, let us condemn him to be jeered at, ridiculed, covered with filth in all the public squares and marketplaces in France's largest cities: imprisonment for life will be the reward of whosoever falls a second time into the same error. Let the most insulting blasphemy, the most atheistic works next be fully and openly authorized, in order to complete the extirpation from the human heart and memory of those appalling pastimes of our childhood; let there be put in circulation the writings most capable of finally illuminating the Europeans upon a matter so important, and let a considerable prize, to be bestowed by the Nation, be awarded to him who, having said and demonstrated everything upon this score, will leave to his countrymen no more than a scythe to mow the land clean of all those phantoms, and a steady heart to hate them. In six months, the whole will be done; your infamous god will be as naught, and all that without ceasing to be just, jealous of the esteem of others without ceasing to be honest men; for it will have been sensed that the real friend of his country must in no way be led about by chimeras, as is the slave of kings; that it is not, in a word, either the frivolous hope of a better world nor fear of the greatest ills

Nature sends us that must lead a republican, whose only guide is virtue and whose one restraint is conscience.

MANNERS

After having made it clear that theism is in no wise suitable to a republican government, it seems to me necessary to prove that French manners are equally unsuitable to it. This article is the more crucial, for the laws to be promulgated will issue from manners, and will mirror them.

Frenchmen, you are too intelligent to fail to sense that new government will require new manners. That the citizens of a free State conduct themselves like a despotic king's slaves is unthinkable: the differences of their interests, of their duties, of their relations amongst one another essentially determine an entirely different manner of behaving in the world; a crowd of minor faults and of little social indelicacies, thought of as very fundamental indeed under the rule of kings whose expectations rose in keeping with the need they felt to impose curbs in order to appear respectable and unapproachable to their subjects, are due to become as nothing with us; other crimes with which we are acquainted under the names of regicide and sacrilege, in a system where kings and religion will be unknown, in the same way must be annihilated in a republican State. In according freedom of conscience and of the press, consider, citizens—for it is practically the same thing—whether freedom of action must not be granted too: excepting direct clashes with the underlying principles of government, there remain to you it is impossible to say how many fewer crimes to punish, because in fact there are very few criminal actions in a society whose foundations are liberty and equality. Matters well weighed and things closely inspected, only that is really criminal which rejects the law; for Nature, equally dictating vices and virtues to us, in reason of our constitution, yet more philosophically, in reason of the need Nature has of the one and the other, what she inspires in us would become a very reliable gauge by which to adjust exactly what is good and bad. But, the better to develop my thoughts upon so important a question, we will classify the different acts in man's life that until the present it has pleased us to call criminal, and we will next square them to the true obligations of a republican.

In every age, the duties of man have been considered under the following three categories:

1. Those his conscience and his credulity impose upon him, with what regards a supreme being;
2. Those he is obliged to fulfill toward his brethren;
3. Finally, those that relate only to himself.

The certainty in which we must be that no god meddles in our affairs and that, as necessary creatures of Nature, like plants and animals, we are here because it would be impossible for us not to be—, this unshakable certainty, it is clear enough, at one stroke erases the first group of duties, those, I wish to say, toward the divinity to which we erroneously believe ourselves beholden; and with them vanish all religious crimes, all those comprehended under the indefinite names of *impiety, sacrilege, blasphemy, atheism,* etc., all those, in brief, which Athens so unjustly punished in Alcibiades, and France in the unfortunate Labarre. If there is anything extravagant in this world it is to see men, in whom only shallowness of mind and poverty of ideas give rise to a notion of god and to what this god expects of them, nevertheless wish to determine what pleases and what angers their imagination's ridiculous phantom. It would hence not be merely to tolerate indifferently each of the cults that I should like to see us limit ourselves; I should like there to be perfect freedom to deride them all; I should like men, gathered in no matter what temple to invoke the eternal who wears their image, to be seen as so many comics in a theater, at whose antics everyone may go to laugh. Regarded in any other light, religions become serious, and then important once again; they will soon stir up and patronize opinions, and no sooner will people fall to disputing over religions than some will be beaten into favoring religions.[12] Equality

---

12 Each nation declares its religion the best of all and relies, to persuade one of it, upon an endless number of proofs not only in disagreement with one another, but nearly all contradictory. In our profound ignorance, what is the one which may please god, supposing now that there is a god? We should, if we are wise, either protect them all and equally, or proscribe them all in the same way; well, to proscribe them is certainly the surer, since we have the moral assurance that all are mummeries, no one of which can be more pleasing than another to a god who does not exist.

once wrecked by the preference or protection tendered one of them, the government will soon disappear, and out of the reconstituted *theocracy* the *aristocracy* will be reborn in a trice. I cannot repeat it to you too often: no more gods, Frenchmen, no more gods, lest under their fatal influence you wish to be plunged back into all the horrors of despotism; but it is only by jeering that you will destroy them; all the dangers they bring in their wake will instantly be revived en masse if you pamper or ascribe any consequence to them. Carried away by anger, you overthrow their idols? Not for a minute; have a bit of sport with them, and they will crumble to bits; once withered, the opinion will collapse of its own accord.

I trust I have said enough to make plain that no laws ought to be decreed against religious crimes, for that which offends an illusion offends nothing, and it would be the height of inconsistency to punish those who outrage or who despise a creed or a cult whose priority to all others is established by no evidence whatsoever. No, that would necessarily be to exhibit a partiality and, consequently, to influence the scales of equality, that foremost law of your new government.

We move on to the second class of man's duties, those which bind him to his fellows; this is of all the classes the most extensive.

Excessively vague upon man's relations with his brothers, Christian morals propose bases so filled with sophistries that we are completely unable to accept them, since, if one is pleased to erect principles, one ought scrupulously to guard against founding them upon sophistries. This absurd morality tells us to love our neighbor as ourselves. Assuredly, nothing would be more sublime were it ever possible for what is false to be beautiful. The point is not at all to love one's brethren as oneself, since that is in defiance of all the laws of Nature, and since hers is the sole voice which must direct all the actions in our life; it is only a question of loving others as brothers, as friends given us by Nature, and with whom we should be able to live much better in a republican State, wherein the disappearance of distances must necessarily tighten the bonds.

May humanity, fraternity, benevolence prescribe our reciprocal obligations, and let us individually fulfill them with the simple degree of energy Nature has given us to this end; let us do so without blaming, and above all without punishing, those who, of chillier temper or more acrimonious humor, do not notice in these yet very touching social ties all the sweetness and gentleness others discover therein; for, it will be agreed, to seek to impose universal laws would be a palpable absurdity: such a proceeding would be as ridiculous as that of the general who would have all his soldiers dressed in a uniform of the same size; it is a terrible injustice to require that men of unlike character all be ruled by the same law: what is good for one is not at all good for another.

That we cannot devise as many laws as there are men must be admitted; but the laws can be lenient, and so few in number, that all men, of whatever character, can easily observe them. Furthermore, I would demand that this small number of laws be of such a sort as to be adaptable to all the various characters; they who formulate the code should follow the principle of applying more or less, according to the person in question. It has been pointed out that there are certain virtues whose practice is impossible for certain men, just as there are certain remedies which do not agree with certain constitutions. Now, would it not be to carry your injustice beyond all limits were you to send the law to strike the man incapable of bowing to the law? Would your iniquity be any less here than in a case where you sought to force the blind to distinguish amongst colors?

From these first principles there follows, one feels, the necessity to make flexible, mild laws and especially to get rid forever of the atrocity of capital punishment, because the law which attempts a man's life is impractical, unjust, inadmissible. Not, and it will be clarified in the sequel, that we lack an infinite number of cases where without offense to Nature (and this I shall demonstrate), men have freely taken one another's lives, simply exercising a prerogative received from their common mother; but it is impossible for the law to obtain the same privileges, since the law, cold and impersonal, is a total stranger to the passions which are able to justify in man the cruel act of murder. Man receives his impressions from Nature, who is able to forgive him this act; the law, on the contrary, always opposed as it is to Nature and receiving nothing from her, cannot be authorized to permit itself the same extravagances: not having the same motives, the law cannot have the same rights. Those are wise and delicate distinctions which escape many people, because very few of them reflect; but they will be grasped and retained by the instructed to whom I recommend them, and will, I hope, exert some influence upon the new code being readied for us.

The second reason why the death penalty must be done away with is that it has never repressed crime; for crime is every day committed at the foot of the scaffold. This punishment is to be got rid of, in a word, because it would be difficult to conceive of a poorer calculation than this, by which a man is put to death for having killed another: under the present arrangement the obvious result is not one man the less but, of a sudden, two; such arithmetic is in use only amongst headsmen and fools. However all that may be, the injuries we can work against our brothers may be reduced to four types: *calumny; theft;* the crimes which, caused by *impurity,* may in a disagreeable sense affect others; and *murder.*

All these were acts considered of the highest importance under the monarchy; but are they quite so serious in a republican State? That is what we are going to analyze with the aid of philosophy's torch, for by its light alone may such an inquiry be undertaken. Let no one tax me with being a dangerous innovator; let no one say that by my writings I seek to blunt the remorse in evildoers' hearts, that my humane ethics are wicked because they augment those same evildoers' penchant for crime. I wish formally to certify here and now, that I have none of these perverse intentions; I set forth the ideas which, since the age when I first began to reason, have identified themselves in me, and to whose expression and realization the infamous despotism of tyrants has been opposed for uncounted centuries. So much the worse for those susceptible to corruption by any idea; so much the worse for them who fasten upon naught but the harmful in philosophic opinions, who are likely to be corrupted by everything. Who knows? They may have been poisoned by reading Seneca and Charron. It is not to them I speak; I address myself only to people capable of hearing me out, and they will read me without any danger.

It is with utmost candor I confess that I have never considered calumny an evil, and especially in a government like our own, under which all of us, bound closer together, nearer one to the other, obviously have a greater interest in becoming acquainted with one another. Either one or the other: calumny attaches to a truly evil man, or it falls upon a virtuous creature. It will be agreed that, in the first case, it makes little difference if one imputes a little more evil to a man known for having done a great deal of it; perhaps indeed the evil which does not exist will bring to light evil which does, and there you have him, the malefactor, more fully exposed than ever before.

We will suppose now that an unwholesome influence reigns over Hanover, but that in repairing to that city where the air is insalubrious, I risk little worse than a bout of fever; may I reproach the man who, to prevent me from going to Hanover, tells me that one perishes upon arriving there? No, surely not; for, by using a great evil to frighten me, he spared me a lesser one.

If, on the contrary, a virtuous man is calumniated, let him not be alarmed; he need but exhibit himself, and all the calumniator's venom will soon be turned back upon the latter. For such a person, calumny is merely a test of purity whence his virtue emerges more resplendent than ever. As a matter of fact, his individual ordeal may profit the cause of virtue in the republic, and add to its sum; for this virtuous and sensitive man, stung by the injustice done him, will apply himself to the cultivation of still greater virtue; he will want to overcome this calumny from which he thought himself sheltered, and his splendid actions will acquire a correspondingly greater degree of energy. Thus, in the first instance, the calumniator produces quite favorable results by inflating the vices of the dangerous object of his attacks; in the second, the results achieved are excellent, for virtue is obliged to offer itself to us entire.

Well now, I am at a loss to know for what reason the calumniator deserves your fear, especially under a regime where it is essential to identify the wicked, and to augment the energy of the good. Let us hence very carefully avoid any declarations prejudicial to calumny; we will consider it both a lantern and a stimulant, and in either case something highly useful. The legislator, all of whose ideas must be as large as the work he undertakes is great, must never be concerned with the effect of that crime which strikes only the individual. It is the general, overall effect he must study; and when in this manner he observes the effects calumny produces, I defy him to find anything punishable in it. I defy him to find any shadow or hint of justice in the law that would punish it; our legislator becomes the man of greatest justice and integrity if, on the contrary, he encourages and rewards it.

Theft is the second of the moral offenses whose examination we proposed.

If we glance at the history of ancient times, we will see theft permitted, nay, recompensed in all the Greek republics; Sparta and Lacedaemon openly favored it; several other peoples regarded it as a virtue in a warrior; it is certain that stealing nourishes courage, strength, skill, tact, in a word, all the virtues useful to a republican system and consequently to our own. Lay partiality aside, and answer me: is theft, whose effect is to distribute wealth more evenly, to be branded as a wrong in our day, under our government which aims at equality? Plainly, the answer is no: it furthers equality and, what is more, renders more difficult the conservation of property. There was once a people who punished not the thief but him who allowed himself to be robbed, in order to teach him to care for his property. This brings us to reflections of a broader scope.

God forbid that I should here wish to assail the pledge to respect property the Nation has just given; but will I be permitted some remarks upon the injustice of this pledge? What is the spirit of the vow taken by all a nation's individuals? Is it not to maintain a perfect equality amongst citizens, to subject them all equally to the law protecting the possessions of all? Well, I ask you now whether that law is truly just which orders the man who has nothing to respect another who has everything? What are the elements of the social contract? Does it not consist in one's yielding a little of his freedom and of his wealth in order to assure and sustain the preservation of each?

Upon those foundations all the laws repose; they justify the punishments inflicted upon him who abuses his liberty; in the same way, they authorize the imposition of conditions; these latter prevent a citizen from protesting when these things are demanded of him, because he knows that by means of what he gives, the rest of what he has is safeguarded for him; but, once again, by what right will he who has nothing be enchained by an agreement which protects only him who has everything? If, by your pledge, you perform an act of equity in protecting the property of the rich, do you not commit one of unfairness in requiring this pledge of the owner who owns nothing? What advantage does the latter derive from your pledge? and how can you expect him to swear to something exclusively beneficial to someone who, through his wealth, differs so greatly from him? Certainly, nothing is more unjust: an oath must have an equal effect upon all the individuals who pronounce it; that it bind him who has no interest in its maintenance is impossible, because it would no longer be a pact amongst free men; it would be the weapon of the strong against the weak, against whom the latter would have to be in incessant revolt. Well, such, exactly, is the situation created by the pledge to respect property the Nation has just required all the citizens to subscribe to under oath; by it only the rich enchain the poor, the rich alone benefit from a bargain into which the poor man enters so thoughtlessly, failing to see that through this oath wrung from his good faith, he engages himself to do a thing that cannot be done with respect to himself.

Thus convinced, as you must be, of this barbarous inequality, do not proceed to worsen your injustice by punishing the man who has nothing for having dared to filch something from the man who has everything: your inequitable pledge gives him a greater right to it than ever. In driving him to perjury by forcing him to make a promise which, for him, is absurd, you justify all the crimes to which this perjury will impel him; it is not for you to punish something for which you have been the cause. I have no need to say more to make you sense the terrible cruelty of chastising thieves. Imitate the wise law of the people I spoke of just a moment ago; punish the man neglectful enough to let himself be robbed; but proclaim no kind of penalty against robbery. Consider whether your pledge does not authorize the act, and whether he who commits it does any more than put himself in harmony with the most sacred of Nature's movements, that of preserving one's own existence at no matter whose expense.

The transgressions we are considering in this second class of man's duties toward his fellows include actions for whose undertaking libertinage may be the cause; among those which are pointed to as particularly incompatible with approved behavior are *prostitution*, *incest*, *rape*, and *sodomy*. We surely must not for one moment doubt that all those known as moral crimes, that is to say, all acts of the sort to which those we have just cited belong, are of total inconsequence under a government whose sole duty consists in preserving, by whatever may be the means, the form essential to its continuance: there you have a republican government's unique morality. Well, the republic being permanently menaced from the outside by the despots surrounding it, the means to its preservation cannot be imagined as *moral means,* for the republic will preserve itself only by war, and nothing is less moral than war. I ask how one will be able to demonstrate that in a state rendered *immoral* by its obligations, it is essential that the individual be *moral?* I will go further: it is a very good thing he is not. The Greek lawgivers perfectly appreciated the capital necessity of corrupting the member-citizens in order that, their *moral dissolution* coming into conflict with the establishment and its values, there would result the *insurrection* that is always indispensable to a political system of perfect happiness which, like republican government, must necessarily excite the hatred and envy of all its foreign neighbors. Insurrection, thought these sage legislators, is not at all a *moral* condition; however, it has got to be a republic's permanent condition. Hence it would be no less absurd than dangerous to require that those who are to insure the perpetual *immoral* subversion of the established order themselves be *moral* beings: for the state of a moral man is one of tranquillity and peace, the state of an *immoral* man is one of perpetual unrest that pushes him to, and identifies him with, the necessary insurrection in which the republican must always keep the government of which he is a member.

We may now enter into detail and begin by analyzing modesty, that fainthearted negative impulse of contradiction to impure affections. Were it among Nature's intentions that man be modest, assuredly she would not have caused him to be born naked; unnumbered peoples, less degraded by civilization than we, go about naked and feel no shame on that account; there can be no doubt that the custom of dressing has had its single origin in harshness of climate and the coquetry of women who would rather provoke desire and secure to themselves its effects than have it caused and satisfied independently of themselves. They further reckoned that Nature having created them not without blemishes, they would be far better assured of all the means needed to please by concealing these flaws behind adornments; thus modesty, far from being a virtue, was merely one of corruption's earliest consequences, one of the first devices of female guile.

Lycurgus and Solon, fully convinced that immodesty's results are to keep the citizen in the *immoral* state indispensable to the mechanics of republican government, obliged girls to exhibit themselves naked at the theater.[13] Rome imitated the example: at the games of Flora they danced naked; the greater part of pagan mysteries were celebrated thus; among some peoples, nudity even passed for a virtue. In any event, immodesty is born of lewd inclinations; what comes of these inclinations comprises the alleged criminality we are discussing, of which prostitution is the foremost effect.

Now that we have got back upon our feet and broken with the host of prejudices that held us captive; now that, brought closer to Nature by the quantity of prejudices we have recently obliterated, we listen only to Nature's voice, we are fully convinced that if anything were criminal, it would be to resist the penchants she inspires in us, rather than to come to grips with them. We are persuaded that lust, being a product of those penchants, is not to be stifled or legislated against, but that it is, rather, a matter of arranging for the means whereby passion may be satisfied in peace. We must hence undertake to introduce order into this sphere of affairs, and to establish all the security necessary so that, when need sends the citizen near the objects of lust, he can give himself over to doing with them all that his passions demand, without ever being hampered by anything, for there is no moment in the life of man when liberty in its whole amplitude is so important to him. Various stations, cheerful, sanitary, spacious, properly furnished and in every respect safe, will be erected in divers points in each city; in them, all sexes, all ages, all creatures possible will be offered to the caprices of the libertines who shall come to divert themselves, and the most

---

13 It has been said the intention of these legislators was, by dulling the passion men experienced for a naked girl, to render more active the one men sometimes experience for their own sex. These sages caused to be shown that for which they wanted there to be disgust, and to be hidden what they thought inclined to inspire sweeter desires; in either case, did they not strive after the objective we have just mentioned? One sees that they sensed the need of immorality in republican manners.

absolute subordination will be the rule of the individuals participating; the slightest refusal or recalcitrance will be instantly and arbitrarily punished by the injured party. I must explain this last more fully, and weigh it against republican manners; I promised I would employ the same logic from beginning to end, and I shall keep my word.

Although, as I told you just a moment ago, no passion has a greater need of the widest horizon of liberty than has this, none, doubtless, is as despotic; here it is that man likes to command, to be obeyed, to surround himself with slaves compelled to satisfy him; well, whenever you withhold from man the secret means whereby he exhales the dose of despotism Nature instilled in the depths of his heart, he will seek other outlets for it, it will be vented upon nearby objects; it will trouble the government. If you would avoid that danger, permit a free flight and rein to those tyrannical desires which, despite himself, torment man ceaselessly: content with having been able to exercise his small dominion in the middle of the harem of sultanas and youths whose submission your good offices and his money procure for him, he will go away appeased and with nothing but fond feelings for a government which so obligingly affords him every means of satisfying his concupiscence; proceed, on the other hand, after a different fashion, between the citizen and those objects of public lust raise the ridiculous obstacles in olden times invented by ministerial tyranny and by the lubricity of our Sardanapaluses[14]—, do that, and the citizen, soon embittered against your regime, soon jealous of the despotism he sees you exercise all by yourself, will shake off the yoke you lay upon him, and, weary of your manner of ruling, will, as he has just done, substitute another for it.

But observe how the Greek legislators, thoroughly imbued with these ideas, treated debauchery at Lacedaemon, at Athens: rather than prohibiting, they sotted the citizen on it; no species of lechery was forbidden him; and Socrates, whom the oracle described

---

[14] It is well known that the infamous and criminal Sartine devised, in the interests of the king's lewdness, the plan of having Dubarry read to Louis XV, thrice each week, the private details, enriched by Sartine, of all that transpired in the evil corners of Paris. This department of the French Nero's libertinage cost the the State three millions.

as the wisest philosopher of the land, passing indifferently from Aspasia's arms into those of Alcibiades, was not on that account less the glory of Greece. I am going to advance somewhat further, and however contrary are my ideas to our present customs, as my object is to prove that we must make all haste to alter those customs if we wish to preserve the government we have adopted, I am going to try to convince you that the prostitution of women who bear the name of honest is no more dangerous than the prostitution of men, and that not only must we associate women with the lecheries practiced in the houses I have set up, but we must even build some for them, where their whims and the requirements of their temper, ardent like ours but in a quite different way, may too find satisfaction with every sex.

First of all, what right have you to assert that women ought to be exempted from the blind submission to men's caprices Nature dictates? and, secondly, by what other right do you defend their subjugation to a continence impossible to their physical structure and of perfect uselessness to their honor?

I will treat each of these questions separately.

It is certain, in a state of Nature, that women are born *vulguivaguous,* that is to say, are born enjoying the advantages of other female animals and belonging, like them and without exception, to all males; such were, without any doubt, both the primary laws of Nature and the only institutions of those earliest societies into which men gathered. *Self-interest, egoism,* and *love* degraded these primitive attitudes, at once so simple and so natural; one thought oneself enriched by taking a woman to wife, and with her the goods of her family: there we find satisfied the first two feelings I have just indicated; still more often, this woman was taken by force, and thereby one became attached to her—there we find the other of the motives in action, and in every case, injustice.

Never may an act of possession be exercised upon a free being; the exclusive possession of a woman is no less unjust than the possession of slaves; all men are born free, all have equal rights: never should we lose sight of those principles; according to which never may there be granted to one sex the legitimate right to lay monopolizing hands upon the other, and never may one of these sexes, or classes, arbitrarily possess the other. Similarly, a woman existing in the purity of Nature's laws cannot allege, as justification for refusing herself to someone who desires her, the love she bears another, because such a response is based upon exclusion, and no man may be excluded from the having of a woman as of the moment it is clear she definitely belongs to all men. The act of possession can only be exercised upon a chattel or an animal, never upon an individual who resembles us, and all the ties which can bind a woman to a man are quite as unjust as illusory.

If then it becomes incontestable that we have received from Nature the right indiscriminately to express our wishes to all women, it likewise becomes incontestable that we have the right to compel their submission, not exclusively, for I should then be contradicting myself, but temporarily.[15] It cannot be denied that we have the right to decree laws that compel woman to yield to the flames of him who would have her; violence itself being one of that right's effects, we can employ it lawfully. Indeed! has Nature not proven that we have that right, by bestowing upon us the strength needed to bend women to our will?

It is in vain women seek to bring to their defense either modesty or their attachment to other men; these illusory grounds are worthless; earlier, we saw how contemptible and factitious is the sentiment of modesty. Love, which may be termed the *soul's madness*, is no more a title by which their constancy may be justified: love, satisfying two persons only, the beloved and the loving, cannot serve the happiness of others, and it is for the sake of the happiness of everyone, and not for an egotistical and privileged happiness, that women have been given to us. All men therefore have an equal right of enjoyment of all women; therefore, there is no man who, in keeping with natural law, may lay claim to a unique and personal right over a woman. The law which will oblige them

---

15 Let it not be said that I contradict myself here, and that after having established, at some point further above, that we have no right to bind a woman to ourselves, I destroy those principles when I declare now we have the right to constrain her; I repeat, it is a question of enjoyment only, not of property: I have no right of possession upon that fountain I find by the road, but I have certain rights to its use; I have the right to avail myself of the limpid water it offers my thirst; similarly, I have no real right of possession over such-and-such a woman, but I have incontestable rights to the enjoyment of her; I have the right to force from her this enjoyment, if she refuses me it for whatever the cause may be.

to prostitute themselves, as often and in any manner we wish, in the houses of debauchery we referred to a moment ago, and which will coerce them if they balk, punish them if they shirk or dawdle, is thus one of the most equitable of laws, against which there can be no sane or rightful complaint.

A man who would like to enjoy whatever woman or girl will henceforth be able, if the laws you promulgate are just, to have her summoned at once to duty at one of the houses; and there, under the supervision of the matrons of that temple of Venus, she will be surrendered to him, to satisfy, humbly and with submission, all the fancies in which he will be pleased to indulge with her, however strange or irregular they may be, since there is no extravagance which is not in Nature, none which she does not acknowledge as her own. There remains but to fix the woman's age; now, I maintain it cannot be fixed without restricting the freedom of a man who desires a girl of any given age.

He who has the right to eat the fruit of a tree may assuredly pluck it ripe or green, according to the inspiration of his taste. But, it will be objected, there is an age when the man's proceedings would be decidedly harmful to the girl's well-being. This consideration is utterly without value; once you concede me the proprietary right of enjoyment, that right is independent of the effects enjoyment produces; from this moment on, it becomes one, whether this enjoyment be beneficial or damaging to the object which must submit itself to me. Have I not already proven that it is legitimate to force the woman's will in this connection? and that immediately she excites the desire to enjoy she has got to expose herself to this enjoyment, putting all egotistical sentiments quite aside? The issue of her well-being, I repeat, is irrelevant. As soon as concern for this consideration threatens to detract from or enfeeble the enjoyment of him who desires her, and who has the right to appropriate her, this consideration for age ceases to exist; for what the object may experience, condemned by Nature and by the law to slake momentarily the other's thirst, is nothing to the point; in this study, we are only interested in what agrees with him who desires. But we will redress the balance.

Yes, we will redress it; doubtless we ought to. These women we have just so cruelly enslaved—there is no denying we must recompense them, and I come now to the second question I proposed to answer.

If we admit, as we have just done, that all women ought to be subjugated to our desires, we may certainly allow then ample satisfaction of theirs. Our laws must be favorable to their fiery temperament. It is absurd to locate both their honor and their virtue in the antinatural strength they employ to resist the penchants with which they have been far more profusely endowed than we; this injustice of manners is rendered more flagrant still since we contrive at once to weaken them by seduction, and then to punish them for yielding to all the efforts we have made to provoke their fall. All the absurdity of our manners, it seems to me, is graven in this shocking paradox, and this brief outline alone ought to awaken us to the urgency of exchanging them for manners more pure.

I say then that women, having been endowed with considerably more violent penchants for carnal pleasure than we, will be able to give themselves over to it wholeheartedly, absolutely free of all encumbering hymeneal ties, of all false notions of modesty, absolutely restored to a state of Nature; I want laws permitting them to give themselves to as many men as they see fit; I would have them accorded the enjoyment of all sexes and, as in the case of men, the enjoyment of all parts of the body; and under the special clause prescribing their surrender to all who desire them, there must be subjoined another guaranteeing them a similar freedom to enjoy all they deem worthy to satisfy them.

What, I demand to know, what dangers are there in this license? Children who will lack fathers? Ha! what can that matter in a republic where every individual must have no other dam than the nation, where everyone born is the motherland's child. And how much more they will cherish her, they who, never having known any but her, will comprehend from birth that it is from her alone all must be expected. Do not suppose you are fashioning good republicans so long as children, who ought to belong solely to the republic, remain immured in their families. By extending to the family, to a restricted number of persons, the portion of affection they ought to distribute amongst their brothers, they inevitably adopt those persons' sometimes very harmful prejudices; such children's opinions, their thoughts are particularized, malformed, and the virtues of a Man of the State become completely inaccessible to them. Finally abandoning their heart altogether to those by whom they have been given breath, they have no devotion left for what will cause them to mature, to understand, and to shine, as if these latter blessings were not more important than the former! If there is the greatest disadvantage in thus letting children imbibe interests from their family often in sharp disagreement with those of their country, there is then the most excellent argument for separating them from their family; and are they not naturally weaned away by the means I suggest, since in absolutely destroying all marital bonds, there are no longer born, as fruits of the woman's pleasure, anything but children to whom knowledge of their father is absolutely forbidden, and with that the possibility of belonging to only one family, instead of being, as they must be, purely *les enfants de la patrie*.

There will then be houses intended for women's libertinage and, like the men's, under the government's protection; in these establishments there will be furnished all the individuals of either sex women could desire, and the more constantly they frequent these places the higher they will be esteemed. There is nothing so barbarous or so ludicrous as to have identified their honor and their virtue with the resistance women show the desires Nature implants in them, and which continually inflame those who are hypocrite enough to pass censure on them. From the most tender age,[16] a girl released from her paternal fetters, no longer having anything to preserve for marriage (completely abolished by the wise laws I advocate), and superior to the prejudices which in former times imprisoned her sex, will therefore, in the houses created for the purpose, be able to indulge in everything to which her constitution prompts her; she will be received respectfully, copiously satisfied, and, returned once again into society, she will be able to tell of the pleasures she tasted quite as publicly as today she speaks of a ball or promenade. O charming sex, you will be free: as do men, you

---

16 The Babylonians scarcely awaited their seventh year to carry their first fruits to the temple of Venus. The first impulse to concupiscence a young girl feels is the moment when Nature bids her prostitute herself, and without any other kind of consideration she must yield instantly Nature speaks; if she resists, she outrages Nature's law.

will enjoy all the pleasures of which Nature makes a duty, from not one will you be withheld. Must the diviner half of humankind be laden with irons by the other? Ah, break those irons; Nature wills it. For a bridle have nothing but your inclinations, for laws only your desires, for morality Nature's alone; languish no longer under brutal prejudices which wither your charms and hold captive the divine impulses of your hearts;[17] like us, you are free, the field of action whereon one contends for Venus' favors is as open to you as it is to us; have no fear of absurd reproaches; pedantry and superstition are things of the past; no longer will you be seen to blush at your charming delinquencies; crowned with myrtle and roses, the esteem we conceive for you will be henceforth in direct proportion to the scale you give your extravagances.

What has just been said ought doubtless to dispense us from examining adultery; nevertheless, let's cast a glance upon it, however nonexistent it be in the eyes of the laws I am establishing. To what point was it not ridiculous in our former institutions to consider adultery criminal! Were there anything absurd in the world, very surely it is the timelessness ascribed to conjugal relations; it appears to me it is but necessary to scrutinize, or sense the weight of, those bonds in order to cease to view as wicked the act which lightens them; Nature, as we remarked recently, having supplied women with a temper more ardent, with a sensibility more profound, than she awarded persons of the other sex, it is unquestionably for women that the marital contract proves more onerous.

Tender women, you ablaze with love's fire, compensate yourselves now, and do so boldly and unafraid; persuade yourselves that there can exist no evil in obedience to Nature's promptings, that it is not for one man she created you, but to please them all, without discrimination. Let no anxiety inhibit you. Imitate the Greek republicans; never did the philosophers whence they had their laws contrive to make adultery a crime for them, and nearly all authorized disorderliness among women. Thomas More proves in his *Utopia*

---

[17] Women are unaware to what point their lasciviousness embellishes them. Let one compare two women of roughly comparable age and beauty, one of whom lives in celibacy, and the other in libertinage: it will be seen by how much the latter exceeds in éclat and freshness; all violence done Nature is far more wearing than the abuse of pleasures; everyone knows beds improve a woman's looks.

that it becomes women to surrender themselves to debauchery, and that great man's ideas were not always pure dreams.[18]

Amongst the Tartars, the more profligate a woman, the more she was honored; about her neck she publicly wore a certain jewelry attesting to her impudicity, and those who were not at all decorated were not at all admired. In Peru, families cede their wives and daughters to the visiting traveler; they are rented at so much the day, like horses, or carriages! Volumes, finally, would not suffice to demonstrate that lewd behavior has never been held criminal amongst the illuminated peoples of the earth. Every philosopher knows full well it is solely to the Christian impostors we are indebted for having puffed it up into crime. The priests had excellent cause to forbid us lechery: this injunction, by reserving to them acquaintance with and absolution for these private sins, gave them an incredible ascendancy over women, and opened up to them a career of lubricity whose scope knew no limits. We know only too well how they took advantage of it and how they would again abuse their powers, were they not hopelessly discredited.

Is incest more dangerous? Hardly. It loosens family ties and the citizen has that much more love to lavish on his country; the primary laws of Nature dictate it to us, our feelings vouch for the fact; and nothing is so enjoyable as an object we have coveted over the years. The most primitive institutions smiled upon incest; it is found in society's origins: it was consecrated in every religion, every law encouraged it. If we traverse the world we will find incest everywhere established. The blacks of the Ivory Coast and Gabon prostitute their wives to their own children; in Judah, the eldest son must marry his father's wife; the people of Chile lie indifferently with their sisters, their daughters, and marry mother and daughter at the same time. I would venture, in a word, that incest ought to be every government's law—every government whose basis is fraternity. How is it that reasonable men were able to carry absurdity to the point of believing that the enjoyment of one's mother, sister or daughter could ever be criminal? Is it not, I ask, an abominable view wherein it is made to appear a crime for a man to place higher

---

[18] The same thinker wished affianced couples to see each other naked before marriage. How many alliances would fail, were this law enforced! It might be declared that the contrary is indeed what is termed purchase of merchandise sight unseen.

value upon the enjoyment of an object to which natural feeling draws him close? One might just as well say that we are forbidden to love too much the individuals Nature enjoins us to love best, and that the more she gives us a hunger for some object, the more she orders us away from it. These are absurd paradoxes; only people bestialized by superstition can believe or uphold them. The community of women I am establishing necessarily leading to incest, there remains little more to say about a supposed misdemeanor whose inexistence is too plainly evident to warrant further pursuit of the matter, and we shall turn our attention to rape, which at first glance seems to be, of all libertinage's excesses, the one which is most dearly established as being wrong, by reason of the outrage it appears to cause. It is certain, however, that rape, an act so very rare and so very difficult to prove, wrongs one's neighbor less than theft, since the latter is destructive to property, the former merely damaging to it. Beyond that, what objections have you to the ravisher? What will you say, when he replies to you that, as a matter of fact, the injury he has committed is trifling indeed, since he has done no more than place a little sooner the object he has abused in the very state in which she would soon have been put by marriage and love.

But sodomy, that alleged crime which will draw the fire of heaven upon cities addicted to it, is sodomy not a monstrous deviation whose punishment could not be severe enough? Ah, sorrowful it is to have to reproach our ancestors for the judiciary murders in which, upon this head, they dared indulge themselves. We wonder that savagery could ever reach the point where you condemn to death an unhappy person all of whose crime amounts to not sharing your tastes. One shudders to think that scarce forty years ago the legislators' absurd thinking had not evolved beyond this point. Console yourselves, citizens; such absurdities are to cease: the intelligence of your lawmakers will answer for it. Thoroughly enlightened upon this weakness occurring in a few men, people deeply sense today that such error cannot be criminal, and that Nature, who places such slight importance upon the essence that flows in our loins, can scarcely be vexed by our choice when we are pleased to vent it into this or that avenue.

What single crime can exist here? For no one will wish to

maintain that all the parts of the body do not resemble each other, that there are some which are pure, and others defiled; but, as it is unthinkable such nonsense be advanced seriously, the only possible crime would consist in the waste of semen. Well, is it likely that this semen is so precious to Nature that its loss is necessarily criminal? Were that so, would she every day institute those losses? and is it not to authorize them to permit them in dreams, to permit them in the act of taking one's pleasure with a pregnant woman? Is it possible to imagine Nature having allowed us the possibility of committing a crime that would outrage her? Is it possible that she consent to the destruction by man of her own pleasures, and to his thereby becoming stronger than she? It is unheard of—into what an abyss of folly one is hurled when, in reasoning, one abandons the aid of reason's torch! Let us abide in our unshakable assurance that it is as easy to enjoy a woman in one manner as in another, that it makes absolutely no difference whether one enjoys a girl or a boy, and as soon as it is clearly understood that no inclinations or tastes can exist in us save the ones we have from Nature, that she is too wise and too consistent to have given us any which could ever offend her.

The penchant for sodomy is the result of physical formation to which we contribute nothing and which we cannot alter. At the most tender age, some children reveal that penchant, and it is never corrected in them. Sometimes it is the fruit of satiety; but even in this case, is it less Nature's doing? Regardless of how it is viewed it is her work, and, in every instance, what she inspires must be respected by men. If, were one to take an exact inventory, it should come out that this taste is infinitely more affecting than the other that the pleasures resulting from it are far more lively, and that for this reason its exponents are a thousand times more numerou than its enemies, would it not then be possible to conclude that, fa from affronting Nature, this vice serves her intentions, and that she is less delighted by our procreation than we so foolishly believe Why, as we travel about the world, how many peoples do we not see holding women in contempt! Many are the men who strictly avoi employing them for anything but the having of the child necessar to replace them. The communal aspect of life in republics alway renders this vice more frequent in that form of society; but it is no dangerous. Would the Greek legislators have introduced it into their republics had they thought it so? Quite the contrary; they deemed it necessary to a warlike race. Plutarch speaks with enthusiasm of the battalion of lovers: for many a year they alone defended Greece's freedom. The vice reigned amongst comrades-in-arms, and cemented their unity. The greatest of men lean toward sodomy. At the time it was discovered, the whole of America was found inhabited by people of this taste. In Louisiana, amongst the Illinois, Indians in feminine garb prostituted themselves as courtesans. The blacks of Benguéla publicly keep men; nearly all the seraglios of Algiers are today exclusively filled with young boys. Not content to tolerate love for young boys, the Thebans made it mandatory; the philosopher of Chaeronea prescribed sodomy as the surest way to a youth's affection.

We know to what extent it prevailed in Rome, where they had public places in which young boys, costumed as girls, and girls as boys, prostituted themselves. In their letters, Martial, Catullus, Tibullus, Horace, and Virgil wrote to men as though to their mistresses; and we read in Plutarch[19] that women must in no way figure in men's love. The Amasians of Crete used to abduct boys, and their initiation was distinguished by the most singular ceremonies. When they were taken with love for one, they notified the parents upon what day the ravisher wished to carry him off; the youth put up some resistance if his lover failed to please him; in the contrary case, they went off together, and the seducer restored him to his family as soon as he had made use of him; for in this passion as in that for women, one always has too much when one has had enough. Strabo informs us that on this very island, seraglios were peopled with boys only; they were prostituted openly.

Is one more authority required to prove how useful this vice is in a republic? Let us lend an ear to Jerome the Peripatetic: "The love of youths," says he, "spread throughout all of Greece, for it instilled in us strength and courage, and thus stood us in good stead when we drove the tyrants out; conspiracies were formed amongst lovers, and they were readier to endure torture than denounce their accomplices; such patriots sacrificed everything to the

---

[19] The *Moralities:* "On Love."

State's prosperity; it was beheld as a certain thing, that these attachments steadied the republic, women were declaimed against, and to entertain connections with such creatures was a frailty reserved to despots." Pederasty has always been the vice of warrior races. From Caesar we learn that the Gauls were to an extraordinary degree given to it. The wars fought to sustain the republic brought about the separation of the two sexes, and hence the propagation of the vice, and when its consequences, so useful to the State, were recognized, religion speedily blessed it. That the Romans sanctified the amours of Jupiter and Ganymede is well known. Sextus Empiricus assures us that this caprice was compulsory amongst the Persians. At last, the women, jealous and contemned, offered to render their husbands the same service they received from young boys; some few men made the experiment, and returned to their former habits, finding the illusion impossible. The Turks, greatly inclined toward this depravity Mohammed consecrated in the Koran, were nevertheless convinced that a very young virgin could well enough be substituted for a youth, and rarely did they grow to womanhood without having passed through the experience. Sextus Quintus and Sanchez allowed this debauch; the latter even undertook to show it was of use to procreation, and that a child created after this preliminary exercise was infinitely better constituted thanks to it. Finally, women found restitution by turning to each other. This latter fantasy doubtless has no more disadvantages than the other, since nothing comes of the refusal to reproduce, and since the means of those who have a bent for reproduction are powerful enough for reproduction's adversaries never to be able to harm population. Amongst the Greeks, this female perversion was also supported by policy: the result of it was that, finding each other sufficient, women sought less communication with men and their detrimental influence in the republic's affairs was thus held to a minimum. Lucian informs us of what progress this license promoted, and it is not without interest we see it exemplified in Sappho.

In fine, these are perfectly inoffensive manias; were women to carry them even further, were they to go to the point of caressing monsters and animals, as the example of every race teaches us, no ill could possibly result therefrom, because corruption of manners often of prime utility to a government, cannot in any sense harm it, and we must demand enough wisdom and enough prudence of our legislators to be entirely sure that no law will emanate from them that would repress perversions which, being determined by constitution and being inseparable from physical structure, cannot render the person in whom they are present any more guilty than the person Nature created deformed.

In the second category of man's crimes against his brethren, there is left to us only murder to examine, and then we will move on to man's duties toward himself. Of all the offenses man may commit against his fellows, murder is without question the cruelest, since it deprives man of the single asset he has received from Nature, and its loss is irreparable. Nevertheless, at this stage several questions arise, leaving aside the wrong murder does him who becomes its victim.

1. As regards the laws of Nature only, is this act really criminal?
2. Is it criminal with what regards the laws of politics?
3. Is it harmful to society?
4. What must be a republican government's attitude toward it?
5. Finally, must murder be repressed by murder?

Each of these questions will be treated separately; the subject is important enough to warrant thorough consideration; our ideas touching murder may surprise for their boldness. But what does that matter? Have we not acquired the right to say anything? The time has come for the ventilation of great verities; men today will not be content with less. The time has come for error to disappear; that blindfold must fall beside the heads of kings. From Nature's point of view, is murder a crime? That is the first question posed.

It is probable that we are going to humiliate man's pride by lowering him again to the rank of all of Nature's other creatures, but the philosopher does not flatter small human vanities; ever in turning pursuit of truth, he discerns it behind stupid notions of pride, lays it bare, elaborates upon it, and intrepidly shows it to the astonished world.

What is man? and what difference is there between him and other plants, between him and all the other animals of the world?

None, obviously. Fortuitously placed, like them, upon this globe, he is born like them; like them, he reproduces, rises, and falls; like them he arrives at old age and sinks like them into nothingness at the close of the life span Nature assigns each species of animal, in accordance with its organic construction. Since the parallels are so exact that the inquiring eye of philosophy is absolutely unable to perceive any grounds for discrimination, there is then just as much evil in killing animals as men, or just as little, and whatever be the distinctions we make, they will be found to stem from our pride's prejudices, than which, unhappily, nothing is more absurd. Let us all the same press on to the question. You cannot deny it is one and the same, to destroy a man or a beast; but is not the destruction of all living animals decidedly an evil, as the Pythagoreans believed, and as they who dwell on the banks of Ganges yet believe? Before answering that, we remind the reader that we are examining the question only in terms of Nature and in relation to her; later on, we will envisage it with reference to men.

Now then, what value can Nature set upon individuals whose making costs her neither the least trouble nor the slightest concern? The worker values his work according to the labor it entails and the time spent creating it. Does man cost Nature anything? And, under the supposition that he does, does he cost her more than an ape or an elephant? I go further: what are the regenerative materials used by Nature? Of what are composed the beings which come into life? Do not the three elements of which they are formed result from the prior destruction of other bodies? If all individuals were possessed of eternal life, would it not become impossible for Nature to create any new ones? If Nature denies eternity to beings, it follows that their destruction is one of her laws. Now, once we observe that destruction is so useful to her that she absolutely cannot dispense with it, and that she cannot achieve her creations without drawing from the store of destruction which death prepares for her, from this moment onward the idea of annihilation which we attach to death ceases to be real; there is no more veritable annihilation; what we call the end of the living animal is no longer a true finis, but a simple transformation, a transmutation of matter, what every modern philosopher acknowledges as one of Nature's fundamental laws. According to these irrefutable principles, death is hence no more than a change of form, an imperceptible passage from one existence into another, and that is what Pythagoras called metempsychosis.

These truths once admitted, I ask whether it can ever be proposed that destruction is a crime? Will you dare tell me, with the design of preserving your absurd illusions, that transmutation is destruction? No, surely not; for, to prove that, it would be necessary to demonstrate matter inert for an instant, for a moment in repose. Well, you will never detect any such moment. Little animals are formed immediately a large animal expires, and these little animals' lives are simply one of the necessary effects determined by the large animal's temporary sleep. Given this, will you dare suggest that one pleases Nature more than another? To support that contention, you would have to prove what cannot be proven: that elongated or square are more useful, more agreeable to Nature than oval or triangular shapes; you would have to prove that, with what regards Nature's sublime scheme, a sluggard who fattens in idleness is more useful than the horse, whose service is of such importance, or than a steer, whose body is so precious that there is no part of it which is not useful; you would have to say that the venomous serpent is more necessary than the faithful dog.

Now, as not one of these systems can be upheld, one must hence consent unreservedly to acknowledge our inability to annihilate Nature's works; in light of the certainty that the only thing we do when we give ourselves over to destroying is merely to effect an alteration in forms which does not extinguish life, it becomes beyond human powers to prove that there may exist anything criminal in the alleged destruction of a creature, of whatever age, sex, or species you may suppose it. Led still further in our series of inferences proceeding one from the other, we affirm that the act you commit in juggling the forms of Nature's different productions is of advantage to her, since thereby you supply her the primary material for her reconstructions, tasks which would be compromised were you to desist from destroying.

Well, let *her* do the destroying, they tell you; one ought to let her do it, of course, but they are Nature's impulses man follows when he indulges in homicide; it is Nature who advises him, and the man who destroys his fellow is to Nature what are the plague and famine, like them sent by her hand which employs every possible means more speedily to obtain of destruction this primary matter, itself absolutely essential to her works.

Let us deign for a moment to illumine our spirit by philosophy's sacred flame; what other than Nature's voice suggests to us personal hatreds, revenges, wars, in a word, all those causes of perpetual murder? Now, if she incites us to murderous acts, she has need of them; that once grasped, how may we suppose ourselves guilty in her regard when we do nothing more than obey her intentions?

But that is more than what is needed to convince any enlightened reader, that for murder ever to be an outrage to Nature is impossible.

Is it a political crime? We must avow, on the contrary, that it is, unhappily, merely one of policy's and politics' greatest instruments. Is it not by dint of murders that France is free today? Needless to say, here we are referring to the murders occasioned by war, not to the atrocities committed by plotters and rebels; the latter, destined to the public's execration, have only to be recollected to arouse forever general horror and indignation. What study, what science, has greater need of murder's support than that which tends only to deceive, whose sole end is the expansion of one nation at another's expense? Are wars, the unique fruit of this political barbarism, anything but the means whereby a nation is nourished, whereby it is strengthened, whereby it is buttressed? And what is war if not the science of destruction? A strange blindness in man, who publicly teaches the art of killing, who rewards the most accomplished killer, and who punishes him who for some particular reason does away with his enemy! Is it not high time errors so savage be repaired?

Is murder then a crime against society? But how could that reasonably be imagined? What difference does it make to this murderous society, whether it have one member more, or less? Will its laws, its manners, its customs be vitiated? Has an individual's death ever had any influence upon the general mass? And after the loss of the greatest battle, what am I saying? after the obliteration of half the world—or, if one wishes, of the entire world—would the little number of survivors, should there be any, notice even the faintest difference in things? No, alas. Nor would Nature notice any either, and the stupid pride of man, who believes everything created for him, would be dashed indeed, after the total extinction of the human species, were it to be seen that nothing in Nature had changed, and that the stars' flight had not for that been retarded. Let us continue.

What must the attitude of a warlike and republican state be toward murder?

Dangerous it should certainly be, either to cast discredit upon the act, or to punish it. Republican mettle calls for a touch of ferocity: if he grows soft, if his energy slackens in him, the republican will be subjugated in a trice. A most unusual thought comes to mind at this point, but if it is audacious it is also true, and I will mention it. A nation that begins by governing itself as a republic will only be sustained by virtues because, in order to attain the most, one must always start with the least. But an already old and decayed nation which courageously casts off the yoke of its monarchical government in order to adopt a republican one, will only be maintained by many crimes; for it is criminal already, and if it were to wish to pass from crime to virtue, that is to say, from a violent to a pacific, benign condition, it should fall into an inertia whose result would soon be its certain ruin. What happens to the tree you would transplant from a soil full of vigor to a dry and sandy plain? All intellectual ideas are so greatly subordinate to Nature's physical aspect that the comparisons supplied us by agriculture will never deceive us in morals.

Savages, the most independent of men, the nearest to Nature, daily indulge in murder which amongst them goes unpunished. In Sparta, in Lacedaemon, they hunted Helots, just as we in France go on partridge shoots. The freest of people are they who are most friendly to murder: in Mindanao, a man who wishes to commit a murder is raised to the rank of warrior brave, he is straightway decorated with a turban; amongst the Caraguos, one must have killed seven men to obtain the honors of this headdress: the inhabitants of Borneo believe all those they put to death will serve them when they themselves depart life; devout Spaniards made a vow to St. James of Galicia to kill a dozen Americans every day; in the kingdom of Tangut, there is selected a strong and vigorous young man: on certain days of the year he is allowed to kill whomever he encounters! Was there ever a people better disposed to murder than the Jews? One sees it in every guise, upon every page of their history.

Now and again, China's emperor and mandarins take measures to stir up a revolt amongst the people, in order to derive, from these maneuvers, the right to transform them into horrible slaughters. May that soft and effeminate people rise against their tyrants; the latter will be massacred in their turn, and with much greater justice; murder, adopted always, always necessary, will have but changed its victims; it has been the delight of some, and will become the felicity of others.

An infinite number of nations tolerates public assassinations; they are freely permitted in Genoa, Venice, Naples, and throughout Albania; at Kachoa on the San Domingo River, murderers, undisguised and unashamedly, upon your orders and before your very eyes cut the throat of the person you have pointed out to them; Hindus take opium to encourage themselves to murder; and then, rushing out into the street, they butcher everyone they meet; English travelers have found this idiosyncracy in Batavia, too.

What people were at once greater and more bloodthirsty than the Romans, and what nation longer preserved its splendor and freedom? The gladiatorial spectacles fed its bravery, it became warlike through the habit of making a game of murder. Twelve or fifteen hundred victims filled the circus' arena every day, and there the women, crueler than the men, dared demand that the dying fall gracefully and be sketched while still in death's throes. The Romans moved from that to the pleasures of seeing dwarfs cut each other to pieces; and when the Christian cult, then infecting the world, came to persuade men there was evil in killing one another, the tyrants immediately enchained that people, and everyone's heroes became their toys.

Everywhere, in short, it was rightly believed that the murderer —that is to say, the man who stifled his sensibilities to the point of killing his fellow man, and of defying public or private vengeance —everywhere, I say, it was thought such a man could only be very courageous, and consequently very precious to a warlike or republican community. We may discover certain nations which, yet more ferocious, could only satisfy themselves by immolating children, and very often their own, and we will see these actions universally adopted, and upon occasion even made part of the law. Several savage tribes kill their children immediately they are born. Mothers, on the banks of the Orinoco, firm in the belief their daughters were born only to be miserable, since their fate was to become wives in this country where women were found insufferable, immolated them as soon as they were brought into the light. In Taprobane and in the kingdom of Sopit, all deformed children were immolated by their own parents. If their children are born on certain days of the week, the women of Madagascar expose them to wild beasts. In the republics of Greece, all the children who came into the world were carefully examined, and if they were found not to conform to the requirements determined by the republic's defense, they were sacrificed on the spot: in those days, it was not deemed essential to build richly furnished and endowed houses for the preservation of mankind's scum.[20] Up until the transferal of the seat of the Empire, all the Romans who were not disposed to feed their off-spring flung them upon the dung heaps. The ancient legislators had no scruple about condemning children to death, and never did one of their codes repress the rights of a father over his family. Aristotle urged abortion; and those ancient republicans, filled with enthusiasm, with patriotic fervor, failed to appreciate this commiseration for the individual person that one finds in modern nations: they loved their children less, but their country more. In all the cities of China, one finds every morning an incredible number of children abandoned in the streets; a dung cart picks them up at dawn, and they are tossed into a moat; often, midwives themselves disencumbered mothers by instantly plunging their issue into vats of boiling water, or by throwing it into the river. In Peking, infants were put into little reed baskets that were left on the canals; every day, these canals were skimmed clean, and the famous traveler Duhalde calculates as above thirty thousand the number of infants collected in the course of each search.

---

[20] It must be hoped the nation will eliminate this expense, the most useless of all; every individual born lacking the qualities to become useful someday to the republic, has no right to live, and the best thing for all concerned is to deprive him of life the moment he receives it.

It cannot be denied that it is extraordinarily necessary, extremely politic to erect a dike against overpopulation in a republican system; for entirely contrary reasons, the birth rate must be encouraged in a monarchy; there, the tyrants being rich only through the number of their slaves, they assuredly have to have men; but do not doubt for a minute that populousness is a genuine vice in a republican government. However, it is not necessary to butcher people to restrain it, as our modern decemvirs used to say; it is but a question of not leaving it the means of extending beyond the limits its happiness prescribes. Beware of too great a multiplication in a race whose every member is sovereign, and be certain that revolutions are never but the effect of a too numerous population. If, for the State's splendor, you accord your warriors the right to destroy men, for the preservation of that same State grant also unto each individual the right to give himself over as much as he pleases, since this he may do without offending Nature, to ridding himself of the children he is unable to feed, or to whom the government cannot look for assistance; in the same way, grant him the right to rid himself, at his own risk and peril, of all enemies capable of harming him, because the result of all these acts, in themselves of perfect inconsequence, will be to keep your population at a moderate size, and never large enough to overthrow your regime. Let the monarchists say a State is great only by reason of its extreme population: this State will forever be poor, if its population surpasses the means by which it can subsist, and it will flourish always if, kept trimly within its proper limits, it can make traffic of its superfluity. Do you not prune the tree when it has overmany branches? and do not too many shoots weaken the trunk? Any system which deviates from these principles is an extravagance whose abuses would conduct us directly to the total subversion of the edifice we have just raised with so much trouble; but it is not at the moment the man reaches maturity one must destroy him in order to reduce population. It is unjust to cut short the days of a well-shaped person; it is not unjust, I say, to prevent the arrival in the world of a being who will certainly be useless to it. The human species must be purged from the cradle; what you foresee as useless to society is what must be stricken out of it; there you have the only reasonable means to the diminishment of a population, whose excessive size is, as we have just proven, the source of certain trouble.

The time has come to sum up.

Must murder be repressed by murder? Surely not. Let us never impose any other penalty upon the murderer than the one he may risk from the vengeance of the friends or family of him he has killed. "I grant you pardon," said Louis XV to Charolais who, to divert himself, had just killed a man; "but I also pardon whoever will kill you." All the bases of the law against murderers may be found in that sublime motto.[21]

Briefly, murder is a horror, but an often necessary horror, never criminal, which it is essential to tolerate in a republican State. I have made it clear the entire universe has given an example of it; but ought it be considered a deed to be punished by death? They who respond to the following dilemma will have answered the question:

Is it or is it not a crime?

If it is not, why make laws for its punishment? And if it is, by what barbarous logic do you, to punish it, duplicate it by another crime?

We have now but to speak of man's duties toward himself. As the philosopher only adopts such duties in the measure they conduce to his pleasure or to his preservation, it is futile to recommend their practice to him, still more futile to threaten him with penalties if he fails to adopt them.

The only offense of this order man can commit is suicide. I will not bother demonstrating here the imbecility of the people who make of this act a crime; those who might have any doubts upon the matter are referred to Rousseau's famous letter. Nearly all early governments, through policy or religion, authorized suicide. Before the Areopagites, the Athenians explained their reasons

---

[21] The Salic Law only punished murder by exacting a simple fine, and as the guilty one easily found ways to avoid payment, Childebert, king of Austrasia, decreed, in a writ published at Cologne, the death penalty, not against the murderer, but against him who would shirk the murderer's fine. Ripuarian Law similarly ordained no more against this act than a fine proportionate to the individual killed. A priest was extremely costly: a leaden tunic, cut to his measurements, was tailored for the assassin, and he was obliged to produce the equivalent of this tunic's weight in gold; in default of which the guilty one and his family remained slaves of the Church.

for self-destruction; then they stabbed themselves. Every Greek government tolerated suicide; it entered into the ancient legislators' scheme; one killed oneself in public, and one made of one's death a spectacle of magnificence.

The Roman Republic encouraged suicide; those so greatly celebrated instances of devotion to country were nothing other than suicides. When Rome was taken by the Gauls, the most illustrious senators consecrated themselves to death; as we imitate that spirit, we adopt the same virtues. During the campaign of '92, a soldier, grief-stricken to find himself unable to follow his comrades to the Jemappes affair, took his own life. Keeping ourselves at all times to the high standard of those proud republicans, we will soon surpass their virtue: it is the government that makes the man. Accustomed for so long to despotism, our courage was utterly crippled; despotism depraved our manners; we are being reborn; it will shortly be seen of what sublime actions the French genius and character are capable when they are free; let us maintain, at the price of our fortunes and our lives, this liberty which has already cost us so many victims, of whom we regret not one if we attain our objective; every one of them sacrificed himself voluntarily; let us not permit their blood to have been shed in vain; but union . . . union, or we will lose the fruit of all our struggles. Upon the victories we have just achieved let us seat excellent laws; our former legislators, still slaves of the despot we have just slaughtered, had given us nothing, but laws worthy of that tyrant they continued to reverence: let us re-do their work, let us consider that it is at last for republicans we are going to labor; may our laws be gentle, like the people they must rule.

In pointing out, as I have just done, the nullity, the indifference of an infinite number of actions our ancestors, seduced by a false religion, beheld as criminal, I reduce our labor to very little. Let as create few laws, but let them be good; rather than multiplying hindrances, it is purely a question of giving an indestructible quality to the law we employ, of seeing to it that the laws we promulgate have, as ends, nothing but the citizen's tranquillity, his happiness and the glory of the republic. But, Frenchmen, after having driven the enemy from your lands, I should not like your zeal to broad cast your principles to lead you further afield; it is only with fire and steel you will be able to carry them to the four corners of the earth. Before taking upon yourselves such resolutions, remember the unsuccess of the crusades. When the enemy will have fled across the Rhine, heed me, guard your frontiers, and stay at home behind them. Revive your trade, restore energy and markets to your manufacturing; cause your arts to flourish again, encourage agriculture, both so necessary in a government such as yours, and whose aim must be to provide for everyone without standing in need of anyone. Leave the thrones of Europe to crumble of themselves: your example, your prosperity will soon send them flying, without your having to meddle in the business at all.

Invincible within, and by your administration and your laws a model to every race, there will not be a single government which will not strive to imitate you, not one which will not be honored by your alliance; but if, for the vainglory of establishing your principles outside your country, you neglect to care for your own felicity at home, despotism, which is no more than asleep, will awake, you will be rent by intestine disorder, you will have exhausted your monies and your soldiers, and all that, all that to return to kiss the manacles the tyrants, who will have subjugated you during your absence, will impose upon you; all you desire may be wrought without leaving your home: let other people observe you happy, and they will rush to happiness by the same road you have traced for them.[22]

EUGENIE, *to Dolmancé*—Now, it strikes me as a very solidly composed document, that one, and it seems to me in such close agreement with your principles, at least with many of them, that I should be tempted to believe you its author.

DOLMANCE—Indeed my thinking does correspond with some part of these reflections, and my discourses—they've proven it to you—even lend to what has just been read to us the appearance of a repetition. . . .

---

[22] Let it be remembered that foreign warfare was never proposed save by the infamous Dumouriez.

EUGENIE—That I did not notice; wise and good words cannot be too often uttered; however, I find several amongst these principles a trifle dangerous.

DOLMANCE—In this world there is nothing dangerous but pity and beneficence; goodness is never but a weakness of which the ingratitude and impertinence of the feeble always force honest folk to repent. Let a keen observer calculate all of pity's dangers, and let him compare them with those of a staunch, resolute severity, and he will see whether the former are not the greater. But we are straying, Eugénie; in the interests of your education, let's compress all that has just been said into this single word of advice: Never listen to your heart, my child; it is the most untrustworthy guide we have received from Nature; with greatest care close it up to misfortune's fallacious accents; far better for you to refuse a person whose wretchedness is genuine than to run the great risk of giving to a bandit, to an intriguer, or to a caballer: the one is of a very slight importance, the other may be of the highest disadvantage.

LE CHEVALIER—May I be allowed to cast a glance upon the foundations of Dolmancé's principles? for I would like to try to annihilate them, and may be able to. Ah, how different they would be, cruel man, if, stripped of the immense fortune which continually provides you with the means to gratify your passions, you were to languish a few years in that crushing misfortune out of which your ferocious mind dares to fashion knouts wherewith to lash the wretched! Cast a pitying look upon them, and stifle not your soul to the point where the piercing cries of need shall never more be heard by you; when your frame, weary from naught but pleasure, languorously reposes upon swansdown couches, look ye at those others wasted by the drudgeries that support your existence, and at their bed, scarcely more than a straw or two for protection against the rude earth whereof, like beasts, they have nothing but the chill crust to lie down upon; cast a glance at them while surrounded by succulent meats wherewith every day twenty of Comus' students awake your sensuality, cast a glance, I say, at those wretches in yonder wood, disputing with wolves the dry soil's bitter root; when the most affecting objects of Cythera's temple are with game charms, laughter led to your impure bed, consider that poor luck less fellow stretched out near his grieving wife: content with the pleasures he reaps at the breast of tears, he does not even suspect the existence of others; look ye at him when you are denying yourself nothing, when you are swimming in the midst of glut, in a sea of surfeit; behold him, I say, doggedly lacking even the basic necessities of life; regard his disconsolate family, his trembling wife who tenderly divides herself between the cares she owes her husband, languishing near her, and those Nature enjoins for love's offspring, deprived of the possibility to fulfill any of those duties so sacred unto her sensitive heart; if you can do it, without a tremor hear her beg of you the leavings your cruelty refuses her!

Barbaric one, are these not at all human beings like you? and if they are of your kind, why should you enjoy yourself when they lie dying? Eugénie, Eugénie, never slay the sacred voice of Nature in your breast: it is to benevolence it will direct you despite yourself when you extricate from out of the fire of passions that absorb it the clear tenor of Nature. Leave religious principles far behind you—very well, I approve it; but abandon not the virtues sensibility inspires in us; 'twill never be but by practicing them we will taste the sweetest, the most exquisite of the soul's delights. A good deed will buy pardon for all your mind's depravities, it will soothe the remorse your misconduct will bring to birth and, forming in the depths of your conscience a sacred asylum whereunto you will sometimes repair, you will find there consolation for the excesses into which your errors will have dragged you. Sister, I am young, yes, I am libertine, impious, I am capable of every mental obscenity, but my heart remains to me, it is pure and, my friends, it is with it I am consoled for the irregularities of this my age.

DOLMANCE—Yes, Chevalier, you are young, your speeches illustrate it; you are wanting in experience; the day will come, and await it, when you will be seasoned; then, my dear, you will no longer speak so well of mankind, for you will have its acquaintance. Twas men's ingratitude dried out my heart, their perfidy which destroyed in me those baleful virtues for which, perhaps, like you, I was also born. Now, if the vices of the one establish these dangerous virtues in the other, is it not then to render youth a great service when one throttles those virtues in youth at an early hour? Oh, my friend, how you do speak to me of remorse! Can remorse exist in the soul of him who recognizes crime in nothing? Let your principles weed it out of you if you dread its sting; will it be possible to repent of an action with whose indifference you are profoundly penetrated? When you no longer believe evil anywhere exists, of what evil will you be able to repent?

LE CHEVALIER—It is not from the mind remorse comes; rather, 'tis the heart's issue, and never will the intellect's sophistries blot out the soul's impulsions.

DOLMANCE—However, the heart deceives, because it is never anything but the expression of the mind's miscalculations; allow the latter to mature and the former will yield in good time; we are constantly led astray by false definitions when we wish to reason logically: I don't know what the heart is, not I: I only use the word to denote the mind's frailties. One single, one unique flame sheds its light in me: when I am whole and well, sound and sane, I am never misled by it; when I am old, hypochondriacal, or pusillanimous, it deceives me; in which case I tell myself I am sensible, but in truth I am merely weak and timid. Once again, Eugénie, I say it to you: be not abused by this perfidious sensibility; be well convinced of it, it is nothing but the mind's weakness; one weeps not save when one is afraid, and that is why kings are tyrants. Reject, spurn the Chevalier's insidious advice; in telling you to open your heart to all of misfortune's imaginary ills, he seeks to fashion for you a host of troubles which, not being your own, would soon plunge you into an anguish and that for no purpose. Ah, Eugénie, believe me when I tell you that the delights born of apathy are worth much more than those you get of your sensibility; the latter can only touch the heart in one sense, the other titillates and overwhelms all of one's being. In a word, is it possible to compare permissible pleasures with pleasures which, to far more piquant delights, join those inestimable joys that come of bursting socially imposed restraints and of the violation of every law?

EUGENIE—You triumph, Dolmancé, the laurel belongs to you. The Chevalier's harangue did but barely brush my spirit, yours seduces and entirely wins it over. Ah, Chevalier, take my advice speak rather to the passions than to the virtues when you wish to persuade a woman.

MADAME DE SAINT-ANGE, *to the Chevalier*—Yes, my friend, fuck us to be sure, but let us have no sermons from you: you'll not convert us, and you might upset the lessons with which we desire to saturate this charming girl's mind.

EUGENIE—Upset? Oh, no, no; your work is finished; what fools call corruption is by now firmly enough established in me to leave not even the hope of a return, and your principles are far too thoroughly riven into my heart ever to be destroyed by the Chevalier's casuistries.

DOLMANCE—She is right, let us not discuss it any longer, Chevalier; you would come off poorly in this debate, and we wish nothing from you but excellence.

LE CHEVALIER—So be it; we are met here for a purpose very different, I know, from the one I wished to achieve; let's go directly to that destination, I agree with you; I'll save my ethics for others who, less besotted than you, will be in a better way to hear me.

MADAME DE SAINT-ANGE—Yes, dear brother, yes, exactly, give us nothing but your fuck; we'll forgo your morals; they are too gentle and mild for roués of our ilk.

EUGENIE—I greatly fear, Dolmancé, that this cruelty you recommend with such warmth may somewhat influence your pleasures; I believe I have already remarked something of the sort: you are hard when you take your pleasure; and I too might be able to confess to feeling a few dispositions to viciousness. . . . In order to clear my thoughts on the matter, please do tell me with what kind of an eye you view the object that serves your pleasures?

DOLMANCE—As absolutely null, that is how I view it, my dear; whether it does or does not share my enjoyment, whether it feels contentment or whether it doesn't, whether apathy or even pain, provided I am happy, the rest is absolutely all the same to me.

EUGENIE—Why, it is even preferable to have the object experience pain, is it not?

DOLMANCE—To be sure, 'tis by much to be preferred; I have given you my opinion on the matter; this being the case, the repercussion within us is much more pronounced, and much more energetically and much more promptly launches the animal spirits in the direction necessary to voluptuousness. Explore the seraglios of Africa, those of Asia, those others of southern Europe, and discover whether the masters of these celebrated harems are much concerned, when their pricks are in the air, about giving pleasure to the individuals they use; they give orders, and they are obeyed, they enjoy and no one dares make them answer; they are satisfied, and the others retire. Amongst them are those who would punish as a lack of respect the audacity of partaking of their pleasure. The king of Acahem pitilessly commands to be decapitated the woman who, in his presence, has dared forget herself to the point of sharing his pleasure, and not infrequently the king performs the beheading himself. This despot, one of Asia's most interesting, is exclusively guarded by women; he never gives them orders save by signs; the cruelest death is the reward reserved for her who fails to understand him, and the tortures are always executed either by his hand or before his eyes.

All that, Eugénie, is founded entirely upon the principles I have already developed for you. What is it one desires when taking one's pleasure? that everything around us be occupied with nothing but ourselves, think of naught but of us, care for us only. If the objects we employ know pleasure too, you can be very sure they are less concerned for us than they are for themselves, and lo! our own pleasure consequently disturbed. There is not a living man who does not wish to play the despot when he is stiff: it seems to him his joy is less when others appear to have as much as he; by an impulse of pride, very natural at this juncture, he would like to be the only one in the world capable of experiencing what he feels: the idea of seeing another enjoy as he enjoys reduces him to a kind of equality with that other, which impairs the unspeakable charm despotism causes him to feel.[23] 'Tis false as well to say there is pleasure i

---

[23] The poverty of the French language compels us to employ words which, today, our happy government, with so much good sense, disfavors; we hope our enlightened readers will understand us well and will not at all confound absurd political despotism with the very delightful despotism of libertinage's passions.

affording pleasure to others; that is to serve them, and the man who is erect is far from desiring to be useful to anyone. On the contrary, by causing them hurt he experiences all the charms a nervous personality relishes in putting its strength to use; 'tis then he dominates, is a *tyrant;* and what a difference is there for the *amour-propre!* Think not that it is silent during such episodes.

The act of enjoyment is a passion which, I confess, subordinates all others to it, but which simultaneously unites them. This desire to dominate at this moment is so powerful in Nature that one notices it even in animals. See whether those in captivity procreate as do those others that are free and wild; the camel carries the matter further still: he will engender no more if he does not suppose himself alone: surprise him and, consequently, show him a master, and he will fly, will instantly separate himself from his companion. Had it not been Nature's intent that man possess this feeling of superiority, she would not have created him stronger than the beings she destines to belong to him at those moments. The debility to which Nature condemned woman incontestably proves that her design is for man, who then more than ever enjoys his strength, to exercise it in all the violent forms that suit him best, by means of tortures, if he be so inclined, or worse. Would pleasure's climax be a kind of fury were it not the intention of this mother of humankind that behavior during copulation be the same as behavior in anger? What well-made man, in a word, what man endowed with vigorous organs does not desire, in one fashion or in another, to molest his partner during his enjoyment of her? I know perfectly well that whole armies of idiots, who are never conscious of their sensations, will have much trouble understanding the systems I am establishing; but what do I care for these fools? 'Tis not to them I am speaking; soft-headed women-worshipers, I leave them prostrate at their insolent Dulcineas' feet, there let them wait for the sighs that will make them happy and, basely the slaves of the sex they ought to dominate, I abandon them to the vile delights of wearing the chains wherewith Nature has given them the right to overwhelm others! Let these beasts vegetate in the abjection which defiles them—'twould be in vain to preach to them!—, but let them not denigrate what they are incapable of understanding, and let them be persuaded that those who wish to establish their principles pertinent to this subject only upon the free outbursts of a vigorous and untrammeled imagination, as do we, you, Madame, and I, those like ourselves, I say, will always be the only ones who merit to be listened to, the only ones proper to prescribe laws unto them and to give lessons! . . .

Goddamn! I've an erection! . . . Get Augustin to come back here, if you please. (*They ring; he reappears.*) 'Tis amazing how this fine lad's superb ass does preoccupy my mind while I talk! All my ideas seem involuntarily to relate themselves to it. . . . Show my eyes that masterpiece, Augustin . . . let me kiss it and caress it, oh! for a quarter of an hour. Hither, my love, come, that I may, in your lovely ass, render myself worthy of the flames with which Sodom sets me aglow. Ah, he has the most beautiful buttocks . . . the whitest! I'd like to have Eugénie on her knees; she will suck his prick while I advance; in this manner, she will expose her ass to the Chevalier, who'll plunge into it, and Madame de Saint-Ange, astride Augustin's back, will present her buttocks to me: I'll kiss them; armed with the cat-o'-nine-tails, she might surely, it should seem to me, by bending a little, be able to flog the Chevalier who, thanks to this stimulating ritual, might resolve not to spare our student. (*The position is arranged.*) Yes, that's it; let's do our best, my friends; indeed, it is a great pleasure to commission you to execute *tableaux;* in all the world, there's not an artist fitter than you to realize them! . . . This rascal does have a nipping tight ass! . . . 'tis all I can do to get a foothold in it. Would you do me the great kindness, Madame, of allowing me to bite and pinch your lovely flesh while I'm at my fuckery?

MADAME DE SAINT-ANGE—As much as you like, my friend; but, I warn you, I am ready to take my revenge: I swear that, for every vexation you give me, I'll blow a fart into your mouth.

DOLMANCE—By God, now! that is a threat! . . . quite enough to drive me to offend you, my dear. (*He bites her.*) Well! Let's see if you'll keep your word. (*He receives a fart.*) Ah, fuck, delicious! delicious! . . . (*He slaps her and immediately receives another fart.*) Oh, 'tis divine, my angel! Save me a few for the critical moment . . . and, be sure of it, I'll then treat you with the extremest cruelty . . . most barbarously I'll use you. . . . Fuck! I can tolerate this no longer . . . I discharge! . . . (*He bites her, strikes her, and she farts uninterruptedly.*) Dost see how I deal with you, my fine fair bitch! . . . how I dominate you . . . once again here . . . and there . . . and let the final insult be to the very idol at which I sacrificed! (*He bites her asshole; the circle of debauchees is broken.*) And the rest of you—what have you been up to, my friends?

EUGENIE, *spewing forth the fuck from her mouth and her ass*—Alas! dear master . . . you see how your disciples have accommodated me! I have a mouthful of fuck and half a pint in my ass, 'tis all I am disgorging on both ends.

DOLMANCE, *sharply*—Hold there! I want you to deposit in my mouth what the Chevalier introduced into your behind.

EUGENIE, *assuming a proper position*—What an extravagance!

DOLMANCE—Ah, there's nothing that can match fuck drained out of the depths of a pretty behind . . . 'tis a food fit for the gods. (*He swallows some.*) Behold, 'tis neatly wiped up, eh? (*Moving to Augustin's ass, which he kisses.*) Mesdames, I am going to ask your permission to spend a few moments in a nearby room with this young man.

MADAME DE SAINT-ANGE—But can't you do here all you wish to do with him?

DOLMANCE, *in a low and mysterious tone*—No; there are certain things which strictly require to be veiled.

EUGENIE—Ah, by God, tell us what you'd be about!

MADAME DE SAINT-ANGE—I'll not allow him to leave if he does not.

DOLMANCE—You then wish to know?

EUGENIE—Absolutely.

DOLMANCE, *dragging Augustin*—Very well, Mesdames, I am going . . . but, indeed, it cannot be said.

MADAME DE SAINT-ANGE—Is there, do you think, any conceivable infamy we are not worthy to hear of and execute?

LE CHEVALIER—Wait, sister. I'll tell you. (*He whispers to the two women.*)

EUGENIE, *with a look of revulsion*—You are right, 'tis hideous.

MADAME DE SAINT-ANGE—Why, I suspected as much.

DOLMANCE—You see very well I had to be silent upon this caprice; and you grasp now that one must be alone and in the deepest shadow in order to give oneself over to such turpitudes.

EUGENIE—Do you want me to accompany you? I'll frig you while you amuse yourself with Augustin.

DOLMANCE—No, no, this is an *affaire d'honneur* and should take place between men only; a woman would only disturb us. . . . At your service in a moment, dear ladies. (*He goes out, taking Augustin with him.*)

DIALOGUE THE SIXTH

MADAME DE SAINT-ANGE, EUGENIE, LE CHEVALIER

MADAME DE SAINT-ANGE—Indeed, brother, your friend is greatly a libertine.

LE CHEVALIER—Then I've not deceived you in presenting him as such.

EUGENIE—I am persuaded there is not his equal anywhere in the world. . . . Oh, my dearest, he is charming; I do hope we will see him often.

MADAME DE SAINT-ANGE—I hear a knock . . . who might it be? . . . I gave orders . . . it must be very urgent. Go see what it is, Chevalier, if you will be so kind.

LE CHEVALIER—A letter Lafleur has brought; he left hastily, saying he remembered the instructions you had given him, but that the matter appeared to him as important as it was pressing.

MADAME DE SAINT-ANGE—Ah ha! what's this? 'Tis your father, Eugénie!

EUGENIE—My father! . . . then we are lost! . . .

MADAME DE SAINT-ANGE—Let's read it before we get upset. (*She reads.*)

349

Would you believe it, my dear lady? my unbearable wife, alarmed by my daughter's journey to your house, is leaving immediately, with the intention of bringing Eugénie home. She imagines all sorts of things ... which, even were one to suppose them real, would, in truth, be but very ordinary and human indeed. I request you to punish her impertinence with exceeding rigor; yesterday, I chastised her for something similar: the lesson was not sufficient. Therefore, mystify her well, I beseech you on bended knee, and believe that, no matter to what lengths you carry things, no complaint will be heard from me. . . . 'Tis a very long time this whore's been oppressing me ... indeed. . . . Do you follow me? what you do will be well done: that is all I can say to you. She will arrive shortly after my letter; keep yourself in readiness. Adieu; I should indeed like to be numbered in your company. Do not, I beg of you, return Eugénie to me until she is instructed. I am most content to leave the first gatherings to your hands, but be well convinced however that you will have labored in some sort in my behalf.

Why, there, Eugénie! you see? There is nothing over which to be disturbed; it must be admitted, though, that the little wife in question is a mightily insolent one.

EUGENIE—The slut! Ha! since Papa gives us a free hand, we must, by God, receive the creature in the manner she deserves.

MADAME DE SAINT-ANGE—Hither, kiss me, my heart. How comforted I am thus to perceive such dispositions in you! . . . Well, be at ease; I guarantee you we will not spare her. Eugénie, you desired a victim, and behold! here is one both Nature and fate are giving you.

EUGENIE—We will enjoy the gift, my dear, I swear to you we'll put her to use!

MADAME DE SAINT-ANGE—How eager I am to know how Dolmancé will react to the news.

DOLMANCE, *entering with Augustin*—'Tis the best news possible, Madame; I was not so far away I could not overhear; Madame de Mistival's arrival is very opportune. . . . You are firmly determined, I trust, to satisfy her husband's expectations?

EUGENIE, *to Dolmancé*—Satisfy them? . . . to surpass them, my love . . . oh, may the earth sink beneath me if you see me falter whatever be the horrors to which you condemn the tramp! . . . Dear friend, entrust to me the supervision of the entire proceedings. . . .

DOLMANCE—Allow your friend and me to take charge; you others need merely obey the orders we give you . . . oh, the insolent creature! I've never seen anything like it! . . .

MADAME DE SAINT-ANGE—Clumsy fool! Well, shall we rather more decently deck ourselves in order to receive her?

DOLMANCE—On the contrary; from the instant she enters, nothing must prevent her from being very sure of the manner in which we have been spending the time with her daughter. Let us all be rather in the greatest disorder.

MADAME DE SAINT-ANGE—I hear sounds; 'tis she! . . . Courage, Eugénie; remember our principles. . . . Ah, by God! 'twill be a delightful scene! . . .

DIALOGUE THE SEVENTH AND LAST

MADAME DE SAINT-ANGE, EUGENIE, LE CHEVALIER, AUGUSTIN, DOLMANCE, MADAME DE MISTIVAL

MADAME DE MISTIVAL, *to Madame de Saint-Ange*—I beg your forgiveness, Madame, for arriving unannounced at your house; but I hear that my daughter is here and as her few years do not yet permit her to venture abroad alone, I beg you, Madame, to be so very good as to return her to me, and not to disapprove my request or behavior.

MADAME DE SAINT-ANGE—This behavior is eminently impolite, Madame; one would say, upon hearing your words, that your daughter is in bad hands.

MADAME DE MISTIVAL—Faith! if one must judge by the state I find her in, and you, Madame, and your company, I believe I am not greatly mistaken in supposing her in no good sort while she is here.

DOLMANCE—Madame, this is an important beginning and, without being exactly informed of the degree of familiarity which obtains between Madame de Saint-Ange and you, I see no reason to pretend that I would not, were I in her place, already have had you pitched out of the window.

MADAME DE MISTIVAL—I do not completely understand what you mean by "pitched out of the window." Be advised, Monsieur, that I am not a woman to be pitched out of windows; I have no idea who you are, but from your language and the state I observe you to be in, it is not impossible to arrive at a speedy conclusion concerning your manners. Eugénie! Follow me.

EUGENIE—I beg your pardon, Madame, but I cannot enjoy that honor.

MADAME DE MISTIVAL—What! my daughter resists me!

DOLMANCE—Nay, 'tis worse yet: 'tis a case of formal dis-obedience, as you observe, Madame. Believe me, do not tolerate it in her. Would you like me to have whips brought in to punish this intractable child?

EUGENIE—I should be greatly afraid, were they to be sent for, that they would be employed rather upon Madame than upon me.

MADAME DE MISTIVAL—Impertinent creature!

DOLMANCE, *approaching Madame de Mistival*—Softly, my sweet, we'll have no invectives here; all of us are Eugénie's pro-tectors, and you might regret your hastiness with her.

MADAME DE MISTIVAL—What! my daughter is to disobey me and I am not to be able to make her sensible of the rights I have over her!

DOLMANCE—And what, if you please, are these rights, Madame? Do you flatter yourself they are legitimate? When Monsieur de Mistival, or whoever it was, spurted into your vagina the several drops of fuck that brought Eugénie into being, did you then, in the act, have her in mind? Eh? I dare say you did not. Well, then, how can you expect her to be beholden to you today for your having discharged when years ago someone fucked your nasty cunt? Take notice, Madame: there is nothing more illusory than fathers' and mothers' sentiments for their children, and children's for the authors of their days. Nothing supports, nothing justifies, nothing establishes such feelings, here in currency, there held in contempt, for there are countries where parents kill their children, others where the latter cut the throats of those whence they have breath. Were reciprocal love to have some natural sanction, consanguinity's power would no longer be chimerical and, without being seen, without mutually being known, parents would distinguish, would adore their sons and, reversibly, these would discern their unknown fathers, would fly into their arms and would do them reverence. Instead of which, what is it we see? Reciprocal hatreds inveterate; children who, even before reaching the age of reason, have never been able to suffer the sight of their fathers; fathers sending away their children because never could they endure their approach. Those alleged instincts are hence fictitious, absurd; self-interest only invents them, usage prescribes, habit sustains, but never did Nature engrave them in our hearts. Tell me: do animals know these feelings? no, surely not; however, 'tis always them one must consult when one wishes to be acquainted with Nature. O fathers! have no qualms regarding the so-called injustices your passions or your interest leads you to work upon these beings, for you nonexistent, to which a few drops of your sperm has given life; to them you owe nothing, you are in the world not for them but for yourselves: great fools you would be to be troubled about, to be occupied with anything but your own selves; for yourselves alone you ought to live; and you, dear children, you who are far more exempted—if it is possible to be far more exempted—from this filial piety whose basis is a true chimera, you must be persuaded also that you owe nothing to those individuals whose blood hatched you out of the darkness. Pity, gratitude, love—not one of these sentiments is their due; they who have given you existence have not a single right to require them from you; they labor for themselves only: let them look after themselves; but the greatest of all the duperies would be to give them either the help or the ministry no relationship can possibly oblige you to give; no law enjoins you, there is no prescription and if, by chance, you should hear some inner voice speaking to you—whether it is custom that inspires these announcements, whether it is your character's moral effect that produces these twinges—, unhesitatingly, remorselessly throttle those absurd sentiments . . . local sentiments, the fruit of geographical accident, climate, which Nature repudiates and reason disavows always!

MADAME DE MISTIVAL—But the care I have lavished upon her, the education I have given her! . . .

DOLMANCE—Why, as for the care, 'tis never but the effect of convention or of vanity; having done no more for her than what is dictated by the customs of the country you inhabit, assuredly, Eugénie owes you nothing. As for her education, it appears to have been damnably poor, for we here have been obliged to replace all the principles you had put into her head; not one of the lot you gave her provides for her happiness, not one is not absurd or illusory. You spoke to her of God as if there were some such thing; of virtue as if it were necessary; of religion as if every religious cult were something other than the result of the grossest imposture and the most signal imbecility; of Jesus Christ as if that rascal were anything but a cheat and a bandit. You have told her that it is sinful to *fuck,* whereas to *fuck* is life's most delicious act; you have wished to give her good manners, as if a young girl's happiness were not inseparable from debauchery and immorality, as if the happiest of all women had not incontestably to be she who wallows most in filth and in libertinage, she who most and best defies every prejudice and who most laughs reputation to scorn. Ah, Madame, disabuse yourself: you have done nothing for your daughter, in her regard you have not fulfilled a single one of the obligations Nature dictates: Eugénie owes you naught but hatred.

MADAME DE MISTIVAL—Oh merciful heaven! my Eugénie is doomed, 'tis evident. . . . Eugénie, my beloved Eugénie, for the last time heed the supplications of her who gave you your life; these are orders no longer, but prayers; unhappily, it is only too true that you are amidst monsters here; tear yourself from this perilous commerce and follow me; I ask it of you on my knees! (*She falls to her knees.*)

DOLMANCE—Ah, very pretty! a tearful scene! . . . To it, Eugénie! Be tender.

EUGENIE, *half-naked, as the reader surely must remember*—Here you are, my dear little Mamma, I bring you my buttocks. . . . There they are, positively at the level of your lips; kiss them, my sweet, suck them, 'tis all Eugénie can do for you. . . . Remember,

Dolmancé: I shall always show myself worthy of having been your pupil.

MADAME DE MISTIVAL, *thrusting Eugénie away, with horror*— Monster! I disown you forever, you are no longer my child!

EUGENIE—Add a few curses to it, if you like, my dearest Mother, in order to render the thing more touching yet, and you will see me equally phlegmatic.

DOLMANCE—Softly, Madame, softly; there is insult here; in our view, you have just rather too harshly repulsed Eugénie; I told you that she is in our safekeeping: a punishment is needed for this crime; have the kindness to undress yourself, strip to the skin, so as to receive what your brutality deserves.

MADAME DE MISTIVAL—Undress myself! . . .

DOLMANCE—Augustin, act as this lady's maid-in-waiting, since she resists. (*Augustin goes brutally to work; Madame de Mistival seeks to protect herself.*)

MADAME DE MISTIVAL, *to Madame de Saint-Ange*—My God, where am I? Are you aware, Madame, of what you are allowing to be done to me in your house? Do you suppose I shall make no complaint?

MADAME DE SAINT-ANGE—It is by no means certain you will be able to.

MADAME DE MISTIVAL—Great God! then I am to be killed here!

DOLMANCE—Why not?

MADAME DE SAINT-ANGE—One moment, gentlemen. Before exposing this charming beauty's body to your gaze, it would be well for me to forewarn you of the condition you are going to find it in. Eugénie has just whispered the entire story into my ear: yesterday, her husband used the whip on her, all but broke his arm beating her for some minor domestic mismanagement . . . and, Eugénie assures me, you are going to find her ass' cheeks looking like moiré taffeta.

DOLMANCE, *immediately Madame de Mistival is naked*—Well, by God, 'tis the absolute truth! I don't believe I've ever seen a body more mistreated than this . . . but, by Jesus! she's got as many cuts before as she has behind! . . . Yet . . . I believe I espy a very fine ass here. (*He kisses and fondles it.*)

MADAME DE MISTIVAL—Leave me alone, leave me, else I'll cry for help!

MADAME DE SAINT-ANGE, *coming up to her and seizing her by the arm*—Listen to me, whore! I'm going to explain everything to you! . . . You are a victim sent us by your own husband; you have got to submit to your fate; nothing can save you from it . . . what will it be? I've no idea; perhaps you'll be hanged, wheeled, quartered, racked, burned alive; the choice of torture depends upon your daughter: 'tis she will give the order for your period; but, my whore, you are going to suffer . . . oh, yes, you will not be immolated until after having undergone an infinite number of preliminary embarrassments. As for your cries, I warn you they will be to no purpose: one could slaughter a steer in this chamber without any risk of having his bellowings overheard. Your horses, your servants have already left; once again, my lovely one, your husband authorizes what we are doing, and your coming here is nothing but a trap baited for your simplicity and into which, you observe, you could not have fallen better.

DOLMANCE—I hope that Madame is now perfectly tranquilized.

EUGENIE—Thus to be forewarned is certainly to have been the object of a very ample consideration.

DOLMANCE, *still feeling and slapping her buttocks*—Indeed, Madame, 'tis clear you have a warm friend in Madame de Saint-Ange. . . . Where, these days, does one come across such candor? What forthrightness in her tone when she addresses you! . . . Eugénie, come here and place your buttocks beside your mother's. . . I'd like to make a comparison of your asses. (*Eugénie obeys.*) My goodness! yours is splendid, my dear, but, by God, Mamma's is not bad either . . . not yet . . . in another instant I'll be amusing myself fucking you both. . . . Augustin, lay a hand upon Madame.

MADAME DE MISTIVAL—Merciful heavens! what an outrage!

DOLMANCE, *continuing throughout to realize his projects, and beginning them with an embuggery of the mother*—Why, not at all! Nothing easier! . . . Look ye! You scarcely felt it! . . . Ha! 'tis clear your husband has many times trod the path! Your turn now, Eugénie. . . . What a difference! . . . There, I'm content; I simply wished to volley the ball a little, to put myself into shape . . . well, a little order now. First, Mesdames, you, Saint-Ange, and you, Eugénie, have the goodness to arm yourselves with artificial pricks in order, one after the other, to deal this respectable lady, now in the cunt, now in the ass . . . the most fearsome strokes. The Chevalier, Augustin, and I, acting with our own members, will relieve you with a prompt exactitude. I am going to begin and, as you may well believe, it is once again her ass which will receive my homage. During the games, parenthetically, each is invited to decide for himself what torture he wishes to inflict upon her; but bear it in mind: the suffering must increase gradually, so as not to kill her off beforetimes. . . . Augustin, dear boy, console me, by buggering me, for the obligation I am under to sodomize this ancient cow. Eugénie, let me kiss your beautiful behind while I bugger mamma, and you, Madame, bring yours near, so that I can handle it . . . socratize it. One must be walled round by asses when 'tis an ass one fucks.

EUGENIE—What, my friend, what are you going to do to this bitch? While losing your sperm, to what do you intend to condemn her?

DOLMANCE, *all the while plying his whip*—The most natural thing in the world: I am going to depilate her and lacerate her thighs with pincers.

MADAME DE MISTIVAL, *understanding this dual vexation*—The monster! Criminal! he is mutilating me! . . . oh, God Almighty!

DOLMANCE—Implore him not, my dove: he will remain deaf to your voice, as he is to that of every other person: never has this powerful figure bothered to entangle himself in an affair concerning merely an ass.

MADAME DE MISTIVAL—Oh, how you are hurting me!

DOLMANCE—Incredible effects of the human mind's idiosyncrasies! . . . You suffer, my best beloved, you weep and, wondrous thing! I discharge . . . ah, double whore! I'd strangle you if I did not wish to leave the pleasure of it to others. She's yours, Saint-Ange. (*Madame de Saint-Ange embuggers and encunts her with her dildo; she bestows a few blows of her fist upon her; the Chevalier succeeds her; he too avails himself of the two avenues and, as he discharges, boxes her ears. 'Tis Augustin who comes next: he acts in like wise and ends with a few digs with his fingers, pokes, pulls, and punches. During these various attacks, Dolmancé has sent his engine straying about all the agents' asses, the while urging them on with his remarks.*) Well, pretty Eugénie, fuck your mother, first of all, encunt her.

EUGENIE—Come, dear lovely Mamma, come, let me serve you as a husband. 'Tis a little thicker than your spouse's, is it not, my dear? Never mind, 'twill enter. . . . Ah, Mother dear, you cry, you scream, scream when your daughter fucks you! . . . And you, Dolmancé, you bugger me! . . . Here I am: at one stroke incestuous, adulteress, sodomite, and all that in a girl who only lost her maidenhead today! . . . What progress, my friends! . . . with what rapidity I advance along the thorny road of vice! . . . Oh, right enough, I am a doomed girl! . . . I believe, dear Mother, you are discharging. . . . Dolmancé, look at her eyes! she comes, it's certain, is it not? Ah, whore! I'm going to teach you to be a libertine . . . well, bitch, what do you think of that? (*She squeezes, twists, wrenches her mother's breasts.*) Ah, fuck, Dolmancé . . . fuck, my gentle friend, I am dying! . . . (*As she discharges, Eugénie showers ten or twelve jarring blows upon her mother's breast and sides.*)

MADAME DE MISTIVAL, *about to lose consciousness*—Have pity upon me, I beg of you . . . I . . . I am not well . . . I am fainting. . . (*Madame de Saint-Ange seems to wish to aid her; Dolmancé lifts a restraining hand.*)

DOLMANCE—Why, no, leave her in her swoon: there is nothing so lubricious as to see a woman who has fainted; we'll flog her: that should restore her to her senses. . . . Eugénie, come, stretch out upon your victim's body . . . 'tis here I wish to discover whether you are steadfast. Chevalier, fuck her as she lies upon her failing mother, and let her frig us, Augustin and me, with each of her hands. You, Saint-Ange, frig her while she's being fucked.

LE CHEVALIER—Indeed, Dolmancé, 'tis horrible, what you have us do; this at once outrages Nature, heaven, and the most sacred laws of humanity.

DOLMANCE—Nothing diverts me like the weighty outbursts of the Chevalier's virtuousness; but in all we are doing, where the devil does he see the least outrage to Nature, to heaven, and to mankind? My friend, it is from Nature roués obtain the principles they put into action; I've told you a thousand times over that Nature, who for the perfect maintenance of the laws of her general equilibrium, has sometimes need of vices and sometimes of virtues, inspires now this impulse, now that one, in accordance with what she requires; hence, we do no kind of evil in surrendering ourselves to these impulses, of whatever sort you may suppose them to be. With what regards heaven, my dear Chevalier, I beg of you, let us no more dread its effects: one single motor is operative in this universe, and that motor is Nature. The miracles—rather, the physical effects—of this mother of the human race, differently interpreted by men, have been deified by them under a thousand forms, each more extraordinary than the other; cheats and intriguers, abusing their fellows' credulity, have propagated their ridiculous daydreams, and that is what the Chevalier calls heaven, that is what he fears offending! . . . Humanity's laws are violated, he adds, by the petty stuff and nonsense in which we are indulging ourselves this afternoon. Get it into your head once and for all, my simple and very fainthearted fellow, that what fools call *humaneness* is nothing but a weakness born of fear and egoism; that this chimerical virtue, enslaving only weak men, is unknown to those whose character is formed by stoicism, courage, and philosophy. Then act, Chevalier, act and fear nothing; were we to pulverize this whore, there'd not be a suspicion of crime in the thing: it is impossible for man to commit a crime; when Nature inculcated in him the irresistible desire to commit crime, she most prudently arranged to put beyond his reach those acts which could disturb her operations or conflict with her will. Ha, my friend, be sure that all the rest is entirely permitted, and that she has not been so idiotic as to give us the power of discomfiting her or of disturbing her workings. The blind instruments of her inspirations, were she to order us to set fire to the universe, the only crime possible would be in resisting her: all the criminals on earth are nothing but the agents of her caprices . . . well, Eugénie, take your place. But what do I see? . . . she's turning pale! . . .

EUGENIE, *lying down upon her mother*—Turning pale! I! God no! you'll very soon see the contrary! (*The attitude is executed; Madame de Mistival remains unconscious. When the Chevalier has discharged, the group is broken.*)

DOLMANCE—What! the bitch is not yet awake! Whips! I say, bring me whips! . . . Augustin, run and gather me a handful of thorns from the garden. (*While waiting, he slaps her face.*) Oh, upon my soul, I fear she may be dead; nothing seems to have any effect upon her.

EUGENIE, *with irritation*—Dead! dead! what's this? Then I'll have to go about wearing black this summer, and I have had the prettiest dresses made for me!

MADAME DE SAINT-ANGE—Ah! the little monster! (*She bursts into laughter.*)

DOLMANCE, *taking the thorns from Augustin, who returns*—We shall see whether this final remedy will not have some results. Eugénie, suck my prick while I labor to restore a mother to you and, Augustin, do you give me back the blows I am going to strike this stricken lady. I should not be sorry, Chevalier, to see you embugger your sister: you would adopt such a posture as to permit me to kiss your buttocks during the operation.

LE CHEVALIER—Well, let's comply with it, since there seems no way of persuading this scoundrel that all he is having us do is appalling. (*The stage is set; as the whipping of Madame de Mistival proceeds, she comes slowly to life.*)

DOLMANCE—Why, do you see the medicine's effects? I told you it would not fail us.

MADAME DE MISTIVAL, *opening her eyes*—Oh heavens! why do you recall me from the grave's darkness? Why do you plunge me again into life's horrors?

DOLMANCE, *whipping her steadily*—Indeed, mother dear, it is because much conversation remains to be held. Must you not hear your sentence pronounced? must it not be executed?... Come, let's gather round our victim: let her kneel in the center of the circle and, trembling, hear what will be announced to her. Madame de Saint-Ange, will you please begin. (*The following speeches are pronounced while the actors are in full action.*)

MADAME DE SAINT-ANGE—I condemn her to be hanged.

LE CHEVALIER—Cut into eighty thousand pieces, after the manner of the Chinese.

AUGUSTIN—As for me, by Gar, I'd let her get off with being broken alive.

EUGENIE—Into my pretty little mamma's body there will be driven wicks garnished with sulphur and I will undertake to set them afire, one by one. (*The circle is dissolved.*)

DOLMANCE, *coolly*—Well, my friends, as your leader and instructor, I shall lighten the sentence; but the difference which will be discovered between what I decree and what you have demanded, this difference, I say, is that your sentences would be in the nature of the effects of mordant practical joking; mine, on the contrary, is going to be the cause of a little knavery. I have, waiting outside, a valet, and he is furnished with what is perhaps one of the loveliest members to be found in all of Nature; however, it distills disease for 'tis eaten by one of the most impressive cases of syphillis I have yet anywhere encountered; I'll have my man come in: we'll have a coupling: he'll inject his poison into each of the two natural conduits that ornament this dear and amiable lady, with this consequence: that so long as this cruel disease's impressions shall last, the whore will remember not to trouble her daughter when Eugénie has herself fucked. (*Everyone applauds; the valet is called in; Dolmancé speaks now to him.*) Lapierre, fuck this woman; she i exceptionally healthy; this amusement might cure you: at least, there may be some precedent for the miracle's success.

LAPIERRE—In front of everyone, Monsieur?

DOLMANCE—Are you afraid to exhibit your prick?

LAPIERRE—No, by God! for it's very attractive. . . . Let's to it, Madame, be so good as to ready yourself.

MADAME DE MISTIVAL—Oh, my God! what a hideous damnation!

EUGENIE—Better that than to die, Mamma; at least I'll be able to wear some gay dresses this summer.

DOLMANCE—Meanwhile, we might amuse ourselves; my opinion would be for us all to flagellate one another: Madame de Saint-Ange will thrash Lapierre, so as to insure Madame de Mistival's obtaining a good encuntment; I'll flay Madame de Saint-Ange, Augustin will whip me, Eugénie will have at Augustin an herself will be very vigorously beaten by the Chevalier. (*All o, which is arranged. When Lapierre has finished cunt-fucking, his master orders him to fuck Madame de Mistival's ass, and he does so. When all is completed, Dolmancé continues.*) Capital! Out with you, Lapierre. Wait. Here are five *louis*. Ha! by God, that was a better inoculation than Tronchin made in all his life!

MADAME DE SAINT-ANGE—I believe it is now of the highest importance to provide against the escape of the poison circulating in Madame's veins; consequently, Eugénie must very carefully sew your cunt and ass so that the virulent humor, more concentrated, less subject to evaporation and not at all to leakage, will more promptly cinder your bones.

EUGENIE—Excellent idea! Quickly, quickly, fetch me needle and thread! . . . Spread your thighs, Mamma, so I can stitch you together—so that you'll give me no more little brothers and sisters. (*Madame de Saint-Ange gives Eugénie a large needle, through whose eye is threaded a heavy red waxed thread; Eugénie sews.*)

MADAME DE MISTIVAL—Oh, my God! the pain!

DOLMANCE, *laughing like a madman*—By God! excellent idea indeed! it does you honor, my dear; it would never have occurred to me.

EUGENIE, *from time to time pricking the lips of the cunt, occasionally stabbing its interior and sometimes using her needle on her mother's belly and* mons veneris.) Pay no attention to it, Mamma. I am simply testing the point.

LE CHEVALIER—The little whore wants to bleed her to death!

DOLMANCE, *causing himself to be frigged by Madame de Saint-Ange, as he witnessess the operation*—Ah, by God! how this extravagance stiffens me! Eugénie, multiply your stitches, so that the seam will be quite solid.

EUGENIE—I'll take, if necessary, over two hundred of them. . . . Chevalier, frig me while I work.

LE CHEVALIER, *obeying*—I've never seen a girl as vicious as this one!

EUGENIE, *much inflamed*—No invectives, Chevalier, or I'll prick you! Confine yourself to tickling me in the correct manner. A little asshole, if you please, my friend; have you only one hand? I can see no longer, my stitches go everywhere. . . . Look at it! do you see how my needle wanders . . . to her thighs, her tits. . . . Oh, fuck! what pleasure! . . .

MADAME DE MISTIVAL—You are tearing me to pieces, vile creature! . . . Oh, how I blush that it was I who gave you life!

EUGENIE—Come, come, be quiet, Mother dear; it's finished.

DOLMANCE, *emerging, with a great erection, from Madame de Saint-Ange's hands*—Eugénie, allow me to do the ass; that part belongs to me.

MADAME DE SAINT-ANGE—You're too stiff, Dolmancé, you'll make a martyr of her.

DOLMANCE—What matter! have we not written permission to make of her what we please? (*He turns Madame de Mistival upon her stomach, catches up the needle, and begins to sew her asshole.*)

MADAME DE MISTIVAL, *screaming like a banshee*—Aië! aië! aië!

DOLMANCE, *driving the needle deep into her flesh*—Silence, bitch! or I'll make a hash of your buttocks. . . . Eugénie, frig me. . . .

EUGENIE—Willingly, but upon condition you prick her more energetically, for, you must admit, you are proceeding with strange forbearance. (*She frigs him.*)

MADAME DE SAINT-ANGE—Work upon those two great cheeks for me!

DOLMANCE—Patience, I'll soon have her carved like a shank of beef; Eugénie, you are forgetting your lessons: you capped my prick!

EUGENIE—'Tis because this bitch's sufferings are inflaming my imagination to the point I no longer know exactly what I am doing.

DOLMANCE—Sweet fucking God! I'm beginning to go out of my mind! Saint-Ange, have Augustin bugger you in front of my eyes while your brother flies into your cunt, and above all dress me a panorama of asses: the picture will finish me. (*He stabs Madame de Mistival's buttocks while the posture he has called for is arranged.*) Here, Mamma dear, take this . . . and again that! . . . (*He drives his needle into at least twenty places.*)

MADAME DE MISTIVAL—Oh pardon me, Monsieur, I beg your pardon a thousand thousand times over . . . you are killing me. . . .

DOLMANCE, *wild with pleasure*—I should like to . . . 'tis an age since I have had such an erection; never would I have thought it possible after so many consecutive ejaculations.

MADAME DE SAINT-ANGE, *executing the called-for attitude*—Are we as we should be, Dolmancé?

DOLMANCE—Augustin, turn a little to the right; I don't see enough ass; have him lean forward: I must see the hole.

EUGENIE—Ah fuck! look at the bugger bleed!

DOLMANCE—Rather a good deal of blood, isn't there? Well, are the rest of you ready? As for myself, one minute more and I'll spray life's very balm upon the wounds I have just opened.

MADAME DE SAINT-ANGE—Yes, my heart, yes . . . I am coming . . . we arrive at the end at the same time. . . .

DOLMANCE, *who has finished his task, does nothing but increase his stabbing of the victim's buttocks as he discharges*—Ah triple bloody fucking God! . . . my sperm flows . . . 'tis lost, by bleeding little Jesus! . . . Eugénie, direct it upon the flanks I have just mutilated . . . oh fuck! fuck! 'tis done . . . over . . . I've no more . . . oh, why must weakness succeed passions so alive? . . .

MADAME DE SAINT-ANGE—Fuck! fuck me, brother, I discharge! . . . (*To Augustin:*) Stir yourself, great fucking-john! Don't you know that it is when I come that you've got to sink your tool deepest into my ass? . . . Ah, sacred name of God! how sweet it is, thus to be fucked by two men . . . (*The group disperses.*)

DOLMANCE—And now all's been said. (*To Madame de Mistival:*) Hey! whore, you may clothe yourself and leave when you wish. I must tell you that your husband authorized the doing of all that has just been done to you. We told you as much; you did not believe it. (*He shows her the letter.*) May this example serve to remind you that your daughter is old enough to do what she pleases; that she likes to fuck, loves to fuck, that she was born to fuck, and that, if you do not wish to be fucked yourself, the best thing for you to do is to let her do what she wants. Get out; the Chevalier will escort you home. Salute the company, whore! on your knees, bow down before your daughter, and beseech her pardon for your abominable use of her. . . . You, Eugénie, bestow two good smacks upon Madame your Mother and as soon as she gains the threshold, help her cross it with a few lusty kicks aimed at her ass. (*All this is done.*) Farewell, Chevalier; don't fuck Madame on the highway: remember, she's sewn up and has got the pox.

After the Chevalier's departure and Madame de Mistival's.) And now, good friends, let's to dinner, and afterward the four of us will retire for the night . . . in the same bed. Well, we've had a he active day. I never dine so heartily, I never sleep so soundly as when I have, during the day, sufficiently befouled myself with what ur fools call crimes.

The Marquis de Sade

Part Three

Two Moral Tales

Eugénie
de Franval
(1788)

In his famous Catalogue raisonné[1] *of 1788, drawn up with obvious pride in the Bastille less than a year before it was stormed, Sade made note of a work entitled* Eugénie de Franval, *which he described in the following manner:*

> 7.[2] Eugénie de Franval, *which might also be called or the Misfortunes of Incest. In all the literature of Europe there are neither any stories or novels wherein the dangers of libertinage are exposed with such force, no work wherein the dark-hued class of fiction [genre sombre] is carried to such frightening and pathetic extremes. This story offers a sublime characterization of a clergyman; a personage well-suited to reconcile the ungodly and debauched with virtue and religion.*

Sade originally intended to include Eugénie de Franval *in a projected multivolume work which was to be entitled* Contes et fabliaux du XVIIIᵉ siècle, par un troubadour provençal.[3] *Of this work, Sade noted:*

> *This work comprises four volumes, with an engraving for each tale; these short tales are interspersed in such a manner that an adventure which is gay, and even*

---

[1] *Of which the full title is:* Catalogue raisonné des œuvres de M. de S•••
à l'époque du 1ᵉʳ octobre 1788, *and the subtitle:* Cette collection contient quinze volumes in-8° avec estampes. *The fifteen volumes of which he gives the breakdown do not, of course, contain the clandestine works he was disinclined to acknowledge.*

[2] Eugénie *was to appear as the seventh tale in the fourth volume of Sade's stories and novellas.*

[3] *Sade, of course, was from Provence.*

*naughty but still well within the limits of modesty and
decency, will follow immediately upon a serious or
tragic adventure....* [4]

*Many of the manuscripts slated for this work were
lost or destroyed when the Bastille was stormed,* [5] *however,
and Sade was obliged to abandon his initial plan of publication. It was not until the year VIII (1800) that he com-
piled a new work, using those tales he had managed to save
or recover, a volume for which he gave up the idea of alter-
nating gay and somber stories, eliminating the gay.* [6] *Sade
entitled the work* Les Crimes de l'Amour, *and prefaced it
by a fascinating essay on the novel,* Idée sur les romans, *in
which, turning his back on much of the French fiction of his
day, he paid special homage to the robust genius of Fielding
and Richardson.*

The eleven stories which comprise Les Crimes de l'A-
mour *are uneven in quality, but at least one of them, Eugénie de Franval, qualifies as among the best of Sade's
shorter fictions. We present it here in its entirety, augmented by certain passages which did not figure in the original edition but which Maurice Heine discovered in Sade's
rough drafts and included in a later edition.* [7]

---

[4] *D.-A.-F. de Sade:* Historiettes, Contes et fabliaux/Dorci, *Paris, Jean-
Jacques Pauvert, 1957.*

[5] *In a letter to Gaufridy, dated late in May, 1790, Sade relates his tale
of woe concerning his removal from the Bastille. "I was taken out bare
as the back of my hand, and all my effects, that is more than a hundred
louis' worth of furniture, clothing, and linen, six hundred volumes some of
which very expensive and, what is irreparable,* fifteen volumes of my
manuscript works, *ready for the printer—manuscripts over which I daily
weep tears of blood—were placed under seals."*

[6] *Perhaps, said the anonymous reviewer of the work in the* Journal de
Paris *on 6 Brumaire (28 October) of that same year, because the author
"doubtless thought that this hue was better suited to us now and for some
time to come, since in this realm [of tragedy] reality still continues to
surpass fiction."*

[7] *These passages appear in italics herein.*

To instruct man and correct his morals: such is the sole goal we set for ourselves in this story. In reading it, may the reader be steeped in the knowledge of the dangers which forever dog the steps of those who, to satisfy their desires, will stop at nothing! May they be persuaded that the best education, wealth, talent, and the gifts of Nature are likely to lead one astray unless they are buttressed and brought to the fore by self-restraint, good conduct, wisdom, and modesty. Such are the truths we intend to relate. May the reader show himself indulgent for the monstrous details of the hideous crime we are obliged to describe; but is it possible to make others detest such aberrations unless one has the courage to lay them bare, without the slightest embellishment?

It is rare that everything conspires in one person to lead him to prosperity; does Nature shower her gifts upon him? Then Fortune refuses him her gifts. Does Fortune lavish her favors upon him? Then Nature proves niggardly. It would appear that the hand of Heaven has wished to show us that, in each individual as in the most sublime operations, the laws of equilibrium are the prime laws of the Universe, those which at the same time govern everything that happens, everything that vegetates, and everything that breathes.

Franval lived in Paris, the city of his birth, and possessed, among a variety of other talents, an income of four hundred thousand *livres,* a handsome figure, and a face to match. But beneath this seductive exterior was concealed a plethora of vices, and unfortunately among them those which, when adopted and practiced, quickly lead to crime. Franval's initial shortcoming was an imagination the disorderliness of which defies description; this is

a shortcoming that one cannot correct; its effects only worsen wit
age. The less one can do, the more one undertakes; the less on
acts, the more one invents; each period of one's life brings ne
ideas to the fore, and satiety, far from dampening one's ardo
paves the way for even more baleful refinements.

As we have said, Franval was generously endowed with a
the charm of youth and all the talents which embellish it; but s
great was his contempt of both moral and religious duties that i
had become impossible for his tutors to inculcate any of them i
him.

In an age when the most dangerous, the most insidious book
are available to children, as well as to their fathers and their tutor
when rashness of thought passes for philosophy, when incredulit
passes for strength, and libertinage is mistaken for imagination
Franval's wit provoked approving laughter. He may have bee
scolded immediately afterward, but later he was praised for i
Franval's father, an ardent advocate of fashionable sophisms, wa
the first to encourage his son to think *soundly* on all these matter
He even went so far as to personally lend his son the works mo
liable to corrupt him all the more quickly. In the light of whic
what teacher would have dared to inculcate principles different fro
those of the household wherein the young Franval was obliged
please?

Be that as it may, Franval lost his parents while he was sti
very young, and when he was nineteen an elderly uncle, who al
died shortly thereafter, bequeathed him, upon the occasion of h
marriage, the full wealth due him from his inheritance.

With such a fortune, Monsieur de Franval should have ha
not the slightest difficulty in finding a wife. An infinite number
possible matches were proposed, but since Franval had begged h
uncle to arrange a match for him with a girl younger than he, ar
with as few relatives as possible, the old man directed his attentio
to a Mademoiselle de Farneille, the daughter of a financier, who ha
lost her father and whose only family was her widowed mothe
The girl was actually quite young, only fifteen, but she had six
thousand very real *livres* annual income and one of the most charr
ing and delightful faces in all Paris . . . one of those virgin-lil
faces in which the qualities of candor and charm vie with each oth

eneath the delicate features of love and feminine grace. Her long
ond hair cascaded down below her waist and her large blue
es bespoke both tenderness and modesty; she had a slender, lithe,
d graceful figure, skin that was lily-white, and the freshness of
ses about her. She was blessed with many talents, was possessed
f a lively but slightly melancholy imagination—that gentle melan-
oly which predisposes one to a love of books and a taste for
litude, attributes which Nature seems to accord to those whom
e has fated for misfortune, as though to make it less bitter for
em by the somber and touching pleasure it brings them, a pleasure
hich makes them prefer tears to the frivolous joy of happiness,
hich is a much less active and less pervasive force.

Madame de Farneille, who was thirty-two at the time of her
ughter's marriage, was also a witty and winning woman, but
rhaps a trifle too reserved and severe. Desirous to see her only
ild happy, she had consulted all of Paris about this marriage. And
ce she no longer had any family, she was obliged to rely for
vice on a few of those cold friends who care not a whit about
ything. They succeeded in convincing her that the young man
o was being proposed for her daughter was, beyond any shadow
a doubt, the best match she could make in Paris, and that she
uld be utterly and unpardonably foolish if she were to turn it
wn. And so the marriage took place, and the young couple,
althy enough to take their own house, moved into it within a few
ys.

Young Franval's heart did not contain any of those vices of
ity, disorder, or irresponsibility which prevent a man from ma-
ing before the age of thirty. Possessed of a fair share of self-
nfidence, and being an orderly man who was at his best in
naging the affairs of a household, Franval had all the qualities
cessary for this aspect of a happy life. His vices, of a different
der altogether, were rather the failings of maturity than the
iscretions of youth: he was artful, scheming, cruel, base, self-
ntered, given to maneuvering, deceitful, and cunning—all of this
concealed not only by the grace and talent we have previously
ntioned but also by his eloquence, his uncommon wit, and his
st pleasing appearance. Such was the man we shall be dealing
h.

Mademoiselle de Farneille, who in accordance with the custo[m] had only known her husband at most a month prior to their ma[r]riage, was taken in by this sparkling exterior, and she had becom[e] his dupe. She idolized him, and the days were not long enough f[or] her to feast her adoring eyes upon him; so great was her adorati[on] in fact, that had any obstacles intervened to trouble the sweetne[ss] of a marriage in which, she said, she had found her only happine[ss] in life, her health, and even her life, might have been endangere[d.]

As for Franval, a philosopher when it came to women as [he] was with regard to everything else in life, coolness and impassivi[ty] marked his attitude toward this charming young woman.

"The woman who belongs to us," he would say, "is a sort [of] individual whom custom has given us in bondage. She must [be] gentle, submissive . . . utterly faithful and obedient; not that [I] especially share the common prejudice concerning the dishonor [a] wife can impose upon us when she imitates our debaucheries. [It's] merely that a man does not enjoy seeing another usurp his righ[ts.] Everything else is a matter of complete indifference, and adds n[ot] a jot to happiness."

With such sentiments in a husband, it is easy to predict tha[t a] life of roses is not what lies in store for the poor girl who is marri[ed] to him. Honest, sensible, well-bred, lovingly anticipating the eve[ry] desire of the only man in the world she cared about, Madame [de] Franval bore her chains during the early years without ever s[us]pecting her enslavement. It was easy for her to see that she w[as] merely gleaning meager scraps in the fields of Hymen, but, still t[oo] happy with what little he left her, she devoted her every attenti[on] and applied herself scrupulously to make certain that during th[ose] brief moments when Franval acknowledged her tenderness [he] would at least find everything that she believed her beloved husba[nd] required to make him happy.

And yet the best proof that Franval had not been complete[ly] remiss in his duties was the fact that, during the first year of th[eir] marriage, his wife, then aged sixteen and a half, gave birth to [a] daughter even more beautiful than her mother, a child whom h[er] father straightway named Eugénie—Eugénie, both the horror a[nd] the wonder of Nature.

Monsieur de Franval, who doubtless had formed the m[ost]

odious designs upon the child the moment she was born, immediately separated her from her mother. Until she was seven, Eugénie was entrusted to the care of some women on whom Franval could rely, and they confined themselves to inculcating in her a good disposition and to teaching her to read. They scrupulously avoided imparting to her the slightest knowledge of any religious or moral principles of the sort that a girl of that age normally receives.

Madame de Farneille and her daughter, who were grieved and shocked by such conduct, reproached Monsieur de Franval for it. He replied imperturbably that his plan was to make his daughter happy, and he had no intention of filling her mind with chimeras designed solely to frighten men without ever proving of the least worth to them. He also said that a girl who needed nothing more than to learn how to make herself pleasing and attractive would be well advised to remain ignorant of such nonsense, for such fantasies would only disturb the serenity of her life without adding a grain of truth to her moral character or a grain of beauty to her body. Such remarks were sorely displeasing to Madame de Farneille, who was increasingly attracted to celestial ideas the more she withdrew from worldly pleasures. Piety is a failing inherent in periods of advancing age or declining health. In the tumult of the passions, we generally feel but slight concern over a future we gauge to be extremely remote, but when passions' language becomes less compelling, when we advance on the final stages of life, when in a word everything leaves us, then we cast ourselves back into the arms of the God we have heard about when we were children. And if, according to philosophy, these latter illusions are fully as fantastic as the others, they are at least not as dangerous.

Franval's mother-in-law had no close relatives, she herself had little or no influence, and at the very most a few casual friends who proved less than that when put to the test. Having to do battle against an amiable, young, well-situated son-in-law, she very wisely decided that it would be simpler to limit herself to remonstrating than to undertake more vigorous measures with a man who could ruin the mother and cause the daughter to be confined if they should dare to pit themselves against him. In consideration of which a few remonstrances were all she ventured, and as soon as she saw that they were to no avail, she fell silent.

Franval, certain of his superiority and perceiving that they were afraid of him, soon threw all restraint to the winds and, only thinly disguising his activities simply for the sake of appearances, he advanced straight toward his terrible goal.

When Eugénie was seven years old, Franval took her to his wife; and that loving mother, who had not seen her child since the day she had brought her into the world, could not get her fill of fondling and caressing her. For two hours she hugged the child to her breast, smothering her with kisses and bathing her with her tears. She wanted to learn all her little talents and accomplishments; but Eugénie had none except the ability to read fluently, to be blessed with perfect health, and to be as pretty as an angel. Madame de Franval was once again plunged into despair when she realized that it was only too true that her daughter was quite ignorant of the most basic principles of religion.

"What are you doing, Sir," she said to her husband. "Do you mean to say you are bringing her up only for this world? Deign to reflect that she, like all of us, is destined to dwell but a second here, afterward to plunge into an eternity, which will be disastrous if you deprive her of the wherewithal to find happiness at the feet of Him from whom all life cometh."

"If Eugénie knows nothing, Madame," Franval replied, "if these maxims are carefully concealed from her, there is no way she could be made unhappy; for if they are true, the Supreme Being is too just to punish her for her ignorance, and if they are false, what need is there to speak to her about them? As for the rest of her education, please have confidence in me. Starting today I shall be her tutor, and I promise you that in a few years your daughter will surpass all the children her own age."

Madame de Franval wished to pursue the matter further; calling the heart's eloquence to the aid of reason, a few tears expressed themselves for her. But Franval, who was not in the least moved by the tears, did not seem even to notice them. He had Eugénie taken away, and informed his wife that if she tried to interfere in any way with the education he planned to give his daughter, or if she attempted to inculcate in the girl principles different from those with which he intended to nourish her, she would by so doing deprive herself of the pleasure of seeing her daughter, whom he would send to one of those châteaux from which she would not re-emerge. Madame de Franval, accustomed to submission, heard his words in silence. She begged her husband not to separate her from such a cherished possession and, weeping, promised not to interfere in any way with the education that was being prepared for her.

From that moment on, Mademoiselle de Franval was installed in a very lovely apartment adjacent to that of her father, with a highly intelligent governess, an assistant governess, a chambermaid, and two girl companions her own age, solely intended for Eugénie's amusement. She was given teachers of writing, drawing, poetry, natural history, elocution, geography, astronomy, Greek, English, German, Italian, fencing, dancing, riding and music. Eugénie arose at seven every day, in summer as well as winter. For breakfast she had a large piece of rye bread, which she took with her out into the garden. She ran and played there till eight, when she came back inside and spent a few moments with her father in his apartment, while he acquainted her with the little tricks and games that society indulges in. Till nine she worked on her lessons; at nine her first tutor arrived. Between then and two she was visited by no less than five teachers. She ate lunch with her two little friends and her head governess. The dinner was composed of vegetables, fish, pastries, and fruit; never any meat, soup, wine, liqueurs, or coffee. From three to four, Eugénie went back out again to play with her companions. There they exercised together, playing tennis, ball, skittles, battledore and shuttlecock, or seeing how far they could run and jump. They dressed according to the seasons; they wore nothing that constricted their waists, never any of those ridiculous corsets equally dangerous for the stomach and chest which, impairing the breathing of a young person, perforce attack the lungs. From four to six, Mademoiselle de Franval received other tutors; and as all had not been able to appear the same day, the others came the following day. Three times a week, Eugénie went to the theater with her father, in the little grilled boxes that were rented for her by the year. At nine o'clock she returned home and dined. All she then had to eat were vegetables and fruit. Four times a week, from ten to eleven, she played with her two governesses and her maid, read from one or more novels, and then went to bed. The three other days, those when Franval did not dine out, she spent alone in her father's apartment, and Franval devoted this period to what he termed *his conferences*. During these sessions he inculcated in his daughter his maxims on morality and religion, presenting to her on the one hand what some men thought on these matters, and then on the other expounding his own views.

Possessed of considerable intelligence, a vast range of knowledge, a keen mind, and passions that were already awakening, it is easy to judge the progress that these views made in Eugénie's soul. But since the shameful Franval's intention was not only to strengthen her mind, these lectures rarely concluded without inflaming her heart as well; and this horrible man succeeded so well in finding the means to please his daughter, he corrupted her so cleverly, he made himself so useful both to her education and her pleasures, he so ardently anticipated her every desire that Eugénie, even in the most brilliant circles, found no one as attractive as her father. And even before he made his intentions explicit, the innocent and pliant creature had filled her young heart with all the sentiments of friendship, gratitude, and tenderness which must inevitably lead to the most ardent love. She had eyes only for Franval; she paid no attention to anyone but him, and rebelled at any idea that might separate her from him. She would gladly have lavished upon him not her honor, not her charms—all these sacrifices would have seemed far too meager for the object of her idolatry—but her blood, her very life, if this tender friend of her heart had demanded it.

Mademoiselle de Franval's feelings for her mother, her respectable and wretched mother, were not quite the same. Her father, by skillfully conveying to his daughter that Madame de Franval, being his wife, demanded certain ministrations from him which often prevented him from doing for his dear Eugénie everything his heart dictated, had discovered the secret of implanting in the heart of this young person much more hate and jealousy than the sort of respectable and tender sentiments that she ought to have felt for such a mother.

"My friend, my brother," Eugénie sometimes used to say to Franval, who did not want his daughter to employ other expressions with him, "this woman you call your wife, this creature who, you tell me, brought me into this world, is indeed most demanding, since in wishing to have you always by her side, she deprives me of the happiness of spending my life with you. . . . It is quite obvious to me that you prefer her to your Eugénie. As for me, I shall never love anything that steals your heart away from me."

"You are wrong, my dear friend," Franval replied. "No one in this world will ever acquire over me rights as strong as yours. The ties which bind this woman and your best friend—the fruit of usage and social convention, which I view philosophically—will never equal the ties between us. . . . You will always be my favorite, Eugénie; you will be the angel and the light of my life, the hearth of my heart, the moving force of my existence."

"Oh! how sweet these words are!" Eugénie replied. "Repeat them to me often, my friend. . . . If only you knew how happy these expressions of your tenderness make me!"

And taking Franval's hand and clasping it to her heart, she went on:

"Here, feel, I can feel them all there. . . ."

"Your tender caresses assure me it's true," Franval answered, pressing her in his arms. . . . And thus, without a trace of remorse, the perfidious wretch concluded his plans for the seduction of this poor girl.

Eugénie's fourteenth year was the time Franval had set for the consummation of his crime. Let us shudder! . . . He did it.

The very day that she reached that age, or rather the day she completed her fourteenth year, they were both in the country, without the encumbering presence of family or other intrusions. The Count, having that day attired his daughter in the manner that vestal virgins had been clothed in ancient times upon the occasion of their consecration to the goddess Venus, brought her upon the stroke of eleven o'clock into a voluptuous drawing room wherein the daylight was softened by muslin curtains and the furniture was bedecked with flowers. In the middle of the room was a throne of roses; Franval led his daughter over to it.

"Eugénie," he said to her, helping her to sit down upon it, "to-day be the queen of my heart and allow me, on bended knee, to worship and adore thee."

"You adore me, my brother, when it is to you that I owe

everything, you who are the author of my days, who has formed me. . . . Ah! let me rather fall down at your feet; that is the only place I belong, and the only place I aspire to with you."

"Oh my dear, my tender Eugénie," said the Count, seating himself beside her on the flower-strewn chairs which were to serve as the scene of his triumph, "if indeed it is true that you owe me something, if your feelings toward me are as sincere as you say they are, do you know by what means you can persuade me of your sincerity?"

"What are they, my brother? Tell them to me quickly, so that I may be quick to seize them."

"All these many charms, Eugénie, that Nature has lavished upon you, all these physical charms with which She has embellished you—these you must sacrifice to me without a moment's delay."

"But what is it you ask of me? Are you not already the master of everything? Does not what you have wrought belong to you? Can another delight in your handiwork?"

"But you are not unaware of people's prejudices. . . ."

"You have never concealed them from me."

"I do not wish to flout them without your consent."

"Do you not despise them as much as I?"

"Surely, but I do not want to be your tyrant, and even less your seducer. The services I am soliciting, nay the rewards I request, I wish to be won through love, and through love alone. You are familiar with the world and with its ways; I have never concealed any of its lures from you. My habit of keeping other men from your eyes, so that I alone will be the constant object of your vision, has become a hoax, a piece of trickery unworthy of me. If in the world there exists a being whom you prefer to me, name him without delay, I shall go to the ends of the earth to find him and straightway lead him back here into your arms. In a word, it is your happiness I seek, my angel, yours much more than mine. These gentle pleasures you can give me will be nothing to me, if they are not the concrete proof of your love. Therefore, Eugénie, make up your mind. The time has come for you to be immolated, and immolated you must be. But you yourself must name the priest who shall perform the sacrifice; I renounce the pleasures which this title assures me if it is not your heart and soul which offer them to me.

And, still worthy of your heart, if 'tis not I whom you most prefer, still I shall, by bringing you him whom you can love and cherish, at least have merited your tender affection though I may not have won the citadel of your heart. And, failing to become Eugénie's lover, I shall still be her friend."

"You will be everything, my brother, you will be everything," Eugénie said, burning with love and desire. *"To whom do you wish me to sacrifice myself if it is not to him whom I solely adore! What creature in the entire universe can be more worthy than you of these meager charms that you desire . . . and over which your burning hands are already roaming with great ardor! Can't you see by the fire which inflames me that I am just as eager as you to know these pleasures of which you have spoken? Ah! do, do what you will, my dear brother, my best friend, make Eugénie your victim; immolated by your beloved hands, she will always be triumphant."*

The fervent Franval who, considering the character we know him to possess, had draped himself in so much delicacy only in order to seduce his daughter all the more subtly, soon abused her credulity and, with all the obstacles eliminated or overcome both by the principles with which he had nourished that open and impressionable heart and by the cunning with which he had ensnared her at this final moment, he concluded his perfidious conquest and himself became with impunity the ravisher of that virginity of which Nature and the bonds of blood had made him the trusted defender.

Several days passed in mutual intoxication. Eugénie, old enough to experience the pleasures of love, her appetite whetted by his doctrines, yielded herself to its transports. Franval taught her all its mysteries; he traced for her all its paths and byways. The more he paid obeisance, the more complete became his conquest. She would have wished to receive him in a thousand temples simultaneously; she accused her friend's imagination of being too timid, of not throwing all caution to the winds. And she had the feeling that he was hiding something from her. She complained of her age, and of a kind of ingenuousness which perhaps kept her from being seductive enough. And if she wished to further her amorous education, it was to insure that no means of inflaming her lover remained unknown to her.

They returned to Paris, but the criminal pleasures which this perverse man had reveled in had too delightfully flattered his moral and physical faculties for that trait of character, inconstancy, which generally caused him to break off his other affairs, to have the least effect in breaking the bonds of this one. He had fallen hopelessly in love, and from this dangerous passion there inevitably ensued the cruelest abandonment of his wife. . . . Alas! what a victim. Madame de Franval, who was then thirty-one, was in the full flower of her beauty. An impression of sadness, the sort which inevitably follows upon the sorrows which consumed her, made her even more attractive. Bathed in her own tears, a constant prey to melancholy, her beautiful hair carelessly scattered over an alabaster throat, her lips lovingly pressed against the portraits of her faithless daughter and tyrant-husband, she resembled one of those beautiful virgins whom Michelangelo was wont to portray in the throes of sorrow. As yet she was still unaware of that which was destined to crown her affliction. The manner in which Eugénie was being educated, the essential things to which Madame de Franval was not privy or those she was told only to make her hate them; the certainty that these duties, despised by Franval, would never be permitted to her daughter; the little time she was allowed to spend with the young person; the fear that the peculiar education that Eugénie was being given might sooner or later lead her into the paths of crime; and, finally, Franval's wild conduct, his daily harshness toward her—she whose only concern in life was to anticipate his every wish, who knew no other charms than those resulting from her having interested or pleased him: these alone, for the moment, were the only causes of her distress. But imagine with what sorrow and pain this tender soul would be afflicted when she learned the full truth!

Meanwhile, Eugénie's education continued. She herself had expressed a desire to follow her masters until she was sixteen, and her talents, the broad scope of her knowledge, the graces which daily developed in her—all these further tightened Franval's fetters. It was easy to see that he had never loved anyone the way he loved Eugénie.

On the surface, nothing in Eugénie's daily routine had been changed save the time of the lectures. These private discussions with her father occurred much more frequently and lasted far into the night. Eugénie's governess was the only person privy to the affair, and they trusted her sufficiently not to be worried about her indiscretion. There were also a few changes in Eugénie's meal schedule: now she ate with her parents. In a house like Franval's, this circumstance soon placed Eugénie in a position to meet people and to be courted with a view toward marriage. Several men did ask for her hand. Franval, certain of his daughter's heart and feeling he had nothing to fear from these requests, had nonetheless failed to realize that this virtual flood of proposals might end by revealing everything.

In one conversation with her daughter—a favor so devoutly desired by Madame de Franval and so rarely obtained—this tender mother informed Eugénie that Monsieur de Colunce had asked for her hand.

"You know the gentleman," Madame de Franval said. "He loves you; he is young, agreeable, and one day he will be rich. He awaits your consent . . . naught but your consent. What will my answer be?"

Taken aback, Eugénie reddened and replied that as yet she did not feel inclined toward marriage, but suggested the matter be referred to her father; his wish would be her command.

Seeing in this reply nothing but candor pure and simple, Madame de Franval waited patiently for a few days until at last she found an occasion to speak to her husband about it. She communicated to him the intentions of the Colunce family, and those of young Colunce himself, and told him what his daughter's reply had been.

As one can imagine, Franval already knew everything; but he made little effort to disguise his feelings.

"Madame," he said dryly to his wife, "I must ask you to refrain from interfering in matters pertaining to Eugénie. I should have imagined that you would have surmised, from the care you saw me take to keep her away from you, how deeply I desired to make certain that anything relating to her should in no wise concern you. I reiterate my orders on this subject. I trust you will not forget them again."

"But what, Sir, shall I reply," she answered, "since the request has been made through me?"

"You will say that I appreciate the honor, and that my daughter has certain congenital defects which make marriage impossible for her."

"But, Monsieur, these defects are not real. Why should I then falsely saddle her with them, and why deprive your daughter of the happiness she may find in marriage?"

"Has marriage then made you so profoundly happy, Madame?"

"Doubtless all other wives have not failed so signally to win their husband's devotion, or" (and this was accompanied by a sigh) "all husbands are not like you."

"Wives . . . wives are faithless, jealous, imperious, coquettish, or pious. . . . Husbands are treacherous, inconstant, cruel, or despotic. There, Madame, you have the summary of everyone on earth. Do not expect to find a paragon."

"Still, everyone gets married."

"True, the fools and ne'er-do-wells. In the words of one philosopher, 'People get married only when they do not know what they are doing, or when they no longer know what to do.' "

"Then you think the human race should be allowed to die out?"

"And why not? A planet whose only product is poison cannot be rooted out too quickly."

"Eugénie will not be grateful to you for your excessive sternness toward her."

"Has she evinced any desire to marry this young man?"

"She said that your wishes were her commands."

"In that case, Madame, my commands are that you pursue this matter no further."

And Monsieur de Franval left the room after reiterating most vigorously to his wife that she never speak to him on the subject again.

Madame de Franval did not fail to inform her mother of the conversation that she had just had with her husband, and Madame de Farneille, a more subtle soul and one more versed in the effects

of the passions than was her attractive daughter, immediately suspected something unnatural was involved.

Eugénie saw her grandmother very seldom, no more than an
hour, on festive or important occasions, and always in the presence
of her father. Desirous of clarifying the matter, Madame de
Farneille sent word to her son-in-law asking him to accord her the
presence of her granddaughter one day, and requesting that he
might allow her to stay one entire afternoon, in order to distract
her, she said, from a migraine headache from which she was suffering. Franval sent back an irritable reply saying that there was
nothing Eugénie feared more than the vapors, but that he would
nonetheless bring her personally to her grandmother whenever the
latter desired. He added, however, that Eugénie would not be able
to remain for very long, since she was obliged to go from her grandmother's to a physics course which she was assiduously following.

When they arrived at Madame de Farneille's, she did not
hide from her son-in-law her astonishment at his refusal of the
proposed marriage.

"I imagine that you safely can allow your daughter to persuade me herself," Madame de Farneille went on, "of this defect
which, according to you, must deprive her of marriage."

"Whether this defect is real or not, Madame," said Franval,
who was slightly surprised by his mother-in-law's resolution, "the
fact is that it would cost me a small fortune to marry my daughter,
and I am still too young to consent to such sacrifices. When she is
twenty-five, she may do as she wishes. Until then, she cannot count
on me or my support."

"And do you feel the same way, Eugénie?" said Madame de
Farneille.

"With this one difference," Eugénie said with considerable
firmness. "My father has given me permission to marry when I am
twenty-five. But to you both here present, Madame, I swear that I
shall never in my life take advantage of this permission, which with
my way of thinking would only lead to unhappiness."

"At your age one does not have 'a way of thinking,' said
Madame de Farneille, "and there is something quite out of the
ordinary in all this, which I intend to ferret out."

"I urge you to try, Madame," Franval said, leading his

daughter away. "In fact, you would be well advised to seek the services of your clergy to help you in solving the enigma. And when all your powers have scraped and delved and you are at last enlightened in the matter, please let me know whether or not I was right in opposing Eugénie's marriage."

Franval's sarcasm concerning his mother-in-law's ecclesiastical advisers was aimed at a respectable personage whom it will be appropriate to introduce at this point, since the sequence of events will soon show him in action.

He was the confessor both of Madame de Farneille and her daughter, one of the most virtuous men in all France: honest, benevolent, a paragon of candor and wisdom, Monsieur de Clervil, far from having all the vices of men of the cloth, was possessed only of gentle and useful qualities. The rod and the staff of the poor, the sincere friend of the wealthy, the consoler of the wretched and downtrodden, this worthy man combined all the gifts which make a person agreeable, all the virtues which make one sensitive.

When consulted, Clervil replied as a man of good common sense that before taking a stand in the matter they would have to unravel the reasons why Monsieur de Franval was opposed to his daughter's marriage; and although Madame de Farneille offered a few remarks suggesting the possibility of an affair—one which in fact existed all too concretely—the prudent confessor rejected these ideas. And finding them too outrageously insulting both for Madame de Franval and for her husband, he indignantly refused even to consider the possibility.

"Crime is such a distressing thing, Madame," this honest man was sometimes wont to say, "it is so highly unlikely that a decent person should voluntarily exceed all the bounds of modesty and virtue, that it is never with anything but the most extreme repugnance that I make up my mind to ascribe such wrongs to someone. Be wary in suspecting the presence of vice. Our suspicions are often the handiwork of our pride and vanity, and almost always the fruit of a secret comparison that takes place in the depths of our soul: we hasten to assign evil, for this gives us the right to feel superior. If we reflect seriously upon the matter, would it not be better to leave a secret sin forever hidden rather than to dream up imaginary ones because of our unforgivable haste, and thus, for no reason, to sully in our eyes people who have never committed any wrongs save those which our pride has ascribed to them? And would our world not be a better place if this principle were always followed? Is it not infinitely less necessary to punish a crime than it is essential to prevent it from spreading? By leaving it in the darkness it seeks, have we not as it were annihilated it? Scandal noised abroad is certain scandal, and the recital of it awakens the passions of those who are inclined toward the same kind of crime. Crime being inevitably blind, the guilty party of the as yet undiscovered crime flatters himself that he will be luckier than the criminal whose crime has been found out. 'Tis not a lesson he has been given, but a counsel, and he gives himself over to excesses that he might never have dared to indulge in without the rash revelations . . . falsely mistaken for justice, but which, in reality, are nothing more than ill-conceived severity, or vanity in disguise."

This initial conference therefore led to no other resolution than the decision to investigate carefully the reasons for Franval's aversion to the marriage of his daughter, and the reasons why Eugénie shared his opinions. It was decided not to undertake anything until these motives were discovered.

"Well, Eugénie," Franval said to his daughter that evening, "now can you see for yourself that they want to separate us? And do you think they'll succeed, my child? . . . Will they succeed in breaking the sweetest bonds in my life?"

"Never . . . never! Don't be afraid, my dearest friend! These bonds in which you delight are as precious to me as they are to you. You did not deceive me when you formed them; you clearly warned me how they would shock the morality of our society. But I was hardly frightened at the idea of breaking a custom which, varying from clime to clime, cannot therefore be sacred. I wanted these bonds; I wove them without remorse. Therefore you need have no fear that I shall break them."

"Alas, who knows? . . . Colunce is younger than I. . . . He has everything a man needs to win you. Eugénie, leave off listening to a vestige of madness which doubtless blinds you. Age and the torch of reason will soon dispel the aura and lead to regrets, you'll confide them to me, and I shall never forgive myself for having been the cause of them."

"No," Eugénie said firmly, "no, I have made up my mind to love no one but you. I should deem myself the most miserable of women if I were obliged to marry. . . . Can you imagine," she went on heatedly, "me, me married to a stranger who, unlike you, would not have double reason to love me and whose feelings therefore would at best be no stronger than his desire. . . . Abandoned and despised by him, what would become of me thereafter? A prude, a sanctimonious person, or a whore? No, no, I prefer being your mistress, my friend. Yes, I love you a hundred times better than being reduced to playing one or the other of these infamous roles in society. . . . But what is the cause of all this commotion?" Eugénie went on bitterly. "Do you know what it is, my friend? *Who* is the cause of it? . . . Your wife? . . . She and she alone. Her implacable jealousy . . . You may be sure of it: these are the only reasons behind the disasters that threaten us. . . . Oh, I don't blame her: everything is simple . . . everything conceivable . . . one can resort to anything when it is a question of keeping you. What would I not do if I were in her place, and someone were trying to steal your affections from me?"

Deeply moved, Franval showered his daughter with a thousand kisses. And Eugénie, finding the encouragement in these criminal caresses to plumb more forcefully the depths of her appalling soul, chanced to mention to her father, with an unforgivable impudence, that the only way for either one of them to escape her mother's surveillance would be to give her a lover. The idea amused Franval. But being a much more evil person than his daughter, and wishing to prepare imperceptibly this young heart for all the impressions of hatred for his wife that he desired to implant therein, he answered that he found this vengeance far too mild, adding that there were plenty of other means of making a woman miserable when she put her husband into a bad humor.

Several weeks passed, during which Franval and his daughter finally decided to put into effect the first plan conceived for the despair of this monster's virtuous wife, rightly believing that before going on to more drastic and shameful acts, they should at least try to give her a lover. For not only would this furnish material for all the other acts, but, if it succeeded, it would necessarily oblige Madame de Franval to cease concerning herself with the faults of others, since she would have her own to worry about. For the execution of this project, Franval cast a careful eye upon all the young men he knew and, after considerable reflection, came to the conclusion that only Valmont could serve as his man.

Valmont was thirty years old, had a charming face, considerable intelligence and a vivid imagination, and no principles whatever. He was, consequently, ideally suited to play the role they were going to offer him. One day Franval invited him to dinner and, as they were leaving the table, he took him aside:

"My friend," he said to him, "I have always believed you worthy of me. The time has come to prove that I have not erred in my judgment. I demand a proof of your sentiments . . . a most extraordinary proof."

"What kind of proof, my dear fellow? Explain yourself, and never for a moment doubt of my eagerness to be of service to you!"

"What do you think of my wife?"

"A delightful creature. And if you weren't her husband, I would long since have made her my mistress."

"This consideration is most delicate and discerning, Valmont, but it does not touch me."

"What do you mean?"

"I am going to astound you . . . 'tis precisely because you are fond of me, and because I am Madame de Franval's husband, that I demand that you become her lover."

"Are you mad?"

"No, but given to whimsy . . . capricious. You've been aware of these qualities in me for a long time. I want to bring about the downfall of virtue, and I maintain that you are the one to snare it."

"What nonsense!"

"Not in the least, 'tis a masterpiece of reason."

"What! You mean you really want me to make you a . . . ?"

"Yes, I want it, I demand it, and I shall cease to consider you my friend if you refuse me this favor. . . . I shall help you. . . . I'll arrange it so that you can be alone with her . . . more and more often, if need be . . . and you will take advantage of these occasions. And the moment I am quite certain of my destiny, I shall, if you like, throw myself at your feet to thank you for your obliging kindness."

"Franval, don't take me for an utter fool. There's something most strange about all this. . . . I refuse to lift a finger until you tell me the whole truth."

"All right . . . but I suspect you're a trifle squeamish . . . I doubt you have sufficient strength of mind to hear all the details of this matter. . . . You're still a prey to prejudice . . . still gallant, I venture to say, eh? . . . If I tell you everything you'll tremble like a child and refuse to do anything further."

"Me, tremble? . . . In all honesty I must say I'm overwhelmed by the way you judge me. Listen, my friend, I want you to know that there is no aberration in the world, not a single vice, however strange or abnormal, that is capable of alarming my heart for even a moment."

"Valmont, have you ever taken the trouble to cast a careful eye on Eugénie from time to time?"

"Your daughter?"

"Or, if you prefer, my mistress."

"Ah, you scoundrel! Now I understand."

"This is the first time in my life I find you perceptive."

"What? On your word of honor, you're in love with your daughter?"

"Yes, my friend, exactly as Lot! I have always held the Holy Scriptures in highest esteem, as I have always been persuaded that one accedes to Heaven by emulating its heroes! . . . Ah! my friend, Pygmalion's madness no longer amazes me. . . . Is the world not full of such weaknesses? Was it not necessary to resort to such methods to populate the world? And what was then not a sin, can it now have become one? What nonsense! You mean to say that a lovely girl cannot tempt me because I am guilty of having sired her? That what ought to bind me more intimately to her should become the very reason for my removal from her? 'Tis because she resembles me, because she is flesh of my flesh, that is to say that she is the embodiment of all the motives upon which to base the most ardent love, that I should regard her with an icy eye? . . . Ah, what sophistry! . . . How totally absurd! Let fools abide by such ridiculous inhibitions, they are not made for hearts such as ours. The dominion of beauty, the holy rights of love are oblivious to futile human conventions. In their ascendancy they annihilate these conventions as the rays of the rising sun purge the earth of the shrouds which cloak it by night. Let us trample underfoot these abominable prejudices, which are always the enemies of happiness. If at times they beguile the reason, it has always been at the expense of the most exquisite pleasures. . . . May we forever despise them!"

"I'm convinced," Valmont responded, "and I am willing to admit that your Eugénie must be a delightful mistress. A beauty more lively than her mother's, even though she does not possess, as does your wife, that languor which seizes the soul with such voluptuousness. But Eugénie has that piquant quality which breaks and subdues us, which, as it were, seems to subjugate anything which would like to offer resistance. While one seems to yield, the other demands; what one allows, the other offers. Of the two, I much prefer the latter."

"But it's not Eugénie I'm giving you, but her mother."

"And what reasons do you have for resorting to such methods?"

"My wife is jealous, an albatross on my neck. She's forever spying on me. She wants Eugénie to marry. I must saddle my wife with sins in order to conceal my own. Therefore you must have her . . . amuse yourself with her for a time . . . and then you'll betray her. Let me surprise you in her arms . . . and then I shall punish her or, using this discovery as a weapon, I shall barter it in return for an armistice on both our parts. But no love, Valmont; with ice in your veins, capture and win her, but do not let her gain mastery over you. If you let sentiments become involved, my plans are as good as finished."

"Have no fear: she would be the first woman who had aroused my heart."

Thus our two villains came to a mutual agreement, and it was resolved that in a very few days Valmont would undertake to seduce Madame de Franval, with full permission to employ anything he wished in order to succeed . . . even the avowal of Franval's love, as the most powerful means of inducing this virtuous woman to seek vengeance.

Eugénie, to whom the plan was revealed, thought it monstrously amusing. The infamous creature even dared declare that if Valmont should succeed, to make her happiness as complete as possible she would like to verify with her own eyes her mother's disgrace, she absolutely had to witness that paragon of virtue incontestably yielding to the charms of a pleasure that she so rigorously condemned in others.

At last the day arrived when the most virtuous, the best, and most wretched of women was not only going to receive the most painful blow that anyone can be dealt but also when her hideous husband was destined to outrage her, abandoning her—handing her over himself—to him by whom he had agreed to be dishonored. . . . What madness! . . . What utter disdain of all principles. With what view in mind does Nature create hearts as depraved as these? . . .

A few preliminary conversations had set the stage for the present scene. Furthermore, Valmont was on close enough terms with Franval so that his wife had not the slightest compunction about remaining alone with him, as indeed she had done on more than one occasion in the past. The three of them were sitting in the drawing room. Franval rose and said:

"I must leave. An important matter requires my presence. . . . 'Tis to leave you in the care of your governess," he said, laughing, "leaving you with Valmont. The man's a pillar of virtue. But if he should forget himself, please be kind enough to inform me. I still do not love him enough to yield him my rights. . . ."

And the insolent fellow departed.

After exchanging a few banalities, the aftereffects of Franval's little joke, Valmont said that he had found his friend changed during the past six months.

"I haven't dared broach the subject, to ask him the reasons," Valmont said, "but he seems to be upset and distressed."

"One thing which is certain," Madame de Franval replied, "is that he is upsetting and distressing those around him."

"Good heavens! What are you saying? . . . that my friend has been treating you badly?"

"If it were still only that!"

"Be so good as to inform me, you know how devoted I am . . . my inviolable attachment."

"A series of frightful disorders ... moral corruption, in short every kind of wrong ... would you believe it? We received a most advantageous offer to marry our daughter ... and he refused. ..."

And here the artful Valmont averted his eyes, the expression of a man who has understood ... who sighs to himself ... and is afraid to explain.

"What is the matter, Monsieur," Madame de Franval resumed, "what I have told you does not surprise you? Your silence is most singular."

"Ah, Madame, is it not better to remain silent than to say things which will bring despair to someone one loves?"

"And what, may I ask, is that enigma? Explain yourself, I beg of you."

"How can you expect me not to shudder if I should be the one who causes the scales to fall from your eyes," Valmont said, warmly seizing one of her hands.

"Oh, Monsieur," Madame de Franval went on, with great animation, "either explain yourself or say not another word, I beseech you. The situation you leave me in is terrible."

"Perhaps less terrible than the state to which you yourself reduce me," said Valmont, casting a look of love at the woman he was intent on seducing.

"But what does all that mean, Sir? You begin by alarming me, you make me desire an explanation, then daring to insinuate certain things that I neither can nor should endure, you deprive me of the means of learning from you what upsets me so cruelly. Speak, Sir, speak or you shall reduce me to utter despair."

"Very well, Madame, since you demand it I shall be less obscure, even though it costs me dearly to break your heart. ... Learn, if you must, the cruel reason behind your husband's refusal to Monsieur Colunce's request ... Eugénie ..."

"Yes?"

"Well, the fact is, Madame, that Franval adores her. Today less her father than her lover, he would rather give up his own life than give up Eugénie."

Madame de Franval had not heard this fatal revelation without reacting, and she fell down in a faint. Valmont hastened to her assistance, and as soon as she had come to her senses he pursued:

"You see, Madame, the cost of the disclosure you demanded. . . . I would have given anything in the world to . . ."

"Leave me, Monsieur, leave me," said Madame de Franval, who was in a state difficult to describe. "After a shock such as this I need to be alone for a while."

"And you expect me to leave you in this situation? Ah, your grief is too fully felt in my own heart for me not to ask you the privilege of sharing it with you. I have inflicted the wound. Let me bind it up."

"Franval, in love with his daughter! Just Heaven! This creature whom I have borne in my womb, 'tis now she who breaks my heart so grievously! . . . So horrible, so shocking a crime! . . . Ah, Monsieur, is it possible? . . . Are you quite certain?"

"Madame, had I the slightest doubt I should have remained silent. I would a hundred times rather have preferred not to tell you anything than to alarm you in vain. 'Tis from your own husband I have the certitude of this infamy, which he confided to me. In any event, try and be calm, I beg of you. Rather let us concentrate now on the means of breaking off this affair than on those of bringing it to light. And you alone hold the key to this rupture. . . ."

"Ah, tell me this minute what it is. This crime horrifies me."

"Madame, a husband of Franval's character is not brought back by virtue. He is little disposed to believe in the virtue of women. Virtue, he maintains, is the fruit of their pride or their temperament, and what they do to remain faithful to us is done more to satisfy themselves than either to please or enchain us. . . . You will excuse me, Madame, if I say that on this point I must admit that I tend to share his opinion. Never in my experience has a wife succeeded in destroying her husband's vices by means of virtue. What would prick him, what would stimulate him much more would be a conduct approximating his own, and by this would you bring him more quickly back to you. Jealousy would be the inevitable result; how many hearts have been restored to love by this infallible means. Your husband, then seeing that this virtue to which he is accustomed, and which he has been so insolent as to despise, is rather the work of reflection than of the organs' insouciance, will really learn to esteem it in you, at the very moment when he believes you capable of discarding it. He imagines . . . he dares to say that if you have never had any lovers, it is because you have never been assaulted. Prove to him that this is a decision which lies solely in your own hands . . . to revenge yourself for his wrongdoings and his contempt. Perhaps, according to your strict principles, you will have committed a minor sin. But think of all the sins you will have prevented! Think of the husband you will have steered back to you! And for no more than the most minor outrage to the goddess you revere, what a disciple you will have brought back into her temple. Ah, Madame, I appeal only to your reason. By the conduct I dare to prescribe to you, you will bring Franval back forever, you will captivate him eternally. The reverse conduct —the one you have been following—sends him flying away from you. He will escape you, never to return. Yes, Madame, I dare to affirm that either you do not love your husband or you should cease this hesitation."

Madame de Franval, very much taken aback by this declaration, remained silent for some time. Then, remembering Valmont's earlier looks, and his initial remarks, she managed to reply adroitly:

"Monsieur, let us presume that I follow the advice you give me; upon whom do you think I should cast my eye to upset my husband further?"

"Ah, my dear, my divine friend," Valmont cried, oblivious to the trap she had set for him, "upon the one man in the world who loves you most, upon him who has adored you since first he set eyes upon you and who swears at your feet to die beneath your sway. . . ."

"Leave, Monsieur," Madame de Franval said imperiously, "leave and never let me see you again. Your ruse has been discovered. You accuse my husband of wrongs of which he can only be innocent merely to advance your own treacherous schemes of seduction. And let me tell you that even were he guilty, the means you offer me are too repugnant to my heart for me to entertain them for a moment. Never do the failings of a husband justify or exonerate those of a wife. For her they must become the reasons for even greater virtue, so that the Just and Righteous man, whom the Almighty will come upon in the afflicted cities on the verge of suffering the effects of his wrath, may divert the flames which are about to consume them."

Upon these words Madame de Franval left the room and, calling for Valmont's servants, obliged him to withdraw, much ashamed of his initial efforts.

Although this attractive woman had seen through Valmont's ruses, what he had said coincided so well with her own and her mother's fears that she resolved to do everything within her power to ascertain these cruel facts. She paid a visit to Madame de Farneille, recounted to her everything that had happened and returned, her mind made up as to the steps that we are going to see her undertake.

It has long been said, and rightfully so, that we have no greater enemies than our own servants; forever jealous, always envious, they seem to seek to lighten the burden of their own yoke by discovering wrongs in us which, then placing us in a position inferior to themselves, allow them for the space of a few moments at least to gratify their vanity by assuming a superiority over us which fate has denied them.

Madame de Franval bribed one of Eugénie's servants: the promise of a fixed pension, a pleasant future, the appearance of doing a good deed—all swayed this creature and she promised to arrange it the following night so that Madame de Franval could dispel all doubts as to her unhappiness.

The moment arrived. The wretched mother was admitted to a room adjoining the room wherein, each night, her perfidious husband outraged both his nuptial bonds and the bonds of Heaven. Eugénie was with her father; several candles remained lighted on a corner cupboard; they were going to illuminate this crime. . . . The altar was prepared, the victim took her place upon it, he who performs the sacrifice followed her. . . .

Madame de Franval was no longer sustained by anything save her despair, her outraged love, and her courage. . . . She burst open the doors restraining her, she hurled herself into the room, and there, her face bathed in tears, she fell on her knees at the feet of the incestuous Franval:

"Oh, you," she cried, addressing herself to Franval, "you who fill my life with misery and sorrow, I have not deserved such treatment. . . . However you have insulted and wronged me, I still worship you. See my tears, and do not dismiss my appeal: I ask you to have mercy on this poor wretched child who, deceived by her own weakness and your seduction, thinks she can find happiness in shamelessness and crime. . . . Eugénie, Eugénie, do you want to thrust a sword into the heart of her who brought you into the world? No longer consent to be the accomplice of this heinous crime whose full horror has been concealed from you! Come . . . let me fold you in my waiting arms. Look at your wretched mother on her knees before you, begging you not to outrage both your honor and Nature. . . . But if you both refuse," the distraught woman went on, bearing a dagger to her heart, "this is the means I shall employ to escape the dishonor with which you are trying to cover me. I shall make my blood flow and stain you here, and you will have to consummate your crimes upon my sad body."

That Franval's hardened heart was able to resist this spectacle, those who are beginning to know this scoundrel will have no trouble believing; but that Eugénie remained unmoved by it is quite inconceivable.

"Madame," said this corrupted girl with the cruelest show of impassivity, "I must admit I find it hard to believe you in full possession of your reason, after the scene you have just made in your husband's room. Is he not the master of his own actions? And when he approves of mine, what right have you to blame them? Do we worry our heads or pry into your indiscretions with Monsieur Valmont? Do we disturb you in the exercise of your pleasures? Therefore deign to respect ours, or do not be surprised if I urge your husband to take whatever steps are required to oblige you to do so. . . ."

At this point Madame de Franval could no longer control her patience, and the full force of her anger was turned against the unworthy creature who could so forget herself as to speak to her in such terms. Struggling to her feet, Madame de Franval threw herself furiously upon her daughter, but the odious and cruel Franval, seizing his wife by the hair, dragged her in a rage away from her daughter out of the room. He threw her violently down the stairs of the house, and she fell, bloody and unconscious, at the door of one of the chambermaids' rooms. Awakened by this terrible noise, the maid quickly saved her mistress from the wrath of her tyrant, who was already on his way downstairs to finish off his hapless victim. . . .

They took her to her room, locked her in, and began to administer to her, while the monster who had just treated her with such utter fury flew back to his detestable companion to spend the night as peacefully as though he had not debased himself lower than the most ferocious beasts by assaults so execrable, so designed to degrade and humiliate her . . . so horrible, in a word, that we blush at the necessity of having to reveal them.

Poor Madame de Franval no longer had any illusions left, and there was no other for her to espouse. It was all too clear that her husband's heart, that is, the most beloved possession of her life, had been taken from her. And by whom? By the very person who owed her the most respect, and who had just spoken to her with utter insolence. She also began to suspect strongly that the whole adventure with Valmont had been nothing more than a detestable trap set to ensnare her in a web of guilt, if 'twere possible or, failing that, to ascribe the guilt to her in any event, in order to counterbalance, and hence justify, the thousand times more serious wrongs which they dared to heap upon her.

Nothing could have been more certain. Franval, informed of Valmont's failure, had prevailed upon him to replace the truth by imposture and indiscretion, and to noise it abroad that he was Madame de Franval's lover. And they had decided that they would forge abominable letters which would document, in the most unequivocal manner, the existence of the illicit commerce in which, however, poor Madame de Franval had actually refused to involve herself.

Meanwhile, in deep despair, Madame de Franval, whose body was covered with numerous wounds, fell seriously ill. Her barbarous husband, refusing to see her and not even bothering to inform himself of her condition, left with Eugénie for the country, on the pretense that since there was fever in the house he did not care to expose his daughter to it.

During her illness, Valmont several times came to call at her door, but was each time refused admission. Locked in her room with her mother and Monsieur de Clervil, Madame de Franval absolutely refused to see anyone else. Consoled by such dear friends as these, who were so fully worthy of being able to influence her, and nourished back to health by their loving care, forty days later Madame de Franval was in a condition to see people again. At which time Franval brought his daughter back to Paris and, with Valmont, mapped out a campaign intended to counter the one it appeared that Madame de Franval and her friends were preparing to direct against him.

Our scoundrel paid his wife a visit as soon as he judged she was well enough to receive him.

"Madame," he said coldly, "you must be aware of my concern for your condition. I cannot conceal from you the fact that your condition is the sole factor restraining Eugénie. She was determined to bring a complaint against you for the way you have treated her. However she may be persuaded of the basic respect due a mother by her daughter, still she cannot ignore the fact that this same mother threw herself on her daughter with a drawn dagger. Such a violent and unseemly act, Madame, could well open the eyes of the government to your conduct and, inevitably, pose a serious threat to both your honor and your liberty."

"I was not expecting such recriminations, Monsieur," Madame de Franval replied. "And when my daughter, seduced by you, becomes at the same time guilty of incest, adultery, libertinage, and ingratitude—ingratitude of the most odious sort—toward her who brought her into the world, . . . yes, I must confess, I did not imagine that after this complexity of horrors that I would be the one against whom a complaint would be brought. It takes all your cunning, all your wickedness, Monsieur, to accuse innocence the while excusing crime with such audacity."

"I am not unaware, Madame, that the pretense for your scene was the odious suspicion you dared to formulate regarding me. But chimeras do not justify crimes. What you have imagined is false. But, unfortunately, what you have done is only too real. You evinced astonishment at the reproaches my daughter directed at you at the time of your affair with Valmont. But, Madame, she has only discovered the irregularities of your conduct since they have been the talk of all Paris. This affair is so well known, and the proofs of it unfortunately so solid, that those who speak to you about it are at the very most guilty of indiscretion, but not of calumny."

"I, Sir," said this respectable woman, rising to her feet, indignantly, "*I* have an affair with Valmont! Just Heaven! 'Tis you who have said it!" (Breaking into tears:)

"Ungrateful wretch! This is how you repay my tenderness. . . . This is my recompense for having loved you so. It is not enough for you to outrage me so cruelly. It is not enough that you seduce my daughter. You have to go even further and, by ascribing crimes which for me would be more terrible than death, dare to justify your own. . . ." (Regaining her composure:) "You say, Monsieur, that you have the proofs of this affair. All right, show them. I demand that they be made public, and I shall force you to show them to everyone if you refuse to show them to me."

"No, Madame, I shall not show them to the whole world; it is not generally the husband who openly displays this sort of thing; he bemoans it, and conceals it as best he can. But if you demand it, Madame, I shall certainly not refuse you. . . ." (And then taking a letter case from his pocket:) "Sit down," he said, "this must be verified calmly. Ill-humor and loss of temper would be harmful but would not convince me. Therefore, I beg you to keep control of yourself, and let us discuss this with composure."

Madame de Franval, thoroughly convinced of her innocence, did not know what to make of these preparatory remarks. And her surprise, mingled with fright, kept her in a state of extreme agitation.

"First of all, Madame," said Franval, emptying one side of the letter case, "here is all your correspondence with Valmont over the past six months. Do not accuse this worthy gentleman either of imprudence or indiscretion. He is doubtless too honorable a man to have dared fail you so badly. But one of his servants, more adroit than Valmont is attentive, discovered the secret way to procure for me this precious monument to your extreme fidelity and your eminent virtue." (Then, leafing through the letters which he spread out on the table:) "Please allow me," he went on, "to choose one from among many of these ordinary displays of chitchat by an overheated woman . . . overheated, I might add, by a most attractive man; one, I say, which seemed to me more lascivious and decisive than the others. Here it is, Madame:

My boring husband is dining tonight in his *maisonette* on the outskirts of Paris with that horrible creature . . . a creature it is impossible brought into the world. Come, my love, come and comfort me for all the sorrows which these two monsters give me. . . . What am I saying? Is this not the greatest service they could be doing me at present, and will that affair not prevent my husband from discovering ours? Let him then tighten the bonds as much as he likes; but at least let him not bethink himself to desire breaking those which attach me to the only man whom I have ever adored in this world.

"Well, Madame?"

"Well, Monsieur, I must say I admire you," Madame de Franval replied. "Each day adds to the incredible esteem you so richly deserve. And however many fine qualities I have recognized in you hitherto, I confess I was yet unaware you were also a forger and a slanderer."

"Ah, so you deny the evidence?"

"Not in the least. All I ask is to be persuaded. We shall have judges appointed . . . experts. And, if you agree, we shall ask that the most severe penalty be exacted against whichever of the two parties is found guilty."

"That is what I call effrontery! Well, the truth is I prefer it to sorrow. . . . Now, where were we? Ah, yes; that you have a lover, Madame," said Franval, shaking out the other side of the letter case, "a lover with a handsome face, and a *boring husband,* is most assuredly nothing so extraordinary. But that at your age you are supporting this lover—at my expense—I trust you will allow me not to find this quite so simple. . . . And yet here are 100,000 *écus* in notes, either paid by you or made out in your hand in favor of Valmont. Please run through them, I beg of you," this monster added, showing them to her without allowing her to touch them. . . .

To Zaide, jeweler

By the present note I hereby agree to pay the sum of twenty-two thousand *livres* on the account of Monsieur de Valmont, by arrangement with him.

FARNEILLE DE FRANVAL

"Here's another made out to Jamet, the horse merchant, for six thousand *livres*. This is for the team of dark bay horses which today are both Valmont's delight and the admiration of all Paris. . . . Yes, Madame, the whole package comes to three hundred thousand, two hundred and eighty-three *livres,* and ten *sous,* a third of which total you still owe, and the balance of which you have most loyally paid. . . . Well, Madame?"

"Ah, Monsieur, this fraud is too crude and vulgar to cause me the least concern. To confound those who have invented it against me, I demand but one thing: that the people in whose names I have, so it is alleged, made out these documents, appear personally and swear under oath that I have had dealings with them."

"They will, Madame, of that you may be sure. Do you think they themselves would have warned me of your conduct if they were not determined to back up their claims? Indeed, without my intervention, one of them would have signed a writ against you today. . . ."

At this point poor Madame de Franval's beautiful eyes filled with bitter tears. Her courage failed to sustain her any longer, and she fell into a fit of despair with the most frightful symptoms: she began to strike her head against the marble objects around her, bruising her face horribly.

"Monsieur," she cried out, throwing herself at her husband's feet, "please do away with me, I beseech you, by means less slow and less torturous. Since my life is an obstacle to your crimes, end it with a single blow . . . refrain though from inching me into my grave. . . . Am I guilty of having loved you? of having rebelled against what was so cruelly stealing your heart from me? . . . Well then, barbarian, punish me for these transgressions. Yes, take this metal shaft," she said, throwing herself on her husband's sword, "and pierce my breast with it, with no pity. But at least let me die worthy of your esteem, let me take as my sole consolation to the grave the certainty that you believe me incapable of the infamies of which you accuse me . . . solely to cover your own. . . ."

She was on her knees at Franval's feet, her head and bust thrown back, her hands wounded and bleeding from the naked steel she had tried to seize and thrust into her breast. This lovely breast was laid bare, her hair was in disarray, its strands soaked by the tears that flowed abundantly. Never had sorrow been more pathetic and more expressive, never had it been seen in a more touching, more noble, and more attractive garb.

"No, Madame," Franval said, resisting her movement, "no, 'tis not your death I desire, but your punishment. I can understand your repentance, your tears do not surprise me, you are furious at having been discovered. I approve of this frame of mind, which leads me to believe you plan to amend your ways, a change that the fate I have in mind for you, and because of which I must depart in order to give it my every care, will doubtless precipitate."

"Stop, Franval," the unhappy woman cried, "do not voice abroad the news of your dishonor, nor tell the world that you are a perjurer, a forger, a slanderer, and guilty of incest into the bargain. . . . You wish to have done with me, I shall run away, I shall leave in search of some refuge where your very memory shall disappear from my mind. . . . You will be free, you can exercise your criminal desires with impunity. . . . Yes, I shall forget you, if I can, oh heartless man. Or, if your painful image remains graven in my heart, if it still pursues me in my distant darkness, I shall not obliterate it, traitor, that effort is beyond my abilities; no, I shall not obliterate it, but I shall punish my own blindness, and shall bury in the horror of the grave the guilty altar which committed the error of holding you too dear. . . ."

With these words, the final outcry of a soul overwhelmed by a recent illness, the poor woman fainted and fell unconscious to the floor. The cold shadows of death spread over the roses of her beautiful complexion, already withered by the stings of despair. She appeared little more than a lifeless mass, from which, however, grace, modesty, and seemliness . . . all the attributes of virtue, had refused to flee. The monster left the room and repaired to his own chambers, there to enjoy, with his guilty daughter, the terrible triumph which vice, or rather low villainy, dared to win over innocence and unhappiness.

Franval's abominable daughter infinitely savored the details of this encounter. She only wished she could have seen them. She would have liked to carry the horror even further and see Valmont vanquish her mother's resistance, and then have Franval surprise them in the act. What means, if that were to happen, what means of justification would their victim then have had left? And was it not important for them to deprive her of any and all means? Such was Eugénie.

Meanwhile, Franval's poor wife had only the refuge of her mother's breast for her tears, and it was not long before she revealed to her the reasons for her latest sorrow. It was at this juncture that Madame de Farneille came to the conclusion that Monsieur de Clervil's age, his calling, and his personal prestige perhaps might exercise a certain good influence on her son-in-law. Nothing is more confident than adversity. As best she could, she apprised this worthy ecclesiastic of the truth about Franval's chaotic conduct; she convinced him of the truth which he had hitherto been disinclined to believe, and she beseeched him above all to employ with such a scoundrel only that persuasive eloquence which appeals to the heart rather than to the head. And after he had talked with this traitor, she suggested that Monsieur de Clervil solicit a meeting with Eugénie, during which he could similarly put to use whatever he should deem most appropriate toward enlightening the poor child as to the abyss that had opened beneath her feet and, if possible, to bring her back to her mother's heart and to the path of virtue.

Franval, informed that Clervil intended to request to see both him and his daughter, had time enough to conspire with Eugénie, and when they had settled on their plans they sent word to Madame de Farneille that both were prepared to hear him out. The credulous Madame de Franval held out the highest hopes for the eloquence of this spiritual guide. The wretched are wont to seize at straws with such avidity, in order to procure for themselves a pleasure which the truth disowns, that they fabricate most cunningly all sorts of illusions!

Clervil arrived. It was nine in the morning. Franval received him in the room where he was accustomed to spending the night with his daughter. He had embellished it with every imaginable elegance, but had nonetheless allowed it to retain a certain disorder which bore witness to his criminal pleasures. In a neighboring room, Eugénie could hear everything, the better to prepare herself for the conversation with her which was due to follow.

"It is only most reluctantly, and with the greatest fear of disturbing you, Monsieur," Clervil began, "that I dare to present myself before you. Persons of our calling are commonly so much a burden to those who, like yourself, spend their lives tasting the pleasures of this world, that I reproach myself for having consented to Madame de Farneille's desires and having requested to converse with you for a moment or two."

"Please sit down, Monsieur, and so long as reason and justice hold sway in your conversation, you need never fear of boring me."

"Sir, you are beloved of a young wife full of charm and virtue and whom, it is alleged, you make most miserable. Having as arms naught but her innocence and her candor, and with only a mother's ear to hear her complaints, still idolizing you despite your wrongs, you can easily imagine the frightful position in which she finds herself!"

"If you please, Monsieur, I should like us to get down to the facts. I have the feeling you are skirting the issue; pray tell me, what is the purpose of your mission?"

"To bring you back to happiness, if that is possible."

"Therefore, if I find myself happy in my present situation, may I assume that you should have nothing further to say to me?"

"It is impossible, Monsieur, to find happiness in the exercise of crime."

"I agree. But the man who, through profound study and mature reflection, has been able to bring his mind to the point where he does not see evil in anything, where he contemplates the whole of human endeavor with the most supreme indifference and considers every action of which man is capable as the necessary result of a power, whatever its nature, which is at times good and at times bad, but always imperious, inspires us alternately with what men approve and what they condemn, but never anything that disturbs or troubles it—that man, I say, and I'm sure you will agree, can be just as happy living the way I do as you are in your chosen calling. Happiness is ideal, it is the work of the imagination. It is a manner of being moved which relies solely upon the way we see and feel. Except for the satisfaction of needs, there is nothing which makes all men equally happy. Not a day goes by but that we see one person made happy by something that supremely displeases another. Therefore, there is no certain or fixed happiness, and the only happiness possible for us is the one we form with the help of our organs and our principles."

"I know that, Monsieur, but though our mind may deceive

us, our conscience never leads us astray, and here is the book wherein Nature has inscribed all our duties."

"And do we not manipulate this factitious conscience at will? Habit bends it, it is for us like soft wax which our fingers shape as they choose. If this book were as certain as you pretend, would man not be endowed with an invariable conscience? From one end of the earth to the other, would not all of man's actions be the same for him? And yet is such truly the case? Does the Hottentot tremble at what terrifies the Frenchman? And does the Frenchman not do daily what would be punishable in Japan? No, Monsieur, no, there is nothing real in the world, nothing deserving of praise or approbation, nothing worthy of being rewarded or punished, nothing which, unjust here, is not quite lawful five hundred leagues away. In a word, no wrong is real, no good is constant."

"Do not believe it, Sir. Virtue is not an illusion. It is not a matter of ascertaining whether something is good here, or bad a few degrees farther away, in order to assign it a precise determination of crime or virtue, and to make certain of finding happiness therein by reason of the choice one has made of it. Man's only happiness resides in his complete submission to the laws of his land. He has either to respect them or to be miserable, there is no middle ground between their infraction and misfortune. 'Tis not, if you prefer to state it in these terms, these things in themselves which give rise to the evils which overwhelm us whenever we allow ourselves free reign to indulge in these forbidden practices, 'tis rather the conflict between these things—which may be intrinsically either good or bad—and the social conventions of the society in which we live. One can surely do no harm by preferring to stroll along the boulevards than along the Champs Elysées. And yet if a law were passed forbidding our citizens from frequenting the boulevards, whosoever should break this law might be setting in motion an eternal chain of misfortunes for himself, although in breaking it he had done something quite simple. Moreover, the habit of breaking ordinary restrictions soon leads to the violation of more serious ones, and from error to error one soon arrives at crimes of a nature to be punished in any country under the sun and to inspire fear in any reasonable creature on earth, no matter in what clime he may dwell. If man does not have a universal conscience, he at least has a national conscience, relative to the existence that we have received from Nature, and in which her hand inscribes our duties in letters which we cannot efface without danger. For example, Monsieur, your family accuses you of incest. It makes no difference what sophistries you employ to justify this crime or lessen the horror, or what specious arguments you apply to it or what authorities you call upon by buttressing these arguments with examples drawn from neighboring countries, the fact remains that this crime, which is only a crime in certain countries, is most assuredly dangerous wherever the law forbids it. It is no less certain that it can give rise to the most frightful consequences, as well as other crimes necessitated by this first one . . . crimes, I might add, of a sort to be deemed abominable by all men. Had you married your daughter on the banks of the Ganges, where such marriages are permitted, perhaps you might have committed only a minor wrong. But in a country where these unions are forbidden, by offering this revolting spectacle to the public . . . and to the eyes of a woman who adores you and who, by this treacherous act, is being pushed to the edge of the grave, you are no doubt committing a frightful act, a crime which tends to break the holiest bonds of Nature: those which, attaching your daughter to her who gave her life, ought to make this person the most respected, the most sacred of all objects to her. You oblige this girl to despise her most precious duties, you cause her to hate the very person who bore her in her womb; without realizing it, you are preparing weapons that she may one day direct against you. In every doctrine you offer her, in every principle you inculcate in her, your condemnation is inscribed. And if one day her arm is raised against you in an attempt against your life, 'tis you who will have sharpened the dagger."

"Your way of reasoning, so different from that of most men of the cloth," Franval replied, "compels me to trust in you, Monsieur. I could deny your accusations. I hope that the frankness with which I reveal myself to you will also oblige you to believe the wrongs I impute to my wife when, to expose them, I employ the same truthfulness with which I intend to characterize my own confessions. Yes, Monsieur, I love my daughter, I love her passionately, she is my mistress, my wife, my daughter, my confidante, my friend, my only God on earth; in fine, she possesses all the homage that any heart can ever hope to obtain, and all homage of which my heart is capable is due her. These sentiments will endure as long as I live. Being unable to give them up, I doubtless must therefore justify them.

"A father's first duty toward his daughter is undeniably— I'm sure you will agree, Monsieur—to procure for her the greatest happiness possible. If he does not succeed in this task, then he has failed in his obligations toward her; if he does succeed, then he is blameless. I have neither seduced nor constrained Eugénie—this is a noteworthy consideration, which I trust you will not forget. I did not conceal the world from her. I expounded for her the good and bad sides of marriage, the roses and the thorns it contains. It was then I offered myself, and left her free to choose. She had adequate time to reflect on the matter. She did not hesitate: she claimed that she could find happiness only with me. Was I wrong to give her, in order to make her happy, what she appeared in full knowledge to desire above all else?"

"These sophistries justify nothing, Monsieur. You were wrong to give your daughter the slightest inclination that the person she could not prefer without crime might become the object of her happiness. No matter how lovely a fruit might appear, would you not regret having offered it to someone if you knew that lurking within its flesh was death? No, Monsieur, no: in this whole wretched affair you have had only one object in mind, and that object was you, and you have made your daughter both an accomplice and a victim. These methods are inexcusable. . . . And what wrongs, in your eyes, do you ascribe to that virtuous and sensitive wife whose heart you twist and break at will? What wrongs, unjust man, except the wrong of loving you?"

"This is the point I wish to discuss with you, Sir, and 'tis here I expect and hope for your confidence. After the full candor to which I have treated you, in making a full confession of all that is ascribed to me, I trust I have some right to expect such confidence."

And then Franval, showing Clervil the forged letters and notes he had attributed to his wife, swore to him that nothing was more authentic than these documents, and than the affair between

Madame de Franval and the person who was the subject of the papers.

Clervil was familiar with the entire matter.

"Well, Monsieur," he said firmly to Franval, "was I not right to tell you that an error viewed at first as being without consequence in itself can, by accustoming us to exceed limits, lead us to the most extravagant excesses of crime and wickedness? You have begun with an act which, in your eyes, you deemed totally inoffensive, and you see to what infamous lengths you are obliged to go in order to justify or conceal it? Follow my advice, Monsieur, throw these unpardonable atrocities into the fire and, I beg of you, let us forget them, let us forget they ever existed."

"These documents are authentic, Monsieur."

"They are false."

"You can only be in doubt about them. Is that sufficient reason for you to contradict me?"

"Pardon me, Monsieur, but the only reason I have to suppose they are authentic is your word on the matter, and you have good reason indeed for buttressing your accusation. As for believing them false, I have your wife's word for it, and she too would have good reason to tell me if they were authentic, if they actually were. This, Sir, is how I judge. Self-interest is the vehicle for all man's actions, the wellspring of everything he does. Wherever I can discover it, the torch of truth immediately lights up. This rule has never once failed me, and I have been applying it for forty years. And furthermore, will your wife's virtue not annihilate this loathsome calumny in everyone's eyes? And is it possible that your wife, with her frankness and her candor, with indeed the love for you which still burns within her, could ever have committed such abominable acts as those you charge her with? No, Monsieur, this is not how crime begins. Since you are so familiar with its effects, you should maneuver more cleverly."

"That, Sir, is abusive language."

"You'll forgive me, Monsieur, but injustice, calumny, libertinage revolt my soul so completely that I sometimes find it hard to control the agitation which these horrors incite in me. Let us burn these papers, Monsieur, I most urgently beseech you . . . burn them for your honor and your peace of mind."

"I never suspected, Monsieur," said Franval, getting to his feet, "that in the exercise of your ministry one could so easily become an apologist . . . the protector of misconduct and of adultery. My wife is dishonoring me, she is ruining me. I have proved it to you. Your blindness concerning her makes you prefer to accuse me and rather suppose that 'tis I who am the slanderer than she the treacherous and debauched woman. All right, Monsieur, the law shall decide. Every court in France shall resound with my accusations, I shall come bearing proof, I shall publish my dishonor, and then we shall see whether you will still be guileless enough, or rather foolish enough, to protect so shameless a creature against me."

"I shall leave you now, Monsieur," Clervil said, also getting to his feet. "I did not realize to what extent the faults of your mind had so altered the qualities of your heart and that, blinded by an unjust desire for revenge, you had become capable of coolly maintaining what could only derive from delirium. . . . Ah! Monsieur, how all this has persuaded me all the more that when man oversteps the bounds of his most sacred duties, he soon allows himself to annihilate all the others. . . . If further reflection should bring you back to your senses, I beg of you to send word to me, Monsieur, and you will always find, in your family as well as in myself, friends disposed to receive you. May I be allowed to see Mademoiselle your daughter for a moment?"

"You, Sir, may do as you like. I would only suggest, nay urge you that when talking with her you either employ more eloquent means or draw upon sounder resources in presenting these luminous truths to her, truths in which I was unfortunate enough to perceive naught but blindness and sophistries."

Clervil went into Eugénie's room. She awaited him dressed in the most elegant and most coquettish negligee. This sort of indecency, the fruit of self-neglidence and of crime, reigned unashamedly in her every gesture and look, and the perfidious girl, insulting the graces which embellished her in spite of herself, combined both the qualities susceptible of inflaming vice and those certain to revolt virtue.

Since it was not appropriate for a girl to engage in so detailed a discussion as a philosopher such as Franval had done, Eugénie confined herself to persiflage. She gradually became openly provocative, but upon seeing that her seductions were in vain, and that a man as virtuous as the one with whom she was dealing had not the slightest intention of allowing himself to be ensnared in her trap, she adroitly cut the knots holding the veil of her charms and, before Clervil had the time to realize what she was doing, she had arranged herself in a state of great disorder.

"The wretch," she cried at the top of her lungs, "take this monster away from me! And, above all, let not my father know of his crime. Just Heaven! I was expecting pious counsel from him . . . and the vile man assaulted my modesty. . . . Look," she cried to the servants who had hastened to her room upon hearing her cries, "look at the condition this shameless creature has put me in. Look at them, look at these benevolent disciples of a divinity they insult and outrage. Scandal, debauchery, seduction: there is the trinity of their morality, while we, dupes of their false virtue, are foolish enough to go on worshiping them."

Clervil, although extremely annoyed by such a scene, nonetheless succeeded in concealing his emotions. And as he left the room he said, with great self-possession, to the crowd around him:

"May heaven preserve this unfortunate child. . . . May it make her better if it can, and let no one in this house offend her sentiments of virtue more than I have done . . . sentiments that I came here less to defile than to revive in her heart."

Such were the only fruits which Madame de Farneille and her daughter culled from a negotiation they had approached so hopefully. They were far from realizing the degradations that crime works in the souls of the wicked: what might have some effect on others only embitters them, and it is in the very lessons of good that they find encouragement to do evil.

From then on, everything turned more venomous on both sides. Franval and Eugénie clearly saw that Madame de Franval would have to be persuaded of her alleged wrongs, in a way that would no longer allow her to doubt of the matter. And Madame de Farneille, in concert with her daughter, concocted serious plans to abduct Eugénie. They discussed the project with Clervil; this worthy man refused to have any part of such drastic resolutions. He had, he said, been too badly treated in this affair to be able to undertake anything more than imploring forgiveness for the guilty, and this he urgently did pray for, steadfastly refusing to involve himself in any other duty or effort of mediation. How sublime were his sentiments! Why is it that this nobility is so rare among men of the cloth? Or why had so singular a man chosen so soiled a calling?

Let us begin with Franval's endeavors.

Valmont reappeared.

"You're an imbecile," Eugénie's guilty lover said to him, "you are unworthy of being my student. And if you do not come off better in a second meeting with my wife, I shall trumpet your name all over Paris. You must have her, my friend, and I mean really have her, my eyes must be persuaded of her defeat . . . in fine, I must be able to deprive that loathsome creature of any means of excuse and of defense."

"And what if she resists?" Valmont responded.

"Then employ violence . . . I shall make certain that there is no one around. . . . Frighten her, threaten her, what does it matter? . . . I shall consider all the means of your triumph as so many favors I owe you."

"Listen," Valmont then said, "I agree to everything you propose, I give you my word of honor that your wife will yield. But I require one condition, and if you refuse it then I refuse to play the game. We agreed that jealousy is to have no part in our arrangements, as you know. I therefore demand that you accord me half an hour with Eugénie. You have no idea how I shall act after I have enjoyed the pleasure of your daughter's company for a short while. . . ."

"But Valmont . . ."

"I can understand your fears. But if you deem me your friend I shall not forgive you for them. All I aspire to is the charm of seeing Eugénie alone and talking with her for a few moments."

"Valmont," said Franval, somewhat astonished, "you place too high a fee on your services. I am as fully aware as you of the ridiculous aspects of jealousy, but I idolize the girl you are referring to, and I should rather give up my entire fortune than yield her favors."

"I am not claiming them, so set your mind at rest."

And Franval, who realized that, among all his friends and

acquaintances, there was none capable of serving his purposes so well as Valmont, was adamantly opposed to letting him escape:

"All right," he said, a trifle testily, "but I repeat that your services come very dear, and by discharging them in this manner you have relieved me from any obligation toward you, and from any gratitude."

"Oh! gratitude is naught but the price paid for honest favors. It will never be kindled in your heart for the services I am going to render you. And I shall even go so far as to predict that these selfsame services will cause us to quarrel before two months are up. Come, my friend, I know the ways of men . . . their faults and failings, and everything they involve. Place the human animal, the most wicked animal of all, in whatever situation you choose, and I shall predict every last result that will perforce ensue. . . . Therefore I wish to be paid in advance, or the game is off."

"I accept," said Franval.

"Very well then," Valmont replied. "Now everything depends on you. I shall act whenever you wish."

"I need a few days to make my preparations," Franval said. "But within four days at the most I am with you."

Monsieur de Franval had raised his daughter in such a way that he had no misgivings about any excessive modesty on her part which would cause her to refuse to participate in the plans he was formulating with his friend. But he was jealous, and this Eugénie knew. She loved him at least as much as he adored her, and as soon as she knew what was in the offing she confessed to Franval that she was terribly afraid this tête-à-tête with Valmont might have serious repercussions. Franval, who believed he knew Valmont well enough to be persuaded that all this would only provide certain nourishments for his head without any danger to his heart, reassured his daughter as best he could, and went about his preparations.

It was then that Franval learned, from servants in whom he had complete confidence and whom he had planted in the service of his mother-in-law, that Eugénie was in the gravest danger and that Madame de Farneille was on the verge of obtaining a writ to have her taken away from him. Franval had no doubt but that the whole plot was Clervil's work. And momentarily putting aside his plans involving Valmont, he turned his complete attention to ridding himself of this poor ecclesiastic whom he wrongly judged to be the instigator of everything. He sowed his gold; this powerful weapon of every vice is properly planted in a thousand different hands, and finally six trustworthy scoundrels are ready and willing to do his bidding.

One evening when Clervil, who was wont to dine rather frequently with Madame de Farneille, was leaving her house alone and on foot, he was surrounded and seized. . . . He was told that the arrest was made upon the orders of the government, and shown a forged document. Then he was thrown into a post chaise and he was driven in all haste to the prison of an isolated château which Franval owned in the depths of the Ardennes. There the poor man was turned over to the concierge of the château as a scoundrel who was plotting to kill his master. And the most careful precautions were taken to make certain that this unfortunate victim, whose only wrong was to have shown himself overly indulgent toward those who outraged him so cruelly, could never again be seen.

Madame de Farneille was on the brink of despair. She had not the slightest doubt but that the whole affair was the work of her son-in-law. Her efforts to ascertain the whereabouts of Clervil slowed those touching upon Eugénie's abduction. Having at her disposal only a limited amount of money, and with only a few friends, it was difficult to pursue two equally important undertakings at once. And furthermore, Franval's drastic action had forced them onto the defensive. They directed all their energies, therefore, toward finding the father confessor. But all their efforts were in vain; our villain had executed his plan so cleverly that it became impossible to uncover the slightest trace.

Madame de Franval, who had not seen her husband since their last scene, was hesitant to question him. But the intensity of one's interest in a matter destroys any other considerations, and she finally found the courage to ask her tyrant if he planned to add to the already long list of grievances of which he was guilty on her behalf by depriving her mother of the best friend she had in the world. The monster protested his innocence. He even carried hypocrisy so far as to offer to help in the search. And seeing that he needed to mollify his wife's hardened heart and mind in preparation for the scene with Valmont, he again promised her that he would do everything in his power to find Clervil. He even caressed his credulous wife, and assured her that, no matter how unfaithful he might be to her, he found it impossible, deep in his heart, not to adore her. And Madame de Franval, always gentle and accommodating, always pleased by anything which brought her closer to a man who was dearer to her than life itself, gave herself over to all the desires of this perfidious husband; she anticipated them, served them, shared them all, without daring, as she should have, to profit from the occasion in order at least to extract a promise from this barbarian to improve his ways, one which would not precipitate his poor wife each day into an abyss of torment and sorrow. But even had she extracted such a promise, would her efforts have been crowned with success? Would Franval, so false in every other aspect of his life, have been any more sincere in the one which, according to him, was only attractive to the extent one could go beyond certain set limits. He would doubtless have made all sorts of promises solely for the pleasure of being able to break them; and perhaps he might even have made her demand that he swear to them, so that to his other frightful pleasures he might add that of perjury.

Franval, absolutely at peace, turned all his attention to troubling others. Such was his vindictive, turbulent, impetuous nature when he was disturbed; desiring to regain his tranquillity at any cost whatever, he would awkwardly obtain it only by those means most likely to make him lose it again. And if he regained it? Then he bent all his physical and moral faculties to making certain he lost it again. Thus, in a state of perpetual agitation, he either had to forestall the artifices he obliged others to employ against him, or else he had to use some of his own against them.

Everything was arranged to Valmont's satisfaction; his tête-à-tête took place in Eugénie's apartment and lasted for the better part of an hour.

There, in the ornate room, Eugénie, on a pedestal, portrayed a young savage weary of the hunt, leaning on the trunk of a palm tree whose soaring branches concealed an infinite number of lights arranged in such a way that their reflections, which shone only on the beautiful girl's physical charms, accentuated them most artfully. The sort of miniature theater wherein this tableau vivant *appeared was surrounded by a six-foot-wide moat which was filled with water and acted as a barrier which prevented anyone from approaching her on any side. At the edge of this circumvallation was placed the throne of a knight, with a silk cord leading from the base of the pedestal to the chair. By manipulating this string, the person in the chair could cause the pedestal to turn in such a manner that the object of his admiration could be viewed from every angle by him, and the arrangement was such that, no matter which way he turned her, she was always delightful to behold. The Count, concealed behind a decorative shrub, was in a position to view both his mistress and his friend. According to the agreement, Valmont was free to examine Eugénie for half an hour. . . . Valmont took his place in the chair . . . he is beside himself; never, he maintains, has he seen so many allurements in one person. He yields to the transports which inflame him, the constantly moving cord offers him an endless succession of new angles and beauties. Which should he prefer above all others, to which shall he sacrifice himself? He cannot make up his mind: Eugénie is such a wondrous beauty! Meanwhile the fleeting minutes pass; for time, in such circumstances, passes quickly. The hour strikes, the knight abandons himself, and the incense flies to the feet of a god whose sanctuary is forbidden him. A veil descends, it is time to leave the room.*

"Well, are you content now?" Franval said, rejoining his friend.

"She is a delightful creature," Valmont replied. "But Franval, if I may offer you one piece of advice, never chance such a thing with any other man. And congratulate yourself for the sentiments I have for you in my heart, which protect you from all danger."

"I am counting on them," Franval said rather seriously. "And now, you must act as soon as you can."

"I shall prepare your wife tomorrow. . . . It is your feeling that a preliminary conversation is required. . . . Four days later you can be sure of me."

They exchanged vows and took leave of each other.

But after his hour with Eugénie, Valmont had not the slightest desire to seduce Madame de Franval or further to assure his friend of a conquest of which he had become only too envious. Eugénie had made such a profound impression upon him that he was unable to put her out of his mind, and he was resolved to have her, no matter what the cost, as his wife. Recollecting upon the matter in tranquillity, once he was no longer repelled by the idea of Eugénie's affair with her father, Valmont was quite certain that his fortune was equal to that of Colunce and that he had just as much right to demand her hand in marriage. He therefore presumed that were he to offer himself as her husband, he could not be refused. He also concluded that by acting zealously to break Eugénie's incestuous bonds, by promising her family that he could not but succeed in such an undertaking, he would inevitably obtain the object of his devotion. There would, of course, be a duel to be fought with Franval, but Valmont was confident that his courage and skill would successfully overcome that obstacle.

Twenty-four hours sufficed for these reflections, and 'twas with these thoughts crowding through his mind that Valmont set off to visit Madame de Franval. She had been informed of his impending call. It will be recalled that in her last conversation with her husband, she had almost become reconciled with him; or, rather, having yielded to the insidious cunning of this traitor, she was no longer in a position to refuse to see Valmont. As an objection to such a visit, she brought up the remarks and the ideas that Franval had advanced, and the letters he had shown her; but he, with seeming unconcern, had more than reassured her that the surest way of convincing people that there was absolutely nothing to her alleged affair with Valmont was to see him exactly as before; to refuse to do so, he assured her, would only lend credence to their suspicions. The best proof a woman can provide of her chastity, he told her, was to continue seeing in public the man to whom her name had been linked. All this was so much sophistry, and Madame de Franval was perfectly well aware of it. Still, she was hoping for some explanation from Valmont, and her desire to obtain it, coupled with her desire not to anger her husband, had blinded her to all the good reasons that should normally have kept her from seeing Valmont.

Thus Valmont arrived to pay his call, and Franval quickly

left them alone as he had the previous time: the explanations and clarifications were sure to be lively and long. Valmont, his head bursting with the ideas which had filled it during the previous twenty-four hours, cut short the formalities and came straight to the point.

"Oh, Madame! Do not think of me as the same man who, the last time he saw you, conducted himself so guiltily in your eyes," he hastened to say. "Then I was the accomplice of your husband's wrongdoings; today I come to repair those wrongs. Have confidence in me, Madame, I beseech you to believe my word of honor that I have come here neither to lie to you nor to deceive you in any way."

Then he confessed to the forged letters and promissory notes and apologized profusely for having allowed himself to be implicated in the affair. He warned Madame of the new horrors they had demanded of him, and as a proof of his candor, he confessed his feelings for Eugénie, revealed what had already been done, and pledged his word to break off everything, to abduct Eugénie from Franval and spirit her away to one of Madame de Farneille's estates in Picardy, if both these worthy ladies would grant him the permission to do so, and as a reward would bestow on him in marriage the girl whom he would thus have rescued from the edge of the abyss.

Valmont's declarations and confessions had such a ring of truth about them that Madame de Franval could not help but be convinced. Valmont was an excellent match for her daughter. After Eugénie's wretched conduct, had she even a right to expect as much? Valmont would assume the responsibility for everything; there was no other way to put a stop to this frightful crime which was driving her to distraction. Moreover, could she not flatter herself that, once the only affair which could really become dangerous both for her and her husband had been broken off, his sentiments might once again be directed toward her? This last consideration tipped the scales in favor of Valmont's plan, and she gave her consent, but only on condition that Valmont give her his word not to fight a duel with her husband and that, after he had delivered Eugénie into Madame de Farneille's hands, he would go abroad and remain there until Franval's fury had abated sufficiently to console himself for the loss of his illicit love and finally consent to the marriage. Valmont agreed to everything; and for her part, Madame de Franval assured him of her mother's full co-operation and promised that she would in no wise oppose or obstruct any of the decisions they came to together. Upon which Valmont left, after again apologizing for having acted so basely against her by participating in her unprincipled husband's schemes.

Madame de Farneille, who was immediately apprised of the affair, left the following day for Picardy, and Franval, caught up in the perpetual whirlwind of his pleasures, counting solidly on Valmont and no longer fearful of Clervil, cast himself into the trap prepared for him with the same guilelessness which he had so often desired to see in others when, in his turn, he had been making his preparations to ensnare them.

For about six months Eugénie, who was now just shy of turning seventeen, had been going out alone or in the company of a few of her female friends. On the eve of the day when Valmont, in accordance with the arrangements made with her father, was to launch his assault upon Madame de Franval, Eugénie had gone alone to see a new play at the Comédie-Française. She likewise left the theater alone, having arranged to meet her father at a given place from which they were to drive elsewhere to dine together. . . . Shortly after her carriage had left the Faubourg Saint-Germain, ten masked men stopped the horses, opened the carriage door, seized Eugénie, and bundled her into a post chaise beside Valmont who, taking every precaution to keep her from crying out, ordered the post chaise to set off with all possible speed, and in the twinkling of an eye they were out of Paris.

Unfortunately, it had been impossible to get rid of Eugénie's retainers or her carriage, and as a result Franval was notified very quickly. Valmont, to make a safe escape, had counted both on Franval's uncertainty as to the route he would take and the two or three hour advance that he would necessarily have. If only he could manage to reach Madame de Farneille's estate, that was all he would need, for from there two trustworthy women and a stage-coach were waiting for Eugénie to drive her toward the border, to a sanctuary with which even he was unfamiliar. Meanwhile, Valmont would go immediately to Holland, returning only to marry

Eugénie when Madame de Farneille and her daughter informed him there were no further obstacles. But fate allowed these well-laid plans to come to grief through the designs of the horrible scoundrel with whom we are dealing.

When the news reached him, Franval did not lose a second. He rushed to the post house and asked for what routes horses had been given since six o'clock that evening. At seven, a traveling coach had departed for Lyon; at eight, a post chaise for Picardy. Franval did not hesitate: the coach for Lyon was certainly of no interest to him, but a post chaise heading toward a province where Madame de Farneille had an estate, yes, that was it: to doubt it would have been madness.

He therefore promptly had the eight best horses at the post hitched up to the carriage in which he was riding, ordered saddles for his servants and, while the horses were being harnessed, purchased and loaded some pistols. And then he set off like an arrow, drawn by love, despair, and a thirst for revenge. When he stopped to change horses at Senlis, he learned that the post chaise he was pursuing had only just left. . . . Franval ordered his men to proceed at top speed. Unfortunately for him, he overtook the post chaise; both he and his servants, with drawn pistols, stopped Valmont's coach, and as soon as the impetuous Franval recognized his adversary, he blew his brains out before Valmont had a chance to defend himself, seized Eugénie, who was faint with fright, tossed her into his own carriage, and was back in Paris before ten o'clock the following morning. Not in the least apprehensive about all that had just happened, Franval devoted his full attention to Eugénie. . . . Had the traitorous Valmont tried to take advantage of the circumstances? Was Eugénie still faithful, and were his guilty bonds still intact and unsullied? Mademoiselle de Franval reassured her father: Valmont had done no more than reveal his plans to her and, full of hope that he would soon be hers in marriage, he refrained from profaning the altar whereon he wished to offer his pure vows.

Franval was reassured by her solemn oaths. . . . But what about his wife? . . . Was she aware of these machinations? was she involved in them in any way? Eugénie, who had had ample time to inform herself on this matter, guaranteed that the entire plot had been the work of her mother, upon whom she showered the most odious names. She also declared that that fateful meeting between Valmont and her mother, wherein the former was, so Franval thought, preparing to serve him so well, had in fact been the meeting during which Valmont had most shamelessly betrayed him.

"Ah!" said Franval, beside himself with anger, "if only he had a thousand lives . . . I would wrench them from him one after the other. . . . And my wife! Here I was trying to lull her, and she was the first to deceive me . . . that creature people think so soft and gentle . . . that angel of virtue! . . . Ah, traitor, you female traitor, you will pay dearly for your crime. . . . My revenge calls for blood, and, if I must, I shall draw it with my own lips from your treacherous veins. . . . Do not be upset, Eugénie," Franval went on in a state of great agitation, "yes, calm yourself, you need some rest. Go and take a few hours' rest, and I shall take care of everything."

Meanwhile Madame de Farneille, who had stationed spies along the road, was soon informed of everything that had just happened. Knowing that her granddaughter had been recaptured and Valmont killed, she lost not a moment returning to Paris. . . . Furious, she immediately called her advisers together; they pointed out to her that Valmont's murder was going to deliver Franval into her hands, and that the influence she feared was shortly going to vanish and she would straightway regain control over both her daughter and Eugénie. But they counseled her to avoid a public scandal, and, for fear of a degrading trial, to solicit a writ that would put her son-in-law out of the way.

Franval was immediately informed of this counsel and of the proceedings that were being taken as a result. Having learned both that his crime was known and that his mother-in-law was, so they told him, only waiting to take advantage of his disaster, Franval left with all dispatch for Versailles, where he saw the Minister and disclosed the whole affair to him. The Minister's reply was to advise Franval to waste no time leaving for one of his estates in Alsace, near the Swiss border.

Franval returned home at once, having made up his mind not to leave without both his wife and his daughter, for a number of reasons: to make sure he would not miss out on his plans for revenge and the punishment he had reserved for his wife's treason, and also to be in possession of hostages dear enough to Madame de Farneille's heart so that she would not dare, at least politically, to instigate actions against him. But would Madame de Franval agree to accompany him to Valmor, the estate to which the Minister had suggested he retire? Feeling herself guilty of that kind of treason which had been the cause of everything which had happened, would she be willing to leave for such a distant place? Would she dare to entrust herself without fear to the arms of her outraged husband? Such were the considerations which worried Franval. To ascertain exactly where he stood, Franval at once went in to see his wife, who already knew everything.

"Madame," he said to her coldly, "you have plunged me into an abyss of woe by your thoughtless indiscretions. While I condemn the effects, I nonetheless applaud the cause, which surely stems from your love both for your daughter and myself. And since the initial wrongs are mine, I must forget the second. My dear and tender wife, who art half my life," he went on, falling to his knees, "will you consent to a reconciliation which nothing can ever again disturb? I come here to offer you that reconciliation, and to seal it here is what I place in your hands. . . ."

So saying he lays at his wife's feet all the forged papers and false correspondence with Valmont.

"Burn all these, my dear friend, I beseech you," the traitor went on, with feigned tears, "and forgive what jealousy drove me to. Let us banish all this bitterness between us. Great are my wrongs, that I confess. But who knows whether Valmont, to assure the success of his plans, has not painted an even darker picture of me than I truly deserve. . . . If he dared tell you that I have ever ceased to love you . . . that you were other than the most precious object in the world, and the one most worthy of respect—ah, my dear angel, if he sullied himself with calumnies such as these, then I say I have done well to rid the world of such a rogue and imposter!"

"Oh! Monsieur," Madame de Franval said in tears, "is it possible even to conceive the atrocities you devised against me? How do you expect me to have the least confidence in you after such horrors?"

"Oh! most tender and loving of women, my fondest desire is that you love me still! What I desire is that, accusing my head alone for the multitude of my sins, you convince yourself that this heart, wherein you reign eternally, has ever been incapable of betraying you. . . . Yes, I want you to know that there is not one of my errors which has not brought me closer to you. . . . The more I withdrew from my dear wife, and the greater the distance between us became, the more I came to realize how impossible it was to replace her in any realm whatsoever. Neither the pleasures nor the sentiments equaled those that my inconstancy caused me to lose with her, and in the very arms of her image I regretted reality. . . . Oh! my dear, my divine friend, where else could I find a heart such as yours? Where else savor the pleasures one culls only in your arms? Yes, I forsake all my errors, my failings . . . henceforth I wish to live only for you in this world . . . to restore in your wounded heart that love which my wrongs destroyed . . . wrongs whose very memory I now abjure."

It was impossible for Madame de Franval to resist such tender effusions on the part of the man she still adored. Is it possible to hate what one has loved so dearly? Can a woman of her delicate and sensitive soul have naught but cold, unfeeling looks for the object which was once so precious to her, cast down at her feet, weeping bitter tears of remorse? She broke down and began to sob. . . .

"I who have never ceased adoring you, you cruel and wicked man," she said, pressing her husband's hands to her heart, " 'tis I whom you have wantonly driven to despair. Ah! Heaven is my witness that of all the scourges with which you might have afflicted me, the fear of losing your heart, of being suspected by you, became the most painful of all to bear. . . . And what object do you choose to outrage me with? . . . My daughter . . . 'tis with her hands you pierce my heart . . . do you wish to oblige me to hate her whom Nature has made so dear to me?"

"Listen to me," Franval said, his tone waxing ever more ardent, "I want to bring her back to you on her knees, humbled, I want her to abjure, as I have done, both her shamelessness and her sins; I want her to obtain, as I have, your pardon. Let us henceforth concern ourselves, all three of us, with nothing but our mutual happiness. I am going to return your daughter to you . . . return my wife to me . . . and let us flee."

"Flee, Great God!"

"My adventure is stirring up trouble . . . tomorrow may already be too late. . . . My friends, the Minister, everyone has advised me to take a voyage to Valmor. . . . Please come with me, my love! Is it possible that at the very moment when I prostrate myself before you asking for your forgiveness you could break my heart by your refusal?"

"You frighten me. . . . What, this adventure . . ."

". . . is being treated not as a duel but as a murder."

"Dear God! And I am the cause of it! . . . Give me your orders, do: dispose of me as you will, my dear husband. I am ready to follow you, to the ends of the earth, if need be. . . . Ah! I am the most wretched woman alive!"

"Consider yourself rather the most fortunate, since every moment of my life is henceforth going to be dedicated to changing into flowers the thorns which in the past I have strewn in your path. . . . Is a desert not enough, when two people love each other? Moreover, this is a situation which cannot last forever. I have friends who have been apprised . . . who are going to act."

"But my mother . . . I should like to see her. . . ."

"No, my love, above all not that. I have positive proof that 'tis she who is stirring up Valmont's family against me, and that, with them, 'tis she who is working toward my destruction. . . ."

"She is incapable of such baseness. Stop imagining such perfidious horrors. Her soul, totally disposed toward love, has never known deceit. . . . You never did appreciate her, Franval. If only you had learned to love her as I do! In her arms we both would have found true happiness on earth. She was the angel of peace that Heaven offered to the errors of your life. Your injustice rejected her proffered heart, which was always open to tenderness, and by inconsequence or caprice, by ingratitude or libertinage, you voluntarily turned your back on the best and most loving friend that Nature ever created for you. . . . Is it true then, you really don't want me to see her?"

"No. I'm afraid I must insist. Time is too precious! You will write her, you will describe my repentance to her. Perhaps she will be moved by my remorse . . . perhaps I shall one day win back her love and esteem. The storm will one day abate, and we shall come back to Paris, and there, in her arms, we shall revel in her forgiveness and tenderness. . . . But now, let us be off, dear friend, we must be gone within the hour at most, the carriage awaits without. . . ."

Terrified, Madame de Franval did not dare raise any further objections. She went about her preparations. Were not Franval's slightest wishes her commands? The traitor flew back to his daughter and brought her back to her mother. There the false creature throws herself at her mother's feet with full as much perfidy as had her father. She weeps, she implores her forgiveness, and she obtains it. Madame de Franval embraces her; how difficult it is to forget one is a mother, no matter how one's children have sinned against her. In a sensitive soul, the voice of Nature is so imperious that the slightest tear from these sacred objects of a mother's affection is enough to make her forget twenty years of faults and failings.

They set off for Valmor. The extreme haste with which this voyage had been prepared justified in Madame de Franval's eyes, which were still as blind and credulous as ever, the paucity of servants that they took along with them. Crime shuns a plethora of eyes, and fears them all; feeling its security possible only in the darkness of mystery, it envelops itself in shadow whenever it desires to act.

When they reached the country estate, nothing was changed, all was as he had promised: constant attentions, respect, solicitous care, evidence of tenderness on the one hand . . . and on the other, the most ardent love—all this was lavished on poor Madame de Franval, who easily succumbed to it. At the end of the world, far removed from her mother, in the depths of a terrible solitude, she was happy because, as she would say, she had her husband's heart again and because her daughter, constantly at her knees, was concerned solely with pleasing her.

Eugénie's room and that of her father were no longer adjoining. Franval's room was at the far end of the château, Eugénie's was next to her mother's. At Valmor, the qualities of decency, regularity, and modesty replaced to the utmost degree all the disorders of the capital. Night after night Franval repaired to his wife's room and there, in the bosom of innocence, candor, and love, the scoundrel shamelessly dared to nourish her hopes with his horrors. Cruel enough not to be disarmed by those naive and ardent caresses which the most delicate of women lavished upon him, it was at the torch of love itself that the villain lighted the torch of vengeance.

As one can easily imagine, however, Franval's attentions toward Eugénie had not diminished. In the morning, while her mother was occupied with her toilet, Eugénie would meet her father at the far end of the garden, and from him she would receive the necessary instructions and the favors which she was far from willing to cede completely to her rival.

No more than a week after their arrival in this retreat, Franval learned that Valmont's family was prosecuting him unremittingly, and that the affair was going to be dealt with in a most serious manner. It was becoming difficult, so they said, to pass it off as a duel, for unfortunately there had been too many witnesses. Furthermore, so Franval was informed, beyond any shadow of a doubt Madame de Farneille was leading the pack of her son-in-law's enemies, her clear intention being to complete his ruin by putting him behind bars or obliging him to leave France, and thus to restore to her as soon as possible the two beloved creatures from whom she was presently separated.

Franval showed these missives to his wife. She at once took out pen and paper to calm her mother, to urge her to see matters in a different light, and to depict for her the happiness she had been enjoying ever since misfortune had succeeded in mollifying the soul of her poor husband. Furthermore, she assured her mother that all her efforts to force her back to Paris with her daughter would be quite in vain, for she had resolved not to leave Valmor until her husband's difficulties had been settled, and ended by saying that if ever the malice of his enemies or the absurdity of his judges should cause a warrant for his arrest to be issued which was degrading to him, she had fully made up her mind to accompany him into exile.

Franval thanked his wife. But having not the least desire to sit and wait for the fate that was being prepared for him, he informed her that he was going to spend some time in Switzerland. He would leave Eugénie in her care, and he begged both women, nay made them promise, not to leave Valmor so long as his fate was still in doubt. No matter what fate might decide for him, he said, he would still return to spend twenty-four hours with his dear wife, to consult with her as to the means for returning to Paris if nothing stood in the way or, if fortune had turned against him, for leaving to go and live somewhere in safety.

Having taken these decisions, Franval, who had not for a moment forgotten that the sole cause of his misfortunes was his wife's rash and imprudent plot with Valmont, and who was still consumed with a desire for revenge, sent word to his daughter that he was waiting for her in the remote part of the park. He locked himself in an isolated summer house with her, and after having made her swear blind obedience to everything he was going to order her to do, he kissed her and spoke to her in the following manner:

"You are about to lose me, my daughter, perhaps forever."

And seeing tears welling up into Eugénie's eyes:

"Calm yourself, my angel," he said to her, "our future happiness is in your hands, and in yours alone. Only you can determine whether we can again find the happiness that once was ours, whether it be in France or somewhere else. You, Eugénie, I trust are as persuaded as one can possibly be that your mother is the sole cause of our misfortunes. You know that I have not lost sight of my plans for revenge. If I have concealed these plans from my wife, you have been aware of my reasons and have approved of them; in fact 'twas you who helped me fashion the blindfold with which it seemed prudent to cover her eyes. The time has come to act, Eugénie, the end is at hand. Your future peace of mind and body depends on it, and what you are going to undertake will assure mine forever as well. You will, I trust, hear me out, and you are too intelligent a girl to be in the least alarmed by what I am about to propose. Yes, my child, the time has come to act, and act we must, without delay and without remorse, and this must be your work.

"Your mother has wished to make you miserable, she has defiled the bonds to which she lays claim, and by so doing she has lost all rights to them. Henceforth she is not only no longer anything more than an ordinary woman for you, but she has even become your worst, your mortal enemy. Now, the law of Nature most deeply graven in our hearts is that we must above all rid ourselves, if we can, of those who conspire against us. This sacred law, which constantly moves and inspires us, does not instill within us the love of our neighbor as being above the love we owe ourselves. First ourselves, then the others: this is Nature's order of progression. Consequently, we must show no respect, no quarter for others as soon as they have shown that our misfortune or our ruin is the object of their desires. To act differently, my daughter, would be to show preference for others above ourselves, and that would be absurd. Now, let me come to the reasons behind the action I shall counsel you to take.

"I am obliged to leave, and you know the reasons why. If I leave you with this woman, Eugénie, within the space of a month her mother will have enticed her back to Paris, and since, after the scandal that has just occurred, you can no longer marry, you can rest assured that these two cruel persons will gain ascendancy over you only to send you to a convent, there to weep over your weakness and repent of our pleasures. 'Tis your grandmother who hounds and pursues me, Eugénie, 'tis she who joins hands with my enemies to complete my destruction. Can such zeal, such methods have any purpose other than to regain possession of you, and can you doubt that once she has you she will have you confined? The worse things go with me, the more those who are persecuting and tormenting us will grow strong and increasingly influential. Now, it would be wrong to doubt that, inwardly, your mother is the brains behind this group, as it would be wrong to doubt that, once I have gone, she will rejoin them. And yet this faction desires my ruin only in order to make you the most wretched woman alive. Therefore we must lose no time in weakening it, and it will be deprived of its most sturdy pillar if your mother is removed from it. Can we opt for another course of action? Can I take you with me? Your mother will be most annoyed, will run back to her mother, and from that day on, Eugénie, we will never know another moment's peace. We will be persecuted and pursued from place to place, no country will have the right to offer us asylum, no refuge on the face of the earth will be held sacred . . . inviolable, in the eyes of the monsters whose fury will pursue us. Do you have any idea how far these odious arms of despotism and tyranny can stretch when they have the weight of gold behind them and are directed by malice? But with your mother dead, on the contrary, Madame de Farneille, who loves her more than she loves you and who has acted solely for her sake in this whole endeavor, seeing her faction deprived of the only person to whom she was really attached in the group, will abandon everything, will stop goading my enemies and arousing them against me. At this juncture, one of two things will happen: either the Valmont incident will be settled and we shall be able to return to Paris in safety, or else the case will become more serious, in which case we shall be obliged to leave France and go to another country, but at least we shall be safe from Madame de Farneille's machinations. But as long as her daughter is still alive, Madame de Farneille will have but a single purpose in mind, and that will be our ruin, because, once again, she believes that her daughter's happiness can be obtained only at the price of our downfall.

"No matter from what angle we view our situation, then, you will see that Madame de Franval is the constant thorn in the side of our security, and her loathsome presence is the most certain obstacle to our happiness.

"Eugénie, Eugénie," Franval continued warmly, taking his daughter's hands in his, "my dear Eugénie, you do love me. Do you therefore consent to lose forever the person who adores you, for fear of an act as essential to our interests? My dear and loving Eugénie, you must decide: you can keep only one of us. You are obliged to kill one of your parents, only the choice of which heart you shall choose as the target of your dagger yet remains. Either your mother must perish, or else you must give me up. . . . What am I saying? You will have to slit my throat. . . . Alas, could I live without you? Do you think it would be possible for me to live without my Eugénie? Could I endure the memory of the pleasures I have tasted in these arms, these delightful pleasures that I shall have lost forever? Your crime, Eugénie, your crime is the same in either case: either you must destroy a mother who loathes you and who lives only to make you unhappy, or else you must murder a father whose every breath is drawn only for you. Choose, Eugénie, go ahead and choose, and if 'tis I you condemn, then do not hesitate, ungrateful daughter: show no pity when you pierce this heart whose only wrong has been to love you too deeply; strike, and I shall bless the blows you strike, and with my last breath I shall say again how I adore you."

Franval fell silent, to hear what his daughter would reply, but she seemed to be lost in deep thought. Finally she threw herself into her father's arms.

"Oh, you, you whom I shall love all my life, can you doubt of the choice I shall make? Can you suspect my courage? Arm me at once, and she who, by her terrible deeds and the threat she poses to your safety, is proscribed will soon fall beneath my blows. Instruct me, Franval, tell me what to do; leave, since your safety demands it, and I shall act while you are gone. I shall keep you apprised of everything. But no matter what turn things may take, once our enemy has been disposed of, do not leave me alone in this château. . . . Come back for me, or send for me to come and join you wherever you may be."

"My darling daughter," said Franval, kissing this monster who had shown herself to be an all too apt pupil of his seductions, "I knew that I would find in you all the sentiments of love and steadfastness of purpose necessary to our mutual happiness. . . . Take this box. Death lies within its lid. . . ."

Eugénie took the fatal box and repeated her promises to her father. Other decisions were taken: it was decided that Eugénie would await the outcome of the trial, and that the decision as to whether the projected crime would take place or not would be dependent upon whether the decision was for or against her father. . . . They took leave of each other, Franval went to pay a call upon his wife, and there carried audacity and deceit so far as to inundate her with his tears, the while receiving from this heavenly angel, without once giving himself away, the touching caresses so full of candor which she lavished upon him. Then, having been given her solemn promise that she would most assuredly remain in Alsace with Eugénie no matter what the outcome of his case, the scoundrel mounted his horse and rode away, leaving behind him the innocence and virtue which his crimes had sullied so long.

Franval proceeded to Basel, and there procured lodgings, for at Basel he was safe from any legal actions that might be instituted against him and at the same time was as close to Valmor as one could possibly be, so that his letters might maintain Eugénie in the

frame of mind he desired to keep her in while he was away.
. . . Basel and Valmor were about twenty-five leagues apart, and
although the road between them went through the Black Forest,
communications were easy enough, so that he was able to receive
news of his daughter once a week. As a measure of precaution,
Franval brought an enormous sum of money with him, but more in
paper than in cash. Let us leave him then, getting settled in Switzerland, and return to his wife.

Nothing could have been purer or more sincere than this excellent woman's intentions. She had promised her husband to remain
in the country until he had given her further orders, and nothing in
the world could have made her change her mind, as she was wont to
assure Eugénie every day. . . . Unfortunately too far removed from
her mother to place her trust in this worthy woman, still a party to
Franval's injustice—the seeds of which he nourished by his letters
sent regularly once a week—Eugénie did not for a moment entertain the thought that she could have a worse enemy in the world
than her mother. And yet there was nothing her mother did not
do to try and break down the invincible antipathy that this ungrateful child kept buried deep in her heart. She showered friendship
and caresses on her, she expressed tender satisfaction with her over
her husband's fortunate change of heart, she even went so far in her
manifestations of gentleness and meekness as to thank Eugénie at
times and give her all the credit for the happy conversion. And then
she would grieve at being the innocent cause of the new calamities
that were threatening Franval; far from accusing Eugénie, she put
the entire onus on herself and, clasping Eugénie to her heart, she
would tearfully ask her whether she could ever forgive her mother.
. . . Eugénie's heart remained hardened to these angelic advances,
and her perverse soul was deaf to the voice of Nature, for vice had
closed off every avenue by which one might reach her. . . . Coldly
withdrawing from her mother's arms, she would look at her with
eyes that were often wild and would say to herself, by way of
encouragement: *How false this woman is . . . how full of deceit and
treachery. The day she had me abducted she caressed me in exactly
the same way.* But these unjust reproaches were naught but the
abominable sophisms with which crime steadies and supports itself
whenever it tries to smother the conscience. Madame de Franval,

whose motives in having Eugénie abducted were her own happiness and peace of mind, and in the interest of virtue, had, it is true, concealed her plans. But such pretense is condemned only by the guilty party who is deceived by it, and in no wise offends probity. Thus Eugénie resisted all her mother's proffered tenderness because she wanted to commit an atrocity, and not in the least because of any wrongs on the part of a mother who had surely committed none with regard to her.

Toward the end of the first month of their stay at Valmor, Madame de Farneille wrote to her daughter that her husband's case was becoming increasingly serious and that, in view of the fear of an unfavorable decision by the court, the return of both Madame de Franval and Eugénie had become a matter of urgent necessity, not only to make an impression on the public, which was spreading the worst kind of gossip, but also to join forces with her and together seek some sort of arrangement that might be able to disarm the forces of justice, and answer for the culprit without sacrificing him.

Madame de Franval, who had resolved not to conceal anything from her daughter, immediately showed her this letter. Staring coldly at her mother, Eugénie asked her evenly what she intended to do in view of this sad news?

"I don't know," Madame de Franval replied. "But the fact is I wonder what good we are doing here? Would we not be serving my husband's interests far better by taking my mother's advice?"

" 'Tis you who are in full charge, Madame," Eugénie replied. "My role is to obey, and you may rest assured of my obedience."

But Madame de Franval, clearly seeing from the curt manner of her daughter's reply that she was dead set against it, told her that she was going to wait, that she would write again, and that Eugénie could be quite sure that if ever she were to fail to follow Franval's intentions, it would only be when she was completely certain that she could serve him better in Paris than at Valmor.

Another month passed in this manner, during which Franval continued to write both to his wife and daughter, and from whom he received letters that could not help but please him, since he saw in those from his wife naught but the most perfect acquiescence to his every desire, and in those from his daughter an unwavering determination to carry out the projected crime as soon as the turn of events required it, or whenever Madame de Franval seemed on the verge of complying with her mother's solicitations.

For, as Eugénie noted in one of her letters, "If I see in your wife naught but the qualities of honesty and candor, and if the friends working on your case in Paris succeed in bringing it to a happy conclusion, I shall turn over to you the task you have entrusted me and you can accomplish it yourself when we are together, if you deem it advisable then. But of course if you should in any case order me to act, and should find it indispensable that I do so, then I shall assume the full responsibility for it by myself, of that you may be sure."

In his reply, Franval approved of everything she reported to him, and these were the last two letters he received and sent. The following mail brought him no more. Franval grew worried. And when the succeeding mail proved equally unsatisfactory, he grew desperate, and since his natural restlessness no longer allowed him to wait for further mails, he immediately decided to pay a personal visit to Valmor to ascertain the reasons for the delays in the mails that were upsetting him so cruelly.

He set off on horseback, followed by a faithful valet. He had calculated his voyage to arrive the second day, late enough at night not to be recognized by anyone. At the edge of the woods which surrounds the Valmor château and which, to the east, joins the Black Forest, six well-armed men stopped Franval and his servant and demanded their money. These rogues had been well informed; they knew with whom they were dealing and were fully aware that Franval, being implicated in an unpleasant affair, never traveled without his paper money and immense amounts of gold. . . . The servant resisted, and was laid out lifeless at the feet of his horse. Franval, drawing his sword, leapt to the ground and attacked these scurvy creatures. He wounded three of them, but found himself surrounded by the others. They stripped him of everything he had, without however being able to disarm him, and as soon as they had despoiled him the thieves escaped. Franval followed them, but the brigands had vanished so swiftly with their booty and horses that it was impossible to tell in which direction they had gone.

The weather that night was miserable. The cutting blast of the north wind was accompanied by a driving hail—all the elements seemed to be conspiring against this poor wretch. There are perhaps cases in which Nature, revolted by the crimes of the person she is pursuing, desires to overwhelm him with all the scourges at Her command before drawing him back again into her bosom. . . . Franval, half-naked but still holding onto his sword, directed his footsteps as best he could away from this baleful place, and toward Valmor. But as he was ill-acquainted with this estate, which he had visited only the one time we have seen him there, he lost his way on the darkened roads of this forest with which he was totally unfamiliar. . . . Completely exhausted, and racked by pain and worry, tormented by the storm, he threw himself to the ground; and there the first tears he had ever shed in his life flowed abundantly from his eyes. . . .

"Ill-fated man," he cried out, "now is everything conspiring to crush me at last . . . to make me feel the pangs of remorse. It took the hand of disaster to pierce my heart. Deceived by the blandishments of good fortune, I should have always gone on failing to recognize it. Oh you, whom I have outraged so grievously, you who at this very moment are perhaps becoming the victim of my fury and barbarous plans, you my adorable wife . . . does the world, vainglorious of your existence, still possess you? Has the hand of Heaven put a stop to my horrors? . . . Eugénie! my too credulous daughter . . . too basely seduced by my abominable cunning . . . has Nature softened your heart? . . . Has she suspended the cruel effects of my ascendancy and your weakness? Is there still time? Is there still time, Just Heaven? . . ."

Suddenly the plaintive and majestic sound of several pealing bells, rising sadly heavenward, came to add to the horror of his fate. . . . He was deeply affected . . . he grew terrified. . . .

"What is this I hear?" he cried out, getting to his feet. "Barbarous daughter . . . is it death? . . . is it vengeance? . . . Are the Furies of hell come then to finish their work? Do these sounds announce to me . . . ? Where am I? Can I hear them? . . . Finish, oh Heaven, finish the task of destroying the culprit. . . ."

And, prostrating himself:

"Almighty God, suffer me to join my voice to those who at this moment are imploring Thee . . . see my remorse and Thy power, and pardon me for disowning Thee. I beseech Thee to grant me this prayer, the first prayer I dare to direct at Thee! Supreme Being, preserve virtue, protect her who was Thy most beautiful image on this earth. I pray that these sounds, these mournful sounds, may not be those I fear and dread."

And Franval, completely distraught, no longer aware of what he was doing nor where he was going, his speech but an incoherent mumble, followed whatever path he chanced across. . . . He heard someone . . . he regained control of himself and listened. . . . It was a man on horseback.

"Whoever you are," Franval called out, advancing toward this man, "whoever you may be, take pity on a poor wretch whom pain and sorrow has rendered distraught. I am ready to take my own life. . . . Instruct me, help me, if you are a man, and a man of any compassion . . . deign to save me from myself."

"Good God!" replied a voice too well-known to poor Franval. "What! You here? . . . For the sake of all that is holy, leave, go away!"

And Clervil—for 'twas he, this worthy mortal, who had escaped from Franval's prison, whom fate had sent toward this miserable creature in the saddest moment of his life—Clervil jumped down off his horse and fell into the arms of his enemy.

"So 'tis you, Monsieur," Franval said, clasping the honorable man to his breast, "you upon whom I have wrought so many horrible acts which weigh so heavily on my conscience?"

"Calm yourself, Monsieur, you must calm yourself. I put away from me all the misfortunes that have recently surrounded me, nor do I remember those which you wished to inflict upon me when Heaven allows me to serve you . . . and I am going to be of service to you, Monsieur, doubtless in a manner which will be rather cruel, but necessary. . . . Here, let us sit down at the foot of this cypress, for now its sinister boughs alone shall be a fitting wreath for you. Oh, my dear Franval, what reverses of fortune I must acquaint you with! . . . Weep, my friend, for tears will relieve you, and I must cause even more bitter tears to flow from your eyes. . . . Your days of delight are over . . . they have vanished as a dream. And all you have left to you are days of sorrow and grief."

"Oh, Monsieur, I understand you . . . those bells . . ."

"Those bells are bearing the homage, the prayers of the inhabitants of Valmor to the feet of Almighty God, for He has allowed them to know an angel only so that they might pity and mourn her all the more."

At which point Franval, placing the tip of his sword at his heart, was about to cut the frail thread of his days, but Clervil forestalled this desperate act:

"No, no, my friend," he cried, " 'tis not death that is needed, but reparation. Hear what I have to say, I have much to tell you, and to tell it, an atmosphere of calm is required."

"Very well, Monsieur, speak. I am listening. Plunge the dagger by slow degrees into my heart. It is only just that he who has tried to torment others should in his turn be oppressed."

"I shall be brief as regards myself, Monsieur," Clervil said. "After several months of the frightful detention to which you subjected me, I was fortunate enough to move my guard to pity. I strongly advised him meticulously to conceal the injustice which you committed regarding me. He will not reveal it, my dear Franval, he will never reveal that secret."

"Oh, Monsieur . . ."

"Hear me out. I repeat that I have much to tell you. Upon my return to Paris I learned of your sorry adventure . . . your departure. . . . I shared Madame de Farneille's tears, which were more sincere than you ever believed. Together with this worthy lady, I conspired to persuade Madame de Franval to bring Eugénie back to us, her presence being more necessary in Paris than in Alsace. . . . You had forbidden her to leave Valmor . . . she obeyed you. She apprised us of these orders and of her reluctance to contradict them. She hesitated as long as she could. You were found guilty, Franval, and the sentence still stands. You have been sentenced to death as guilty of a highway murder. Neither Madame de Farneille's entreaties nor the efforts of your family and friends could alter the decision of justice: you have been worsted . . . dishonored forever . . . you are ruined . . . all your goods and estates have been seized. . . ." (And in response to a second, violent movement on Franval's part:) "Listen to me, Monsieur, hear me out, I say, I demand this of you in expiation of your crimes; I demand it too in the name of Heaven, which may still be moved to forgiveness by your repentance. At this time we wrote to Madame de Franval to apprise her of all this: her mother informed her that, as her presence had become absolutely indispensable, she was sending me to Valmor to persuade her once and for all to return to Paris. I set off immediately after the letter was posted, but unfortunately it reached Valmor before me. When I arrived, it was already too late; your horrible plot had succeeded only too well; I found Madame de Franval dying. . . . Oh, Monsieur, what base, what foul villainy! . . . But I am touched by your abject state, I shall refrain from reproaching you any further for your crimes. Let me tell you everything. Eugénie was unable to bear the sight, and when I arrived her repentance was already expressed by a flood of tears and bitter sobs. . . . Oh, Monsieur, how can I describe to you the cruel effect of this varied scene. Your wife, disfigured by convulsions of pain, was dying. . . . Eugénie, having been reclaimed by Nature, was uttering frightful cries, confessing her guilt, invoking death, wanting to kill herself, in turn falling at the feet of those whom she was imploring and fastening herself to the breast of her mother, trying desperately to revive her with her own breath, to warm her with her tears, to move her by the spectacle of her remorse; such, Monsieur, was the sinister scene that struck my eyes when I arrived at Valmor.

"When I entered the house, Madame de Franval recognized me. She pressed my hands in hers, wet them with her tears, and uttered a few words which I had great difficulty hearing, for they could scarcely escape from her chest which was constricted from the effects of the poison. She forgave you. . . . She implored Heaven's forgiveness for you, and above all she asked for her daughter's forgiveness. . . . See then, barbarous man, that the final thoughts, the final prayers of this woman whose heart you broke and whose virtue you vilified were yet for your happiness.

"I gave her every care I could, and revived the flagging spirits of the servants to do the same, I called upon the most celebrated practitioners of medicine available . . . and I employed all my resources to console your Eugénie. Touched by the terrible state she was in, I felt I had no right to refuse her my consolations. But nothing succeeded. Your poor wife gave up the ghost amid such convulsions and torments as are impossible to describe. At that fatal moment, Monsieur, I witnessed one of the sudden effects of remorse which till then had been unknown to me. Eugénie threw herself on her mother and died at the same moment as she. We all thought she had merely fainted. . . . No, all her faculties were extinguished. The situation had produced such a shock to her vital organs that they had all ceased simultaneously to function, and she actually died from the violent impact of remorse, grief, and despair. . . . Yes, Monsieur, both are lost to you. And the bells which you yet hear pealing are celebrating simultaneously two creatures, both of whom were born to make you happy, whom your hideous crimes have made the victims of their attachment to you, and whose bloody images will pursue you to your grave.

"Oh, my dear Franval, was I wrong then in times past to try and save you from the abyss into which your passions were plunging you? Will you still condemn, still cover with ridicule the votaries of virtue? And are virtue's disciples wrong to burn incense at its altars when they see crime so surrounded by troubles and scourges?"

Clervil fell silent. He glanced at Franval and saw that he was petrified with sorrow. His eyes were fixed and from them tears were flowing, but no expression managed to cross his lips. Clervil asked him why he had found him in this half-naked state. In two words, Franval related to him what had happened.

"Ah, Monsieur," cried the generous Clervil, "how happy I am, even in the midst of all the horrors which surround me, to be able at least to ease your situation. I was on my way to Basel in search of you, I was going to acquaint you with all that had happened, I was going to offer you the little I possess. . . . Take it, I beg you to. As you know, I am not rich, but here are a hundred *louis*, my life's savings, they are all I own. I demand that you . . ."

"Oh noble and generous man," Franval cried, embracing the knees of that rare and honorable friend, "why me? Do I need anything, after the losses I have suffered? And from you, you whom I have treated so miserably, 'tis you who fly to my help."

"Must we remember past wrongs when misfortune overwhelms him who has done them to us? When this happens, the only revenge we owe is to alleviate his suffering. And what point is there in adding to his grief when his heart is burdened with his own reproaches? . . . Monsieur, that is the voice of Nature. You can see that the sacred cult of a Supreme Being does not run counter to it as you had supposed, since the counsel offered by the one is naught but the holy writ of the other."

"No," said Franval, getting to his feet, "no, Monsieur, I no longer have need for anything at all. Since Heaven has left me this one last possession," he went on, displaying his sword, "teach me what use I must put it to. . . ." (Looking at the sword:) "This, my dear, my only friend, this is the same sword that my saintly wife seized one day to plunge into her breast when I was overwhelming her with horrors and calumnies. . . . 'Tis the very same. . . . Perhaps I may even discover traces of her sacred blood on it . . . blood which my own must efface. . . . Come, let us walk awhile, until we come to some cottages wherein I may inform you of my last wishes . . . and then we shall take leave of each other forever. . . ."

They began walking, keeping a look out for a road that would lead them to some habitation. . . . Night still enveloped the forest in its darkest veils. Suddenly the sound of mournful hymns was heard, and the men saw several torches rending the dark shadows and lending the scene a tinge of horror that only sensitive souls will understand. The pealing of bells grew louder, and to these mournful accents, which were still only scarcely audible, were joined flashes of lightning, which had hitherto been absent from the sky, and the ensuing thunder which mingled with the funereal sounds they had previously heard. The lightning which flashed across the skies, occasionally eclipsing the sinister flames of the torches, seemed to be vying with the inhabitants of the earth for the right to conduct to her grave this woman whom the procession was accompanying. Everything gave rise to horror, everything betokened desolation, and it seemed that Nature herself had donned the garb of eternal mourning.

"What is this?" said Franval, who was deeply moved.

"Nothing, nothing," Clervil said, taking his friend's hand and leading him in another direction.

"Nothing? No, you're misleading me. I want to see what it is. . . ."

He dashed forward . . . and saw a coffin.

"Merciful Heaven," he cried. "There she is; it is she, it is she. God has given me one last occasion to see her. . . ."

At the bidding of Clervil, who saw that it was impossible to calm the poor man down, the priests departed in silence. . . . Completely distraught, Franval threw himself on the coffin, and from it he seized the sad remains of the woman whom he had so gravely offended. He took the body in his arms and laid it at the foot of a tree, and in a state of delirium threw himself upon it, crying in utter despair:

"Oh you whose life has been snuffed out by my barbarous cruelty, oh touching creature whom I still adore, see at your feet your husband beseeching your pardon and your forgiveness. Do not imagine that I ask this in order to outlive you. No, no, 'tis in order that the Almighty, touched by your virtues, might deign to forgive me as you have done, if such be possible. . . . You must have blood, my sweet wife, you must have blood to be avenged . . . and avenged you shall be. . . . Ah! first see my tears and witness my repentance; I intend to follow you, beloved shade . . . but who will receive my tortured soul if you do not intercede for it? Rejected alike from the arms of God and from your heart, do you wish to see it condemned to the hideous tortures of Hell when it is so sincerely repentant of its crimes? Forgive, dear soul, forgive these crimes and see how I avenge them."

With these words Franval, eluding Clervil's gaze, plunged the sword he was holding twice through his body. His impure blood flowed onto his victim and seemed to sully her much more than avenge her.

"Oh my friend," he said to Clervil, "I am dying, but I am dying in the bosom of remorse. . . . Apprise those who remain behind both of my deplorable end and of my crimes, tell them that is the way that a man who is a miserable slave of his passions must die, a man vile enough to have stifled in his heart the cry of duty and of Nature. Do not deny me half of my wretched wife's coffin without my remorse I would not have been worthy of sharing it but now my remorse renders me full worthy of that favor, and demand it. Adieu."

Clervil granted poor Franval's dying wish, and the procession continued on its way. An eternal refuge soon swallowed up a husband and wife born to love each other, a couple fashioned for happiness and who would have savored it in its purest form if crim and its frightful disorders had not, beneath the guilty hand of one of the two, intervened to change their life from a garden of delight into a viper's nest.

The worthy ecclesiastic soon carried back to Paris the frightful details of these different calamities. No one was distressed by the death of Franval; only his life had been a cause of grief. But his wife was mourned, bitterly mourned. And indeed what creature is more precious, more appealing in the eyes of men than the person who has cherished, respected, and cultivated the virtues of the earth and, at each step of the way, has found naught but misfortune and grief?

Justine,
or Good Conduct Well Chastised
(1791)

*T*he most famous of all Sade's works is the novel Justine.
It is also probably the one he cared most about—Sade
dedicated it to the faithful companion of the last twenty-
five years of his existence, Marie-Constance Quesnet. It was
also the book which caused him the most difficulty with the
authorities during his lifetime.

Sade finished the first draft of this "philosophical
novel" while he was a prisoner in the Bastille. Working
uninterruptedly over the two-week period from June 23 to
July 8, 1787, in his cell in the "Second Liberty," Sade
completed the hundred-and-thirty-eight-page manuscript,
which he entitled Les Infortunes de la Vertu. Originally intended to become a part of the volume he was then preparing, Contes et fabliaux du XVIIIᵉ siècle, this "first Justine"
underwent considerable revision in the course of the following year, and Sade soon determined to strike it from his list
of tales and make it a work unto itself.

Writing to his lawyer-friend Reinaud on June 12,
1791, a little more than a year after the Revolutionary
government had rendered him his liberty, Sade noted: "At
the moment a novel of mine is being printed, but it is a
work too immoral to be sent to so pious and so decent a
man as yourself. I needed money, my publisher said that
he wanted it well spiced, and I gave it to him fit to plague
the devil himself. It is called Justine, or Good Conduct Well
Chastised. Burn it and do not read it, if perchance it falls
into your hands. I am disclaiming the authorship. . . ."

In fact, the original edition of Justine—the author's
first work published during his lifetime—did not bear his

name. Printed in Paris, chez Girouard[1] on the rue du Bout-du-Monde, Justine first appeared in two octavo volumes, with a frontispiece depicting Virtue between Licentiousness and Irreligion, and at the place on the title page generally reserved for the publisher's imprint there appeared the vague description: In Holland, At Associated Booksellers.

What of the admission by the author that he wrote the novel to order? This, as Lely points out, seems hardly likely. First, the general outline and somber pessimism of the 1791 Justine *were already evident in the 1787 version. Second, the novel does figure in the* Catalogue raisonné *which Sade himself drew up roughly three years before its publication. And finally—perhaps the most convincing argument of all—Sade dedicated the novel, as we have noted, to his dear friend Marie-Constance Quesnet, an indication that he himself valued the work highly, well understood its importance, and would never have dared compromise the merit of the work by spicing it to suit the publisher's taste.*

"Will it not be felt," writes Sade in his dedication, "that Virtue, however beautiful, becomes the worst of all possible attitudes when it is found too feeble to contend with Vice and that, in an entirely corrupted age, the safest course is to follow the others?" If this be the impression, says Sade, it is wrong: this work is intended to combat such "dangerous sophistries," such "false philosophy," and show how Virtue afflicted may turn a thoroughly depraved and corrupt spirit wherein there yet remain a few good principles, back toward the path of righteousness.

During the decade following its publication, Justine *went through six printings (one of which, actually done in Paris, bore as the unlikely place of publication: "Philadelphia"), eloquent testimony to its early popularity. Doubtless prompted by its success, an enterprising Paris publisher, Nicolas Massé, brought out, in 1797, the monumental ten-volume work entitled* La Nouvelle Justine . . . suivie de l'Histoire de Juliette, sa soeur, *which was freely offered, at*

---

[1] *Girouard was later to perish, under the Reign of Terror, on January 8, 1794.*

least for a year following its publication, in the leading Paris bookstores. Then, in the waning two years of the eighteenth century, searches and seizures began, ending with the arrest, on March 6, 1801, of the man who was purported to be, but adamantly denied he was, the author of both works. On that day, both Sade and Massé were arrested on the latter's premises. A search of Massé's offices revealed a number of manuscripts in Sade's handwriting, as well as printed volumes of Justine and Juliette annotated in his hand. Massé, after being detained for twenty-four hours, was released upon condition that he reveal the whereabouts of his stock of Juliette, and there is evidence to indicate that the publisher, to save himself, had denounced Sade to the police. Be that as it may, Sade was once again incarcerated, first in Sainte-Pélagie and then, two years later, in the Charenton Asylum, where he was to remain a prisoner until the end of his life.

O thou my friend! The prosperity of Crime is like unto the lightning, whose traitorous brilliancies embellish the atmosphere but for an instant, in order to hurl into death's very depths the luckless one they have dazzled.

TO MY DEAR FRIEND

Yes, Constance, it is to thee I address this work; at once the example and honor of thy sex, with a spirit of profoundest sensibility combining the most judicious and the most enlightened of minds, thou art she to whom I confide my book, which will acquaint thee with the sweetness of the tears Virtue sore beset doth shed and doth cause to flow. Detesting the sophistries of libertinage and of irreligion, in word and deed combatting them unweariogly, I fear not that those necessitated by the order of personages appearing in these Memoires will put thee in any peril; the cynicism remarkable in certain portraits (they were softened as much as ever they could be) is no more apt to frighten thee; for it is only Vice that trembles when Vice is found out, and cries scandal immediately it is attacked. To bigots Tartuffe was indebted for his ordeal; Justine's will be the achievement of libertines, and little do I dread them: they'll not betray my intentions, these thou shalt perceive; thy opinion is sufficient to make my whole glory and after having pleased thee I must either please universally or find consolation in a general censure.

The scheme of this novel (yet, 'tis less a novel than one might suppose) is doubtless new; the victory gained by Virtue over Vice, the rewarding of good, the punishment of evil, such is the usual scheme in every other work of this species: ah! the lesson cannot be too often dinned in our ears!

But throughout to present Vice triumphant and Virtue a victim of its sacrifices, to exhibit a wretched creature wandering from one misery to the next; the toy of villainy; the target of every debauch; exposed to the most barbarous, the most monstrous caprices; driven witless by the most brazen, the most specious sophistries; prey to the most cunning seductions, the most irresistible suborna-

tions; for defense against so many disappointments, so much bane and pestilence, to repulse such a quantity of corruption having nothing but a sensitive soul, a mind naturally formed, and considerable courage: briefly, to employ the boldest scenes, the most extraordinary situations, the most dreadful maxims, the most energetic brush strokes, with the sole object of obtaining from all this one of the sublimest parables ever penned for human edification; now, such were, 'twill be allowed, to seek to reach one's destination by a road not much traveled heretofore.

Have I succeeded, Constance? Will a tear in thy eye determine my triumph? After having read Justine, wilt say: "Oh, how these renderings of crime make me proud of my love for Virtue! How sublime does it appear through tears! How 'tis embellished by misfortunes!"

Oh, Constance! may these words but escape thy lips, and my labors shall be crowned.

*T*he very masterpiece of philosophy would be to develop the means Providence employs to arrive at the ends she designs for man, and from this construction to deduce some rules of conduct acquainting this wretched two-footed individual with the manner wherein he must proceed along life's thorny way, forewarned of the strange caprices of that fatality they denominate by twenty different titles, and all unavailingly, for it has not yet been scanned nor defined.

If, though full of respect for social conventions and never overstepping the bounds they draw round us, if, nonetheless, it should come to pass that we meet with nothing but brambles and briars, while the wicked tread upon flowers, will it not be reckoned —save by those in whom a fund of incoercible virtues renders deaf to these remarks—, will it not be decided that it is preferable to abandon oneself to the tide rather than to resist it? Will it not be felt that Virtue, however beautiful, becomes the worst of all attitudes when it is found too feeble to contend with Vice, and that, in an entirely corrupted age, the safest course is to follow along after the others? Somewhat better informed, if one wishes, and abusing the knowledge they have acquired, will they not say, as did the angel Jesrad in *Zadig,* that there is no evil whereof some good is not born? and will they not declare, that this being the case, they can give themselves over to evil since, indeed, it is but one of the fashions of producing good? Will they not add, that it makes no difference to the general plan whether such-and-such a one is by preference good or bad, that if misery persecutes virtue and prosperity accompanies crime, those things being as one in Nature's view, far better to join company with the wicked who flourish, than to be counted amongst the virtuous who founder? Hence, it is im-

457

portant to anticipate those dangerous sophistries of a false philosophy; it is essential to show that through examples of afflicted virtue presented to a depraved spirit in which, however, there remain a few good principles, it is essential, I say, to show that spirit quite as surely restored to righteousness by these means as by portraying this virtuous career ornate with the most glittering honors and the most flattering rewards. Doubtless it is cruel to have to describe, on the one hand, a host of ills overwhelming a sweet-tempered and sensitive woman who, as best she is able, respects virtue, and, on the other, the affluence of prosperity of those who crush and mortify this same woman. But were there nevertheless some good engendered of the demonstration, would one have to repent of making it? Ought one be sorry for having established a fact whence there resulted, for the wise man who reads to some purpose, so useful a lesson of submission to providential decrees and the fateful warning that it is often to recall us to our duties that Heaven strikes down beside us the person who seems to us best to have fulfilled his own?

Such are the sentiments which are going to direct our labors, and it is in consideration of these intentions that we ask the reader's indulgence for the erroneous doctrines which are to be placed in the mouths of our characters, and for the sometimes rather painful situations which, out of love for truth, we have been obliged to dress before his eyes.

Madame la Comtesse de Lorsange was one of those priestesses of Venus whose fortune is the product of a pretty face and much misconduct, and whose titles, pompous though they are, are not to be found but in the archives of Cythera, forged by the impertinence that seeks, and sustained by the fool's credulity that bestows, them; brunette, a fine figure, eyes of a singular expression, that modish unbelief which, contributing one further spice to the passions, causes those women in whom it is suspected to be sought after that much more diligently; a trifle wicked, unfurnished with any principle, allowing evil to exist in nothing, lacking however that amount of depravation in the heart to have extinguished its sensibility; haughty, libertine; such was Madame de Lorsange.

Nevertheless, this woman had received the best education;

daughter of a very rich Parisian banker, she had been brought up, together with a sister named Justine, by three years younger than she, in one of the capital's most celebrated abbeys where, until the ages of twelve and fifteen years, the one and the other of the two sisters had been denied no counsels, no masters, no books, and no polite talents.

At this period crucial to the virtue of the two maidens, they were in one day made bereft of everything: a frightful bankruptcy precipitated their father into circumstances so cruel that he perished of grief. One month later, his wife followed him into the grave. Two distant and heartless relatives deliberated what should be done with the young orphans; a hundred crowns apiece was their share of a legacy mostly swallowed up by creditors. No one caring to be burdened with them, the convent's door was opened, their dowry was put into their hands, and they were left at liberty to become what they wished.

Madame de Lorsange, at the time called Juliette, whose mind and character were to all intents and purposes as completely formed then as at thirty, the age she had attained at the opening of the tale we are about to relate, seemed nothing but overjoyed to be put at large; she gave not a moment's thought to the cruel events which had broken her chains. As for Justine, aged as we have remarked, twelve, hers was of a pensive and melancholy character, which made her far more keenly appreciate all the horrors of her situation. Full of tenderness, endowed with a surprising sensibility instead of with her sister's art and finesse, she was ruled by an ingenuousness, a candor that were to cause her to tumble into not a few pitfalls. To so many qualities this girl joined a sweet countenance, absolutely unlike that with which Nature had embellished Juliette; for all the artifice, wiles, coquetry one noticed in the features of the one, there were proportionate amounts of modesty, decency, and timidity to be admired in the other; a virginal air, large blue eyes very soulful and appealing, a dazzling fair skin, a supple and resilient body, a touching voice, teeth of ivory and the loveliest blond hair, there you have a sketch of this charming creature whose naive graces and delicate traits are beyond our power to describe.

They were given twenty-four hours to leave the convent; into their hands, together with their five score crowns, was thrown the responsibility to provide for themselves as they saw fit. Delighted to be her own mistress, Juliette spent a minute, perhaps two, wiping away Justine's tears, then, observing it was in vain, she fell to scolding instead of comforting her; she rebuked Justine for her sensitiveness; she told her, with a philosophic acuity far beyond her years, that in this world one must not be afflicted save by what affects one personally; that it was possible to find in oneself physical sensations of a sufficiently voluptuous piquancy to extinguish all the moral affections whose shock could be painful; that it was all the more essential so to proceed, since true wisdom consists infinitely more in doubling the sum of one's pleasures than in increasing the sum of one's pains; that, in a word, there was nothing one ought not do in order to deaden in oneself that perfidious sensibility from which none but others profit while to us it brings naught but troubles. But it is difficult to harden a gentle good heart, it resists the arguments of a toughened bad mind, and its solemn satisfactions console it for the loss of the *bel-esprit*'s false splendors.

Juliette, employing other resources, then said to her sister, that with the age and the figure they both of them had, they could not die of hunger—she cited the example of one of their neighbors' daughters who, having escaped from her father's house, was presently very royally maintained and far happier, doubtless, than if she had remained at home with her family; one must, said Juliette, take good care to avoid believing it is marriage that renders a girl happy; that, a captive under the hymeneal laws, she has, with much ill-humor to suffer, a very slight measure of joys to expect; instead of which, were she to surrender herself to libertinage, she might always be able to protect herself against her lovers' moods, or be comforted by their number.

These speeches horrified Justine; she declared she preferred death to ignominy; whatever were her sister's reiterated urgings, she adamantly refused to take up lodging with her immediately she saw Juliette bent upon conduct that caused her to shudder.

After each had announced her very different intentions, the two girls separated without exchanging any promises to see each another again. Would Juliette, who, so she affirmed, intended to become a lady of consequence, would Juliette consent to receive a little girl whose virtuous but base inclinations might be able to bring her into dishonor? and, on her side, would Justine wish to jeopardize her morals in the society of a perverse creature who was bound to become public debauchery's toy and the lewd mob's victim? And so each bid an eternal adieu to the other, and they left the convent on the morrow.

During early childhood caressed by her mother's dressmaker, Justine believes this woman will treat her kindly now in this hour of her distress; she goes in search of the woman, she tells the tale of her woes, she asks employment . . . she is scarcely recognized; and is harshly driven out the door.

"Oh Heaven!" cries the poor little creature, "must my initial steps in this world be so quickly stamped with ill-fortune? That woman once loved me; why does she cast me away today? Alas! 'tis because I am poor and an orphan, because I have no more means and people are not esteemed save in reason of the aid and benefits one imagines may be had of them." Wringing her hands, Justine goes to find her curé; she describes her circumstances with the vigorous candor proper to her years. . . . She was wearing a little white garment, her lovely hair was negligently tucked up under her bonnet, her breast, whose development had scarcely begun, was hidden beneath two or three folds of gauze, her pretty face had somewhat of pallor owing to the unhappiness consuming her, a few tears rolled from her eyes and lent to them an additional expressiveness. . . .

"You observe me, Monsieur," said she to the saintly ecclesiastic . . . "Yes, you observe me in what for a girl is a most dreadful position; I have lost my father and mother. . . . Heaven has taken them from me at an age when I stand in greatest need of their assistance. . . . They died ruined, Monsieur; we no longer have anything. There," she continued, "is all they left me," and she displayed her dozen *louis*, "and nowhere to rest my poor head. . . . You will have pity upon me, Monsieur, will you not? You are Religion's minister and Religion was always my heart's virtue; in the name of that God I adore and whose organ you are, tell me, as if you were a second father unto me, what must I do? . . . what must become of me?"

The charitable priest clapped an inquisitive eye upon Justine,

and made her answer, saying that the parish was heavily loaded;
that it could not easily take new charges unto its bosom, but that if
Justine wished to serve him, if she were prepared for hard toil,
there would always be a crust of bread in his kitchen for her. And
as he uttered those words, the gods' interpreter chucked her under
the chin; the kiss he gave her bespoke rather too much worldliness
for a man of the church, and Justine, who had understood only too
well, thrust him away. "Monsieur," said she, "I ask neither alms
of you nor a position as your scullion; it was all too recently I took
leave of an estate loftier than that which might make those two
favors desirable; I am not yet reduced to imploring them; I am
soliciting advice whereof my youth and my misfortunes put me in
need, and you would have me purchase it at an excessively inflated
price." Ashamed thus to have been unmasked, the pastor promptly
drove the little creature away, and the unhappy Justine, twice rejected on the first day of her condemnation to isolation, now enters
a house above whose door she spies a shingle; she rents a small
chamber on the fourth floor, pays in advance for it, and, once established, gives herself over to lamentations all the more bitter because she is sensitive and because her little pride has just been compromised cruelly.

We will allow ourselves to leave her in this state for a short
while in order to return to Juliette and to relate how, from the very
ordinary condition in which she sets forth, no better furnished
with resources than her sister, she nevertheless attains, over a
period of fifteen years, the position of a titled woman, with an income of thirty thousand pounds, very handsome jewels, two or
three houses in the city, as many in the country and, at the present
moment, the heart, the fortune and the confidence of Monsieur de
Corville, Councilor to the State, an important man much esteemed
and about to have a minister's post. Her rise was not, there can
be no question of it, unattended by difficulties: 'tis by way of the
most shameful, most onerous apprenticeship that these ladies attain
their objectives; and 'tis in all likelihood a veteran of unnumbered
campaigns one may find today abed with a Prince: perhaps she yet
carries the humiliating marks of the brutality of the libertines into
whose hands her youth and inexperience flung her long ago.

Upon leaving the convent, Juliette went to find a woman whose name she had once heard mentioned by a youthful friend; perverted was what she desired to be and this woman was to pervert her; she arrived at her house with a small parcel under her arm, clad in a blue dressing gown nicely disarrayed, her hair straggling carelessly about, and showing the prettiest face in the world, if it is true that for certain eyes indecency may have its charms; she told her story to this woman and begged her to afford her the sanctuary she had provided her former friend.

"How old are you?" Madame Duvergier demanded.

"I will be fifteen in a few days, Madame," Juliette replied.

"And never hath mortal . . ." the matron continued.

"No, Madame, I swear it," answered Juliette.

"But, you know, in those convents," said the old dame, "sometimes a confessor, a nun, a companion . . . I must have conclusive evidence."

"You have but to look for it," Juliette replied with a blush.

And, having put on her spectacles, and having scrupulously examined things here and there, the duenna declared to the girl:

"Why, you've only to remain here, pay strict attention to what I say, give proof of unending complaisance and submissiveness to my practices, you need but be clean, economical, and frank with me, be prudent with your comrades and fraudulent when dealing with men, and before ten years' time I shall have you fit to occupy the best second-story apartment: you'll have a commode, pier-glass mirrors before you and a maid behind, and the art you will have acquired from me will give you what you need to procure yourself the rest."

These suggestions having left her lips, Duvergier lays hands on Juliette's little parcel; she asks her whether she does not have some money, and Juliette having too candidly admitted she had a hundred crowns, the dear mother confiscates them, giving her new boarding guest the assurance her little fortune will be chanced at the lottery for her, but that a girl must not have money. "It is," says she, "a means to doing evil, and in a period as corrupt as ours, a wise and well-born girl should carefully avoid all which might lure her into any snares. It is for your own good I speak, my little one," adds the duenna, "and you ought to be grateful for what I am doing."

The sermon delivered, the newcomer is introduced to her colleagues; she is assigned a room in the house, and on the next day her maidenhead is put on sale.

Within four months the merchandise is sold successively to about one hundred buyers; some are content with the rose, others more fastidious or more depraved (for the question has not yet been decided) wish to bring to full flower the bud that grows adjacently. After each bout, Duvergier makes a few tailor's readjustments and for four months it is always the pristine fruits the rascal puts on the block. Finally, at the end of this harassing novitiate, Juliette obtains a lay sister's patents; from this moment onward, she is a recognized girl of the house; thereafter she is to share in its profits and losses. Another apprenticeship; if in the first school, aside from a few extravagances, Juliette served Nature she altogether ignores Nature's laws in the second, where a complete shambles is made of what she once had of moral behavior; the triumph she obtains in vice totally degrades her soul; she feel that, having been born for crime, she must at least commit i grandly and give over languishing in a subaltern's role, which, al though entailing the same misconduct, although abasing her equally brings her a slighter, a much slighter profit. She is found agreeabl by an elderly gentleman, much debauched, who at first has her com merely to attend to the affairs of the moment; she has the skil to cause herself magnificently to be kept; it is not long before sh is appearing at the theater, at promenades, amongst the elite, th very *cordon bleu* of the Cytherean order; she is beheld, mentioned desired, and the clever creature knows so well how to manage he affairs that in less than four years she ruins six men, the poorest o whom had an annuity of one hundred thousand crowns. Nothin more is needed to make her reputation; the blindness of fashionabl people is such that the more one of these creatures has demon strated her dishonesty, the more eager they are to get upon he list; it seems that the degree of her degradation and her corruptio becomes the measure of the sentiments they dare display for he

Juliette had just attained her twentieth year when a certai Comte de Lorsange, a gentleman out of Anjou, about forty yea of age, became so captivated by her he resolved to bestow his nam upon her; he awarded her an income of twelve thousand pounds an assured her of the rest of his fortune were he to be the first to die; he gave her, as well, a house, servants, lackeys, and the sort of mundane consideration which, in the space of two or three years, succeeded in causing her beginnings to be forgot.

It was at this point the fell Juliette, oblivious of all the fine feelings that had been hers by birthright and good education, warped by bad counsel and dangerous books, spurred by the desire to enjoy herself, but alone, and to have a name but not a single chain, bent her attentions to the culpable idea of abridging her husband's days. The odious project once conceived, she consolidated her scheme during those dangerous moments when the physical aspect is fired by ethical error, instants when one refuses oneself much less, for then nothing is opposed to the irregularity of vows or to the impetuosity of desires, and the voluptuousness one experiences is sharp and lively only by reason of the number of the restraints whence one bursts free, or their sanctity. The dream dissipated, were one to recover one's common-sense mood the thing would be of but mediocre import, 'tis the story of mental wrongdoing; everyone knows very well it offends no one; but, alas! one sometimes carries the thing a little farther. What, one ventures to wonder, what would not be the idea's realization, if its mere abstract shape has just exalted, has just so profoundly moved one? The accursed reverie is vivified, and its existence is a crime.

Fortunately for herself, Madame de Lorsange executed it in such secrecy that she was sheltered from all pursuit and with her husband she buried all traces of the frightful deed which precipitated him into the tomb.

Once again become free, and a countess, Madame de Lorsange returned to her former habits; but, believing herself to have some figure in the world, she put somewhat less of the indecent in her deportment. 'Twas no longer a kept girl, 'twas a rich widow who gave pretty suppers at which the Court and the City were only too happy to be included; in a word, we have here a correct woman who, all the same, would to bed for two hundred *louis,* and who gave herself for five hundred a month.

Until she reached the age of twenty-six, Madame de Lorsange made further brilliant conquests: she wrought the financial downfall of three foreign ambassadors, four Farmers-general, two bishops, a cardinal, and three knights of the King's Order; but as it is rarely one stops after the first offense, especially when it has turned out very happily, the unhappy Juliette blackened herself with two additional crimes similar to the first: one in order to plunder a lover who had entrusted a considerable sum to her, of which the man's family had no intelligence; the other in order to capture a legacy of one hundred thousand crowns another one of her lovers granted her in the name of a third, who was charged to pay her that amount after his death. To these horrors Madame de Lorsange added three or four infanticides. The fear of spoiling her pretty figure, the desire to conceal a double intrigue, all combined to make her resolve to stifle the proof of her debauches in her womb; and these misdeeds, like the others, unknown, did not prevent our adroit and ambitious woman from finding new dupes every day.

It is hence true that prosperity may attend conduct of the very worst, and that in the very thick of disorder and corruption, all of what mankind calls happiness may shed itself bountifully upon life; but let this cruel and fatal truth cause no alarm; let honest folk be no more seriously tormented by the example we are going to present of disaster everywhere dogging the heels of Virtue; this criminal felicity is deceiving, it is seeming only; independently of the punishment most certainly reserved by Providence for those whom success in crime has seduced, do they not nourish in the depths of their soul a worm which unceasingly gnaws, prevents them from finding joy in these fictive gleams of meretricious well-being, and, instead of delights, leaves naught in their soul but the rending memory of the crimes which have led them to where they are? With what regards the luckless one fate persecutes, he has his heart for his comfort, and the interior ecstasies virtues procure bring him speedy restitution for the injustice of men.

Such was the state of affairs with Madame de Lorsange when Monsieur de Corville, fifty, a notable wielding the influence and possessing the privileges described further above, resolved entirely to sacrifice himself for this woman and to attach her to himself forever. Whether thanks to diligent attention, whether to maneuver, whether to policy on the part of Madame de Lorsange, he succeeded, and there had passed four years during which he dwelt with her, entirely as if with a legitimate wife, when the acquisition of a very handsome property not far from Montargis obliged both of them to go and spend some time in the Bourbonnais.

One evening, when the excellence of the weather had induced them to prolong their stroll beyond the bounds of their estate and toward Montargis, too fatigued, both, to attempt to return home as they had left, they halted at the inn where the coach from Lyon stops, with the intention of sending a man by horse to fetch them a carriage. In a cool, low-ceilinged room in this house, looking out upon a courtyard, they took their ease and were resting when the coach we just mentioned drew up at the hostelry.

It is a commonplace amusement to watch the arrival of a coach and the passengers' descent: one wagers on the sort of persons who are in it, and if one has gambled upon a whore, an officer, a few abbots and a monk, one is almost certain to win. Madame de Lorsange rises, Monsieur de Corville follows her; from the window they see the well-jolted company reel into the inn. There seemed to be no one left in the carriage when an officer of the mounted constabulary, stepping to the ground, received in his arms, from one of his comrades poised high on top of the coach, a girl of twenty-six or twenty-seven, dressed in a worn calico jacket and swathed to the eyes in a great black taffeta mantle. She was bound hand and foot like a criminal, and in such a weakened state, she would surely have fallen had her guards not given her support. A cry of surprise and horror escaped from Madame de Lorsange: the girl turned and revealed, together with the loveliest figure imaginable, the most noble, the most agreeable, the most interesting visage, in brief, there were there all the charms of a sort to please, and they were rendered yet a thousand times more piquant by that tender and touching air innocence contributes to the traits of beauty.

Monsieur de Corville and his mistress could not suppress their interest in the miserable girl. They approached, they demanded of one of the troopers what the unhappy creature had done.

"She is accused of three crimes," replied the constable, " 'tis a question of murder, theft and arson; but I wish to tell your lordship that my comrade and I have never been so reluctant to take a criminal into custody; she's the most gentle thing, d'ye know, and seems to be the most honest too."

"Oh, la," said Monsieur de Corville, "it might easily be one of those blunders so frequent in the lower courts . . . and where were these crimes committed?"

"At an inn several leagues from Lyon, it's at Lyon she was tried; in accordance with custom she's going to Paris for confirmation of the sentence and then will be returned to Lyon to be executed."

Madame de Lorsange, having heard these words, said in lowered voice to Monsieur de Corville, that she fain would have from the girl's own lips the story of her troubles, and Monsieur de Corville, who was possessed of the same desire, expressed it to the pair of guards and identified himself. The officers saw no reason not to oblige, everyone decided to stay the night at Montargis; comfortable accomodations were called for; Monsieur de Corville declared he would be responsible for the prisoner, she was unbound, and when she had been given something to eat, Madame de Lorsange, unable to control her very great curiosity, and doubtless saying to herself, "This creature, perhaps innocent, is, however, treated like a criminal, whilst about me all is prosperity. . . . I who am soiled with crimes and horrors"; Madame de Lorsange I say, as soon as she observed the poor girl to be somewhat restored, to some measure reassured by the caresses they hastened to bestow upon her, besought her to tell how it had fallen out that she, with so very sweet a face, found herself in such a dreadful plight.

"To recount you the story of my life, Madame," this lovely one in distress said to the Countess, "is to offer you the most striking example of innocence oppressed, is to accuse the hand of Heaven, is to bear complaint against the Supreme Being's will, is, in a sense, to rebel against His sacred designs. . . . I dare not. . . ." Tears gathered in this interesting girl's eyes and, after having given vent to them for a moment, she began her recitation in these terms.

Permit me to conceal my name and birth, Madame; without being illustrious, they are distinguished, and my origins did not destine me to the humiliation to which you see me reduced. When very young I lost my parents; provided with the slender inheritance they had left me, I thought I could expect a suitable position and, refusing to accept all those which were not, I gradually spent, at Paris where I was born, the little I possessed; the poorer I became, the more I was despised; the greater became my need of support, the less I was able to hope for it; but from amongst all the severities to which I was exposed at the beginning of my woeful career, from amongst all the terrible proposals that were made me, I will cite to you what befell me at the home of Monsieur Dubourg, one of the capital's richest tradesmen. The woman with whom I had lodgings had recommended him to me as someone whose influence and wealth might be able to meliorate the harshness of my situation; after having waited a very long time in this man's antechamber, I was admitted; Monsieur Dubourg, aged forty-eight, had just risen out of bed, and was wrapped in a dressing gown which barely hid his disorder; they were about to prepare his coiffure; he dismissed his servants and asked me what I wanted with him.

"Alas, Monsieur," I said, greatly confused, "I am a poor orphan not yet fourteen years old and I have already become familiar with every nuance of misfortune; I implore your commiseration, have pity upon me, I beseech you," and then I told in detail of all my ills, the difficulty I was having to find a place, perhaps I even mentioned how painful it was for me to have to take one, not having been born for a menial's condition. My suffering throughout it all, how I exhausted the little substance I had . . . failure to obtain work, my hope he would facilitate matters and help me find the wherewithal to live; in sum, I said everything that is dictated by the eloquence of wretchedness, always swift to rise in a sensitive soul. . . . After having listened to me with many distractions and much yawning, Monsieur Dubourg asked whether I had always been well-behaved. "I should be neither so poor nor so embarrassed, Monsieur," I answered him, "had I wished to cease to be."

"But," said Dubourg upon hearing that, "but what right have you to expect the wealthy to relieve you if you are in no way useful to them?"

"And of what service are you speaking, Monsieur? I asked nothing more than to render those decency and my years will permit me fulfill."

"The services of a child like yourself are of no great use in a household," Dubourg replied to me. "You have neither the age nor the appearance to find the place you are seeking. You would be better advised to occupy yourself with giving men pleasure and to labor to discover someone who will consent to take care of you; the virtue whereof you make such a conspicuous display is worthless in this world; in vain will you genuflect before its altars, its ridiculous incense will nourish you not at all. The thing which least flatters men, that which makes the least favorable impression upon them, for which they have the most supreme contempt, is good behavior in your sex; here on earth, my child, nothing but what brings in gain or insures power is accounted; and what does the virtue of women profit us! It is their wantonness which serves and amuses us; but their chastity could not interest us less. When, to be brief, persons of our sort give, it is never except to receive; well, how may a little girl like yourself show gratitude for what one does for her if it is not by the most complete surrender of all that is desired of her body!"

"Oh, Monsieur," I replied, grown heavy of heart and uttering a sigh, "then uprightness and benevolence are to be found in man no longer!"

"Precious little," Dubourg rejoined. "How can you expect them still to exist after all the wise things that have been said and written about them? We have rid ourselves of this mania of obliging others gratuitously; it was recognized that charity's pleasures are nothing but sops thrown to pride, and we turned our thoughts to stronger sensations; it has been noticed, for example, that with a child like you, it is infinitely preferable to extract, by way of dividends upon one's investment, all the pleasures lechery is able to offer—much better these delights than the very insipid and futile ones said to come of the disinterested giving of help; his reputation for being a liberal man, an alms-giving and generous man, is not, even at the instant when he most enjoys it, comparable to the slightest sensual pleasure."

"Oh, Monsieur, in the light of such principles the miserable must therefore perish!"

"Does it matter? We have more subjects in France than are needed; given the mechanism's elastic capacities for production, the State can easily afford to be burdened by fewer people."

"But do you suppose children respect their fathers when they are thus despised by them?"

"And what to a father is the love of the children who are a nuisance to him?"

"Would it then have been better had they been strangled in the cradle?"

"Certainly, such is the practice in numerous countries; it was the custom of the Greeks, it is the custom in China: there, the offspring of the poor are exposed, or are put to death. What is the good of letting those creatures live who, no longer able to count upon their parents' aid either because they are without parents or because they are not wanted or recognized by them, henceforth are useful for nothing and simply weigh upon the State: that much surplus commodity, you see, and the market is glutted already; bastards, orphans, malformed infants should be condemned to death immediately they are pupped: the first and the second because, no longer having anyone who wishes or who is able to take care of them, they are mere dregs which one day can have nothing but an undesirable effect upon the society they contaminate; the others because they cannot be of any usefulness to it; the one and the other of these categories are to society what are excrescences to the flesh, battening upon the healthy members' sap, degrading them, enfeebling them; or, if you prefer, they are like those vegetable parasites which, attaching themselves to sound plants, cause them to deteriorate by sucking up their nutritive juices. It's a shocking outrage, these alms destined to feed scum, these most luxuriously appointed houses they have the madness to construct quite as if the human species were so rare, so precious one had to preserve it down to its last vile portion! But enough of politics whereof, my child, you are not likely to understand anything; why lament your fate? for it is in your power, and yours only, to remedy it."

"Great Heavens! at the price of what!"

"At the price of an illusion, of something that has none but the value wherewith your pride invests it. Well," continued this barbarian, getting to his feet and opening the door, "that is all I can do for you; consent to it, or deliver me from your presence; I have no fondness for beggars. . . ."

My tears flowed fast, I was unable to check them; would you believe it, Madame? they irritated rather than melted this man. He shut the door and, seizing my dress at the shoulder, he said most brutally he was going to force from me what I would not accord him voluntarily. At this cruel moment my misery endowed me with courage; I freed myself from his grasp and rushed toward the door:

"Odious man," said I as I fled from him, "may the Heaven you have so grievously offended some day punish your execrable heartlessness as it merits to be. You are worthy neither of the riches you have put to such vile use, nor of the very air you breathe in a world you defile with your barbarities."

I lost no time telling my hostess of the reception given me by the person to whom she had sent me; but what was my astonishment to have this wretch belabor me with reproaches rather than share my sorrow.

"You idiotic chit!" said she in a great rage, "do you imagine men are such great dupes as to dole out alms to little girls such as you without requiring something for their money? Monsieur Dubourg's behavior was far too gentle; in his place I should not have allowed you to leave without having had satisfaction from you. But since you do not care to profit from the aid I offer you, make your own arrangements as you please; you owe me money: pay it tomorrow; otherwise, it's to jail."

"Madame, have pity—"

"Yes, yes, pity; one need only have pity and one starves to death."

"But what would you have me do?"

"You must go back to Dubourg; you must appease him; you must bring home money to me; I will visit him, I will give him notice; if I am able, I'll repair the damage your stupidity has caused; I will convey your apologies, but keep it in mind, you had better improve your conduct."

Ashamed, desperate, knowing not which way to turn, seeing myself savagely repulsed by everyone, I told Madame Desroches (that was my landlady's name) that I had decided to do whatever had to be done to satisfy her. She went to the financier's house and upon her return advised me that she had found him in a very irritable mood, that it had not been without an effort she had managed to incline him in my favor, that by dint of supplications she had at least persuaded him to see me again the following morning, but that I would have to keep a strict watch over my behavior, because, were I to take it into my head to disobey him again, he himself would see to it I was imprisoned forever.

All atremble, I arrived; Dubourg was alone and in a state yet more indecent than on the previous day. Brutality, libertinage, all the characteristics of the debauchee glittered in his cunning glances.

"Thank Desroches," he said harshly, "for it is as a favor to her I intend to show you an instant's kindness; you must surely be aware how little you deserve it after your performance yesterday. Undress yourself and if you once again manifest the least resistance to my desires, two men, waiting for you in the next room, will conduct you to a place whence you will never emerge alive."

"Oh Monsieur," say I, weeping, clutching the wicked man's knees, "unbend, I beseech you; be so generous as to relieve me without requiring what would be so costly I should rather offer you my life than submit to it. . . . Yes, I prefer to die a thousand times over than violate the principles I received in my childhood. . . . Monsieur, Monsieur, constrain me not, I entreat you; can you conceive of gleaning happiness in the depths of tears and disgust? Dare you suspect pleasure where you see naught but loathing? No sooner shall you have consummated your crime than my despair will overwhelm you with remorse. . . ."

But the infamies to which Dubourg abandoned himself prevented me from continuing; that I was able to have believed myself capable of touching a man who was already finding, in the very spectacle of my suffering, one further vehicle for his horrible passions! Would you believe it, Madame? becoming inflamed by the shrill accents of my pleadings, savoring them inhumanly, the wretch disposed himself for his criminal attempts! He gets up, and exhibiting himself to me in a state over which reason is seldom triumphant, and wherein the opposition of the object which causes reason's downfall is but an additional ailment to delirium, he seizes me brutally, impetuously snatches away the veils which still conceal what he burns to enjoy; he caresses me. . . . Oh! what a picture, Great God! What unheard-of mingling of harshness . . . and lewdness! It seemed that the Supreme Being wished, in that first of my encounters, to imprint forever in me all the horror I was to have for a kind of crime whence there was to be born the torrent of evils that have beset me since. But must I complain of them? No, needless to say; to his excesses I owe my salvation; had there been less debauchery in him, I were a ruined girl; Dubourg's flames were extinguished in the fury of his enterprises, Heaven intervened in my behalf against the monster before he could commit the offenses he was readying for, and the loss of his powers, before the sacrifice could occur, preserved me from being its victim.

The consequence was Dubourg became nothing if not more insolent; he laid upon me the blame for his weakness' mistakes, wanted to repair them with new outrages and yet more mortifying invectives; there was nothing he did not say to me, nothing he did not attempt, nothing his perfidious imagination, his adamantine character and the depravation of his manners did not lead him to undertake. My clumsiness made him impatient: I was far from wishing to participate in the thing, to lend myself to it was as much as I could do, my remorse remained lively. However, it was all for naught, submitting to him, I ceased to inflame him; in vain he passed successively from tenderness to rigor . . . from groveling to tyranny . . . from an air of decency to the profligate's excesses, in vain, I say, there was nothing for it, we were both exhausted, and happily he was unable to recover what he needed to deliver more dangerous assaults. He gave it up, made me promise to come the next day, and to be sure of me he refused absolutely to give me anything above the sum I owed Desroches. Greatly humiliated by the adventure and firmly resolved, whatever might happen to me, not to expose myself a third time, I returned to where I was lodging. I announced my intentions to Desroches, paid her, and heaped maledictions upon the criminal capable of so cruelly exploiting my misery. But my imprecations, far from drawing the wrath of God down upon him, only added to his good fortune; and a week later I learned this signal libertine had just obtained a general trusteeship from the Government, which would augment his revenues by more than five hundred thousand pounds per annum. I was absorbed in the reflections such unexpected inconsistencies of fate inevitably give rise to, when a momentary ray of hope seemed to shine in my eyes.

Desroches came to tell me one day that she had finally located a house into which I could be received with pleasure provided my comportment remained of the best. "Great Heaven, Madame," I cried, transported, throwing myself into her arms, "that condition is the one I would stipulate myself—you may imagine how happy I am to accept it." The man I was to serve was a famous Parisian usurer who had become rich, not only by lending money upon collateral, but even by stealing from the public every time he thought he could do so in safety. He lived in the rue Quincampoix, had a third-story flat, and shared it with a creature of fifty years he called his wife and who was at least as wicked as he.

"Thérèse," this miser said to me (such was the name I had taken in order to hide my own), "Thérèse, the primary virtue in this house is probity; if ever you make off with the tenth part of a penny, I'll have you hanged, my child, d'ye see. The modest ease my wife and I enjoy is the fruit of our immense labors, and of our perfect sobriety. . . . Do you eat much, little one?"

"A few ounces of bread each day, Monsieur," I replied, "water, and a little soup when I am lucky enough to get it."

"Soup! Bleeding Christ! Soup! Behold, deary," said the usurer to his dame, "behold and tremble at the progress of luxury: it's looking for circumstances, it's been dying of hunger for a year, and now it wants to eat soup; we scarcely have it once a week, on Sunday, we who work like galley slaves: you'll have three ounces of bread a day, my daughter, plus half a bottle of river water, plus one of my wife's old dresses every eighteen months, plus three crowns' wages at the end of each year, if we are content with your services, if your economy responds to our own and if, finally, you make the house prosper through orderliness and arrangement. Your duties are mediocre, they're done in jig time; 'tis but a question of washing and cleaning this six-room apartment thrice a week, of making our beds, answering the door, powdering my wig, dressing my wife's hair, looking after the dog and the parakeet, lending a hand in the kitchen, washing the utensils, helping my wife whenever she prepares us a bite to eat, and daily devoting four or five hours to the washing, to mending stockings, hats, and other little household odds and ends; you observe, Thérèse, 'tis nothing at all, you will have ample free time to yourself, we will permit you to employ it to your own interest, provided, my child, you are good, discreet and, above all, thrifty, that's of the essence."

You may readily imagine, Madame, that one had to be in the

frightful state I indeed was in to accept such a position; not only was there infinitely more work to be done than my strength permitted me to undertake, but should I be able to live upon what was offered me? However, I was careful to raise no difficulties and was installed that same evening.

Were my cruel situation to permit me to amuse you for an instant, Madame, when I must think of nothing but gaining your compassion, I should dare describe some of the symptoms of avarice I witnessed while in that house; but a catastrophe so terrible for me was awaiting me during my second year there that it is by no means easy to linger over entertaining details before making you acquainted with my miseries.

Nevertheless, you will know, Madame, that, for light in Monsieur du Harpin's apartment, there was never any but what he got from the street lamp which, happily, was placed opposite his room; never did Monsieur or Madame use linen; what I washed was hoarded away, it was never touched; on the sleeves of Monsieur's coat, as well as upon Madame's dress, were old gauntlet cuffs sewn over the material, and these I removed and washed every Saturday evening; no sheets; no towels, and that to avoid laundry expenses. Never was wine drunk in her house, clear water being, declared Madame du Harpin, the natural drink of man, the healthiest and least dangerous. Every time bread was sliced, a basket was put beneath the knife so that whatever fell would not be lost; into this container went, also, and with exactitude all the scraps and leavings that might survive the meal, and this compound, fried up on Sunday together with a little butter, made a banquet for the day of rest; never was one to beat clothing or too energetically dust the furniture for fear of wearing it out, instead, very cautiously, one tickled about with a feather. Monsieur's shoes, and Madame's as well, were double-soled with iron, they were the same shoes that had served them on their wedding day; but a much more unusual custom was the one they had me practice once a week: there was in the apartment a rather large room whose walls were not papered; I was expected to take a knife and scrape and shave away a certain quantity of plaster, and this I next passed through a fine sieve; what resulted from this operation became the powder wherewith every morning I sprinkled Monsieur's peruke and

Madame's hair, done up in a bun. Ah! wouldst to God those had been the only turpitudes of which this evil pair had made habits! Nothing's more normal than the desire to conserve one's property; but what is not normal is the desire to augment it by the accession of the property of others. And it was not long before I perceived that it was only thus du Harpin acquired his wealth.

Above us there lodged a solitary individual of considerable means who was the owner of some handsome jewels, and whose belongings, whether because of their proximity or because they had passed through my master's hands, were very well known to him; I often heard him express regrets to his wife over the loss of a certain gold box worth fifty or sixty *louis,* which article would infallibly have remained his, said he, had he proceeded with greater cleverness. In order to console himself for the sale of the said box, the good Monsieur du Harpin projected its theft, and it was to me he entrusted the execution of his plan.

After having delivered a long speech upon the indifference of robbery, upon, indeed, its usefulness in the world, since it maintains a sort of equilibrium which totally confounds the inequality of property; upon the infrequence of punishment, since out of every twenty thieves it could be proven that not above two dies on the gallows; after having demonstrated to me, with an erudition of which I had not dreamt Monsieur du Harpin capable, that theft was honored throughout Greece, that several races yet acknowledge it, favor it, and reward it for a bold deed simultaneously giving proof of courage and skill (two virtues indispensable to a warlike nation), after having, in a word, exalted his personal influence which would extricate me from all embarrassments in the event I should be detected, Monsieur du Harpin tendered me two lock picks, one to open the neighbor's front door, the other his secretary within which lay the box in question; incessantly he enjoined me to get him this box and, in return for so important a service, I could expect, for two years, to receive an additional crown.

"Oh Monsieur!" I exclaimed, shuddering at his proposal, "is it possible a master dare thus corrupt his domestic! What prevents me from turning against you the weapons you put into my hands?

and what defense will you have if someday I make you the victim of your own principles?"

Du Harpin, much confused, fell back upon a lame subterfuge: what he was doing, said he, was being done with the simple intention of testing me; how fortunate that I had resisted this temptation, he added . . . how I should have been doomed had I succumbed, etc. I scoffed at this lie; but I was soon enough aware of what a mistake it had been to answer him with such asperity: malefactors do not like to find resistance in those they seek to seduce; unfortunately, there is no middle ground or median attitude when one is so unlucky as to have been approached by them: one must necessarily thereupon become either their accomplices, which is exceedingly dangerous, or their enemies, which is even more so. Had I been a little experienced, I would have quit the house forthwith, but it was already written in Heaven that every one of the honest gestures that was to emanate from me would be answered by misfortunes.

Monsieur du Harpin let more than a month drift by, that is to say, he waited until the end of my second year with him, and waited without showing the least hint of resentment at the refusal I had given him, when one evening, having just retired to my room to taste a few hours of repose, I suddenly heard my door burst open and there, not without terror, I saw Monsieur du Harpin and four soldiers of the watch standing by my bed.

"Perform your duty, Sirrah," said he to the men of the law, "this wretch has stolen from me a diamond worth a thousand crowns, you will find it in her chamber or upon her person, the fact is certain."

"I have robbed you, Monsieur!" said I, sore troubled and springing from my bed, "I! Great Heaven! Who knows better than you the contrary to be true! Who should be more deeply aware than you to what point I loathe robbery and to what degree it is unthinkable I could have committed it."

But du Harpin made a great uproar to drown out my words; he continued to order perquisitions, and the miserable ring was discovered in my mattress. To evidence of this strength there was nothing to reply; I was seized instantly, pinioned, and led to prison without being able to prevail upon the authorities to listen to one word in my favor.

The trial of an unfortunate creature who has neither influence nor protection is conducted with dispatch in a land where virtue is thought incompatible with misery, where poverty is enough to convict the accused; there, an unjust prepossession causes it to be supposed that he who ought to have committed a crime did indeed commit it; sentiments are proportioned according to the guilty one's estate; and when once gold or titles are wanting to establish his innocence, the impossibility that he be innocent then appears self-evident.[1]

I defended myself, it did no good, in vain I furnished the best material to the lawyer whom a protocol of form required be given me for an instant or two; my employer accused me, the diamond had been discovered in my room; it was plain I had stolen it. When I wished to describe Monsieur du Harpin's awful traffic and prove that the misfortune that had struck me was naught but the fruit of his vengeance and the consequence of his eagerness to be rid of a creature who, through possession of his secret, had become his master, these pleadings were interpreted as so many recriminations, and I was informed that for twenty years Monsieur du Harpin had been known as a man of integrity, incapable of such a horror. I was transferred to the Conciergerie, where I saw myself upon the brink of having to pay with my life for having refused to participate in a crime; I was shortly to perish; only a new misdeed could save me: Providence willed that Crime serve at least once as an aegis unto Virtue, that crime might preserve it from the abyss which is some-day going to engulf judges together with their imbecility.

I had about me a woman, probably forty years old, as celebrated for her beauty as for the variety and number of her villainies; she was called Dubois and, like the unlucky Thérèse, was on the eve of paying the capital penalty, but as to the exact form of it the judges were yet mightily perplexed: having rendered herself guilty of every imaginable crime, they found themselves virtually obliged to invent a new torture for her, or to expose her to one whence we ordinarily exempt our sex. This woman had become

---

[1] O ages yet to come! You shall no longer be witness to these horrors and infamies abounding!

interested in me, criminally interested without doubt, since the basis of her feelings, as I learned afterward, was her extreme desire to make a proselyte of me.

Only two days from the time set for our execution, Dubois came to me; it was at night. She told me not to lie down to sleep, but to stay near her side. Without attracting attention, we moved as close as we could to the prison door. "Between seven and eight," she said, "the Conciergerie will catch fire, I have seen to it; no question about it, many people will be burned; it doesn't matter, Thérèse," the evil creature went on, "the fate of others must always be as nothing to us when our own lives are at stake; well, we are going to escape here, of that you can be sure; four men—my confederates—will join us and I guarantee you we will be free."

I have told you, Madame, that the hand of God which had just punished my innocence, employed crime to protect me; the fire began, it spread, the blaze was horrible, twenty-one persons were consumed, but we made a successful sally. The same day we reached the cottage of a poacher, an intimate friend of our band who dwelt in the forest of Bondy.

"There you are, Thérèse," Dubois says to me, "free. You may now choose the kind of life you wish, but were I to have any advice to give you, it would be to renounce the practice of virtue which, as you have noticed, is the courting of disaster; a misplaced delicacy led you to the foot of the scaffold, an appalling crime rescued you from it; have a look about and see how useful are good deeds in this world, and whether it is really worth the trouble immolating yourself for them. Thérèse, you are young and attractive, heed me, and in two years I'll have led you to a fortune; but don't suppose I am going to guide you there along the paths of virtue: when one wants to get on, my dear girl, one must stop at nothing; decide, then, we have no security in this cottage, we've got to leave in a few hours."

"Oh Madame," I said to my benefactress, "I am greatly indebted to you, and am far from wishing to disown my obligations: you saved my life; in my view, 'tis frightful the thing was achieved through a crime and, believe me, had I been the one charged to commit it, I should have preferred a thousand deaths to the anguish of participating in it; I am aware of all the dangers I risk in trusting myself to the honest sentiments which will always remain in my heart; but whatever be the thorns of virtue, Madame, I prefer them unhesitatingly and always to the perilous favors which are crime's accompaniment. There are religious principles within me which, may it please Heaven, will never desert me; if Providence renders difficult my career in life, 'tis in order to compensate me in a better world. That hope is my consolation, it sweetens my griefs, it soothes me in my sufferings, it fortifies me in distress, and causes me confidently to face all the ills it pleases God to visit upon me. That joy should straightway be extinguished in my soul were I perchance to besmirch it with crime, and together with the fear of chastisements in this world I should have the painful anticipation of torments in the next, which would not for one instant procure me the tranquillity I thirst after."

"Those are absurd doctrines which will have you on the dung heap in no time, my girl," said Dubois with a frown; "believe me: forget God's justice, His future punishments and rewards, the lot of those platitudes lead us nowhere but to death from starvation. O Thérèse, the callousness of the Rich legitimates the bad conduct of the Poor; let them open their purse to our needs, let humaneness reign in their hearts and virtues will take root in ours; but as long as our misfortune, our patient endurance of it, our good faith, our abjection only serves to double the weight of our chains, our crimes will be their doing, and we will be fools indeed to abstain from them when they can lessen the yoke wherewith their cruelty bears us down. Nature has caused us all to be equals born, Thérèse; if fate is pleased to upset the primary scheme of the general law, it is up to us to correct its caprices and through our skill to repair the usurpations of the strongest. I love to hear these rich ones, these titled ones, these magistrates and these priests, I love to see them preach virtue to us. It is not very difficult to forswear theft when one has three or four times what one needs to live; it is not very necessary to plot murder when one is surrounded by nothing but adulators and thralls unto whom one's will is law; nor is it very hard to be temperate and sober when one has the most succulent dainties constantly within one's reach; they can well contrive to be sincere when there is never any apparent advantage in falsehood. . . . But we, Thérèse, we whom the barbaric Providence you are mad enough to idolize, has condemned to slink in the dust of humiliation as doth the serpent in grass, we who are beheld with disdain only because we are poor, who are tyrannized because we are weak; we, who must quench our thirst with gall and who, wherever we go, tread on the thistle always, you would have us shun crime when its hand alone opens up unto us the door to life, maintains us in it, and is our only protection when our life is threatened; you would have it that, degraded and in perpetual abjection, while this class dominating us has to itself all the blessings of fortune, we reserve for ourselves naught but pain, beatings, suffering, nothing but want and tears, brandings and the gibbet. No, no, Thérèse, no; either this Providence you reverence is made only for our scorn, or the world we see about us is not at all what Providence would have it. Become better acquainted with your Providence, my child, and be convinced that as soon as it places us in a situation where evil becomes necessary, and while at the same time it leaves us the possibility of doing it, this evil harmonizes quite as well with its decrees as does good, and Providence gains as much by the one as by the other; the state in which she has created us is equality: he who disturbs is no more guilty than he who seeks to re-establish the balance; both act in accordance with received impulses, both have to obey those impulses and enjoy them."

I must confess that if ever I was shaken it was by this clever woman's seductions; but a yet stronger voice, that of my heart to which I gave heed, combatted her sophistries; I declared to Dubois that I was determined never to allow myself to be corrupted. "Very well!" she replied, "become what you wish, I abandon you to your sorry fate; but if ever you get yourself hanged, which is an end you cannot avoid, thanks to the fatality which inevitably saves the criminal by sacrificing the virtuous, at least remember before dying never to mention us."

While we were arguing thus, Dubois' four companions were drinking with the poacher, and as wine disposes the malefactor's heart to new crimes and causes him to forget his old, our bandits no sooner learned of my resolution than, unable to make me their accomplice, they decided to make me their victim; their principles, their manners, the dark retreat we were in, the security they thought they enjoyed, their drunkenness, my age, my innocence—everything encouraged them. They get up from table, they confer in whispers, they consult Dubois, doings whose lugubrious mystery makes me shiver with horror, and at last there comes an order to me then and there to satisfy the desires of each of the four; if I go to it cheerfully, each will give me a crown to help me along my way; if they must employ violence, the thing will be done all the same; but the better to guard their secret, once finished with me they will stab me, and will bury me at the foot of yonder tree.

I need not paint the effect this cruel proposition had upon me, Madame, you will have no difficulty understanding that I sank to my knees before Dubois, I besought her a second time to be my protectress: the low creature did but laugh at my tears:

"Oh by God!" quoth she, "here's an unhappy little one. What! you shudder before the obligation to serve four fine big boys one after another? Listen to me," she added, after some reflection, "my sway over these dear lads is sufficiently great for me to obtain a reprieve for you upon condition you render yourself worthy of it."

"Alas! Madame, what must I do?" I cried through my tears; "command me; I am ready."

"Join us, throw in your lot with us, and commit the same deeds, without show of the least repugnance; either that, or I cannot save you from the rest." I did not think myself in a position to hesitate; by accepting this cruel condition I exposed myself to further dangers, to be sure, but they were the less immediate; perhaps I might be able to avoid them, whereas nothing could save me from those with which I was actually menaced.

"I will go everywhere with you, Madame," was my prompt answer to Dubois, "everywhere, I promise you; shield me from the fury of these men and I shall never leave your side while I live."

"Children," Dubois said to the four bandits, "this girl is one of the company, I am taking her into it; I ask you to do her no ill, don't put her stomach off the *métier* during her first days in it; you see how useful her age and face can be to us; let's employ them to our advantage rather than sacrifice them to our pleasures."

But such is the degree of energy in man's passions nothing can subdue them. The persons I was dealing with were in no state to heed reason: all four surrounded me, devoured me with their fiery glances, menaced me in a still more terrible manner; they were about to lay hands on me, I was about to become their victim.

"She has got to go through with it," one of them declared, "it's too late for discussion: was she not told she must give proof of virtues in order to be admitted into a band of thieves? and once a little used, won't she be quite as serviceable as she is while a virgin?"

I am softening their expressions, you understand, Madame, I am sweetening the scene itself; alas! their obscenities were such that your modesty might suffer at least as much from beholding them unadorned as did my shyness.

A defenseless and trembling victim, I shuddered; I had barely strength to breathe; kneeling before the quartet, I raised my feeble arms as much to supplicate the men as to melt Dubois' heart. . . .

"An instant," said one who went by the name of Coeur-de-fer and appeared to be the band's chief, a man of thirty-six years, of a bull's strength and bearing the face of a satyr; "one moment, friends: it may be possible to satisfy everyone concerned; since this little girl's virtue is so precious to her and since, as Dubois states it very well, this quality otherwise put into action could become worth something to us, let's leave it to her; but we have got to be appeased; our mood is warm, Dubois, and in the state we are in, d'ye know, we might perhaps cut your own throat if you were to stand between us and our pleasures; let's have Thérèse instantly strip as naked as the day she came into the world, and next let's have her adopt one after the other all the positions we are pleased to call for, and meanwhile Dubois will sate our hungers, we'll burn our incense upon the altars' entrance to which this creature refuses us."

"Strip naked!" I exclaimed, "Oh Heaven, what is it thou doth require of me? When I shall have delivered myself thus to your eyes, who will be able to answer for me? . . ."

But Coeur-de-fer, who seemed in no humor either to grant me more or to suspend his desires, burst out with an oath and struck me in a manner so brutal that I saw full well compliance was my last resort. He put himself in Dubois' hands, she having been put by his in a disorder more or less the equivalent of mine and, as soon as I was as he desired me to be, having made me crouch down upon all fours so that I resembled a beast, Dubois took in hand a very monstrous object and led it to the peristyles of first one and then the other of Nature's altars, and under her guidance the blows it delivered to me here and there were like those of a battering ram thundering at the gates of a besieged town in olden days. The shock of the initial assault drove me back; enraged, Coeur-de-fer threatened me with harsher treatments were I to retreat from these; Dubois is instructed to redouble her efforts, one of the libertines grasps my shoulders and prevents me from staggering before the concussions: they become so fierce I am in blood and am able to avoid not a one.

"Indeed," stammers Coeur-de-fer, "in her place I'd prefer to open the doors rather than see them ruined this way, but she won't have it, and we're not far from the capitulation. . . . Vigorously . . . vigorously, Dubois. . . ."

And the explosive eruption of this debauchee's flames, almost as violent as a stroke of lightning, flickers and dies upon ramparts ravaged without being breached.

The second had me kneel between his legs and while Dubois administered to him as she had to the other, two enterprises absorbed his entire attention: sometimes he slapped, powerfully but in a very nervous manner, either my cheeks or my breasts; sometimes his impure mouth fell to sucking mine. In an instant my face turned purple, my chest red. . . . I was in pain, I begged him to spare me, tears leapt from my eyes; they roused him, he accelerated his activities; he bit my tongue, and the two strawberries on my breasts were so bruised that I slipped backward, but was kept from falling. They thrust me toward him, I was everywhere more furiously harassed, and his ecstasy supervened. . . .

The third bade me mount upon and straddle two somewhat separated chairs and, seating himself betwixt them, excited by Dubois, lying in his arms, he had me bend until his mouth was directly below the temple of Nature; never will you imagine, Madame, what this obscene mortal took it into his head to do; willy-nilly, I was obliged to satisfy his every need. . . . Just Heaven! what man, no matter how depraved, can taste an instant of pleasure in such things. . . . I did what he wished, inundated him, and my complete submission procured this foul man an intoxication of which he was incapable without this infamy.

The fourth attached strings to all parts of me to which it was possible to tie them, he held the ends in his hand and sat down seven or eight feet from my body; Dubois' touches and kisses excited him prodigiously; I was standing erect: 'twas by sharp tugs now on this string, now on some other that the savage irritated his pleasures; I swayed, I lost balance again and again, he flew into an ecstasy each time I tottered; finally, he pulled all the cords at once, I fell to the floor in front of him: such was his design: and my forehead, my breast, my cheeks received the proofs of a delirium he owed to none but this mania.

That is what I suffered, Madame, but at least my honor was respected even though my modesty assuredly was not. Their calm restored, the bandits spoke of regaining the road, and that same night we reached Tremblai with the intention of approaching the woods of Chantilly, where it was thought a few good prizes might be awaiting us.

Nothing equaled my despair at being obliged to accompany such persons, and I was only determined to part with them as soon as I could do so without risk. The following day we lay hard by Louvres, sleeping under haystacks; I felt in need of Dubois' support and wanted to pass the night by her side; but it seemed she had planned to employ it otherwise than protecting my virtue from the attacks I dreaded; three of the thieves surrounded her and before my very eyes the abominable creature gave herself to all three simultaneously. The fourth approached me; it was the captain. "Lovely Thérèse," said he, "I hope you shall not refuse me at least the pleasure of spending the night with you?" and as he perceived my extreme unwillingness, "fear not," he went on; "we'll have a chat together, and I will attempt nothing without your consent.

"O Thérèse," cried he, folding me in his arms, " 'tis all foolishness, don't you know, to be so pretentious with us. Why are you concerned to guard your purity in our midst? Even were we to agree to respect it, could it be compatible with the interests of the band? No need to hide it from you, my dear; for when we settle down in cities, we count upon your charms to snare us some dupes."

"Why, Monsieur," I replied, "since it is certain I should prefer death to these horrors, of what use can I be to you, and why do you oppose my flight?"

"We certainly do oppose it, my girl," Coeur-de-fer rejoined, "you must serve either our pleasures or our interests; your poverty imposes the yoke upon you, and you have got to adapt to it. But, Thérèse, and well you know it, there is nothing in this world that cannot be somehow arranged: so listen to me, and accept the management of your own fate: agree to live with me, dear girl, consent to belong to me and be properly my own, and I will spare you the baneful role for which you are destined."

"I, Sir, I become the mistress of a—"

"Say the word, Thérèse, out with it: a scoundrel, eh? Oh, I admit it, but I have no other titles to offer you; that our sort does not marry you are doubtless well aware: marriage is one of the sacraments Thérèse, and full of an undiscriminating contempt for them all, with none do we ever bother. However, be a little reasonable; that sooner or later you lose what is so dear to you is an indispensable necessity, hence would it not be better to sacrifice it to a single man who thereupon will become your support and protector, is that not better, I say, than to be prostituted to everyone?"

"But why must it be," I replied, "that I have no other alternative?"

"Because, Thérèse, we have got you, and because the stronger is always the better reason; La Fontaine made the remark ages ago. Truthfully," he continued rapidly, "is it not a ridiculous extravagance to assign, as you do, such a great value to the most futile of all things? How can a girl be so dull-witted as to believe that virtue may depend upon the somewhat greater or lesser diameter of one of her physical parts? What difference does it make to God or man whether this part be intact or tampered with? I will go further: it being the intention of Nature that each individual fulfill on this earth all of the purposes for which he has been formed, and women existing only to provide pleasure for men, it is plainly to outrage her thus to resist the intention she has in your regard. It is to wish to be a creature useless in this world and consequently one contemptible. This chimerical propriety, which they have had the absurdity to present to you as a virtue and which, since infancy, far from being useful to Nature and society, is an obvious defiance of the one and the other, this propriety, I say, is no more than a reprehensible stubbornness of which a person as mettlesome and full of intelligence as you should not wish to be guilty. No matter; continue to hear me out, dear girl, I am going to prove my desire to please you and to respect your weakness. I will not by any means touch that phantom, Thérèse, whose possession causes all your delight; a girl has more than one favor to give, and one can offer to Venus in many a temple; I will be content with the most mediocre; you know, my dear, near the Cyprean altar, there is situate an obscure grot into whose solitude Love retires, the more energetically to seduce us: such will be the altar where I will burn my incense; no disadvantages there, Thérèse; if pregnancies affright you, 'tis not in this manner they can come about, never will your pretty figure be deformed this way; the maidenhead so cherished by you will be preserved unimpaired, and whatever be the use to which you decide to put it, you can propose it unattainted. Nothing can betray a girl from this quarter, however rude or multiple the attacks may be; as soon as the bee has left off sucking the pollen, the rose's calix closes shut again; one would never imagine it had been opened. There exist girls who have known ten years of pleasure this way, even with several men, women who were just as much married as anyone else after it all, and on their wedding nights they proved quite as virgin as could be wished. How many fathers, what a multitude of brothers have thuswise abused their daughters and sisters without the latter having become on that account any the less worthy of a later hymeneal sacrifice! How many confessors have not employed the same route to satisfaction, without parents experiencing the mildest disquiet; in one word, 'tis the mystery's asylum, 'tis there where it connects itself with love by ties of prudence. . . . Need I tell you further, Thérèse, that although this is the most secret temple it is howbeit the most voluptuous; what is necessary to happiness is found nowhere else, and that easy vastness native to the adjacent aperture falls far short of having the piquant charms of a locale into which one does not enter without effort, where one takes up one's abode only at the price of some trouble; women themselves reap an advantage from it, and those whom reason compels to know this variety of pleasure, never pine after the others. Try it, Thérèse, try, and we shall both be contented."

"Oh Monsieur," I replied, "I have no experience of the thing;

but I have heard it said that this perversion you recommend outrages women in a yet more sensitive manner. . . . It more grievously offends Nature. The hand of Heaven takes its vengeance upon it in this world, Sodom provides the example."

"What innocence, my dear, what childishness," the libertine retorted; "who ever told you such a thing? Yet a little more attention, Thérèse, let me proceed to rectify your ideas.

"The wasting of the seed destined to perpetuate the human species, dear girl, is the only crime which can exist—such is the hypothesis; according to it, this seed is put in us for the sole purpose of reproduction, and if that were true I would grant you that diverting it is an offense. But once it is demonstrated that her situating this semen in our loins is by no means enough to warrant supposing that Nature's purpose is to have all of it employed for reproduction, what then does it matter, Thérèse, whether it be spilled in one place or in another? Does the man who diverts it perform a greater evil than Nature who does not employ all of it? Now, do not those natural losses, which we can imitate if we please, occur in an abundance of instances? Our very ability to provoke them, firstly, is an initial proof that they do not offend Nature in the slightest. It would be contrary to all the equity and profound wisdom we everywhere recognize in her laws for them to permit what might affront her; secondly, those losses occur a hundred hundred million times every day, and she instigates them herself; nocturnal pollutions, the inutility of semen during the periods of woman's pregnancy, are they not authorized by her laws, enjoined by them, and do they not prove that, very little concerned for what may result from this liquid to which we so foolishly attach a disproportionate value, she permits us its waste with the same indifference she herself causes it every day to be wasted; she tolerates reproduction, yes, but much is wanting to prove reproduction is one of her intentions; she lets us go ahead with our reproducing to be sure, but it being no more to her advantage than our abstaining therefrom, the choice we happen to make is as one to her. Is it not clear that leaving us the power to create, not to create, or to destroy, we will not delight her at all or disappoint her any more by adopting toward the one or the other the attitude which suits us best; and what could be more self-evident than that the course we choose, being but the result of her power over us and the influence upon us of her actions, will far more surely please than it will risk offending her. Ah, Thérèse! believe me, Nature frets very little over those mysteries we are great enough fools to turn into worship of her. Whatever be the temple at which one sacrifices, immediately she allows incense to be burned there, one can be sure the homage offends her in no wise; refusals to produce, waste of the semen employed in production, the obliteration of that seed when it has germinated, the annihilation of that germ even long after its formation, all those, Thérèse, are imaginary crimes which are of no interest to Nature and at which she scoffs as she does at all the rest of our institutions which offend more often than they serve her."

Coeur-de-fer waxed warm while expounding his perfidious maxims, and I soon beheld him again in the state which had so terrified me the night before; in order to give his lesson additional impact, he wished instantly to join practice to precept; and, my resistances notwithstanding, his hands strayed toward the altar into which the traitor wanted to penetrate. . . . Must I declare, Madame, that, blinded by the wicked man's seductions; content, by yielding a little, to save what seemed the more essential; reflecting neither upon his casuistries' illogicalities nor upon what I was myself about to risk since the dishonest fellow, possessing gigantic proportions, had not even the possibility to see a woman in the most permissible place and since, urged on by his native perversity, he most assuredly had no object but to maim me; my eyes as I say, perfectly blind to all that, I was going to abandon myself and become criminal through virtue; my opposition was weakening; already master of the throne, the insolent conqueror concentrated all his energies in order to establish himself upon it; and then there was heard the sound of a carriage moving along the highway. Upon the instant, Coeur-de-fer forsakes his pleasures for his duties; he assembles his followers and flies to new crimes. Not long afterward, we hear cries, and those bandits, all bloodied over, return triumphant and laden with spoils.

"Let's decamp smartly," says Coeur-de-fer, "we've killed three men, the corpses are on the road, we're safe no longer." The booty is divided, Coeur-de-fer wants me to have my share; it comes to twenty *louis,* which I am compelled to accept. I tremble at the obligation to take such money; however, we are in a hurry, everyone snatches up his belongings and off we go.

The next day we find ourselves out of danger and in the forest of Chantilly; during supper, the men reckon what their latest operation has been worth to them, and evaluate the total capture at no more than two hundred *louis*.

"Indeed," says one of them, "it wasn't worth the trouble to commit three murders for such a little sum."

"Softly, my friends," Dubois answers, "it was not for the sake of their purses I exhorted you not to spare those travelers, it was solely in the interests of our security; the law's to be blamed for these crimes, the fault's not ours; so long as thieves are hanged like murderers, thefts shall never be committed without assassinations. The two misdeeds are punished equally; why then abstain from the second when it may cover up the first? What makes you suppose, furthermore," the horrid creature continued, "that two hundred *louis* are not worth three killings? One must never appraise values save in terms of our own interests. The cessation of the victims' existences is as nothing compared to the continuation of ours, not a mite does it matter to us whether any individual is alive or in the grave; consequently, if one of the two cases involves what in the smallest way affects our welfare, we must, with perfect unremorse, determine the thing in our own favor; for in a completely indifferent matter we should, if we have any wits and are master of the situation, undoubtedly act so as to turn it to the profitable side, entirely neglecting whatever may befall our adversary; for there is no rational commensuration between what affects us and what affects others; the first we sense physically, the other only touches us morally, and moral feelings are made to deceive; none but physical sensations are authentic; thus, not only do two hundred *louis* suffice for three murders, but even thirty *centimes* would have sufficed, for those thirty *centimes* would have procured a satisfaction which, although light, must necessarily affect us to a much more lively degree than would three men murdered, who are nothing to us, and by the wrongs done whom we are not in the least touched, no, not even scratched; our organic feebleness, careless thinking, the accursed prejudices in which we were brought up, the vain terrors of religion and law, those are what hamper idiots and confound their criminal careers, those are what prevent them from arriving at greatness; but every strong and healthy individual, endowed with an energetically organized mind, who preferring himself to others, as he must, will know how to weigh their interests in the balance against his own, will laugh God and mankind to the devil, will brave death and mock at the law, fully aware that it is to himself he must be faithful, that by himself all must be measured, will sense that the vastest multitude of wrongs inflicted upon others cannot offset the least enjoyment lost to himself or be as important as his slightest pleasure purchased by an unheard-of host of villainies. Joy pleases him, it is in him, it is his own, crime's effect touches him not, is exterior to him; well, I ask, what thinking man will not prefer what causes his delectation to what is alien to him? who will not consent to commit this deed whereof he experiences nothing unpleasant, in order to procure what moves him most agreeably?"

"Oh Madame," I said to Dubois, asking her leave to reply to her execrable sophistries, "do you not at all feel that your damnation is writ in what you have just uttered? At the very most, such principles could only befit the person powerful enough to have nothing to dread from others; but we, Madame, perpetually in fear and humiliated; we, proscribed by all honest folk, condemned by every law, should we be the exponents of doctrines which can only whet the sword blade suspended above our heads? Would we find ourselves in this unhappy position were we in the center of society; were we to be where, that is to say, we ought to be, without our misconduct and delivered from our miseries, do you fancy such maxims could be any more fitting to us? How would you have him not perish who through blind egoism wishes all alone to strive against the combined interests of others? Is not society right never to suffer in its midst the man who declares himself hostile to it? And can the isolated individual fight against everyone? Can he flatter himself he is happy and tranquil if, refusing to submit to the social contract, he does not consent to give up a little of his happiness to insure the rest? Society is maintained only by the ceaseless interexchange of considerations and good works, those are the bonds which cement the edifices; such a one who instead of positive acts offers naught but crimes, having therefore to be dreaded, will necessarily be attacked if he is the strongest, laid low by the first he offends if he is the weakest; but destroyed at any rate, for there is in man a powerful instinct which compels him to safeguard his peace and quiet and to strike whosoever seeks to trouble them; that is why the long endurance of criminal associations is virtually impossible: their well-being suddenly confronted by cold steel, all the others must promptly unite to blunt the threatening point. Even amongst ourselves, Madame, I dare add; how can you lull yourself into believing you can maintain concord amongst ourselves when you counsel each to heed nothing but his own self-interest? Would you have any just complaints to make against the one of us who wanted to cut the throats of the others, who did so in order to monopolize for himself what has been shared by his colleagues? Why, 'tis a splendid panegyric to Virtue, to prove its necessity in even a criminal society ... to prove for a certainty that this society would disintegrate in a trice were it not sustained by Virtue!"

"Your objections, Thérèse," said Coeur-de-fer, "not the theses Dubois has been expounding, are sophistries; our criminal fraternities are not by any means sustained by Virtue; rather by self-interest, egoism, selfishness; this eulogy of Virtue, which you have fabricated out of a false hypothesis, miscarries; it is not at all owing to virtuousness that, believing myself, let us suppose, the strongest of the band, I do not use a dagger on my comrades in order to appropriate their shares, it is because, thereupon finding myself all alone, I would deprive myself of the means which assure me the fortune I expect to have with their help; similarly, this is the single motive which restrains them from lifting their arms against me. Now this motive, as you, Thérèse, perfectly well observe, is purely selfish, and has not even the least appearance of virtue; he who wishes to struggle alone against society's interests must, you say, expect to perish; will he not much more certainly perish if, to enable him to exist therein, he has nothing but his misery and is abandoned by others? What one terms the interest of society is simply the mass of individual interests unified, but it is never otherwise than by ceding that this private interest can accommodate and blend with the general interest; well, what would you have him cede who has nothing he can relinquish? And he who had much? Agree that he should see his error grow apace with the discovery that he was giving infinitely more than he was getting in return; and, such being the case, agree that the unfairness of the bargain should prevent him from concluding it. Trapped in this dilemma, the best thing remaining for this man, don't you agree, is to quit this unjust society, to go elsewhere, and to accord prerogatives to a different society of men who, placed in a situation comparable to his, have their interest in combating, through the coordination of their lesser powers, the broader authority that wished to extract from the poor man what little he possessed in exchange for nothing at all. But you will say, thence will be born a state of perpetual warfare. Excellent! is that not the perpetual state of Nature? Is it not the only state to which we are really adapted? All men are born isolated, envious, cruel and despotic; wishing to have everything and surrender nothing, incessantly struggling to maintain either their rights or achieve their ambition, the legislator comes up and says to them: Cease thus to fight; if each were to retreat a little, calm would be restored. I find no fault with the position implicit in the agreement, but I maintain that two species of individuals cannot and ought not submit to it, ever; those who feel they are the stronger have no need to give up anything in order to be happy, and those who find themselves the weaker also find themselves giving up infinitely more than what is assured them. However, society is only composed of weak persons and strong; well, if the pact must perforce displease both weak and strong, there is great cause to suppose it will fail to suit society, and the previously existing state of warfare must appear infinitely preferable, since it permitted everyone the free exercise of his strength and his industry, whereof he would discover himself deprived by a society's unjust pact which takes too much from the one and never accords enough to the other; hence, the truly intelligent person is he who, indifferent to the risk of renewing the state of war that reigned prior to the contract, lashes out in irrevocable violation of that contract, violates it as much and often as he is able, full certain that what he will gain from these ruptures will always be more important than what he will lose if he happens to be a member of the weaker class; for such he was when he respected the treaty; by breaking it he may become one of the stronger; and if the laws return him to the class whence he wished to emerge, the worst that can befall him is the loss of his life, which is a misfortune infinitely less great than that of existing in opprobrium and wretchedness. There are then two positions available to us: either crime, which renders us happy, or the noose, which prevents us from being unhappy. I ask whether there can be any hesitation, lovely Thérèse, and where will your little mind find an argument able to combat that one?"

"Oh Monsieur," I replied with the vehemence a good cause inspires, "there are a thousand; but must this life be man's unique concern? Is this existence other than a passage each of whose stages ought only, if he is reasonable, to conduct him to that eternal felicity, the prize vouchsafed by Virtue? I suppose together with you (but this, however, is rare, it conflicts with all reason's informations, but never mind), I will for an instant grant you that the villain who abandons himself to crime may be rendered happy by it in this world, but do you imagine God's justice does not await that dishonest man, that he will not have to pay in another world for what he does in this? Ah! think not the contrary, Monsieur, believe it not," I added, tears in my eyes, " 'tis the misfortunate one's sole consolation, take it not away from us; forsaken by mankind, who will avenge us if not God?"

"Who? No one, Thérèse, absolutely no one; it is in no wise necessary that the misfortunate be avenged; they flatter themselves with the notion because they would like to be, the idea comforts them, but it is not on that account the less false: better still, it is essential that the misfortunate suffer; their humiliation, their anguishes are included in what Nature decrees, and their miserable existence is useful to the general scheme, as is that of the prosperity which crushes them; such is the truth which should stifle remorse in the tyrant's soul or in the malefactor's; let him not constrain himself; let him blindly, unthinkingly deliver himself up to causing every hurt the idea for which may be born in him, it is only Nature's voice which suggests this idea; such is the only fashion in which she makes us her laws' executors. When her secret inspirations dispose us to evil, it is evil she wishes, it is evil she requires, for the sum of crimes not being complete, not sufficient to the laws of equilibrium, the only laws whereby she is governed, she demands that there be crimes to dress the scales; therefore let him not be afraid, let him not pause, whose brain is driven to concerting ill; let him unheeding commit wrong immediately he discerns the impulsion, it is only by lagging and snuffling he outrages Nature. But let us ignore ethics for a moment, since it's theology you want. Be advised then, young innocent, that the religion you fall back upon, being nothing but the relationship between man and God, nothing but the reverence the creature thinks himself obliged to show his creator, is annihilated instantly this creator's existence is itself proven illusory.

"Primitive man, terrified by the phenomena which harried him, had necessarily to believe that a sublime being unknown to him had the direction of their operation and influence; it is native to weakness to suppose strength and to fear it; the human mind, then too much in its infancy to explore, to discover in Nature's depths the laws of motion, the unique springs of the entire mechanism that struck him with awe, found it simpler to fancy a motor in this Nature than to view Nature as her own mover, and without considering that he would have to go to much more trouble to edify, to define this gigantic master, than through the study of Nature to find the cause of what amazed him, he acknowledged this sovereign being, he elaborated rituals to worship it: from this moment each nation composed itself an overlord in conformance with its peculiar characteristics, its knowledge, and its climate; soon there were as many religions on earth as races and peoples and not long after, as many Gods as families; nevertheless, behind all these idols it was easy to recognize the same absurd illusion, first fruit of human blindness. They appareled it differently, but it was always the same thing. Well, tell me, Thérèse, merely because these idiots talk drivel about the erection of a wretched chimera and about the mode of serving him, must it follow that an intelligent man has got to renounce the certain and present happiness of life; like Aesop's dog, must he abandon the bone for the shadow and renounce his real joys for hallucinations? No, Thérèse, no, there is no God, Nature sufficeth unto herself; in no wise hath she need of an author; once supposed, that author is naught but a decayed version of herself, is merely what we describe in school by the phrase, a begging of the question. A God predicates a creation, that is to say, an instant when there was nothing, or an instant when all was in chaos. If one or the other of these states was evil, why did your God allow it to subsist? Was it good? Then why did he change it? But if all is now good a last, your God has nothing left to do; well, if he is useless, how can he be powerful? And if he is not powerful, how can he be God? If, in a word, Nature moves herself, what do we want with a motor? and if the motor acts upon matter by causing it to move, how is it not itself material? Can you conceive the effect of the mind upon matter and matter receiving motion from the mind which itself has no movement? Examine for one cold-blooded instant all the ridiculous and contradictory qualities wherewith the fabricators of this execrable chimera have been obliged to clothe him; verify for your own self how they contradict one another, annul one another, and you will recognize that this deific phantom, engendered by the fear of some and the ignorance of all, is nothing but a loathsome platitude which merits from us neither an instant of faith nor a minute's examination; a pitiable extravagance, disgusting to the mind, revolting to the heart, which ought never to have issued from the darkness save to plunge back into it, forever to be drowned.

"May the hope or fear of a world to come, bred of those primordial lies, trouble you not, Thérèse, and above all give over endeavoring to forge restraints for us out of this stuff. Feeble portions of a vile crude matter, upon our death, that is to say, upon the conjointure of the elements whereof we are composed with the elements composing the universal mass, annihilated forever, regardless of what our behavior has been, we will pass for an instant into Nature's crucible thence to spring up again under other shapes, and that without there being any more prerogatives for him who madly smoked up Virtue's effigy, than for the other who wallowed in the most disgraceful excesses, because there is nothing by which Nature is offended and because all men, equally her womb's issue, during their term having acted not at all save in accordance with her impulsions, will all of them meet with after their existence, both the same end and the same fate."

I was once again about to reply to these appalling blasphemies when we heard the clatter of a horseman not far away.

"To arms!" shouted Coeur-de-fer, more eager to put his systems into action than to consolidate their bases.

The men leapt into life . . . and an instant later a luckless traveler was led into the copse where we had our camp.

Questioned upon his motive for traveling alone and for being so early abroad, upon his age, his profession, the rider answered that his name was Saint-Florent, one of the most important merchants of Lyon, that he was thirty-six years old, that he was on his way back from Flanders where he had been concerned with affairs relative to his business, that he had not much hard money upon his person, but many securities. He added that his valet had left him the preceding day and that, to avoid the heat, he was journeying at night with the intention of reaching Paris the next day, where he would secure a new domestic, and would conclude some of his transactions; that, moreover, he was following an unfamiliar road, and, apparently, he must have lost his way while dozing on his horse. And having said that, he asked for his life, in return offering all he possessed. His purse was examined, his money was counted, the prize could not have been better. Saint-Florent had near unto a half a million, payable upon demand at the capital, had also a few gems and about a hundred gold *louis*. . . .

"Friend," said Coeur-de-fer, clapping his pistol to Saint-Florent's nose, "you understand, don't you, that after having robbed you, we cannot leave you alive."

"Oh Monsieur," I cried, casting myself at the villain's feet, "I beseech you not to present me the horrible spectacle, upon my reception into your band, of this poor man's death; allow him to live, do not refuse me this first request I ask of you."

And quickly resorting to a most unusual ruse, in order to justify the interest I appeared to take in the captive:

"The name Monsieur has just given himself," I added with warmth, "causes me to believe we are nearly related. Be not astonished, Monsieur," I went on, now addressing the voyager, "be not at all surprised to find a kinsman in these circumstances; I will explain it all to you. In the light of this," I continued, once again imploring our chief, "in the light of this, Monsieur, grant me the unlucky creature's life, I will show my gratitude for the favor by the completest devotion to all that will be able to serve your interests."

"You know upon what conditions I can accord you what you ask, Thérèse," Coeur-de-fer answered; "you know what I demand from you . . ."

"Ah, very well, Monsieur, I will do everything," I cried,

throwing myself between Saint-Florent and our leader, who was still about to kill him. "Yes, I will do anything; spare him."

"Let him live," said Coeur-de-fer, "but he has got to join us, that last clause is crucial, I can do nothing if he refuses to comply with it, my comrades would be against me."

Surprised, the merchant, understanding nothing of this consanguinity I was establishing, but observing his life saved if he were to consent to the proposal, saw no cause for a moment's hesitation. He was provided with meat and drink, as the men did not wish to leave the place until daybreak.

"Thérèse," Coeur-de-fer said to me, "I remind you of your promise, but, since I am weary tonight, rest quietly beside Dubois, I will summon you toward dawn and if you are not prompt to come, taking this knave's life will be my revenge for your deceit."

"Sleep, Monsieur, sleep well," I replied, "and believe that she whom you have filled with gratitude has no desire but to repay it."

However, such was far from my design, for if ever I believed deception permitted, it was certainly upon this occasion. Our rascals, greatly overconfident, kept at their drinking and fell into slumber, leaving me entirely at liberty beside Dubois who, drunk like the others, soon closed her eyes too.

Then seizing my opportunity as soon as the bandits surrounding us were overcome with sleep:

"Monsieur," I said to the young Lyonnais, "the most atrocious catastrophe has thrown me against my will into the midst of these thieves, I detest both them and the fatal instant that brought me into their company. In truth, I have not the honor to be related to you; I employed the trick to save you and to escape, if you approve it, with you, from out of these scoundrels' clutches; the moment's propitious," I added, "let us be off; I notice your pocketbook, take it back, forget the money, it is in their pockets; we could not recover it without danger: come, Monsieur, let us quit this place. You see what I am doing for you, I put myself into your keeping; take pity on me; above all, be not more cruel than these men; deign to respect my honor, I entrust it to you, it is my unique treasure, they have not ravished it away from me."

It would be difficult to render the declarations of gratitude I had from Saint-Florent. He knew not in what terms to express his thanks; but we had no time to talk; it was a question of flight. With a dextrous movement, I retrieve the pocketbook, return it to him, and treading softly we walk through the copse, leaving the horse for fear the sound of his hoofs might rouse the men; with all possible dispatch we reach the path which is to lead us out of the forest. We had the good luck to be out of it by daybreak, without having been followed by anyone; before ten o'clock we were in Luzarches and there, free from all anxiety, we thought of nothing but resting ourselves.

There are moments in life when one finds that despite one's riches, which may be great, one nevertheless lacks what is needed to live; such was Saint-Florent's case: five hundred thousand francs might be awaiting him in Paris, but he now had not a coin on his person; mindful of this, he paused before entering the inn. . . .

"Be easy, Monsieur," I said upon perceiving his embarrassment, "the thieves have not left me without money, here are twenty *louis,* take them, please, use them, give what remains to the poor; nothing in the world could make me want to keep gold acquired by murder."

Saint-Florent, whose refinements of character I at the time did not exactly appreciate, was absolutely unwilling to accept what I tendered him; he asked me what my expectations were, said he would make himself bound to fulfill them, and that he desired nothing but the power to acquit himself of his indebtedness to me.

"It is to you I owe my life and fortune, Thérèse," he added, kissing my hands, "I can do no better than to lay them both at your feet; receive them, I beseech you, and permit the God of marriage to tighten the knots of friendship."

I know not whether it was from intuition or chilliness of temper, but I was so far from believing that what I had done for the young man could motivate such sentiments as these he expressed for me, that I allowed him to read in my countenance the refusal I dared not articulate; he understood, insisted no further, and limited himself to asking what he could do for me.

"Monsieur," said I, "if my behavior is really not without merit in your view, for my entire recompense I ask nothing more than to proceed to Lyon with you and to have you find me a place in some correct household, where my modesty will have no more to suffer."

"You could do nothing better," said Saint-Florent, "and no one is in a better position than I to render this service; I have twenty relatives in the city," and the young trader then besought me to divulge my reasons for having left Paris where I had mentioned to him I was born. I told my story with equal amounts of confidence and ingenuousness.

"Oh, if it is but that," said the young man, "I will be of use to you before we reach Lyon; fear not, Thérèse, your troubles are over; the affair will be hushed; you will not be sought after and, certainly, less in the asylum where I wish to leave you than in any other. A member of my family dwells near Bondy, a charming region not far from here; I am sure it will be a pleasure for her to have you with her; I will introduce you tomorrow."

In my turn filled with gratitude, I approve a project which seems so well suited to me; we repose at Luzarches for the rest of the day and on the morrow, it is our plan, we will gain Bondy, but six leagues distant.

"The weather is fine," Saint-Florent says to me, "trust me, Thérèse; it will be most enjoyable to go afoot; we will reach my relative's estate, will tell of our adventure, and this manner of arriving, I should think, will make you appear in a still more interesting light."

Having not the faintest suspicion of this monster's designs, and far from imagining that I was to be less safe with him than I had been when in the infamous company I had left, I agree to everything; we dine together; he not so much as murmurs when for the night I take a chamber separate from his, and after having waited until the warmest part of the day is past, certain of what he tells me, that four or five hours will suffice to bring us to his relative's, we leave Luzarches and strike out on foot for Bondy.

It was toward four o'clock in the afternoon when we entered the forest. Until then Saint-Florent had not once contradicted himself: always the same propriety, always the same eagerness to prove his sentiments for me; I should not have thought myself more secure had I been with my father. The shades of night began to descend upon the forest and to inspire that kind of religious horror which at once causes the birth of fear in timorous spirits and criminal projects in ferocious hearts. We followed mere paths; I was walking ahead, I turned to ask Saint-Florent whether these obscure trails were really the ones we ought to be following, whether perchance he had not lost his bearings, whether he thought we were going to arrive soon.

"We have arrived, whore," the villain replied, toppling me with a blow of his cane brought down upon my head; I fell unconscious. . . .

Oh, Madame, I have no idea what that man afterward said or did; but the state I was in when I returned to my senses advised me only too well to what point I had been his victim. It was darkest night when I awoke; I was at the foot of a tree, away from any road, injured, bleeding . . . dishonored, Madame; such had been the reward of all I had just done for the unlucky man; and carrying infamy to its ultimate degree, the wretch, after having done to me all he had wished, after having abused me in every manner, even in that which most outrages Nature, had taken my purse . . . containing the same money I had so generously offered him. He had torn my clothing, most of it lay in shreds and ribbons about me, I was virtually naked, and several parts of my body were lacerated, clawed; you may appreciate my situation: there in the depths of the night, without resources, without honor, without hope, exposed to every peril: I wished to put an end to my days: had a weapon been presented to me, I would have laid hands on it and abridged this unhappy life full only of plagues for me . . . the monster! What did I do to him, I asked myself, to have deserved such cruel treatment at his hands? I save his life, restore his fortune to him, he snatches away what is most dear to me! A savage beast would have been less cruel! O man, thus are you when you heed nothing but your passions! Tigers that dwell in the wildest jungles would quail before such ignominies . . . these first pangs of suffering were succeeded by some few minutes of exhaustion; my eyes, brimming over with tears, turned mechanically toward the sky; my heart did spring to the feet of the Master who dwelleth there . . . that pure glittering vault . . . that imposing stillness of the night . . . that terror which numbed my senses . . . that image of Nature in peace, nigh unto my whelmed, distraught soul . . . all distilled a somber horror into me, whence there was soon born the need to pray. I cast myself down, kneeling before that potent God denied by the impious, hope of the poor and the downtrodden.

"Holy Majesty, Saintly One," I cried out in tears, "Thou Who in this dreadful moment deign to flood my soul with a celestial joy, Who doubtless hath prevented me from attempting my life; O my Protector and my Guide, I aspire to Thy bounties, I implore Thy clemency, behold my miseries and my torments, my resignation, and hear Thou my entreaties: Powerful God! Thou knowst it, I am innocent and weak, I am betrayed and mistreated; I have wished to do well in imitation of Thee, and Thy will hath punished it in me: may Thy will be done, O my God! all its sacred effects are cherished by me, I respect them and cease to complain of them; but if however I am to find naught but stings and nettles terrestrially, is it to offend Thee, O my Sovereign Master, to supplicate Thy puissance to take me into Thy bosom, in order untroubled to adore Thee, to worship Thee far away from these perverse men who, alas! have made me meet with evils only, and whose bloodied and perfidious hands at their pleasure drown my sorrowful days in a torrent of tears and in an abyss of agonies."

Prayer is the misfortunate's sweetest comfort; strength re-enters him once he has fulfilled this duty. My courage renewed, I raised myself up, I gathered together the rags the villain had left me, and I hid myself in a thicket so as to pass the night in less danger. The security I believed I enjoyed, the satisfaction I had just tasted by communing with my God, all combined to help me rest a few hours, and the sun was already risen high when I opened my eyes. For the wretched, the instant of awakening is hideous: the imagination, refreshed by sleep's sweet ministrations, very rapidly and lugubriously fills with the evils these moments of deceiving repose have smoothed into oblivion.

Very well, I said as I examined myself, it is then true that there are human creatures Nature reduces to the level of wild beasts! Lurking in this forest, like them flying the sight of man, what difference now exists between them and me? Is it worth being born for a fate so pitiable? . . . And my tears flowed abundantly as I meditated in sorrow; I had scarcely finished with my reflections when I heard sounds somewhere about; little by little, two men hove into view. I pricked up my ears:

"Come, dear friend," said one of them, "this place will suit us admirably; the cruel and fatal presence of an aunt I abhor will not prevent me from tasting a moment with you the pleasures I cherish."

They draw near, they station themselves squarely in front of me and so proximately that not one of their words, not one of their gestures is able to escape me, and I observe . . . Just Heaven, Madame, said Thérèse, interrupting herself, is it possible that destiny has placed me in none but situations so critical that it becomes quite as difficult for Virtue to hear them recited as for modesty to describe them? That horrible crime which equally outrages both Nature and social conventions, that heinous deed, in a word, which the hand of God has so often smitten, rationalized, legitimized by Coeur-de-fer, proposed by him to the unhappy Thérèse, despite her wishes consummated against her by the butcher who has just immolated her, in brief, I did see that revolting execration carried out before my own eyes, together with all the impure gropings and fumblings, all the frightful episodes the most meditated depravity can devise. One of the men, he who gave himself, was twenty-four years old, of such a bearing and presence one might suppose him of an elevated degree, the other, of about the same age, appeared to be one of his domestics. The act was scandalous and prolonged. Bending over, supported by his hands, leaning upon the crest of a little hillock facing the thicket where I lay, the young master exposed naked to his companion in debauch the impious sacrificial altar, and the latter, whom the spectacle filled with ardor, caressed the idol, ready to immolate it with a spear far more awful and far more colossal than the one wherewith the captain of the brigands of Bondy had menaced me; but, in no wise intimidated, the young master seemed prepared unhesitatingly to brave the shaft that was presented to him; he teased it, he excited it, covered it with kisses; seized it, plunged it into himself, was in an ecstasy as he swallowed it up; aroused by criminal caresses, the infamous creature writhed and struggled under the iron and seemed to regret it was not yet more terrible; he withstood its blows, he rose to anticipate them, he repelled them. . . . A tender couple lawfully

connected would not have caressed one another so passionately
. . . their mouths were pressed together, their sighs intermingled,
their tongues entwined, and I witnessed each of them, drunk with
lust, bring his perfidious horrors to completion in the very vortex
of delight. The homage is renewed, and in order to fire the incense
nothing is neglected by him who cries aloud his demand for it;
kisses, fingerings, pollutions, debauchery's most appalling refinements, everything is employed to revive sinking strength, and it all
succeeds in reanimating them five times in swift succession; but that
without either of them changing his role. The young lord was constantly the woman and although there was about him what suggested the possibility he could have acted the man in his turn, he had
not for one instant even the appearance of wishing to. If he visited
the altar corresponding to the one in him where sacrifices were
performed, it was in the other idol's behalf, and there was never
any indication the latter was threatened by assault.

Ah, how slowly the time seemed to pass! I dared not budge
for fear of detection; at last, the criminal actors in this indecent
drama, no doubt surfeited, got up and were prepared to start
along the road that was to take them home, when the master drew
near the bush which hid me; my bonnet betrayed me . . . he caught
sight of it. . . .

"Jasmin," said he to his valet, "we are discovered . . . a girl
has beheld our mysteries. . . . Come hither, flush the bitch into the
open, let's find out why she is here."

I did not put them to the trouble of dragging me from my
sanctuary; I stepped forward immediately and, falling at their
feet,

"Oh, Messieurs!" I cried, stretching my arms toward them,
"deign to have pity upon an unhappy creature whose fate more
deserves your compassion than you may think; there are very few
misfortunes which can equal mine; do not let the posture wherein
you discover me cause any suspicion to be born in you; it is rather
the consequence of my misery than of my faults; do not augment
the ills which overwhelm me, be so kind as to diminish them by
making available to me the means to escape the furies that hound
me."

The Comte de Bressac (that was the name of the young man

into whose hands I had fallen) possessed a mind containing a great fund of wickedness and libertinage; no very abundant amount of sympathy dwelled in his heart. Unfortunately, it is only too common to find men in whom pity has been obliterated by libertinage, whose ordinary effect is to harden: whether it be that the major part of his excesses necessitates apathy in the soul, or that the violent shock passion imparts to the nervous system decreases the vigor of its action, the fact always remains that a libertine is rarely a man of sensibility. But in addition to this harshness native to the species whose character I am sketching, there was also in Monsieur de Bressac a disgust for our sex so inveterate, a hatred so powerful for all that distinguishes it, that I encountered considerable difficulty introducing the affections into his soul wherewith I strove to move him.

"My little dove," said the Count, severity in his tone, "if you are looking for dupes, improve your style; neither my friend nor I ever sacrifice at your sex's impure temple; if it is money you are begging, look for people who are fond of good works, we never perform any of that description. . . . But, wretch, out with it: did you see what passed between Monsieur and me?"

"I saw you conversing together upon the sward," I replied, "nothing more, Monsieur, I assure you."

"I should like to believe it," said the Count, "for your own good; were I to imagine you had seen anything else, never would you emerge alive from where we are. . . . Jasmin, it is early, we have time to hear the girl's adventures, and afterward we will see what's to be done with her."

The young men sit down, they order me to sit near them, and thereupon very ingenuously I make them acquainted with all the woes that have afflicted me from the day of my birth.

"Well, Jasmin," said Monsieur de Bressac as soon as I had finished, "for once let us be just: the equitable Thémis has doomed this creature, let us not suffer the Goddess' designs to be thwarted so cruelly: let us expose the delinquent to the death penalty she has incurred: this little murder, far from being a crime, will merely take its place as a reparation in the moral scheme; since sometimes we have the misfortune to disturb that order, let us at least courageously make amends when the occasion arises. . . ."

And the cruel men, having laid hands upon me, dragged me toward the wood, laughing at my tears and screams.

"We'll tie each of her members to a tree—we need four trees placed in a rectangle," said Bressac, tearing off my clothes.

Then by means of their cravats, their handkerchiefs, their braces, they make cords wherewith I am tied instantly, in keeping with their plan, that is to say in the cruelest and most painful position imaginable. I cannot express to you what I suffered; it seemed they were rending me limb from limb and that my belly, facing downward and strained to the utmost, was about to split at any moment; sweat drenched my forehead, I no longer existed save through the violence of pain; had it ceased to compress my nerves, a mortal anguish would surely have seized me: the villains were amused by my posture, they considered me and applauded.

"Well, that's enough," Bressac said at last, "for the time being she may get off with a fright.

"Thérèse," he continued as he untied my hands and commanded me to dress myself, "show a little judgment and come along with us; if you attach yourself to me you shall never have reason to regret it. My aunt requires a second maid; I am going to present you to her and, upon the basis of your story, undertake to interest her in you; I shall make myself answerable for your conduct; but should you abuse my kindness, were you to betray my confidence, or were you not to submit yourself to my intentions, behold these four trees, Thérèse, behold the plot of earth they encompass: it might serve you for a sepulcher: bear it in mind that this dreadful place is no more than a league's distance from the château to which I am going to lead you and that, upon the least provocation, I will bring you back here at once."

I forgot my sufferings instantly, I embraced the Count's knees, tears streaming down my cheeks, I swore to behave myself well; but quite as insensible to my joy as to my pain,

"Let us be off," said Bressac, "your actions will speak for you, they alone will govern your fate."

We advance; Jasmin and his master exchange whispered remarks; I follow them humbly, without saying a word. In less than an hour we arrive at Madame la Marquise de Bressac's château, whose magnificence and the multitude of servants it contains make me see that whatever the post I must hold in the house, it will surely be more advantageous to me than that of drudge to Monsieur du Harpin. I am made to wait in an office where Jasmin most obligingly offers me everything conducive to my comfort. The young Count seeks out his aunt, acquaints her with what he has done, and a half-hour later himself comes to introduce me to the Marquise.

Madame de Bressac was a woman of forty-six years, still very beautiful, and who seemed highly respectable and sensible, although into her principles and remarks somewhat of austerity had entrance; for two years she had been the widow of the young Count's uncle, who had married her without any fortune beyond the fine name he brought with him. All the riches Monsieur de Bressac was able to hope for depended upon this aunt; what had come down to him from his father barely gave him the wherewithal to buy his pleasures: to which income Madame de Bressac joined a considerable allowance, but that scarcely sufficed; nothing is so expensive as the delights to which the Count was addicted; perhaps they are purchased at a cheaper rate than others, but they far more rapidly multiply. Fifty thousand crowns was the Marquise's revenue, and young Monsieur de Bressac was its sole heir. All efforts to induce him to find a profession or an occupation had failed; he could not adapt himself to whatever diverted his attentions from libertinage. The Marquise passed three months of the year's twelve in the country; the rest of the time she lived in Paris; and these three months which she required her nephew to spend with her, were a kind of torture for a man who hated his aunt and considered as wasted every moment he passed outside the city which was the home of his pleasures.

The young Count bade me relate to the Marquise the matter with which I had just made him acquainted, and as soon as I was done:

"Your candor and naïveté," Madame de Bressac said to me, "do not permit me to think you untruthful. I will inquire after no other information save what will authorize me to believe you are really the daughter of the man you indicate; if it is so, then I knew your father, and that will be one more reason to take an interest in you. As for the du Harpin affair, I will assume responsibility for settling it with two visits paid to the Chancellor; he has been my friend for ages. In all the world there is no man of greater integrity; we have but to prove your innocence to him: all the charges leveled against you will crumble and be withdrawn. But consider well, Thérèse: what I promise you now will not be yours save at the price of flawless conduct; thus, you see that the effects of the gratitude I require will always redound to your profit." I cast myself at the Marquise's feet, assured her she would be contented with me; with great kindness she raised me up and upon the spot gave me the post of second chambermaid in her service.

At the end of three days, the information Madame de Bressac had sought from Paris arrived; it corresponded with what I desired; the Marquise praised me for having in no wise imposed upon her, and every thought of unhappiness vanished from my mind, to be replaced by nothing but hope for the sweetest consolations it was permitted me to expect; but it did not consort with the designs of Heaven that the poor Thérèse should ever be happy, and if fortuitously there were born unto her some few moments of calm, it was only to render more bitter those of distress that were to succeed them.

We were no sooner arrived in Paris than Madame de Bressac hastened to work in my behalf: the first president judge wished to see me, he heard with interest the tale of my misfortunes; du Harpin's calumnies were recognized, but it was in vain they undertook to punish him; having made a great success of trafficking in counterfeit banknotes, whereby he ruined three or four families, and whence he amassed nearly two millions, he had just removed to England; as regarded the burning of the Palace prisons, they were convinced that although I had profited from the event, I was in no way to blame for causing it and the case against me was dropped, the officiating magistrates being agreed, so I was assured, that there was no need to employ further formalities; I asked no questions, I was content to learn what I was told, and you will see shortly whether I was mistaken.

You may readily imagine that as a consequence of what she did for me, I became very fond of Madame de Bressac; had she not shown me every kindness as well, had not such steps as those she had taken obligated me forever to this precious protectress? However, it was by no means the young Count's intention that I become so intimately attached to his aunt. . . . But this seems the moment for a portrait of the monster.

Monsieur de Bressac had the charms of youth and the most attractive countenance too; if there were some defects in his figure or his features, it was because they had a rather too pronounced tendency toward that nonchalance, that softness which properly belongs only to women; it seemed that, in lending him the attributes of the feminine sex, Nature had introduced its tastes into him as well. . . . Yet what a soul lurked behind those effeminate graces! All the vices which characterize the villain's genius were to be encountered in his: never had wickedness, vindictiveness, cruelty, atheism, debauchery, contempt for all duties and principally those out of which Nature is said to fashion our delights, never had all these qualities been carried to such an extreme. In the midst of all his faults predominated another: Monsieur de Bressac detested his aunt. The Marquise did everything conceivable to restore her nephew to the paths of virtue; perhaps she put too much rigorousness into her attempts; the result, however, was that the Count, further inflamed by that very rigor's effects, only the more impetuously gave himself up to his predilections and the poor Marquise gained nothing from her persecutions but his redoubled hate.

"Do not imagine," the Count would often tell me, "that it is of her own accord my aunt acts in all that concerns you, Thérèse; believe me, were it not for my constant badgering she would quickly forget what she has promised to do for you. She would have you feel indebted to her, but all she has done is owing exclusively to me; yes, Thérèse, exactly, it is to me alone you are beholden, and the thanks I expect from you should appear the more disinterested, for although you've a pretty face, it is not, and you know it very well, after your favors I aspire; no, Thérèse, the services I await from you are of a radically different sort, and when you are well convinced of what I have accomplished in behalf of your tranquillity, I hope I will find what I think I have the right to expect from your spirit."

So obscure were these speeches I knew not how to answer; however, reply to him I did, on a chance, as it were, and perhaps with too great a facility. Must I confess it? Alas! yes; to conceal my shortcomings would be to wrong your confidence and poorly to respond to the interest my misfortunes have quickened in you. Hear then, Madame, of the one deliberate fault with which I have to reproach myself. . . . What am I saying, a fault? It was a folly, an extravagance . . . there has never been one to equal it; but at least it is not a crime, it is merely a mistake, for which I alone have been punished, and of which it surely does not seem that the equitable hand of Heaven had to make use in order to plunge me into the abyss which yawned beneath me soon afterward. Whatever the foul treatment to which the Comte de Bressac had exposed me the first day I had met him, it had, all the same, been impossible to see him so frequently without feeling myself drawn toward him by an insuperable and instinctive tenderness. Despite all my recollections of his cruelty, all my thoughts upon his disinclinations toward women, upon the depravity of his tastes, upon the gulf which separated us morally, nothing in the world was able to extinguish this nascent passion, and had the Count called upon me to lay down my life, I would have sacrificed it for him a thousand times over. He was far from suspecting my sentiments . . . he was far, the ungrateful one, from divining the cause of the tears I shed every day; nevertheless, it was out of the question for him to be in doubt of my eagerness to fly to do his every bidding, to please him in every possible way, it could not have been he did not glimpse, did not have some inkling of my attentions; doubtless, because they were instinctive, they were also mindless, and went to the point of serving his errors, of serving them as far as decency permitted, and always of hiding them from his aunt. This behavior had in some sort won me his confidence, and all that came from him was so precious to me, I was so blinded by the little his heart offered me, that I sometimes had the weakness to believe he was not indifferent to me. But how promptly his excessive disorders disabused me: they were such that even his health was affected. I several times took the liberty to represent to him the dangers of his conduct, he would hear me out patiently, then end by telling me that one does not break oneself of the vice he cherished.

"Ah, Thérèse!" he exclaimed one day, full of enthusiasm, "if only you knew this fantasy's charms, if only you could understand what one experiences from the sweet illusion of being no more than a woman! incredible inconsistency! one abhors that sex, yet one wishes to imitate it! Ah! how sweet it is to succeed, Thérèse, how delicious it is to be a slut to everyone who would have to do with you and carrying delirium and prostitution to their ultimate period, successively, in the very same day, to be the mistress of a porter, a marquis, a valet, a friar, to be the beloved of each one after the other, caressed, envied, menaced, beaten, sometimes victorious in their arms, sometimes a victim and at their feet, melting them with caresses, reanimating them with excesses. . . . Oh no, Thérèse, you do not understand what is this pleasure for a mind constructed like mine. . . . But, morals aside, if you are able to imagine this divine whimsy's physical sensations, there is no withstanding it, it is a titillation so lively, it is of so piquant a voluptuousness . . . one becomes giddy, one ceases to reason, stammers; a thousand kisses one more tender than the next do not inflame us with an ardor in any way approaching the drunkenness into which the agent plunges us; enlaced in his arms, our mouth glued to his, we would that our entire being were incorporated into his; we would not make but a single being with him; if we dare complain, 'tis of being neglected; we would have him, more robust than Hercules, enlarge us, penetrate us; we would have that precious semen, shot blazing to the depths of our entrails, cause, by its heat and its strength, our own to leap forth into his hands. . . . Do not suppose, Thérèse, we are made like other men; 'tis an entirely different structure we have; and, in creating us, Heaven has ornamented the altars at which our Celadons sacrifice with that very same sensitive membrane which lines your temple of Venus; we are, in that sector, as certainly women as you are in your generative sanctuary; not one of your pleasures is unknown to us, there is not one we do not know how to enjoy, but we have in addition to them our own, and it is this delicious combination which makes us of all men on earth the most sensitive to pleasure, the best created to experience it; it is this enchanting combination which renders our tastes incorrigible, which would turn us into enthusiasts and frenetics were one to have the stupidity to punish us . . . which makes us worship, unto the grave itself, the charming God who enthralls us."

Thus the Count expressed himself, celebrating his eccentricities; when I strove to speak to him of the Being to whom he owed everything, and of the grief such disorders caused his respectable aunt, I perceived nothing in him but spleen and ill-humor and especially impatience at having to see, in such hands and for so long, riches which, he would say, already ought to belong to him; I saw nothing but the most inveterate hatred for that so gentle woman, nothing but the most determined revolt against every natural sentiment. It would then be true that when in one's tastes one has been able so formally to transgress that law's sacred instinct, the necessary consequence of this original crime is a frightful penchant to commit every other.

Sometimes I employed the means Religion provides; almost always comforted by it, I attempted to insinuate its sweetnesses into this perverse creature's soul, more or less certain he could be restrained by those bonds were I to succeed in having him strike at the lure; but the Count did not long tolerate my use of such weapons. A declared enemy of our most holy mysteries, a stubborn critic of the purity of our dogmas, an impassioned antagonist of the idea of a Supreme Being's existence, Monsieur de Bressac, instead of letting himself be converted by me, sought rather to work my corruption.

"All religions start from a false premise, Thérèse," he would say; "each supposes as necessary the worship of a Creator, but that creator never existed. In this connection, put yourself in mind of the sound precepts of that certain Coeur-de-fer who, you told me, used to labor over your mind as I do; nothing more just, nor more precise, than that man's principles, and the degradation in which we have the stupidity to keep him does not deprive him of the right to reason well.

"If all Nature's productions are the resultant effects of the laws whereof she is a captive; if her perpetual action and reaction suppose the motion necessary to her essence, what becomes of the sovereign master fools gratuitously give her? that is what your sagacious instructor said to you, dear girl. What, then, are religions if not the restraint wherewith the tyranny of the mightier sought to enslave the weaker? Motivated by that design, he dared say to him whom he claimed the right to dominate, that a God had forged the irons with which cruelty manacled him; and the latter, bestialized by his misery, indistinctly believed everything the former wished. Can religions, born of these rogueries, merit respect? Is there one of them, Thérèse, which does not bear the stamp of imposture and of stupidity? What do I descry in them all? Mysteries which cause reason to shudder, dogmas which outrage Nature, grotesque ceremonies which simply inspire derision and disgust. But if amongst them all there were one which most particularly deserves our scorn and hatred, O Thérèse, is it not that barbaric law of the Christianity into which both of us were born? Is there any more odious? one which so spurs both the heart and mind to revolt? How is it that rational men are still able to lend any credence to the obscure mutterings, to the alleged miracles of that appalling cult's vile originator? Has there ever existed a rowdy scoundrel more worthy of public indignation! What is he but a leprous Jew who, born of a slut and a soldier in the world's meanest stews, dared fob himself off for the spokesman of him who, they say, created the universe! With such lofty pretensions, you will have to admit, Thérèse, at least a few credentials are necessary. But what are those of this ridiculous Ambassador? What is he going to do to prove his mission? Is the earth's face going to be changed? are the plagues which beset it going to be annihilated? is the sun going to shine upon it by night as well as by day? vices will soil it no more? Are we going to see happiness reign at last? . . . Not at all; it is through hocus-pocus, antic capers, and puns[2] that God's envoy announces himself to the world; it is in the elegant society of manual laborers, artisans, and streetwalkers that Heaven's minister comes to manifest his grandeur; it is by drunken carousing with these, bedding with those, that God's friend, God himself, comes to bend the toughened sinner to his laws; it is by inventing nothing for his farces but what can satisfy either his lewdness or his gourmand's guts that the knavish fellow demonstrates his mission; however all that may be, he makes his fortune; a few beef-witted satellites gravitate toward the villain; a sect is formed; this crowd's dogmas manage to seduce some Jews; slaves of the Roman power, they joyfully embrace a religion which, ridding them of their shackles, makes them subject to none but a metaphysical tyranny. Their motives become evident, their indocility unveils itself, the seditious louts are ar-

---

[2] The Marquis de Bièvre never made one quite as clever as the Nazarene's to his disciple: "Thou art Peter and upon this Rock I will build my Church"; and they tell us that witty language is one of our century's innovations!

rested; their captain perishes, but of a death doubtless much too merciful for his species of crime, and through an unpardonable lapse of intelligence, this uncouth boor's disciples are allowed to disperse instead of being slaughtered cheek to jowl with their leader. Fanaticism gets minds in its grip, women shriek, fools scrape and scuffle, imbeciles believe, and lo! the most contemptible of beings, the most maladroit quacksalver, the clumsiest impostor ever to have made his entrance, there he is: behold! God, there's God's little boy, his papa's peer; and now all his dreams are consecrated! and now all his epigrams are become dogmas! and all his blunders mysteries! His fabulous father's breast opens to receive him and that Creator, once upon a time simple, of a sudden becomes compound, triple, to humor his son, this lad so worthy of his greatness; but does that sacred God stick at that? No, surely not, his celestial might is going to bestow many another and greater favor. At the beck and call of a priest, of, that is to say, an odd fellow foul with lies, the great God, creator of all we behold, is going to abase himself to the point of descending ten or twelve million times every morning in a morsel of wheat paste; this the faithful devour and assimilate, and God Almighty is lugged to the bottom of their intestines where he is speedily transmuted into the vilest excrements, and all that for the satisfaction of the tender son, odious inventor of this monstrous impiety which had its beginnings in a cabaret supper. He spake, and it was ordained. He said: this bread you see will be my flesh; you will digest it as such; now, I am God; hence, God will be digested by you; hence, the Creator of Heaven and Earth will be changed, because I have spoken, into the vilest stuff the body of man can exhale, and man will eat his God, because this God is good and because he is omnipotent. However, these blatherings increase; their growth is attributed to their authenticity, their greatness, their sublimity to the puissance of him who introduced them, while in truth the commonest causes double their existence, for the credit error acquires never proved anything but the presence of swindlers on the one side and of idiots on the other. This infamous religion finally arrives on the throne, and it is a weak, cruel, ignorant and fanatical emperor who, enveloping it in the royal mantle, soils the four corners of the earth with it. O Thérèse, what weight are these arguments to carry with an inquiring and philosophic mind? Is the sage able to see anything in this appalling heap of fables but the disgusting fruit of a few men's imposture and the diddled credulity of a vast number? had God willed it that we have some religion or other, and had he been truly powerful or, to frame it more suitably, had there truly been a God, would it have been by these absurd means he would have imparted his instructions to us? Would it have been through the voice of a contemptible bandit he would have shown how it were necessary to serve him? Were he supreme, were he mighty, were he just, were he good, this God you tell me about, would it be through enigmas and buffooneries he would wish to teach me to serve and know him? Sovereign mover of the stars and the heart of man, may he not instruct us by employing the one or convince us by graving himself in the other? Let him, one of these days, upon the Sun indite the law, writ out in letters of fire, the law as he wants us to understand it, in the version that pleases him; then from one end of the universe to the other, all mankind will read it, will behold it at once, and thereafter will be guilty if they obey it not. But to indicate his desires nowhere but in some unknown corner of Asia; to select for witnesses the craftiest and most visionary of people, for alter ego the meanest artisan, the most absurd, him of the greatest rascality; to frame his doctrine so confusedly it is impossible to make it out; to limit knowledge of it to a small group of individuals; to leave the others in error and to punish them for remaining there. . . . Why, no, Thérèse, no, these atrocities are not what we want for our guidance; I should prefer to die a thousand deaths rather than believe them. When atheism will wish for martyrs, let it designate them; my blood is ready to be shed. Let us detest these horrors, Thérèse; let the most steadfast outrages cement the scorn which is patently their due. . . . My eyes were barely open when I began to loathe these coarse reveries; very early I made it a law unto myself to trample them in the dust, I took oath to return to them never more; if you would be happy, imitate me; as do I, hate, abjure, profane the foul object of this dreadful cult; and this cult too, created for illusion, made like him to be reviled by everyone who pretends to wisdom."

"Oh! Monsieur," I responded, weeping, "you would deprive an unfortunate of her fondest hope were you to wither in her heart this religion which is her whole comfort. Firmly attached to its teachings, absolutely convinced that all the blows leveled against it are nothing but libertinage's effects and the passions', am I to sacrifice, to blasphemies, to sophistries horrible to me, my heart's sweetest sustenance?"

I added a thousand other arguments to this one, they merely caused the Count to laugh, and his captious principles, nourished by a more male eloquence, supported by readings and studies I, happily, had never performed, daily attacked my own principles, without shaking them. Madame de Bressac, that woman filled with piety and virtue, was not unaware her nephew justified his wild behavior with every one of the day's paradoxes; she too often shuddered upon hearing them; and as she condescended to attribute somewhat more good sense to me than to her other women, she would sometimes take me aside and speak of her chagrin.

Meanwhile, her nephew, champing at the bit, had reached the point where he no longer bothered to hide his malign intentions; not only had he surrounded his aunt with all of that dangerous *canaille* which served his pleasures, but he had even carried boldness so far as to declare to her, in my presence, that were she to take it into her head to frustrate his appetite, he would convince her of their charm by practicing them before her very eyes.

I trembled; I beheld this conduct with horror. I strove to rationalize my reactions by attributing their origin to personal motives, for I wished to stifle the unhappy passion which burned in my soul; but is love an illness to be cured? All I endeavored to oppose to it merely fanned its flames, and the perfidious Count never appeared more lovable to me than when I had assembled before me everything which ought to have induced me to hate him.

I had remained four years in this household unrelentingly persecuted by the same sorrows, forever consoled by the same sweetnesses, when this abominable man, finally believing himself sure of me, dared disclose his infamous schemes. We were in the country at the time, I alone attended upon the Marquise, her first maid-in-waiting had obtained leave to remain in Paris through the summer to look after some of her husband's business. One evening shortly after I had retired, and as I was taking some air upon the balcony of my room, being unable to bring myself to go to bed because of the extreme heat, I suddenly heard the Count knock; he wished to have a word or two with me. Alas! the moments that cruel author of my ills accorded me of his presence were too precious for me to dare refuse him one; he enters, carefully closes the door and flings himself into an armchair.

"Listen to me, Thérèse," and there is a note of embarrassment in his voice, "I have things of the greatest importance to say to you; swear to me you will never reveal any of them."

"Monsieur," I reply, "do you think me capable of abusing your confidence?"

"You have no idea what you would be risking were you to prove to me I had made a mistake in trusting you!"

"The most frightful of all my woes should be to lose your trust, I have no need of greater menaces. . . ."

"Ah then, Thérèse, I have condemned my aunt to die . . . and it is your hand I must employ."

"My hand!" I cried, recoiling in fright, "have you been able, Monsieur, to conceive such projects? . . . no, dispose of my life if you must, but imagine not you will ever obtain from me the horror you propose."

"Hear me, Thérèse," says the Count, reasoning with me calmly, "I indeed foresaw your distaste for the idea but, as you have wit and verve, I flattered myself with the belief I could vanquish your feelings . . . could prove to you that this crime, which seems to you of such enormity, is, at bottom, a very banal affair.

"Two misdeeds present themselves, Thérèse, to your not very philosophic scrutiny: the destruction of a creature bearing a resemblance to us, and the evil with which this destruction is augmented when the said creature is one of our near kinsmen. With regard to the crime of destroying one's fellow, be persuaded, dear girl, it is purely hallucinatory; man has not been accorded the power to destroy; he has at best the capacity to alter forms, but lacks that required to annihilate them: well, every form is of equal worth in Nature's view; nothing is lost in the immense melting pot where variations are wrought: all the material masses which fall into it spring incessantly forth in other shapes, and whatsoever be our interventions in this process, not one of them, needless to say, outrages her, not one is capable of offending her. Our depredations revive her power; they stimulate her energy, but not one attenuates her; she is neither impeded nor thwarted by any. . . . Why! what difference does it make to her creative hand if this mass of flesh today wearing the conformation of a bipedal individual is reproduced tomorrow in the guise of a handful of centipedes? Dare one say that the construction of this two-legged animal costs her any more than that of an earthworm, and that she should take a greater interest in the one than in the other? If then the degree of attachment, or rather of indifference, is the same, what can it be to her if, by one man's sword, another man is trans-speciated into a fly or a blade of grass? When they will have convinced me of the sublimity of our species, when they will have demonstrated to me that it is really so important to Nature, that her laws are necessarily violated by this transmutation, then I will be able to believe that murder is a crime; but when the most thoughtful and sober study has proven to me that everything that vegetates upon this globe is of equal value in her eyes, I shall never concede that the alteration of one of these creatures into a thousand others can in any sense upset her intentions or sort ill with her desires. I say to myself: all men, all animals, all plants growing, feeding, destroying and reproducing themselves by the same means, never undergoing a real death, but a simple variation in what modifies them; all, I say, appearing today in one form and several years or hours later in another, all may, at the will of the being who wishes to move them, change a thousand thousand times in a single day, without one of Nature's directives being affected for one instant—what do I say? without this transmuter having done anything but good, since, by dismantling the individuals whose basic components again become necessary to Nature, he does naught by this action, improperly qualified as criminal, but render her the creative energy of which she is necessarily deprived by him who, through brutish indifference, dares not undertake any shuffling, as it were, of the deck. . . . O Thérèse, it is man's pride alone erects murder as a crime. This vain creature, imagining himself the most sublime of the globe's inhabitants, its most essential, takes his departure from this false principle in order to affirm that the deed which results in his undoing can be nothing but an infamy; but his vanity, his lunacy alter the laws of Nature not one jot; no person exists who in the depths of his heart does not feel the most vehement desire to be rid of those by whom he is hampered, troubled, or whose death may be of some advantage to him; and do you suppose, Thérèse, that the difference between this desire and its effect is very great? Now, if these impressions come to us from Nature, can it be presumed they irritate her? Would she inspire in us what would cause her downfall? Ah, be at ease, dear girl, we experience nothing that does not serve her; all the impulses she puts in us are the agents of her decrees; man's passions are but the means she employs to attain her ends. If she stands in need of more individuals, she inspires lust in us and behold! there are creations; when destructions become necessary to her, she inserts vengeance, avarice, lechery, ambition into our hearts and lo! you have murders; but she has not ceased to labor in her own behalf, and whatever we do, there can be no question of it, we are the unthinking instruments of her caprices.

"Ah, no, Thérèse, no! Nature does not leave in our hands the possibility of committing crimes which would conflict with her economy; has it ever been known to happen that the weakest were able to offend the mightiest? What are we in comparison to her? Can she, when she created us, have placed in us what would be capable of hurting her? Can that idiotic supposition consort with the sublime and sure manner in which we see her attain her ends? Ah! were murder not one of the human actions which best fulfilled her intentions, would she permit the doing of murder? May to imitate then be to injure her? Can she be incensed to see man do to his brethren what she herself does to him every day? Since it is proven that she cannot reproduce without destructions, is it not to act in harmony with her wishes to multiply them unceasingly? The man who moves in this direction, who plunges ahead with all possible zeal, will incontestably be the one who serves her best, since it will be he who most co-operates with the schemes she manifests constantly. The primary and most beautiful of Nature's qualities is motion, which agitates her at all times, but this motion is simply a perpetual consequence of crimes, she conserves it by means of crimes only; the person who most nearly resembles her, and therefore the most perfect being, necessarily will be the one whose most active agitation will become the cause of many crimes; whereas, I repeat, the inactive or indolent person, that is to say, the virtuous person, must be in her eyes—how may there be any doubt of it?—the least perfect since he tends only to apathy, to lethargy, to that inactivity which would immediately plunge everything back into chaos were his star to be in the ascendant. Equilibrium must be preserved; it can only be preserved by crimes; therefore, crimes serve Nature; if they serve her, if she demands them, if she desires them, can they offend her? And who else can be offended if she is not?

"But my aunt is the creature I am going to destroy. . . . Oh, Thérèse, in a philosopher's view how frivolous are these consanguinary ties! Forgive me, but I do not even wish to discuss them, so futile are they. These contemptible chains, fruit of our laws and our political institutions—can they mean anything to Nature?

"Desert your prejudices, Thérèse, leave them behind, and serve me; your fortune is made."

"Oh Monsieur!" I replied, terrified by the Comte de Bressac, "your mind invents this theory of an impassive, indifferent Nature; deign rather to heed your heart, and you will hear it condemn all libertinage's false reasonings. Is not that heart, to whose tribunal I recommend you, the sanctuary where this Nature you outrage wishes to be heard and respected? If she engraves upon it the extreme horror of the crime you meditate, will you grant me it is a damnable one? Passions, I know, are blinding you at the present moment, but once they subside, how will you not be torn by remorse? The greater your sensitivity, the more cruelly shall it sting you. . . . Oh Monsieur! preserve, respect this tender, invaluable friend's life; sacrifice it not; you would perish of despair! Every day . . . at every instant you would be visited by the image of this cherished aunt, she whom your unthinking rage would have hurled into her tomb; you would hear her plaintive voice still pronouncing those sweet names that were your childhood's joy; she would be present during your waking hours and appear to torture you in your dreams; she would open with her bloodstained fingers the wounds wherewith you would have mutilated her; thereafter not one happy moment would shine for you while you dwelt upon this earth; you would become a stranger to pleasures; your every idea would be of trouble; a celestial arm, whose might you do not appreciate, would avenge the days you would have obliterated, by envenoming your own, and without having tasted happiness from your felonies, you would be slain by mortal sorrow for having dared accomplish them."

As I uttered these words tears returned to my eyes, I sank to my knees before the Count; by all that is most holy I did implore him to let fade into oblivion an infamous aberration I swore to him all my life I would conceal. . . . But I did not know the man with whom I was dealing; I knew not to what point passions had enthroned crime in that perverse soul. The Count rose and spoke in a voice of ice.

"I see very well I was mistaken, Thérèse," said he. "I regret it, perhaps as much on your account as on my own; no matter, I shall discover other means, and it will be much you shall have lost without your mistress gaining anything."

The threat changed all my ideas; by not accepting the criminal role proposed to me, I was exposing myself to great personal risk and my protectress was infallibly to perish; by consenting to be his accomplice, I would shield myself from the Count's wrath and would assuredly save his aunt; an instant's reflection convinced me I should agree to everything. But as so rapid a reversal would have appeared suspicious, I strove to delay my capitulation; I obliged the Count to repeat his sophistries often; little by little I took on an air of not knowing what to reply: Bressac believed me vanquished; I justified my weakness by the potency of his art and in the end I surrendered. The Count sprang into my arms. Ah, how I should have been overjoyed had his movement been inspired by another motive. . . . What is it I am saying? The time had passed: his horrible conduct, his barbarous designs had annihilated all the feelings my weakling heart had dared conceive, and I saw in him nothing but a monster. . . .

"You are the first woman I have ever held in my arms," said the Count, "and truly, it is with all my soul. . . . You are delicious, my child; a gleam of wisdom seems to have penetrated into your mind! That this charming mind has lain in darkness for so long! Incredible."

Next, we came to facts. In two or three days, as soon, that is, as an opportunity presented itself, I was to drop a dose of poison—Bressac gave me the package that contained it—into the cup of chocolate Madame customarily took in the morning. The

Count assured my immunity against all consequences and directly I consummated the deed, handed me a contract providing me with an annuity of two thousand crowns; he signed these promises without characterizing the state in which I was to enjoy their benefits; we separated.

In the midst of all this, something most singular occurred, something all too able to reveal the atrocious soul of the monster with whom I had to deal; I must not interrupt myself for a moment for, no doubt, you are awaiting the denouement of the adventure in which I had become involved.

Two days following the conclusion of our criminal pact, the Count learned that an uncle, upon whose succession he had not in the least counted, had just left him an income of eighty thousand pounds. . . . "O Heaven!" I said to myself upon hearing the news, "is it then in thuswise celestial justice punishes the basest conspiracy!" And straightway repenting this blasphemy spoken against Providence, I cast myself upon my knees and implored the Almighty's forgiveness, and happily supposed that this unexpected development should at least change the Count's plans. . . . What was my error!

"Ah, my dear Thérèse," he said that same evening, having run to my room, "how prosperity does rain down upon me! Often I have told you so: the idea of a crime or an execution is the surest means to attract good fortune; none exists save for villains."

"What!" I responded, "this unhoped for bounty does not persuade you, Monsieur, patiently to await the death you wished to hasten?"

"Wait?" the Count replied sharply, "I do not intend to wait two minutes, Thérèse; are you not aware I am twenty-eight? Well, it is hard to wait at my age. . . . No, let this affect our scheme not in the slightest, give me the comfort of seeing everything brought to an end before the time comes for us to return to Paris. . . . Tomorrow, at the very latest the day after tomorrow, I beseech you. There has been delay enough: the hour approaches for the payment of the first quarter of your annuity . . . for performing the act which guarantees you the money. . . ."

As best I could, I disguised the fright this desperate eagerness inspired in me, and I renewed my resolution of the day before, well persuaded that if I were not to execute the horrible crime I had engaged to commit, the Count would soon notice I was playing a trick upon him and that, if I were to warn Madame de Bressac, whatever would be her reaction to the project's disclosure, the young Count, observing himself deceived one way or another, would promptly resort to more certain methods which, causing his aunt equally to perish, would also expose me to all her nephew's vengeance. There remained the alternative of consulting the law, but nothing in the world could have induced me to adopt it; I decided to forewarn the Marquise; of all possible measures, that seemed the best, and I elected it.

"Madame," I said to her on the morrow of my last interview with the Count, "Madame, I have something of the highest importance to reveal, but however vital its interest to you, I shall not broach it unless, beforehand, you give me your word of honor to bear no resentment against your nephew for what Monsieur has had the audacity to concert. . . . You will act, Madame, you will take the steps prudence enjoins, but you will say not a word. Deign to give me your promise; else I am silent."

Madame de Bressac, who thought it was but a question of some of her nephew's everyday extravagances, bound herself by the oath I demanded, and I disclosed everything. The unhappy woman burst into tears upon learning of the infamy. . . . "The monster!" she cried, "have I ever done anything that was not for his good? Had I wished to thwart his vices, or correct them, what other motive than his own happiness could have constrained me to severity! And is it not thanks to me he inherits this legacy his uncle has just left him? Ah, Thérèse, Thérèse, prove to me that it is true, this project . . . put me in a way that will prevent me from doubting; I need all that may aid in extinguishing the sentiments my unthinking heart dares yet preserve for the monster. . . ." And then I brought the package of poison into view; it were difficult to furnish better proof; yet the Marquise wished to experiment with it; we made a dog swallow a light dose, shut up the animal, and at the end of two hours it was dead after being seized by frightful convulsions. Any lingering doubt by now dispelled, Madame de Bressac came to a decision; she bade me give her the rest of the

poison and immediately sent a courier with a letter to the Duc de
Sonzeval, related to her, asking him to go directly, but in secrecy, to
the Secretary of State, and to expose the atrocity of a nephew
whose victim she might at any moment become; to provide himself
with a *lettre de cachet;* to make all possible haste to come and
deliver her from the wretch who had so cruelly plotted to take her
life.

But the abominable crime was to be consummated; some inconceivable permission must have been granted by Heaven that
virtue might be made to yield to villainy's oppressions: the animal
upon which we had experimented revealed everything to the Count:
he heard it howling; knowing of his aunt's fondness for the beast,
he asked what had been done to it; those to whom he spoke knew
nothing of the matter and made him no clear answer; from this
moment, his suspicions began to take shape; he uttered not a word,
but I saw that he was disquieted; I mentioned his state to the
Marquise, she became further upset, but could think of nothing to
do save urge the courier to make yet greater haste, and, if possible,
still more carefully to hide the purpose of his mission. She advised
her nephew that she was writing to Paris to beg the Duc de
Sonzeval to waste not a moment to take up the matter of the
recently deceased uncle's inheritance for if no one were to appear to
claim it, there was litigation to be feared; she added that she had
requested the Duke to come and give her a complete account of the
affair, in order that she might learn whether or not she and her
nephew would be obliged to make a journey to Paris. Too skillful a
physiognomist to fail to notice the embarrassment in his aunt's face,
to fail to observe, as well, some confusion written upon mine, the
Count smiled at everything and was no less on his guard. Under the
pretext of taking a promenade, he leaves the château; he lies in
wait for the courier at a place the man must inevitably pass. The
messenger, far more a creature of the Count than his aunt's trustworthy minion, raises no objections when his master demands to
see the dispatches he is carrying, and Bressac, once convinced of
what no doubt he calls my treachery, gives the courier a hundred
louis, together with instructions never to appear again at the
Marquise's. He returns to the château, rage in his heart; however,
he restrains himself; he encounters me, as usual he cajoles me, asks

whether it shall not be tomorrow, points out it is essential the deed be performed before the Duke's arrival, then goes to bed with a tranquil air about which nothing is to be remarked. At the time I knew nothing, I was the dupe of everything. Were the appalling crime to be committed—as the Count's actions informed me later—he would of course have to commit it himself; but I did not know how; I conjectured much; what good would it do to tell you what I imagined? Rather, let us move ahead to the cruel manner in which I was punished for not having wished to undertake the thing. On the day after the messenger was intercepted, Madame drank her chocolate as she always did, dressed, seemed agitated, and sat down at table; scarcely was I out of the dining room when the Count accosted me.

"Thérèse," and nothing could have been more phlegmatic than his manner as he spoke, "I have found a more reliable method than the one I proposed to attain our objectives, but numerous details are involved, and I dare not come so often to your room; at precisely five o'clock be at the corner of the park, I'll join you, we will take a walk together in the woods; while on our promenade I'll explain it all."

I wish to affirm, Madame, that, whether because of the influence of Providence, whether owing to an excessive candor, whether to blindness, nothing gave me a hint of the terrible misery awaiting me; I believed myself so safe, thanks to the Marquise's secret arrangements, that I never for a moment imagined that the Count had been able to discover them; nevertheless I was not entirely at ease.

"Le parjure est vertu quand on promit le crime," one of our tragic poets has said; but perjury is always odious to a delicate and sensitive spirit which finds itself compelled to resort to it. My role embarrassed me.

However that may be, I came to the rendezvous; the Count was not late in getting there; he came up to me very gay and easy, and we set off into the forest; the while he but laughed banteringly and jested, as was his habit when we were together. When I sought to guide the conversation to the subject which he had desired to discuss, he told me to wait yet a little, he said he feared we might be observed, it did not seem to him we were in a safe enough place;

very gradually, without my perceiving it, we approached the four trees to which I had been so cruelly bound long ago. Upon seeing the place, a quiver ran through me: all the horror of my fate rose up before my eyes, and fancy whether my terror was not doubled when I caught sight of the preparations which had been made in that horrible place. Ropes hung from one of the trees; huge mastiffs were leashed to each of the other three and seemed to be waiting for nothing but me in order to fall to sating the hunger announced by their gaping foam-flecked jaws; one of the Count's favorites guarded them.

Whereupon the perfidious creature ceased to employ all but the very foulest epithets.

"Scum," quoth he, "do you recognize that bush whence I dragged you like a wild beast only to spare a life you deserved to lose? Do you recognize these trees unto which I threatened to lash you were you ever to give me cause to repent my kindness? Why did you agree to perform the task I demanded, if you intended to betray me to my aunt? and how could you imagine it was virtue you served by imperiling the freedom of him to whom you owe all your happiness? By necessity placed between two crimes, why have you chosen the more abominable?"

"Alas! I did not choose the less . . ."

"But you should have refused," the Count continued, in his rage seizing one of my arms and shaking me furiously, "yes, certainly, refused, and not consented to betray me."

Then Monsieur de Bressac told me how he had gone about the interception of Madame's messages, and how the suspicion had been born which had led him to decide to stop them.

"What has your duplicity done for you, unworthy creature? You have risked your life without having saved my aunt's: the die is cast, upon my return to the château I will find a fortune awaiting me, but you must perish; before you expire you must learn that the virtuous road is not always the safest, and that there are circumstances in this world when complicity in crime is preferable to informing." And without giving me time to reply, without giving evidence of the least pity for the frightful situation I was in, he dragged me toward the tree destined for me and by which his valet stood expectantly. "Here she is," he said, "the creature who wanted to poison my aunt and who may already have committed the terrible crime in spite of my efforts to prevent it; no doubt, it would have been better to have put her into the hands of justice, but the law would have taken away her life, and I prefer to leave it to her in order that she have longer to suffer."

The two villains then lay hands on me, in an instant they strip me naked. "Pretty buttocks," said the Count in a tone of cruelest irony, brutally handling those objects, "superb flesh . . . excellent lunch for the dogs." When no article of clothing is left upon me, I am secured to the tree by a rope attached around my waist; so that I may defend myself as best I can, my arms are left free, and enough slack is provided for me to advance or retreat about two yards. The arrangements completed, the Count, very much moved, steps up to have a look at my expression, he turns and passes around me; his savage way of handling me seems to say that his murderous fingers would like to dispute the rage of his mastiff's steel teeth. . . .

"Come," says he to his lieutenant, "free the animals, the time has arrived."

They are loosed, the Count excites them, all three fling themselves upon my poor body, one would think they were sharing it in such wise that not one of its parts would be exempt from assault; in vain I drive them back, they bite and tear me with renewed fury, and throughout this horrible scene, Bressac, the craven Bressac, as if my torments had ignited his perfidious lust . . . the beastly man gives himself up, while he regards me, to his companion's criminal caresses.

"Enough," said he after several minutes had gone by, "that will do. Tie up the dogs and let's abandon this creature to her sweet fate.

"Well indeed, Thérèse," says he as he severs my bonds, "virtue is not to be practiced at some expense; a pension of two thousand crowns, would that not have been worth more than the bites you are covered with?"

But in my state I can scarcely hear him; I slump to the foot of the tree and am about to lose consciousness.

"It is most generous of me to save your life," continues the traitor whom my sufferings inflame, "at least take good care how you make use of this favor. . . ."

Then he orders me to get up, dress, and quit the place at once. As my blood is flowing everywhere, in order that my few clothes, the only clothes I have, not be stained, I gather some grass to wipe myself; Bressac paces to and fro, much more preoccupied with his thoughts than concerned with me.

My swollen flesh, the blood that continues to stream from my multiple wounds, the atrocious pain I am enduring, everything makes the operation of dressing well nigh impossible; never once does the dishonest man who has just put me into this horrible state . . . him for whom I once would have sacrified my life, never once does he deign to show me the least hint of sympathy. When at length I am ready:

"Go wherever you wish," says he; "you must have some money left, I will not take it from you, but beware of reappearing at any one of my houses in the city or the country: there are two excellent reasons for not doing so: you may just as well know, first of all, that the affair you thought finished is not at all over. They informed you that the law was done with you; they told you what is not true; the warrant for your arrest still holds, the case is still warm: you were left in this situation so that your conduct might be observed. In the second place, you are going to pass, insofar as the public is concerned, for the Marquise's murderer; if she yet breathes, I am going to see to it she carries this notion into the grave, the entire household will share it; and there you have two trials still to face instead of one: instead of a vile usurer, you have for an adversary a rich and powerful man who is determined to hound you into Hell itself if you misuse the life his compassion leaves to you."

"Oh Monsieur!" was my response, "whatever have been your severities with me, fear not that I will retaliate; I thought myself obliged to take steps against you when it was a question of your aunt's life; but where only the unhappy Thérèse is involved, I shall never do anything. Adieu, Monsieur, may your crimes render you as happy as your cruelties have made me to suffer; and no matter what the fate reserved to me by Heaven, while it shall prolong my deplorable life, I shall only employ my days in uttering prayers for you."

The Count raised his head; he could not avoid glancing at me upon hearing these words, and, as he beheld me quavering and covered with tears and doubtless was afraid lest he be moved by what he saw, the cruel one went away, and I saw him nevermore.

Entirely delivered unto my agony, I fell back again and lay by the tree; there, giving free reign to my hurt, I made the forest resound with my groans; I pressed my stricken frame against the earth, and shed upon the sward all my tears.

"O my God," I cried out, "Thou hast so willed it; it was grained in Thy eternal decrees that the innocent were to fall unto the guilty and were to be their prey: dispose of me, O Lord, I am yet far away from what Thou didst suffer for us; may those I endure, as I adore Thee, render me worthy someday of what rewards Thou keepeth for the lowly, when he hath Thee before him in his tribulations, and let his anguishes be unto Thy greater glorification!"

Night was closing: it was almost beyond my power to move; I was scarcely able to stand erect; I cast my eyes upon the thicket where four years earlier I had slept a night when I had been in circumstances almost as unhappy! I dragged myself along as best I could, and having reached the very same spot, tormented by my still bleeding wounds, overwhelmed by my mind's anxieties and the sorrows of my heart, I passed the cruelest night imaginable.

By dawn, thanks to my youth and my vigorous temperament, some of my strength was restored; greatly terrified by the proximity of that baneful château, I started away from it without delay; I left the forest, and resolved at any price to gain the first habitation which might catch my eye, I entered the town of Saint-Marcel, about five leagues distant from Paris; I demanded the address of a surgeon, one was given me; I presented myself and besought him to dress my wounds; I told him that, in connection with some affair at whose source lay love, I had fled my mother's house, quit Paris, and during the night had been overtaken in the forest by bandits who in revenge for my resistance to their desires, had set their dogs upon me. Rodin, as this artist was called, examined me with the greatest attention, found nothing dangerous about my injuries; had I come to him directly, he said, he would have been able to guarantee that in the space of a fortnight he would have me as fresh and whole as I had been before my adventure; however, the night passed in the open and my worry had infected my wounds, and I could not expect to be well in less than a month. Rodin found space in his own house to lodge me, took all possible care of me, and on the thirtieth day there no longer existed upon my body a single vestige of Monsieur de Bressac's cruelties.

As soon as I was fit to take a little air, my first concern was to find in the town some girl sufficiently adroit and intelligent to go to the Marquise's château and find out what had taken place there since my departure. This apparently very dangerous inquisitiveness would without the slightest doubt have been exceedingly misplaced; but here it was not a question of mere curiosity. What I had earned while with the Marquise remained in my room; I had scarcely six *louis* about me, and I possessed above forty at the château. I did not suppose the Count would be unkind enough to refuse me what was so legitimately mine. Persuaded that, his first fury once passed, he would not wish to do me such an injustice, I wrote a letter calculated to touch him as deeply as possible. I was careful to conceal my address and I begged him to send back my old clothes together with the small sum that would be found in my chamber. A lively and spirited peasant girl of twenty-five undertook to deliver my letter and promised to do her best to bring me back all the information she could garner upon the various subjects about which I gave her to understand I needed to be enlightened. I insisted, that above all else, she hide the name of the place where I was, that she not breathe a word of me in whatever form or connection, and that she say she had taken the letter from a man who had brought it from somewhere fifteen leagues away. Jeannette left, and twenty-four hours later she came back with the reply; it still exists, I have it here, Madame, but before you read it, deign to learn what had transpired at the Count's château since I had been out of it.

Having fallen seriously ill the very day I left, the Marquise de Bressac had been seized by frightful pains and convulsions, and had died the next morning; the family had rushed to the château and the nephew, seemingly gripped in the greatest desolation, had declared that his aunt had been poisoned by a chambermaid who had taken flight the same day. Inquiries were made, and they had the intention to put the wretch to death were she to be found; as for the rest, the Count discovered that the inheritance had made him much wealthier than he had ever anticipated he would be; the Marquise's strongbox, pocketbook, and gems, all of them objects of which no one had known anything, put the nephew, apart from his revenues, in possession of more than six hundred thousand francs in chattels or cash. Behind his affected grief, the young man had, it was said, considerable trouble concealing his delight, and the relatives, convoked for the autopsy demanded by the Count, after having lamented the unhappy Marquise's fate and sworn to avenge her should the culprit fall into their hands, had left the young man in undisputed and peaceful possession of his villainy. Monsieur de Bressac himself had spoken to Jeannette, he had asked a number of questions to which the girl had replied with such frankness and decision that he had resolved to give her his response without pressing her further. There is the fatal letter, said Thérèse, handing it to Madame de Lorsange, yes, there it is, Madame, sometimes my heart has need of it and I will keep it until I die; read it, read it without shuddering, if you can.

Madame de Lorsange, having taken the note from our lovely adventuress' hands, read therein the following words:

> The criminal capable of having poisoned my aunt is brazen indeed to dare thus write to me after her execrable deed; better still is the care with which she conceals her retreat; for she may be sure she will be discomfited if she is discovered. But what is it she has the temerity to demand? What are these references to money? Does what she left behind equal the thefts she committed, either during her sojourn in the house or while consummating her final crime? Let her avoid sending a second request similar to this, for she is advised her ambassador will be arrested and held until the law acquaints itself with the place where the guilty party is taking cover.

Madame de Lorsange returned the note to Thérèse; "Continue, my dear child," said she, "the man's behavior is horrifying; to be swimming in gold and to deny her legitimate earnings to a poor creature who merely did not want to commit a crime, that is a gratuitous infamy entirely without example."

Alas! Madame, Thérèse continued, resuming her story, I was in tears for two days over that dreadful letter; I was far more afflicted by the thought of the horrible deed it attested than by the refusal it contained. Then, I groaned, then I am guilty, here am

I a second time denounced to justice for having been overly respect-ful of the law! So be it, I repent nothing, I shall never know the least remorse so long as my soul is pure, and may I never be responsible for any evil other than that of having too much heeded the equitable and virtuous sentiments which will never abandon me.

I was, however, simply unable to believe that the pursuits and inquiries the Count mentioned were really true, for they seemed highly implausible: it would be so dangerous for him to have me brought into court that I imagined there was far greater reason for him to be frightened at the prospect of having to confront me, than I had cause to tremble before his menaces. These reflections led me to decide to stay where I was and to remain, if possible, until the augmentation of my funds might allow me to move on; I communicated my plan to Rodin, who approved it, and even sug-gested I keep my chamber in his house; but first of all, before I speak of what I decided to do, it is necessary to give you an idea of this man and his entourage.

Rodin was forty years of age, dark-haired, with shaggy eye-brows, a sparkling bright eye; there was about him what bespoke strength and health but, at the same time, libertinage. In wealth he was risen far above his native station, possessing from ten to twelve thousand pounds a year; owing to which, if Rodin practiced his surgical art, it was not out of necessity, but out of taste; he had a very attractive house in Saint-Marcel which, since the death of his wife two years previously, he shared with two girls, who were his servants, and with another, who was his own daughter. This young person, Rosalie by name, had just reached her fourteenth year; in her were gathered all the charms most capable of exciting admira-tion: the figure of a nymph, an oval face, clear, lovely, extraor-dinarily animated, delicate pretty features, very piquant as well, the prettiest mouth possible, very large dark eyes, soulful and full of feeling, chestnut-brown hair falling to below her waist, skin of an incredible whiteness . . . aglow, smooth, already the most beautiful throat in all the world, and, furthermore, wit, vivacity, and one of the most beautiful souls Nature has yet created. With respect to the companions with whom I was to serve in this household, they were two peasant girls: one of them was a governess, the other the cook. She who held the first post could have been twenty-five, the other eighteen or twenty, and both were extremely attractive; their looks suggested a deliberate choice, and this in turn caused the birth of some suspicions as to why Rodin was pleased to accommodate me. What need has he of a third woman? I asked myself, and why does he wish them all to be pretty? Assuredly, I continued, there is something in all this that little conforms with the regular manners from which I wish never to stray; we'll see.

In consequence, I besought Monsieur Rodin to allow me to extend my convalescence at his home for yet another week, declaring that, at the end of this time, he would have my reply to what he had very kindly proposed.

I profited from this interval by attaching myself more closely to Rosalie, determined to establish myself in her father's house only if there should prove to be nothing about it whence I might be obliged to take umbrage. With these designs, I cast appraising glances in every direction, and, on the following day, I noticed that this man enjoyed an arrangement which straightway provoked in me furious doubts concerning his behavior.

Monsieur Rodin kept a school for children of both sexes; during his wife's lifetime he had obtained the required charter and they had not seen fit to deprive him of it after he had lost her. Monsieur Rodin's pupils were few but select: in all, there were but fourteen girls and fourteen boys: he never accepted them under twelve and they were always sent away upon reaching the age of sixteen; never had monarch prettier subjects than Rodin. If there were brought to him one who had some physical defect or a face that left something to be desired, he knew how to invent twenty excuses for rejecting him, all his arguments were very ingenious, they were always colored by sophistries to which no one seemed able to reply; thus, either his corps of little day students had incomplete ranks, or the children who filled them were always charming. These youngsters did not take their meals with him, but came twice a day, from seven to eleven in the morning, from four to eight in the afternoon. If until then I had not yet seen all of this little troupe it was because, having arrived at Rodin's during the holidays, his scholars were not attending classes; toward the end of my recovery they reappeared.

Rodin himself took charge of the boys' instruction, his governess looked after that of the girls, whom he would visit as soon as he had completed his own lessons; he taught his young pupils writing, arithmetic, a little history, drawing, music, and for all that no other master but himself was employed.

I early expressed to Rosalie my astonishment that her father, while performing his functions as a doctor, could at the same time act as a schoolmaster; it struck me as odd, said I, that being able to live comfortably without exercising either the one or the other of these professions, he devoted himself to both. Rosalie, who by now had become very fond of me, fell to laughing at my remark; the manner in which she reacted to what I said only made me the more curious, and I besought her to open herself entirely to me.

"Listen," said that charming girl, speaking with all the candor proper to her age, and all the naïveté of her amiable character; "listen to me, Thérèse, I am going to tell you everything, for I see you are a well brought up girl . . . incapable of betraying the secret I am going to confide to you.

"Certainly, dear friend, my father could make ends meet without pursuing either of these two occupations; and if he pursues both at once, it is because of the two motives I am going to reveal to you. He practices medicine because he has a liking for it; he takes keen pleasure in using his skill to make new discoveries, he has made so many of them, he has written so many authoritative texts based upon his investigations that he is generally acknowledged the most accomplished man in France at the present time; he worked for twenty years in Paris, and for the sake of his amusements he retired to the country. The real surgeon at Saint-Marcel is someone named Rombeau whom he has taken under his tutelage and with whom he collaborates upon experiments; and now, Thérèse, would you know why he runs a school? . . . libertinage, my child, libertinage alone, a passion he carries to its extremes. My father finds in his pupils of either sex objects whose dependence submits them to his inclinations, and he exploits them. . . . But wait a moment . . . come with me," said Rosalie, "today is Friday, one of the three days during the week when he corrects those who have misbehaved; it is in this kind of punishment my father takes his pleasure; follow me, I tell you, you shall see how he behaves. Everything is visible from a closet in my room which adjoins the one where he concludes his business; let's go there without making any noise, and above all be careful not to say a word both about what I am telling you and about what you are going to witness."

It was a matter of such great importance to familiarize my-self with the customs of this person who had offered me asylum, that I felt I could neglect nothing which might discover them to me; I follow hard upon Rosalie's heels, she situates me near a par-tition, through cracks between its ill-joined boards one can view everything going on in the neighboring room.

Hardly have we taken up our post when Rodin enters, leading a fourteen-year-old girl, blond and as pretty as Love; the poor creature is sobbing away, all too unhappily aware of what awaits her; she comes in with moans and cries; she throws herself down before her implacable instructor, she entreats him to spare her, but his very inexorability fires the first sparks of the unbending Rodin's pleasure, his heart is already aglow, and his savage glances spring alive with an inner light. . . .

"Why, no, no," he cries, "not for one minute, this happens far too frequently, Julie, I repent my forbearance and leniency, their sole result has been repeated misconduct on your part, but could the gravity of this most recent example of it possibly allow me to show clemency, even supposing I wished to? A note passed to a boy upon entering the classroom!"

"Sir, I protest to you, I did not—"

"Ah! but I saw it, my dear, I saw it."

"Don't believe a word of it," Rosalie whispered to me, "these are trifles he invents by way of pretext; that little creature is an angel, it is because she resists him he treats her harshly."

Meanwhile, Rodin, greatly aroused, had seized the little girl's hands, tied them to a ring fitted high upon a pillar standing in the middle of the punishment room. Julie is without any defense . . . any save the lovely face languishingly turned toward her execu-tioner, her superb hair in disarray, and the tears which inundate the most beautiful face in the world, the sweetest . . . the most in-teresting. Rodin dwells upon the picture, is fired by it, he covers those supplicating eyes with a blindfold, approaches his mouth and dares kiss them, Julie sees nothing more, now able to proceed as he wishes, Rodin removes the veils of modesty, her blouse is unbuttoned, her stays untied, she is naked to the waist and yet further below. . . . What whiteness! What beauty! These are roses strewn upon lilies by the Graces' very hands . . . what being is so heartless, so cruel as to condemn to torture charms so fresh . . . so poignant? What is the monster that can seek pleasure in the depths of tears and suffering and woe? Rodin contemplates . . . his inflamed eye roves, his hands dare profane the flowers his cruelties are about to wither; all takes place directly before us, not a detail can escape us: now the libertine opens and peers into, now he closes up again those dainty features which enchant him; he offers them to us under every form, but he confines himself to these only: although the true temple of Love is within his reach, Rodin, faithful to his creed, casts not so much as a glance in that direction, to judge by his behavior, he fears even the sight of it; if the child's posture exposes those charms, he covers them over again; the slightest disturbance might upset his homage, he would have nothing distract him . . . finally, his mounting wrath exceeds all limits, at first he gives vent to it through invectives, with menaces and evil language he affrights this poor little wretch trembling before the blows wherewith she realizes she is about to be torn; Rodin is beside himself, he snatches up a cat-o'-nine-tails that has been soaking in a vat of vinegar to give the thongs tartness and sting. "Well there," says he, approaching his victim, "prepare yourself, you have got to suffer"; he swings a vigorous arm, the lashes are brought whistling down upon every inch of the body exposed to them; twenty-five strokes are applied; the tender pink rosiness of this matchless skin is in a trice run into scarlet.

Julie emits cries . . . piercing screams which rend me to the soul; tears run down from beneath her blindfold and like pearls shine upon her beautiful cheeks; whereby Rodin is made all the more furious. . . . He puts his hands upon the molested parts, touches, squeezes, worries them, seems to be readying them for further assaults; they follow fast upon the first, Rodin begins again, not a cut he bestows is unaccompanied by a curse, a menace, a reproach . . . blood appears . . . Rodin is in an ecstasy; his delight is immense as he muses upon the eloquent proofs of his ferocity. He can contain himself no longer, the most indecent condition manifests his overwrought state; he fears not to bring everything out of hiding, Julie cannot see it . . . he moves to the breech and hovers there, he would greatly like to mount as a victor, he dares not, instead, he begins to tyrannize anew; Rodin whips with might and main and finally manages, thanks to the leathern stripes, to open this asylum of the Graces and of joy. . . . He no longer knows who he is or where; his delirium has attained to such a pitch the use of reason is no longer available to him; he swears, he blasphemes, he storms, nothing is exempt from his savage blows, all he can reach is treated with identical fury, but the villain pauses nevertheless, he senses the impossibility of going further without risking the loss of the powers which he must preserve for new operations.

"Dress yourself," he says to Julie, loosening her bonds and readjusting his own costume, "and if you are once again guilty of similar misconduct, bear it firmly in mind you will not get off quite so lightly."

Julie returns to her class, Rodin goes into the boys' and immediately brings back a young scholar of fifteen, lovely as the day; Rodin scolds him; doubtless more at his ease with the lad, he wheedles and kisses while lecturing him.

"You deserve to be punished," he observes, "and you are going to be."

Having uttered these words, he oversteps the last bounds of modesty with the child; for in this case, everything is of interest to him, nothing is excluded, the veils are drawn aside, everything is palpated indiscriminately; Rodin alternates threats, caresses, kisses, curses; his impious fingers attempt to generate voluptuous sentiments in the boy and, in his turn, Rodin demands identical ministrations.

"Very well," cries the satyr, spying his success, "there you are in the state I forbade. . . . I dare swear that with two more movements you'd have the impudence to spit at me. . . ."

But too sure of the titillations he has produced, the libertine advances to gather a homage, and his mouth is the temple offered to the sweet incense; his hands excite it to jet forth, he meets the spurts, devours them, and is himself ready to explode, but he wishes to persevere to the end.

"Ah, I am going to make you pay for this stupidity!" says he and gets to his feet.

He takes the youth's two hands, he clutches them tight, and offers himself entirely to the altar at which his fury would perform a sacrifice. He opens it, his kisses roam over it, his tongue drives deep into it, is lost in it. Drunk with love and ferocity, Rodin mingles the expressions and sentiments of each. . . .

"Ah, little weasel!" he cries, "I must avenge myself upon the illusion you create in me."

The whips are picked up, Rodin flogs; clearly more excited by the boy than he was by the vestal, his blows become both much more powerful and far more numerous: the child bursts into tears, Rodin is in seventh heaven, but new pleasures call, he releases the boy and flies to other sacrifices. A little girl of thirteen is the boy's successor, and she is followed by another youth who is in turn abandoned for a girl; Rodin whips nine: five boys, four girls; the last is a lad of fourteen, endowed with a delicious countenance: Rodin wishes to amuse himself, the pupil resists; out of his mind with lust, he beats him, and the villain, losing all control of himself, hurls his flame's scummy jets upon his young charge's injured parts, he wets him from waist to heels; enraged at not having had strength enough to hold himself in check until the end, our corrector releases the child very testily, and after warning him against such tricks in the future, he sends him back to the class: such are the words I heard, those the scenes which I witnessed.

"Dear Heaven!" I said to Rosalie when this appalling drama came to its end, "how is one able to surrender oneself to such excesses? How can one find pleasure in the torments one inflicts?"

"Ah," replied Rosalie, "you do not know everything. Listen," she said, leading me back into her room, "what you have seen has perhaps enabled you to understand that when my father discovers some aptitudes in his young pupils, he carries his horrors much further, he abuses the girls in the same manner he deals with the boys." Rosalie spoke of that criminal manner of conjugation whereof I myself had believed I might be the victim with the brigands' captain into whose hands I had fallen after my escape from the Conciergerie, and by which I had been soiled by the merchant from Lyon. "By this means," Rosalie continued, "the girls are not in the least dishonored, there are no pregnancies to fear, and nothing prevents them from finding a husband; not a year

goes by without his corrupting nearly all the boys in this way, an
at least half the other children. Of the fourteen girls you have seen
eight have already been spoiled by these methods, and he has taken
his pleasure with nine of the boys; the two women who serve him
are submitted to the same horrors. . . . O Thérèse!" Rosalie added
casting herself into my arms, "O dear girl, and I too, yes I, h
seduced me in my earliest years; I was barely eleven when I be
came his victim . . . when, alas! I was unable to defend mysel
against him."

"But Mademoiselle," I interrupted, horrified, "at least Re
ligion remained to you . . . were you unable to consult a confesso
and avow everything?"

"Oh, you do not know that as he proceeds to pervert us h
stifles in each of us the very seeds of belief, he forbids us all religiou
devotions, and, furthermore, could I have done so? he had in
structed me scarcely at all. The little he had said pertaining to thes
matters had been motivated by the fear that my ignorance migh
betray his impiety. But I had never been to confession, I had no
made my First Communion; so deftly did he cover all these thing
with ridicule and insinuate his poisonous self into even our smalles
ideas, that he banished forever all their duties out of them whom h
suborned; or if they are compelled by their families to fulfill thei
religious duties, they do so with such tepidness, with such complete
indifference, that he has nothing to fear from their indiscretion; bu
convince yourself, Thérèse, let your own eyes persuade you," sh
continued, very quickly drawing me back into the closet whence w
had emerged; "come hither: that room where he chastises hi
students is the same wherein he enjoys us; the lessons are over now
it is the hour when, warmed by the preliminaries, he is going t
compensate himself for the restraint his prudence sometimes im
poses upon him; go back to where you were, dear girl, and wit
your own eyes behold it all."

However slight my curiosity concerning these new abomina
tions, it was by far the better course to leap back into the close
rather than have myself surprised with Rosalie during the classe
Rodin would without question have become suspicious. And so
took my place; scarcely was I at it when Rodin enters his daughter
room, he leads her into the other, the two women of the hou

arrive; and thereupon the impudicious Rodin, all restraints upon his behavior removed, free to indulge his fancies to the full, gives himself over in a leisurely fashion and undisguisedly to committing all the irregularities of debauchery. The two peasants, completely nude, are flogged with exceeding violence; while he plies his whip upon the one the other pays him back in kind, and during the intervals when he pauses for rest, he smothers with the most uninhibited, the most disgusting caresses, the same altar in Rosalie who, elevated upon an armchair, slightly bent over, presents it to him; at last, there comes this poor creature's turn: Rodin ties her to the stake as he tied his scholars, and while one after another and sometimes both at once his domestics flay him, he beats his daughter, lashes her from her ribs to her knees, utterly transported by pleasure. His agitation is extreme: he shouts, he blasphemes, he flagellates: his thongs bite deep everywhere, and wherever they fall, there immediately he presses his lips. Both the interior of the altar and his victim's mouth . . . everything, the before-end excepted, everything is devoured by his suckings; without changing the disposition of the others, contenting himself with rendering it more propitious, Rodin by and by penetrates into pleasure's narrow asylum; meanwhile, the same throne is offered by the governess to his kisses, the other girl beats him with all her remaining strength, Rodin is in seventh heaven, he thrusts, he splits, he tears, a thousand kisses, one more passionate than the other, express his ardor, he kisses whatever is presented to his lust: the bomb bursts and the libertine besotted dares taste the sweetest of delights in the sink of incest and infamy. . . .

Rodin sat down to dine; after such exploits he was in need of restoratives. That afternoon there were more lessons and further corrections, I could have observed new scenes had I desired, but I had seen enough to convince myself and to settle upon a reply to make to this villain's offers. The time for giving it approached. Two days after the events I have described, he himself came to my room to ask for it. He surprised me in bed. By employing the excuse of looking to see whether any traces of my wounds remained, he obtained the right, which I was unable to dispute, of performing an examination upon me, naked, and as he had done the same thing twice a day for a month and had never given any offense

to my modesty I did not think myself able to resist. But this time
Rodin had other plans; when he reaches the object of his worship,
he locks his thighs about my waist and squeezes with such force
that I find myself, so to speak, quite defenseless.

"Thérèse," says he, the while moving his hands about in
such a manner as to erase all doubt of his intents, "you are fully
recovered, my dear, and now you can give me evidence of the
gratitude with which I have beheld your heart overflowing; nothing
simpler than the form your thanks would take; I need nothing beyond this," the traitor continued, binding me with all the strength
at his command. ". . . Yes, this will do, merely this, here is my
recompense, I never demand anything else from women . . . but,"
he continued, " 'tis one of the most splendid I have seen in all my
life . . . What roundness, fullness! . . . unusual elasticity! . . . what
exquisite quality in the skin! . . . Oh my! I absolutely must put
this to use. . . ."

Whereupon Rodin, apparently already prepared to put his
projects into execution, is obliged, in order to proceed to the next
stage, to relax his grip for a moment; I seize my opportunity and
extricating myself from his clutches,

"Monsieur," I say, "I beg you to be well persuaded that there
is nothing in the entire world which could engage me to consent to
the horrors you seem to wish to commit. My gratitude is due to
you, indeed it is, but I will not pay my debt in a criminal coin. Need
less to say, I am poor and most unfortunate; but no matter; here
is the small sum of money I possess," I continue, producing my
meager purse, "take what you esteem just and allow me to leave
this house, I beg of you, as soon as I am in a fitting state to go."

Rodin, confounded by the opposition he little expected from
a girl devoid of means and whom, according to an injustice very
ordinary amongst men, he supposed dishonest by the simple fact
she was sunk in poverty; Rodin, I say, gazed at me attentively.

"Thérèse," he resumed after a minute's silence, "Thérèse,
it is hardly appropriate for you to play the virgin with me; I have
so it would seem to me, some right to your complaisance; but, however, it makes little difference: keep your silver but don't leave me;
I am highly pleased to have a well-behaved girl in my house, the
conduct of these others I have about me being far from impeccable

. . . Since you show yourself so virtuous in this instance, you will be equally so, I trust, in every other. My interests would benefit therefrom; my daughter is fond of you, just a short while ago she came and begged me to persuade you not to go; and so rest with us, if you will, I invite you to remain."

"Monsieur," I replied, "I should not be happy here; the two women who serve you aspire to all the affection you are able to give them; they will not behold me without jealousy, and sooner or later I will be forced to leave you."

"Be not apprehensive," Rodin answered, "fear none of the effects of these women's envy, I shall be quite capable of keeping them in their place by maintaining you in yours, and you alone will possess my confidence without any resultant danger to yourself. But in order to continue to deserve it, I believe it would be well for you to know that the first quality, the foremost, I require in you, Thérèse, is an unassailable discretion. Many things take place here, many which do not sort with your virtuous principles; you must be able to witness everything, hear all and never speak a syllable of it. . . . Ah, Thérèse, remain with me, stay here, Thérèse, my child, it will be a joy to have you; in the midst of the many vices to which I am driven by a fiery temper, an unrestrainable imagination and a much rotted heart, at least I will have the comfort of a virtuous being dwelling close by, and upon whose breast I shall be able to cast myself as at the feet of a God when, glutted by my debauches, I . . ." "Oh Heaven!" I did think at this moment, "then Virtue is necessary, it is then indispensable to man, since even the vicious one is obliged to find reassurance in it and make use of it as of a shelter." And then, recollecting Rosalie's requests that I not leave her, and thinking to discern some good principles in Rodin, I resolved to stay with him.

"Thérèse," Rodin said to me several days later, "I am going to install you near my daughter; in this way, you will avoid all frictions with the other two women, and I intend to give you three hundred pounds wages."

Such a post was, in my situation, a kind of godsend; inflamed by the desire to restore Rosalie to righteousness, and perhaps even her father too were I able to attain some influence over him, I repented not of what I had just done . . . Rodin, having had me dress myself, conducted me at once to where his daughter was; Rosalie received me with effusions of joy, and I was promptly established.

Ere a week was gone by I had begun to labor at the conversions after which I thirsted, but Rodin's intransigence defeated all my efforts.

"Do not believe," was the response he made to my wise counsels, "that the kind of deference I showed to the virtue in you proves that I either esteem virtue or have the desire to favor it over vice. Think nothing of the sort, Thérèse, 'twould be to deceive yourself; on the basis of what I have done in your regard, anyone who was to maintain, as consequential to my behavior, the importance or the necessity of virtue would fall into the very largest error, and sorry I would be were you to fancy that such is my fashion of thinking. The rustic hovel to which I repair for shelter when, during the hunt, the excessive heat of the sun's rays falls perpendicularly upon me, that hut is certainly not to be mistaken for a superior building: its worth is merely circumstantial; I am exposed to some sort of danger, I find something which affords protection, I use it, but is this something the grander on that account? can it be the less contemptible? In a totally vicious society, virtue would be totally worthless; our societies not being entirely of this species, one must absolutely either play with virtue or make use of it so as to have less to dread from its faithful followers. If no one adopts the virtuous way, it becomes useless; I am then not mistaken when I affirm that it owes its necessity to naught but opinion or circumstances; virtue is not some kind of mode whose value is incontestable, it is simply a scheme of conduct, a way of getting along, which varies according to accidents of geography and climate and which, consequently, has no reality, the which alone exhibits its futility. Only what is constant is really good; what changes perpetually cannot claim that characterization: that is why they have declared that immutability belongs to the ranks of the Eternal's perfections; but virtue is completely without this quality: there is not, upon the entire globe, two races which are virtuous in the same manner; hence, virtue is not in any sense real, nor in any wise intrinsically good and in no sort deserves our reverence. How is it to be employed? as a prop, as a device: it is politic to adopt the virtue of the country one inhabits, so that those who practice it, either because they have a taste for it or who have to cultivate it because of their station, will leave you in peace, and so that this virtue which happens to be respected in your area will guarantee you, by its conventional preponderance, against the assaults delivered by them who profess vice. But, once again, all that is at the dictation of variable circumstances, and nothing in all that assigns a real merit to virtue. There are, furthermore, such virtues as are impossible to certain men; now, how are you going to persuade me that a virtue in conflict or in contradiction with the passions is to be found in Nature? And if it is not in Nature and natural, how can it be good? In those men we are speaking of there will certainly be vices opposed to these virtues, and these vices will be preferred by these men, since they will be the only modes . . . the only schemes of being which will be thoroughly agreeable to their peculiar physical constitutions or to their uncommon organs; in this hypothesis, there would then be some very useful vices: well, how can virtue be useful if you demonstrate to me that what is contrary to virtue is useful? In reply to that, one hears that virtue is useful to others, and that in this sense it is good; for if it is posited that I must do only what is good to others, in my turn I will receive only good. And this argument is pure sophistry: in return for the small amount of good I receive at the hands of others thanks to the virtue they practice, my obligation to practice virtue in my turn causes me to make a million sacrifices for which I am in no wise compensated. Receiving less than I give, I hence conclude a very disadvantageous bargain, I experience much more ill from the privations I endure in order to be virtuous, than I experience good from those who do it to me; the arrangement being not at all equitable, I therefore must not submit to it, and certain, by being virtuous, not to cause others as much pleasure as I receive pain by compelling myself to be good, would it not be better to give up procuring them a happiness which must cost me so much distress? There now remains the harm I may do others by being vicious and the evil I myself would suffer were everyone to resemble me. Were we to acknowledge an efficient circulation of vices, I am certainly running a grave danger, I concede it; but the grief experienced by what I risk is offset by the pleasure I receive from causing others to be

menaced: and there, you see, equality is re-established: and everyone is more or less equally happy: which is not the case and cannot
be the case in a society where some are good and others are bad, because, from this mixture, perpetual pitfalls result, and no pitfalls
exist in the other instance. In the heterogeneous society, all interests
are unalike: there you have the source of an infinite number of
miseries; in the contrary association, all interests are identical,
each individual composing it is furnished with the same proclivities,
the same penchants, each one marches together with all the others
and to the same goal; they are all happy. But, idiots complain to
you, evil does not make for happiness. No, not when everyone has
agreed to idolize good; but merely cease to prize, instead deflate,
heap abuse upon what you call good, and you will no longer
revere anything but what formerly you had the idiocy to call evil;
and every man will have the pleasure of committing it, not at all
because it will be permitted (that might be, upon occasion, a reason
for the diminishment of its appeal), but because the law will no
longer punish it, and it is the law, through the fear it inspires,
which lessens the pleasure Nature has seen to it we take in crime. I
visualize a society where it will be generally admitted that incest
(let us include this offense together with all the others), that incest,
I say, is criminal: those who commit incest will be unhappy, because
opinion, laws, beliefs, everything will concert to chill their pleasure;
those who desist from doing this evil, those who, because of these
restraints, will not dare, will be equally unhappy: thus, the law
that proscribes incest will have done nothing but cause wretchedness. Now, I visualize another society neighboring the first; in this
one incest is no crime at all: those who do not desist will not be
unhappy, and those who desire it will be happy. Hence, the society
which permits this act will be better suited to mankind than the
one in which the act is represented as a crime; the same pertains to
all other deeds clumsily denominated criminal; regard them from
this point of view, and you create crowds of unhappy persons;
permit them, and not a complaint is to be heard; for he who
cherishes this act, whatever it happens to be, goes about performing
it in peace and quiet, and he who does not care for it either remains
in a kind of neutral indifference toward it, which is certainly not
painful, or finds restitution for the hurt he may have sustained by

resorting to a host of other injuries wherewith in his turn he belabors whosoever has aggrieved him: thus everyone in a criminal society is either very happy indeed, or else in a paradise of unconcern; consequently, there's nothing good, nothing respectable, nothing that can bring about happiness in what they call virtue. Let those who follow the virtuous track be not boastingly proud of the concessions wrung from us by the structural peculiarities of our society; 'tis purely a matter of circumstance, an accident of convention that the homages demanded of us take a virtuous form; but in fact, this worship is a hallucination, and the virtue which obtains a little pious attention for a moment is not on that account the more noble."

Such was the infernal logic of Rodin's wretched passions; but Rosalie, gentle and less corrupt, Rosalie, detesting the horrors to which she was submitted, was a more docile auditor and more receptive to my opinions. I had the most ardent desire to bring her to discharge her primary religious duties; but we would have been obliged to confide in a priest, and Rodin would not have one in the house; he beheld them, and the beliefs they professed, with horror: nothing in the world would have induced him to suffer one to come near his daughter; to lead the girl to a confessor was equally impossible: Rodin never allowed Rosalie to go abroad unless he accompanied her. We were therefore constrained to bide our time until some occasion might present itself; and while we waited I instructed the young person; by giving her a taste for virtue, I inspired in her another for Religion, I revealed to her its sacred dogmas and its sublime mysteries, and I so intimately attached these two sentiments to her youthful heart that I rendered them indispensable to her life's happiness.

"O Mademoiselle," I said one day, my eyes welling with tears at her compunction, "can man blind himself to the point of believing that he is not destined to some better end? Is not the fact he has been endowed with the capacity of consciousness of his God sufficient evidence that this blessing has not been accorded him save to meet the responsibilities it imposes? Well, what may be the foundation of the veneration we owe the Eternal, if it is not that virtue of which He is the example? Can the Creator of so many wonders have other than good laws? And can our hearts be pleasing unto Him if their element is not good? It seems to me that, for sensitive spirits, the only valid motives for loving that Supreme Being must be those gratitude inspires. Is it not a favor thus to have caused us to enjoy the beauties of this Universe? and do we not owe Him some gratitude in return for such a blessing? But a yet stronger reason establishes, confirms the universal chain of our duties; why should we refuse to fulfill those required by His decrees, since they are the very same which consolidate our happiness amongst mortals? Is it not sweet to feel that one renders oneself worthy of the Supreme Being simply by practicing those virtues which must bring about our contentment on earth, and that the means which render us worthy to live amongst our brethren are the identical ones which give us the assurance of a rebirth, in the life still to come, close by the throne of God! Ah, Rosalie! how blind are they who would strive to ravish away this our hope! Mistaken, benighted, seduced by their wretched passions, they prefer to deny eternal verities rather than abandon what may render them deserving of them. They would rather say, 'These people deceive us,' than admit they deceive themselves; the lingering thought of what they are preparing themselves to lose troubles them in their low riot and sport; it seems to them less dreadful to annihilate hope of Heaven, than to be deprived of what would acquire it for them! But when those tyrannical passions finally weaken and fade in them, when the veil is torn away, when there is no longer anything left in their disease-eaten hearts to counter the imperious voice of that God their delirium disregardingly misprized, Oh Rosalie! what must it be, this cruel awakening! and how much its accompanying remorse must inflate the price to be paid for the instant's error that blinded them! Such is the condition wherein man has got to be in order to construe his proper conduct: 'tis neither when in drunkenness, nor when in the transport produced by a burning fever, he ought to be believed or his sayings marked, but when his reason is calmed and enjoys its full lucid energy he must seek after the truth, 'tis then he divines and sees it. 'Tis then with all our being we yearn after that Sacred One of Whom we were once so neglectful; we implore Him, He becomes our whole solace; we pray to Him, He hears our entreaties. Ah, why then should I deny Him, why should I be unheeding of this Object so necessary to happiness? Why should I prefer to say with the misguided man, There is no God, while the heart of the reasoning part of humankind every instant offers me proofs of this Divine Being's existence? Is it then better to dream amongst the mad than rightly to think with the wise? All derives nevertheless from this initial principle: immediately there exists a God, this God deserves to be worshiped, and the primary basis of this worship indisputably is Virtue."

From these elementary truths I easily deduced the others and the deistic Rosalie was soon made a Christian. But by what means, I repeat, could I join a little practice to the morality? Rosalie, bound to obey her father, could at the very most do no more than display her disgust for him, and with a man like Rodin might that not become dangerous? He was intractable; not one of my doctrines prevailed against him; but although I did not win him over, he for his part at least did not shake me.

However, such an academy, dangers so permanent, so real, caused me to tremble for Rosalie, so much so in fact that I could not find myself in any wise guilty in engaging her to fly from this perverse household. It seemed to me that to snatch her from her incestuous father were a lesser evil than to leave her prey to all the risks she must run by staying with him. I had already delicately hinted at the idea and perhaps I was not so very far from success when all of a sudden Rosalie vanished from the house; all my efforts to find out where she was failed. When I interrogated his women or Rodin himself I was told she had gone to pass the summer months with a relative who lived ten leagues away. When I made inquiries around the neighborhood, they were at first astonished to hear such a question from a member of the household, then, as had Rodin and his domestics, they would answer that she had been seen, everyone had bade her farewell the day before, the day she had left; I received the same replies everywhere. I asked Rodin why this departure had been kept secret from me; why had I not been allowed to accompany my mistress? He assured me the unique reason had been to avoid a scene difficult for both Rosalie and me, and that I would certainly see the person I loved very soon. I had to be content with these answers, but it was more difficult to be convinced of their truth. Was it presumable that Rosalie—and how great was her affection for me!—could have consented to leave me without so much as one word? and according to what I knew of Rodin's character, was there not much to fear for the poor girl's fate? I resolved to employ every device to learn what had become of her, and in order to find out, every means seemed justifiable.

The following day, noticing I was alone in the house, I carefully investigated every corner of it; I thought I caught the sound of moans emanating from a very obscure cellar. . . . I approached; a pile of firewood seemed to be blocking a narrow door at the end of a passageway; by removing the obstructions I am able to advance . . . further noises are to be heard . . . I believe I detect a voice . . . I listen more carefully . . . I am in doubt no longer.

"Thérèse," I hear at last, "O Thérèse, is it you?"

"Yes, my dear, my most tender friend," I cry, recognizing Rosalie's accents. . . . "Yes, 'tis Thérèse Heaven sends to your rescue . . ."

And my numerous questions scarcely allow this interesting girl time to reply. At length I learn that several hours before her disappearance, Rombeau, Rodin's friend and colleague, had examined her naked and that she had received an order from her father to ready herself to undergo, at Rombeau's hands, the same horrors Rodin exposed her to every day; that she had resisted; that Rodin, furious, had seized her and himself presented her to his companion's frantic attacks; that, next, the two men had spoken together in whispers for a very long time, leaving her naked the while, and periodically renewing their probings, they had continued to amuse themselves with her in the same criminal fashion and had maltreated her in a hundred different ways; that, after this session, which had lasted four or five hours, Rodin had finally said he was going to send her to the country to visit one of her family, but that she must leave at once and without speaking to Thérèse, for reasons he would explain the day afterward, for he intended to join her immediately. He had given Rosalie to understand he meant to marry her and this accounted for the examination Rombeau had given her, which was to determine whether she were capable of becoming a mother. Rosalie had indeed left under an old woman's guardianship; she had crossed through the town, in passing said farewell to several acquaintances; but immediately night had fallen, her conductress had led her back to her father's house;

she had entered at midnight. Rodin, who was waiting for her, had seized her, had clapped his hand over her mouth to stifle her voice and, without a word, had plunged her into this cellar where, in truth, she had been decently well fed and looked after.

"I have everything to fear," the poor thing added; "my father's conduct toward me since he put me here, his discourses, what preceded Rombeau's examination, everything, Thérèse, everything suggests that these monsters are going to use me in one of their experiments, and that your poor Rosalie is doomed."

After copious tears had flowed from my eyes, I asked the unhappy girl whether she knew where the key to the cellar was kept; she did not; but she did not believe their custom was to take it with them. I sought for it everywhere; in vain; and by the time the hour arrived for me to return upstairs I had been able to give the dear child no more by way of aid than consoling words, a few hopes, and many tears. She made me swear to come back the next day; I promised, even assuring her that if by that time I had discovered nothing satisfactory regarding her, I would leave the house directly, fetch the police and extricate her, at no matter what price, from the terrible fate threatening her.

I went up; Rombeau was dining with Rodin that evening. Determined to stick at nothing to clarify my mistress' fate, I hid myself near the room where the two friends were at table, and their conversation was more than enough to convince me of the horror of the project wherewith both were occupied.

It was Rodin who was speaking: "Anatomy will never reach its ultimate state of perfection until an examination has been performed upon the vaginal canal of a fourteen- or fifteen-year-old child who has expired from a cruel death; it is only from the contingent contraction we can obtain a complete analysis of a so highly interesting part."

"The same holds true," Rombeau replied, "for the hymeneal membrane; we must, of course, find a young girl for the dissection. What the deuce is there to be seen after the age of puberty? nothing; the menstrual discharges rupture the hymen, and all research is necessarily inexact; your daughter is precisely what we need; although she is fifteen, she is not yet mature; the manner in which we have enjoyed her has done no damage to the membranous tissue, and we will be able to handle her with complete immunity from interference. I am delighted you have made up your mind at last."

"Oh, I certainly have," Rodin rejoined; "I find it odious that futile considerations check the progress of science; did great men ever allow themselves to be enslaved by such contemptible chains? And, when Michelangelo wished to render a Christ after Nature, did he make the crucifixion of a young man the occasion for a fit of remorse? Why no: he copied the boy in his death agonies. But where it is a question of the advance of our art, how absolutely essential such means become! And how the evil in permitting them dwindles to insignificance! Only think of it! you sacrifice one, but you save a million, perhaps; may one hesitate when the price is so modest? Is the murder operated by the law of a species different from the one we are going to perform? and is not the purpose of those laws, which are commonly found so wise, the sacrifice of one in order to save a thousand?"

"But what other way can one approach the problem?" Rombeau demanded; "there is certainly no other by which to obtain any information. In those hospitals where I worked as a young man I saw similar experiments by the thousand; but in view of the ties which attach you to this creature, I must confess I was afraid you would hesitate."

"What! because she is my daughter? A capital reason!" Rodin roared, "and what rank do you then fancy this title must allot her in my heart? I place roughly the same value (weighing the matter very nicely) upon a little semen which has hatched its chick, and upon that I am pleased to waste while enjoying myself. One has the power to take back what one has given; amongst no race that has ever dwelled upon earth has there been any disputing the right to dispose of one's children as one sees fit. The Persians, the Medes, the Armenians, the Greeks enjoyed this right in its fullest latitude. The constitution decreed by Lycurgus, that paragon of lawgivers, not only accorded fathers every right over their offspring, but even condemned to death those children parents did not care to feed, or those which were discovered malformed. A great proportion of savage peoples kill their young immediately they are born. Nearly all the women of Asia, Africa, and America practice abortions, and are not for that reason covered with discredit; Cook discovered the custom widespread in all the South Sea islands. Romulus permitted infanticide; the law of the twelve tables similarly tolerated it and until the era of Constantine the Romans exposed or killed their children with impunity. Aristotle recommended this pretended crime; the Stoic sect regarded it as praiseworthy; it is still very much in use in China. Every day one counts, lying in the streets and floating in the canals of Peking, more than ten thousand individuals immolated or abandoned by their parents, and in that wisely-governed empire whatever be the child's age, a father need but put it into the hands of a judge to be rid of it. According to the laws of the Parthians, one killed one's son, one's daughter, or one's brother, even at the age of nubility; Caesar discovered the custom universal amongst the Gauls; several passages in the Pentateuch prove that amongst the children of God one was allowed to kill one's children; and, finally, God Himself ordered Abraham to do just that. It was long believed, declares a celebrated modern author, that the prosperity of empires depends upon the slavery of children; this opinion is supported by the healthiest logic. Why! a monarch will fancy himself authorized to sacrifice twenty or thirty thousand of his subjects in a single day to achieve his own ends, and a father is not to be allowed, when he esteems it propitious, to become the master of his children's lives! What absurdity! O folly! Oh what is this inconsistency, this feebleness in them upon whom such chains are binding! A father's authority over his children, the only real one, the one that serves as basis to every other, that authority is dictated to us by the voice of Nature herself, and the intelligent study of her operations provides examples of it at every turn and instant. Czar Peter was in no doubt as to this right; he used it habitually and addressed a public declaration to all the orders of his empire, in which he said that, according to laws human and divine, a father had the entire and absolute right to sentence his children to death, without appeal and without consulting the opinion of anyone at all. It is nowhere but in our own barbarous France that a false and ludicrous pity has presumed to suppress this prerogative. No," Rodin pursued with great feeling, "no, my friend, I will never understand how a father, who had the kindness to provide it with life, may not be at liberty to bestow death upon his issue. 'Tis the ridiculous value we attach to this life which eternally makes us speak drivel about the kind of deed to which a man resorts in order to disencumber himself of a fellow creature. Believing that existence is the greatest of all goods, we stupidly fancy we are doing something criminal when we convey someone away from its enjoyment; but the cessation of this existence, or at least what follows it, is no more an evil than life is a good; or rather, if nothing dies, if nothing is destroyed, if nothing is lost to Nature, if all the decomposed parts of any body whatsoever merely await dissolution to reappear immediately under new forms, how indifferent is this act of murder! and how dare one find any evil in it? In this connection I ought to act according to nothing but my own whim; I ought to regard the thing as very simple indeed, especially so when it becomes necessary to an act of such vital importance to mankind . . . when it can furnish such a wealth of knowledge: henceforth it is an evil no longer, my friend, it is no longer a crime, no, not a petty misdemeanor, it is the best, the wisest, the most useful of all actions, and crime would exist only in refusing oneself the pleasure of committing it."

"Ha!" said Rombeau, full of enthusiasm for these appalling maxims, "I applaud you, my dear fellow, your wisdom enchants me, but your indifference is astonishing; I thought you were amorous—"

"I? in love with a girl? . . . Ah, Rombeau! I supposed you knew me better; I employ those creatures when I have nothing better to hand: the extreme penchant I have for pleasures of the variety you have watched me taste makes very precious to me all the temples at which this sort of incense can be offered, and to multiply my devotions, I sometimes assimilate a little girl into a pretty little boy; but should one of these female personages unhappily nourish my illusion for too long, my disgust becomes energetically manifest, and I have never found but one means to satisfy it deliciously . . . you understand me, Rombeau; Chilpéric, the most voluptuous of France's kings, held the same views. His boisterous organ proclaimed aloud that in an emergency one could make use of a woman, but upon the express condition one exterminated her immediately one had done with her.[3] For five years this

---

[3] Cf. a work entitled *The Jesuits in Fine Fettle.*

little wench has been serving my pleasures; the time has come for her to pay for my loss of interest by the loss of her existence."

The meal ended; from those two madmen's behavior, from their words, their actions, their preparations, from their very state, which bordered upon delirium, I was very well able to see that there was not a moment to be lost, and that the hour of the unhappy Rosalie's destruction had been fixed for that evening. I rushed to the cellar, resolved to deliver her or die.

"O dear friend," I cried, "there is not an instant to waste . . . the monsters . . . it is to be tonight . . . they are going to come. . . ."

And upon saying that, I make the most violent efforts to batter down the door. One of my blows dislodges something, I reach out my hand, it is the key, I seize it, I hasten to open the door . . . I embrace Rosalie, I urge her to fly, I promise to follow her, she springs forward . . . Just Heaven! It was again decreed that Virtue was to succumb, and that sentiments of the tenderest commiseration were going to be brutally punished; lit by the governess, Rodin and Rombeau appeared of a sudden, the former grasped his daughter the instant she crossed the threshold of the door beyond which, a few steps away, lay deliverance.

"Ah, wretch, where are you going?" Rodin shouts, bringing her to a halt while Rombeau lays hands upon me. . . . "Why," he continues, glancing at me, "here's the rascal who has encouraged your flight! Thérèse, now we behold the results of your great virtuous principles . . . the kidnaping of a daughter from her father!"

"Certainly," was my steadfast reply, "and I must do so when that father is so barbarous as to plot against his daughter's life."

"Well, well! Espionage and seduction," Rodin pursued; "all a servant's most dangerous vices; upstairs, up with you, I say, the case requires to be judged."

Dragged by the two villains, Rosalie and I are brought back to the apartments; the doors are bolted. The unlucky daughter of Rodin is tied to the posts of a bed, and those two demoniacs turn all their rage upon me, their language is of the most violent, the sentence pronounced upon me appalling: it is nothing less than a question of a vivisection in order to inspect the beating of my heart, and upon this organ to make observations which cannot practicably be made upon a cadaver. Meanwhile, I am undressed, and subjected to the most impudicious fondlings.

"Before all else," says Rombeau, "my opinion is a stout attack ought to be delivered upon the fortress your lenient proceedings have respected. . . . Why, 'tis superb! do you mark that velvet texture, the whiteness of those two half-moons defending the portal! never was there a virgin of such freshness."

"Virgin! but so she is, or nearly," says Rodin, "once raped, and then it was despite her wishes; since then, untouched. Here, let me take the wheel a moment . . ." and the cruel one added to Rombeau's his homage made up of those harsh and savage caresses which degrade rather than honor the idol. Had whips been available I should have been cruelly dealt with; whips were indeed mentioned, but none were found, they limited themselves to what the bare hand could achieve; they set me afire . . . the more I struggled, the more rigidly I was held; when however I saw them about to undertake more serious matters, I flung myself prostrate before my executioners and offered them my life.

"But when you are no longer a virgin," said Rombeau, "what is the difference? What are these qualms? we are only going to violate you as you have been already and not the least peccadillo will sit on your conscience; you will have been vanquished by force . . ." and comforting me in this manner, the infamous one placed me on a couch.

"No," spoke up Rodin, interrupting his colleague's effervescence, of which I was on the brink of becoming the victim, "no, let's not waste our powers with this creature; remember we cannot further postpone the operations scheduled for Rosalie, and our vigor is necessary to carry them out; let's punish this wretch in some other manner."

Upon saying which, Rodin put an iron in the fire. "Yes," he went on, "let's punish her a thousand times more than we would were we to take her life, let's brand her; this disgrace, joined to all the sorry business about her body, will get her hanged if she does not first die of hunger; until then she will suffer, and our more prolonged vengeance will become the more delicious."

Wherewith Rombeau seized me, and the abominable Rodin

applied behind my shoulder the red-hot iron with which thieves are marked.

"Let her dare appear in public, the whore," the monster continued, exhibiting the ignominious letter, "and I'll sufficiently justify my reasons for sending her out of the door with such secrecy and promptitude."

They bandage me, dress me, and fortify me with a few drops of brandy, and under the cover of night the two scientists conduct me to the forest's edge and abandon me cruelly there after once again having sketched what dangers a recrimination would expose me to were I to dare bring complaint in my present state of disgrace.

Anyone else might have been little impressed by the menace; what would I have to fear as soon as I found the means to prove that what I had just suffered had been the work not of a tribunal but of criminals? But my weakness, my natural timidity, the frightful memory of what I had undergone at Paris and recollections of the château de Bressac—it all stunned me, terrified me; I thought only of flight, and was far more stirred by anguish at having to abandon an innocent victim to those two villains, who were without doubt ready to immolate her, than I was touched by my own ills. More irritated, more afflicted morally than in physical pain, I set off at once; but, completely unoriented, never stopping to ask my way, I did but swing in a circle around Paris and on the fourth day of traveling I found I had got no further than Lieursaint. Knowing this road would lead me to the southern provinces, I resolved to follow it and try to reach those distant regions, fancying to myself that the peace and calm so cruelly denied me in those parts of France where I had grown up were, perhaps, awaiting me in others more remote; fatal error! how much there remained of grief and pain yet to experience.

Whatever had been my trials until that time, at least I was in possession of my innocence. Merely the victim of a few monsters' attempts, I was still able to consider myself more or less in the category of an honest girl. The fact was I had never been truly soiled save by a rape operated five years earlier, and its traces had healed . . . a rape consummated at an instant when my numbed state had not even left me the faculty of sensation. Other than that, what was there with which I could reproach myself? Nothing, oh! nothing, doubtless; and my heart was chaste, I was overweeningly proud of it, my presumption was to be punished; the outrages awaiting me were to be such that in a short while it would no longer be possible, however slight had been my participation, for me to form the same comforting ideas in the depths of my heart.

This time I had my entire fortune about me; that is to say, about a hundred crowns, comprising the total of what I had saved from Bressac's clutches and earned from Rodin. In my extreme misery I was able to feel glad that this money, at least, had not been taken from me; I flattered myself with the notion that through the frugality, temperance, and economy to which I was accustomed, this sum would amply suffice until I was so situated as to be able to find a place of some sort. The execration they had just stamped upon my flesh did not show, I imagined I would always be able to disguise it and that this brand would be no bar to making my living. I was twenty-two years old, in good health, and had a face which, to my sorrow, was the object of eulogies all too frequent; I possessed some virtues which, although they had brought me unremitting injury, nevertheless, as I have just told you, were my whole consolation and caused me to hope that Heaven would finally grant me, if not rewards, at least some suspension of the evils they had drawn down upon me. Full of hope and courage, I kept my road until I gained Sens, where I rested several days. A week of this and I was entirely restored; I might perhaps have found work in that city but, penetrated by the necessity of getting further away, I resumed my journeying with the design of seeking my fortune in Dauphiné; I had heard this province much spoken of, I fancied happiness attended me there, and we are going to see with what success I sought it out.

Never, not in a single one of my life's circumstances, had the sentiments of Religion deserted me. Despising the vain casuistries of strong-headed thinkers, believing them all to emanate from libertinage rather than consequent upon firm persuasion, I had dressed my conscience and my heart against them and, by means of the one and the other, I had found what was needed in order to make them stout reply. By my misfortunes often forced to neglect my pious duties, I would make reparation for these faults whenever I could find the opportunity.

I had just, on the 7th of August, left Auxerre; I shall never forget that date. I had walked about two leagues: the noonday heat beginning to incommode me, I climbed a little eminence crowned by a grove of trees; the place was not far removed from the road, I went there with the purpose of refreshing myself and obtaining a few hours of sleep without having to pay the expense of an inn, and up there I was in greater safety than upon the highway. I established myself at the foot of an oak and, after a frugal lunch, I drifted off into sweet sleep. Well did I rest, for a considerable time, and in a state of complete tranquillity; and then, opening my eyes, it was with great pleasure I mused upon the landscape which was visible for a long distance. From out of the middle of a forest that extended upon the right, I thought I could detect, some three or four leagues from where I was, a little bell tower rising modestly into the air. . . . "Beloved solitude," I murmured, "what a desire I have to dwell a time in thee; and thou afar," said I, addressing the abbey, "thou must be the asylum of a few gentle, virtuous recluses who are occupied with none but God . . . with naught but their pious duties; or a retreat unto some holy hermits devoted to Religion alone . . . men who, far removed from that pernicious society where incessant crime, brooding heavily, threatfully over innocence, degrades it, annihilates it . . . ah! there must all virtues dwell, of that I am certain, and when mankind's crimes exile them out of the world, 'tis thither they go in that isolated place to commune with the souls of those fortunate ones who cherish them and cultivate them every day."

I was absorbed in these thoughts when a girl of my age, keeper of a flock of sheep grazing upon the plateau, suddenly appeared before my eyes; I question her about that habitation, she tells me what I see is a Benedictine monastery occupied by four solitary monks of peerless devotion, whose continence and sobriety are without example. Once a year, says the girl, a pilgrimage is made to a miraculous Virgin who is there, and from Her pious folk obtain all their hearts' desire. Singularly eager immediately to go and implore aid at the feet of this holy Mother of God, I ask the girl whether she would like to come and pray with me; 'tis impossible, she replies, for her mother awaits her; but the road there is easy. She indicates it to me, she assures me the superior of the house, the most respectable, the most saintly of men, will receive me with perfect good grace and will offer me all the aid whereof I can possibly stand in need. "Dom Sévérino, so he is called," continues the girl, "is an Italian closely related to the Pope, who overwhelms him with kindnesses; he is gentle, honest, correct, obliging, fifty-five years old, and has spent above two-thirds of his life in France . . . you will be satisfied with him, Mademoiselle," the shepherdess concluded, "go and edify yourself in that sacred quiet, and you will only return from it improved."

This recital only inflamed my zeal the more, I became unable to resist the violent desire I felt to pay a visit to this hallowed church and there, by a few acts of piety, to make restitution for the neglect whereof I was guilty. However great was my own need of charities, I gave the girl a crown, and set off down the road leading to Saint Mary-in-the-Wood, as was called the monastery toward which I directed my steps.

When I had descended upon the plain I could see the spire no more; for guide I had nothing but the forest ahead of me, and before long I began to fear that the distance, of which I had forgotten to inform myself, was far greater than I had estimated at first; but was in nowise discouraged. I arrived at the edge of the forest and, some amount of daylight still remaining, I decided to forge on, considering I should be able to reach the monastery before nightfall. However, not a hint of human life presented itself to my gaze, not a house, and all I had for road was a beaten path I followed virtually at random; I had already walked at least five leagues without seeing a thing when, the Star having completely ceased to light the universe, it seemed I heard the tolling of a bell. . . . I harken, I move toward the sound, I hasten, the path widens ever so little, at last I perceive several hedges and soon afterward the monastery; than this isolation nothing could be wilder, more rustic, there is no neighboring habitation, the nearest is six leagues removed, and dense tracts of forest surround the house on all sides; it was situated in a depression, I had a goodly distance to descend in order to get to it, and this was the reason I had lost sight of the tower; a gardener's cabin nestled against the monastery's walls; it was there one applied before entering. I demanded of this gate-keeper whether it were permitted to speak to the superior; he asked to be informed of my errand; I advised him that a religious duty had drawn me to this holy refuge and that I would be well repaid for all the trouble I had experienced to get to it were I able to kneel an instant before the feet of the miraculous Virgin and the saintly ecclesiastics in whose house the divine image was preserved. The gardener rings and I penetrate into the monastery; but as the hour is advanced and the fathers are at supper, he is some time in returning. At last he reappears with one of the monks:

"Mademoiselle," says he, "here is Dom Clément, steward to the house; he has come to see whether what you desire merits inter-rupting the superior."

Clément, whose name could not conceivably have been less descriptive of his physiognomy, was a man of forty-eight years, of an enormous bulk, of a giant's stature; somber was his expression, fierce his eye; the only words he spoke were harsh, and they were expelled by a raucous voice: here was a satyric personage indeed, a tyrant's exterior; he made me tremble. . . . And then despite all I could do to suppress it, the remembrance of my old miseries rose to smite my troubled memory in traits of blood. . . .

"What do you want?" the monk asked me; his air was surly, his mien grim; "is this the hour to come to a church? . . . Indeed, you have the air of an adventuress."

"Saintly man," said I, prostrating myself, "I believed it was always the hour to present oneself at God's door; I have hastened from far off to arrive here; full of fervor and devotion, I ask to confess, if it is possible, and when what my conscience contains is known to you, you will see whether or not I am worthy to humble myself at the feet of the holy image."

"But this is not the time for confession," said the monk, his manner softening; "where are you going to spend the night? We have no hospice . . . it would have been better to have come in the morning." I gave him the reasons which had prevented me from doing so and, without replying, Clément went to report to the superior. Several minutes later the church was opened, Dom

Sévérino himself approached me, and invited me to enter the temple with him.

Dom Sévérino, of whom it would be best to give you an idea at once, was, as I had been told, a man of fifty-five, but endowed with handsome features, a still youthful quality, a vigorous physique, herculean limbs, and all that without harshness; a certain elegance and pliancy reigned over the whole and suggested that in his young years he must have possessed all the traits which constitute a splendid man. There were in all the world no finer eyes than his; nobility shone in his features, and the most genteel, the most courteous tone was there throughout. An agreeable accent which colored every one of his words enabled one to identify his Italian origin and, I admit it, this monk's outward graces did much to dispel the alarm the other had caused me.

"My dear girl," said he very graciously, "although the hour is unseasonable and though it is not our usage to receive so late, I will however hear your confession, and afterward we will confer upon the means whereby you may pass the night in decency; tomorrow you will be able to bow down before the sacred image which brings you here."

We enter the church; the doors are closed; a lamp is lit near the confessional. Sévérino bids me assume my place, he sits down and requests me to tell him everything with complete confidence.

I was perfectly at ease with a man who seemed so mild-mannered, so full of gentle sympathy. I disguised nothing from him: I confessed all my sins; I related all my miseries; I even uncovered the shameful mark wherewith the barbaric Rodin had branded me. Sévérino listened to everything with keenest attention, he even had me repeat several details, wearing always a look of pity and of interest; but a few movements, a few words betrayed him nevertheless—alas! it was only afterward I pondered them thoroughly. Later, when able to reflect calmly upon this interview, it was impossible not to remember that the monk had several times permitted himself certain gestures which dramatized the emotion that had heavy entrance into many of the questions he put to me, and those inquiries not only halted complacently and lingered lovingly over obscene details, but had borne with noticeable insistence upon the following five points:

1. Whether it were really so that I were an orphan and had been born in Paris. 2. Whether it were a certainty I were bereft of kin and had neither friends, nor protection, nor, in a word, anyone to whom I could write. 3. Whether I had confided to anyone, other than to the shepherdess who had pointed out the monastery to me, my purpose in going there, and whether I had not arranged some rendezvous upon my return. 4. Whether it were certain that I had known no one since my rape, and whether I were fully sure the man who had abused me had done so on the side Nature condemns as well as on the side she permits. 5. Whether I thought I had not been followed and whether anyone, according to my belief, might have observed me enter the monastery.

After I had answered these questions in all modesty, with great sincerity, and most naively:

"Very well," said the monk, rising and taking me by the hand, "come, my child, tomorrow I shall procure you the sweet satisfaction of communing at the feet of the image you have come to visit; let us begin by supplying your primary needs," and he led me toward the depths of the church. . . .

"Why!" said I, sensing a vague inquietude arise in me despite myself, "what is this, Father? Why are we going inside?"

"And where else, my charming pilgrim?" answered the monk, introducing me into the sacristy. "Do you really fear to spend the night with four saintly anchorites? Oh, we shall find the means to succor you, my dearest angel, and if we do not procure you very great pleasures, you will at least serve ours in their most extreme amplitude." These words sent a thrill of horror through me; I burst out in a cold sweat, I fell to shivering; it was night, no light guided our footsteps, my terrified imagination raised up the specter of death brandishing its scythe over my head; my knees were buckling . . . and at this point a sudden shift occurred in the monk's speech. He jerked me upright and hissed:

"Whore, pick up your feet and get along; no complaints, don't try resistance, not here, it would be useless."

These cruel words restore my strength, I sense that if I falter I am doomed, I straighten myself. "O Heaven!" I say to the traitor, "must I then be once again my good sentiments' victim, must the desire to approach what is most respectable in Religion be once again punished as a crime! . . ."

We continue to walk, we enter obscure byways, I know not where I am, where I am going. I was advancing a pace ahead of Dom Sévérino; his breathing was labored, words flowed incoherently from his lips, one might have thought he was drunk; now and again he stopped me, twined his left arm about my waist while his right hand, sliding beneath my skirts from the rear, wandered impudently over that unseemly part of ourselves which, likening us to men, is the unique object of the homages of those who prefer that sex for their shameful pleasures. Several times the libertine even dared apply his mouth to these areas' most secluded lair; and then we recommenced our march. A stairway appears before us; we climb thirty steps or forty, a door opens, brightness dazzles my eyes, we emerge into a charmingly appointed, magnificently illuminated room; there, I see three monks and four girls grouped around a table served by four other women, completely naked. At the spectacle I recoil, trembling; Sévérino shoves me forward over the threshold and I am in the room with him.

"Gentlemen," says he as we enter, "allow me to present you with one of the veritable wonders of the world, a Lucretia who simultaneously carries upon her shoulder the mark stigmatizing girls who are of evil repute, and, in her conscience, all the candor, all the naïveté of a virgin. . . . One lone violation, friends, and that six years ago; hence, practically a vestal . . . indeed, I do give her to you as such . . . the most beautiful, moreover . . . Oh Clément! how that cheerless countenance of yours will light up when you fall to work on those handsome masses . . . what elasticity, my good fellow! what rosiness!"

"Ah, fuck!" cried the half-intoxicated Clément, getting to his feet and lurching toward me: "we are pleasantly met, and let us verify the facts."

I will leave you for the briefest possible time in suspense about my situation, Madame, said Thérèse, but the necessity to portray these other persons in whose midst I discovered myself obliges me to interrupt the thread of my story. You have been made acquainted with Dom Sévérino, you suspect what may be his predilections;

alas! in these affairs his depravation was such he had never tasted other pleasures—and what an inconsistency in Nature's operations was here! for with the bizarre fantasy of choosing none but the straiter path, this monster was outfitted with faculties so gigantic that even the broadest thoroughfares would still have appeared too narrow for him.

As for Clément, he has been drawn for you already. To the superficies I have delineated, join ferocity, a disposition to sarcasm, the most dangerous roguishness, intemperance in every point, a mordant, satirical mind, a corrupt heart, the cruel tastes Rodin displayed with his young charges, no feelings, no delicacy, no religion, the temperament of one who for five years had not been in a state to procure himself other joys than those for which savagery gave him an appetite—and you have there the most complete characterization of this horrid man.

Antonin, the third protagonist in these detestable orgies, was forty; small, slight of frame but very vigorous, as formidably organized as Sévérino and almost as wicked as Clément; an enthusiast of that colleague's pleasures, but giving himself over to them with a somewhat less malignant intention; for while Clément, when exercising this curious mania, had no objective but to vex, to tyrannize a woman, and could not enjoy her in any other way, Antonin using it with delight in all its natural purity, had recourse to the flagellative aspect only in order to give additional fire and further energy to her whom he was honoring with his favors. In a word, one was brutal by taste, the other by refinement.

Jérôme, the eldest of the four recluses, was also the most debauched; every taste, every passion, every one of the most bestial irregularities were combined in this monk's soul; to the caprices rampant in the others, he joined that of loving to receive what his comrades distributed amongst the girls, and if he gave (which frequently happened), it was always upon condition of being treated likewise in his turn: all the temples of Venus were, what was more, as one to him, but his powers were beginning to decline and for several years he had preferred that which, requiring no effort of the agent, left to the patient the task of arousing the sensations and of producing the ecstasy. The mouth was his favorite temple, the shrine where he liked best to offer, and while he was in the pursuit of those choice pleasures, he would keep a second woman active: she warmed him with the lash. This man's character was quite as cunning, quite as wicked as that of the others; in whatever shape or aspect vice could exhibit itself, certain it was immediately to find a spectator in this infernal household. You will understand it more easily, Madame, if I explain how the society was organized. Prodigious funds had been poured by the Order into this obscene institution, it had been in existence for above a century, and had always been inhabited by the four richest monks, the most powerful in the Order's hierarchy, they of the highest birth and of a libertinage of sufficient moment to require burial in this obscure retreat, the disclosure of whose secret was well provided against as my further explanations will cause you to see in the sequel; but let us return to the portraits.

The eight girls who were present at the supper were so much separated by age I cannot describe them collectively, but only one by one; that they were so unlike with respect to their years astonished me—I will speak first of the youngest and continue in order.

This youngest one of the girls was scarcely ten: pretty but irregular features, a look of humiliation because of her fate, an air of sorrow and trepidation.

The second was fifteen: the same trouble written over her countenance, a quality of modesty degraded, but a bewitching face, of considerable interest all in all.

The third was twenty: pretty as a picture, the loveliest blond hair; fine, regular, gentle features; she appeared less restive, more broken to the saddle.

The fourth was thirty: she was one of the most beautiful women imaginable; candor, quality, decency in her bearing, and all a gentle spirit's virtues.

The fifth was a girl of thirty-six, six months pregnant; darkhaired, very lively, with beautiful eyes, but having, so it seemed to me, lost all remorse, all decency, all restraint.

The sixth was of the same age: a tall creature of grandiose proportions, a true giantess, fair of face but whose figure was already ruined in excess flesh; when I first saw her she was naked, and I was readily able to notice that not one part of her body was unstamped by signs of the brutality of those villains whose pleasures her unlucky star had fated her to serve.

The seventh and eighth were two very lovely women of about forty.

Let us continue with the story of my arrival in this impure place.

I did tell you that no sooner had I entered than each one approached me: Clément was the most brazen, his foul lips were soon glued to my mouth; I twisted away in horror, but I was advised all resistance was pure affectation, pretense, and useless; I should do best by imitating my companions.

"You may without difficulty imagine," declared Dom Séverino, "that a recalcitrant attitude will be to no purpose in this inaccessible retreat. You have, you say, undergone much suffering; but that greatest of all woes a virtuous girl can know is yet missing from the catalogue of your troubles. Is it not high time that lofty pride be humbled? and may one still expect to be nearly a virgin at twenty-two? You see about you companions who, upon entering here, like yourself thought to resist and who, as prudence will bid you to do, ended by submitting when they noticed that stubbornness could lead them to incur penalties; for I might just as well declare to you, Thérèse," the superior continued, showing me scourges, ferules, withes, cords, and a thousand other instruments of torture, "yes, you might just as well know it: there you see what we use upon unmanageable girls; decide whether you wish to be convinced. What do you expect to find here? Mercy? we know it not; humaneness? our sole pleasure is the violation of its laws. Religion? 'tis as naught to us, our contempt for it grows the better acquainted with it we become; allies . . . kin . . . friends . . . judges? there's none of that in this place, dear girl, you will discover nothing but cruelty, egoism, and the most sustained debauchery and impiety. The completest submissiveness is your lot, and that is all; cast a glance about the impenetrable asylum which shelters you: never has an outsider invaded these premises: the monastery could be taken, searched, sacked, and burned, and this retreat would still be perfectly safe from discovery: we are in an isolated outbuilding, as good as buried within the six walls of incredible thickness surrounding us entirely, and here you are, my child, in the midst of four libertines who surely have no inclination to spare you and whom your entreaties, your tears, your speeches, your genuflections, and your outcries will only further inflame. To whom then will you have recourse? to what? Will it be to that God you have just implored with such earnestness and who, by way of reward for your fervor, only precipitates you into further snares, each more fatal than the last? to that illusory God we ourselves outrage all day long by insulting his vain commandments? . . . And so, Thérèse, you conceive that there is no power, of whatever species you may suppose, which could possibly deliver you out of our hands, and there is neither in the category of things real nor in that of miracles, any sort of means which might permit you successfully to retain this virtue you yet glory in; which might, in fine, prevent you from becoming, in every sense and in every manner, the prey of the libidinous excesses to which we, all four of us, are going to abandon ourselves with you. . . . Therefore, little slut, off with your clothes, offer your body to our lusts, let it be soiled by them instantly or the severest treatment will prove to you what risks a wretch like yourself runs by disobeying us."

This harangue . . . this terrible order, I felt, left me no shifts, but would I not have been guilty had I failed to employ the means my heart prompted in me? my situation left me this last resource: I fall at Dom Sévérino's feet, I employ all a despairing soul's eloquence to supplicate him not to take advantage of my state or abuse it; the bitterest tears spring from my eyes and inundate his knees, all I imagine to be of the strongest, all I believe the most pathetic, I try everything with this man. . . . Great God! what was the use? could I have not known that tears merely enhance the object of a libertine's coveting? how was I able to doubt that everything I attempted in my efforts to sway those savages had the unique effect of arousing them. . . . "Take the bitch," said Sévérino in a rage, "seize her, Clément, let her be naked in a minute, and let her learn that it is not in persons like ourselves that compassion stifles Nature." My resistance had animated Clément, he was foaming at the mouth: he took hold of me, his arm shook nervously; interspersing his actions with appalling blasphemies, he had my clothing torn away in a trice.

"A lovely creature," came from the superior, who ran his

fingers over my flanks, "may God blast me if I've ever seen one better made; friends," the monk pursued, "let's put order into our procedures; you know our formula for welcoming newcomers: she might be exposed to the entire ceremony, don't you think? let's omit nothing; and let's have the eight other women stand around us to supply our wants and to excite them."

A circle is formed immediately, I am placed in its center and there, for more than two hours, I am inspected, considered, handled by those four monks, who, one after the other, pronounce either encomiums or criticisms.

You will permit me, Madame, our lovely prisoner said with a blush, to conceal a part of the obscene details of this odious ritual; allow your imagination to figure all that debauch can dictate to villains in such instances; allow it to see them move to and fro between my companions and me, comparing, confronting, contrasting, airing opinions, and indeed it still will not have but a faint idea of what was done in those initial orgies, very mild, to be sure, when matched against all the horrors I was soon to experience.

"Let's to it," says Séverino, whose prodigiously exalted desires will brook no further restraint and who in this dreadful state gives the impression of a tiger about to devour its prey, "let each of us advance to take his favorite pleasure." And placing me upon a couch in the posture expected by his execrable projects and causing me to be held by two of his monks, the infamous man attempts to satisfy himself in that criminal and perverse fashion which makes us to resemble none but the sex we do not possess while degrading the one we have; but either the shameless creature is too strongly proportioned, or Nature revolts in me at the mere suspicion of these pleasures; Séverino cannot overcome the obstacles; he presents himself, and he is repulsed immediately. . . . He spreads, he presses, thrusts, tears, all his efforts are in vain; in his fury the monster lashes out against the altar at which he cannot speak his prayers; he strikes it, he pinches it, he bites it; these brutalities are succeeded by renewed challenges; the chastened flesh yields, the gate cedes, the ram bursts through; terrible screams rise from my throat; the entire mass is swifty engulfed, and darting its venom the next moment, robbed then of its strength, the snake gives ground before the movements I make to expel it, and Sévérino weeps with rage. Never in my life have I suffered so much.

Clément steps forward; he is armed with a cat-o'-nine-tails; his perfidious designs glitter in his eyes.

" 'Tis I," says he to Sévérino, " 'tis I who shall avenge you, Father, I shall correct this silly drab for having resisted your pleasures." He has no need of anyone else to hold me; with one arm he enlaces me and forces me, belly down, across his knees; what is going to serve his caprices is nicely discovered. At first, he tries a few blows, it seems they are merely intended as a prelude; soon inflamed by lust, the beast strikes with all his force; nothing is exempt from his ferocity; everything from the small of my back to the lower part of my thighs, the traitor lays cuts upon it all; daring to mix love with these moments of cruelty, he fastens his mouth to mine and wishes to inhale the sighs agony wrests from me . . . my tears flow, he laps them up, now he kisses, now he threatens, but the rain of blows continues; while he operates, one of the women excites him; kneeling before him, she works with each hand at diverse tasks; the greater her success, the more violent the strokes delivered me; I am nigh to being rent and nothing yet announces the end of my sufferings; he has exhausted every possibility, still he drives on; the end I await is to be the work of his delirium alone; a new cruelty stiffens him: my breasts are at the brute's mercy, he irritates them, uses his teeth upon them, the cannibal snaps, bites, this excess determines the crisis, the incense escapes him. Frightful cries, terrifying blasphemies, shouts characterize its spurtings, and the monk, enervated, turns me over to Jérôme.

"I will be no more of a threat to your virtue than Clément was," said this libertine as he caressed the blood-spattered altar at which Clément had just sacrificed, "but I should indeed like to kiss the furrows where the plow passed; I too am worthy to open them, and should like to pay them my modest respects; but I should like even more," went on the old satyr, inserting a finger where Sévérino had lodged himself, "I should like to have the hen lay, and 'twould be most agreeable to devour its egg . . . does one exist? Why, yes indeed, by God! . . . Oh, my dear, dear little girl! how very soft . . ."

His mouth takes the place of his finger. . . I am told what I have to do, full of disgust I do it. In my situation, alas, am I permitted to refuse? The infamous one is delighted . . . he swallows, then, forcing me to kneel before him, he glues himself to me in this position; his ignominious passion is appeased in a fashion that cannot justify any complaint on my part. While he acts thus, the fat woman flogs him, another puts herself directly above his mouth and acquits herself of the same task I have just been obliged to execute.

" 'Tis not enough," says the monster, "each one of my hands has got to contain . . . for one cannot get one's fill of these goodies." The two prettiest girls approach; they obey: there you have the excesses to which satiety has led Jérôme. At any rate, thanks to impurities he is happy, and at the end of half an hour, my mouth finally receives, with a loathing you must readily appreciate, this evil man's disgusting homage.

Antonin appears. "Well," says he, "let's have a look at this so very spotless virtue; I wonder whether, damaged by a single assault, it is really what the girl maintains." His weapon is raised and trained upon me; he would willingly employ Clément's devices: I have told you that active flagellation pleases him quite as much as it does the other monk but, as he is in a hurry, the state in which his colleague has put me suffices him: he examines this state, relishes it, and leaving me in that attitude of which they are all so fond, he spends an instant pawing the two hemispheres poised at the entrance; in a fury, he rattles the temple's porticos, he is soon at the sanctuary; although quite as violent as Séverino's, Antonin's assault, launched against a less narrow passage, is not as painful to endure; the energetic athlete seizes my haunches and, supplying the movements I am unable to make, he shakes me, pulls me to him vivaciously; one might judge by this Hercules' redoubling efforts that, not content to be master of the place, he wishes to reduce it to a shambles. Such terrible attacks, so new to me, cause me to succumb; but unconcerned for my pain, the cruel victor thinks of nothing but increasing his pleasure; everything embraces, everything conspires to his voluptuousness; facing him, raised upon my flanks, the fifteen year-old girl, her legs spread open, offers his mouth the altar at which he sacrifices in me: leisurely, he pumps that precious natural juice whose emission Nature has only lately granted the young child; on her knees, one of the older women bends toward my vanquisher's loins, busies herself about them and with her impure tongue animating his desires, she procures them their ecstasy while, to inflame himself yet further, the debauchee excites a woman with either hand; there is not one of his senses which is not tickled, not one which does not concur in the perfection of my delirium; he attains it, but my unwavering horror for all these infamies inhibits me from sharing it. . . . He arrives there alone; his jets, his cries, everything proclaims it and, despite myself, I am flooded with the proofs of a fire I am but one of six to light; and thereupon I fall back upon the throne which has just been the scene of my immolation, no longer conscious of my existence save through my pain and my tears . . . my despair and my remorse.

However, Dom Séverino orders the women to bring me food; but far from being quickened by these attentions, an access of furious grief assails my soul. I, who located all my glory, all my felicity in my virtue, I who thought that, provided I remained well-behaved at all times, I could be consoled for all fortune's ills, I cannot bear the horrible idea of seeing myself so cruelly sullied by those from whom I should have been able to expect the greatest comfort and aid: my tears flowed in abundance, my cries made the vault ring; I rolled upon the floor, I lacerated my breast, tore my hair, invoked my butchers, begged them to bestow death upon me . . . and, Madame, would you believe it? this terrible sight excited them all the more.

"Ah!" said Séverino, "I've never enjoyed a finer spectacle: behold, good friends, see the state it puts me in; it is really unbelievable, what feminine anguish obtains from me."

"Let's go back to work," quoth Clément, "and in order to teach her to bellow at fate, let the bitch be more sharply handled in this second assault."

The project is no sooner conceived than put into execution; up steps Séverino, but his speeches notwithstanding, his desires require a further degree of irritation and it is only after having used Clément's cruel measures that he succeeds in marshaling the forces necessary to accomplish his newest crime. Great God! What excess of ferocity! Could it be that those monsters would carry it to the point of selecting the instant of a crisis of moral agony as violent as that I was undergoing, in order to submit me to so barbarous a physical one! " 'Twould be an injustice to this novice," said Clément, "were we not to employ in its major form what served us so well in its merely episodic dimension," and thereupon he began to act, adding: "My word upon it, I will treat her no better than did you." "One instant," said Antonin to the superior whom he saw about to lay hands upon me again; "while your zeal is exhaled into this pretty maiden's posterior parts, I might, it seems to me, make an offering to the contrary God; we will have her between us two."

The position was so arranged I could still provide Jérôme with a mouth; Clément fitted himself between my hands, I was constrained to arouse him; all the priestesses surrounded this frightful group; each lent an actor what she knew was apt to stir him most profoundly; however, it was I supported them all, the entire weight bore down upon me alone; Sévérino gives the signal, the other three follow close after him and there I am a second time infamously defiled by the proofs of those blackguards' disgusting luxury.

"Well," cries the superior, "that should be adequate for the first day; we must now have her remark that her comrades are no better treated than she." I am placed upon an elevated armchair and from there I am compelled to witness those other horrors which are to terminate the orgies.

The monks stand in queue; all the sisters file before them and receive whiplashes from each; next, they are obliged to excite their torturers with their mouths while the latter torment and shower invectives upon them.

The youngest, she of ten, is placed upon a divan and each monk steps forward to expose her to the torture of his choice; near her is the girl of fifteen; it is with her each monk, after having meted out punishment, takes his pleasure; she is the butt; the eldest woman is obliged to stay in close attendance upon the monk presently performing, in order to be of service to him either in this operation or in the act which concludes it. Sévérino uses only his hands to molest what is offered him and speeds to engulf himself in the sanctuary of his whole delight and which she whom they have posted nearby presents to him; armed with a handful of nettles, the eldest woman retaliates upon him for what he has a moment ago done to the child; 'tis in the depths of painful titillations the libertine's transports are born. . . . Consult him; will he confess to cruelty? But he has done nothing he does not endure in his turn.

Clément lightly pinches the little girl's flesh; the enjoyment offered within is beyond his capabilities, but he is treated as he has dealt with the girl, and at the feet of the idol he leaves the incense he lacks the strength to fling into its sanctuary.

Antonin entertains himself by kneading the fleshier parts of the victim's body; fired by her convulsive struggling, he precipitates himself into the district offered to his chosen pleasures. In his turn he is mauled, beaten, and ecstasy is the fruit of his torments.

Old Jérôme employs his teeth only, but each bite leaves a wound whence blood leaps instantly forth; after receiving a dozen, the target tenders him her open mouth; therein his fury is appeased while he is himself bitten quite as severely as he did bite.

The saintly fathers drink and recover their strength.

The thirty-six-year-old woman, six months pregnant, as I have told you, is perched upon a pedestal eight feet high; unable to pose but one leg, she is obliged to keep the other in the air; round about her, on the floor, are mattresses garnished three feet deep with thorns, splines, holly; a flexible rod is given to her that she may keep herself erect; it is easy to see, on the one hand, that it is to her interest not to tumble, and on the other, that she cannot possibly retain her balance; the alternatives divert the monks; all four of them cluster around her, during the spectacle each has one or two women to excite him in divers manners; great with child as she is, the luckless creature remains in this attitude for nearly a quarter of an hour; at last, strength deserts her, she falls upon the thorns, and our villains, wild with lust, one last time step forward to lavish upon her body their ferocity's abominable homage . . . the company retires.

The superior put me into the keeping of the thirty-year-old girl of whom I made mention; her name was Omphale; she was charged to instruct me, to settle me in my new domicile. But that night I neither saw nor heard anything. Annihilated, desperate, I thought of nothing but to capture a little rest. In the room where I had been installed I noticed other women who had not been at the supper; I postponed consideration of these new objects until the following day, and occupied myself with naught else but repose. Omphale left me to myself; she went to put herself to bed; scarcely had I stepped into mine when the full horror of my circumstances presented itself to me in yet more lively colors: I could not dispel the thought of the execrations I had suffered, nor of those to which I had been a witness. Alas! if at certain times those pleasures had occurred to my wandering imagination, I had thought them chaste, as is the God Who inspires them, given by Nature in order to comfort human beings; I had fancied them the product of love and delicacy. I had been very far from believing that man, after the example of savage beasts, could only relish them by causing his companion to shudder . . . then, returning to my own black fate . . . "O Just Heaven," I said to myself, "it is then absolutely certain that no virtuous act will emanate from my heart without being answered at once by an agonizing echo! And of what evil was I guilty, Great God! in desiring to come to accomplish some religious duties in this monastery? Do I offend Heaven by wanting to pray? Incomprehensible decrees of Providence, deign," I continued, "deign to open wide my eyes, cause me to see if you do not wish me to rebel against you!" Bitterest tears followed these musings, and I was still inundated with them when daylight appeared; then Omphale approached my bed.

"Dear companion," she said, "I come to exhort you to be courageous; I too wept during my first days, but now the thing has become a habit; as have I, you will become accustomed to it all; the beginnings are terrible: it is not simply the necessity to sate these debauchees' hungers which is our life's torture, it is the loss of our freedom, it is the cruel manner in which we are handled in this terrible house."

The wretched take comfort in seeing other sufferers about them. However trenchant were my anguishes, they were assuaged for an instant; I begged my companion to inform me of the ills I had to expect.

"In a moment," my instructress said, "but first get up and let me show you about our retreat, observe your new companions; then we'll hold our conversation."

Following Omphale's suggestion, I began by examining the

chamber we were in. It was an exceedingly large chamber, containing eight little beds covered with clean calico spreads; by each bed
was a partitioned dressing room; but all the windows which lit both
these closets and the room itself were raised five feet above the
floor and barred inside and out. In the middle of the room was a large
table, secured to the floor, and it was intended for eating or work;
three doors bound and braced with iron closed the room; on our side
no fittings or keyholes were to be seen; on the other, enormous bolts.

"And this is our prison?"

"Alas! yes, my dear," Omphale replied; "such is our unique
dwelling place; not far from here, the eight other girls have a
similar room, and we never communicate with each other save
when the monks are pleased to assemble us all at one time."

I peered into the alcove destined for me; it was eight feet
square, daylight entered it, as in the great room, by a very high
window fitted all over with iron. The only furniture was a bidet, a
lavatory basin and a *chaise percée.* I re-emerged; my companions,
eager to see me, gathered round in a circle: they were seven, I made
the eighth. Omphale, inhabiting the other room, was only in this to
indoctrinate me; were I to wish it, she would remain with me, and
one of the others would take her place in her own chamber; I asked
to have the arrangement made. But before coming to Omphale's
story, it seems to me essential to describe the seven new companions
fate had given me; I will proceed according to age, as I did with
the others.

The youngest was twelve years old: a very animated, very
spirited physiognomy, the loveliest hair, the prettiest mouth.

The second was sixteen: she was one of the most beautiful
blondes imaginable, with truly delicious features and all the grace,
all the sweetness of her age, mingled with a certain interesting quality, the product of her sadness, which rendered her yet a thousand
times more beautiful.

The third was twenty-three; very pretty, but an excessive effrontery, too much impudence degraded, so I thought, the charms
Nature had endowed her with.

The fourth was twenty-six: she had the figure of Venus; but
perhaps her forms were rather too pronounced; a dazzling fair

skin; a sweet, open, laughing countenance, beautiful eyes, a mouth a trifle large but admirably furnished, and superb blond hair.

The fifth was thirty-two; she was four months pregnant; with an oval, somewhat melancholic face, large soulful eyes; she was very pale, her health was delicate, she had a harmonious voice but the rest seemed somehow spoiled. She was naturally libertine: she was, I was told, exhausting herself.

The sixth was thirty-three; a tall strapping woman, the loveliest face in the world, the loveliest flesh.

The seventh was thirty-eight; a true model of figure and beauty: she was the superintendent of my room; Omphale forewarned me of her malicious temper and, principally, of her taste for women.

"To yield is the best way of pleasing her," my companion told me; "resist her, and you will bring down upon your head every misfortune that can befall you in this house. Bear it in mind."

Omphale asked permission of Ursule, which was the superintendent's name, to instruct me; Ursule consented upon condition I kiss her. I approached: her impure tongue sought to attach itself to mine, and meanwhile her fingers labored to determine sensations she was far indeed from obtaining. However, I had to lend myself to everything, my own feelings notwithstanding, and when she believed she had triumphed, she sent me back to my closet where Omphale spoke to me in the following manner:

"All the women you saw yesterday, my dear Thérèse, and those you have just seen, are divided into four classes, each containing four girls; the first is called the children's class: it includes girls ranging from the most tender age to those of sixteen; a white costume distinguishes them.

"The second class, whose color is green, is called the youthful class; it contains girls of from sixteen to twenty-one.

"The third is the class of the age of reason; its vestments are blue; its ages are from twenty-one to thirty, and both you and I belong to it.

"The fourth class, dressed in reddish brown, is intended for those of mature years; it is composed of anyone over thirty.

"These girls are either indiscriminately mingled at the Reverend Fathers' suppers, or they appear there by class: it all depends upon the whims of the monks but, when not at the meals, they are mixed in the two dormitories, as you are able to judge by those who are lodged in ours.

"The instruction I have to give you," said Omphale, "divides under the headings of four primary articles; in the first, we will treat of what pertains to the house; in the second we will place what regards the behavior of the girls, their punishment, their feeding habits, etc., etc., etc.; the third article will inform you of the arrangement of these monks' pleasures, of the manner in which the girls serve them; the fourth will contain observations on personnel changes.

"I will not, Thérèse, describe the environs of this frightful house, for you are as familiar with them as I; I will only discuss the interior; they have shown it all to me so that I can give a picture of it to newcomers, whose education is one of my chores, and in whom, by means of this account, I am expected to dash all hope of escape. Yesterday Séverino explained some of its features and he did not deceive you, my dear. The church and the pavilion form what is properly called the monastery; but you do not know where the building we inhabit is situated and how one gets here; 'tis thus: in the depths of the sacristy, behind the altar, is a door hidden in the wainscoting and opened by a spring; this door is the entrance to a narrow passage, quite as dark as it is long, whose windings your terror, upon entering, prevented you from noticing; the tunnel descends at first, because it must pass beneath a moat thirty feet deep, then it mounts after the moat and, leveling out, continues at a depth of no more than six feet beneath the surface; thus it arrives at the basements of our pavilion having traversed the quarter of a league from the church; six thick enclosures rise to baffle all attempts to see this building from the outside, even were one to climb into the church's tower; the reason for this invisibility is simple: the pavilion hugs the ground, its height does not attain twenty-five feet, and the compounded enclosures, some stone walls, others living palisades formed by trees growing in strait proximity to each other, are, all of them, at least fifty feet high: from whatever direction the place is observed it can only be taken for a dense clump of trees in the forest, never for a habitation; it is, hence, as I have said, by means of a trap door opening into the cellars one emerges from the obscure corridor of which I gave you some idea and of which you cannot possibly have any recollection in view of the state you must have been while walking through it. This pavilion, my dear, has, in all, nothing but basements, a ground floor, an entresol, and a first floor; above it there is a very thick roof covered with a large tray, lined with lead, filled with earth, and in which are planted evergreen shrubberies which, blending with the screens surrounding us, give to everything a yet more realistic look of solidity; the basements form a large hall in the middle, around it are distributed eight smaller rooms of which two serve as dungeons for girls who have merited incarceration, and the other six are reserved for provisions; above are located the dining room, the kitchens, pantries, and two cabinets the monks enter when they wish to isolate their pleasures and taste them with us out of their colleagues' sight; the intervening story is composed of eight chambers, whereof four have each a closet: these are the cells where the monks sleep and introduce us when their lubricity destines us to share their beds; the four other rooms are those of the serving friars, one of whom is our jailer, another the monks' valet, a third the doctor, who has in his cell all he needs for emergencies, and the fourth is the cook; these four friars are deaf and dumb; it would be difficult to expect, as you observe, any comfort or aid from them; furthermore, they never pass time in our company and it is forbidden to accost or attempt to communicate with them. Above the entresol are two seraglios; they are identical; as you see, each is a large chamber edged by eight cubicles; thus, you understand, dear girl, that, supposing one were to break through the bars in the casement and descend by the window, one would still be far from being able to escape, since there would remain five palisades, a stout wall, and a broad moat to get past: and were one even to overcome these obstacles, where would one be? In the monastery's courtyard which, itself securely shut, would not afford, at the first moment, a very safe egress. A perhaps less perilous means of escape would be, I admit, to find, somewhere in our basements, the opening to the tunnel that leads out; but how are we to explore these underground cellars, perpetually locked up as we are? were one even to be able to get down there, this opening would still not be found, for it enters the building in some hidden corner unknown to us and itself barricaded by grills to which they alone have the key. However, were all these difficulties vanquished, were one in the corridor, the route would still not be any the more certain for us, for it is strewn with traps with which only they are familiar and into which anyone who sought to traverse the passageways would inevitably fall without the guidance of the monks. And so you must renounce all thought of escape, for it is out of the question, Thérèse; believe me, were it thinkable, I should long have fled this detestable place, but that cannot be. They who come here never leave save upon their death; and thence is born this impudence, this cruelty, this tyranny these villains use with us; nothing inflames them, nothing stimulates their imagination like the impunity guaranteed them by this impregnable retreat; certain never to have other witnesses to their excesses than the very victims they feast upon, sure indeed their perversities will never be revealed, they carry them to the most abhorrent extremes; delivered of the law's restraints, having burst the checks Religion imposes, unconscious of those of remorse, there is no atrocity in which they do not indulge themselves, and by this criminal apathy their abominable passions are so much more agreeably pricked that nothing, they say, incenses them like solitude and silence, like helplessness on one hand and impunity on the other. The monks regularly sleep every night in this pavilion, they return here at five in the afternoon and go to the monastery the following morning at nine, except for one of the four, chosen daily, who spends the day here: he is known as the Officer of the Day. We will soon see what his duties are. As for the four subaltern friars, they never budge from here; in each chamber we have a bell which communicates with the jailer's cell; the superintendent alone has the right to ring for him but, when she does so in time of her need or ours, everyone comes running instantly; when they return each day, the fathers themselves bring the necessary victuals and give them to the cook, who prepares our meals in accordance with their instructions; there is an artesian well in the basements, abundant wines of every variety in the cellars. We pass on to the second article which relates to the girls' manners, bearing, nourishment, punishment, etc.

"Our number is always maintained constant; affairs are so managed that we are always sixteen, eight in either chamber, and, as you observe, always in the uniform of our particular class; before the day is over you will be given the habit appropriate to the one you are entering; during the day we wear a light costume of the color which belongs to us; in the evening, we wear gowns of the same color and dress our hair with all possible elegance. The superintendent of the chamber has complete authority over us, disobedience to her is a crime; her duty is to inspect us before we go to the orgies and if things are not in the desired state she is punished as well as we. The errors we may commit are of several kinds. Each has its particular punishment, and the rules, together with the list of what is to be expected when they are broken, are displayed in each chamber; the Officer of the Day, the person who comes, as I explained a moment ago, to give us orders, to designate the girls for the supper, to visit our living quarters, and to hear the superintendents' complaints, this monk, I say, is the one who, each evening, metes out punishment to whoever has merited it: here are the crimes together with the punishments exacted for them.

"Failure to rise in the morning at the prescribed hour, thirty strokes with the whip (for it is almost always with whipping we are punished; it were perfectly to be expected that an episode in these libertines' pleasures would have become their preferred mode of correction). The presentation during the pleasurable act, either through misunderstanding or for whatsoever may be the reason, of one part of the body instead of some other which was desired, fifty strokes; improper dress or an unsuitable coiffure, twenty strokes; failure to have given prior notice of incapacitation due to menstruation, sixty strokes; upon the day the surgeon confirms the existence of a pregnancy, one hundred strokes are administered; negligence, incompetence, or refusal in connection with luxurious proposals, two hundred strokes. And how often their infernal wickedness finds us wanting on that head, without our having made the least mistake! How frequently it happens that one of them will suddenly demand what he very well knows we have just accorded another and cannot immediately do again! One undergoes the punishment nonetheless; our remonstrances, our pleadings are never heeded; one must either comply or suffer the consequences. Imperfect behavior in the chamber, or disobedience shown the superintendent, sixty strokes; the appearance of tears, chagrin, sorrow, remorse, even the look of the slightest return to Religion, two hundred strokes. If a monk selects you as his partner when he wishes to taste the last crisis of pleasure and if he is unable to achieve it, whether the fault be his, which is most common, or whether it be yours, upon the spot, three hundred strokes; the least hint of revulsion at the monks' propositions, of whatever nature these propositions may be, two hundred strokes; an attempted or concerted escape or revolt, nine days' confinement in a dungeon, entirely naked, and three hundred lashes each day; caballing, the instigation of plots, the sowing of unrest, etc., immediately upon discovery, three hundred strokes; projected suicide, refusal to eat the stipulated food or the proper quantity, two hundred strokes; disrespect shown toward the monks, one hundred eighty strokes. Those only are crimes; beyond what is mentioned there, we can do whatever we please, sleep together, quarrel, fight, carry drunkenness, riot and gourmandizing to their furthest extremes, swear, blaspheme: none of that makes the faintest difference, we may commit those faults and never a word will be said to us; we are rated for none but those I have just mentioned. But if they wish, the superintendents can spare us many of these unpleasantnesses; however, this protection, unfortunately, can be purchased only by complacencies frequently more disagreeable than the sufferings for which they are substitutes; these women, in both chambers, have the same taste, and it is only by according them one's favors that one enters into their good graces. Spurn one of them, and she needs no additional motive to exaggerate her report of your misdeeds, the monks the superintendents serve double their powers, and far from reprimanding them for their injustice, unceasingly encourage it in them; they are themselves bound by all those regulations and are the more severely chastised if they are suspected of leniency: not that the libertines need all that in order to vent their fury upon us, but they welcome excuses; the look of legitimacy that may be given to a piece of viciousness renders it more agreeable in their eyes, adds to its piquancy, its charm. Upon arriving here each of us is provided with a little store of linen; we are given everything by the half-dozen, and our supplies are renewed every year, but we are obliged to surrender what we bring here with us; we are not permitted to keep the least thing. The complaints of the four friars I spoke of are heard just as are the superintendents'; their mere delation is sufficient to procure our punishment; but they at least ask nothing from us and there is less to be feared from that quarter than from the superintendents who, when vengeance informs their maneuvers, are very demanding and very dangerous. Our food is excellent and always copious; were it not that their lust derives benefits thence, this article might not be so satisfactory, but as their filthy debauches profit thereby, they spare themselves no pains to stuff us with food: those who have a bent for flogging seek to fatten us, and those, as Jérôme phrased it yesterday, who like to see the hen lay, are assured by means of abundant feeding, of a greater yield of eggs. Consequently, we eat four times a day; at breakfast, between nine and ten o'clock we are regularly given *volaille au riz,* fresh fruit or compotes, tea, coffee, or chocolate; at one o'clock, dinner is served; each table of eight is served alike; a very good soup, four entrées, a roast of some kind, four second courses, dessert in every season. At five-thirty an afternoon lunch of pastries and fruit arrives. There can be no doubt of the evening meal's excellence if it is taken with the monks; when we do not join them at table, as often happens, since but four of us from each chamber are allowed to go, we are given three roast plates and four entremets; each of us has a daily ration of one bottle of white wine, one of red, and an half-bottle of brandy; they who do not drink that much are at liberty to distribute their quota to the others; among us are some great gourmands who drink astonishing amounts, who get regularly drunk, all of which they do without fear of reprimand; and there are, as well, some for whom these four meals still do not suffice; they have but to ring, and what they ask for will be brought them at once.

"The superintendents require that the food be consumed, and if someone persists in not wishing to eat, for whatever reason, upon the third infraction that person will be severely punished; the monks' supper is composed of three roast dishes, six entrées followed by a cold plate and eight entremets, fruit, three kinds of wine, coffee and liqueurs: sometimes all eight of us are at table with them, sometimes they oblige four of us to wait upon them, and these four dine afterward; it also happens from time to time that they take only four girls for supper; they are, ordinarily, an entire class; when our number is eight, there are always two from each class. I need hardly tell you that no one ever visits us; under no circumstances is any outsider ever admitted into this pavilion. If we fall ill, we are entrusted to the surgeon friar only, and if we die, we leave this world without any religious ministrations; our bodies are flung into one of the spaces between the circumvallations, and that's an end to it; but, and the cruelty is signal, if the sick one's condition becomes too grave or if there is fear of contagion, they do not wait until we are dead to dispose of us; though still alive, we are carried out and dropped in the place I mentioned. During the eighteen years I have been here I have seen more than ten instances of this unexampled ferocity; concerning which they declare it is better to lose one than endanger sixteen; the loss of a girl, they continue, is of very modest import, and it may be so easily repaired there is scant cause to regret it. Let us move on to the arrangements concerning the monks' pleasures and to all of what pertains to the subject.

"We rise at exactly nine every morning, and in every season; we retire at a later or an earlier hour, depending upon the monks' supper. Immediately we are up, the Officer of the Day comes on his rounds; he seats himself in a large armchair and each of us is obliged to advance, stand before him with our skirts raised upon the side he prefers; he touches, he kisses, he examines, and when everyone has carried out this duty, he identifies those who are to participate at the evening's exercises: he prescribes the state in which they must be, he listens to the superintendent's report, and the punishments are imposed. Rarely does the officer leave without a luxurious scene in which all eight usually find roles. The superintendent directs these libidinous activities, and the most entire submission on our part reigns during them. Before breakfast it often occurs that one of the Reverend Fathers has one of us called from bed; the jailer friar brings a card bearing the name of the person desired, the Officer of the Day sees to it she is sent, not even he has the right to withhold her, she leaves and returns when dismissed. This first ceremony concluded, we breakfast; from this moment till evening we have no more to do; but at seven o'clock in summer, at six in winter, they come for those who have been designated; the jailer friar himself escorts them, and after the supper they who have not been retained for the night come back to the seraglio. Often, all return; other girls have been selected for the night, and they are advised several hours in advance in what costume they must make their appearance; sometimes only the Girls of the Watch sleep out of the chamber."

"Girls of the Watch?" I interrupted. "What function this?"

"I will tell you," my historian replied.

"Upon the first day of every month each monk adopts a girl who must serve a term as his servant and as the target of his shameful desires; only the superintendents are exempted, for they have the task of governing their chambers. The monks can neither exchange girls during the month, nor make them serve two months in succession; there is nothing more cruel, more taxing than this drudgery, and I have no idea how you will bear up under it. When five o'clock strikes, the Girl of the Watch promptly descends to the monk she serves and does not leave his side until the next day, at the hour he sets off for the monastery. She rejoins him when he comes back; she employs these few hours to eat and rest, for she must remain awake all night throughout the whole of the term she spends with her master; I repeat to you, the wretch remains constantly on hand to serve as the object of every caprice which may enter the libertine's head; cuffs, slaps, beatings, whippings, hard language, amusements, she has got to endure all of it; she must remain standing all night long in her patron's bedroom, at any instant ready to offer herself to the passions which may stir that tyrant; but the cruelest, the most ignominious aspect of this servitude is the terrible obligation she is under to provide her mouth or her breast for the relief of the one and the other of the monster's needs: he never uses any other vase: she has got to be the willing recipient of everything and the least hesitation or recalcitrance is straightway punished by the most savage reprisals. During all the scenes of lust these are the girls who guarantee pleasure's success, who guide and manage the monks' joys, who tidy up whoever has become covered with filth: for example, a monk dirties himself while enjoying a woman: it is his aide's duty to repair the disorder; he wishes to be excited? the task of rousing him falls to the wretch who accompanies him everywhere, dresses him, undresses him, is ever at his elbow, who is always wrong, always at fault, always beaten; at the suppers her place is behind her master's chair or, like a dog, at his feet under the table, or upon her knees, between his thighs, exciting him with her mouth; sometimes she serves as his cushion, his seat, his torch; at other times all four of them will be grouped around the table in the most lecherous, but, at the same time, the most fatiguing attitudes.

"If they lose their balance, they risk either falling upon the thorns placed near by, or breaking a limb, or being killed, such cases have been known; and meanwhile the villains make merry, enact debauches, peacefully get drunk upon meats, wines, lust, and upon cruelty."

"O Heaven!" said I to my companion, trembling with horror, "is it possible to be transported to such excesses! What infernal place is this!"

"Listen to me, Thérèse, listen, my child, you have not yet heard it all, not by any means," said Omphale. "Pregnancy, reverenced in the world, is the very certitude of reprobation amongst these villains; here, the pregnant woman is given no dispensations: brutalities, punishments, and watches continue; on the contrary, a gravid condition is the certain way to procure oneself troubles, sufferings, humiliations, sorrows; how often do they not by dint of blows cause abortions in them whose fruits they decide not to harvest, and when indeed they do allow the fruit to ripen, it is in order to sport with it: what I am telling you now should be enough to warn you to preserve yourself from this state as best you possibly can."

"But is one able to?"

"Of course, there are certain devices, sponges. . . But if Antonin perceives what you are up to, beware of his wrath; the safest way is to smother whatever might be the natural impression by striving to unhinge the imagination, which with monsters like these is not difficult.

"We have here as well," my instructress continued, "certain dependencies and alliances of which you probably know very little and of which it were well you had some idea; although this has more to do with the fourth article—with, that is to say, the one that treats of our recruitings, our retrenchments, and our exchanges —I am going to anticipate for a moment in order to insert the following details.

"You are not unaware, Thérèse, that the four monks composing this brotherhood stand at the head of their Order; all belong to distinguished families, all four are themselves very rich: independently of the considerable funds allocated by the Benedictines for the maintenance of this bower of bliss into which everyone hopes to enter in his turn, they who do arrive here contribute a large proportion of their property and possessions to the foundation already established. These two sources combined yield more than a hundred thousand crowns annually which is devoted solely to finding recruits and meeting the house's expenses; they have a dozen discreet and reliable women whose sole task is to bring them every month a new subject, no younger than twelve nor older than thirty. The conscriptee must be free of all defects and endowed with the greatest possible number of qualities, but principally with that of eminent birth. These abductions, well paid for and always effected a great distance from here, bring no consequent discomfitures; I have never heard of any that resulted in legal action; their extreme caution protects them against everything. They do not absolutely confine themselves to virgins: a girl who has been seduced already or a married woman may prove equally pleasing, but a forcible abduction has got to take place, rape must be involved, and it must be definitely verified; this circumstance arouses them; they wish to be certain their crimes cost tears; they would send away any girl who was to come here voluntarily; had you not made a prodigious defense, had they not recognized a veritable fund of virtue in you, and, consequently, the possibility of crime, they would not have kept you twenty-four hours. Everyone here, Thérèse, comes of a distinguished line; my dear friend, you see before you the only daughter of the Comte de * * *, carried off from Paris at the age of twelve and destined one day to have a dowry of a hundred thousand crowns: I was ravished from the arms of my governess who was taking me by carriage, unoccupied save for ourselves, from my father's country seat to the Abbey of Panthemont where I was brought up; my guardian disappeared; she was in all likelihood bought; I was fetched hither by post chaise. The same applies to all the others. The girl of twenty belongs to one of the noblest families of Poitou. The one sixteen years old is the daughter of the Baron de * * *, one of the greatest of the Lorraine squires;

Counts, Dukes, and Margraves are the fathers of the girls of
twenty-three, twelve, and thirty-two; in a word, there is not one
who cannot claim the loftiest titles, not one who is not treated with
the greatest ignominy. But these depraved men are not content
to stop at these horrors; they have wished to bring dishonor into
the very bosom of their own family. The young lady of twenty-six,
without doubt one of the most beautiful amongst us, is Clément's
daughter; she of thirty-six is the niece of Jérôme.

"As soon as a new girl has arrived in this cloaca, as soon as
she has been sealed in here forever to become a stranger to the
world, another is immediately retrenched: such is our sufferings'
complement; the cruelest of our afflictions is to be in ignorance of
what happens to us during these terrible and disquieting dismissals.
It is absolutely impossible to say what becomes of one upon leaving
this place. From all the evidence we in our isolation are able to
assemble, it seems as if the girls the monks retire from service
never appear again; they themselves warn us, they do not conceal
from us that this retreat is our tomb, but do they assassinate us?
Great Heaven! Would murder, the most execrable of crimes, would
murder be for them what it was for that celebrated Maréchal de
Retz,[4] a species of erotic entertainment whose cruelty, exalting
their perfidious imaginations, were able to plunge their senses into
a more intense drunkenness! Accustomed to extracting joy from
suffering only, to know no delectation save what is derived from
inflicting torment and anguish, would it be possible they were
distracted to the point of believing that by redoubling, by amelio-
rating the delirium's primary cause, one would inevitably render it
more perfect; and that, without principles as without faith, wanting
manners as they are lacking in virtues, the scoundrels, exploiting
the miseries into which their earlier crimes plunged us, were able
to find satisfaction in the later ones which snatch our lives away
from us. . . . I don't know. . . . If one questions them upon the
matter, they mumble unintelligibilities, sometimes responding negatively, sometimes in the affirmative; what is certain is that not one
of those who has left, despite the promises she made us to denounce
these men to the authorities and to strive to procure our liberation

---

[4] See *L'Historie de Bretagne* by Dom Lobineau. (*Maréchal de Retz:* Gilles de Rai,
marshal of Charles VII's army.—*Tr.*)

not one, I say, has ever kept her word. . . . Once again: do they placate us, dissuade us, or do they eliminate the possibility of our preferring charges? What we ask those who arrive for news of them who have gone, they never have any to communicate. What becomes of these wretches? That is what torments me, Thérèse, that is the fatal incertitude which makes for the great unhappiness of our existence. I have been in this house for eighteen years, I have seen more than two hundred girls depart from it. . . . Where are they? All of them having sworn to help us, why has not one kept her vow?

"Nothing, furthermore, justifies our retirement; age, loss of looks, this is not what counts: caprice is their single rule. They will dismiss today the girl they most caressed yesterday, and for ten years they will keep another of whom they are the most weary: such is the story of this chamber's superintendent; she has been twelve years in the house, and to preserve her I have seen them get rid of fifteen-year-old children whose beauty would have rendered the very Graces jealous. She who left a week ago was not yet sixteen; lovely as Venus herself, they had enjoyed her for less than a year, but she became pregnant and, as I told you Thérèse, that is a great sin in this establishment. Last month they retired one of sixteen, a year ago one of twenty, eight months pregnant; and, recently, another when she began to feel the first pangs of childbirth. Do not imagine that conduct has any bearing upon the matter: I have seen some who flew to do their every bidding and who were gone within six months' time; others sullen, peevish, fantastical whom they kept a great number of years; hence, it is useless to prescribe any kind of behavior to our newly arrived; those monsters' whimsy bursts all circumscriptions, and caprice forms the unique law by which their actions are determined.

"When one is going to be dismissed, one is notified the same morning, never earlier: as usual, the Officer of the Day makes his appearance at nine o'clock and says, let us suppose, 'Omphale, the monastery is sending you into retirement; I will come to take you this evening.' Then he continues about his business. But you do not present yourself for his inspection; he examines the others, then he leaves; the person about to be released embraces her comrades, she makes a thousand promises to strive in their behalf, to bring charges, to bruit abroad what transpires in the monastery: the hour strikes, the monk appears, the girl is led away, and not a word is heard of her. Supper takes place in the usual fashion; we have simply been able to remark that upon these days the monks rarely reach pleasure's ultimate episodes, one might say they proceed gingerly and with unwonted care. However, they drink a great deal more, sometimes even to inebriation; they send us to our chamber at a much earlier hour, they take no one to bed with them, even the Girls of the Watch are relegated to the seraglios."

"Very well," I say to my companion, "if no one has helped you it is because you have had to deal with frail, intimidated creatures, or women with children who dared not attempt anything for you. That they will kill us is not my fear; at least, I don't believe they do: that reasoning beings could carry crime to that point ... it is unthinkable ... I know that full well. ... After what I have seen and undergone I perhaps ought not defend mankind as I do, but, my dear, it is simply inconceivable that they can execute horrors the very idea of which defies the imagination. Oh dear companion!" I pursued with great emotion, "would you like to exchange that promise which for my part I swear I will fulfill! ... Do you wish it?"

"Yes."

"Ah, I swear to you in the name of all I hold most holy, in the name of the God Who makes me to breathe and Whom only I adore ... I vow to you I will either die in the undertaking or destroy these infamies ... will you promise me the same?"

"Do not doubt it," Omphale replied, "but be certain of these promises' futility; others more embittered than you, stauncher, no less resolute and not so scrupulous, in a word, friends who would have shed their last drop of blood for us, have not kept identical vows; and so, dear Thérèse, and so allow my cruel experience to consider ours equally vain and to count upon them no more."

"And the monks," I said, "do they also vary, do new ones often come here?"

"No," answered Omphale, "Antonin has been here ten years, Clément eighteen, Jérôme thirty, Séverino twenty-five. The superior was born in Italy, he is closely allied to the Pope with whom he is in intimate contact; only since his arrival have the so-called miracles of the Virgin assured the monastery's reputation and prevented scandalmongers from observing too closely what takes place here; but when he came the house was already furnished as presently you see it to be; it has subsisted in the same style and upon this footing for above a century, and all the superiors who have governed it have perpetuated a system which so amicably smiles upon their pleasures. Sévérino, the most libertine man of our times, has only installed himself here in order to lead a life consonant with his tastes. He intends to maintain this abbey's secret privileges as long as he possibly can. We belong to the diocese of Auxerre, but whether or not the bishop is informed, we never see him, never does he set foot in the monastery: generally speaking, very few outsiders come here except toward the time of the festival which is that of Notre Dame d'Août; according to the monks, ten persons do not arrive at this house over the period of a twelvemonth; however, it is very likely that when strangers do present themselves, the superior takes care to receive them with hospitality; by appearances of religion and austerity he imposes upon them, they go away content, the monastery is eulogized, and thus these villains' impunity is established upon the people's good faith and the credulity of the devout."

Omphale had scarcely concluded her instruction when nine o'clock tolled; the superintendent called us to come quickly, and the Officer of the Day did indeed enter. 'Twas Antonin; according to custom, we drew ourselves up in a line. He cast a rapid glance upon the group, counted us, and sat down; then, one by one, we went forward and lifted our skirts, on the one side as high as the navel, on the other up to the middle of the back. Antonin greeted the homage with the blasé unconcern of satiety; then, clapping an eye upon me, he asked how I liked this newest of my adventures. Getting no response but tears, "She'll manage," he said with a laugh; "in all of France there's not a single house where girls are finished as nicely as they are in this." From the superintendent's hands he took the list of girls who had misbehaved, then, addressing himself to me again, he caused me to shudder; each gesture, each movement which seemed to oblige me to submit myself to these libertines was for me as a sentence of death. Antonin commanded me to sit on the edge of a bed and when I was in this posture he bade the superintendent uncover my breast and raise my skirt to above my waist; he himself spread my legs as far apart as possible, he seats himself before this prospect, one of my companions comes and takes up the same pose on top of me in such a way that it is the altar of generation instead of my visage which is offered to Antonin; with these charms raised to the level of his mouth he readies himself for pleasure. A third girl, kneeling before him, begins to excite him with her hands, and a fourth, completely naked, with her fingers indicates where he must strike my body. Gradually, this girl begins to arouse me and what she does to me Antonin does as well, with both his hands, to two other girls on his left and right. One cannot imagine the language, the obscene speeches by which that debauchee stimulates himself; at last he is in the state he desires, he is led to me, but everyone follows him, moves with him, endeavors to inflame him yet further while he takes his pleasure; his naked hind parts are exposed, Omphale takes possession of them and neglects nothing in order to irritate him: rubbings, kisses, pollutions, she employs them all; completely afire, Antonin leaps toward me. . . . "I wish to stuff her this time," he says, beside himself. . . . These moral deviations determine the physical. Antonin, who has the habit of uttering terrible cries during the final instants of drunkenness, emits dreadful ones; everyone surrounds, everyone serves him, everyone labors to enrich his ecstasy, and the libertine attains it in the midst of the most bizarre episodes of luxury and depravation.

These groupings were frequent; for when a monk indulged in whatever form of pleasure, all the girls regularly surrounded him in order to fire all his parts' sensations, that voluptuousness might, if one may be forgiven the expression, more surely penetrate into him through every pore.

Antonin left, breakfast was brought in; my companions forced me to eat, I did so to please them. We had not quite finished when the superior entered: seeing us still at table, he dispensed us from ceremonies which were to have been identical with those we had just executed for Antonin. "We must give a thought to dressing her," said he, looking at me; and then he opened a wardrobe and threw upon my bed several garments of the color appropriate to my class, and several bundles of linen as well.

"Try that on," he said, "and give me what belongs to you."

I donned the new clothes and surrendered my old; but, in anticipation of having to give them up, I had, during the night, prudently removed my money from my pockets and had concealed it in my hair. With each article of clothing I took off, Sévérino's ardent stare fell upon the feature newly exposed, and his hands wandered to it at once. At length, when I was half-naked, the monk seized me, put me in the position favorable to his pleasure, that is to say, in the one exactly opposite to the attitude Antonin had made me assume; I wish to ask him to spare me, but spying the fury already kindled in his eyes, I decide the obedient is the safer way; I take my place, the others form a ring around me, Sévérino is able to see nothing but a multitude of those obscene altars in which he delights; his hands converge upon mine, his mouth fastens upon it, his eyes devour it . . . he is at the summit of pleasure.

With your approval, Madame, said the beautiful Thérèse, I shall limit myself to a foreshortened account of the first month I spent in that monastery, that is, I will confine myself to the period's principal anecdotes; the rest would be pure repetition; the monotony of that sojourn would make my recital tedious; immediately afterward, I should, it seems to me, move on to the events which finally produced my emergence from this ghastly sewer.

I did not attend supper that first day; I had simply been elected to pass the night with Dom Clément. In accordance with custom, I was outside his cell some few minutes before he was expected to return to it; the jailer opened the door, then locked it when I had gone in.

Clément arrives as warm with wine as lust, he is followed by the twenty-six year-old girl who, at the time was officiating as his watch; previously informed of what I am to do, I fall to my knees as soon as I hear him coming; he nears me, considers me in my humbled posture, then commands me to rise and kiss him upon the mouth; he savors the kiss for several moments and imparts to it all the expression . . . all the amplitude one could possibly conceive. Meanwhile, Armande, as his thrall was named, undresses me by stages; when the lower part of the loins, with which she had begun, is exposed, she bids me turn around and display to her uncle the area his tastes cherish. Clément examines it, feels it, then, reposing himself in an armchair, orders me to bring it close so that he can kiss it; Armande is upon her knees, rousing him with her mouth,

Clément places his at the sanctuary of the temple I present to him and his tongue strays into the path situate at its center; his hands fasten upon the corresponding altar in Armande but, as the clothing the girl is still wearing impedes him, he commands her to be rid of it, this is soon done, and the docile creature returns to her uncle to take up a position in which, while exciting him with only the hand, she finds herself better within reach of Clément's. The impure monk uninterruptedly occupied with me in like fashion, then tells me to give the largest possible vent to whatever winds may be hovering in my bowels, and these I am to direct into his mouth; this eccentricity struck me as revolting, but I was at the time far from perfect acquaintance with all the irregularities of debauch: I obey and straightway feel the effect of this intemperance. More excited, the monk becomes more impassioned: he suddenly applies bites to six different places upon the fleshy globes I have put at his disposal: I emit a cry and start forward involuntarily, whereat he stands, advances toward me, rage blazing in his eyes, and demands whether I know what I am risking by unsettling him. . . . I make a thousand apologies, he grasps the corset still about my torso, rips it away, and my blouse too, in less time than it takes to tell. . . . Ferociously he seizes my breasts, spouting invectives as he squeezes, wrings, crushes them; Armande undresses him, and there we are, all three of us, naked. Upon Armande his attention comes to bear for a moment: he deals her savage blows with his fists; kisses her mouth, nibbles her tongue and lips, she screams; pain now and again sends the girl into uncontrollable gales of weeping; he has her stand upon a chair and extracts from her just what he desired from me; Armande satisfies him, with one hand I excite him, and, during this luxury, I whip him gently with the other, he also bites Armande, but she holds herself somehow in check, not daring to stir a hair. The monster's tooth-marks are soon printed upon the lovely girl's flesh; they are to be seen in a number of places; brusquely wheeling upon me: "Thérèse," he says, "you are going to suffer cruelly"— he had no need to tell me so, for his eyes declared it but too emphatically. "You are going to be lashed everywhere," he continues, "everywhere, without exception," and as he spoke he again laid hands upon my breasts and mauled them brutally, he bruised their extremities with his fingertips and occasioned me very sharp pain; I dared not say a word for fear of irritating him yet more, but sweat bathed my forehead and, willy-nilly, my eyes filled with tears; he turns me about, makes me kneel on the edge of a chair upon whose back I must keep my hands without removing them for a single instant; he promises to inflict the gravest penalties upon me if I lift them; seeing me ready and well within range, he orders Armande to fetch him some birch rods, she presents him with a handful, slender and long; Clément snatches them, and recommending that I not stir, he opens with a score of stripes upon my shoulders and the small of my back; he leaves me for an instant, returns to Armande, brings her back, she too is made to kneel upon a chair six feet from where I am; he declares he is going to flog us simultaneously and the first of the two to release her grip, utter a cry, or shed a tear will be exposed on the spot to whatever torture he is pleased to inflict: he bestows the same number of strokes upon Armande he has just given me, and positively upon the identical places, he returns to me, kisses everything he has just left off molesting, and raising his sticks, says to me, "Steady, little slut, you are going to be used like the last of the damned." Whereupon I receive fifty strokes, all of them directed between the region bordered by the shoulders and the small of the back. He dashes to my comrade and treats her likewise: we pronounce not a word; nothing may be heard but a few stifled groans, we have enough strength to hold back our tears. There was no indication as to what degree the monk's passions were inflamed; he periodically excited himself briskly, but nothing rose. Returning now to me, he spent a moment eyeing those two fatty globes then still intact but about to undergo torture in their turn; he handled them, he could not prevent himself from prying them apart, tickling them, kissing them another thousand times. "Well," said he, "be courageous . . ." and a hail of blows descended upon these masses, lacerating them to the thighs. Extremely animated by the starts, the leaps, the grinding of teeth, the contortions the pain drew from me, examining them, battening upon them rapturously, he comes and expresses, upon my mouth which he kisses with fervor, the sensations agitating him. . . . "This girl entertains me," he cries, "I have never flogged another with as much pleasure," and he goes back to his niece whom he treats with the same barbarity; there remained the space between the upper thigh and the calves and this he struck with identical vehemence: first the one of us, then the other. "Ha!" he said, now approaching me, "let's change hands and visit this place here"; now wielding a cat-o'-nine-tails he gives me twenty cuts from the middle of my belly to the bottom of my thighs; then wrenching them apart, he slashed at the interior of the lair my position bares to his whip. "There it is," says he, "the bird I am going to pluck": several thongs having, through the precautions he had taken, penetrated very deep, I could not suppress my screams. "Well, well!" said the villain, "I must have found the sensitive area at last; steady there, calm yourself, we'll visit it a little more thoroughly"; however, his niece is put in the same posture and treated in the same manner; once again he reaches the most delicate region of a woman's body; but whether through habit, or courage, or dread of incurring treatment yet worse, she has enough strength to master herself, and about her nothing is visible beyond a few shivers and spasmodic twitchings. However, there was by now a slight change in the libertine's physical aspect, and although things were still lacking in substance, thanks to strokings and shakings a gradual improvement was being registered.

"On your knees," the monk said to me, "I am going to whip your titties."

"My titties, oh my Father!"

"Yes, those two lubricious masses which never excite me but I wish to use them thus," and upon saying this, he squeezed them, he compressed them violently.

"Oh Father! They are so delicate! You will kill me!"

"No matter, my dear, provided I am satisfied," and he applied five or six blows which, happily, I parried with my hands. Upon observing that, he binds them behind my back; nothing remains with which to implore his mercy but my countenance and my tears, for he has harshly ordered me to be silent. I strive to melt him . . . but in vain, he strikes out savagely at my now unprotected bosom; terrible bruises are immediately writ out in black and blue; blood appears as his battering continues, my suffering wrings tears from me, they fall upon the vestiges left by the monster's rage, and render them, says he, yet a thousand times more interesting . . . he kisses those marks, he devours them and now and again returns to my mouth, to my eyes whose tears he licks up with lewd delight. Armande takes her place, her hands are tied, she presents breasts of alabaster and the most beautiful roundness; Clément pretends to kiss them, but to bite them is what he wishes. . . . And then he lays on and that lovely flesh, so white, so plump, is soon nothing more in its butcher's eyes but lacerations and bleeding stripes. "Wait one moment," says the berserk monk, "I want to flog simultaneously the most beautiful of behinds and the softest of breasts." He leaves me on my knees and, bringing Armande toward me, makes her stand facing me with her legs spread, in such a way that my mouth touches her womb and my breasts are exposed between her thighs and below her behind; by this means the monk has what he wants before him: Armande's buttocks and my titties in close proximity: furiously he beats them both, but my companion, in order to spare me blows which are becoming far more dangerous for me than for her, has the goodness to lower herself and thus shield me by receiving upon her own person the lashes that would inevitably have wounded me. Clément detects the trick and separates us: "She'll gain nothing by that," he fumes, "and if today I have the graciousness to spare that part of her, 'twill only be so as to molest some other at least as delicate." As I rose I saw that all those infamies had not been in vain: the debauchee was in the most brilliant state; and it made him only the more furious; he changes weapons—opens a cabinet where several martinets are to be found and draws out one armed with iron tips. I fall to trembling. "There, Thérèse," says he showing me the martinet, "you'll see how delicious it is to be whipped with this . . . you'll feel it, you'll feel it, my rascal, but for the instant I prefer to use this other one . . ." It was composed of small knotted cords, twelve in all; at the end of each was a knot somewhat larger than the others, about the size of a plum pit. "Come there! Up! The cavalcade! . . . the cavalcade!" says he to his niece; she, knowing what is meant, quickly gets down on all fours, her rump raised as high as possible, and tells me to imitate her; I do. Clément leaps upon my back, riding facing my rear; Armande, her own presented to him, finds herself directly ahead of Clément: the villain then discovering us both well within reach, furiously cuts at the charms we offer him; but, as this position obliges us to open as wide as possible that delicate part of ourselves which distinguishes our sex from men's, the barbarian aims stinging blows in this direction: the whip's long and supple strands, penetrating into the interior with much more facility than could withes or ferules, leave deep traces of his rage; now he strikes one, now his blows fly at the other; as skilled a horseman as he is an intrepid flagellator, he several times changes his mount; we are exhausted, and the pangs of pain are of such violence that it is almost impossible to bear them any longer. "Stand up," he tells us, catching up the martinet again, "yes, get up and stand in fear of me"—his eyes glitter, foam flecks his lips—like persons distracted, we run about the room, here, there, he follows after us, indiscriminately striking Armande, myself; the villain brings us to blood; at last he traps us both between the bed and the wall: the blows are redoubled: the unhappy Armande receives one upon the breast which staggers her, this last horror determines his ecstasy, and while my back is flailed by its cruel effects, my loins are flooded by the proofs of a delirium whose results are so dangerous.

"We are going to bed," Clément finally says to me; "that has perhaps been rather too much for you, Thérèse, and certainly not enough for me; one never tires of this mania notwithstanding the fact it is a very pale image of what one should really like to do; ah, dear girl! you have no idea to what lengths this depravity leads us, you cannot imagine the drunkenness into which it plunges us, the violent commotion in the electrical fluid which results from the irritation produced by the suffering of the object that serves our passions; how one is needled by its agonies! The desire to increase them . . . 'tis, I know, the reef upon which the fantasy is doomed to wreck, but is this peril to be dreaded by him who cares not a damn for anything?"

Although Clément's mind was still in the grip of enthusiasm, I observed that his senses were much more calm, and by way of reply to what he had just said, I dared reproach him his tastes' depravation, and the manner in which this libertine justified them merits inclusion, it seems to me, amidst the confessions you wish to have from me.

"Without question the silliest thing in the world, my dear Thérèse," Clément said to me, "is to wish to dispute a man's tastes, to wish to contradict, thwart, discredit, condemn, or punish them if they do not conform either with the laws of the country he inhabits on with the prejudices of social convention. Why indeed! Will it never be understood that there is no variety of taste, however bizarre, however outlandish, however criminal it may be supposed, which does not derive directly from and depend upon the kind of organization we have individually received from Nature? That posed, I ask with what right one man will dare require another either to curb or get rid of his tastes or model them upon those of the social order? With what right will the law itself, which is created for man's happiness only, dare pursue him who cannot mend his ways, or who would succeed in altering his behavior only at the price of forgoing that happiness whose protection the law is obliged to guarantee him? Even were one to desire to change those tastes could one do so? Have we the power to remake ourselves? Can we become other than what we are? Would you demand the same thing from someone born a cripple? and is this inconformity of our tastes anything in the moral sphere but what the ill-made man's imperfection is in the physical?

"Shall we enter into details? Why, very well. The keen mind I recognize in you, Thérèse, will enable you to appreciate them. I believe you have been arrested by two irregularities you have re-marked in us: you are astonished at the piquant sensation experi-enced by some of our friends where it is a question of matters commonly beheld as fetid or impure, and you are similarly surprised that our voluptuous faculties are susceptible of powerful excitation by actions which, in your view, bear none but the emblem of fe-rocity; let us analyze both these tastes and attempt, if 'tis possible, to convince you that there is nothing simpler or more normal in this world than the pleasures which are their result.

"Extraordinary, you declare, that things decayed, noisome, and filthy are able to produce upon our senses the irritation essen-tial to precipitate their complete delirium; but before allowing oneself to be startled by this, it would be better to realize, Thérèse, that objects have no value for us save that which our imagination imparts to them; it is therefore very possible, bearing this constant truth well in mind, that not only the most curious but even the vilest and most appalling things may affect us very appreciably. The human imagination is a faculty of man's mind whereupon, through the senses' agency, objects are painted, whereby they are modified, and wherein, next, ideas become formed, all in reason of the initial glimpsing of those external objects. But this imagination, itself the result of the peculiar organization a particular individual is endowed with, only adopts the received objects in such-and-such a manner and afterward only creates ideas according to the effects produced by perceived objects' impact: let me give you a comparison to help you grasp what I am exposing. Thérèse, have you not seen those differently formed mirrors, some of which diminish objects, others of which enlarge them; some give back frightful images of things, some beautify things; do you now imagine that were each of these types of mirrors to possess both a creative and an objective faculty, they would not each give a completely different portrait of the same man who stands before them, and would not that portrait be different thanks to the manner in which each mirror had perceived the object? If to the two faculties we have just ascribed to the mirror, there were added a third of sensation, would not this man, seen by it in such-and-such a manner, be the source of that one kind of feeling the mirror would be able, indeed would be obliged, to conceive for the sort of being the mirror had perceived? The mirror sees the man as beautiful, the mirror loves the man; another mirror sees the man as frightful and hates him, and it is always the same being who produces various impressions.

"Such is the human imagination, Thérèse; the same object is represented to it under as many forms as that imagination has various facets and moods, and according to the effect upon the imagination received from whatsoever be the object, the imagination is made to love or to hate it; if the perceived object's impact strikes it in an agreeable manner, the object is loved, preferred, even if this object has nothing really attractive about it; and if the object, though of a certain high value in the eyes of someone else, has only struck in a disagreeable manner the imagination we are discussing, hostility will be the result, because not one of our sentiments is formed save in reason of what various objects produce upon the imagination; these fundamentals once grasped, should not by any means be cause for astonishment that what distinctly pleases some is able to displease others, and, conversely, that the most extraordinary thing is able to find admirers. . . . The cripple also discovers certain mirrors which make him handsome.

"Now, if we admit that the senses' joy is always dependent upon the imagination, always regulated by the imagination, one must not be amazed by the numerous variations the imagination is apt to suggest during the pleasurable episode, by the infinite multitude of different tastes and passions the imagination's various extravagances will bring to light. Luxurious though these tastes may be, they are never intrinsically strange; there is no reason to find a mealtime eccentricity more or less extraordinary than a bedroom whim; and in the one and the other, it is not more astonishing to idolize what the common run of mankind holds detestable than it is to love something generally recognized as pleasant. To like what others like proves organic conformity, but demonstrates nothing in favor of the beloved object. Three-quarters of the universe may find the rose's scent delicious without that serving either as evidence upon which to condemn the remaining quarter which might find the smell offensive, or as proof that this odor is truly agreeable.

"If then in this world there exist persons whose tastes conflict with accepted prejudices, not only must one not be surprised by the fact, not only must one not scold these dissenters or punish them, but one must aid them, procure them contentment, remove obstacles which impede them, and afford them, if you wish to be just, all the means to satisfy themselves without risk; because they are no more responsible for having this curious taste than you are responsible for being live-spirited or dull-witted, prettily made or knock-kneed. It is in the mother's womb that there are fashioned the organs which must render us susceptible of such-and-such a fantasy; the first objects which we encounter, the first conversations we overhear determine the pattern; once tastes are formed nothing in the world can destroy them. Do what it will, education is incapable of altering the pattern, and he who has got to be a villain just as surely becomes a villain, the good education you give him notwithstanding; quite as he, however much he has lacked good example, flies unerringly toward virtue if his organs dispose him to the doing of good. Both have acted in accordance with their organic structure, in accordance with the impressions they have received from Nature, and the one is no more deserving of punishment than the other is of reward.

"Curiously enough, so long as it is merely a question of trifles, we are never in the least astonished by the differences existing among tastes; but let the subject take on an erotic tincture, and listen to the word spread about! rumors fly, women, always thoughtful of guarding their rights—women whose feebleness and inconsequence make them especially prone to seeing enemies everywhere about—, women, I say, are all constantly trembling and quivering lest something be snatched away from them and if, when taking one's pleasure, one unfortunately puts practices to use which conflict with woman-worship, lo! there you have crimes which merit the noose. And what an injustice! Must sensual pleasure render a man better than life's other pleasures? In one word, must our penchants be any more concentrated upon the temple of generation, must it necessarily more certainly awaken our desires, than some other part of the body either the most contrary to or at the furthest remove from it? than some emanation of the body either the most fetid or the most disgusting? It should not, in my opinion, appear any more astonishing to see a man introduce singularity into his libertine pleasures than it should appear strange to see him employ the uncommon in any other of life's activities. Once again, in either case, his singularity is the result of his organs: is it his fault if what affects you is naught to him, or if he is only moved by what repels you? What living man would not instantly revise his tastes, his affections, his penchants and bring them into harmony with the general scheme, what man, rather than continue a freak, would not prefer to be like everyone else, were it in his power to do so? It is the most barbarous and most stupid intolerance to wish to fly at such a man's throat; he is no more guilty toward society, regardless of what may be his extravagances, than is, as I have just said, the person who came blind and lame into the world. And it would be quite as unjust to punish or deride the latter as to afflict or berate the other. The man endowed with uncommon tastes is sick; if you prefer, he is like a woman subject to hysterical vapors. Has the idea to punish such a person ever occurred to us? let us be equally fair when dealing with the man whose caprices startle us; perfectly like unto the ill man or the woman suffering from vapors, he is deserving of sympathy and not of blame; that is the moral apology for the persons whom we are discussing; a physical explanation will

without doubt be found as easily, and when the study of anatomy
reaches perfection they will without any trouble be able to demonstrate the relationship of the human constitution to the tastes which
it affects. Ah, you pedants, hangmen, turnkeys, lawmakers, you
havepate rabble, what will you do when we have arrived there?
what is to become of your laws, your ethics, your religion, your
gallows, your Gods and your Heavens and your Hell when it shall
be proven that such a flow of liquids, this variety of fibers, that
degree of pungency in the blood or in the animal spirits are sufficient
to make a man the object of your givings and your takings away?
We continue. Cruel tastes astonish you.

"What is the aim of the man who seeks his joy? is it not to
give his senses all the irritation of which they are susceptible in
order, by this means, better and more warmly to reach the ultimate
crisis . . . the precious crisis which characterizes the enjoyment as
good or bad, depending upon the greater or lesser activity which
occurs during the crisis? Well, is one not guilty of an untenable
sophistry when one dares affirm it is necessary, in order to amel-
iorate it, that it be shared with the woman? Is it not plain enough
that the woman can share nothing with us without taking something
from us? and that all she makes away with must necessarily be had
by her at our expense? And what then is this necessity, I ask, that a
woman enjoy herself when we are enjoying ourselves? in this
arrangement is there any sentiment but pride which may be flattered? and does one not savor this proud feeling in a far more
piquant manner when, on the contrary, one harshly constrains this
woman to abandon her quest for pleasure and to devote herself to
making you alone feel it? Does not tyranny flatter the pride in a
far more lively way than does beneficence? In one word, is not he
who imposes much more surely the master than he who shares?
But how could it ever have entered a reasonable man's head that
delicacy is of any value during enjoyment? 'Tis absurd, to maintain
it is necessary at such a time; it never adds anything to the pleasure
of the senses, why, I contend that it detracts therefrom. To love
and to enjoy are two very different things: the proof whereof is
that one loves every day without enjoying, and that even more often
one enjoys without loving. Anything by way of consideration for
the woman one stirs into the broth has got to dilute its strength

and impair its flavor for the man; so long as the latter spends his time giving enjoyment, he assuredly does not himself do any enjoying, or his enjoyment is merely intellectual, that is to say, chimerical and far inferior to sensual enjoyment. No, Thérèse, no, I will not cease repeating it, there is absolutely no necessity that, in order to be keen, an enjoyment must be shared; and in order that this kind of pleasure may be rendered piquant to the utmost, it is, on the contrary, very essential that the man never take his pleasure save at the expense of the woman, that he take from her (without regard for the sensation she may experience thereby) everything which may in any way improve or increase the voluptuous exercise he wants to relish, and this without the slightest concern for whatever may be the effects of all this upon the woman, for preoccupation of that sort will prove bothersome to him; he either wants the woman to partake of pleasure, and thereupon his joys are at an end; or he fears lest she will suffer, and he is hurled into confusion, all's brought to a stop. If egoism is Nature's fundamental commandment, it is very surely most of all during our lubricious delights that this celestial Mother desires us to be most absolutely under its rule; why, it's a very small evil, is it not, that, in the interests of the augmentation of the man's lecherous delights he has got either to neglect or upset the woman's; for if this upsetting of her pleasure causes him to gain any, what is lost to the object which serves him affects him in no wise, save profitably: it must be a matter of indifference to him whether that object is happy or unhappy, provided it be delectable to him; in truth, there is no relation at all between that object and himself. He would hence be a fool to trouble himself about the object's sensations and forget his own; he would be entirely mad if, in order to modify those sensations foreign to him, he were to renounce improvement of his. That much established, if the individual in question is, unhappily, organized in such a fashion he cannot be stirred save by producing painful sensations in the object employed, you will admit he is forced to go ruthlessly to work, since the point of it all is to have the best possible time, the consequences for the object being entirely excluded from consideration. . . . We will return to the problem; let us continue in an orderly fashion.

"Isolated enjoyment therefore has its charms, it may therefore have more of them than all other kinds; why! if it were not so, how should the aged and so many deformed or defective persons be able to enjoy themselves? for they know full well they are not loved nor lovable; perfectly certain it is impossible to share what they experience, is their joy any the less powerful on that account? Do they desire even the illusion? Behaving with utter selfishness in their riots, you will observe them seeking pleasure, you will see them sacrifice everything to obtain it, and in the object they put to use never other than passive properties. Therefore, it is in no wise necessary to give pleasures in order to receive them; the happy or unhappy situation of the victim of our debauch is, therefore, absolutely as one from the point of view of our senses, there is never any question of the state in which his heart or mind may be; it matters not one whit, the object may be pleased by what you do to it, the object may suffer, it may love or detest you: all these considerations are nullified immediately it is only a question of your sensation. Women, I concede, may establish contrary theories, but women, who are nothing but machines designed for voluptuousness, who ought to be nothing but the targets of lust, are untrustworthy authorities whenever one has got to construct an authentic doctrine upon this kind of pleasure. Is there a single reasonable man who is eager to have a whore partake of his joy? And, however, are there not millions of men who amuse themselves hugely with these creatures? Well, there you have that many individuals convinced of what I am urging, who unhesitatingly put it into practice, and who scorn those who use good principles to legitimate their deeds, those ridiculous fools, the world is stuffed to overflowing with them, who go and come, who do this and that, who eat, who digest, without ever sensing a thing.

"Having proven that solitary pleasures are as delicious as any others and much more likely to delight, it becomes perfectly clear that this enjoyment, taken in independence of the object we employ, is not merely of a nature very remote from what could be pleasurable to that object, but is even found to be inimical to that object's pleasure: what is more, it may become an imposed suffering, a vexation, or a torture, and the only thing that results from this abuse is a very certain increase of pleasure for the despot who does the tormenting or vexing; let us attempt to demonstrate this.

"Voluptuous emotion is nothing but a kind of vibration produced in our soul by shocks which the imagination, inflamed by the remembrance of a lubricious object, registers upon our senses, either through this object's presence, or better still by this object's being exposed to that particular kind of irritation which most profoundly stirs us; thus, our voluptuous transport—this indescribable convulsive needling which drives us wild, which lifts us to the highest pitch of happiness at which man is able to arrive—is never ignited save by two causes: either by the perception in the object we use of a real or imaginary beauty, the beauty in which we delight the most, or by the sight of that object undergoing the strongest possible sensation; now, there is no more lively sensation than that of pain; its impressions are certain and dependable, they never deceive as may those of the pleasure women perpetually feign and almost never experience; and, furthermore, how much self-confidence, youth, vigor, health are not needed in order to be sure of producing this dubious and hardly very satisfying impression of pleasure in a woman. To produce the painful impression, on the contrary, requires no virtues at all: the more defects a man may have, the older he is, the less lovable, the more resounding his success. With what regards the objective, it will be far more certainly attained since we are establishing the fact that one never better touches, I wish to say, that one never better irritates one's senses than when the greatest possible impression has been produced in the employed object, by no matter what devices; therefore, he who will cause the most tumultuous impression to be born in a woman, he who will most thoroughly convulse this woman's entire frame, very decidedly will have managed to procure himself the heaviest possible dose of voluptuousness, because the shock resultant upon us by the impressions others experience, which shock in turn is necessitated by the impression we have of those others, will necessarily be more vigorous if the impression these others receive be painful, than if the impression they receive be sweet and mild; and it follows that the voluptuous egoist, who is persuaded his pleasures will be keen only insofar as they are entire, will therefore impose, when he has it in his power to do so, the strongest possible dose of pain upon the employed object, fully certain that what by way of voluptuous pleasure he extracts will be his only by dint of the very lively impression he has produced."

"Oh, Father," I said to Clément, "these doctrines are dreadful, they lead to the cultivation of cruel tastes, horrible tastes."

"Why, what does it matter?" demanded the barbarian; "and, once again, have we any control over our tastes? Must we not yield to the dominion of those Nature has inserted in us as when before the tempest's force the proud oak bends its head? Were Nature offended by these proclivities, she would not have inspired them in us; that we can receive from her hands a sentiment such as would outrage her is impossible, and, extremely certain of this, we can give ourselves up to our passions, whatever their sort and of whatever their violence, wholly sure that all the discomfitures their shock may occasion are naught but the designs of Nature, of whom we are the involuntary instruments. And what to us are these passions' consequences? When one wishes to delight in any action whatsoever, there is never any question of consequences."

"I am not speaking to you of consequences," I put in abruptly, "but of the thing itself; if indeed you are the stronger and if through atrocious principles of cruelty you love to take your pleasure only by means of causing suffering with the intention of augmenting your sensations, you will gradually come to the point of producing them with such a degree of violence that you will certainly risk killing the employed object."

"So be it; that is to say that, by means of tastes given me by Nature, I shall have carried out the intentions of Nature who, never affecting her creations save through destructions, never inspires the thought of the latter in me save when she is in need of the former; that is to say that from an oblong portion of matter I shall have formed three or four thousand round or square ones. Oh Thérèse, is there any crime here? Is this the name with which to designate what serves Nature? Is it in man's power to commit crimes? And when, preferring his own happiness to that of others, he overthrows or destroys whatever he finds in his path, has he done anything but serve Nature whose primary and most imperious inspirations enjoin him to pursue his happiness at no matter whose expense? The doctrine of brotherly love is a fiction we owe to Christianity and not to Nature; the exponent of the Nazarene's cult, tormented, wretched and consequently in an enfeebled state which prompted him to cry out for tolerance and compassion, had no choice but to allege this fabulous relationship between one person and another; by gaining acceptance for the notion he was able to save his life. But the philosopher does not acknowledge these gigantic rapports; to his consideration, he is alone in the universe, he judges everything subjectively, he only is of importance. If he is thoughtful of or caresses another for one instant, it is never but in strait connection with what profit he thinks to draw from the business; when he is no longer in need of others, when he can forcefully assert his empire, he then abjures forever those pretty humanitarian doctrines of doing good deeds to which he only submitted himself for reasons of policy; he no longer fears to be selfish, to reduce everyone about him, and he sates his appetites without inquiring to know what his enjoyments may cost others, and without remorse."

"But the man you describe is a monster."

"The man I describe is in tune with Nature."

"He is a savage beast."

"Why, is not the tiger or the leopard, of whom this man is, if you wish, a replica, like man created by Nature and created to prosecute Nature's intentions? The wolf who devours the lamb accomplishes what this common mother designs, just as does the malefactor who destroys the object of his revenge or his lubricity."

"Oh, Father, say what you will, I shall never accept this destructive lubricity."

"Because you are afraid of becoming its object—there you have it: egoism. Let's exchange our roles and you will fancy it very nicely. Ask the lamb, and you will find he does not understand why the wolf is allowed to devour him; ask the wolf what the lamb is for: to feed me, he will reply. Wolves which batten upon lambs, lambs consumed by wolves, the strong who immolate the weak, the weak victims of the strong: there you have Nature, there you have her intentions, there you have her scheme: a perpetual action and reaction, a host of vices, a host of virtues, in one word, a perfect equilibrium resulting from the equality of good and evil on earth; the equilibrium essential to the maintenance of the stars, of vegetation and, lacking which, everything would be instantly in ruins. O

Thérèse, mightily astonished she would be, this Nature, were she to be able to converse with us for a moment and were we to tell her that these crimes which serve her, these atrocities she demands and inspires in us are punished by laws they assure us are made in imitation of hers. 'Idiots' she would reply to us, 'sleep, eat, and fearlessly commit whatever crimes you like whenever you like: every one of those alleged infamies pleases me, and I would have them all, since it is I who inspire them in you. It is within your province to regulate what annoys me and what delights, indeed! be advised that there is nothing in you which is not my own, nothing I did not place in you for reasons it is not fitting you be acquainted with; know that the most abominable of your deeds is, like the most virtuous of some other, but one of the manners of serving me. So do not restrain yourself, flout your laws, a fig for your social conventions and your Gods; listen to me and to none other, and believe that if there exists a crime to be committed against me it is the resistance you oppose, in the forms of stubbornness or casuistries, to what I inspire in you.' "

"Oh, Just Heaven!" I cried, "you make me shudder! Were there no crimes against Nature, whence would come that insurmountable loathing we experience for certain misdeeds?"

"That loathing is not dictated by Nature," the villain replied with feeling, "its one source is in the total lack of habit; does not the same hold true for certain foods? Although they are excellent, is not our repugnance merely caused by our being unaccustomed to them? would you dare say, upon the basis of your prejudices or ignorance, that they are good or bad? If we make the effort, we will soon become convinced and will find they suit our palate; we have a hostility toward medicaments, do we not, although they are salutary; in the same fashion, let us accustom ourselves to evil and it will not be long before we find it charming; this momentary revulsion is certainly a shrewdness, a kind of coquetry on the part of Nature, rather than a warning that the thing outrages her: thus she prepares the pleasures of our triumph; she even manages thus to augment those of the deed itself: better still, Thérèse, better still: the more the deed seems appalling to us, the more it is in contradiction with our manners and customs, the more it runs headlong against restraints and shatters them, the more it conflicts with social conventions and affronts them, the more it clashes with what we mistake for Nature's laws, then the more, on the contrary, it is useful to this same Nature. It is never but by way of crimes that she regains possession of the rights Virtue incessantly steals away from her. If the crime is slight, if it is at no great variance with Virtue, its weight will be less in re-establishing the balance indispensable to Nature; but the more capital the crime, the more deadly, the more it dresses the scales and the better it offsets the influence of Virtue which, without this, would destroy everything. Let him then cease to be in a fright, he who meditates a crime or he who has just committed one: the vaster his crime, the better it will serve Nature."

These frightful theories soon led me to think of Omphale's doubts upon the manner in which we left the terrible house we were in. And it was then I conceived the plans you will see me execute in the sequel. However, to complete my enlightenment I could not prevent myself from putting yet a few more questions to Father Clément.

"But surely," I said, "you do not keep your passions' unhappy victims forever; you surely send them away when you are wearied of them?"

"Certainly, Thérèse," the monk replied; "you only entered this establishment in order to leave it when the four of us agree to grant your retirement. Which will most certainly be granted."

"But do you not fear," I continued, "lest the younger and less discreet girls sometimes go and reveal what is done here?"

" 'Tis impossible."

"Impossible?"

"Absolutely."

"Could you explain . . ."

"No, that's our secret, but I can assure you of this much: that whether you are discreet or indiscreet, you will find it perfectly impossible ever to say a word about what is done here when you are here no longer. And thus you see, Thérèse, I recommend no discretion to you, just as my own desires are governed by no restraining policy. . . ."

And, having uttterd these words, the monk fell asleep. From that moment onward, I could no longer avoid realizing that the most violent measures were used with those unhappy ones of us who were retrenched and that this terrible security they boasted of was only the fruit of our death. I was only the more confirmed in my resolve; we will soon see its effect.

As soon as Clément was asleep, Armande came near to me.

"He will awake shortly," she said; "he will behave like a madman: Nature only puts his senses to sleep in order to give them, after a little rest, a much greater energy; one more scene and we will have peace until tomorrow."

"But you," I said to my companion, "aren't you going to sleep a little while?"

"How can I?" Armande replied, "when, were I not to remain awake and standing by his side, and were my negligence to be perceived, he would be the man to stab me to death."

"O Heaven!" I sighed, "why! even as he sleeps the villain would that those around him remain in a state of suffering!"

"Yes," my companion responded, "it is the very barbarity of the idea which procures the furious awakening you are going to witness; upon this he is like unto those perverse writers whose corruption is so dangerous, so active, that their single aim is, by causing their appalling doctrines to be printed, to immortalize the sum of their crimes after their own lives are at an end; they themselves can do no more, but their accursed writings will instigate the commission of crimes, and they carry this sweet idea with them to their graves: it comforts them for the obligation, enjoined by death, to relinquish the doing of evil."

"The monsters!" I cried. . . .

Armande, who was a very gentle creature, kissed me as she shed a few tears, then went back to pacing about the roué's bed.

Two hours passed and then the monk did indeed awake in a prodigious agitation and seized me with such force I thought he was going to strangle me; his respiration was quick and labored, his eyes glittered, he uttered incoherent words which were exclusively blasphemous or libertine expressions; he summoned Armande, called for whips, and started in again with his flogging of us both, but in a yet more vigorous manner than before having gone to sleep. It seemed as if he wished to end matters with me; shrill cries burst from his mouth; to abridge my sufferings, Armande excited him violently, he lost his head entirely, and finally made rigid by the most violent sensations, the monster lost both his ardor and his desires together with smoking floods of semen.

Nothing transpired during the rest of the night; upon getting up, the monk was content to touch and examine each of us; and as he was going to say Mass, we returned to the seraglio. The superintendent could not be prevented from desiring me in the inflamed state she swore I must be in; exhausted I indeed was and, thus weakened, how could I defend myself? She did all she wished, enough to convince me that even a woman, in such a school, soon losing all the delicacy and restraint native to her sex, could only, after those tyrants' example, become obscene and cruel.

Two nights later, I slept with Jérôme; I will not describe his horrors to you; they were still more terrifying. What an academy, great God! by week's end I had finally made the circuit, and then Omphale asked me whether it were not true that of them all, Clément was the one about whom I had the most to complain.

"Alas!" was my response, "in the midst of a crowd of horrors and messes of filth which now disgust and now revolt, it is very difficult to pronounce upon these villains' individual odiousness; I am mortally weary of them all and would that I were gone from here, whatever be the fate that awaits me."

"It might be possible that you will soon be satisfied," my companion answered; "we are nearing the period of the festival: this circumstance rarely takes place without bringing them victims; they either seduce girls by means of the confessional, or, if they can, they cause them to disappear: which means so many new recruits, each of whom always supposes a retrenchment."

The famous holiday arrived . . . will you be able to believe, Madame, what monstrous impieties the monks were guilty of during this event! They fancied a visible miracle would double the brilliance of their reputation; and so they dressed Florette, the youngest of the girls, in all the Virgin's attire and adornments; by means of concealed strings they tied her against the wall of the niche and ordered her to elevate her arms very suddenly and with compunction toward heaven simultaneously the host was raised. As the little creature was threatened with the cruelest chastising if she were to speak a single word or mismanage in her role, she carried it off marvelously well, and the fraud enjoyed all the success that could possibly have been expected. The people cried aloud the miracle, left rich offerings to the Virgin, and went home more convinced than ever of the efficacity of the celestial Mother's mercies. In order to increase their impiety, our libertines wanted to have Florette appear at the orgies that evening, dressed in the same costume that had attracted so many homages, and each one inflamed his odious desires to submit her, in this guise, to the irregularity of his caprices. Aroused by this initial crime, the sacrilegious ones go considerably further: they have the child stripped naked, they have her lie on her stomach upon a large table; they light candles, they place the image of our Saviour squarely upon the little girl's back and upon her buttocks they dare consummate the most redoubtable of our mysteries. I swooned away at this horrible spectacle, 'twas impossible to bear the sight. Sévérino, seeing me unconscious, says that, to bring me to heel, I must serve as the altar in my turn. I am seized; I am placed where Florette was lying; the sacrifice is consummated, and the host . . . that sacred symbol of our august Religion . . . Sévérino catches it up and thrusts it deep into the obscene locale of his sodomistic pleasures . . . crushes it with oaths and insults . . . ignominiously drives it further with the intensified blows of his monstrous dart and as he blasphemes, spurts, upon our Saviour's very Body, the impure floods of his lubricity's torrents. . . .

I was insensible when they drew me from his hands; I had to be carried to my room, where for a week I shed uninterrupted tears over the hideous crime for which, against my will, I had been employed. The memory still gnaws at my soul, I never think back upon that scene without shuddering. . . . In me, Religion is the effect of sentiment; all that offends or outrages it makes my very heart bleed.

The end of the month was close at hand when one morning toward nine Sévérino entered our chamber; he appeared greatly aroused; a certain crazed look hovered in his eyes; he examines us, one after the other, places us in his cherished attitude, and especially lingers over Omphale; for several minutes he stands, contemplating her in the posture she has assumed, he excites himself, mutters dully, secretly, kisses what is offered him, allows everyone to see he is in a state to consummate, and consummates nothing;

next, he has her straighten up, casts upon her glances filled with rage and wickedness; then, swinging his foot, with all his strength he kicks her in the belly, she reels backward and falls six yards away.

"The company is retrenching you, whore," he says, "we are tired of you, be ready by this afternoon. I will come to fetch you myself." And he leaves.

When he is gone Omphale gets up and, weeping, casts herself into my arms.

"Ah!" she says, "by the infamy, by the cruelty of the preliminaries . . . can you still blind yourself as to what follows? Great God! what is to become of me?"

"Be easy," I say to the miserable girl, "I have made up my mind about everything; I only await the opportunity; it may perhaps present itself sooner than you think; I will divulge these horrors; if it is true the measures they take are as cruel as we have reason to believe, strive to obtain some delays, postpone it, and I will wrest you from their clutches."

In the event Omphale were to be released, she swore in the same way to aid me, and both of us fell to weeping. The day passed, nothing happened during it; at five o'clock Sévérino returned.

"Well," he asked Omphale, "are you ready?"

"Yes, Father," she answered between sobs, "permit me to embrace my friends."

" 'Tis useless," replied the monk; "we have no time for lachrymose scenes; they are waiting for us; come." Then she asked whether she were obliged to take her belongings with her.

"No," said the superior; "does not everything belong to the house? You have no further need of any of it"; then, checking himself, as might one who has said too much:

"Those old clothes have become useless; you will have some cut to fit your size, they will be more becoming to you; be content to take along only what you are wearing."

I asked the monk whether I might be allowed to accompany Omphale to the door of the house; his reply was a glance that made me recoil in terror. . . . Omphale goes out, she turns toward us eyes filled with uneasiness and tears, and the minute she is gone I fling myself down upon the bed, desperate.

Accustomed to these occurrences or blind to their significance, my companions were less affected by Omphale's departure than I; the superior returned an hour later to lead away the supper's girls of whom I was one—we were only four: the girl of twelve, she of sixteen, she of twenty-three, and me. Everything went more or less as upon other days; I only noticed that the Girls of the Watch were not on hand, that the monks often whispered in each other's ears, that they drank much, that they limited themselves violently to exciting desires they did not once consummate, and that they sent us away at an early hour without retaining any of us for their own beds. . . . I deduced what I could from what I observed, because, under such circumstances, one keeps a sharp eye upon everything, but what did this evidence augur? Ah, such was my perplexity that no clear idea presented itself to my mind but it was not immediately offset by another; recollecting Clément's words, I felt there was everything to fear . . . of course; but then, hope . . . that treacherous hope which comforts us, which blinds us, and which thus does us almost as much ill as good . . . hope finally surged up to reassure me. . . . Such a quantity of horrors were so alien to me that I was simply unable to conceive of them. In this terrible state of confusion, I lay down in bed; now I was persuaded Omphale would not fail to keep her word; and the next instant I was convinced the cruel devices they would use against her would deprive her of all power to help us, and that was my final opinion when I saw an end come to the third day of having heard nothing at all.

Upon the fourth I found myself again called to supper; the company was numerous and select: the eight most beautiful women were there that evening, I had been paid the honor of being included amongst them; the Girls of the Watch attended too. Immediately we entered we caught sight of our new companion.

"Here is the young lady the corporation has destined to re-place Omphale, Mesdemoiselles," said Séverino.

And as the words escaped his lips he tore away the mantlets and lawn which covered the girl's bust, and we beheld a maiden of fifteen, with the most agreeable and delicate face: she raised her lovely eyes and graciously regarded each of us; those eyes were still moist with tears, but they contained the liveliest expression; her figure was supple and light, her skin of a dazzling whiteness, she had the world's most beautiful hair, and there was something so seductive about the whole that it was impossible not to feel oneself automatically drawn to her. Her name was Octavie; we were soon informed she was a girl of the highest quality, born in Paris, and had just emerged from a convent in order to wed the Comte de * * *: she had been kidnaped while en route in the company of two governesses and three lackeys; she did not know what had become of her retinue; it had been toward nightfall and she alone had been taken; after having been blindfolded, she had been brought to where we were and it had not been possible to know more of the matter.

As yet no one had spoken a word to her. Our libertine quartet, confronted by so much charm, knew an instant of ecstasy; they had only the strength to admire her. Beauty's dominion commands respect; despite his heartlessness, the most corrupt villain must bow before it or else suffer the stings of an obscure remorse; but monsters of the breed with which we had to cope do not long languish under such restraints.

"Come, pretty child," quoth the superior, impudently drawing her toward the chair in which he was settled, "come hither and let's have a look to see whether the rest of your charms match those Nature has so profusely distributed in your countenance."

And as the lovely girl was sore troubled, as she flushed crimson and strove to fend him off, Sévérino grasped her rudely round the waist.

"Understand, my artless one," he said, "understand that what I want to tell you is simply this: get undressed. Strip. Instantly."

And thereupon the libertine slid one hand beneath her skirts while he grasped her with the other. Clément approached, he raised Octavie's clothes to above her waist and by this maneuver exposed the softest, the most appetizing features it is possible anywhere to find; Sévérino touches, perceives nothing, bends to scrutinize more narrowly, and all four agree they have never seen anything as beautiful. However, the modest Octavie, little accustomed to usage of this sort, gushes tears, and struggles.

"Undress, undress," cries Antonin, "we can't see a thing this way."

He assists Sévérino and in a trice we have displayed to us all the maiden's unadorned charms. Never, without any doubt, was there a fairer skin, never were there more happily modeled forms. . . . God! the crime of it! . . . So many beauties, such chaste freshness, so much innocence and daintiness—all to become prey to these barbarians! Covered with shame, Octavie knows not where to fly to hide her charms, she finds naught but hungering eyes everywhere about, nothing but brutal hands which sully those treasures; the circle closes around her, and, as did I, she rushes hither and thither; the savage Antonin lacks the strength to resist; a cruel attack determines the homage, and the incense smokes at the goddess' feet. Jérôme compares her to our young colleague of sixteen, doubtless the seraglio's prettiest; he places the two altars of his devotion one next to the other.

"Ha! what whiteness! what grace!" says he as he fingers Octavie, "but what gentility and freshness may be discerned in this other one: indeed," continues the monk all afire, "I am uncertain"; then imprinting his mouth upon the charms his eyes behold, "Octavie," he cries, "to you the apple, it belongs to none but you, give me the precious fruit of this tree my heart adores. . . . Ah, yes! yes, one of you, give it me, and I will forever assure beauty's prize to who serves me sooner."

Sévérino observes the time has come to meditate on more serious matters; absolutely in no condition to be kept waiting, he lays hands upon the unlucky child, places her as he desires her to be; not yet being able to have full confidence in Octavie's aid, he calls for Clément to lend him a hand. Octavie weeps and weeps unheeded; fire gleams in the impudicious monk's glance; master of the terrain, one might say he casts about a roving eye only to consider the avenues whereby he may launch the fiercest assault; no ruses, no preparations are employed; will he be able to gather these so charming roses? will he be able to battle past the thorns? Whatever the enormous disproportion between the conquest and the assailant, the latter is not the less in a sweat to give fight; a piercing cry announces victory, but nothing mollifies the enemy's chilly heart; the more the captive implores mercy, the less quarter is granted her, the more vigorously she is pressed; the ill-starred one fences in vain: she is soon transpierced.

"Never was laurel with greater difficulty won," says Sévérino, retreating, "I thought indeed that for the first time in my life I would fall before the gate . . . ah! 'twas never so narrow, that way, nor so hot; 'tis the God's own Ganymede."

"I had better bring her round to the sex you have just soiled," cries Antonin, seizing Octavie where she is, and not wishing to let her stand up; "there's more than one breach to a rampart," says he, and proudly, boldly marching up, he carries the day and is within the sanctuary in no time at all. Further screams are heard.

"Praise be to God," quoth the indecent man, "I thought I was alone; and would have doubted of my success without a groan or two from the victim; but my triumph is sealed. Do you observe? Blood and tears."

"In truth," says Clément, who steps up with whip in hand, "I'll not disturb her sweet posture either, it is too favorable to my desires." Jérôme's Girl of the Watch and the twenty-year-old girl hold Octavie: Clément considers, fingers; terrified, the little girl beseeches him, and is not listened to.

"Ah, my friends!" says the exalted monk, "how are we to avoid flogging a schoolgirl who exhibits an ass of such splendor!"

The air immediately resounds to the whistle of lashes and the thud of stripes sinking into lovely flesh; Octavie's screams mingle with the sounds of leather, the monk's curses reply: what a scene for these libertines surrendering themselves to a thousand obscenities in the midst of us all! They applaud him, they cheer him on; however, Octavie's skin changes color, the brightest tints incarnadine join the lily sparkle; but what might perhaps divert Love for an instant, were moderation to have direction of the sacrifice, becomes, thanks to severity, a frightful crime against Love's laws; nothing stops or slows the perfidious monk, the more the young student complains, the more the professor's harshness explodes; from the back to the knee, everything is treated in the same way, and it is at last upon his barbaric pleasures' blood-drenched vestiges the savage quenches his flames.

"I shall be less impolite, I think," says Jérôme, laying hands upon the lovely thing and adjusting himself between her coral lips; "where is the temple where I would sacrifice? Why, in this enchanting mouth. . . ."

I fall silent. . . . 'Tis the impure reptile withering the rose—my figure of speech relates it all.

The rest of the *soirée* would have resembled all the others had it not been for the beauty and the touching age of this young maiden who more than usually inflamed those villains and caused them to multiply their infamies; it was satiety rather than commiseration that sent the unhappy child back to her room and gave er, for a few hours at least, the rest and quiet she needed.

I should indeed have liked to have been able to comfort her that first night, but, obliged to spend it with Sévérino, it may well ave been I on the contrary who stood in the greater need of help, or I had the misfortune, no, not to please, the word would not be uitable, no, but in a most lively manner to excite that sodomite's famous passions; at this period he desired me almost every night; eing exhausted on this particular one, he conducted some researches; doubtless afraid the appalling sword with which he was ndowed would not cause me an adequate amount of pain, he ancied, this time, he might perforate me with one of those rticles of furniture usually found in nunneries, which decency forids me from naming and which was of an exorbitant thickness; ere, one was obliged to be ready for anything. He himself made e weapon penetrate into his beloved shrine; thanks to powerful ows, it was driven very deep; I screamed; the monk was amused, fter a few backward and forward passes, he suddenly snapped e instrument free and plunged his own into the gulf he had just g open . . . what whimsy! Is that not positively the contrary of erything men are able to desire! But who can define the spirit of ertinage? For a long time we have realized this to be an enigma Nature; she has not yet pronounced the magic word.

In the morning, feeling somewhat renewed, he wanted to try t another torture: he produced a far more massy machine: this e was hollow and fitted with a high-pressure pump that squirted incredibly powerful stream of water through an orifice which ve the jet a circumference of over three inches; the enormous inrument itself was nine inches around by twelve long. Sévérino aded it with steaming hot water and prepared to bury it in my ont end; terrified by such a project, I throw myself at his knees to k for mercy, but he is in one of those accursed situations where pity cannot be heard, where far more eloquent passions stifle it an substitute an often exceedingly dangerous cruelty. The monk threat ens me with all his rage if I do not acquiesce; I have to obey. Th perfidious machine penetrates to the two-thirds mark and the tear ing it causes combined with its extreme heat are about to depriv me of the use of my senses; meanwhile, the superior, showering a uninterrupted stream of invectives upon the parts he is molesting has himself excited by his follower; after fifteen minutes of rubbin which lacerates me, he releases the spring, a quart of nearly boilin water is fired into the last depths of my womb . . . I fall into a fain Séverino was in an ecstasy . . . he was in a delirium at least th equal of my agony.

"Why," said the traitor, "that's nothing at all. When I r cover my wits, we'll treat those charms much more harshly . . . salad of thorns, by Jesus! well peppered, a copious admixture vinegar, all that tamped in with the point of a knife, that's wha they need to buck them up; the next mistake you make, I condem you to the treatment," said the villain while he continued to hand the object of his worship; but two or three homages after the pr ceeding night's debauches had near worked him to death, and I wa sent packing.

Upon returning to my chamber I found my new companion tears; I did what I could to soothe her, but it is not easy to adju to so frightful a change of situation; this girl had, furthermore, great fund of religious feeling, of virtue, and of sensitivity; owir to it, her state only appeared to her the more terrible. Ompha had been right when she told me seniority in no way influenced r tirement; that, simply by the monks' caprice, or by their fear ulterior inquiries, one could undergo dismissal at the end of a wee as easily as at the end of twenty years. Octavie had not been wi us four months when Jérôme came to announce her departure; though 'twas he who had most enjoyed her during her sojourn the monastery, he who had seemed to cherish her and seek her mo than any other, the poor child left, making us the same promis Omphale had given; she kept them just as poorly.

From that moment on, my every thought was bent upon t plan I had been devising since Omphale's departure; determined do everything possible to escape from this den of savages, nothir that might help me succeed held any terrors for me. What was there to dread by putting my scheme into execution? Death. And were I to remain, of what could I be certain? Of death. And successful flight would save me; there could be no hesitation for there was no alternative; but it were necessary that, before I launched my enterprise, fatal examples of vice rewarded be yet again reproduced before my eyes; it was inscribed in the great book of fate, in that obscure tome whereof no mortal has intelligence, 'twas set down there, I say, that upon all those who had tormented me, humiliated me, bound me in iron chains, there were to be heaped unceasing bounties and rewards for what they had done with regard to me, as if Providence had assumed the task of demonstrating to me the inutility of virtue. . . . Baleful lessons which however did not correct me, no, I wavered not; lessons which, should I once again escape from the blade poised above my head, will not prevent me from forever remaining the slave of my heart's Divinity.

One morning, quite unexpectedly, Antonin appeared in our chamber and announced that the Reverend Father Sévérino, allied to the Pope and his protégé, had just been named General of the Benedictine Order by His Holiness. The next day that monk did in effect depart, without taking his leave of us; 'twas said another was expected to replace him, and he would be far superior in debauch to all who remained; additional reasons to hasten ahead with my plans.

The day following Sévérino's departure, the monks decided to retrench one more of my companions; I chose for my escape the very day when sentence was pronounced against the wretched girl, so that the monks, preoccupied with her, would pay less attention to me.

It was the beginning of spring; the length of the nights still somewhat favored my designs: for two months I had been preparing them, they were completely unsuspected; little by little I sawed through the bars over my window, using a dull pair of scissors I had found; my head could already pass through the hole; with sheets and linen I had made a cord of more than sufficient length to carry me down the twenty or twenty-five feet Omphale had told me was the building's height. When they had taken my old belongings, I had been careful, as I told you, to remove my little fortune which came to about six *louis*, and these I had always kept hidden with extreme caution; as I left, I put them into my hair, and nearly all of our chamber having left for that night's supper, finding no one about but one of my companions who had gone to bed as soon as the others had descended, I entered my cabinet; there, clearing the hole I had scrupulously kept covered at all times, I knotted my cord to one of the undamaged bars, then, sliding down outside, I soon touched the ground—'twas not this part which troubled me: the six enclosures of stone and trees my companion had mentioned were what intrigued me far more.

Once there, I discovered that each concentric space between one barrier and the next was no more than eight feet wide, and it was this proximity which assured a casual glance that there was nothing in the area but a dense cluster of trees. The night was very dark; as I turned round the first alley to discover where I might not find a gap in the palisade, I passed beneath the dining hall, which seemed deserted; my inquietude increased; however, I continued my search and thus at last came abreast the window to the main underground room, located directly below that in which the orgies were staged. Much light flooded from the basement, I was bold enough to approach the window and had a perfect view of the interior. My poor companion was stretched out upon a trestle table, her hair in disarray; she was doubtless destined for some terrible torture by which she was going to find freedom, the eternal end of her miseries. . . . I shuddered, but what my glances fell upon soon astonished me more: Omphale had either not known everything, or had not told all she knew; I spied four naked girls in the basement, and they certainly did not belong to our group; and so there were other victims of these monsters' lechery in this horrible asylum . . . other wretches unknown to us. . . . I fled away and continued my circuit until I was on the side opposite the basement window; not yet having found a breach, I resolved to make one; all unobserved, I had furnished myself with a long knife; I set to work; despite my gloves, my hands were soon scratched and torn; but nothing daunted me; the hedge was two feet thick, I opened a passage, went through, and entered the second ring; there, I was surprised to find nothing but soft earth underfoot; with each step I sank in ankle deep: the further I advanced into these copses, the more profound the darkness became. Curious to know whence came the change of terrain, I felt about with my hands ... O Just Heaven! my fingers seized the head of a cadaver! Great God! I thought, whelmed with horror, this must then be the cemetery, as indeed I was told, into which those murderers fling their victims; they have scarcely gone to the bother of covering them with earth! ... this skull perhaps belongs to my dear Omphale, perhaps it is that of the unhappy Octavie, so lovely, so sweet, so good, and who while she lived was like unto the rose of which her charms were the image. And I, alas! might that this have been my resting place! Wouldst that I had submitted to my fate! What had I to gain by going on in pursuit of new pitfalls? Had I not committed evil enough? Had I not been the occasion of a number of crimes sufficiently vast? Ah! fulfill my destiny! O Earth, gape wide and swallow me up! Ah, 'tis madness, when one is so forsaken, so poor, so utterly abandoned, madness to go to such pains in order to vegetate yet a few more instants amongst monsters! ... But no! I must avenge Virtue in irons. ... She expects it of my courage. ... Let her not be struck down ... let us advance: it is essential that the universe be ridded of villains as dangerous as these. Ought I fear causing the doom of three or four men in order to save the millions of individuals their policy or their ferocity sacrifice?

And therewith I pierce the next hedge; this one was thicker than the first: the further I progressed, the stouter they became. The hole was made, however, but there was firm ground beyond ... nothing more betrayed the same horrors I had just encountered; and thus I arrived at the brink of the moat without having met with the wall Omphale had spoken of; indeed, there turned out to be none at all, and it is likely that the monks mentioned it merely to add to our fear. Less shut in when beyond the sextuple enclosure, I was better able to distinguish objects: my eyes at once beheld the church and the bulk of the adjacent building; the moat bordered each of them; I was careful not to attempt to cross it at this point; I moved along the edge and finally discovering myself opposite one of the forest roads, I resolved to make my crossing there and to dash down that road as soon as I had climbed up the other side of the ditch; it was very deep but, to my good fortune, dry and lined with brick, which eliminated all possibilities of slipping; then I leapt: a little dazed by my fall, it was a few moments before I got to my feet . . . I went ahead, got to the further side without meeting any obstacle, but how was I to climb it! I spent some time seeking a means and at last found one where several broken bricks at once gave me the opportunity to use the others as steps and to dig foot-holds in order to mount; I had almost reached the top when something gave way beneath my weight and I fell back into the moat under the debris I dragged with me; I thought myself dead; this involuntary fall had been more severe than the other; I was, as well, entirely covered with the material which had followed me; some had struck my head . . . it was cut and bleeding. O God! I cried out in despair, go no further; stay there; 'tis a warning sent from Heaven; God does not want me to go on: perhaps I am de-ceived in my ideas, perhaps evil is useful on earth, and when God's hand desires it, perhaps it is a sin to resist it! But, soon revolted by that doctrine, the too wretched fruit of the corruption which had surrounded me, I extricated myself from the pile of rubble on top of me and finding it easier to climb by the breach I had just made, for now there were new holes, I try once again, I take courage, a moment later I find myself at the crest. Because of all this I had strayed away from the path I had seen, but having taken careful note of its position, I found it again, and began to run. Before day-break I reached the forest's edge and was soon upon that little hill from which, six long months before, I had, to my sorrow, espied that frightful monastery; I rest a few minutes, I am bathed in perspiration; my first thought is to fall upon my knees and beg God to forgive the sins I unwillingly committed in that odious asylum of crime and impurity; tears of regret soon flowed from my eyes. Alas! I said, I was far less a criminal when last year I left this same road, guided by a devout principle so fatally deceived! O God! In what state may I now behold myself! These lugubrious reflections were in some wise mitigated by the pleasure of discovering I was free; I continued along the road toward Dijon, supposing it would only be in that capital my complaints could be legitimately lodged. . . .

At this point Madame de Lorsange persuaded Thérèse to catch her breath for a few minutes at least; she needed the rest; the

motion she put into her narrative, the wounds these dreadful re-
itals reopened in her soul, everything, in short, obliged her to re-
ort to a brief respite. Monsieur de Corville had refreshments
rought in, and after collecting her forces, our heroine set out again
o pursue her deplorable adventures in great detail, as you shall see.

$\mathcal{B}$y the second day all my initial fears of pursuit had dissipated; the weather was extremely warm and, following my thrifty habit, I left the road to find a sheltered place where I could eat a light meal that would fortify me till evening. Off the road to the right stood a little grove of trees through which wound a limpid stream; this seemed a good spot for my lunch. My thirst quenched by this pure cool water, nourished by a little bread, my back leaning against a tree trunk, I breathed deep draughts of clear, serene air which relaxed me and was soothing. Resting there, my thoughts dwelled upon the almost unexampled fatality which, despite the thorns strewn thick along the career of Virtue, repeatedly brought me back, whatever might happen, to the worship of that Divinity and to acts of love and resignation toward the Supreme Being from Whom Virtue emanates and of Whom it is the image. A kind of enthusiasm came and took possession of me; alas! I said to myself, He abandons me not, this God I adore, for even at this instant I find the means to recover my strength. Is it not to Him I owe this merciful favor? And are there not persons in the world to whom it is refused? I am then not completely unfortunate because there are some who have more to complain of than I. . . . Ah! am I not much less so than the unlucky ones I left in that den of iniquity and vice from which God's kindness caused me to emerge as if by some sort of miracle? . . . And full of gratitude I threw myself upon my knees, raised my eyes, and fixing the sun, for it seemed to me the Divinity's most splendid achievement, the one which best manifests His greatness, I was drawing from that Star's sublimity new motives for prayer and good works when all of a sudden I felt myself seized by two men who, having cast something over my head to

627

prevent me from seeing and crying out, bound me like a criminal and dragged me away without uttering a word.

And thus had we walked for nearly two hours during which I knew not whither my escorts were taking me when one of them, hearing me gasp for air, proposed to his comrade that I be freed of the sack covering my head; he agreed, I drank in fresh air and observed that we were in the midst of a forest through which we were traveling along a fairly broad although little frequented road. A thousand dark ideas rushed straightway into my mind. I feared I was being led back to their odious monastery.

"Ah," I say to one of my guides, "ah Monsieur, will you tell me where I am being conducted? May I not ask what you intend to do with me?"

"Be at ease, my child," the man replied, "and do not let the precautions we are obliged to take cause you any fright; we are leading you to a good master; weighty considerations engage him to procure a maid for his wife by means of this mysterious process, but never fear, you will find yourself well off."

"Alas! Messieurs," I answered, "if 'tis my welfare for which you labor it is to no purpose I am constrained; I am a poor orphan, no doubt much to be commiserated; I ask for nothing but a place and since you are giving me one, I have no cause to run away, do I?"

"She's right," said one of my escorts, "let's make her more comfortable; untie everything but her hands."

They do so and we resume our march. Seeing me calmed, they even respond to my questions, and I finally learn that I am destined to have for master one Comte de Gernande, a native of Paris, but owning considerable property in this country and rich to the tune of five hundred thousand pounds a year, all of which he consumes alone—so said one of my guides.

"Alone?"

"Yes, he is a solitary man, a philosopher: he never sees a soul; but on the other hand he is one of Europe's greatest epicures; there is not an eater in all the world who can hold a candle to him. But I'll say no more about it; you'll see."

"But what do these cautious measures signify, Monsieur?"

"Well, simply this. Our master has the misfortune to have a wife who has become insane; a strict watch must be kept over her, she never leaves her room, no one wishes to be her servant; it would have done no good to propose the work to you, for had you been forewarned you'd never have accepted it. We are obliged to carry girls off by force in order to have someone to exercise this unpleasant function."

"What? I will be made this lady's captive?"

"Why, forsooth, yes, you will, and that's why we have you tied this way; but you'll get on . . . don't fret, you'll get on perfectly; apart from this annoyance, you'll lack nothing."

"Ah! Merciful Heaven! what thralldom!"

"Come, come, my child, courage, you'll get out of it someday and you'll have made your fortune."

My guide had no sooner finished speaking than we caught sight of the château. It was a superb and vast building isolated in the middle of the forest, but this great edifice which could have accommodated hundreds of persons, seemed to be inhabited hardly at all. I only noticed a few signs of life coming from kitchens situated in the vaults below the central part of the structure; all the rest was as deserted as the château's site was lonely. No one was there to greet us when we entered; one of my guides went off in the direction of the kitchens, the other presented me to the Count. He was at the far end of a spacious and superb apartment, his body enveloped in an oriental satin dressing gown, reclining upon an ottoman, and having hard by him two young men so indecently, or rather so ridiculously, costumed, their hair dressed with such elegance and skill, that at first I took them for girls; a closer inspection allowed me to recognize them for two youths, one of about fifteen, the other perhaps sixteen. Their faces struck me as charming, but in such a state of dissipated softness and weariness, that at the outset I thought they were ill.

"My Lord, here is a girl," said my guide, "she seems to us to be what might suit you: she is properly bred and gentle and asks only to find a situation; we hope you will be content with her."

" 'Tis well," the Count said with scarcely a glance in my direction; "you, Saint-Louis, will close the doors when you go out and you will say that no one is to enter unless I ring."

Then the Count rose to his feet and came up to examine me. While he makes a detailed investigation I can describe him to you:

the portrait's singularity merits an instant's attention. Monsieur de Gernande was at that time a man of fifty, almost six feet tall and monstrously fat. Nothing could be more terrifying than his face, the length of his nose, his wicked black eyes, his large ill-furnished mouth, his formidable high forehead, the sound of his fearful raucous voice, his enormous hands; all combined to make a gigantic individual whose presence inspired much more fear than reassurance. We will soon be able to decide whether the morals and actions of this species of centaur were in keeping with his awesome looks. After the most abrupt and cavalier scrutiny, the Count demanded to know my age.

"I am twenty-three, Monsieur," I replied.

And to this first question he added some others of a personal nature. I made him privy to everything that concerned me; I did not even omit the brand I had received from Rodin, and when I had represented my misery to him, when I had proven to him that unhappiness had constantly dogged my footsteps:

"So much the better," the dreadful man replied, "so much the better, it will have made you more pliable—adaptability counts heavily toward success in this household—; I see nothing to regret in the wretchedness that hounds an abject race of plebeians Nature has doomed to grovel at our feet throughout the period allotted them to live on the same earth as we. Your sort is more energetic and less insolent, the pressures of adversity help you fulfill your duties toward us."

"But, Monsieur, I told you that I am not of mean birth."

"Yes, yes, I have heard that before, they always pass themselves off for all kinds of things when in fact they are nothing or miserable. Oh indeed, pride's illusions are of the highest usefulness to console fortune's ills, and then, you see, it is up to us to believe what we please about these lofty estates beaten down by the blows of destiny. Pish, d'ye know, it's all the same to me if you fancy yourself a princess. To my consideration you have the look and more or less the costume of a servant, and as such you may enter my hire, if it suits you. However," the hard-hearted man continued, "your welfare, your happiness—they are your concern, they depend on your performance: a little patience, some discretion, and in a few years you will be sent forth in a way to avoid further service."

Then he took one after the other of my arms, rolled my sleeves to the elbows, and examined them attentively while asking me how many times I had been bled.

"Twice, Monsieur," I told him, rather surprised at the question, and I mentioned when and under what circumstances it had happened. He pressed his fingers against the veins as one does when one wishes to inflate them, and when they were swollen to the desired point, he fastened his lips to them and sucked. From that instant I ceased to doubt libertinage was involved in this dreadful person's habits, and tormenting anxieties were awakened in my heart.

"I have got to know how you are made," continued the Count, staring at me in a way that set me to trembling; "the post you are to occupy precludes any corporeal defects; show me what you have about you."

I recoiled; but the Count, all his facial muscles beginning to twitch with anger, brutally informed me that I should be ill-advised to play the prude with him, for, said he, there are infallible methods of bringing women to their senses.

"What you have related to me does not betoken a virtue of the highest order; and so your resistance would be quite as misplaced as ludicrous."

Whereupon he made a sign to his young boys who, approaching immediately, fell to undressing me. Against persons as enfeebled, as enervated as those who surrounded me, it is certainly not difficult to defend oneself; but what good would it have done? The cannibal who had cast me into their hands could have pulverized me, had he wished to, with one blow of his fist. I therefore understood I had to yield: an instant later I was unclothed; 'twas scarcely done when I perceived I was exciting those two Ganymedes to gales of laughter.

"Look ye, friend," said the younger, "a girl's a pretty thing, eh? But what a shame there's that cavity there."

"Oh!" cried the other, "nothing nastier than that hole, I'd not touch a woman even were my fortune at stake."

And while my fore end was the subject of their sarcasms, the Count, an intimate partisan of the behind (unhappily, alas! like every libertine), examined mine with the keenest interest: he handled it brutally, he browsed about with avidity; taking handfuls of flesh between his fingers, he rubbed and kneaded them to the point of drawing blood. Then he made me walk away from him, halt, walk backward in his direction, keeping my behind turned toward him while he dwelled upon the sight of it. When I had returned to him, he made me bend, stoop, squat, stand erect, squeeze and spread. Now and again he slipped to his knees before that part which was his sole concern. He applied kisses to several different areas of it, even a few upon that most secret orifice; but all his kisses were distinguished by suction, his lips felt like leeches. While he was applying them here and there and everywhere he solicited numerous details concerning what had been done to me at the monastery of Saint Mary-in-the-Wood, and without noticing that my recitations doubled his warmth, I was candid enough to give them all with naïveté. He summoned up one of his youths and placing him beside me, he untied the bow securing a great red ribbon which gathered in white gauze pantaloons, and brought to light all the charms this garment concealed. After some deft caresses bestowed upon the same altar at which, in me, the Count had signaled his devotion, he suddenly exchanged the object and fell to sucking that part which characterized the child's sex. He continued to finger me whether because of habit in the youth, whether because of the satyr's dexterity, in a very brief space Nature, vanquished, caused there to flow into the mouth of the one what was ejected from the member of the other. That was how the libertine exhausted the unfortunate children he kept in his house, whose number we will shortly see; 'twas thus he sapped their strength, and that was what caused the languor in which I beheld them to be. And now let us see how he managed to keep women in the same state of prostration and what was the true cause of his own vigor's preservation.

The homage the Count rendered me had been protracted, but during it not a trace of infidelity to his chosen temple had he revealed; neither his glances, nor his kisses, nor his hands, nor his desires strayed away from it for an instant; after having sucked the other lad and having in likewise gathered and devoured his sperm:

"Come," he said to me, drawing me into an adjacent room

before I could gather up my clothes, "come, I am going to show you how we manage."

I was unable to dissimulate my anxiety, it was terrible; but there was no other way to put a different aspect upon my fate, I had to quaff to the lees the potion in the chalice tendered to me.

Two other boys of sixteen, quite as handsome, quite as peaked as the first two we had left in the salon, were working upon a tapestry when we entered the room. Upon our entrance they rose.

"Narcisse," said the Count to one of them, "here is the Countess' new chambermaid; I must test her; hand me the lancets."

Narcisse opens a cupboard and immediately produces all a surgeon's gear. I allow your imagination to fancy my state; my executioner spied my embarrassment, and it merely excited his mirth.

"Put her in place, Zéphire," Monsieur de Gernande said to another of the youths, and this boy approached me with a smile.

"Don't be afraid, Mademoiselle," said he, "it can only do you the greatest good. Take your place here."

It was a question of kneeling lightly upon the edge of a tabouret located in the middle of the room; one's arms were elevated and attached to two black straps which descended from the ceiling.

No sooner have I assumed the posture than the Count steps up scalpel in hand: he can scarcely breathe, his eyes are alive with sparks, his face smites me with terror; he ties bands about both my arms, and in a flash he has lanced each of them. A cry bursts from between his teeth, it is accompanied by two or three blasphemies when he catches sight of my blood; he retires to a distance of six feet and sits down. The light garment covering him is soon deployed; Zéphire kneels between his thighs and sucks him; Narcisse, his feet planted on his master's armchair, presents the same object to him to suckle he is himself having drained by Zéphire. Gernande gets his hands upon the boy's loins, squeezes them, presses them to him, but quits them long enough to cast his inflamed eyes toward me. My blood is escaping in floods and is falling into two white basins situated underneath my arms. I soon feel myself growing faint.

"Monsieur, Monsieur," I cry, "have pity on me, I am about to collapse."

I sway, totter, am held up by the straps, am unable to fall; but my arms having shifted, and my head slumping upon my shoulder, my face is now washed with blood. The Count is drunk with joy . . . however, I see nothing like the end of his operation approaching, I swoon before he reaches his goal; he was perhaps only able to attain it upon seeing me in this state, perhaps his supreme ecstasy depended upon this morbid picture. . . . At any rate, when I returned to my senses I found myself in an excellent bed, with two old women standing near me; as soon as they saw me open my eyes, they brought me a cup of bouillon and, at three-hour intervals, rich broths; this continued for two days, at the end of which Monsieur de Gernande sent to have me get up and come for a conversation in the same salon where I had been received upon my arrival. I was led to him; I was still a little weak and giddy, but otherwise well; I arrived.

"Thérèse," said the Count, bidding me be seated, "I shall not very often repeat such exercises with you, your person is useful for other purposes; but it was of the highest importance I acquaint you with my tastes and the manner in which you will expire in this house should you betray me one of these days, should you be unlucky enough to let yourself be suborned by the woman in whose society you are going to be placed.

"That woman belongs to me, Thérèse, she is my wife and that title is doubtless the most baleful she could have, since it obliges her to lend herself to the bizarre passion whereof you have been a recent victim; do not suppose it is vengeance that prompts me to treat her thus, scorn, or any sentiment of hostility or hatred; it is merely a question of passion. Nothing equals the pleasure I experience upon shedding her blood . . . I go mad when it flows; I have never enjoyed this woman in any other fashion. Three years have gone by since I married her, and for three years she has been regularly exposed every four days to the treatment you have undergone. Her youth (she is not yet twenty), the special care given her, all this keeps her aright; and as the reservoir is replenished at the same rate it is tapped, she has been in fairly good health since the regime began. Our relations being what they are, you perfectly well appreciate why I can neither allow her to go out nor to receive visitors. And so I represent her as insane and her mother, the only

iving member of her family, who resides in a château six leagues
rom here, is so firmly convinced of her derangement that she dares
iot even come to see her. Not infrequently the Countess implores
ny mercy, there is nothing she omits to do in order to soften me;
iut I doubt whether she shall ever succeed. My lust decreed her
'ate, it is immutable, she will go on in this fashion so long as she
s able; while she lives she will want nothing and as I am incredibly
ond of what can be drained from her living body, I will keep her
.live as long as possible; when finally she can stand it no more, well,
ush, Nature will take its course. She's my fourth; I'll soon have a
ifth. Nothing disturbs me less than to lose a wife. There are so
nany women about, and it is so pleasant to change.

"In any event, Thérèse, your task is to look after her. Her
,lood is let once every ninety-six hours; she loses two bowls of it
ach time and nowadays no longer faints, having got accustomed to
t. Her prostration lasts twenty-four hours; she is bedridden one
lay out of every four, but during the remaining three she gets on
olerably well. But you may easily understand this life displeases
ier; at the outset there was nothing she would not try to deliver
ierself from it, nothing she did not undertake to acquaint her
nother with her real situation: she seduced two of her maid-
ervants whose maneuvers were detected early enough to defeat
heir success: she was the cause of these two unhappy creatures'
iuin, today she repents what she did and, recognizing the irremedi-
ble character of her destiny, she is co-operating cheerfully and has
iromised not to make confederates of the help I hire to care for
er. But this secret and what becomes of those who conspire to be-
ray me, these matters, Thérèse, oblige me to put no one in her
eighborhood but persons who, like yourself, have been impressed;
nd thus inquiries are avoided. Not having carried you off from
nyone's house, not having to render an account of you to anyone
t all, nothing stands in the way of my punishing you, if you deserve
o be, in a manner which, although you will be deprived of mortal
reath, cannot nevertheless expose me to interrogations or embroil
ie in any unpleasantnesses. As of the present moment you inhabit
he world no longer, since the least impulse of my will can cause
ou to disappear from it. What can you expect at my hands? Happi-
ess if you behave properly, death if you seek to play me false.

Were these alternatives not so clear, were they not so few, I would
ask for your response; but in your present situation we can dispense
with questions and answers. I have you, Thérèse, and hence you
must obey me. . . . Let us go to my wife's apartment."

Having nothing to object to a discourse as precise as this, I
followed my master: we traversed a long gallery, as dark, as solitary as the rest of the château; a door opens, we enter an antechamber where I recognize the two elderly women who waited
upon me during my coma and recovery. They got up and introduced
us into a superb apartment where we found the unlucky Countess
doing tambour brocade as she reclined upon a chaise longue; she
rose when she saw her husband.

"Be seated," the Count said to her, "I permit you to listen to
me thus. Here at last we have a maid for you, Madame," he continued, "and I trust you will remember what has befallen the others
—and that you will not try to plunge this one into an identical misfortune."

"It would be useless," I said, full eager to be of help to this
poor woman and wishing to disguise my designs, "yes, Madame, I
dare certify in your presence that it would be to no purpose, you
will not speak one word to me I shall not report immediately to
his Lordship, and I shall certainly not jeopardize my life in order
to serve you."

"I will undertake nothing, Mademoiselle, which might force
you into that position," said this poor woman who did not yet
grasp my motives for speaking in this wise; "rest assured: I solicit
nothing but your care."

"It will be entirely yours, Madame," I answered, "but beyond
that, nothing."

And the Count, enchanted with me, squeezed my hand as he
whispered: "Nicely done, Thérèse, your prosperity is guaranteed if
you conduct yourself as you say you will." The Count then showed
me to my room which adjoined the Countess' and he showed me a
well that the entirety of this apartment, closed by stout doors and
double grilled at every window, left no hope of escape.

"And here you have a terrace," Monsieur de Gernande went
on, leading me out into a little garden on a level with the apartment, "but its elevation above the ground ought not, I believe, give

you the idea of measuring the walls; the Countess is permitted to take fresh air out here whenever she wishes, you will keep her company . . . adieu."

I returned to my mistress and, as at first we spent a few moments examining one another without speaking, I obtained a good picture of her—but let me paint it for you.

Madame de Gernande, aged nineteen and a half, had the most lovely, the most noble, the most majestic figure one could hope to see, not one of her gestures, not a single movement was without gracefulness, not one of her glances lacked depth of sentiment: nothing could equal the expression of her eyes, which were a beautiful dark brown although her hair was blond; but a certain languor, a lassitude entailed by her misfortunes, dimmed their *éclat,* and thereby rendered them a thousand times more interesting; her skin was very fair, her hair very rich; her mouth was very small, perhaps too small, and I was little surprised to find this defect in her: 'twas a pretty rose not yet in full bloom; but teeth so white . . . lips of a vermillion . . . one might have said Love had colored them with tints borrowed from the goddess of flowers; her nose was aquiline, straight, delicately modeled; upon her brow curved two ebony eyebrows; a perfectly lovely chin; a visage, in one word, of the finest oval shape, over whose entirety reigned a kind of attractiveness, a naïveté, an openness which might well have made one take this adorable face for an angelic rather than mortal physiognomy. Her arms, her breasts, her flanks were of a splendor . . . of a round fullness fit to serve as models to an artist; a black silken fleece covered her *mons veneris,* which was sustained by two superbly cast thighs; and what astonished me was that, despite the slenderness of the Countess' figure, despite her sufferings, nothing had impaired the firm quality of her flesh: her round, plump buttocks were as smooth, as ripe, as firm as if her figure were heavier and as if she had always dwelled in the depths of happiness. However, frightful traces of her husband's libertinage were scattered thickly about; but, I repeat, nothing spoiled, nothing damaged . . . the very image of a beautiful lily upon which the honeybee has inflicted some scratches. To so many gifts Madame de Gernande added a gentle nature, a romantic and tender mind, a heart of such sensibility! . . . well-educated, with talents . . . a native art for seduction which no one but her infamous husband could resist, a charming timbre in her voice and much piety: such was the unhappy wife of the Comte de Gernande, such was the heavenly creature against whom he had plotted; it seemed that the more she inspired ideas, the more she inflamed his ferocity, and that the abundant gifts she had received from Nature only became further motives for that villain's cruelties.

"When were you last bled, Madame?" I asked in order to have her understand I was acquainted with everything.

"Three days ago," she said, "and it is to be tomorrow. . . ." Then, with a sigh: ". . . yes, tomorrow . . . Mademoiselle, tomorrow you will witness the pretty scene."

"And Madame is not growing weak?"

"Oh, Great Heaven! I am not twenty and am sure I shall be no weaker at seventy. But it will come to an end, I flatter myself in the belief, for it is perfectly impossible for me to live much longer this way: I will go to my Father, in the arms of the Supreme Being I will seek a place of rest men have so cruelly denied me on earth."

These words clove my heart; wishing to maintain my role, I disguised my trouble, but upon the instant I made an inward promise to lay down my life a thousand times, if necessary, rather than leave this ill-starred victim in the clutches of this monstrous debauchee.

The Countess was on the point of taking her dinner. The two old women came to tell me to conduct her into her cabinet; I transmitted the message; she was accustomed to it all, she went out at once, and the two women, aided by the two valets who had carried me off, served a sumptuous meal upon a table at which my place was set opposite my mistress. The valets retired and the women informed me that they would not stir from the antechamber so as to be near at hand to receive whatever might be Madame's orders. I relayed this to the Countess, she took her place and, with an air of friendliness and affability which entirely won my heart, invited me to join her. There were at least twenty dishes upon the table.

"With what regards this aspect of things, Mademoiselle, you see that they treat me well."

"Yes, Madame," I replied, "and I know it is the wish of Monsieur le Comte that you lack nothing."

"Oh yes! But as these attentions are motivated only by cruelty, my feelings are scarcely of gratitude."

Her constant state of debilitation and perpetual need of what would revive her strength obliged Madame de Gernande to eat copiously. She desired partridge and Rouen duckling; they were brought to her in a trice. After the meal, she went for some air on the terrace, but upon rising she took my arm, for she was quite unable to take ten steps without someone to lean upon. It was at this moment she showed me all those parts of her body I have just described to you; she exhibited her arms: they were covered with small scars.

"Ah, he does not confine himself to that," she said, "there is not a single spot on my wretched person whence he does not love to see blood flow."

And she allowed me to see her feet, her neck, the lower part of her breasts and several other fleshy areas equally speckled with healed punctures. That first day I limited myself to murmuring a few sympathetic words and we retired for the night.

The morrow was the Countess' fatal day. Monsieur de Gernande, who only performed the operation after his dinner—which he always took before his wife ate hers—had me join him at table; it was then, Madame, I beheld that ogre fall to in a manner so terrifying that I could hardly believe my eyes. Four domestics, amongst them the pair who had led me to the château, served this amazing feast. It deserves a thorough description: I shall give it you without exaggeration. The meal was certainly not intended simply to overawe me. What I witnessed then was an everyday affair.

Two soups were brought on, one a consommé flavored with saffron, the other a ham bisque; then a sirloin of English roast beef, eight hors d'oeuvres, five substantial entrées, five others only apparently lighter, a boar's head in the midst of eight braised dishes which were relieved by two services of entremets, then sixteen plates of fruit; ices, six brands of wine, four varieties of liqueur and coffee. Monsieur de Gernande attacked every dish, and several were polished off to the last scrap; he drank a round dozen bottles of wine, four, to begin with, of Burgundy, four of Champagne with the roasts; Tokay, Mulseau, Hermitage and Madeira were downed

with the fruit. He finished with two bottles of West Indies rum
and ten cups of coffee.

As fresh after this performance as he might have been had he
just waked from sleep, Monsieur de Gernande said:

"Off we go to bleed your mistress; I trust you will let me know
if I manage as nicely with her as I did with you."

Two young boys I had not hitherto seen, and who were of the
same age as the others, were awaiting at the door of the Countess'
apartment; it was then the Count informed me he had twelve
minions and renewed them every year. These seemed yet prettier
than the ones I had seen hitherto; they were livelier . . . we went
in. . . . All the ceremonies I am going to describe now, Madame,
were part of a ritual from which the Count never deviated, they
were scrupulously observed upon each occasion, and nothing ever
changed except the place where the incisions were made.

The Countess, dressed only in a loose-floating muslin robe,
fell to her knees instantly the Count entered.

"Are you ready?" her husband inquired.

"For everything, Monsieur," was the humble reply; "you
know full well I am your victim and you have but to command me."

Monsieur de Gernande thereupon told me to undress his wife
and lead her to him. Whatever the loathing I sensed for all these
horrors, you understand, Madame, I had no choice but to submit
with the most entire resignation. In all I have still to tell you, do
not, I beseech you, do not at any time regard me as anything but a
slave; I complied simply because I could not do otherwise, but
never did I act willingly in anything whatsoever.

I removed my mistress' simar, and when she was naked conducted her to her husband who had already taken his place in a
large armchair: as part of the ritual she perched upon this armchair
and herself presented to his kisses that favorite part over which he
had made such a to-do with me and which, regardless of person or
sex, seemed to affect him in the same way.

"And now spread them, Madame," the Count said brutally.

And for a long time he rollicked about with what he enjoyed
the sight of; he had it assume various positions, he opened it, he
snapped it shut; with tongue and fingertip he tickled the narrow
aperture; and soon carried away by his passions' ferocity, he

plucked up a pinch of flesh, squeezed it, scratched it. Immediately he produced a small wound he fastened his mouth to the spot. I held his unhappy victim during these preliminaries, the two boys, completely naked, toiled upon him in relays; now one, now the other knelt between Gernande's thighs and employed his mouth to excite him. It was then I noticed, not without astonishment, that this giant, this species of monster whose aspect alone was enough to strike terror, was howbeit barely a man; the most meager, the most minuscule excrescence of flesh or, to make a juster comparison, what one might find in a child of three was all one discovered upon this so very enormous and otherwise so corpulent individual; but its sensations were not for that the less keen and each pleasurable vibration was as a spasmodic attack. After this prologue he stretched out upon a couch and wanted his wife, seated astride his chest, to keep her behind poised over his visage while with her mouth she rendered him, by means of suckings, the same service he had just received from the youthful Ganymedes who were simultaneously, one to the left, one to the right, being excited by him; my hands meanwhile worked upon his behind: I titillated it, I polluted it in every sense; this phase of activities lasted more than a quarter of an hour but, producing no results, had to be given up for another; upon her husband's instructions I stretched the Countess upon a chaise longue: she lay on her back, her legs spread as wide as possible. The sight of what she exposed put her husband in a kind of rage, he dwelt upon the perspective . . . his eyes blaze, he curses; like one crazed he leaps upon his wife, with his scalpel pricks her in several places, but these were all superficial gashes, a drop or two of blood, no more, seeped from each. These minor cruelties came to an end at last; others began. The Count sits down again, he allows his wife a moment's respite, and, turning his attention to his two little followers, he now obliges them to suck each other, and now he arranges them in such a way that while he sucks one, the other sucks him, and now again the one he sucked first brings round his mouth to render the same service to him by whom he was sucked: the Count received much but gave little. Such was his satiety, such his impotence that the extremest efforts availed not at all, and he remained in his torpor: he did indeed seem to experience some very violent reverberations, but nothing manifested itself; he several times ordered me to suck his little friends and immediately to convey to his mouth whatever incense I drained from them; finally he flung them one after the other at the miserable Countess. These young men accosted her, insulted her, carried insolence to the point of beating her, slapping her, and the more they molested her, the more loudly the Count praised and egged them on.

Then Gernande turned to me; I was in front of him, my buttocks at the level of his face, and he paid his respects to his God; but he did not abuse me; nor do I know why he did not torment his Ganymedes; he chose to reserve all his unkindness for the Countess. Perhaps the honor of being allied to him established one's right to suffer mistreatment at his hands; perhaps he was moved to cruelty only by attachments which contributed energy to his outrages. One can imagine anything about such minds, and almost always safely wager that what seems most apt to be criminal is what will inflame them most. At last he places his young friends and me beside his wife and enlaces our bodies; here a man, there a woman, etc., all four dressing their behinds; he takes his stand some distance away and muses upon the panorama, then he comes near, touches, feels, compares, caresses; the youths and I were not persecuted, but each time he came to his wife, he fussed and bothered and vexed her in some way or other. Again the scene changes: he has the Countess lie belly down upon a divan and taking each boy in turn, he introduces each of them into the narrow avenue Madame's posture exposes: he allows them to become aroused, but it is nowhere but in his mouth the sacrifice is to be consummated; as one after another they emerge he sucks each. While one acts, he has himself sucked by the other, and his tongue wanders to the throne of voluptuousness the agent presents to him. This activity continues a long time, it irritates the Count, he gets to his feet and wishes me to take the Countess' place; I instantly beg him not to require it of me, but he insists. He lays his wife upon her back, has me superimpose myself upon her with my flanks raised in his direction and thereupon he orders his aides to plumb me by the forbidden passage: he brings them up, his hands guide their introduction; meanwhile, I have got to stimulate the Countess with my fingers and kiss her mouth; as for the Count, his offertory is still the same; as each of the boys cannot act without exhibiting to him one of the sweetest objects of his veneration, he turns it all to his profit and, as with the Countess, he who has just perforated me is obliged to go, after a few lunges and retreats, and spill into his mouth the incense I have warmed. When the boys are finished, seemingly inclined to replace them, the Count glues himself to my buttocks.

"Superfluous efforts," he cries, "this is not what I must have . . . to the business . . . the business . . . however pitiable my state . . . I can hold back no longer . . . come, Countess, your arms!"

He seizes her ferociously, places her as I was placed, arms suspended by two black straps; mine is the task of securing the bands; he inspects the knots: finding them too loose, he tightens them, "So that," he says, "the blood will spurt out under greater pressure"; he feels the veins, and lances them, on each arm, at almost the same moment. Blood leaps far: he is in an ecstasy; and adjusting himself so that he has a clear view of these two fountains, he has me kneel between his legs so I can suck him; he does as much for first one and then the other of his little friends, incessantly eyeing the jets of blood which inflame him. For my part, certain the instant at which the hoped for crisis occurs will bring a conclusion to the Countess' torments, I bring all my efforts to bear upon precipitating this denouement, and I become, as, Madame, you observe, I become a whore from kindness, a libertine through virtue. The much awaited moment arrives at last; I am not familiar with its dangers or violence, for the last time it had taken place I had been unconscious. . . . Oh, Madame! what extravagance! Gernande remained delirious for ten minutes, flailing his arms, staggering, reeling like one falling in a fit of epilepsy, and uttering screams which must have been audible for a league around; his oaths were excessive; lashing out at everyone at hand, his strugglings were dreadful. The two little ones are sent tumbling head over heels; he wishes to fly at his wife, I restrain him: I pump the last drop from him, his need of me makes him respect me; at last I bring him to his senses by ridding him of that fiery liquid, whose heat, whose viscosity, and above all whose abundance puts him in such a frenzy I believe he is going to expire; seven or eight tablespoons would scarcely have contained the discharge, and the thickest gruel would hardly give a notion of its consistency; and with all that, no appearance of an erection at all, rather, the limp look and feel of exhaustion: there you have the contrarieties which, better than might I, explain artists of the Count's breed. The Count ate excessively and only dissipated each time he bled his wife, every four days, that is to say. Would this be the cause of the phenomenon? I have no idea, and not daring to ascribe a reason to what I do not understand, I will be content to relate what I saw.

However, I rush to the Countess, I stanch her blood, untie her, and deposit her upon a couch in a state of extreme weakness; but the Count, totally indifferent to her, without condescending to cast even a glance at this victim stricken by his rage, abruptly goes out with his aides, leaving me to put things in whatever order I please. Such is the fatal apathy which better than all else characterizes the true libertine soul: if he is merely carried away by passion's heat, limned with remorse will be his face when, calmed again, he beholds the baleful effects of delirium; but if his soul is utterly corrupt? then such consequences will affright him not: he will observe them with as little trouble as regret, perhaps even with some of the emotion of those infamous lusts which produced them.

I put Madame de Gernande to bed. She had, so she said, lost much more this time than she ordinarily did; but such good care and so many restoratives were lavished upon her, that she appeared well two days later. That same evening, when I had completed all my chores in the Countess' apartment, word arrived that the Count desired to speak to me; Gernande was taking supper; I was obliged to wait upon him while he fed with a much greater intemperance than at dinner; four of his pretty little friends were seated round the table with him and there, every evening, he regularly drank himself into drunkenness; but to that end, twenty bottles of the most excellent wine were scarcely sufficient and I often saw him empty thirty. And every evening, propped up by his minions, the debauchee went to bed, and took one or two of the boys with him; these were nothing but vehicles which disposed him for the great scene.

But I had discovered the secret of winning this man's very highest esteem: he frankly avowed to me that few women had pleased him so much; and thereby I acquired the right to his confidence, which I only exploited in order to serve my mistress.

One morning Gernande called me to his room to inform me of

some new libertine schemes; after having listened closely and approved enthusiastically, and seeing him in a relatively calm state, I undertook to persuade him to mitigate his poor wife's fate. "Is it possible, Monsieur," I said to him, "that one may treat a woman in this manner, even setting aside all the ties which bind you to her? Condescend to reflect upon her sex's touching graces."

"Oh Thérèse!" the Count answered with alacrity, "why in order to pacify me do you bring me arguments which could not more positively arouse me? Listen to me, my dear girl," he continued, having me take a place beside him, "and whatever the invectives you may hear me utter against your sex, don't lose your temper; no, a reasoned discussion; I'll yield to your arguments if they're logically sound.

"How are you justified, pray tell me, Thérèse, in asserting that a husband lies under the obligation to make his wife happy? and what titles dares this woman cite in order to extort this happiness from her husband? The necessity mutually to render one another happy cannot legitimately exist save between two persons equally furnished with the capacity to do one another hurt and, consequently, between two persons of commensurate strength: such an association can never come into being unless a contract is immediately formed between these two persons, which obligates each to employ against the other no kind of force but what will not be injurious to either; but this ridiculous convention assuredly can never obtain between two persons one of whom is strong and the other weak. What entitles the latter to require the former to treat kindly with him? and what sort of a fool would the stronger have to be in order to subscribe to such an agreement? I can agree not to employ force against him whose own strength makes him to be feared; but what could motivate me to moderate the effects of my strength upon the being Nature subordinates to me? Pity, do you say? That sentiment is fitting for no one but the person who resembles me and as he is an egoist too, pity's effects only occur under the tacit circumstances in which the individual who inspires my commiseration has sympathy for me in his turn; but if my superiority assures me a constant ascendancy over him, his sympathy becoming valueless to me, I need never, in order to excite it, consent to any sacrifice. Would I not be a fool to feel pity for the chicken they slaughtered for my dinner? That object, too inferior to me, lacking any relation to me, can never excite any feelings in me; well, the relationships of a wife to her husband and that of the chicken to myself are of identical consequence, the one and the other are household chattels which one must use, which one must employ for the purpose indicated by Nature, without any differentiation whatsoever. But, I ask, had it been Nature's intention to create your sex for the happiness of ours and vice versa, would this blind Nature have caused the existence of so many ineptitudes in the construction of the one and the other of those sexes? Would she have implanted faults so grave in each that mutual estrangement and antipathy were bound infallibly to be their result? Without going any further in search of examples, be so good as to tell me, Thérèse, knowing my organization to be what it is, what woman could I render happy? and, reversibly, to what man can the enjoyment of a woman be sweet when he is not endowed with the gigantic proportions necessary to satisfy her? In your opinion, will they be moral qualities which will compensate his physical shortcomings? And what thinking being, upon knowing a woman to her depths, will not cry with Euripides: 'That one amongst the Gods who brought women into the world may boast of having produced the worst of all creatures and the most afflicting to man.' If then it is demonstrated that the two sexes do not at all sort agreeably with each other and that there is not one well-founded grievance of the one which could not equally and immediately be voiced by the other, it is therefore false, from this moment, to say that Nature created them for their reciprocal happiness. She may have permitted them the desire to attain each other's vicinity in order to conjugate in the interests of propagation, but in no wise in order to form attachments with the design of discovering a mutual felicity. The weaker therefore having no right to mouth complaints with the object of wresting pity from the stronger and no longer being able to raise the objection that the stronger depends for his happiness upon her, the weaker, I say, has no alternative but to submit; and as, despite the difficulty of achieving that bilateral happiness, it is natural that individuals of both sexes labor at nothing but to procure it for themselves, the weaker must reconcile herself to distilling from her submissiveness the only dose of happiness she can possibly hope to cull, and the stronger must strive after his by whatever oppressive methods he is pleased to employ, since it is proven that the mighty's sole happiness is yielded him by the exercise of his strong faculties, by, that is to say, the most thorough-going tyranny; thus, that happiness the two sexes cannot find with each other they will find, one in blind obedience, the other in the most energetic expression of his domination. Why! were it not Nature's intention that one of the sexes tyrannize the other, would she not have created them equally strong? By rendering one in every particular inferior to the other, has she not adequately indicated that she wills the mightier to exploit the rights she has given him? the more the latter broadens his authority, the more, by means of his preponderance, he worsens the misery of the woman enthralled by her destiny, the better he answers Nature's intentions; the frail being's complaints do not provide a correct basis for analyzing the process; judgments thus come by would be nothing if not vicious, since, to reach them, you would have to appropriate none but the feeble's ideas: the suit must be judged upon the stronger party's power, upon the scope he has given to his power, and when this power's effects are brought to bear upon a woman, one must examine the question, What is a woman? and how has this contemptible sex been viewed in ancient times and in our own by seventy-five per cent of the peoples of this earth?

"Now, what do I observe upon coolly proceeding to this investigation? A puny creature, always inferior to man, infinitely less attractive than he, less ingenious, less wise, constructed in a disgusting manner entirely opposite to what is capable of pleasing a man, to what is able to delight him . . . a being three-quarters of her life untouchable, unwholesome, unable to satisfy her mate throughout the entire period Nature constrains her to childbearing, of a sharp turn of humor, shrill, shrewish, bitter, and thwart; a tyrant if you allow her privileges, mean, vile, and a sneak in bondage; always false, forever mischievous, constantly dangerous; in short, a being so perverse that during several convocations the question was very soberly agitated at the Council of Mâcon whether or not this peculiar creature, as distinct from man as is man from the ape, had any reasonably legitimate pretensions to classification as a human; but this quandary might be merely an error of the times; were women more favorably viewed in earlier ages? Did the Persians, the Medes, the Babylonians, the Greeks, the Romans honor this odious sex we are able to dare make our idol today? Alas! I see it oppressed everywhere, everywhere rigorously banished from affairs, contemned everywhere, vilified, sequestered, locked up; women treated, in a word, like beasts one stables in the barn and puts to use when the need arises. Do I pause a moment at Rome? then I hear the wise Cato exclaim from the heart of the ancient world's capital: 'Were women lacking to men, they would yet hold conversation with the Gods.' I hear a Roman censor begin his harangue with these words: 'Gentlemen, were we ever to find a means to live without women, thereupon unto us should true happiness be known.' I hear the Greek theater resound to these lines intoned: 'O Zeus! what reason was it obliged thee to create women? couldst not have given being to humankind by better devices and wiser, by schemes which in a word would have spared us this female pestilence?' I see this same Greek race hold that sex in such high contempt legislation was needed to oblige a Spartan to reproduce, and one of the penalties decreed in those enlightened republics was to compel a malefactor to garb himself in a woman's attire, that is to say, to wear the raiments of the vilest and most scorned creature of which man had acquaintance.

"But without inquiring for examples in ages at such a great remove from ours, with what sort of an eye is this wretched sex still viewed upon the earth's surface? How is it dealt with? I behold it imprisoned throughout Asia and serving there as slave to the barbarous whims of a despot who molests it, torments it, and turns its sufferings into a game. In America I find a naturally humane race, the Eskimos, practicing all possible acts of beneficence amongst men and treating women with all imaginable severity: I see them humiliated, prostituted to strangers in one part of the world, used as currency in another. In Africa, where without doubt their station is yet further degraded, I notice them toiling in the manner of beasts of burden, tilling the soil, fertilizing it and sowing seed, and serving their husbands on their knees only. Will I follow Captain Cook in his newest discoveries? Is the charming isle of Tahiti, where pregnancy is a crime sometimes meriting death for the mother and almost always for the child, to offer me women enjoying a happier lot? In the other islands this same mariner charted, I find them beaten, harassed by their own offspring, and bullied by the husband himself who collaborates with his family to torment them with additional rigor.

"Oh, Thérèse! let not all this astonish you, nor be more surprised by the general pre-eminence accorded men over their wives in all epochs: the more a people is in harmony with Nature, the better will be its use of her laws; the wife can have no relation to her husband but that of a slave to his master; very decidedly she has no right to pretend to more cherished titles. One must not mistake for a prerogative the ridiculous abuses which, by degrading our sex, momentarily elevates yours: the cause for these travesties must be sought out, enunciated, and afterward one must only the more constantly return to reason's sagacious counsels. Well, Thérèse, here is the cause of the temporary respect your sex once upon a time enjoyed and which it still misuses today while they who perpetuate it are unaware of what they are doing.

"In the Gaul of long ago, that is to say, in that one part of the world where women were not totally treated as slaves, women had the habit of prophesying, of predicting the happy event: the people fancied they plied their trade successfully only because of the intimate commerce they doubtless had with the Gods; whence they were, so to speak, associated with the sacerdotal and enjoyed a measure of the consideration lavished upon priests. French chivalry was founded upon these inanities and finding them favorable to its spirit, adopted them: but what happened next was what happens always: the causes became extinct, the effects were preserved; chivalry vanished, the prejudices it nourished persevered. This ancient veneration accorded for no sound reason could not itself be annihilated when what founded the illusion had dissipated: we no longer stand in awe of witches, but we reverence whores and, what is worse, we continue to kill each other for them. May such platitudes cease to influence these our philosophers' minds, and restoring women to their true position, may the intelligent spirit conceive them, as Nature indicates, as the wisest peoples acknowledge, to be nothing but individuals created for their pleasures, submitted to their caprices, objects whose frailty and wickedness make them deserving of naught but contempt.

"But not only, Thérèse, did all the peoples of the earth enjoy the most extensive rights over their women, there were even to be found certain races which condemned women to death immediately they were born into the world, and of their numbers retained only those few necessary to the race's reproduction. The Arabs known as Koreish interred their daughters at the age of seven upon a mountain near Mecca, because, said they, so vile a sex appeared to them unworthy of seeing the light; in the seraglio of the King of Achem, the most appalling tortures are applied as punishment for the mere suspicion of infidelity, for the slightest disobedience in the service of the prince's lusts, or as soon as his women inspire his distaste; upon the banks of the River Ganges they are obliged to immolate themselves over their husbands' ashes, for they are esteemed of no further purpose in the world once their lords are able to enjoy them no more; in other regions they are hunted like wild beasts, 'tis an honor to kill a quantity of them; in Egypt they are sacrificed to the Gods; they are trampled under foot in Formosa if they become pregnant; German law condemned the man who killed a foreign woman to pay a fine of about ten crowns, nothing at all if the woman was his own or a courtesan; everywhere, to be brief, everywhere, I repeat, I see women humiliated, molested, everywhere sacrificed to the superstition of priests, to the savagery of husbands, to the playfulness of libertines. And because I have the misfortune to live amidst a people still so uncouth as not to dare abolish the most ludicrous of prejudices, I should deprive myself of the rights Nature has granted me! I should forgo all the pleasures to which these privileges give birth! . . . Come, come, Thérèse, that's not just, no, 'tis unfair: I will conceal my behavior because I must, but I will be compensated, in the retreat where I have exiled myself, and silently, for the absurd chains to which I am condemned by legislation, and here I will treat my wife as I like, for I find my right to do so lettered in all the universe's codes, graved in my heart, and sealed in Nature."

"Oh Monsieur," said I, "your conversion is impossible."

"And I advise you not to attempt it, Thérèse," Gernande answered; "the tree is too long out of the nursery; at my age one can advance a few steps in the career of evil, but not one toward good. My principles and my tastes have brought me joy since childhood, they have always been the unique bases of my conduct and actions: I will, who knows? go further, I have the feeling it could be done, but return? never; I have too great a horror for mankind's prejudices, I too sincerely hate their civilization, their virtue and their Gods ever to sacrifice my penchants to them."

From this moment I saw very clearly that nothing remained for me, in order either to extricate myself from this house or to save the Countess, but the employment of stratagems and joint action with her.

During the year I had spent in the house, what I had allowed her to read in my heart was more than sufficient to dispel any doubts she might have of my desire to serve her, and now she could not fail to divine what had at first prompted me to act differently. I became less guarded, then spoke; she assented; we settled upon a plan: it was to inform her mother, to expose the Count's infamies to her eyes. Madame de Gernande was certain that unfortunate lady would hasten with all expedition to sever her daughter's bonds; but how were we to approach her? for we were so securely imprisoned, so closely watched! Accustomed to coping with ramparts, I gauged those upon which the terrace was raised: their height was scarcely thirty feet; there was no other enclosure in sight; once at the foot of the wall I thought one would find oneself already on the road through the forest; but the Countess, having been brought to this apartment at night and never having left it since, was unable to confirm my ideas. I agreed to attempt the descent; the letter Madame de Gernande wrote to her mother could not have been better phrased to melt and persuade her to come to the rescue of her most unhappy daughter; I slipped the letter into my bosom, I embraced that dear and attractive woman, then, as soon as night had fallen, aided by our bed linen, I slid to the ground outside the fortress. What had become of me, O Heaven! I discovered that instead of being outside the enclosure I was simply in a park, and in a park girt by walls which the quantity and dense foliage of trees had camouflaged from sight: these battlements were more than forty feet high, all of them garnished at the top with broken glass, and of a prodigious thickness . . . what was to become of me? Dawn was not far off: what would they think when I was found in a place into which I could not have come without a certain plan of escape?

Would I be able to keep the Count's fury at bay? Was it not very likely that ogre would drink my blood to punish such an offense? To return was out of the question, the Countess had drawn back the sheets; to knock at the door would be still more certainly to betray myself; a little more and I would have lost my head altogether and ceded to the violent effects of my despair. Had I been able to recognize some pity in the Count's soul, I might perhaps have been lulled into hopefulness, but a tyrant, a barbarian, a man who detested women and who, he said, had long been seeking the occasion to immolate one by draining away her blood drop by drop in order to find out how many hours she would be able to last . . . No doubt about it, he was going to put me to the test. Knowing not what would happen or what to do, discovering dangers everywhere, I threw myself down beside a tree, determined to await my fate and silently resigning myself to the Eternal's will. . . . The sun rose at last; merciful Heaven! the first object to present itself to me . . . is the Count himself: it had been frightfully warm during the night, he had stepped out to take a breath of air. He believes he is in error, he supposes this a specter, he recoils, rarely is courage a traitor's virtue: I get trembling to my feet, I fling myself at his knees.

"Thérèse! What are you doing here?" he demands.

"Oh, Monsieur, punish me," I reply, "I am guilty and have nothing to answer you."

Unhappily, in my fright I had forgotten to destroy the Countess' letter: he suspects its existence, asks for it, I wish to deny I have it; but Gernande sees the fatal letter protruding above my kerchief, snatches it, reads it, and orders me to follow him.

We enter the château, descend a hidden stairway leading down to the vaults: the most profound stillness reigns there below ground; after several detours, the Count opens a dungeon and casts me into it.

"Impudent girl," says he, "I gave you warning that the crime you have just committed is punished here by death: therefore prepare yourself to undergo the penalty you have been pleased to incur. When tomorrow I rise from dinner I am going to dispatch you."

Once again I fall prostrate before him but, seizing me by the hair, he drags me along the ground, pulls me several times around my prison, and ends by hurling me against the wall in such a manner I am nigh to having my brains dashed out.

"You deserve to have me open your four veins this instant," says he as he closes the door, "and if I postpone your death, be very sure it is only in order to render it the more horrible."

He has left; I am in a state of the most violent agitation; I shall not describe the night I passed: my tormented imagination together with the physical hurt done me by the monster's initial cruelties made it one of the most dreadful I had ever gone through. One has no conception of what anguish is suffered by the wretch who from hour to hour awaits his ordeal, from whom hope has fled, and who knows not whether this breath he draws may not be his last. Uncertain of the torture, he pictures it in a thousand forms, one more frightful than the other; the least noise he hears may be that of his approaching assassins; the blood freezes in his veins, his heart grows faint, and the blade which is to put a period to his days is less cruel than those terrible instants swollen with the menace of death.

In all likelihood the Count began by revenging himself upon his wife: you will be as convinced of it as I by the event which saved me. For thirty-six hours I lingered in the critical condition I have just described; during that time I was brought no relief; and then my door was opened and the Count appeared: he was alone, fury glittered in his eyes.

"You must be fully cognizant of the death you are going to undergo: this perverse blood has got to be made to seep out of you: you will be bled three times a day, I want to see how long you can survive the treatment. 'Tis an experiment I have been all afire to make, you know; my thanks to you for furnishing me the means."

And, for the time being occupying himself with no passion but his vengeance, the monster made me stretch forth an arm, pricked it and stopped the wound after he had drawn two bowls of blood. He had scarcely finished when cries were heard.

"Oh, my Lord, my Lord!" exclaimed one of the servants who came running up to him, "come as quick as ever you can, Madame is dying, she wishes to speak to you before she gives up her soul."

And the old woman turned and flew back to her mistress.

However habituated one may be to crime, it is rarely that news of its accomplishment does not strike terror into him who has committed it; this fear avenges Virtue: Virtue resumes possession of its rights: Gernande goes out in alarm, he forgets to secure the dungeon's doors; although enfeebled by a forty hours' fast and the blood I have lost, I exploit my opportunity, leap from my cell, find my way unimpeded, traverse the court, the park, and reach the forest without having been perceived. Walk, I say to myself, walk, walk, be courageous; if the mighty scorn the weak, there is an omnipotent God Who shields the latter and Who never abandons them. My head crowded with these ideas, I advance with a stout heart and before night closes I find myself in a cottage four leagues from the château. Some money remained to me, my needs were attended to, in a few hours I was rested. I left at daybreak and, renouncing all plans to register old or new complaints with the authorities, I asked to be directed toward Lyon; the road was pointed out to me and on the eighth day I reached that city, very weak, suffering much, but happy and unpursued; once arrived, I turned all my thoughts to recovery before striking out for Grenoble where, according to one of my persistent notions, happiness awaited me.

One day my eye fell upon a gazette printed in some distant place; what was my surprise to behold crime crowned once again and to see one of the principal authors of my miseries arrived at the pinnacle of success. Rodin, the surgeon of Saint-Michel, that infamous wretch who had punished me with such cruelty for having wished to spare him the murder of his daughter, had just, the newspaper declared, been named First Surgeon to the Empress of Russia with the considerable emoluments accompanying that post. May he prosper, the villain, I muttered to myself, may he be so whilst Providence so wills it; and thou, unhappy creature, suffer, suffer uncomplainingly, since it is decreed that tribulations and pain must be Virtue's frightful share; no matter, I shall never lose my taste for it.

But I was far from done with these striking examples of the triumph of vice, examples so disheartening for Virtue, and the flourishing condition of the personage whose acquaintance I was about to renew was surely to exasperate and amaze me more than any other, since it was that of one of the men at whose hands I had endured the bloodiest outrages. I was exclusively busied with preparing my departure when one evening a lackey clad in gray and completely unknown to me brought me a note; upon presenting it, he said his master had charged him to obtain my response without fail. The missive was worded this way: "A man who has somewhat wronged you, who believes he recognized you in the Place de Bellecour, is most desirous to see you and to make amends for his conduct: hasten to come to meet him; he has things to tell you which may help liquidate his entire indebtedness to you."

The message carried no signature and the lackey offered no explanations. Having declared I was resolved to make no answer at all lest I was informed of who his master was:

"He is Monsieur de Saint-Florent, Mademoiselle," the lackey said; "he has had the honor to know you formerly in the neighborhood of Paris; you rendered him, he maintains, services for which he burns to attest his gratitude. Presently risen to a position of undisputed eminence in this city's commercial circles, he at once enjoys the consideration and the means which put him in a position to prove his regard for you. He awaits you."

My deliberations were soon completed. If this man had other than good intentions, I said to myself, would he be apt to write to me, to have me spoken to in this fashion? He repented his past infamies, was covered with remorse, it was with horror he remembered having torn from me what I cherished most and, by inaugurating a sequence of nightmares, having reduced me to the cruelest circumstances a woman may know . . . yes, yes, no doubt of it, this is repentance, I should be culpable before the Supreme Being were I not to consent to assuage his sufferings. Am I in a position, furthermore, to spurn the support that is proposed here? Rather, ought I not eagerly snatch at all that is offered to relieve me? This man wishes to see me in his town house: his prosperity must surround him with servants before whom he will have to act with enough dignity to prevent him from daring to fail me again, and in my state, Great God! can I inspire anything but sympathy in him? Therefore I assured Saint-Florent's lackey that upon the morrow at eleven o'clock I would take the privilege of going to salute his master; that I congratulated him upon his good fortune, and added that luck had treated me in nothing approaching the same manner.

I returned to my room, but I was so preoccupied with what this man might wish to say to me that I slept not a wink all night; the next day I arrived at the indicated address: a superb mansion, a throng of domestics, that insolent *canaille*'s contemptuous glances at the poverty it scorned, everything afflicts me and I am about ready to retreat when up comes the same liveryman who had spoken to me the previous evening, and, reassuring me, he conducts me into a sumptuous drawing room where, although it is nine years since I have set eyes on him, I perfectly recognize my butcher who has now reached the age of forty-five. He does not rise upon my entrance, but gives the order we be left alone, and gestures me to come and seat myself near the vast armchair where he is enthroned.

"I wanted to see you again, my child," says he with a humiliating tone of superiority, "not that I thought I had much wronged you, not that a troublesome recollection bids me make restitutions from which I believe my position exempts me; but I remember that, however brief was our acquaintance, you exhibited some parts during it: wit and character are needed for what I have to propose to you and if you accept, the need I will then have of you will insure your discovery of the resources which are necessary to you, and upon which it should be in vain you were to count without signifying your agreement."

I wished to reply with some reproaches for the levity of this beginning, but Saint-Florent imposed silence upon me.

"'Tis water under the bridge," says he, "a purely emotional episode, and my principles support the belief I have, that no brake should be applied to passion; when the appetites speak, they must be heard: that's my law. When I was captured by the thieves with whom you were, did you see me burst into tears? Swallow the bitter pill and act with diligence if one is weak, enjoy all one's rights if powerful: that's my doctrine. You were young and pretty, Thérèse, we found ourselves in the middle of a forest, nothing so arouses me sensually as the rape of a young virgin girl; such you were, I raped you; I might perhaps have done worse had what I attempted not met with success and had you put up any resistance. But I raped

you, then left you naked and robbed in the middle of the night, upon
a perilous road: two motives gave rise to that further villainy: I
needed money and had none; as for the other reason which drove
me to do this, 'twould be in vain were I to explain it, Thérèse, it
would surpass your understanding. Only those spirits who are deep-
learned in the heart of man, who have studied its innermost re-
cesses, gained access to the most impenetrable nooks of this dim-lit
labyrinth, they alone might be able to account for this consequence
of an aberration."

"What, Monsieur! the money I gave you . . . the service I had
just rendered you . . . to be paid for what I did in your behalf by
the blackest treachery . . . that may, you think, be understood,
justified?"

"Why yes, Thérèse! yes indeed! the proof an explanation
exists for all I did is that, having just pillaged you, molested you
. . . (for, Thérèse, I did beat you, you know), why! having taken
twenty steps, I stopped and, meditating upon the state in which
I had left you, I at once found strength in these ideas, enough to
perpetrate additional outrages I might not have committed had it
not been for that: you had lost but one maidenhead. . . . I turned,
retraced my steps, and made short work of the other. . . . And so
it is true that in certain souls lust may be born from the womb of
crime! What do I say? it is thus true that only crime awakes and
stiffens lust and that there is not a single voluptuous pleasure it
does not inflame and improve. . . ."

"Oh Monsieur! what horror is this?"

"Could I not have acquitted myself of a still greater? I was
close enough to it, I confess, but I was amply sure you were going
to be reduced to the last extremities: the thought satisfied me, I left
you. Well, Thérèse, let's leave the subject and continue to my
reason for desiring to see you.

"My incredible appetite for both of a little girl's maidenheads
has not deserted me, Thérèse," Saint-Florent pursued; "with this
it is as with all libertinage's other extravagances: the older you
grow, the more deeply they take root; from former misdeeds fresh
desires are born, and new crimes from these desires. There would
be nothing to the matter, my dear, were not the means one employs
to succeed exceedingly culpable. But as the desire of evil is the

primum mobile of our caprices, the more criminal the thing we are led to do, the better our irritation. When one arrives at this stage, one merely complains of the mediocrity of the means: the more encompassing their atrociousness, the more piquant our joy becomes, and thus one sinks in the quagmire without the slightest desire to emerge.

"That, Thérèse, is my own history: two young children are necessary for my daily sacrifices; having once enjoyed them, not only do I never again set eyes upon these objects, but it even becomes essential to my fantasies' entire satisfaction that they instantly leave the city: I should not at all savor the following day's pleasures were I to imagine that yesterday's victims still breathed the same air I inhale; the method for being rid of them is not complicated. Would you believe it, Thérèse? They are my debauches which populate Languedoc and Provence with the multitude of objects of libertinage with which those regions are teeming:[5] one hour after these little girls have served me, reliable emissaries pack them off and sell them to the matchmakers of Montpellier, Toulouse, Nîmes, Aix, and Marseilles: this trade, two-thirds of whose net profits go to me, amply recompenses the outlay required to procure my subjects, and thus I satisfy two of my most cherished passions, lust and greed; but reconnoitering and seduction are bothersome. Furthermore, the kind of subject is of infinite importance to my lubricity: I must have them all procured from those asylums of misery where the need to live and the impossibility of managing to do so eat away courage, pride, delicacy, finally rot the soul, and, in the hope of an indispensable subsistence, steel a person to undertake whatever appears likely to provide it. I have all these nests ransacked, all these dungheaps combed pitilessly: you've no idea what they yield; I would even go further, Thérèse: I say that civil activity, industry, a little social ease would defeat my subornations and divest me of a great pro-

---

[5] Let this not be mistaken for a fable: this wretched figure existed in this same Lyon. What is herein related of his maneuvers is exact and authentic: he cost the honor of between fifteen and twenty thousand unhappy little creatures: upon the completion of each operation, the victim was embarked on the Rhône, and for thirty years the above-mentioned cities were peopled with the objects of this villain's debauchery, with girls undone by him. There is nothing fictitious about this episode but the gentleman's name.

portion of my subjects: I combat these perils with the influence I enjoy in this city, I promote commercial and economic fluctuations or instigate the rise of prices which, enlarging the poverty-stricken class, depriving it, on the one hand, of possibilities of work and on the other rendering difficult those of survival, increases according to a predictable ratio the total number of the subjects misery puts into my clutches. The strategy is a familiar one, Thérèse: these scarcities of firewood, dearths of wheat and of other edibles wherefrom Paris has been trembling for so many years, have been created for the identical purposes which animate me: avarice, libertinage: such are the passions which, from the gilded halls of the rich, extend a multitude of nets to ensnare the poor in their humble dwellings. But whatever skill I employ to press hard in this sector, if dexterous hands do not pluck nimbly in another, I get nothing for my troubles, and the machine goes quite as badly as if I were to cease to exhaust my imagination in devising and my credit in operating. And so I need a clever woman, young and intelligent, who, having herself found her way through misery's thorny pathways, is more familiar than anyone else with the methods for debauching those who are in the toils; a woman whose keen eyes will descry adversity in its darkest caves and attics, whose suborning intelligence will determine destitution's victims to extricate themselves from oppression by the means I make available; a spirited woman, in a word, unscrupulous and ruthless, who will stop at nothing in order to succeed, who will even go to the point of cutting away the scanty reserves which, still bolstering up those wretches' hopes, inhibit them from taking the final step. I had an excellent woman and trustworthy, she has just died: it cannot be imagined to what lengths that brilliant creature carried effrontery; not only did she use to isolate these wretches until they would be forced to come begging on their knees, but if these devices did not succeed in accelerating their fall, the impatient villain would hasten matters by kidnaping them. She was a treasure; I need but two subjects a day, she would have got me ten had I wanted them. The result was I used to be able to make better selections, and the superabundance of raw material consumed by my operations reimbursed me for inflated labor costs. That's the woman I have got to replace, my dear, you'll have four people under your command and ten thousand crowns wages for your trouble; I have had my say, Thérèse; give me your answer, and above all do not let your illusions prevent you from accepting happiness when chance and my hand offer it to you."

"Oh Monsieur," I say to this dishonest man, shuddering at his speech, "is it possible you have been able to conceive such joys and that you dare propose that I serve them? What horrors you have just uttered in my hearing! Cruel man, were you to be miserable for but two days, you would see these doctrines upon humanity swiftly obliterated from your heart: it is prosperity blinds and hardens you: mightily blasé you are before the spectacle of the evils whence you suppose yourself sheltered, and because you hope never to suffer them, you consider you have the right to inflict them; may happiness never come nigh unto me if it can produce this degree of corruption! O Just Heaven! not merely to be content to abuse the misfortunate! To drive audacity and ferocity to the point of increasing it, of prolonging it for the unique gratification of one's desires! What cruelty, Monsieur! the wildest animals do not give us the example of a comparable barbarity."

"You are mistaken, Thérèse, there is no roguery the wolf will not invent to draw the lamb into his clutches: these are natural ruses, while benevolence has nothing to do with Nature: charity is but an appurtenance of the weakness recommended by the slave who would propitiate his master and dispose him to leniency; it never proclaimed itself in man save in two cases: in the event he is weak, or in the event he fears he will become weak; that this alleged virtue is not natural is proven by the fact it is unknown to the man who lives in a state of Nature. The savage expresses his contempt for charity when pitilessly he massacres his brethren from motives of either revenge or cupidity . . . would he not respect that virtue were it etched in his heart? but never does it appear there, never will it be found wherever men are equal. Civilization, by weeding certain individuals out of society, by establishing rank and class, by giving the rich man a glimpse of the poor, by making the former dread any change of circumstances which might precipitate him into the latter's misery, civilization immediately puts the desire into his head to relieve the poor in order that he may be helped in his turn should he chance to lose his wealth; and thus was benevolence born, the fruit of civilization and fear: hence it is merely a circumstantial virtue, but nowise a sentiment originating in Nature, who never inserted any other desire in us but that of satisfying ourselves at no matter what the price. It is thus by confounding every sentiment, it is by continually refusing to analyze a single one of them that these people are able to linger in total darkness about them all and deprive themselves of every pleasurable enjoyment."

"Ah, Monsieur," I interrupted with great emotion, "may there be one any sweeter than the succoring of misfortune? Leaving aside the dread lest someday one have to endure suffering oneself, is there any more substantial satisfaction than that to be had from obliging others? . . . from relishing gratitude's tearful thanks, from partaking of the well-being you have just distributed like manna to the downtrodden who, your own fellow creatures, nevertheless want those things which you take airily for granted; oh! to hear them sing your praise and call you their father, to restore serenity to brows clouded by failure, destitution, and despair; no, Monsieur, not one of this world's lewd pleasures can equal this: it is that of the Divinity Himself, and the happiness He promises to those who on earth will serve Him, is naught other than the possibility to behold or make happy creatures in Heaven. All virtues stem directly from that one, Monsieur; one is a better father, a better son, a better husband when one knows the charm of alleviating misfortune's lot. One might say that like unto the sun's rays, the charitable man's presence sheds fertility, sweetness, and joy everywhere about and upon all, and the miracle of Nature, after this source of celestial light, is the honest, delicate, and sensitive soul whose supreme felicity consists in laboring in behalf of that of others."

"Feeble Phoebus stuff, Thérèse," Saint-Florent smiled; "the character of man's enjoyment is determined by the kind of organs he has received from Nature; a weak individual's, and hence every woman's, incline in the direction of procuring moral ecstasies which are more keenly felt than any other by these persons whose physical constitution happens to be entirely devoid of energy; quite the opposite is the case for vigorous spirits who are far more delighted by powerful shocks imparted to what surround them than they would be by the delicate impressions the feeble creatures by whom they are surrounded inevitably prefer, as befits their constitution; similarly the vigorous spirits delight more in what affects others painfully than in what affects them agreeably: such is the only difference between the cruel and the meek; both groups are endowed with sensibility, but each is endowed with it in a special manner. I do not deny that each class knows its pleasures, but I, together with a host of philosophers, maintain of course that those of the individual constructed in the more vigorous fashion are incontestably more lively than all his adversary's; and, these axioms established, there may and there must be men of one sort who take as much joy in everything cruelty suggests, as the other category of persons tastes delight in benevolence; but the pleasures of the latter will be mild, those of the former keen and strong: these will be the most sure, the most reliable, and doubtless the most authentic, since they characterize the penchants of every man who is still a creature of Nature, and indeed of all children before they have fallen under the sway of civilization; the others will merely be the effect of this civilization and, consequently, of deceiving and vapid delights. Well, my child, since we are met not so much in order to philosophize as to conclude a bargain, be so kind as to give me your final decision . . . do you or do you not accept the post I propose to you?"

"I very decidedly reject it, Monsieur," I replied, getting to my feet, ". . . indeed I am poor . . . oh yes! very poor, Monsieur; but richer in my heart's sentiments than I could be in all fortune's blessings; never will I sacrifice the one in order to possess the other; I may die in indigence, but I will not betray Virtue."

"Get out," the detestable man said to me, "and, above all, should I have anything to fear from your indiscretion, you will be promptly conveyed to a place where I need dread it no longer."

Nothing heartens Virtue like the fear of vice; a good deal less timorous than I should have thought, I dared, upon promising he would have nothing to dread at my hands, remind him of what he had stolen from me in the forest of Bondy and apprise him of my present circumstances which, I said, made this money indispensable to me. The monster gave me harsh answer, declaring it was up to me to earn it and that I had refused.

"No Monsieur, no," I replied firmly, "no, I repeat, I would rather perish a thousand times over than preserve my life at that price."

"And as for myself," Saint-Florent rejoined, "there is in the same way nothing I would not prefer to the chagrin of disbursing unearned money: despite the refusal you have the insolence to give me, I should relish passing another fifteen minutes in your company; and so if you please, we will move into my boudoir and a few moments of obedience will go far to straighten out your pecuniary difficulties."

"I am no more eager to serve your debauches in one sense than in another, Monsieur," I proudly retorted; "it is not charity I ask, cruel man; no, I should not procure you the pleasure of it; what I demand is simply what is my due: that is what you stole from me in the most infamous manner. . . . Keep it, cruel wretch, keep it if you see fit: unpityingly observe my tears; hear, if you are able, hear without emotion need's sorrowing accents, but bear in mind that if you commit this newest outrage, I will have bought, for the price it costs me, the right to scorn you forever."

Furious, Saint-Florent ordered me to leave and I was able to read in his dreadful countenance that, had it not been for what he had confided in me and were he not afraid lest it get abroad, my bold plain speaking might perhaps have been repaid by some brutality. . . . I left. At the same instant they were bringing the debauchee one of the luckless victims of his sordid profligacy. One of those women whose horrible state he had suggested I share was leading into the house a poor little girl of about nine who displayed every attribute of wretchedness and dereliction: she scarcely seemed to have enough strength to keep erect. . . . O Heaven! I thought upon beholding this, is it conceivable that such objects can inspire any feelings but those of pity? Woe unto the depraved one who will be able to suspect pleasures in the womb want consumes, who will seek to gather kisses from lips withered by hunger and which open only to curse him!

Tears spilled from my eyes; I should have liked to snatch that victim from the tiger awaiting her; I dared not. Could I have done it? I returned directly to my hotel, quite as humiliated by the misfortune which attracted such proposals as revolted by the opulence which ventured to make them.

The following day I left Lyon by way of the road to Dauphiné, still filled with the mad faith which allowed me to believe happiness awaited me in that province. Traveling afoot as usual, with a pair of blouses and some handkerchiefs in my pockets, I had not proceeded two leagues when I met an old woman; she approached me with a look of suffering and implored alms. Far from having the miserliness of which I had just received such cruel examples, and knowing no greater worldly happiness than what comes of obliging a poor person, I instantly drew forth my purse with the intention of selecting a crown and giving it to this woman; but the unworthy creature, much quicker than I, although I had at first judged her aged and crippled, leaps nimbly at my purse, seizes it, aims a powerful blow of her fist at my stomach, topples me, and the next I see of her, she has put a hundred yards betwixt us; there she is, surrounded by four rascals who gesture threateningly and warn me not to come near.

"Great God!" I cried with much bitterness, "then it is impossible for my soul to give vent to any virtuous impulse without my being instantly and very severely punished for it!" At this fatal moment all my courage deserted me; today I beg Heaven's forgiveness in all sincerity, for I faltered; but I was blinded by despair. I felt myself ready to give up a career beset with so many obstacles. I envisioned two alternatives: that of going to join the scoundrels who had just robbed me, or that of returning to Lyon to accept Saint-Florent's offer. God had mercy upon me; I did not succumb, and though the fresh hope He quickened in me was misleading, since so many adversities yet lay in store for me, I nevertheless thank Him for having held me upright: the unlucky star which guides me, although innocent, to the gallows, will never lead me to worse than death; other supervision might have brought me to infamy, and the one is far less cruel than the other.

I continue to direct my steps toward Vienne, having decided to sell what remains to me in order to get on to Grenoble: I was walking along sadly when, at a quarter league's distance from this city, I spied a plain to the right of the highway, and in the fields were two riders busily trampling a man beneath their horses' hooves after having left him for dead, the pair rode off at a gallop. This appalling spectacle melted me to the point of tears. "Alas!" I said to myself, "there is an unluckier person than I; health and strength at least remain to me, I can earn my living, and if that poor fellow is not rich, what is to become of him?"

However much I ought to have forbidden myself the self-indulgence of sympathy, however perilous it was for me to surrender to the impulse, I could not vanquish my extreme desire to approach the man and to lavish upon him what care I could offer. I rush to his side, I aid him to inhale some spirits I had kept about me: at last he opens his eyes and his first accents are those of gratitude. Still more eager to be of use to him, I tear up one of my blouses in order to bandage his wounds, to stanch his blood: I sacrificed for this wretched man one of the few belongings I still owned. These first attentions completed, I give him a little wine to drink: the unlucky one has completely come back to his senses, I cast an eye upon him and observe him more closely. Although traveling on foot and without baggage, he had some valuable effects—rings, a watch, a snuff box—but the latter two have been badly damaged during his encounter. As soon as he is able to speak he asks me what angel of charity has come to his rescue and what he can do to express his gratitude. Still having the simplicity to believe that a soul enchained by indebtedness ought to be eternally beholden to me, I judge it safe to enjoy the sweet pleasure of sharing my tears with him who has just shed some in my arms: I instruct him of my numerous reverses, he listens with interest, and when I have concluded with the latest catastrophe that has befallen me, the recital provides him with a glimpse of my poverty.

"How happy I am," he exclaims, "to be able at least to acknowledge all you have just done for me; my name is Roland," the adventurer continues, "I am the owner of an exceedingly fine château in the mountains fifteen leagues hence, I invite you to follow me there; and that this proposal cause your delicacy no alarm, I am going to explain immediately in what way you will be of service to me. I am unwedded, but I have a sister I love passionately: she has dedicated herself to sharing my solitude; I need someone to wait upon her; we have recently lost the person who held that office until now, I offer her post to you."

I thanked my protector and took the liberty to ask him how it chanced that a man such as he exposed himself to the dangers of journeying alone, and, as had just occurred, to being molested by bandits.

"A stout, youthful, and vigorous fellow, for several years," said Roland, "I have been in the habit of traveling this way between the place where I reside and Vienne. My health and pocketbook benefit from walking. It is not that I need avoid the expense of a coach, for I am wealthy, and you will soon see proof of it if you are good enough to return home with me; but thriftiness never hurts. As for those two men who insulted me a short while ago, they are two would-be gentlemen of this canton from whom I won a hundred *louis* last week in a gaming house at Vienne; I was content to accept their word of honor, then I met them today, asked for what they owe me, and you witnessed in what coin they paid me."

Together with this man I was deploring the double misfortune of which he was the victim when he proposed we continue our way.

"Thanks to your attentions I feel a little better," said Roland; "night is approaching, let's get on to a house which should be two leagues away; by means of the horses we will secure tomorrow, we might be able to arrive at my château the same afternoon."

Absolutely resolved to profit from the aid Heaven seemed to have sent me, I help Roland to get up, I give him my arm while we walk, and indeed, after progressing two leagues we find the inn he had mentioned. We take supper together, 'tis very proper and nice; after our meal Roland entrusts me to the mistress of the place, and the following day we set off on two mules we have rented and which are led by a boy from the inn; we reach the frontier of Dauphiné, ever heading into the highlands. We were not yet at our destination when the day ended, so we stopped at Virieu, where my patron showed me the same consideration and provided me with the same care; the next morning we resumed our way toward the mountains. We arrived at their foot toward four in the afternoon; there, the road becoming almost impassable, Roland requested my muleteer not to leave me for fear of an accident, and we penetrated into the gorges. We did but turn, wind, climb for the space of more than four leagues, and by then we had left all habitations and all traveled roads so far behind us I thought myself come to the end of the world; despite myself, I was seized by a twinge of uneasiness; Roland could not avoid seeing it, but he said nothing, and I was made yet more uncomfortable by his silence. We finally came to a castle perched upon the crest of a mountain; it beetled over a dreadful precipice into which it seemed ready to plunge: no road seemed

o lead up to it; the one we had followed, frequently by goats only,
trewn with pebbles and stones, however did at last take us to this
awful eyrie which much more resembled the hideaway of thieves
han the dwelling place of virtuous folk.

"That is where I live," said Roland, noticing I was gazing up
at his castle.

I confessed my astonishment to see that he lived in such isola-
ion.

"It suits me," was his abrupt reply.

This response redoubled my forebodings. Not a syllable is lost
upon the miserable; a word, a shift of inflection and, when 'tis a
question of the speech of the person upon whom one depends, 'tis
nough to stifle hope or revive it; but, being completely unable to
do anything, I held my tongue and waited. We mounted by zigzags;
he strange pile suddenly loomed up before us: roughly a quarter
of a league still separated it from us: Roland dismounted and hav-
ng told me to do likewise, he returned both mules to the boy, paid
him and ordered him to return. This latest maneuver was even more
displeasing to me; Roland observed my anxiety.

"What is the trouble, Thérèse?" he demanded, urging me on
oward his fortress; "you are not out of France; we are on the
Dauphiné border and within the bishopric of Grenoble."

"Very well, Monsieur," I answered; "but why did it ever
ccur to you to take up your abode in a place befitting brigands and
obbers?"

"Because they who inhabit it are not very honest people," said
Roland; "it might be altogether possible you will not be edified by
heir conduct."

"Ah, Monsieur!" said I with a shudder, "you make me
remble; where then are you leading me?"

"I am leading you into the service of the counterfeiters of
whom I am the chief," said Roland, grasping my arm and driving
me over a little drawbridge that was lowered at our approach and
aised immediately we had traversed it; "do you see that well?" he
ontinued when we had entered; he was pointing to a large and deep
grotto situated toward the back of the courtyard, where four
omen, nude and manacled, were turning a wheel; "there are your
ompanions and there your task, which involves the rotation of

that wheel for ten hours each day, and which also involves the
satisfaction of all the caprices I am pleased to submit you and the
other ladies to; for which you will be granted six ounces of black
bread and a plate of kidney beans without fail each day; as for your
freedom, forget it; you will never recover it. When you are dead
from overwork, you will be flung into that hole you notice beside
the well, where the remains of between sixty and eighty other rascals of your breed await yours, and your place will be taken by
somebody else."

"Oh, Great God!" I exclaimed, casting myself at Roland's
feet, "deign to remember, Monsieur, that I saved your life, that
moved by gratitude for an instant, you seemed to offer me happiness and that it is by precipitating me into an eternal abyss of evil
you reward my services. Is what you are doing just? and has no
remorse already begun to avenge me in the depths of your heart?"

"What, pray tell, do you mean by this feeling of gratitude with
which you fancy you have captivated me?" Roland inquired. "Be
more reasonable, wretched creature; what were you doing when you
came to my rescue? Between the two possibilities, of continuing on
your way and of coming up to me, did you not choose the latter
as an impulse dictated by your heart? You therefore gave yourself
up to a pleasure? How in the devil's name can you maintain I am
obliged to recompense you for the joys in which you indulge yourself? And how did you ever get it into your head that a man like myself, who is swimming in gold and opulence, should condescend to
lower himself to owing something to a wretch of your species? Even
had you resurrected me, I should owe you nothing immediately it
were plain you had acted out of selfishness only: to work, slave, to
work; learn that though civilization may overthrow the principles
of Nature, it cannot however divest her of her rights; in the beginning she wrought strong beings and weak and intended that the
lowly should be forever subordinated to the great; human skill and
intelligence made various the positions of individuals, it was no
longer physical force alone that determined rank, 'twas gold; the
richest became the mightiest man, the most penurious the weakest;
if the causes which establish power are not to be found in Nature's
ordinations, the priority of the mighty has always been inscribed
therein, and to Nature it made no difference whether the weak

danced at the end of a leash held by the richest or the most energetic, and little she cared whether the yoke crushed the poorest or the most enfeebled; but these grateful impulses out of which you would forge chains for me, why, Thérèse, Nature recognizes them not; it has never been one of her laws that the pleasure whereunto someone surrenders when he acts obligingly must become a cause for the recipient of his gratuitous kindness to renounce his rights over the donor; do you detect these sentiments you demand in the animals which serve us as examples? When I dominate you by my wealth or might is it natural for me to abandon my rights to you, either because you have enjoyed yourself while obliging me or because, being unhappy, you fancied you had something to gain from your action? Even were service to be rendered by one equal to another, never would a lofty spirit's pride allow him to stoop to acknowledge it; is not he who receives always humiliated? And is this humiliation not sufficient payment for the benefactor who, by this alone, finds himself superior to the other? Is it not pride's delight to be raised above one's fellow? Is any other necessary to the person who obliges? And if the obligation, by causing humiliation to him who receives, becomes a burden to him, by what right is he to be forced to continue to shoulder it? Why must I consent to let myself be humiliated every time my eyes fall upon him who has obliged me? Instead of being a vice, ingratitude is as certainly a virtue in proud spirits as gratitude is one in humble; let them do what they will for me if doing it gives them pleasure, but let them expect nothing from me simply because they have enjoyed themselves."

Having uttered these words, to which Roland gave me no opportunity to reply, he summoned two valets who upon his instructions seized me, despoiled me, and shackled me next to my companions, so was I set to work at once, without a moment's rest after the fatiguing journey I had just made. Then Roland approaches me, he brutally handles all those parts of me designation of which modesty forbids, heaps sarcasms upon me, makes impertinent reference to the damning and little merited brand Rodin printed upon me, then, catching up a bull's pizzle always kept in readiness nearby, he applies twenty cuts to my behind.

"That is how you will be treated, bitch," says he, "when you lag at the job; I'm not giving you this for anything you've already done, but only to show you how I cope with those who make mistakes."

I screamed, struggled against my manacles; my contortions, my cries, my tears, the cruel expressions of my pain merely entertained my executioner. . . .

"Oh, little whore, you'll see other things," says Roland, "you're not by a long shot at the end of your troubles and I want you to make the acquaintance of even the most barbaric refinements of misery."

He leaves me.

Located in a cave on the edge of that vast well were six dark kennels; they were barred like dungeons, and they served us as shelters for the night, which arrived not long after I was enlisted in this dreadful chain gang. They came to remove my fetters and my companions', and after we had been given the ration of water, beans, and dry bread Roland had mentioned, we were locked up.

I was no sooner alone than, undistracted, I abandoned myself to contemplating my situation in all its horror. Is it possible, I wondered, can it be that there are men so hardened as to have stifled in themselves their capacity for gratitude? This virtue to which I surrender myself with such charm whenever an upright spirit gives me the chance to feel it . . . can this virtue be unknown to certain beings, can they be utter strangers to it? and may they who have suppressed it so inhumanly in themselves be anything but monsters?

I was absorbed in these musings when suddenly I heard the door to my cell open; 'tis Roland: the villain has come to complete his outraging of me by making me serve his odious eccentricities: you may well imagine, Madame, that they were to be as ferocious as his other proceedings and that such a man's love-makings are necessarily tainted by his abhorrent character. But how can I abuse your patience by relating these new horrors? Have I not already more than soiled your imagination with infamous recitations? Dare I hazard additional ones?

"Yes, Thérèse," Monsieur de Corville put in, "yes, we insist upon these details, you veil them with a decency that removes all their edge of horror; there remains only what is useful to whoever seeks to perfect his understanding of enigmatic man. You may not fully apprehend how these tableaux help toward the development of the human spirit; our backwardness in this branch of learning may very well be due to the stupid restraint of those who venture to write upon such matters. Inhibited by absurd fears, they only discuss the puerilities with which every fool is familiar, and dare not, by addressing themselves boldly to the investigation of the human heart, offer its gigantic idiosyncrasies to our view."

"Very well, Monsieur, I shall proceed," Thérèse resumed, deeply affected, "and proceeding as I have done until this point, I will strive to offer my sketches in the least revolting colors."

Roland, with whose portrait I ought to begin, was a short, heavy-set man, thirty-five years old, incredibly vigorous and as hirsute as a bear, with a glowering mien and fierce eye; very dark, with masculine features, a long nose, bearded to the eyes, black, shaggy brows; and in him that part which differentiates men from our sex was of such length and exorbitant circumference, that not only had I never laid eyes upon anything comparable, but was even absolutely convinced Nature had never fashioned another as prodigious; I could scarcely surround it with both hands, and its length matched that of my forearm. To this physique Roland joined all the vices which may be the issue of a fiery temperament, of considerable imagination, and of a luxurious life undisturbed by anything likely to distract from one's leisure pursuits. From his father Roland had inherited a fortune; very early on in life he had become surfeited by ordinary pleasures, and begun to resort to nothing but horrors; these alone were able to revive desires in a person jaded by excessive pleasure; the women who served him were all employed in his secret debauches and to satisfy appetites only slightly less dishonest within which, nevertheless, this libertine was able to find the criminal spice wherein above all his taste delighted; Roland kept his own sister as a mistress, and it was with her he brought to a climax the passions he ignited in our company.

He was virtually naked when he entered; his inflamed visage was evidence simultaneously of the epicurean intemperance to which he had just given himself over, and the abominable lust which consumed him; for an instant he considers me with eyes that unstring my limbs.

"Get out of those clothes," says he, himself tearing off what I was wearing to cover me during the night . . . "yes, get rid of all that and follow me; a little while ago I made you sense what you risk by laziness; but should you desire to betray us, as that crime would be of greater magnitude, its punishment would have to be proportionally heavier; come along and see of what sort it would be."

I was in a state difficult to describe, but Roland, affording my spirit no time in which to burst forth, immediately grasped my arm and dragged me out; he pulls me along with his right hand, in his left he holds a little lantern that emits a feeble light; after winding this way and that, we reach a cellar door; he opens it, thrusts me ahead of him, tells me to descend while he closes this first barrier; I obey; a hundred paces further, a second door; he opens and shuts it in the same way; but after this one there is no stairway, only a narrow passage hewn in the rock, filled with sinuosities, whose downward slope is extremely abrupt. Not a word from Roland; the silence affrights me still more; he lights us along with his lantern; thus we travel for about fifteen minutes; my frame of mind makes me yet more sensitive to these subterranean passages' terrible humidity. At last, we had descended to such a depth that it is without fear of exaggeration I assure you the place at which we were to arrive must have been more than a furlong below the surface of the earth; on either side of the path we followed were occasional niches where I saw coffers containing those criminals' wealth: one last bronze door appeared, Roland unlocked it, and I nearly fell backward upon perceiving the dreadful place to which this evil man had brought me. Seeing me falter, he pushed me rudely ahead, and thus, without wishing to be there, I found myself in the middle of that appalling sepulcher. Imagine, Madame, a circular cavern, twenty-five feet in diameter, whose walls, hung in black, were decorated by none but the most lugubrious objects, skeletons of all sizes, crossed bones, several heads, bundles of whips and collections of martinets, sabers, cutlasses, poignards, firearms: such were the horrors one spied on the walls illuminated by a three-wicked oil lamp suspended in one corner of the vault; from a transverse beam dangled a rope which fell to within eight or ten feet of the ground in the center of this dungeon and which, as very soon you will see, was there for no other purpose than to facilitate dreadful expedi tions: to the right was an open coffin wherein glinted an effigy of death brandishing a threatful scythe; a prayer stool was beside it; above it was visible a crucifix bracketed by candles of jet; to the left, the waxen dummy of a naked woman, so lifelike I was for a long time deceived by it; she was attached to a cross, posed with her chest facing it so that one had a full view of her posterior and cruelly molested parts; blood seemed to ooze from several wounds and to flow down her thighs; she had the most beautiful hair in all the world, her lovely head was turned toward us and seemed to implore our mercy; all of suffering's contortions were plainly wrought upon her lovely face, and there were even tears flowing down her cheeks: the sight of this terrible image was again enough to make me think I would collapse; the further part of the cavern was filled by a vast black divan which eloquently bespoke all the atrocities which occurred in this infernal place.

"And here is where you will perish, Thérèse," quoth Roland, "if ever you conceive the fatal notion of leaving my establishment; yes, it is here I will myself put you to death, here I will make you reverberate to the anguishes inflicted by everything of the most appalling I can possibly devise."

As he gave vent to this threat Roland became aroused; his agitation, his disorder made him resemble a tiger about to spring upon its prey: 'twas then he brought to light the formidable member wherewith he was outfitted; he had me touch it, asked me whether I had ever beheld its peer.

"Such as you see it, whore," said he in a rage, "in that shape it has, however, got to be introduced into the narrowest part of your body even if I must split you in half; my sister, considerably your junior, manages it in the same sector; never do I enjoy women in any other fashion," and so as to leave me in no doubt of the locale he had in mind, he inserted into it three fingers armed with exceedingly long nails, the while saying:

"Yes, 'tis there, Thérèse, it will be shortly into this hole I will drive this member which affrights you; it will be run every inch of the way in, it will tear you, you'll bleed and I will be beside myself."

Foam flecked his lips as he spoke these words interspersed with revolting oaths and blasphemies. The hand, which had been prying open the shrine he seemed to want to attack, now strayed over all the adjacent parts; he scratched them, he did as much to my breast, he clawed me so badly I was not to get over the pain for a fortnight. Next, he placed me on the edge of the couch, rubbed alcohol upon that mossy tonsure with which Nature ornaments the altar wherein our species finds regeneration; he set it afire and burned it. His fingers closed upon the fleshy protuberance which surmounts this same altar, he snatched at it and scraped roughly, then he inserted his fingers within and his nails ripped the membrane which lines it. Losing all control over himself, he told me that, since he had me in his lair, I might just as well not leave it, for that would spare him the nuisance of bringing me back down again; I fell to my knees and dared remind him again of what I had done in his behalf. . . . I observed I but further excited him by harping again upon the rights to his pity I fancied were mine; he told me to be silent, bringing up his knee and giving me a tremendous blow in the pit of the stomach which sent me sprawling on the flagstones. He seized a handful of my hair and jerked me erect.

"Very well!" he said, "come now! prepare yourself; it is a certainty, I am going to kill you. . . ."

"Oh, Monsieur!"

"No, no, you've got to die; I do not want to hear you reproach me with your good little deeds; I don't like owing anything to anybody, others have got to rely upon me for everything. . . . You're going to perish, I tell you, get into that coffin, let's see if it fits."

He lifts me, thrusts me into it and shuts it, then quits the cavern and gives me the impression I have been left there. Never had I thought myself so near to death; alas! it was nonetheless to be presented to me under a yet more real aspect. Roland returns, he fetches me out of the coffin.

"You'll be well off in there," says he, "one would say 'twas made for you; but to let you finish peacefully in that box would be a death too sweet; I'm going to expose you to one of a different variety which, all the same, will have its agreeable qualities; so implore your God, whore, pray to him to come posthaste and avenge you if he really has it in him. . . ."

I cast myself down upon the *prie-dieu,* and while aloud I open my heart to the Eternal, Roland in a still crueler manner intensifies upon the hindquarters I expose to him, his vexations and his torments; with all his strength he flogs those parts with a steel-tipped martinet, each blow draws a gush of blood which springs to the walls.

"Why," he continued with a curse, "he doesn't much aid you, your God, does he? and thus he allows unhappy virtue to suffer, he abandons it to villainy's hands; ah! what a bloody fine God you've got there, Thérèse, what a superb God he is! Come," he says, "come here, whore, your prayer should be done," and at the same time he places me upon the divan at the back of that cell; "I told you Thérèse, you have got to die!"

He seizes my arms, binds them to my side, then he slips a black silken noose about my neck; he holds both ends of the cord and, by tightening, he can strangle and dispatch me to the other world either quickly or slowly, depending upon his pleasure.

"This torture is sweeter than you may imagine, Thérèse," says Roland; "you will only approach death by way of unspeakably pleasurable sensations; the pressure this noose will bring to bear upon your nervous system will set fire to the organs of voluptuousness; the effect is certain; were all the people who are condemned to this torture to know in what an intoxication of joy it makes one die, less terrified by this retribution for their crimes, they would commit them more often and with much greater self-assurance; this delicious operation, Thérèse, by causing, as well, the contraction of the locale in which I am going to fit myself," he added as he presented himself to a criminal avenue so worthy of such a villain, "is also going to double my pleasure."

He thrusts, he sweats, 'tis in vain; he prepares the road, 'tis futile; he is too monstrously proportioned, his enterprises are repeatedly frustrated; and then his wrath exceeds all limits; his nails, his hands, his feet fly to revenge him upon the opposition Nature puts up against him; he returns to the assault, the glowing blade slides to the edge of the neighboring canal and smiting vigorously, penetrates to nigh the midway mark; I utter a cry; Roland, enraged by his mistake, withdraws petulantly, and this time hammers at the other gate with such force the moistened dart plunges in, rending me. Roland exploits this first sally's success; his efforts become more violent; he gains ground; as he advances, he gradually tightens the fatal cord he has passed round my neck, hideous screams burst from my lips; amused by them, the ferocious Roland urges me to redouble my howlings, for he is but too confident of their insufficiency, he is perfectly able to put a stop to them when he wishes; their shrill sharp notes inflame him, the noose's pressure is modulated by his degrees of delight; little by little my voice waxes faint; the tightenings now become so intense that my senses weaken although I do not lose the power to feel; brutally shaken by the enormous instrument with which Roland is rending my entrails, despite my frightful circumstances, I feel myself flooded by his lust's jetted outpourings; I still hear the cries he mouths as he discharges; an instant of stupor followed, I knew not what had happened to me, but soon my eyes open again to the light, I find myself free, untied, and my sensory organs seem to come back to life.

"Well, Thérèse," says my butcher, "I dare swear that if you'll tell the truth you'll say you felt pleasure only?"

"Only horror, Monsieur, only disgust, only anguish and despair."

"You are lying, I am fully acquainted with the effects you have just experienced, but what does it matter what they were? I fancy you already know me well enough to be damned certain that when I undertake something with you, the joy you reap from it concerns me infinitely less than my own, and this voluptuousness I seek has been so keen that in an instant I am going to procure some more of it. It is now upon yourself, Thérèse," declares this signal libertine, "it is upon you alone your life is going to depend."

Whereupon he hitches about my neck the rope that hangs from the ceiling; he has me stand upon a stool, pulls the rope taut, secures it, and to the stool he attaches a string whose end he keeps in his hand as he sits down in an armchair facing me; I am given a sickle which I am to use to sever the rope at the moment when, by means of the string, he jerks the stool from beneath my feet.

"Notice, Thérèse," he says when all is ready, "that though you may miss your blow, I'll not miss mine; and so I am not mistaken when I say your life depends upon you."

He excites himself; it is at his intoxication's critical moment he is to snatch away the stool which, removed, will leave me dangling from the beam; he does everything possible to pretend the instant has come; he would be beside himself were I to miss my cue; but do what he will, I divine the crisis, the violence of his ecstasy betrays him, I see him make the telltale movement, the stool flies away, I cut the rope and fall to the ground; there I am, completely detached, and although five yards divide us, would you believe it, Madame? I feel my entire body drenched with the evidence of his delirium and his frenzy.

Anyone but I, taking advantage of the weapon she clutched in her hand, would doubtless have leapt upon that monster; but what might I have gained by this brave feat? for I did not have the keys to those subterranean passages, I was ignorant of their scheme, I should have perished before being able to emerge from them; Roland, furthermore, was armed; and so I got up, leaving the sickle on the ground so that he might not conceive the slightest suspicion of my intentions, and indeed he had none, for he had savored the full extent of pleasure and, far more content with my tractability, with my resignation, than with my agility, he signaled to me and we left.

The next day I cast an appraising eye upon my companions: those four girls ranged from twenty-five to thirty years of age; although bestialized and besotted by misery and warped by excessive drudgery, they still had the remnants of beauty; their figures were handsome, and the youngest, called Suzanne, still had, together with charming eyes, very fine hair; Roland had seized her in Lyon, he had deflowered her, and after having sworn to her family he would marry her, he had brought her to this frightful château, where she had been three years his slave, and during that period she had been especially singled out to be the object of the monster's ferocities: by dint of blows from the bull's pizzle, her buttocks had become as calloused and toughened as would be cow's hide dried in the sun; she had a cancer upon her left breast and an abscess in her matrix which caused her unspeakable suffering; all that was the perfidious Roland's achievement; each of those horrors was the fruit of his lecheries.

It was she who informed me Roland was on the eve of departing for Venice if the considerable sums he had very recently shipped to Spain could be converted into letters of credit he needed for Italy, for he did not want to transport his gold east across the Alps; never did he send any in that direction: it was in a different country from the one he had decided to inhabit that he circulated his false coins; by this device, rich to be sure but only in the banknotes of another kingdom, his rascalities could never be detected in the land where he planned to take up his next abode. But everything could be overthrown within the space of an instant and the retirement he envisioned wholly depended upon this latest transaction in which the bulk of his treasure was compromised. Were Cadiz to accept his false *piasters, sequins,* and *louis,* and against them send him letters negotiable in Venice, Roland would be established for the rest of his days; were the fraud to be detected, one single day would suffice to demolish the fragile edifice of his fortune.

"Alas!" I remarked upon learning these details, "Providence will be just for once. It will not countenance the success of such a monster, and all of us will be revenged. . . ."

Great God! in view of the experience I had acquired, how was I able thus to reason!

Toward noon we were given a two-hour respite, which we always used to good advantage to go for a little individual rest and food in our cells; at two o'clock we were reattached to the wheel and were made to work till nightfall; never were we allowed to enter the château; if we were naked, 'twas not only because of the heat, but so as better to be able to receive the bull's pizzle beatings our savage master periodically came to inflict upon us; in winter we were given pantaloons and a light sweater which so closely hugged the skin that our bodies were not the less exposed to the blows of a villain whose unique pleasure was to beat us half-senseless.

A week passed during which I saw no sign of Roland; on the ninth day he visited us at work and maintained Suzanne and I were improperly applying ourselves to our task; he distributed thirty cuts with the pizzle upon each of us, slashing us from back to calf.

At midnight on that same day, the evil man came to get me in my kennel and, warmed by the sight of what his cruelties had produced, he once again introduced his terrible bludgeon into the shadowy lair I exposed by the posture he made me assume in order to inspect the vestiges of his rage. When his hungers were appeased I thought to profit from his momentary calm to supplicate him to mitigate my lot. Alas! I was unaware that in such a genius, whereas the delirious interlude stimulates the penchant for cruelty into greater activity, the subsequent reflux does not by any means restore the honest man's pacific virtues to it; 'tis a fire more or less quickened by the fuel wherewith it is fed, but one whose embers, though covered with cinder, burn nonetheless.

"And what right have you," Roland replied to me, "to expect me to sweeten your circumstances? Because of the fantasies I am pleased to put into execution with you? But am I to throw myself at your feet and implore you to accord favors for the granting of which you can implore some recompense? I ask nothing from you, I take, and I simply do not see that, because I exercise one right over you, it must result that I have to abstain from demanding a second; there is no love in what I do: love is a chivalric sentiment I hold in sovereign contempt and to whose assaults my heart is always impervious; I employ a woman out of necessity, as one employs a round and hollow vessel for a different purpose but an analogous need; but never according this individual, which my money and authority make subject to me, either esteem or tenderness, owing to myself what I get from her and never exacting from her anything but submission, I cannot be constrained, in the light of all this, to acknowledge any gratitude toward her. I ask them who would like to compel me to be thankful whether a thief who snatches a man's purse in the woods because he, the thief, is the stronger of the two, owes this man any gratitude for the wrong he has just done him; the same holds true for an outrage committed against a woman: it may justify a repetition of the abuse, but never is it a sufficient reason to grant her compensation."

"Oh, Monsieur," I said to him, "to what limits you do carry your villainy!"

"To the ultimate periods," Roland answered; "there is not a single extravagance in the world in which I have not indulged, not a crime I have not committed, and not one that my doctrines do not excuse or legitimate; unceasingly, I have found in evil a kind of attractiveness which always redounds to my lust's advantage; crime ignites my appetites; the more frightful it is, the more it stimulates; in committing it, I enjoy the same sort of pleasure ordinary folk taste in naught but libricity, and a hundred times I have discovered myself, while thinking of crime, while surrendering to it, or just after having executed it, in precisely the same state in which one is when confronted by a beautiful naked woman; it irritates my senses in the same way, and I have committed it in order to arouse myself as, when one is filled with impudicious designs, one approaches a beautiful object."

"Oh, Monsieur! 'tis frightful, what you say, but I have beheld examples of it."

"There are a thousand, Thérèse. It must not be supposed that it is a woman's beauty which best stirs a libertine mind, it is rather the species of crime that the law has associated with possession of her: the proof of which is that the more criminal this possession the more one is inflamed by it; the man who enjoys a woman he steals from her husband, a daughter he snatches from her parents, knows a far greater delectation, no doubt of it, than does the husband who enjoys no one but his wife, and the more the ties one breaks appear to be respected, the more the voluptuousness is compounded. If 'tis one's mother, or one's daughter, so many additional charms to the pleasures experienced; when you've savored all this, then you truly would have interdictions further increase in order to give the violation of them added difficulty and greater charm; now, if pleasure-taking is seasoned by a criminal flavoring, crime, dissociated from this pleasure, may become a joy in itself; there will then be a certain delight in naked crime. Well, it is impossible that what contributes the saline tang not itself be very salty. Thus, let me imagine, the abduction of a girl on one's own account will give a very lively pleasure, but abduction in the interests of someone else will give all that pleasure with which the enjoyment of this girl is improved by rape; the theft of a watch, the rape of a purse will also give the same pleasure, and if I have accustomed my senses to being moved by the rape of some girl *qua* rape, that same pleasure, that same delight will be found again in the seizing of the watch or of the purse, etc.; and that explains the eccentricity in so many honest folk who steal without needing to steal. Nothing more common; from this moment on, one both tastes the greatest pleasure in everything criminal, and, by every imaginable device, one renders simple enjoyments as criminal as they can possibly be rendered; by conducting oneself in this style, one but adds to enjoyment the dash of salt which was wanting and which became indispensable to happiness' perfection. These doctrines lead far, I know; perhaps, Thérèse, I shall even show you how far before too long, but what matter? enjoyment's the thing. Was there, for example, dear girl, anything more ordinary or more natural than for me to enjoy you? But you oppose it, you ask that it stop; it would seem that, in the light of my obligations toward you, I ought to grant what you request; however, I surrender to nothing, I listen to nothing, I slash through all the knots that bind fools, I submit you to my desires, and out of the most elementary, the most monotonous enjoyment I evolve one that is really delicious; therefore submit, Thérèse, submit, and if ever you are reincarnated and return to the world in the guise of the mighty, exploit your privileges in the same way and you will know every one of the most lively and most piquant pleasures."

These words gone out of his mouth, Roland went away and left me to ponder thoughts which, as you may well believe, presented him in no favorable aspect.

I had been six months in this household, from time to time serving the villain's disgraceful debauches, when one night I beheld him enter my prison with Suzanne.

"Come, Thérèse," said he, " 'tis already a long time, I find, since I took you down to that cavern which impressed you so deeply; both of you are going to accompany me there, but don't expect to climb back together, for I absolutely must leave one of you behind; well, we'll see which one fate designates."

I get to my feet, cast alarmed glances at my companion, I see tears rolling from her eyes . . . and we set off.

When we were locked into the underground vault, Roland examined each of us with ferocious eyes; he amused himself by reiterating our sentence and persuading us both that one of the two would certainly remain there below.

"Well," said he, seating himself and having us stand directly before him, "each of you take your turn and set to work exorcising this disabled object; there's a devil in it keeps it limp, and woe unto the one of you who restores its energy."

" 'Tis an injustice," quoth Suzanne; "she who arouses you most should be the one to obtain your mercy."

"Not at all," Roland retorted, "once it is manifest which of you arouses me most, it is established which one's death will give me the greater pleasure . . . and I'm aiming at pleasure, nothing else. Moreover, by sparing her who inflames me the more rapidly, you would both proceed with such industry that you might perhaps plunge my senses into their ecstasy before the sacrifice were consummated, and that must not happen."

" 'Tis to want evil for evil's sake, Monsieur," I said to Roland, "the completion of your ecstasy ought to be the only thing you desire, and if you attain it without crime, why do you want to commit one?"

"Because I only deliciously reach the critical stage in this way, and because I only came down here in order to commit one. I know perfectly well I might succeed without it, but I want it in order to succeed."

And, during this dialogue, having chosen me to begin, I start exciting his behind with one hand, his front with the other, while he touches at his leisure every part of my body offered him by my nakedness.

"You've still a long way to go, Thérèse," said he, fingering my buttocks, "before this fine flesh is in the state of petrified callosity and mortification apparent in Suzanne's; one might light a fire under that dear girl's cheeks without her feeling a thing; but you, Thérèse, you . . . these are yet roses bound in lilies: we'll get to them in good time, in good time."

You simply have no idea, Madame, how much that threat set me at ease; Roland doubtless did not suspect, as he uttered it, the peace it sent flooding through me, for was it not clear that, since he planned to expose me to further cruelties, he was not yet eager to immolate me? I have told you, Madame, that everything the wretched hear drives home, and thenceforth I was reassured. Another increase of happiness! I was performing in vain, and that enormous mass telescoped into itself resisted all my shakings;

Suzanne was in the same posture, she was palpated in the same areas, but as her flesh was toughened in a very different way, Roland treated it with much less consideration; however, Suzanne was younger.

"I am convinced," our persecutor was saying, "that the most awesome whips would now fail to draw a drop of blood from that ass."

He made each of us bend over and, our angle of inclination providing him with the four avenues of pleasure, his tongue danced wriggling into the two narrowest; the villain spat into the others; he turned us about, had us kneel between his thighs in such a manner our breasts found themselves at a level with what of him we were stimulating.

"Oh! as regards breasts," said Roland, "you've got to yield to Suzanne; never had you such fine teats; now then, let's take a look at this noble endowment."

And with those words he pressed the poor girl's breasts till, beneath his fingers, they were covered with bruises. At this point it was no longer I who was exciting him, Suzanne had replaced me; scarcely had she fallen into his clutches when his dart, springing from its quiver, began to menace everything surrounding it.

"Suzanne," said Roland, "behold an appalling triumph. . . . tis your death decreed, Suzanne; I feared as much," added that ferocious man as he nipped and clawed her breasts.

As for mine, he only sucked and chewed them. At length, he placed Suzanne on her knees at the edge of the sofa, he made her bend her head and in this attitude he enjoyed her according to the frightful manner natural to him; awakened by new pains, Suzanne struggles and Roland, who simply wishes to skirmish, is content with a brisk passage of arms, and comes to take refuge in me at the same shrine at which he has sacrificed in my companion whom he does not cease to vex and molest the while.

"There's a whore who excites me cruelly," he says to me, "I don't know what to do with her."

"Oh, Monsieur," say I, "have pity upon her; her sufferings could not be more intense."

"Oh, but you're wrong!" the villain replies, "one might . . . ah! if only I had with me that celebrated Emperor Kié, one of the greatest scoundrels ever to have sat on the Chinese throne,[6] with Kié we'd really be able to perform wonders. Both he and his wife, they say, immolated victims daily and would have them live twenty-four hours in death's cruelest agonies, and in such a state of suffering that they were constantly on the verge of expiring but never quite able to die, for those monsters administered that kind of aid which made them flutter between relief and torture and only brought them back to life for one minute in order to kill them the next. . . . I, Thérèse, I am too gentle, I know nothing of those arts, I'm a mere apprentice."

Roland retires without completing the sacrifice and hurts me almost as much by this precipitous withdrawal as he had upon inserting himself. He throws himself into Suzanne's arms, and joining sarcasm to outrage:

"Amiable creature," he apostrophizes, "with such delight I remember the first instants of our union; never had woman given me such thrilling pleasures, never had I loved one as I did you . . . let us embrace, Suzanne, for we're going to part, perhaps the season of our separation will be long."

"Monster!" my companion retorts, thrusting him away with horror, "begone; to the torments you inflict upon me, join not the despair of hearing your terrible remarks; sate your rage, tigerish one, but at least respect my sufferings."

Roland laid hands on her, stretched her upon the couch, her legs widespread, and the workshop of generation ideally within range.

"Temple of my ancient pleasures," the infamous creature intoned, "you who procured me delights so sweet when I plucked your first roses, I must indeed address to you my farewells. . . ."

The villain! he drove his fingernails into it and, rummaging

---

[6] Kié, the Emperor of China, had a wife as cruel and debauched as he; bloodshed was as naught to them, and for their exclusive pleasure they spilled rivers of it every day; within their palace they had a secret chamber where victims were put to death before their eyes and while they enjoyed themselves. Théo, one of this Prince's successors, had, like him, a very bloodthirsty wife; they invented a brass column and this great cylinder they would heat red hot; unlucky persons were bound to it while the royal couple looked on: "The Princess," writes the historian from whom we have borrowed these touches, "was infinitely entertained by these melancholy victims' contortions and screams; she was not content unless her husband gave her this spectacle frequently." *Hist. des Conj.* vol. 7, page 43.

about inside for a few minutes while screams burst from Suzanne's mouth, he did not withdraw them until they were covered with blood. Glutted and wearied by these horrors, and feeling, indeed, he could restrain himself no longer:

"Come, Thérèse, come," he said, "let's conclude all this with a little scene of funambulism: it'll be cut-the-cord,[7] dear girl."

That was the name he gave that deadly legerdemain of which I gave you a description when I mentioned Roland's cavern for the first time. I mount the three-legged stool, the evil fellow fits the halter about my neck, he takes his place opposite me; although in a frightful state, Suzanne excites him manually; an instant passes, then he snaps the stool from beneath me, but equipped with the sickle, I sever the cord immediately and fall uninjured to the ground.

"Nicely done, very neat," says Roland, "your turn, Suzanne, there it is, and I'll spare you, if you manage as cleverly."

Suzanne takes my place. Oh, Madame, allow me to pass over that dreadful scene's details. . . . The poor thing did not recover from it.

"And now off we go, Thérèse," says Roland, "you'll not return to this place until your time has come."

"Whenever you like, Monsieur, whenever you like," I reply; "I prefer death to the frightful life you have me lead. Are there wretches such as we for whom life can be valuable? . . ."

And Roland locked me into my cell. The next day my companions asked what had become of Suzanne and I told them; they were hardly surprised; all were awaiting the same fate and each,

---

[7] This game, described above, was in great use amongst the Celts from whom we are descended (see Monsieur Pelloutier's *Histoire des Celtes*); virtually all these extravagances of debauchery, these extraordinary libertine passions, some part of which are described in this book and which, how ridiculously! today awaken the law's attention, were, in days bygone, either our ancestors' sports, games far superior to our contemporary amusements, or legalized customs, or again, religious ceremonies; currently, they are transformed into crimes. In how many pious rituals did not the pagans employ flagellation! Several people used these identical tortures, or passions, to initiate their warriors; this was known as *huscanaver* (*viz.*, the religious ceremonies of every race on earth). These pleasantries, whose maximum inconvenience may be at the very most the death of a slut, are capital crimes at the moment. Three cheers for the progress of civilization! How it conspires to the happiness of man, and how much more fortunate than our forebears we are!

like me, seeing therein a term to their suffering, passionately longed for it.

And thus two years went by, Roland indulging in his customary debauchery, I lingering on with the prospect of a cruel death, when one day the news went about the château that not only were our master's expectations satisfied, not only had he received the immense quantity of Venetian funds he had wished, but that he had even obtained a further order for another six millions in counterfeit coin for which he would be reimbursed in Italy when he arrived to claim payment; the scoundrel could not possibly have enjoyed better luck; he was going to leave with an income of two millions, not to mention his hopes of getting more: this was the new piece of evidence Providence had prepared for me. This was the latest manner in which it wished to convince me that prosperity belongs to Crime only and indigence to Virtue.

Matters were at this stage when Roland came to take me to his cavern a third time. I recollect what he threatened me with on my previous visit, I shudder. . . .

"Rest assured," he says, "you've nothing to fear, 'tis a question of something which concerns me alone . . . an uncommon joy I'd like to taste and from which you will incur no risks."

I follow him. When the doors are shut:

"Thérèse," says Roland, "there's no one in the house but you to whom I dare confide the problem; I've got to have a woman of impeccable honesty. . . . I've no one about but you, I confess that I prefer you to my sister. . . .

Taken aback, I entreat him to clarify himself.

"Then listen," says he; "my fortune is made, but whatever be the favors I have received from fate, it can desert me at any instant; I may be trapped, I could be caught while transporting my bullion, and if that misfortune occurs, Thérèse, it's the rope that's waiting for me: 'tis the same delight I am pleased to have women savor: that's the one will serve as my undoing; I am as firmly persuaded as I can possibly be that this death is infinitely sweeter than cruel; but as the women upon whom I have tested its initial anguishes have never really wished to tell me the truth, it is in person I wish to be made acquainted with the sensation. By way of the experience itself I want to find out whether it is not very

certain this asphyxiation impels, in the individual who undergoes it,
the erectory nerve to produce an ejaculation; once convinced this
death is but a game, I'll brave it with far greater courage, for it is
not my existence's cessation terrifies me: my principles are determined upon that head and well persuaded matter can never become
anything but matter again, I have no greater dread of Hell than I
have expectation of Paradise; but a cruel death's torments make me
apprehensive; I don't wish to suffer when I perish; so let's have a
try. You will do to me everything I did to you; I'll strip; I'll mount
the stool, you'll adjust the rope, I'll excite myself for a moment,
then, as soon as you see things assume a certain consistency, you'll
jerk the stool free and I'll remain hanging; you'll leave me there
until you either discern my semen's emission or symptoms of
death's throes; in the latter case, you'll cut me down at once; in the
other, you'll allow Nature to take her course and you'll not detach
me until afterward. You observe, Thérèse, I'm putting my life in
your hands; your freedom, your fortune will be your good conduct's
reward."

"Ah, Monsieur, there's folly in the proposition."

"No, Thérèse, I insist the thing be done," he answered, undressing himself, "but behave yourself well; behold what proof I
give you of my confidence and high regard!"

What possibility of hesitation had I? Was he not my master?
Furthermore, it seemed to me the evil I was going to do him would
be immediately offset by the extreme care I would take to save his
life: I was going to be mistress of that life, but whatever might be
his intentions with respect to me, it would certainly only be in order
to restore it to him.

We take our stations; Roland is stimulated by a few of his
usual caresses; he climbs upon the stool, I put the halter round his
neck; he tells me he wants me to curse him during the process, I am
to reproach him with all his life's horrors, I do so; his dart soon
rises to menace Heaven, he himself gives me the sign to remove the
stool, I obey; would you believe it, Madame? nothing more true
than what Roland had conjectured: nothing but symptoms of
pleasure ornament his countenance and at practically the same instant rapid jets of semen spring nigh to the vault. When 'tis all
shot out without any assistance whatsoever from me, I rush to cut

him down, he falls, unconscious, but thanks to my ministrations he quickly recovers his senses.

"Oh Thérèse!" he exclaims upon opening his eyes, "oh, those sensations are not to be described; they transcend all one can possibly say: let them now do what they wish with me, I stand unflinching before Themis' sword!

"You're going to find me guilty yet another time, Thérèse," Roland went on, tying my hands behind my back, "no thanks for you, but, dear girl, what can one expect? a man doesn't correct himself at my age. . . . Beloved creature, you have just saved my life and never have I so powerfully conspired against yours; you lamented Suzanne's fate; ah well, I'll arrange for you to meet again; I'm going to plunge you alive into the dungeon where she expired."

I will not describe my state of mind, Madame, you fancy what it was; in vain did I weep, groan, I was not heeded. Roland opened the fatal dungeon, he hangs out a lamp so that I can still better discern the multitude of corpses wherewith it is filled; next, he passes a cord under my arms which, as you know, are bound behind my back, and by means of this cord he lowers me thirty feet: I am twenty more from the bottom of the pit: in this position I suffer hideously, it is as if my arms are being torn from their sockets. With what terror was I not seized! what a prospect confronted my eyes! Heaps of bodies in the midst of which I was going to finish my life and whose stench was already infecting me. Roland cinches the rope about a stick fitted above the hole then, brandishing a knife, I hear him exciting himself.

"Well, Thérèse," he cries, "recommend your soul to God, the instant my delirium supervenes will be that when I plunge you into the eternal abyss awaiting you; ah . . . ah . . . Thérèse, ah . . ." and I feel my head covered with proof of his ecstasy; but, happily he has not parted the rope: he lifts me out.

"Ha," says he, "were you afraid?"

"Oh, Monsieur—"

" 'Tis thus you'll die, be sure of it, Thérèse, be sure of it, and 'twas pleasant to familiarize you with your egress."

We climb back to the light. . . . Was I to complain? or be thankful? What a reward for what I had just done for him! Bu

ad the monster not been in a position to do more? Could he not
ave killed me? Oh, what a man!

Roland prepared his departure; on the eve of setting out
e pays me a visit; I fall before his feet, most urgently I beg him to
ree me and to give me whatever little sum of money he would like,
hat I might be able to reach Grenoble.

"Grenoble! Certainly not, Thérèse, you'd denounce us when
ou got there."

"Very well, Monsieur," I say, sprinkling his knees with my
ears, "I swear to you I'll never go there and, to be sure of me,
ondescend to take me to Venice with you; I will perhaps find
entler hearts there than in my native land, and once you are so
ind as to set me free, I swear to you by all that is holy I will never
mportune you."

"I'll not aid you, not a pennyworth of aid will you get from
ne," that peerless rogue answered; "everything connected with
ity, commiseration, gratitude is so alien to my heart that were I
hree times as rich as I am, they'd not see me give one crown to the
oor; the spectacle of misery irritates me, amuses me, and when
am unable to do evil myself, I have a delicious time enjoying that
ccomplished by the hand of destiny. Upon all this I have principles
o which, Thérèse, I adhere faithfully; poverty is part of the
atural order; by creating men of dissimilar strength, Nature has
onvinced us of her desire that inequality be preserved even in
hose modifications our culture might bring to Nature's laws. To
elieve indigence is to violate the established order, to imperil it, it
s to enter into revolt against that which Nature has decreed, it is
o undermine the equilibrium that is fundamental to her sublimest
rrangements; it is to strive to erect an equality very perilous to
ociety, it is to encourage indolence and flatter drones, it is to
each the poor to rob the rich man when the latter is pleased to re-
use the former alms, for it's a dangerous habit, and gratuities en-
ourage it."

"Oh, Monsieur, how harsh these principles are! Would you
peak thus had you not always been wealthy?"

"Who knows, Thérèse? everyone has a right to his opinion,
hat's mine, and I'll not change it. They complain about beggars in
rance: if they wished to be rid of them, the thing could soon be

done; hang seven or eight thousand of 'em and the infamous breed will vanish overnight. The Body Politic should be governed by the same rules that apply to the Body Physical. Would a man devoured by vermin allow them to feed upon him out of sympathy? In our gardens do we not uproot the parasitic plant which harms useful vegetation? Why then should one choose to act otherwise in this case?"

"But Religion," I expostulated, "benevolence, Monsieur, humanity ..."

"... are the chopping blocks of all who pretend to happiness," said Roland; "if I have consolidated my own, it is only upon the debris of all those infamous prejudices of mankind; 'tis by mocking laws human and divine; 'tis by constantly sacrificing the weak when I find them in my path, 'tis by abusing the public's good faith; 'tis by ruining the poor and stealing from the rich I have arrived at the summit of that precipice whereupon sits the temple sacred to the divinity I adore; why not imitate me? The narrow road leading to that shrine is as plainly offered to your eyes as mine; the hallucinatory virtues you have preferred to it, have they consoled you for your sacrifices? 'Tis too late, luckless one, 'tis too late, weep for your sins, suffer, and strive to find in the depths of the phantoms you worship, if any finding there is to be done, what the reverence you have shown them has caused you to lose."

With these words, the cruel Roland leaps upon me and I am again forced to serve the unworthy pleasures of a monster I had such good reason to abhor; this time I thought he would strangle me; when his passions were satisfied, he caught up the bull's pizzle and with it smote me above a hundred blows all over my body, the while assuring me I was fortunate he lacked the time to do more.

On the morrow, before setting out, the wretch presented us with a new scene of cruelty and of barbarity whereof no example is furnished by the annals of Andronicus, Nero, Tiberius, or Wenceslaus. Everyone at the château supposed Roland's sister would leave with him, and he had indeed told her to dress and ready herself for the journey; at the moment of mounting his horse, he leads her toward us. "There's your post, vile creature," says he, ordering her to take off her clothes, "I want my comrades to remember me by leaving them as a token the woman for whom they thought I had a fancy; but as we need only a certain number and as I am going to follow a dangerous road upon which my weapons will perhaps be useful, I must try my pistols upon one of these rascals." Whereupon he loads one of his guns, aims it at each of our breasts, and comes at last to his sister. "Off you go, whore," says he, blasting out her brains, "go advise the devil that Roland, the richest villain on earth, is he who most insolently taunts the hand of Heaven and challenges Satan's own!" The poor girl did not expire at once: she writhed in her death throes for a considerable period: 'twas a hideous spectacle: that infamous scoundrel calmly considered it and did not tear his eyes away until he had left us forever.

Everything changed the day after Roland went away. His successor, a gentle and very reasonable man, had us released at once.

"That is hardly fit work for a frail and delicate sex," he said to us with kindness; "animals should be employed at this machine; our trade is criminal enough without further offending the Supreme Being with gratuitous atrocities."

He installed us in the château and, without requiring me to do so, suggested I assume possession of the duties Roland's sister had performed; the other women were busied cutting out counterfeit coins, a much less fatiguing task, no doubt, and one for which they were rewarded, as was I, with good lodgings and excellent food.

At the end of two months, Dalville, Roland's successor, informed us of his colleague's happy arrival at Venice; there he had established himself and there realized his fortune and there he enjoyed it in peace and quiet, wholly content, full of the felicity he had anticipated. The fate of the man who replaced him was of a distinctly different character. The unfortunate Dalville was honest in his profession, indeed, even more honest than was necessary in order to be destroyed.

One day, while all was calm at the château, while, under the direction of that good master, the work, although criminal, was however being carried on with gaiety, one day the gates were stormed, the moats bridged and the house, before our men had a moment's opportunity to look to their defense, found itself invaded by soldiers of the constabulary, sixty strong. Surrender was our sole alternative; we were shackled like beasts; we were attached to the horses and marches down to Grenoble. "O Heaven!" I said to myself as we entered, " 'tis then the scaffold destiny holds for me in this city wherein I wildly fancied my happiness was to be born. . . . Oh! how deceived is man by his intuitions!"

The court was not long tarrying over the counterfeiters' case; they were all sentenced to the gallows; when the mark that branded me was detected, they scarcely gave themselves the trouble of interrogating me and I was about to be hanged along with the others when I made a last effort to obtain some pity from that famous magistrate who proved to be an honor to his tribunal, a judge of integrity, a beloved citizen, an enlightened philosopher whose wisdom and benevolence will grave his name for all time in letters of gold upon Themis' temple. He listened to me; convinced of my good faith and the authenticity of my wretched plight, he deigned to give my case a little more attention than his cohorts saw fit to lavish upon it. . . . O great man, 'tis to thee I owe an homage: a miserable creature's gratitude would not sit onerously with thee and the tribute she offers thee, by publishing abroad thy goodness of heart, will always be her sweetest joy.

Monsieur S*** himself became my advocate; my testimony was heard, and his male eloquence illumined the mind of the court. The general depositions of the false coiners they were going to execute fortified the zeal of the man who had the kindness to take an interest in me: I was declared an unwilling party to crime, innocent, and fully acquitted of all charges, was set at complete liberty to become what I wished; to those services my protector added a collection he had taken for my relief, and it totaled more than fifty *louis;* I began to see a dawning of happiness at last; my presentiments seemed finally about to be realized and I thought I had reached an end of my tribulations when it pleased Providence to convince me they were still far from their definitive cessation.

Upon emerging from jail I took up lodgings at an inn facing the Isère bridge on the side of the *faubourgs* where, I had been assured, I might find proper quarters. My plan, suggested by the advice of Monsieur S***, was to stay there awhile in order to try to find a situation in the town; in the event the letters of recommendation Monsieur S*** had so kindly given me produced no results, I was to return to Lyon. On the second day I was dining at my inn—'twas what is called table d'hôte—when I noticed I was being closely scrutinized by a tall, very handsomely attired woman who went under a baroness' title; upon examining her in my turn, I believed I recognized her; we both rose and approached each other, we embraced like two people who once knew each other but cannot remember under what circumstances.

Then the baroness drew me aside.

"Thérèse," says she, "am I in error? are you not the person I saved from the Conciergerie ten years ago? have you entirely forgotten your Dubois?"

Little flattered by this discovery, I however replied to it with politeness, but I was dealing with the most subtle, the most adroit woman in contemporary France; there was no way of eluding her. Dubois overwhelmed me with attentions, she said that she, like the entire town, had taken an interest in my fate but that had she known who I really was, she would have resorted to all sorts of measures and made many a representation to the magistrates, amongst whom, she declared, she had several friends. As usual, I was weak, I permitted myself to be led to this woman's room and there I related my sufferings to her.

"My dear friend," said she, renewing her embraces, "if I have desired to see you more intimately, it is to tell you I have made my fortune and that all I possess is at your disposal; look here," she said, opening some caskets brimming with gold and diamonds, "these are the fruits of my industry; had I worshiped Virtue like you, I should be in prison today, or hanged."

"O Madame," I cried, "if you owe all that to naught but crime, Providence, which eventually is always just, will not suffer you to enjoy it for long."

"An error," said Dubois; "do not imagine that Providence invariably favors Virtue; do not let a brief interlude of prosperity blind you to this point. It is as one to the maintenance of Providence's scheme whether 'tis Peter or Paul who follows the evil career while the other surrenders himself to good; Nature must have an equal quantity of each, and the exercise of crime rather than the commission of good is a matter of you've no idea what indifference to her; listen Thérèse, pay a little attention to me," continued that corruptor, seating herself and bidding me take a nearby chair; "you have some wit, my child, and your intelligence will be speedily convinced.

"'Tis not man's election of Virtue which brings him happiness, dear girl, for Virtue, like vice, is nothing beyond a scheme of getting along in the world; 'tis not, hence, a question of adopting one course rather than another; 'tis merely a matter of following the road generally taken; he who wanders away from it is always wrong; in an entirely virtuous world, I would recommend virtue to you, because worldly rewards being associated therewith, happiness would infallibly be connected with it too; in a totally corrupt world, I would never advise anything but vice. He who does not walk along with others has inevitably to perish; everyone he encounters he collides with, and, as he is weak, he has necessarily to be crushed. It is in vain the law wishes to re-establish order and restore men to righteousness; too unjust to undertake the task, too insufficient to succeed in it, those laws will lure you away from the beaten path, but only temporarily; never will they make man abandon it. While the general interest of mankind drives it to corruption, he who does not wish to be corrupted with the rest will therefore be fighting against the general interest; well, what happiness can he expect who is in perpetual conflict with the interest of everyone else? Are you going to tell me it is vice which is at odds with mankind's welfare? I would grant this true in a world composed of equal proportions of good and bad people, because in this instance, the interest of the one category would be in clear contradiction with that of the other; however, that does not hold true in a completely corrupt society; in it, my vices outrage the vicious only and provoke in them other vices which they use to square matters: and thus all of us are happy: the vibration becomes general: we have a multitude of conflicts and mutual injuries whereby everyone, immediately recovering what he has just lost, incessantly discovers himself in a happy position. Vice is dangerous to naught but Virtue which, frail and timorous, dares undertake nothing; but when it shall no longer exist on earth, when its wearisome reign shall reach its end, vice thereafter outraging no one but the vicious, will cause other vices to burgeon but will cause no further damage to the virtuous. How could you help but have foundered a thousand times over in the course of your life, Thérèse? for have you not continually driven up the one-way street all the world has crowded down? Had you turned and abandoned yourself to the tide you would have made a safe port as well as I. Will he who wishes to climb upstream cover as much distance in a day as he who moves with the current? You constantly talk about Providence; ha! what proves to you this Providence is a friend of order and consequently enamored of Virtue? Does It not give you uninterrupted examples of Its injustices and Its irregularities? Is it by sending mankind war, plagues, and famine, is it by having formed a universe vicious in every one of its particulars It manifests to your view Its extreme fondness of good? Why would you have it that vicious individuals displease It since Providence Itself acts only through the intermediary of vices? since all is vice and corruption in Its works? since all is crime and disorder in what It wills? Moreover, whence do we derive those impulses which lead us to do evil? is it not Providence's hand which gives them to us? is there a single one of our sensations which does not come from It? one of our desires which is not Its artifact? is it then reasonable to say that It would allow us or give us penchants for something which might be harmful to It or useless? if then vices serve Providence, why should we wish to disown them, disclaim them, resist them? what would justify our labors to destroy them? and whence comes the right to stifle their voice? A little more philosophy in the world would soon restore all to order and would cause magistrates and legislators to see that the crimes they condemn and punish with such rigor sometimes have a far greater degree of utility than those virtues they preach without practicing and without ever rewarding."

"But when I become sufficiently enfeebled, Madame," I replied, "to be able to embrace your appalling doctrines, how will you manage to suppress the feelings of guilt in my heart whose birth they will cause at every instant?"

"Guilt is an illusion," Dubois answered; "my dear Thérèse, it it naught but the idiotic murmuring of a soul too debilitated to dare annihilate it."

"Annihilate it! May one?"

"Nothing simpler; one repents only of what one is not in the habit of doing; frequently repeat what makes you remorseful and you'll quickly have done with the business; against your qualms oppose the torch of your passions and self-interest's potent laws: they'll be put to rout in a trice. Remorse is no index of criminality; it merely denotes an easily subjugated spirit; let some absurd command be given you, which forbids you to leave this room, and you'll not depart without guilty feelings however certain it is your departure will cause no one any harm. And so it is not true that it is exclusively crime which excites remorse. By convincing yourself of crime's nullity, of its necessity with what regards Nature's universal scheme, it would therefore be as possible to vanquish the guilt one would sense after having committed it as it would be to throttle that which would be born from your leaving this room after having received the illegal order to stay here. One must begin with a precise analysis of everything mankind denominates as criminal; by convincing oneself that it is merely the infraction of its laws and national manners they characterize thus, that what is called crime in France ceases to be crime two hundred leagues away, that there is no act really considered criminal everywhere upon earth, none which, vicious or criminal here, is not praiseworthy and virtuous a few miles hence, that it is all a matter of opinion and of geography and that it is therefore absurd to tie oneself down to practicing virtues which are only vices somewhere else, and to flying from crimes which are excellent deeds in another climate—I ask you now if, after these reflections, I can still retain any feelings of guilt for having committed, either for the sake of pleasure or of self-interest, a crime in France which is nothing but a virtue in China? or if I ought to make myself very miserable or be prodigiously troubled about practicing actions in France which would have me burned in Siam? Now, if remorse exists only in reason of prohibition, if it is never but born of the wreckage of the inhibitory check and in no wise of the committed act, is it so very wise to allow the impulse in itself to subsist? is it not stupid not to extirpate it at once? Let one become accustomed to considering as inconsequential the act which has just excited remorse; let the scrupulously meditated study of the manners and customs of all the world's nations culminate in one's judging the act indifferent; as a result of this research, let one repeat this act, whatever it is, as often as possible; or, better still, let one commit more powerful versions of the act one is concerting so as better to habituate oneself to it, do this, and familiarity together with reason will soon destroy remorse for it; they will rapidly annihilate this shadowy, furtive impulse, issue of naught but ignorance and education. One will straightway feel that there being nothing really criminal in anything whatsoever, there is stupidity in repentance and pusillanimity in not daring to do everything that may be useful or agreeable to us, whatever be the dikes one must breach, the fences one must topple in order to do it. I am forty-five, Thérèse; I committed my first crime at fourteen. That one emancipated me from all the bonds that hampered me; since then I have not ceased to chase fortune throughout a career sown with crimes, there's not a single one I've not done or had done . . . and never have I known any remorse. However that may be, I am reaching my term, yet another two or three neat strokes and I pass from the mediocre condition wherein I was to have spent my life, to an income of above fifty thousand a year. I repeat, my dear, never upon this happily traveled road has remorse made me feel its stings; a catastrophic miscarriage might this instant plunge me from the pinnacle into the abyss, I'd not feel remorse, no: I would lament my want of skill or accuse men, but I should always be at peace with my conscience."

"Very well," I replied, "very well, Madame, but let's spend a moment reasoning in terms of your own principles: what right have you to require that my conscience be as impregnable as yours when since childhood it has not been accustomed to vanquishing the same prejudices? By what title do you require that my mind, which is not constituted like your own, be able to adopt the same systems? You acknowledge sums of good and evil in Nature, you admit that, in consequence, there must be a certain quantity of beings who practice good and another group which devotes itself to evil; the course I elect is hence natural; therefore, how would you be able to demand that I take leave of the rules Nature prescribes to me? You say you find happiness in the career you pursue; very well, Madame, why should it be that I do not also find it in the career I pursue? Do not suppose, furthermore, that the law's vigilance long leaves in peace him who violates its codes, you have just had a striking example of the contrary; of the fifteen scoundrels with whom I was living, fourteen perish ignominiously. . . ."

"And is that what you call a misfortune?" Dubois asked. "But what does this ignominy mean to him who has principles no longer? When one has trespassed every frontier, when in our eyes honor is no more than a hallucination, reputation of perfect indifference, religion an illusion, death a total annihilation; is it then not the same thing, to die on the scaffold or in bed? There are two varieties of rascals in the world, Thérèse: the one a powerful fortune or prodigious influence shelters from this tragic end; the other one who is unable to avoid it when taken. The latter, born unprovided with possessions, must have but one desire if he has any *esprit*: to become rich at no matter what price; if he succeeds, he obtains what he wanted and should be content; if he is put on the rack, what's he to regret since he has nothing to lose? Those laws decreed against banditry are null if they are not extended to apply to the powerful bandit; that the law inspire any dread in the miserable is impossible, for the sword is the miserable man's only resource."

"And do you believe," I broke in, "that in another world Celestial Justice does not await him whom crime has not affrighted in this one?"

"I believe," this dangerous woman answered, "that if there were a God there would be less evil on earth; I believe that since evil exists, these disorders are either expressly ordained by this God, and there you have a barbarous fellow, or he is incapable of preventing them and right away you have a feeble God; in either case, an abominable being, a being whose lightning I should defy and whose laws contemn. Ah, Thérèse! is not atheism preferable to the one and the other of these extremes? that's my doctrine, dear lass, it's been mine since childhood and I'll surely not renounce it while I live."

"You make me shudder, Madame," I said, getting to my feet; "will you pardon me? for I am unable to listen any longer to your sophistries and blasphemies."

"One moment, Thérèse," said Dubois, holding me back, "if I cannot conquer your reason, I may at least captivate your heart. I have need of you, do not refuse me your aid; here are a thousand *louis*: they will be yours as soon as the blow is struck."

Heedless of all but my penchant for doing good, I immediately asked Dubois what was involved so as to forestall, if 'twere possible, the crime she was getting ready to commit.

"Here it is," she said: "have you noticed that young tradesman from Lyon who has been taking his meals here for the past four or five days?"

"Who? Dubreuil?"

"Precisely."

"Well?"

"He is in love with you, he told me so in confidence, your modest and gentle air pleases him infinitely, he adores your candor, your virtue enchants him; this romantic fellow has eight hundred thousand francs in gold or paper, it's all in a little coffer he keeps near his bed; let me give the man to understand you consent to hear him, whether that be true or not; for, does it matter? I'll get him to propose you a drive, you'll take a carriage out of the town, I'll persuade him he will advance matters with you during your promenade; you'll amuse him, you'll keep him away as long as possible, meanwhile I'll rob him, but I'll not flee; his belongings will reach Turin before I quit Grenoble, we will employ all imaginable art to dissuade him from settling his eyes upon us, we'll pretend to assist his searches; however, my departure will be announced, he'll not be surprised thereby, you'll follow me, and the thousand *louis* will be counted out to you immediately we get to the Piedmont."

"Agreed, Madame," I said to Dubois, fully determined to warn Dubreuil of the concerted theft, "but consider," I added in order more thoroughly to deceive this villain, "that if Dubreuil is fond of me, by revealing the business or by giving myself to him, I might get much more from him than you offer me to betray him."

"Bravo," replied Dubois, "that's what I call an adept scholar, I'm beginning to believe Heaven gave you a greater talent for crime than you pretend: ah well," she continued, picking up a quill, "here's my note for twenty thousand crowns, now dare say no to me."

"Not for the world, Madame," quoth I, taking her note, "but, at least, my weakness and my wrong in surrendering to your seductions are to be attributed only to my impecunious circumstances."

"I'd prefer to interpret it as a meritorious act of your

intelligence," said Dubois, "but if you prefer me to blame your poverty, why then, as you like; serve me and you will always be content."

Everything was arranged; the same evening I began in earnest to play my game with Dubreuil, and indeed I discovered he had some taste for me.

Nothing could have been more embarrassing than my situation: I was without any doubt far from lending myself to the proposed crime even had it been worth ten thousand times as much gold; but the idea of denouncing this woman was also painful for me; I was exceedingly loath to expose to death a creature to whom I had owed my freedom ten years before. I should have liked to have been able to find a way of preventing the crime without having it punished, and with anyone else but a consummate villain like Dubois I should have succeeded; here then is what I resolved to do, all the while unaware that this horrible woman's base maneuvers would not only topple the entire edifice of my honorable schemes but even punish me for having dreamt of them.

Upon the day fixed for the projected outing, Dubois invites us both to dine in her room, we accept, and the meal over, Dubreuil and I descend to summon the carriage that has been prepared for us; Dubois does not accompany us, I find myself alone with Dubreuil the moment before we set out.

"Monsieur," I say, speaking very rapidly, "listen closely to me, don't be alarmed, no noise, and above all pay strict attention to what I am going to recommend; have you a reliable friend at this hotel?"

"Yes, I have a young associate upon whom I can count with absolute confidence."

"Then, Monsieur, go promptly and order him not to leave your room for a second while we are on our drive."

"But I have the key to the room; what does this excess of precaution signify?"

"It is more essential than you believe, Monsieur, I beg you to employ it, or else I shall not go out with you; the woman with whom we dined is a bandit, she only arranged our outing in order more easily to rob you while we are gone; make haste, Monsieur, she is watching us, she is dangerous; quickly, turn your key over to your friend, have him go and install himself in your room and let him not budge until we're back. I'll explain the rest as soon as we are in the carriage."

Dubreuil heeds me, presses my hand in token of thanks, flies to give orders relative to the warning he has received, and returns; we leave; when en route, I disclose the entire adventure to him, I recite mine and inform him of the unhappy circumstances in my life which have caused me to make the acquaintance of such a woman. This correct and sensible young man expresses the deepest gratitude for the service I have just so kindly rendered him, he takes an interest in my misfortunes, and proposes to alleviate them with the bestowal of his hand.

"I am only too happy to be able to make you restitution for the wrongs fortune has done you, Mademoiselle," says he; "I am my own master, dependent upon no one, I am going on to Geneva to make a considerable investment with the funds your timely warning has saved me from losing; accompany me to Switzerland; when we arrive there I shall become your husband and you will not appear in Lyon under any other title, or, if you prefer, Mademoiselle, if you have any misgivings, it will only be in my own country I will give you my name."

Such an offer, so very flattering, was one I dared not refuse; but it did not on the other hand become me to accept it without making Dubreuil aware of all that might cause him to repent it; he was grateful for my delicacy and only insisted the more urgently . . . unhappy creature that I was! 'twas necessary that happiness be offered me only in order that I be more deeply penetrated with grief at never being able to seize it! it was then ordained that no virtue could be born in my heart without preparing torments for me!

Our conversation had already taken us two leagues from the city, and we were about to dismount in order to enjoy the fresh air along the bank of the Isère, when all of a sudden Dubreuil told me he felt very ill. . . . He got down, he was seized by dreadful vomitings; I had him climb into the carriage at once and we flew back posthaste to Grenoble. Dubreuil is so sick he has to be borne to his room; his condition startles his associate whom we find there and who, in accordance with instructions, has not stirred from the chamber; a doctor comes, Just Heaven! Dubreuil has been poisoned! I no sooner learn the fatal news than I dash to Dubois' apartment; the infamous creature! she's gone; I rush to my room, my armoire has been forced open, the little money and odds and ends I possess have been removed; Dubois, they tell me, left three hours ago in the direction of Turin. There was no doubt she was the author of this multitude of crimes; she had gone to Dubreuil's door; annoyed to find his room occupied, she revenged herself upon me and had envenomed Dubreuil at dinner so that upon our return, if she had succeeded with her theft, that unhappy young man would be more busied with his own failing life than concerned to pursue her who had made off with his fortune and would let her fly in safety; the accident of his death, occurring, so to speak, while he was in my arms, would make me appear more suspect than herself; nothing directly informed us of the scheme she had contrived, but could it have been different?

And then I rush back to Dubreuil's room; I am not allowed to approach his bedside. "But why?" I demand and am given the reason: the poor man is expiring and is no longer occupied with anyone save his God. However, he exonerates me, he gives assurance of my innocence; he expressly forbids that I be pursued; he dies. Hardly has he closed his eyes when his associate hastens to bring me the news and begs me to be easy. Alas! how could I be? how was I not to weep bitterly for the loss of a man who had so generously offered to extricate me from misery! how was I not to deplore a theft which forced me back into the wretchedness whence I had only a moment before emerged! Frightful creature! I cried; if 'tis to this your principles lead you, is it any wonder they are abhorred and that honest folk punish them! But I was arguing from the injured party's viewpoint and Dubois, who had only reaped happiness therefrom and saw nothing but her interest in what she had undertaken, Dubois, I say, had doubtless reached a very different conclusion.

To Dubreuil's associate, whose name was Valbois, I divulged everything, both what had been concerted against the man we had lost and what had happened to me. He sympathized with me, most sincerely regretted Dubreuil and blamed the overly nice scruples which had prevented me from lodging a complaint instantly I had been advised of Dubois' schemes; we agreed that this monster who needed but four hours to get to another country and security would arrive there before we would be able to organize her pursuit, that to follow her would involve considerable expense, that the inn-keeper, heavily compromised by the proceedings we would launch, by defending himself with vehemence might perhaps end by having me crushed, I . . . who seemed to be living in Grenoble as one who had missed the gallows by a hairsbreadth. These reasons convinced me and even terrified me to the point I resolved to leave the town without even saying farewell to my protector, Monsieur S * * *. Dubreuil's friend approved the idea; he did not conceal from me that if the entire adventure were to be revealed he would be obliged to make depositions which, his precautions notwithstanding, would involve me as much by my intimacy with Dubreuil as in reason of my last outing with his friend; in the light of which he urged me to leave at once without a word to anyone, and I could be perfectly sure that, on his side, he would never take steps against me, whom he believed innocent, and, in all that had just occurred, whom he could only accuse of weakness.

Upon pondering Valbois' opinions, I recognized they were that much better the more certain it appeared I would be beheld with suspicion; the less my guilt, the wiser his suggestions; the one thing that spoke in my behalf, the recommendation I had made to Dubreuil at the outset of our promenade, which had, so they told me, been unsatisfactorily explained by the article of his death, would not appear so conclusive as I might hope; whereupon I promptly made my decision; I imparted it to Valbois.

"Would," said he, "that my friend had charged me with some dispositions favorable to you, I should carry out such requests with the greatest pleasure; I am sorry indeed he did not tell me 'twas to you he owed the advice to guard his room; but he said nothing of the sort, not a word did I have from him, and consequently I am obliged to limit myself to merely complying with his orders. What you have suffered by his loss would persuade me to do something in my own name were I able to, Mademoiselle, but I am just setting up in business, I am young, my fortune is not boundless, I am com-pelled to render an account of Dubreuil to his family and without delay; allow me then to confine myself to the one little service I beg you to accept: here are five *louis* and I have here as well an honest merchant from Chalon-sur-Saône, my native city; she is going to return there after a day and a night's stop at Lyon where she is called by business matters; I put you into her keeping."

"Madame Bertrand," Valbois continued, "here is the young lady I spoke of; I recommend her to you, she wishes to procure herself a situation. With the same earnestness which would apply were she my own sister, I beg you to take all possible steps to find something in our city which will be suitable to her person, her birth, and her upbringing; that until she is properly installed she incur no expense; do see to her requirements and I shall reimburse you immediately I am home."

Valbois besought me leave to embrace me. "Adieu, Mademoiselle," he continued, "Madame Bertrand sets off tomorrow at daybreak; accompany her and may a little more happiness attend you in a city where I shall perhaps soon have the satisfaction of seeing you again."

The courtesy of this young man, who was in no sort indebted to me, brought tears to my eyes. Kind treatment is sweet indeed when for so long one has experienced naught but the most odious. I accepted his gifts, at the same time swearing I was going to work at nothing but to put myself in a way to be able someday to reciprocate. Alas! I thought as I retired, though the exercise of yet another virtue has just flung me into destitution, at least, for the first time in my life, the hope of consolation looms out of this appalling pit of evil into which Virtue has cast me again.

The hour was not advanced; I needed a breath of air and so went down to the Isère embankment, desiring to stroll there for several instants; and, as almost always happens under similar circumstances, my thoughts, absorbing me entirely, led me far. Finding myself, at length, in an isolated place, I sat down, more leisurely to ponder. However, night descended before I thought to return; of a sudden I felt myself seized by three men: one clapped a hand over my mouth, the other two precipitated me into a carriage, climbed in, and for three full hours we sped along, during which time not one of these brigands deigned either to say a word to me or respond to any of my questions. The blinds were drawn down, I saw nothing; the carriage came to a halt before a house, gates swung wide, we entered, the gates clanged to immediately. My abductors pick me up, lead me through several unlit apartments, and finally leave me in one near which is a room wherein I perceive a light.

"Stay here," says one of my ravishers as he withdraws with his companions, "you're soon going to see an old acquaintance."

And they disappear, carefully shutting all the doors. At almost the same time, that leading into the room where I had spied illumination is opened, and carrying a candle in her hand, I see emerge . . . oh, Madame, fancy who it was . . . Dubois . . . Dubois herself, that frightful monster, devoured, no question of it, by the most ardent desire to be revenged.

"Hither, charming girl," said she in an arrogant tone, "come here and receive the reward for the virtues in which you indulged yourself at my expense. . . ." And angrily clutching my hand: ". . . ah, you wretch! I'll teach you to betray me!"

"No, Madame, no," I say in great haste, " I betrayed you not at all: inform yourself: I uttered not one word which could cause you any inquietude, no, I spoke not the least word which might compromise you."

"But did you not offer resistance to the crime I meditated? have you not thwarted its execution, worthless creature! You've got to be chastened. . . ."

And, as we were entering, she had no time to say more. The apartment into which I was made to pass was lit with equal sumptuousness and magnificence; at the further end, reclining upon an ottoman, was a man of about forty, wearing a billowing taffeta dressing robe.

"Monseigneur," said Dubois, presenting me to him, "here is the young lady you wanted, she in whom all Grenoble has become interested . . . the celebrated Thérèse, to be brief, condemned to hang with the counterfeiters, then delivered thanks to her innocence and her virtue. Acknowledge that I serve you with skill, Monseigneur; not four days ago you evinced your extreme desire to immolate her to your passions; and today I put her into your hands; you will perhaps prefer her to that pretty little pensionnaire from the Benedictine convent at Lyon you also desired and who should be arriving any minute: the latter has her physical and moral integrity this one here has nothing but a sentimental chastity; but it is deep-grained in her being and nowhere will you find a creature more heavily ballasted with candor and honesty. They are both at your disposition, Monseigneur: you'll either dispatch each this evening, or one today and the other tomorrow. As for myself, I am leaving you: your kindnesses in my regard engaged me to make you privy to my Grenoble adventure. One man dead, Monseigneur, one dead man; I must fly——"

"Ah no, no, charming woman!" cried the master of the place; "no, stay, and fear nothing while you have my protection! You are as a soul unto my pleasures; you alone possess the art of exciting and satisfying them, and the more you multiply your crimes, the more the thought of you inflames my mind. . . . But this Thérèse is a pretty thing. . . ." and addressing himself to me: "what is your age, my child?"

"Twenty-six, Monseigneur," I replied, "and much grief."

"Ha, yes, grief indeed, lots of distress, excellent, I'm familiar with all that, hugely amusing, just what I like; we're going to straighten everything out, we'll put a stop to these tumbles; I guarantee you that in twenty-four hours you'll be unhappy no longer, ha! . . ." and, with that, dreadful flights of laughter . . . "'tis true, eh, Dubois? I've a sure method for ending a young girl's misfortunes, haven't I?"

"Indeed you do," the odious creature replied; "and if Thérèse weren't a friend of mine, I'd never have brought her to you; but it is only fair I reward her for what she did for me. You'd never imagine how useful this dear thing was to me during my latest enterprise at Grenoble; you, Monseigneur, have had the kindness to accept my expression of gratitude, and, I pray you, repay what I owe her with interest."

The opaque ambiguity of these phrases, what Dubois had said to me upon entering, the species of gentleman with whom I had to do, this other girl whose forthcoming appearance had been announced, all this instantly troubled my imagination to a degree it would be difficult to describe. A cold sweat seeped from my pores and I was about to fall in a swoon—'twas at that instant this man's projects finally became clear to me. He calls me to him, begins with two or three kisses whereby our mouths are obliged to unite; he seeks my tongue, finds and sucks it and his, running deep into my throat, seems to be pumping the very breath from my lungs. He has me bend my head upon his chest, he lifts my hair and closely observes the nape of my neck.

"Oh, 'tis delicious!" he cries, squeezing it vigorously; "I've never seen one so nicely attached; 'twill be divine to make it jump free."

This last remark confirmed all my intimations; I saw very clearly I was once again in the clutches of one of those libertines moved by cruel passions, whose most cherished delights consist in enjoying the agonies or the death of the luckless victims procured them by money; I observed I was in danger of losing my life.

And then a knock at the door; Dubois leaves and an instant later ushers in the young Lyonnaise she had mentioned shortly before. I'll now try to sketch the two personages in whose company you are going to see me for a while. The Monseigneur, whose name and estate I never discovered, was, as I told you, a man of forty years, slender, indeed slight of frame, but vigorously constituted, sinewy, with his muscles almost constantly tensed, powerful biceps showing upon arms that were covered with a growth of thick black hair; everything about him proclaimed strength and good health; his face was animated, his gaze ardent, his eyes small, black, and wicked, there were splendid white teeth in his mouth, and liveliness in his every feature; his height was above average, and this man's amatory goad, which I was to have but too frequent occasion to see and feel, was roughly a foot long and above eight inches around. This incisive, nervous, constantly alerted and oozing instrument, ribboned with great purple veins that rendered its aspect still more formidable, was levitated throughout the séance, which lasted five or six hours; never once did it sink or falter. I had never before or since found a more hirsute man: he resembled those fauns described in fables. His powerful hands ended in fingers whose strength was that of a vice; as for his character, it seemed to me harsh, abrupt, cruel, his mind was inclined to that sarcasm and teasing of a sort calculated to redouble the sufferings one was perfectly well able to see one had to expect such a man would strive to inflict.

The little Lyonnaise was called Eulalie. A glimpse of her was enough to convince one of her distinguished birth and virtue: she was the daughter of one of the city's foremost families from whose house Dubois' criminal hirelings had abducted her under the pretext of conveying her to a rendezvous with the lover she idolized; together with an enchanting forthrightness and naïveté, she possessed one of the most delightful countenances imaginable. Barely sixteen years old, Eulalie had the face of a genuine Madonna; her features were embellished by an enviable innocence and modesty; she had little color but was only the more fetching for that; and the sparkle in her superb eyes endowed her pretty face with all the fire and warmth whereof, at first glance, this pallor seemed to deprive her; her rather generous mouth was filled with the prettiest teeth, her already fully matured breasts seemed yet whiter than her complexion; but she was no sense lacking in plumpness: her form was round and well furnished, all her flesh was firm, sweet, and succulent. Dubois asserted it were impossible to behold a more beautiful ass: little expert in these matters, you will permit me to abstain from judging here. A fine mossy growth shadowed her fore end; majestic blond hair floated about all those charms, rendering them still more piquant; and to complete the masterpiece, Nature, who seemed to have created it for pleasure, had endowed her with the sweetest and most lovable temperament. Tender and delicate flower, thus were you to grace the world for but an instant in order more swiftly to be withered!

"Oh, Madame!" she said upon recognizing Dubois, "is it in this way you have deceived me! . . . Just Heaven! where have you brought me?"

"You shall see, my child," put in the master of the house, abruptly seizing Eulalie, drawing her to him and forthwith beginning his kisses while, upon his orders, I excited him with one hand.

Eulalie sought to protect herself, but, thrusting the girl toward the libertine, Dubois eliminated all possibility of her escape. The sitting was long; for very fresh, new-blown was that flower, and the hornet's desire to drain its pollen was commensurately great. His iterated suckings were succeeded by an inspection of Eulalie's neck; betimes, I palpated his member and felt it throb with growing insistence.

"Well," said Monseigneur, "here are two victims who shall fill my cup of joy to overflowing: Dubois, you shall be well paid, for I am well served. Let's move into my boudoir; follow us, dear woman, come," he continued as he led us away; "you'll leave tonight, but I need you for the party."

Dubois resigns herself, and we pass into the debauchee's pleasure chamber, where we are stripped naked.

Oh, Madame, I shall not attempt to represent the infamies of which I was at once victim and witness. This monster's pleasures were those of the executioner; his unique joy consisted in decapitating. My luckless companion . . . oh, no! Madame . . . no! do not require me to finish . . . I was about to share her fate; spurred on by Dubois, the villain had decided to render my torture yet more horrible when both experienced a need to revive their strength; whereupon they sat down to eat. . . . What a debauch! But ought I complain? for did it not save my life? Besotted with wine, exhausted by overeating, both fell dead drunk and slumbered amidst the litter that remained from their feast. No sooner do I see them collapse than I leap to the skirt and mantle Dubois had just removed in order to appear more immodest in her patron's view; I snatch up a candle and spring toward the stairway: this house, divested, or nearly so, of servants, contains nothing to frustrate my escape, I do encounter someone, I put on a terrified air and cry to him to make all haste to relieve his master who is dying, and I reach the door without meeting further obstacles. I have no acquaintance with the roads, I'd not been allowed to see the one whereby we had come, I take the first I see . . . 'tis the one leading to Grenoble; there is nothing denied us when fortune deigns momentarily to smile upon us; at the inn everyone was still abed, I enter secretly and fly to Valbois' room, knock, Valbois wakes and scarcely recognizes me in my disordered state; he demands to know what has befallen me, I relate the horrors whereof I was simultaneously an observer and object.

"You can have Dubois arrested," I tell him, "she's not far from here, I might even be able to point out the way. . . . Quite apart from all her other crimes, the wretch has taken both my clothing and the five *louis* you gave me."

"O Thérèse," says Valbois, "there's no denying it, you are without doubt the unluckiest girl on earth, but, nevertheless, my honest creature, do you not perceive, amidst all these afflictions which beset you, a celestial arm that saves you? may that be unto you as one additional motive for perpetual virtuousness, for never do good deeds go unrewarded. We will not chase after Dubois, my reasons for letting her go in peace are the same you expounded yesterday, let us simply repair the harm she has done you: here, first of all, is the money she stole from you. In an hour's time I'll have a seamstress bring two complete outfits for you, and some linen.

"But you have got to leave, Thérèse, you must leave this very day, Bertrand expects you, I've persuaded her to delay her departure a few hours more, join her. . . ."

"O virtuous young man," I cried, falling into my benefactor's arms, "may Heaven someday repay you for the kindness you have done me."

"Ah, Thérèse," said Valbois, embracing me, "the happiness you wish me . . . I've enjoyed it already, 'tis presently mine, since your own is my doing . . . fare thee well."

And thus it was I left Grenoble, Madame, and though I had not found in that city all the felicity I had imagined was awaiting me there, at least I had never met in another so many kindly and goodhearted people assembled to sympathize with or assuage my woes.

My conductress and I were in a small covered carriage drawn by one horse we drove from within; we had with us, beside Madame Bertrand's baggage, her baby girl of fifteen months whom she was still suckling and for whom I straightway, to my vast misfortune, formed an attachment quite as deep as was that of the mother who had brought the infant into the world.

She was, this Bertrand, an unattractive person, suspicious, gossipy, noisy, monotonous, and dull-witted. Every night we regularly emptied the carriage and transported everything into our inn and then went to sleep in the same room. Until Lyon, everything went along very smoothly, but during the three days this woman needed for her business dealings, I fell upon someone I was far from expecting to encounter in that city.

Together with girls from the hotel whom I had got to accompany me, I would take walks on the Rhône quay; one day I all of a sudden espied the Reverend Father Antonin formerly of Saint

Mary-in-the-Wood, now superior in charge of his order's establishment located in that city. That monk accosted me and after rebuking me in a very low and still sharper tone for my flight, and having given me to understand I would be running great risks of recapture were he to relay information to the Burgundian monastery, he added, softening his manner, that he would not breathe a word if I should be willing that very instant to come to visit him in his new quarters and to bring with me the girl I was with, who struck him as worth having; then repeating his proposal aloud, and to this other creature: "We shall reward you handsomely, both of you," quoth the monster; "there are ten of us in our house, and I promise you a minimum of one *louis* from each if your complacency is unlimited." I flush crimson upon hearing these words; I spend a moment trying to convince the monk he has made a mistake; failing at that, I attempt to use signs to induce him to be silent, but nothing prevails with this insolent fellow, and his solicitations become only the more heated; at last having received repeated refusals, he demands to know our address; in order to get rid of him, I immediately give a fictitious one, he writes it down, and leaves us with the assurance we will soon meet again.

Upon returning to our inn I explained as best I could the history of this unfortunate acquaintance; but whether my companion was not at all satisfied by what I told her, or whether she may perhaps have been exceedingly annoyed by my virtuous performance which deprived her of an adventure wherefrom she might have earned much, she waggled her tongue, the effects of which were only too plainly revealed by Bertrand's remarks upon the occasion of the deplorable catastrophe I am going to relate to you in a moment; however, the monk never did reappear, and we left Lyon.

Having quit the city late, we could get no further than Villefranche that day, and there we stopped for the night; 'twas in that town, Madame, there took place the horrible event which today causes me to appear before you in a criminal guise, although I was no more a malefactor in that one of my life's fateful circumstances than in any other of those where you have observed me so unjustly assaulted by the blows of fate; and as in many another instance, so this time I was flung into the abyss by nothing other than the good-ness of my heart and the wickedness of men.

Having made Villefranche toward six o'clock in the evening, we supped in haste and retired directly, that we might be able to undertake a longer stage on the morrow; we had not been two hours in bed when a dreadful smell of smoke roused us from sleep; con-vinced the flames are near at hand, we get instantly from bed. Just Heaven! the havoc wrought by the fire was already but too fright-ful; half-naked, we open our door and all around us hear nothing but the fracas of collapsing walls, the noise of burning timbers and woodwork and the shrieks of those who had fallen into the blaze; surrounded by devouring flames we have no idea in which direction to run; to escape their violence, we rush past them and soon find ourselves lost in a milling crush of wretches who, like ourselves, are seeking salvation in flight; at this point I remember that my con-ductress, more concerned for her own than for her child's safety, has not thought of preserving it from death; without a word to the woman, I fly to our chamber, having to pass through the conflagra-tion and to sustain burns in several places: I snatch up the poor little creature, spring forward to restore her to her mother: I advance along a half-consumed beam, miss my footing, instinctively thrust out my hands, this natural reflex forces me to release the precious burden in my arms . . . it slips from my grasp and the unlucky child falls into the inferno before its own mother's eyes; at this instant I am myself seized . . . carried away; too upset to be able to dis-tinguish anything, I am unaware whether 'tis aid or peril which surrounds me but, to my grief, I am but too fully enlightened when flung into a post chaise, I discover myself beside Dubois who, clap-ping a pistol to my head, threatens to blow out my brains if I utter a syllable . . .

"Ah, little villain," says she, "I've got you now and this time for good."

"Oh, Madame! you?" I exclaim. "Here?"

"Everything that has just transpired is my doing," the monster replies, " 'twas by arson I saved your life; and by a fire you're going to lose it: in order to catch you I'd have followed you to Hell had it been necessary. Monseigneur was furious, believe me, when he found out you had escaped; I get two hundred louis for every girl

I procure him, and not only did he not want to pay me for Eulalie, but he menaced me with all his anger could produce were I to fail to bring you back. I discovered I'd missed you by two hours at Lyon; yesterday I reached Villefranche an hour after your arrival, I had the hotel burned by the henchmen I always have in my employ, I wanted to incinerate you or get you back; I've got you, I'm returning you to a house your flight has plunged into trouble and unquiet, and I'm taking you there, Thérèse, to be treated in a cruel manner. Monseigneur swore he'd not have tortures terrible enough for you, and we'll not step from this carriage until we are at his seat. Well, Thérèse, what is your present opinion of Virtue?"

"Oh, Madame! that it is very frequently crime's prey; that it is happy when triumphant; but that it ought to be the unique object of the Heavenly God's rewards even though human atrocities bring about its downfall upon earth."

"You've not long to wait before you know, Thérèse, whether there is really a God who punishes or recompenses the deeds of mortals. . . . Ah! if, in the eternal inexistence you are shortly going to enter, if 'twere possible to cogitate in that state of annihilation, how much you would regret the fruitless sacrifices your inflexible stubbornness has forced you to make to phantoms who have never doled out any but the wages of sorrow. . . . Thérèse, there is yet time left to you: if you wish to be my accomplice I'll save you, for, I avow, 'tis more than I can bear to see you break down ever and ever again upon Virtue's routes all beset by perils. What! are you not yet sufficiently punished for your good behavior and false principles? What kind of misery do you have to know in order to be persuaded to mend your ways? What then are the examples you require in order to be convinced the attitude you have adopted is the worst of all and that, as I have told you a hundred times over, one must expect nothing but calamity when, breasting the crowd's headlong stampede, one wishes to be virtuous and alone in a completely corrupt society. You count upon an avenging God; cease to be a gull, Thérèse, disabuse yourself, the God you fabricate for yourself is but a fiction whose stupid existence is never found elsewhere but in the heads of the crazed; 'tis a phantom invented by human wickedness; the solitary purpose of this illusion is to deceive mankind or to create armed divisions among men. The greatest service it were possible to render humankind would have been instantly to cut the throat of the first impostor who took it into his head to speak of God to men. How much blood that one murder would have spared the universe! Get on, get on with you, Thérèse, perpetually active Nature, Nature acting always, has no need of a master for her government. And if indeed this master did exist, after all the faults and sins with which he has stuffed creation, would he, think you, would he merit anything from us but scorn and outrage? Ah, if he exists, your God, how I do hate him! Thérèse, how I abhor him! Yes, were this existence authentic, I affirm that the mere pleasure of perpetually irritating whatever I found that bore his impress or bespoke his touch would become for me the most precious compensation for the necessity in which I would find myself to acknowledge some belief in him. . . . Once again, Thérèse, do you wish to become my confederate? A superb possibility presents itself, with courage we can execute the thing; I'll save your life if you'll undertake it. This Monseigneur to whose house we are going, and whom you know, lives alone in the country house where he gives his parties; their species, with which you are familiar, requires isolation; a single valet lives with him when he takes up residence there for the sake of his pleasures: the man riding ahead of the coach, you and I, dear girl, that's three of us against two; when that libertine is inflamed by his lecheries, I'll snatch away the saber with which he decapitates his victims, you'll hold him, we'll kill him, and meanwhile my man will have done in the valet. There's money hidden in that house; more than eight hundred thousand francs, Thérèse, I'm sure of it, the thing's well worth the trouble. . . . Choose, clever creature, decide: death or an alliance; if you betray me, if you expose my plan to him, I'll accuse you of having contrived it alone, and don't doubt for a moment that the confidence he has always had in me will tip the balance my way . . . think carefully before you give me your answer: this man is a villain; hence, by assassinating him we merely aid the law whose rigorous treatment he deserves. A day does not go by, Thérèse, without this rascal murdering a girl; is it then to outrage Virtue by punishing Crime? And does the reasonable proposition I make you still alarm your wild principles?"

"Be certain of it, Madame," I answered; "it is not with the

object of chastening crime you propose this deed, it is rather with the sole intention of committing one yourself; consequently there cannot be but great evil in doing what you suggest, and no semblance of legitimacy can appear thereupon; better still, even were you to intend to avenge humanity for this man's horrors, you would still be committing evil by doing so, for this is not a problem which concerns you: there are laws decreed to punish the guilty; let those laws take their course, it is not unto our feeble hands the Supreme Being has entrusted their sword, never might we wield that blade without affronting justice."

"Well, then you'll have to die, worthless creature," retorted the furious Dubois, "you'll die; don't tease yourself with hopes of escaping your fate."

"What matters it to me?" I calmly answered, "I shall be delivered of all the ills that assail me; death holds no terrors for me, 'tis life's last sleep, 'tis the downtrodden's haven of repose. . . ."

And, upon these words, that savage beast sprang at me, I thought she was going to strangle me; she struck several blows upon my breast, but released me, however, immediately I cried out, for she feared lest the postilion hear me.

We were moving along at a brisk pace; the man who was riding ahead arranged for new horses and we stopped only long enough to change teams. As the new pair was being harnessed, Dubois suddenly raised her weapon and clapped it to my heart . . . what was she about to do? . . . Indeed, my exhaustion and my situation had beaten me down to the point of preferring death to the ordeal of keeping it at bay.

We were then preparing to enter Dauphiné, of a sudden six horsemen, galloping at top speed behind our coach, overtook it and, with drawn cutlasses, forced our driver to halt. Thirty feet off the highway was a cottage to which these cavaliers, whom we soon identified as constables, ordered the driver to lead the carriage; when we were alongside it, we were told to get out, and all three of us entered the peasant's dwelling. With an effrontery unthinkable in a woman soiled with unnumbered crimes, Dubois, who found herself arrested, archly demanded of these officers whether she were known to them, and with what right they comported themselves thus with a woman of her rank.

"We have not the honor of your acquaintance, Madame," replied the officer in charge of the squadron; "but we are certain you have in your carriage the wretch who yesterday set fire to the principal hotel in Villefranche"; then, eyeing me closely: "she answers the description, Madame, we are not in error; have the kindness to surrender her to us and to inform us how a person as respectable as you appear to be could have such a woman in your keeping."

"Why, 'tis very readily accounted for," replied Dubois with yet greater insolence, "and, I declare, I'll neither hide her from you nor take her side in the matter if 'tis certain she is guilty of the horrible crime you speak of. I too was staying at that hotel in Villefranche, I left in the midst of all the commotion and as I am getting into my coach, this girl runs up, begs my compassion, says she has just lost everything in the fire, and implores me to take her with me to Lyon where she hopes to be able to find a place. Far less attentive to my reason than to my heart's promptings, I acquiesced, consented to fetch her along; once in the carriage she offered herself as my servant; once again imprudence led me to agree to everything and I have been taking her to Dauphiné where I have my properties and family: 'tis a lesson, assuredly, I presently recognize with utmost clarity all of pity's shortcomings; I shall not again be guilty of them. There she is, gentlemen, there she is; God forbid that I should be interested in such a monster, I abandon her to the law's severest penalties, and, I beseech you, take every step to prevent it from being known that I committed the unfortunate mistake of lending an instant's credence to a single word she uttered."

I wished to defend myself, I wanted to denounce the true villain; my speeches were interpreted as calumniatory recriminations to which Dubois opposed nothing but a contemptuous smile. O fatal effects of misery and biased prepossession, of wealth and of insolence! Were it thinkable that a woman who had herself called Madame la Baronne de Fulconis, who proclaimed a high degree and displayed opulence, who asserted she owned extensive holdings and arrogated a family to herself; were it to be conceived that such a personage could be guilty of a crime wherefrom she did not appear to have the slightest thing to gain? And, on the other hand, did not everything condemn me? I was unprotected, I was poor, 'twas a very sure thing I'd done a fell deed.

The squadron officer read me the catalogue of Bertrand's deposed charges. 'Twas she had accused me; I'd set the inn afire to pillage her with greater ease, and she'd been robbed indeed to her last penny; I'd flung her infant into the flames in order that, blinded by the despair with which this event would overwhelm her, she'd forget all else and give not a thought to my maneuvers; and, further- more, Bertrand had added, I was a girl of suspect virtue and bad habits who had escaped the gallows at Grenoble and whom she had only taken in charge, very foolishly, thanks to the excessive kindness she had shown a young man from her own district, my lover, no doubt. I had publicly and in broad daylight solicited monks in Lyon: in one word, there was nothing the unworthy creature had not ex- ploited in order to seal my doom, nothing that calumny whetted by despair had not invented in order to besmirch me. Upon the woman's insistence, a juridical examination had been conducted on the premises. The fire had begun in a hayloft into which several persons had taken oath I had entered the evening of that fatal day, and that was true. Searching for a water closet to which I had not been very clearly directed by a maid I had consulted, I had entered this loft having failed to locate the sought after place, and there I had remained long enough to make what I was accused of plausible, or at least to furnish probabilities of its truth; and 'tis well known: in this day and age those are proofs. And so, do what I could to defend myself, the officer's single response was to ready his mana- cles.

"But, Monsieur," I expostulated before allowing him to put me in irons, "if I robbed my traveling companion at Villefranche, the money ought to be found upon my person; search me."

This ingenuous defense merely excited laughter; I was assured I'd not been alone, that they were certain I had accomplices to whom, as I fled, I had transferred the stolen funds. Then the malicious Dubois, who knew of the brand which to my misfortune Rodin had burned upon my flesh long ago, in one instant Dubois put all sympathy to rout.

"Monsieur," said she to the officer, "so many mistakes are committed every day in affairs of this sort that you will forgive me for the idea that occurs to me: if this girl is guilty of the atrocity she is accused of it is surely not her first; the character required to execute crimes of this variety is not attained in a night: and so I beg you to examine this girl, Monsieur . . . were you to find, by chance, something upon her wretched body . . . but if nothing denounces her, allow me to defend and protect her."

The officer agreed to the verification . . . it was about to be carried out . . .

"One moment, Monsieur," said I, "stay; this search is to no purpose; Madame knows full well I bear the frightful mark; she also knows very well what misfortune caused it to be put on me: this subterfuge of hers is the crowning horror which will, together with all the rest, be revealed at Themis' own temple. Lead me away, Messieurs: here are my hands, load them with chains; only Crime blushes to carry them, stricken Virtue is made to groan thereby, but is not terrified."

"Truth to tell," quoth Dubois, "I'd never have dreamt my idea would have such success; but as this creature repays my kindness by insidious inculpations, I am willing to return with her if you deem it necessary."

"There's no need whatsoever to do so, Madame la Baronne," rejoined the officer, "this girl is our quarry: her avowals, the mark branded on her body, it all condemns her; we need no one else, and we beg your pardon a thousand times over for having caused you this protracted inconvenience."

I was handcuffed immediately, flung upon the crupper of one of the constables' mounts, and Dubois went off, not before she had completed her insults by giving a few crowns to my guards, which generously bestowed silver was to aid me during my melancholy sojourn while awaiting trial.

O Virtue! I cried when I perceived myself brought to this dreadful humiliation; couldst thou suffer a more penetrating outrage! Were it possible that Crime might dare affront thee and vanquish thee with so much insolence and impunity!

We were soon come to Lyon; upon arrival I was cast into the keep reserved for criminals and there I was inscribed as an arsonist, harlot, child-murderer, and thief.

Seven persons had been burned to death in the hotel; I had

myself thought I might be; I had been on the verge of perishing; but she who had been the cause of this horror was eluding the law's vigilance and Heaven's justice: she was triumphant, she was flying on to new crimes whereas, innocent and unlucky, I had naught for prospect but dishonor, castigation, and death.

For such a long time habituated to calumny, injustice, and wretchedness; destined, since childhood, to acquit myself of not a single virtuous deed or feel a single righteous sentiment without suffering instant retribution therefor, my anguish was rather mute and blunted than rending, and I shed fewer tears than I might have supposed . . . however, as 'tis instinctive in the distressed creature to seek after every possible device to extricate himself from the chasm into which his ill-fortune has plunged him, Father Antonin came to my mind; whatever the mediocre relief I could hope from him, I did not deny to myself I was anxious to see him: I asked for him, he appeared. He had not been informed of by whom he was desired; he affected not to recognize me; whereupon I told the turnkey that it was indeed possible he had forgotten me, having been my confessor only when I was very young, but, I continued, it was as my soul's director I solicited a private interview with him. 'Twas agreed by both parties. As soon as I was alone with this holy man I cast myself at his knees, rained tears upon them and besought him to save me from my cruel situation; I proved my innocence to him; I did not conceal that the culpable proposals he had made me some days before had provoked my young companion's enmity, and presently, said I, she accused me out of spite. The monk listened attentively.

"Thérèse," said he when I was done, "don't lose control of yourself as you customarily do when someone contradicts your damnable prejudices; you notice to what a pass they've brought you, and you can at present readily convince yourself that it's a hundred times better to be a rascal and happy than well-behaved and unprosperous; your case is as bad as it possibly could be, dear girl, there's nothing to be gained by hiding the fact from you: this Dubois you speak of, having the largest benefits to reap from your doom, will unquestionably labor behind the scene to ruin you: Bertrand will accuse you, all appearances stand against you, and, these days, appearances are sufficient grounds for decreeing the death sentence: you are, hence, lost, 'tis plain: one single means might save you: I get on well with the bailiff, he has considerable influence with this city's magistrature; I'm going to tell him you are my niece, and that by this title I am claiming you: he'll dismiss the entire business: I'll ask to send you back to my family; I'll have you taken away, but 'twill be to our monastery and incarceration there, whence you'll never emerge . . . and there, why conceal it? you, Thérèse, will be the bounden slave of my caprices, you'll sate them all without a murmur; as well, you will submit yourself to my colleagues: in a word, you will be as utterly mine as the most subordinated of victims . . . you heed me: the task is hard; you know what are the passions of libertines of our variety; so make up your mind, and make me prompt answer."

"Begone, Father," I replied, horror-struck, "begone, you are a monster to dare so cruelly take advantage of my circumstances in order to force upon me the alternatives of death or infamy; I shall know how to die, if die I must, but 'twill be to die sinless."

"As you like," quoth the cruel man as he prepared to withdraw; "I have never been one to impose happiness upon reluctant people. . . . Virtue has so handsomely served you until the present, Thérèse, you are quite right to worship at its altar . . . good-bye: above all, let it not occur to you to ask for me again."

He was leaving; an unconquerable impulse drew me to his knees yet another time.

"Tiger!" I exclaimed through my tears, "open your granite heart, let my appalling misadventures melt it, and do not, in order to conclude them, do not impose conditions more dreadful to me than death itself. . . ."

The violence of my movements had disturbed what veiled my breast, it was naked, my disheveled hair fell in cascades upon it, it was wetted thoroughly by my tears; I quicken desires in the dishonest man . . . desires he wants to satisfy on the spot; he dares discover to me to what point my state arouses them; he dares dream of pleasures lying in the middle of the chains binding me and beneath the sword which is poised to smite me . . . I was upon my knees . . . he flings me backward, leaps upon me, there we lie upon the wretched straw I use for a bed; I wish to cry out, he stuffs his handkerchief into my mouth; he ties my arms; master of me, the infamous creature examines me everywhere ... everything becomes prey to his gaze, his fingerings, his perfidious caresses; at last, he appeases his desires.

"Listen to me," says he, untying me and readjusting his costume, "you do not want me to be helpful, all very well; I am leaving you; I'll neither aid nor harm you, but if it enters your head to breathe a word of what has just happened, I will, by charging you with yet more enormous crimes, instantly deprive you of all means of defending yourself; reflect carefully before jabbering ... I am taken for your confessor ... now hark: we are permitted to reveal anything and all when 'tis a question of a criminal; fully approve what I am going to say to your warden, or else I'll crush you like a fly."

He knocks, the jailer appears.

"Monsieur," says the traitor, "the nice young lady is in error; she wished to speak to a Father Antonin who is now in Bordeaux; I have no acquaintance of her, never have I even set eyes upon her: she besought me to hear her confession, I did so, I salute you and her and shall always be ready to present myself when my ministry is esteemed important."

Upon uttering these words, Antonin departs and leaves me as much bewildered by his fraudulence as revolted by his libertinage and insolence.

My situation was so dreadful that, whatever it might be, I could ill afford not to employ every means at my disposal; I recollected Monsieur de Saint-Florent: in the light of my behavior toward him, I was incapable of believing this man could underestimate my character; once long ago I had rendered him a most important service, he had dealt most cruelly with me, and therefore I imagined he could not, in my presently critical plight, very well refuse to make reparation for the wrongs he had done me; no, I was sure he would at least have to acknowledge, as best he were able, what I had so generously done in his behalf; passions' heat might have blinded him upon the two occasions I had held commerce with him; there had been some sort of excuse for his former horrors, but in this instance, it seemed to me, no feeling should prevent him from coming to my aid. . . . Would he renew his last proposals? to the assistance I was going to request from him would he attach the condition I must agree to the frightful employments he had outlined to me before? ah, very well! I'd accept and, once free, I should easily discover the means to extricate myself from the abominable kind of existence into which he might have the baseness to lure me. Full of these ideas, I write a letter to him, I describe my miseries, I beg him to visit me; but I had not devoted adequate thought to analyzing this man's soul when I supposed it susceptible of infiltration by beneficence; I either did not sufficiently remember his appalling theories, or my wretched weakness constantly forcing me to use my own heart as the standard by which to judge others, fancied this man was bound to comport himself toward me as I should certainly have done toward him.

He arrives; and, as I have asked to see him alone, he is freely introduced into my cell. From the marks of respect showered profusely upon him it was easy to determine the eminent position he held in Lyon.

"Why, it's you!" said he, casting scornful eyes upon me, "I was deceived by the letter; I thought it written by a woman more honest than you and whom I would have helped with all my heart; but what would you have me do for an imbecile of your breed? What! you're guilty of a hundred crimes one more shocking than the other, and when someone suggests a way for you to earn your livelihood you stubbornly reject the proposal? Never has stupidity been carried to these lengths."

"Oh, Monsieur!" I cried, "I am not in the least guilty."

"Then what the devil must one do in order to be?" the harsh creature sharply rejoined. "The first time in my life I clapped eyes on you, there you were, in the thick of a pack of bandits who wanted to assassinate me; and now it is in the municipal prison I discover you, accused of three or four new crimes and wearing, so they tell me, a mark on your shoulder which proclaims your former misdeeds. If that is what you designate by the word honest, do inform me of what it would require not to be."

"Just Heaven, Monsieur!" I replied, "can you excoriate that period in my life when I knew you, and should it not rather be for me to make you blush at the memory of what passed then? You know very well, Monsieur, the bandits who captured you, and amongst whom you found me, kept me with them by force; they wanted to kill you, I saved your life by facilitating your escape while making mine; and what, cruel man, did you do to thank me for my aid? is it possible you can recall your actions without horror? You yourself wanted to murder me; you dazed me by terrible blows and, profiting from my half-unconscious state, you snatched from me what I prized most highly; through an unexampled refinement of cruelty, you plundered me of the little money I possessed quite as if you had desired to summon humiliation and misery to complete your victim's obliteration! And great was your success, barbaric one! indeed, it has been entire; 'tis you who precipitated me into desolation; 'tis you who made the abyss to yawn, and 'tis thanks to you I fell into it and have not ceased to fall since that accursed moment.

"Nevertheless, Monsieur, I would forget it all, yes, everything is effaced from my memory, I even ask your pardon for daring to upbraid you for what is past, but can you hide from yourself the fact that some recompense, some gratitude is owing to me? Ah, deign not to seal up your heart when the wing of death brushes its shadow over my unhappy days; 'tis not death I fear, but disgrace; save me from the dread horror of a criminal's end: all I demand from you comes to that single mercy, refuse me it not, and both Heaven and my heart will reward you someday."

I was weeping, I was upon my knees before this ferocious man and, far from reading upon his face the effect I thought I should be able to expect from the disturbances I flattered myself I was producing in his soul, I distinguished nothing but a muscular alteration caused by that sort of lust whose germinal origins are in cruelty. Saint-Florent was seated opposite me; his wicked dark eyes considered me in a dreadful manner, and I noticed his hand glide to a certain sector and his fingers begin to perform those certain motions which indicated I was putting him in a state which was by no means that of pity; he concealed himself withal, and, getting to his feet:

"Look here," he said, "your case rests entirely in the hands of Monsieur de Cardoville; I need not tell you what official post he occupies; it suffices that you know your fate depends absolutely upon him; he and I have been intimate friends since childhood; I shall speak to him; if he agrees to a few arrangements, you will be called for at sunset and in order that he may see you, you'll be brought to either his home or mine; such an interrogation, wrapped in secrecy, will make it much simpler to turn matters in your favor, which could not possibly be done here. If he consents to bestow the favor, justify yourself when you have your interview with him, prove your innocence to him in a persuasive manner; that is all I can do for you. Adieu, Thérèse, keep yourself ready for any eventuality and above all do not have me waste my time taking futile measures." Saint-Florent left.

Nothing could have equaled my perplexity; there had been so little harmony between that man's remarks, the character I knew him to have, and his actual conduct, that I dreaded yet further pitfalls; but, Madame, pause a moment and decide whether I was right or wrong; was I in a position to hesitate? for my position was desperate; and was I not obliged to leap at everything which had the semblance of assistance? Hence I decided to accompany the persons who would come to fetch me; should I be compelled to prostitute myself, I would put up what defense I could; was it to death I was to be led? too bad; it would not, at least, be ignominious, and I would be rid of all my sufferings. Nine o'clock strikes, the jailer appears, I tremble.

"Follow me," that Cerberus says; "you are wanted by Messieurs Saint-Florent and de Cardoville; consider well and take advantage, as it befits you, of the favor Heaven offers you; there are many here who might desire such a blessing and who will never obtain it."

Arrayed as best I am able, I follow the warden who puts me into the keeping of two strange tall fellows whose savage aspect doubles my fright; not a word do they utter; the carriage rolls off and we halt before an immense mansion I soon recognize as Saint-Florent's. Silence enshrouds everything; it augments my dread however, my guides grasp my arms, hustle me along, and we climb to the fourth floor; there we discover a number of small decorated apartments; they seem to me very mysterious indeed. As we progress through them every door closes shut behind us, and thus we advance till we reach a remote room in which, I notice, there are no windows; Saint-Florent awaits me, and also the man I am told is Monsieur de Cardoville, in whose hands my case rests; this heavy

set, fleshy personage, provided with a somber and feral countenance, could have been about fifty years of age; although he was in
lounging costume, 'twas readily to be seen he was a gentleman of the
bar. An air of severity seemed to distinguish his entire aspect; it
made a deep impression upon me. O cruel injustice of Providence!
'tis then possible Virtue may be overawed by Crime. The two men
who had led me hither, and whom I was better able to make out by
the gleam of the twenty candles which lit this room, were not above
twenty-five and thirty years old. The first, referred to as La Rose,
was a dark handsome chap with Hercules' own figure; he seemed
to me the elder; the other had more effeminate features, the loveliest chestnut locks and large brown eyes; he was at least five feet
ten inches tall, a very Adonis, had the finest skin to be seen, and was
called Julien. As for Saint-Florent, you are acquainted with him; as
much of coarseness in his traits as in his character, yet, nevertheless,
certain splendid features.

"Everything is secured fast?" Saint-Florent asked Julien.

"We're well shut in, yes, Monsieur," the young man replied;
"your servants are off for the night in accordance with your orders
and the gatekeeper, who alone is on watch, will follow his instructions to admit no one under any circumstances." These few
words enlightened me, I shivered, but what could I have done, confronted as I was by four men?

"Sit down over there, my friends," said Cardoville, kissing the
two men, "we'll call for your co-operation when the need arises."

Whereupon Saint-Florent spoke up: "Thérèse," said he, presenting me to Cardoville, "here is your judge, this is the man upon
whom your fate depends; we have discussed your problem; but it
appears to me that your crimes are of such a nature we will have
much to do to come to terms about them."

"She has exactly forty-two witnesses against her," remarks
Cardoville, who takes a seat upon Julien's knees, who kisses him
upon the lips, and who permits his fingers to stray over the young
man's body in the most immodest fashion; "it's a perfect age since
we condemned anyone to die for crimes more conclusively established."

"I? Conclusively established crimes?"

"Conclusively established or inconclusively established," quoth

Cardoville, getting to his feet and coming up to shout, with much effrontery, at my very nose, "you're going to burn pissing if you do not, with an entire resignation and the blindest obedience, instantly lend yourself to everything we are going to require of you."

"Yet further horrors!" I cried; "ah indeed! 'tis then only by yielding to infamies innocence can escape the snares set for it by the wicked!"

"That's it; 'tis ordained," Saint-Florent broke in; "you know, my dear: the weak yield to the strong's desires, or fall victims to their wickedness: that's all: that's your whole story, Thérèse, therefore obey."

And while he spoke the libertine nimbly pulled up my skirts. I recoiled, fended him off, horrified, but, having reeled backward into Cardoville's arms, the latter grasped my hands and thereupon exposed me, defenseless, to his colleague's assaults. The ribbons holding up my skirts were cut, my bodice torn away, my kerchief, my blouse, all were removed, and in no time I found myself before those monsters' eyes as naked as the day I came into the world.

"Resistance . . ." said one. "Resistance," chimed in the other, both proceeding to despoil me, "the whore fancies she can resist us. . . ." and not a garment was ripped from my body without my receiving a few blows.

When I was in the state they wished, they drew up their chairs, which were provided with protruding armrests; thus a narrow space between the chairs was left and into it I was deposited; and thus they were able to study me at their leisure: while one regarded my fore end, the other mused upon my behind; then they turned me round, and turned me again. In this way I was stared at, handled, kissed for thirty minutes and more; during this examination not one lubricious episode was neglected, and I thought it safe to conjecture, upon the basis of those preliminaries, that each had roughly the same idiosyncrasies.

"Well, now," Saint-Florent said to his friend, "did I not tell you she had a splendid ass!"

"Yes, by God! her behind is sublime," said the jurist who thereupon kissed it; "I've seen damned few buttocks molded like these: why! look ye! solid and fresh at the same time! . . . how d'ye suppose that fits with such a tempestuous career?"

"Why, it's simply that she's never given herself of her own accord; I told you there's nothing as whimsical as this girl's exploits! She's never been had but by rape"—and then he drives his five fingers simultaneously into the peristyle of Love's temple—"but she's been had . . . unfortunately, for it's much too capacious for me: accustomed to virgins, I could never put up with this."

Then, swinging me around, he repeated the same ceremony with my behind wherein he found the same flaws.

"Ah well, you know our secret," said Cardoville.

"And I'll employ it too," replied Saint-Florent; "and you who have no need of the same resource, you, who are content with a factitious activity which, although painful for the woman, nevertheless brings enjoyment of her to perfection, you, I hope, will not have her till I'm done."

"Fair enough," Cardoville answered, "while watching you, I'll busy myself with those preludes so cherished by my lechery; I'll play the girl with Julien and La Rose while you masculinize Thérèse, and, so I think, the one's as good as the other."

"Doubtless a thousand times better; for you've no idea how fed up I am with women! . . . do you suppose I would be capable of enjoying those whores without the help of the auxiliary episodes we both use to add a tart flavor to the business?"

With these words, having afforded me clear evidence their state called for more substantial pleasures, the impudicious creatures rose and made me mount upon a large chair, my forearms leaning upon its back, my knees propped upon its arms, and my behind arched so that it was prominently thrust toward them. I was no sooner placed in this attitude than they stepped out of their breeches, tucked up their shirts, and save for their shoes, they thus discovered themselves completely naked from the waist down; they exhibited themselves to me, passed several times to and fro before my eyes, making boastful display of their behinds of which they were overweeningly proud, for, they declared, they had parts far superior to anything I could offer; indeed, each was womanishly made in this region: 'twas especially Cardoville who was possessed of elegant lines and majestic form, snowy white color and enviable plumpness; they whiled away a minute or two polluting themselves in full view of me, but did not ejaculate: about Cardoville, nothing that was not of the most ordinary; as for Saint-Florent, 'twas monstrous: I shuddered to think that such was the dart which had immolated me. Oh Just Heaven! what need of maidenheads had a man of those dimensions? Could it be anything other than ferocity which governed such caprices? But what, alas! were the other weapons I was going to be confronted by! Julien and La Rose, plainly aroused by these exhibitions, also ridded themselves of their clothes and advanced pike in hand. . . . Oh, Madame! never had anything similar soiled my gaze, and whatever may have been my previous representations, what now I beheld surpassed everything I have been able to describe until the present: 'tis like unto the ascendancy the imperious eagle enjoys over the dove. Our two debauchees soon laid hands upon those menacing spears: they caressed them, polluted them, drew them to their mouths, and the combat straightway became more in earnest. Saint-Florent crouches upon the armchair supporting me; he is so adjusted my widespread buttocks are on an exact level with his mouth; he kisses them, his tongue penetrates into first one then the other temple. Saint-Florent provided Cardoville with amusement, the latter offers himself to the pleasures of La Rose whose terrific member instantly vanishes into the redoubt dressed before him, and Julien, situated beneath Saint-Florent, excites him with his mouth the while grasping his haunches and modulating them before the resolute blows of Cardoville who, treating his friend with intransigent rudeness, does not quit him before having wetted the sanctuary with his incense. Nothing could equal Cardoville's transports when the crisis deprives him of his senses; softly abandoning himself to the man who is serving as husband to him, but pressing hard after him of whom he is making a wife, this dastardly libertine, with hoarse gasps like unto those of a dying man, thereupon pronounces indescribable blasphemies; as for Saint-Florent, measure governs his evolutions, he restrains himself, and the tableau is dissolved without his having performed his *beau geste*.

"Truly," Cardoville says to his comrade, "you still give me as much pleasure as you did when you were fifteen. . . . Indeed," he continues, turning and kissing La Rose, " 'tis true this fine lad knows how to arouse me too. . . . Have you not found me rather gulfy this evening, angelic boy? . . . would you believe it, Saint-Florent 'tis the thirty-sixth time I've had it today . . . only natural that the thing be somewhat dilated; I'm all yours, dear friend," the abominable man pursues, fitting himself into Julien's mouth, his nose glued to my behind, and his own offered to Saint-Florent, "I'm yours for the thirty-seventh." Saint-Florent takes his pleasure with Cardoville, La Rose his with Saint-Florent, and after a quick skirmish the latter burns in his friend the same offering his friend had burned in him. If Saint-Florent's ecstasy was of briefer duration, it was no less intense, less noisy, less criminal than Cardoville's; the one shouted, roared out everything that came to his mouth, the other restricted his transports' scope without their being the less energetic for that; Saint-Florent chose his words with care, but they were simply yet filthier and more impure: distraction and rage, to select precise terms, seemed to characterize the delirium of the one, wickedness and ferocity were the eminent qualities announced in the other's.

"To work, Thérèse, revive us," says Cardoville; "you see the lamps are extinguished, they've got to be lit again."

While Julien enjoyed Cardoville and La Rose Saint-Florent, the two libertines inclined over me and one after the other inserted their languishing instruments into my mouth; while I pumped one, I was obliged to go to the rescue of the other and pollute it with my hands, then I had to anoint the member itself and the adjacent parts with an alcoholic liquid I had been given; but I was not to limit myself to sucking, I had to revolve my tongue about the heads and I was required to nibble them with my teeth while my lips squeezed tightly about them. However, our two patients were being vigorously thumped and jolted; Julien and La Rose shifted in order to increase the sensations produced by entrances and exits. When at length two or three homages had flowed into those impure temples I began to perceive a degree of firmness; although the elder of the two, Cardoville's was the first to manifest solidity; he swung his hand and with all the strength at his command slapped one of my titties: that was my reward. Saint-Florent was not far behind him; he repaid my efforts by nearly tearing one of my ears from my head. They backed away, reviewed the situation, and then warned me to prepare to receive the treatment I richly deserved. An analysis of these libertines' appalling language allowed to me to conclude that vexations were about to descend like a hailstorm upon me. To have besought mercy in the state to which they had just reduced me would have been to have further aroused them: and so they placed me, completely naked as I was, in the center of the circle they formed by all four drawing up chairs. I was obliged to parade from one to the next and to receive the penance each in his turn chose to order me to do; I had no more compassion from the youths than from the older men, but 'twas above all Cardoville who distinguished himself by refined teasings which Saint-Florent, cruel as he was, was unable to duplicate without an effort.

A brief respite succeeded these vicious orgies, I was given a few instants to catch my breath; I had been beaten black and blue, but what surprised me was that they doctored and healed the damage done me in less time than it had taken to inflict it, whereof not the slightest trace remained. The lubricities were resumed.

There were moments when all those bodies seemed to form but one and when Saint-Florent, lover and mistress, received copious quantities of what the impotent Cardoville doled out with sparing economy: the next instant, no longer active but lending himself in every manner, both his mouth and hindquarters served as altars to frightful homages. Cardoville cannot resist such a profusion of libertine scenes. Seeing his friend brilliantly elevated, he comes up to offer himself to Saint-Florent's lust, and the tradesman enjoys him; I sharpen the spears, I steer them in the direction they are to thrust, and my exposed buttocks provide a perspective to the lubricity of some, a target for the bestiality of others. As all this wears on our two libertines become more circumspect, for considerable efforts are the price of reanimation; they emerge unscathed from their joustings and their new state is such to terrify me even more.

"Very well, La Rose," says Saint-Florent, "take the bitch; we'll tighten her up: it's time for the stricturing."

I am not familiar with the expression: a cruel experiment soon reveals its meaning. La Rose seizes me, he places my flanks upon a small circular repentance stool not a foot in diameter: once there, lacking any other support, my legs fall on one side, my head and arms on the other; my four limbs, stretched as far apart as possible, are tied to the floor; the executioner who is going to perform the stricturing catches up a long needle through whose eye he passes

stout waxed thread, and with complete unconcern for either the
blood he is to shed or the sufferings he is going to cause me, the
monster, directly before the two colleagues whom the spectacle
amuses, sews shut the entrance to the temple of Love; when finished, he turns me over, now my belly rests upon the repentance
stool; my limbs hang free, they are attached as before, and the indecent shrine of Sodom is barricaded in the same manner: I do
not speak of my agonies, Madame, you must yourself fancy what
they were, I was on the verge of losing consciousness.

"Splendid, that's how I must have them," quoth Saint-Florent
when I had been turned over again and was lying on my buttocks,
and when, in this posture, he spied well within striking range the
fortress he wanted to invade. "Accustomed to reaping nothing but
the first fruits, how, without this ceremony, should I be able to
harvest any pleasures from this creature?"

Saint-Florent had the most violent erection, they were currying
and drubbing his device to keep it rampant; grasping that pike, he
advances: in order to excite him further, Julien enjoys Cardoville
before his eyes; Saint-Florent opens the attack, maddened by the
resistance he encounters, he presses ahead with incredible vigor,
the threads are strained, some snap. Hell's tortures are as naught
to mine; the keener my agonies, the more piquant seem to be my
tormenter's delights. At length, everything capitulates before his
efforts, I am ripped asunder, the glittering dart sinks to the ultimate depths, but Saint-Florent, anxious to husband his strength,
merely touches bottom and withdraws; I am turned over; the same
obstacles: the savage one scouts them as he stands heating his engine and with his ferocious hands he molests the environs in order
to put the place in fit condition for assault. He presents himself,
the natural smallness of the locale renders his campaign more
arduous to wage, my redoubtable vanquisher soon storms the gates,
tears the entry; I am bleeding; but what does it matter to the
conquering hero? Two vigorous heaves carry him into the sanctuary
and there the villain consummates a dreadful sacrifice whose rack-
ing pains I should not have been able to endure another second.

"My turn," cries up Cardoville, causing me to be untied, "I'll
have no tailoring done, but I'm going to place the dear girl upon
a camping bed which should restore her circulation, and bring out

all the warmth and mobility her temperament or her virtue re
fuse us."

Upon the spot La Rose opens a closet and draws out a cross
made of gnarled, thorny, spiny wood. 'Tis thereon the infamous
debauchee wishes to place me, but by means of what episode will he
improve his cruel enjoyment? Before attaching me, Cardoville in
serts into my behind a silver-colored ball the size of an egg; he
lubricates it and drives it home: it disappears. Immediately it is in
my body I feel it enlarge and begin to burn; without heeding my
complaints, I am lashed securely to this thorn-studded frame
Cardoville penetrates as he fastens himself to me: he presses my
back, my flanks, my buttocks on the protuberances upon which they
are suspended. Julien fits himself into Cardoville; obliged to bear
the weight of these two bodies, and having nothing to support my
self upon but these accursed knots and knurs which gouge into my
flesh, you may easily conceive what I suffered; the more I thrust
up against those who press down upon me, the more I am driven
upon the irregularities which stab and lacerate me. Meanwhile the
terrible globe has worked its way deep into my bowels and is cramp
ing them, burning them, tearing them; I scream again and again
no words exist which can describe what I am undergoing; all the
same and all the while, my murderer frolics joyfully, his mouth
glued to mine, he seems to inhale my pain in order that it may
magnify his pleasures: his intoxication is not to be rendered; but
as in his friend's instance, he feels his forces about to desert him
and like Saint-Florent wants to taste everything before they a
gone entirely. I am turned over again, am made to eject the arden
sphere, and it is set to producing in the vagina itself, the same co
flagration it ignited in the place whence it has just been flushed
the ball enters, sears, scorches the matrix to its depths; I am no
spared, they fasten me belly-down upon the perfidious cross, and far
more delicate parts of me are exposed to molestation by the thorn
excrescences awaiting them. Cardoville penetrates into the for
bidden passage; he perforates it while another enjoys him in sim
ilar wise: and at last delirium holds my persecutor in its grasp, his
appalling shrieks announce the crime's completion; I am inundated
then untied.

"Off you go, dear friends," Cardoville says to the pair

young men, "get your hands on this whore and amuse yourselves in whatever way your whims advise: she's yours, we're done with her." The two youthful libertines seize me. While one entertains himself with the front, the other buries himself in the rear; they change places and change again; I am more gravely torn by their prodigious thickness than I have been by Saint-Florent's artificial barricadings; both he and Cardoville toy with the young men while they occupy themselves with me. Saint-Florent sodomizes La Rose who deals in like manner with me, and Cardoville does as much to Julien who employs a more decent place to excite himself in me. I am the focal point of these execrable orgies, their absolute center and mainspring; La Rose and Julien have each four times done reverence at my altars, whilst Cardoville and Saint-Florent, less vigorous or more enervated, are content with one sacrifice offered to each of my lovers. And then the last measure of seed is sown by La Rose—'twas high time, for I was ready to swoon.

"My comrade has certainly hurt you, Thérèse," says Julien, "and I am going to repair all the damage." He picks up a flask of spirits and several times rubs all my wounds. The traces of my executioners' atrocities vanish, but nothing assuages my pain, and never had I experienced any as sharp.

"What with our skill at making the evidence of our cruelties disappear, the ladies who would like to lodge complaints against us must have the devil's own time getting themselves believed, eh, Thérèse?" says Cardoville. "What proofs do you fancy could be presented to support an accusation?"

"Oh," Saint-Florent interrupts, "the charming Thérèse is in no condition to level charges; on the eve of being immolated herself, we ought to expect nothing but prayers from her."

"Well, she'd be ill-advised to undertake the one or the other," Cardoville replies; "she might inculpate us; but would she be heard? I doubt it; our consequence and eminent stations in this city would scarcely allow anyone to notice suits which, anyhow, always come before us and whereof we are at all times the masters. Her final torture would simply be made crueler and more prolonged. Thérèse must surely sense we have amused ourselves with her person for the natural, common, and uncomplex reason which engages might to abuse feebleness; she must surely sense she cannot escape her sentence, that it must be undergone, that she will undergo it, that it would be in vain she might divulge this evening's absence from jail; she'd not be believed; the jailer—for he's ours—would deny it at once. And so may this lovely and gentle girl, so penetrated with the grandeur of Providence, peacefully offer up to Heaven all she has just suffered and all that yet awaits her; these will be as so many expiations for the frightful crimes which deliver her into the hands of the law; put on your clothes, Thérèse, day is not yet come, the two men who brought you hither are going to conduct you back to your prison."

I wanted to say a word, I wanted to cast myself a suppliant at these ogres' feet, either to unbend their hearts, or ask that their hands smite away my life. But I am dragged off, pitched into a cab, and my two guides climb in after me; we had hardly started off when infamous desires inflamed them again.

"Hold her for me," quoth Julien to La Rose, "I simply must sodomize her; I have never laid eyes on a behind which could squeeze me so voluptuously; I'll render you the same service."

There is nothing I can do to defend myself, the project is executed, Julien triumphs, and it is not without atrocious agonies I sustain this newest attack: the assailant's exorbitant bulk, the lacerated condition of those parts, the fire with which that accursed ball had devoured my intestines, everything combined to make me suffer tortures which La Rose renewed immediately his companion was finished. Before arriving I was thus yet another time victim of those wretched valets' criminal libertinage; we reached our destination at last. The jailer greeted us, he was alone, it was still night, no one saw me enter.

"Go to sleep, Thérèse," said he, restoring me to my cell, "and if ever you wish to tell, it makes no difference whom, that on this night you left prison, remember that I will contradict you, and that this useless accusation will get you nowhere. . . ."

And, said I to myself when I was left alone, I should regret departing this world! I should dread to leave a universe freighted with such monsters! Ah! were the hand of God to snatch me from their clutches at whatever instant and in whatever manner He sees fit! why! I'd complain no more; the unique consolation which may remain to the luckless one bred up in this den of savage beasts, his one comfort is the hope of leaving it soon.

The next day I heard nothing and resolved to abandon myself to Providence, I languished and would touch no food. The day after that, Cardoville came to question me; I could not repress a shudder upon beholding the nonchalance wherewith that scoundrel walked in to execute his judiciary duties—he, Cardoville, the most villainous of mortals, he who, contrary to every article of the justice in which he was cloaked, had just so cruelly abused my innocence and exploited my misery; it was in vain I pled my cause, the dishonest man's artfulness devised more crimes than I could invent defenses; when all the charges had been well established in the view of this iniquitous judge, and when the case was made, he had the impudence to ask me whether I knew in Lyon one Monsieur de Saint-Florent, a wealthy and estimable citizen; I answered that I knew him, yes.

"Excellent," said Cardoville, "no more is needed. This Monsieur de Saint-Florent, whom you declare you know, also has a perfect knowledge of you; he has deposed that he saw you in a band of thieves, that you were the first to steal his money and his pocketbook. He further deposes that your comrades wished to spare his life, that you recommended they take it from him; nevertheless, he managed to escape. Saint-Florent adds that, several years later, having recognized you in Lyon, he yielded to your importunings and permitted you to come to pay him a call at his home upon condition you would give him your word to behave well in future and that, while he was delivering a lecture on manners to you, while he was seeking to persuade you to persist along the paths of righteousness, you carried insolence and crime to the point of choosing these moments of kindness to steal a watch and one hundred *louis* he had left lying upon the mantel. . . ."

And, profiting from the resentment and anger such atrocious calumnies provoked in me, Cardoville ordered the court clerk to write that my silence and my facial expressions were ample acknowledgment of my guilt and were tantamount to a confession.

I threw myself upon the ground, I made the walls resound with my cries, I struck my head against the stone floor, hoping to obtain a speedier death, unable to find vehicles to give expression to my rage: "Villain!" I screamed, "I put my faith in the God of Justice who will revenge me for your crimes; He shall cry out innocence, He shall make you repent your disgraceful abuse of the authority vested in you!" Cardoville rings and tells the jailer to take me away, I appear, says he, to be unsettled by despair and remorse and, at any rate, in no state to follow the interrogation; "But, on the other hand, what remains to be asked or said? The dossier is complete; she has confessed to all her crimes." And the villain leaves peacefully! And divine lightning strikes him not!

The case was tried in short order; motivated and directed by hatred, vengeance, and lust, the court promptly condemned me and I was dispatched to Paris for the confirmation of my sentence. While on this fatal journey, which, though guiltless, I made in the character of the last of criminals, the most bitter and the most dolorous thoughts gathered in my head and completed the desolation of my heart. Under what doom-spelling star must I have been born, I wondered, in order that I be utterly incapable of conceiving a single generous sentiment without immediately being drowned in a sea of misfortunes! And why is it that this enlightened Providence whose justice I am pleased to worship, the while punishing me for my virtues, simultaneously shows me those who crush me with their crimes carried to the pinnacle of happiness!

During my childhood I meet a usurer; he seeks to induce me to commit a theft, I refuse, he becomes rich. I fall amongst a band of thieves, I escape from them with a man whose life I save; by way of thanks, he rapes me. I reach the property of an aristocratic debauchee who has me set upon and devoured by his dogs for not having wanted to poison his aunt. From there I go to the home of a murderous and incestuous surgeon whom I strive to spare from doing a horrible deed: the butcher brands me for a criminal; he doubtless consummates his atrocities, makes his fortune, whilst I am obliged to beg for my bread. I wish to have the sacraments made available to me, I wish fervently to implore the Supreme Being whence howbeit I receive so many ills, and the august tribunal, at which I hope to find purification in our most holy mysteries, becomes the bloody theater of my ignominy: the monster who abuses and plunders me is elevated to his order's highest honors and I fall back into the appalling abyss of misery. I attempt to preserve a woman from her husband's fury, the cruel one wishes to put me to death by draining away my blood drop by drop. I wish to relieve a poor woman, she robs me. I give aid to a man whom adversaries have struck down and left unconscious, the thankless creature makes me turn a wheel like an animal; he hangs me for his pleasure's sake; all fortune's blessings accrue to him, and I come within an ace of dying on the gallows for having been compelled to work for him. An unworthy woman seeks to seduce me for a new crime, a second time I lose the little I own in order to rescue her victim's treasure. A gentleman, a kind spirit wishes to compensate me for all my sufferings by the offer of his hand, he dies in my arms before being able to do anything for me. I risk my life in a fire in order to snatch a child, who does not belong to me, from the flames; the infant's mother accuses and launches legal proceedings against me. I fall into my most mortal enemy's hands; she wishes to carry me off by force and take me to a man whose passion is to cut off heads: if I avoid that villain's sword it is so that I can trip and fall under Themis'. I implore the protection of a man whose life and fortune I once saved; I dare expect gratitude from him, he lures me to his house, he submits me to horrors, and there I find the iniquitous judge upon whom my case depends; both abuse me, both outrage me, both accelerate my doom; fortune overwhelms them with favors, I hasten on to death.

That is what I have received from mankind, that is what I have learned of the danger of trafficking with men; is it any wonder that my soul, stung, whipsawed by unhappiness, revolted by outrage and injustice, aspires to nothing more than bursting from its mortal confines?

A thousand pardons, Madame, said this unlucky girl, terminating her adventures at this point; a thousand times over I ask to be forgiven for having sullied your spirit with such a host of obscenities, for having, in a word, so long abused your patience. I have, perhaps, offended Heaven with impure recitals, I have laid open my old wounds, I have disturbed your ease and rest; farewell, Madame, Godspeed; the Star rises above the horizon, I hear my guards summon me to come, let me run on to meet my destiny, I fear it no more, 'twill abridge my torment: this last mortal instant dreaded only by the favored being whose days have passed unclouded; but the wretched creature who has breathed naught but the venomous effluvia of reptiles, whose tottering feet have trod only upon nettles, who has never beheld the torch of dawn save with feelings like unto those of the lost traveler who, trembling, perceives the thunderbolt's forked track; she from whom cruel accident has snatched away parents, all kin, friends, fortune, protection, aid; she who in all this world has nothing more than tears to quench her thirst and for sustenance her tribulations; she, I say, undismayed sees death advance, she even yearns for it as for a safe haven, a port wherein tranquillity will be born again unto her when she is clasped to the breast of a God too just to permit that innocence, defiled and ground under the heel on earth, may not find recompense for so many evils in another world.

The honest Monsieur de Corville had not heard this tale without profound emotion; as for Madame de Lorsange in whom, as we have said, the monstrous errors of her youth had not by any means extinguished sensibility, as for Madame de Lorsange, she was ready to swoon.

"Mademoiselle," said she to Justine, "it is difficult to listen to you without taking the keenest interest in you; but, and I must avow it! an inexplicable sentiment, one far more tender than this I describe, draws me invincibly toward you and does make of your ills my very own. You have disguised your name, you have concealed your birth, I beg you to disclose your secret to me; think not that it is a vain curiosity which bids me speak thus to you ... Great God! may what I suspect be true? ... O Thérèse! were you Justine? ... were it that you would be my sister!"

"Justine! Madame! 'tis a strange name."

"She would have been your age—"

"Juliette! is it you I hear?" cried the unhappy prisoner, casting herself into Madame de Lorsange's arms; ". . . you . . . my sister . . . ah, I shall die far less miserable, for I have been able to embrace you again! . . ."

And the two sisters, clasped in each other's arms, were prevented by their sobs from hearing one another, and found expression in naught but tears.

Monsieur de Corville was unable to hold back his own; awar

of the overpowering significance of this affair and sensing his involvement in it, he moves into an adjoining room, sits down and
writes a letter to the Lord Chancellor, with fiery strokes, in ardent
ciphers he paints in all its horror the fate of poor Justine, whom
we shall continue to call Thérèse; he takes upon himself responsibility for her innocence, he will guarantee it under oath; he asks
that, until the time her case has been finally clarified, the allegedly
guilty party be confined to no other prison but his château, and
Corville gives his word he will produce her in court the instant the
Chief Justice signals his desire to have her appear there; he makes
himself known unto Thérèse's two guards, entrusts his correspondence to them, makes himself answerable for their prisoner; he
is obeyed, Thérèse is confided to him; a carriage is called for.

"Come, my too unfortunate creature," Monsieur de Corville
says to Madame de Lorsange's interesting sister, "come hither; all
is going to be changed; it shall not be said your virtues ever remained unrewarded and that the beautiful soul you had from Nature ever encountered but steel; follow us, 'tis upon me you depend
henceforth. . . ."

And Monsieur de Corville gave a brief account of what he
had just done.

"Dearly beloved and respectable man," said Madame de Lorsange, casting herself down before her lover, "this is the most
splendid gesture you have performed in your life, it is such as comes
from one who has true acquaintance with the human heart and the
spirit of the law which is the avenger of oppressed innocence. There
she stands, Monsieur, behold, there is your captive; go, Thérèse,
go, run, fly at once and kneel down before this equitable protector
who will not, as have all others, abandon you. O, Monsieur, if those
attachments of love which have bound me to you have been cherished, how much more so are they to become now that they are
strengthened by the most tender esteem. . . ."

And one after the other the two women embraced the knees
of a so generous friend, and upon him they did shed their tears.

A few hours later they arrived at the château; once there,
Monsieur de Corville and Madame de Lorsange both strove with
might and main to raise Thérèse from the ultimate deeps of un-

happiness to the pure sunshine of contentment and well-being. They took greatest joy in giving her to eat of the most succulent foods, they laid her to sleep in the finest of beds, they did urge her to command and they made her will to be done, and into their hospitable proceedings they introduced all the gentility and understanding it were possible to expect from two sensitive souls. She was given medicines for several days, she was bathed, dressed, arrayed in elegant attire, embellished, the two lovers worshiped her, each labored at nothing but to make her forget her sorrows as quickly as might be. An excellent surgeon was fetched; he undertook to make the ignominious mark disappear, and soon the cruel result of Rodin's villainy was effectively gone; and everything responded to the cares her benefactors lavished upon Thérèse: the shadowed memories of misery were already effaced from that amiable girl's brow; already the Graces had re-established their empire thereupon. For the livid tints on her cheeks of alabaster were substituted the rosy hue appropriate to her years; what had been withered by such a multitude of griefs was called back to fresh new life. Laughter, for so many years banished from her lips, reappeared again under the wings of Pleasure. The very best news came from the Court; Monsieur de Corville had put all of France in action, he had reanimated the zeal of Monsieur S* * *, who collaborated with him to publicize Thérèse's ill-treatment and to restore her to a tranquillity to which she was so heavily entitled. At length letters came from the King, they nullified all the legal proceedings unjustly initiated against her, they gave her back the name of an honest citizen, imposed silence upon all the realm's tribunals before which efforts had been made to defame her, and accorded her a thousand crowns a year, interest realized upon the gold seized in the counterfeiters' Dauphiné workshop. They wished to make Cardoville and Saint-Florent answer for their misdeeds but, in accordance with the fatality of the star intending upon all of Thérèse's persecutors, one of them, Cardoville, had just, before his crimes were made known, been named to the administration of the Province of * * *, and the other to general supervision of Colonial Trade; each had already reached his destination, the edicts affected no one but the powerful families who soon found means to quiet the storm and, pacifically installed in Fortune's sanctuary, those monsters' depredations were quickly forgotten.[8]

With what regards Thérèse, as soon as she learned of so many agreeable developments she came well-nigh to expiring from joy; for several days on end the sweetest tears flowed from her eyes and she rejoiced upon her guardians' breasts, and then, all of a sudden, her humor altered, and 'twas impossible to ferret out the cause. She became somber, uneasy, troubled, was given to dreaming, sometimes she burst into weeping before her friends, and was not herself able to explain what was the subject of her woe. "I was not born for such felicity," said she to Madame de Lorsange, ". . . oh, dear sister, 'tis impossible it last much longer." She was assured all her troubles were over, none remained, said they, no more inquietude for her; 'twas all in vain, nothing would quiet her; one might have said that this melancholy creature, uniquely destined for sorrow, and feeling the hand of misery forever raised above her head, already foresaw the final blow whereby she was going to be smitten down.

Monsieur de Corville was still residing on his country estate; 'twas toward summer's end, they had planned an outing when the approach of a dreadful storm obliged them to postpone their promenade; the excessive heat had constrained them to leave all the windows open. Lightning glitters, shakes, hail slashes down, winds blow wrathfully, heaven's fire convulses the clouds, in the most hideous manner makes them to seethe; it seems as if Nature were wearied out of patience with what she has wrought, as if she were ready to confound all the elements that she might wrench new forms from them. Terrified, Madame de Lorsange begs her sister to make all haste and close the shutters; anxious to calm her, Thérèse dashes to the windows which are already being broken; she would do battle with the wind, she gives a minute's fight, is driven back and at that instant a blazing thunderbolt reaches her where she stands in the middle of the room . . . transfixes her.

Madame de Lorsange emits a terrible cry and falls in a faint; Monsieur de Corville calls for help, attentions are given each woman, Madame de Lorsange is revived, but the unhappy Thérèse

---

[8] As for the monks of Saint Mary-in-the-Wood, suppression of the religious orders will expose the atrocious crimes of that horrible crew.

has been struck in such wise hope itself can no longer subsist for her; the lightning entered her right breast, found the heart, and after having consumed her chest and face, burst out through her belly. The miserable thing was hideous to look upon; Monsieur de Corville orders that she be borne away. . . .

"No," says Madame de Lorsange, getting to her feet with the utmost calm; "no, leave her here before my eyes, Monsieur, I have got to contemplate her in order to be confirmed in the resolves I have just taken. Listen to me, Corville, and above all do not oppose the decision I am adopting; for the present, nothing in the world could swerve my designs.

"The unheard of sufferings this luckless creature has experienced although she has always respected her duties, have something about them which is too extraordinary for me not to open my eyes upon my own self; think not I am blinded by that false-gleaming felicity which, in the course of Thérèse's adventures, we have seen enjoyed by the villains who battened upon her. These caprices of Heaven's hand are enigmas it is not for us to sound, but which ought never seduce us. O thou my friend! The prosperity of Crime is but an ordeal to which Providence would expose Virtue, it is like unto the lightning, whose traitorous brilliancies but for an instant embellish the atmosphere, in order to hurl into death's very deeps the luckless one they have dazzled. And there, before our eyes, is the example of it; that charming girl's incredible calamities, her terrifying reversals and uninterrupted disasters are a warning issued me by the Eternal, Who would that I heed the voice of mine guilt and cast myself into His arms. Ah, what must be the punishment I have got to fear from Him, I, whose libertinage, irreligion, and abandon of every principle have stamped every instant of my life! What must I not expect if 'tis thus He has treated her who in all her days had not a single sin whereof to repent! Let us separate, Corville, the time has come, no chain binds us one to the other, forget me, and approve that I go and by an eternal penance abjure, at the Supreme Being's feet, the infamies wherewith I am soiled absolutely. That appalling stroke was necessary to my conversion in this life, it was needed for the happiness I dare hope for in another. Farewell, Monsieur; the last mark of your friendship I ask is that you institute no perquisitions to discover what shall have become of me. Oh, Corville! I await you in a better world, your virtues should lead you unto it; may the atonements I make, to expiate my crimes, in this place where I go to spend the unhappy years that remain to me, permit me to encounter you again someday."

Madame de Lorsange leaves the house immediately; she takes some money with her, leaps into a carriage, to Monsieur de Corville abandons the rest of her ownings after having recommended that they be turned into a pious legacy, and flies to Paris, where she takes a Carmelite's veil; not many years go by before she becomes the example of her order and the edification, as much by her great piety as by the wisdom of her mind and the regularity of her manners.

Monsieur de Corville, worthy of his country's highest posts, attained to them, and, whatever were his honors, he employed them for no end but to bring happiness to the people, glory to his master, whom, "although a minister," he served well, and fortune to his friends.

O you who have wept tears upon hearing of Virtue's miseries; you who have been moved to sympathy for the woe-ridden Justine; the while forgiving the perhaps too heavy brushstrokes we have found ourselves compelled to employ, may you at least extract from this story the same moral which determined Madame de Lorsange! May you be convinced, with her, that true happiness is to be found nowhere but in Virtue's womb, and that if, in keeping with designs it is not for us to fathom, God permits that it be persecuted on Earth, it is so that Virtue may be compensated by Heaven's most dazzling rewards.

Bibliography

I. WORKS PUBLISHED DURING THE AUTHOR'S LIFETIME

LITERARY WORKS

1. *Justine, ou les Malheurs de la Vertu. En Hollande, Chez les Libraires associés* [Paris, Girouard], 1791. Two volumes, 8vo. Frontispiece by Chéry. During Sade's lifetime, there were six further printings between the initial publication and 1801. Sade's re-arrest that year put an end to the reprintings. These subsequent editions were:
   1) *En Hollande* [Paris, Girouard], 1791. Two volumes, 12-mo. Certain copies of this edition include twelve erotic engravings.
   2) *A Londres* [Paris, Cazin], 1792. Two volumes, 18 mo. Frontispiece and five engravings.
   3) *Troisième* [fourth] *édition corrigée et augmentée. Philadelphie* [Paris], 1794. Two volumes, 18mo. Frontispiece and five engravings.
   4) *A Londres* [Paris], 1797. Four volumes, 18mo. Further augmented edition. Six erotic engravings.
   5) *En Hollande* [Paris], 1800. Four volumes, 16mo. Presented as the *Troisième édition corrigée et augmentée*, this is actually a reprint of the original edition.

6) *En Hollande* [Paris], 1801. Four volumes, 16mo. Also presented as the *Troisième édition corrigée et augmentée*, this was a reprinting of the 1800 edition.[1]

2. *Aline et Valcour, ou le Roman philosophique. Ecrit à la Bastille un an avant la Révolution de France. Orné de quatorze gravures. Par le citoyen S***. A Paris, chez Girouard, Libraire, rue du Bout-du-Monde, n° 47, 1793.* Eight volumes, 18mo.
There are actually three different editions of this work, bearing different dates and, in some instances, containing sixteen rather than twelve engravings. Sade announced[2] the book would appear at Easter of 1791, but the instability of the times and the death of Girouard beneath the guillotine in 1794 kept the book from appearing until 1795, which date should be taken as the date of reference of the original edition.

3. *La Philosophie dans le boudoir. Ouvrage posthume de l'auteur de "Justine." A Londres, aux dépens de la Compagnie, MDCCXCV.* Two volumes, 18mo. Frontispiece and four erotic engravings.

4. *La Nouvelle Justine, ou les Malheurs de la Vertu. Ouvrage orné d'un frontispice et de quarante sujets gravés avec soin. En Hollande* [Paris], *1797.* Four volumes, 18mo. These four volumes comprise the first part of the definitive edition of this work, of which the second part, in six volumes, bears the title:

5. *La Nouvelle Justine, ou les Malheurs de la Vertu, suivie de l'Histoire de Juliette, sa soeur* [*ou les Prospérités du vice.*] *Ouvrage orné d'un frontispice et de cent sujets gravés avec soin. En Hollande* [Paris], *1797.*

6. *Oxtiern, ou les malheurs du libertinage, drame en trois actes et en prose par D.-A.-F. S. Représenté au Théâtre Molière,*

---

[1] See the *"Bibliographie des Œuvres de Sade"* drawn up by Robert Valençay in *Les Infortunes de la Vertu*, Paris, Les Editions du Point du Jour, 1946.
[2] In a letter of March 6, 1791.

à Paris, en 1791; et à Versailles, sur celui de la Société Dra-matique, le 22 frimaire, l'an 8 de la République. A Versailles, chez Blaizot, Libraire, rue Satory. An huitième [1800]. One volume, 8vo, 48 pages.

7. *Les Crimes de l'Amour, Nouvelles héroïques et tragiques; précédées d'une Idée sur les romans et ornées de gravures, par D.-A.-F. Sade, auteur d' "Aline et Valcour." A Paris, chez Massé, éditeur-propriétaire, rue Helvétius n° 580. An VIII* [1800]. Four volumes, 12mo. Four frontispieces. This work contains eleven stories, as follows:

Vol. I—*Juliette et Raunai, ou la Conspiration d'Amboise, nouvelle historique; La Double Epreuve.*

Vol. II—*Miss Henriette Stralson, ou les Effets du désespoir, nouvelle anglaise; Faxelange, ou les Torts de l'ambition; Florville et Couvral, ou le Fatalisme.*

Vol. III—*Rodrigue, ou la Tour enchantée, conte allégorique; Laurence et Antonio, nouvelle italienne; Ernestine, nou-velle suédoise.*

Vol. IV—*Dorgeville, ou le Criminel par Vertu; la Comtesse de Sancerre, ou la Rivale de sa fille, anecdote de la Cour de Bourgogne; Eugénie de Franval.*

8. *L'Auteur de "Les Crimes de l'Amour" à Villeterque, follicu-laire. Paris, Massé, an XI* [1803]. 12 mo, 20 pages.

9. *La Marquise de Gange. Paris, Béchet, Libraire, quai des Augustins, n° 63, 1813.* Two volumes, 12mo.

POLITICAL PAMPHLETS

1. *Adresse d'un citoyen de Paris, au roi des Français. Paris, Girouard, no date* [1791]. 8vo, 8 pages.

2. *Section des Piques. Observations présentées à l'Assemblée administrative des hôpitaux. 28 octobre 1792. De l'Impri-*

merie de la Section des Piques, rue Saint-Fiacre, nº 2., 8vo, 4 pages.

3. *Section des Piques. Idée sur le mode de la sanction des Loix; par un citoyen de cette Section. De l'Imprimerie de la rue Saint-Fiacre nº 2, 2 novembre 1792. 8vo, 16 pages.*

4. *Pétition des Sections de Paris à la Convention nationale. De l'imprimerie de la Section des Piques.* No date [1793]. *8vo, 4 pages.*

5. *Section des Piques. Extraits des Régistres des délibérations de l'Assemblée générale et permanente de la Section des Piques. De l'Imprimerie de la Section des Piques, 1793. 8vo, 8 pages.*

6. *La Section des Piques à ses Frères et Amis de la Société de la Liberté et de l'Egalité, à Saintes, département de la Charente-Inférieure. De l'Imprimerie de la Section des Piques, 1793. 8vo, 4 pages.*

7. *Section des Piques. Discours prononcé par la Section des Piques, aux mânes de Marat et de Le Pelletier, par Sade, citoyen de cette section et membre de la Société populaire. De l'Imprimerie de la Section des Piques, 1793. 8vo, 8 pages.*

8. *Pétition de la Section des Piques, aux représentans du peuple français. De l'Imprimerie de la Section des Piques, 1793. 8vo, 8 pages.*

II. PRINCIPAL POSTHUMOUS PUBLICATIONS

1. *Dorci ou la Bizarrerie du sort, conte inédit par le marquis de Sade, publié sur le manuscrit avec une notice sur l'auteur* [signed A. F. (Anatole France)]. Paris, Charavay frères, éditeurs, 1881. 16mo, 64 pages.

2. *Historiettes, Contes et fabliaux de Donatien-Alphonse-François, marquis de Sade, publiés pour la première fois sur les manuscrits autographes inédits par Maurice Heine. A Paris, pour les membres de la Société du Roman Philosophique, 1926. 4to, 340 pages.*

Contains the following works: HISTORIETTES—*Le Serpent; La Saillie gasconne; L'Heureuse Feinte; Le M. . . puni; L'Evêque embourbé; Le Revenant; Les Harangueurs provençaux; Attrapez-moi toujours de même; L'Epoux complaisant; Aventure incompréhensible; La Fleur de châtaignier.* CONTES ET FABLIAUX—*L'Instituteur philosophe; La Prude, ou la Rencontre imprévue; Emilie de Tourville, ou la Cruauté fraternelle; Augustine de Villeblanche, ou le Stratagème de l'amour; Soit fait ainsi qu'il est requis; Le Président mystifié; La Marquise de Thélème, ou les Effets du libertinage; Le Talion; Le Cocu de lui-même, ou le Raccommodement imprévu; Il y a place pour deux; L'Epoux corrigé; le Mari prêtre, conte provençal; La Châtelaine de Longueville, ou la Femme vengée; Les Filous.* APPENDICE—*Les Dangers de la bienfaisance (Dorci).*

3. *Dialogue entre un prêtre et un moribond, par Donatien-Alphonse-François, marquis de Sade, publié pour la première fois sur le manuscrit autographe inédit, avec un avant-propos et des notes par Maurice Heine.* [Paris], Stendhal et Compagnie, 1926. Small 4to, 62 pages.

4. *Correspondance inédite du Marquis de Sade, de ses proches et de ses familiers, publiée avec une introduction, des annales et des notes par Paul Bourdin.* Paris, Librairie de France, 1929. Small 4to, 452 pages.

5. *Marquis de Sade. Les Infortunes de la Vertu. Texte établi sur le manuscrit original autographe et publié pour la première fois avec une introduction par Maurice Heine.* Paris, Editions Fourcade, 1930. 8vo, 206 pages.

6. *Les 120 Journées de Sodome, ou l'Ecole du libertinage, par le marquis de Sade. Edition critique établie sur le manuscrit*

original autographe par Maurice Heine. A Paris, par S. et C., aux dépens des Bibliophiles souscripteurs, 1931–1935. Three volumes, 4to, 500 pages (uninterrupted pagination throughout the three volumes).[3]

7. *Marquis de Sade. L'Aigle, Mademoiselle. . . , Lettres publiées pour la première fois sur les manuscrits autographes inédits avec une Préface et un Commentaire par Gilbert Lely.* Paris, Les Editions Georges Artigues, 1949. One volume, 16mo, 222 pages.

8. *Marquis de Sade. Histoire secrète d'Isabelle de Bavière, reine de France. Publiée pour la première fois sur le manuscrit autographe inédit avec un avant-propos par Gilbert Lely.* Paris, Librairie Gallimard, 1953. One volume, 16mo, 336 pages.

9. *Marquis de Sade. Le Carillon de Vincennes. Lettres inédites publiées avec des notes par Gilbert Lely.* Paris, "Arcanes," 1953. One volume, 16mo, 106 pages.

10. *Marquis de Sade. Cahiers personnels (1803–04). Publiés pour la première fois sur les manuscrits autographes inédits avec une préface et des notes par Gilbert Lely.* Paris, Corréa, 1953. One volume, 12mo, 130 pages.

11. *Marquis de Sade. Monsieur le 6. Lettres inédites (1778–1784) publiées et annotées par Georges Daumas. Preface de Gilbert Lely.* Paris, Julliard, 1954. One volume, 16mo, 288 pages.

12. *Marquis de Sade. Cent onze Notes pour La Nouvelle Justine. Collection "Le Terrain vague," no. IV.* [Paris 1956.] Small 4to, 158 pages (unnumbered).

---

[3] An earlier edition of *The 120 Days*, edited by Dr. Eugen Dühren, was published in 1904. The version is so riddled with errors, however, that Maurice Heine's 1931-1935 edition must rightly figure as the original edition of this work.

III. PRINCIPAL UNPUBLISHED MANUSCRIPTS

1. *Œuvres diverses* (*1764–1769*). Contains the one-act play *Le Philosophe soi-disant;* the epistolary work *Voyage de Hollande;* various letters, couplets, etc. Until the discovery of this notebook, Sade's earliest writing was thought to date from 1782.

2. *Les Jumelles ou le Choix difficile.* Two-act comedy in verse.

3. *Le Prévaricateur ou le Magistrat du temps passé.* Five-act comedy in verse.

4. *Jeanne Laisné, ou le Siège de Beauvais.* Five-act tragedy in verse.

5. *L'Ecole des jaloux ou la Folle Epreuve.* One-act comedy in *vers libres.*

6. *Le Misanthrope par amour ou Sophie et Desfrancs.* Five-act comedy in *vers libres.*

7. *Le Capricieux, ou l'Homme inégal.* Five-act comedy in verse.

8. *Les Antiquaires.* One-act comedy in prose.

9. *Henriette et Saint-Clair, ou la Force du Sang.* Prose drama in five acts.

0. *Franchise et Trahison.* Prose drama in three acts.

1. *Fanny, ou les Effets du désespoir.* Prose drama in three acts.

2. *La Tour mysterieuse.* Opéra-comique in one act.

3. *L'Union des arts ou les Ruses de l'amour.* A play in alexandrines, prose and *vers libres.* In the *Catalogue raisonné* of 1788, this work was to comprise six parts and a final *Divertissement.* In the extant manuscript, the *Divertissement* and one play, *La Fille malheureuse,* are missing.

4. *Les Fêtes de l'amitié.* Two acts incorporating prose, verse, and vaudeville.

15. *Adélaïde de Brunswick, princesse de Saxe, événement du XI*
    siècle. Novel.

IV. PRINCIPAL UNPUBLISHED MANUSCRIPTS EITHER
DESTROYED OR NOT RECOVERED[4]

1. *L'Egarement de l'infortune.* Three-act prose drama.

2. *Tancrède.* One-act lyric play in alexandrine verse with music
   interspersed.

3. *La Fille malheureuse.* One-act comedy in prose.

4. *La Fine Mouche.* Tale.

5. *L'Heureux Echange.* Tale.

6. *La Force du Sang.* Tale.

7. *Les Inconvénients de la pitié.* Tale (first draft).

8. *Les Reliques.* Tale.

9. *Le Curé de Prato.* Tale.

10. *La Marquise de Thélème.* Tale (first draft).

11. *Le Portefeuille d'un homme de lettres.* Of this projected
    four-volume work, there exists eleven *historiettes* published
    by Maurice Heine, an *avertissement,* the *Voyage de Hollande*
    previously cited, and various fragments.

12. *La Liste du Suisse. Historiette.*

13. *La Messe trop chère. Historiette.*

14. *L'Honnête Ivrogne. Historiette.*

15. *N'y allez jamais sans lumière. Historiette.*

---

[4] Numbers 1 through 17 represent works mentioned in the 1788 *Catalogue raisonné;*
numbers 18 through 20 are works seized at Sade's publisher, Massé, on 15 *Ventôse,*
An IX; number 21 is the projected ten-volume work burned at the *Préfecture de*
Police after Sade's death.

16. *La justice vénitienne. Historiette.*

17. *Adélaïde de Miramas, ou le Fanatisme protestan. Historiette.*

18. *Les Délassements du libertin, ou la Neuvaine de Cythère.*

19. *Les Caprices, ou un peu de tout.* Political work.

20. *Les Conversations du château de Charmelle.* The first draft of *Les Journées de Florbelle.*

21. *Les Journées de Florbelle, ou la Nature dévoilée, suivies des Mémoires de l'abbé de Modose et des Aventures d'Emilie de Volnange servant de preuves aux assertions, ouvrage orné de deux cents gravures.* This immense work, contained in over a hundred notebooks, according to Lely's estimate, was burned by the police at the request and in the presence of Sade's son, Donatien-Claude-Armand.